P9-DEW-926

This Rough Magic

Mercedes Lackey
Eric Flint
Dave Freer

THIS ROUGH MAGIC

This is a work of fiction. All the characters and events portrayed in this book are fictional, and any resemblance to real people or incidents is purely coincidental.

Copyright © 2003 by Mercedes Lackey, Eric Flint & Dave Freer

All rights reserved, including the right to reproduce this book or portions thereof in any form.

A Baen Books Original

Baen Publishing Enterprises
P.O. Box 1403
Riverdale, NY 10471
www.baen.com

ISBN: 0-7434-9909-3

Cover art by Larry Dixon

First paperback printing, June 2005

Library of Congress Cataloging-in-Publication Number:
2003019966

Distributed by Simon & Schuster
1230 Avenue of the Americas
New York, NY 10020

Production & design by Windhaven, Auburn, NH (www.windhaven.com)
Typeset by Bell Road Press, Sherwood, OR
Printed in the United States of America

ENTER THE LION

The elderly patriarch of Venice came forward through the crowd of Senators. He reached the front of the hall where Benito and Locovico stood. "This is a specific instruction from the Grand Metropolitan in Rome himself," he said loudly.

Well, thought Benito. *This reduces my chances of being lynched. I'm not sure what it's all about, but it's welcome.*

The Patriarch continued. "Know all of you that as far as we have been able to determine, the island of Corfu is under siege with great magical forces concentrated on it. The practitioners of sacred magic in Rome have detected demonism at work here." He turned to the now-gaping Enrico Licosa. "This entire story reeks of the snares and deceits of the Evil One."

The Senate was in a hubble-bubble of frightened whispers now. Benito heard shreds of "the Devil himself . . ."

Then another man stood up. This one Benito recognized: Andrea Recchia. His son and Benito had had a small affray consisting largely of Benito giving the handsome scion of the house a black eye and a broken nose. By the look on his face Benito could tell he thought this was payback time.

"If you ask me, fellow senators, you need look no further for the Devil's helpers than that man"—pointing at Benito—"who has broken his exile—a clear breach of our ancient laws."

The hall erupted into a bedlam. Or—started to.

The great doors exploded inward, with the sound of a thousand bombards. Benito looked up to see Marco. But this was not entirely his brother at all. He was completely overshadowed by a great golden figure with wide-spread wings that overfilled the doorway.

And it spoke in a roar, a roar that was also words. The windows and wall trembled and some of the *Case Vecchie* dropped to their knees. **"What fools are you, who threaten my city?"**

In this series:

The *Shadow of the Lion*
(Mercedes Lackey, Eric Flint & Dave Freer)
This Rough Magic
(Mercedes Lackey, Eric Flint & Dave Freer)
A Mankind Witch
by Dave Freer (forthcoming)

For a complete listing of Baen titles
by these authors, please go to our website at:
www.baen.com

To Bishop Bartolomé de las Casas
(1474–1566 a.d.)

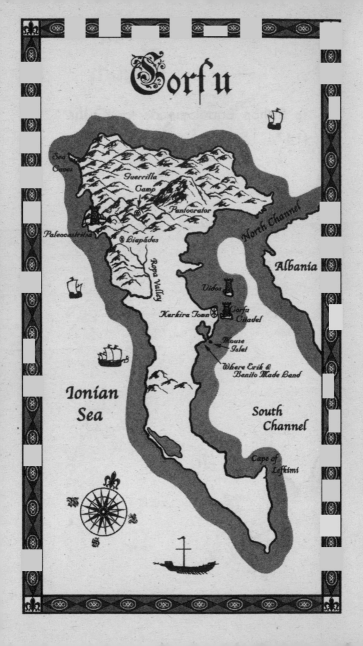

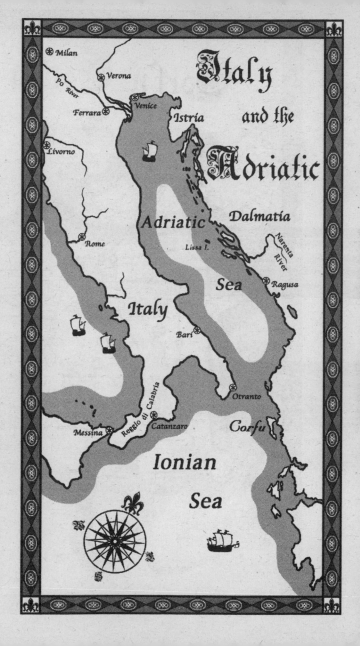

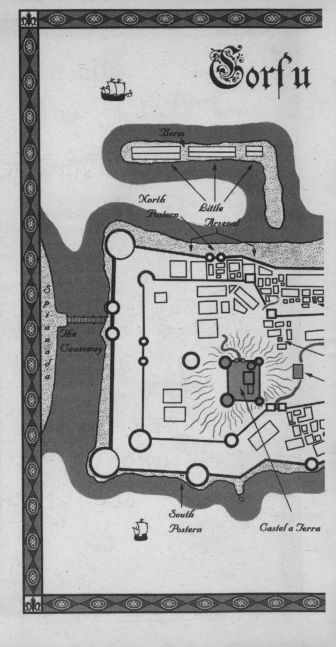

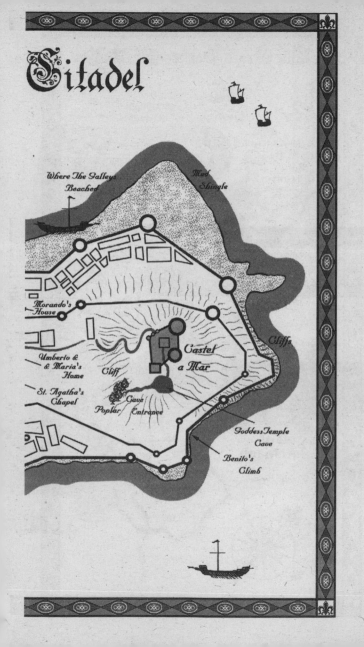

Citadel

Where The Galleys Beached

Mud Shingle

Morando's House

Umberto & & Maria's Home

St. Agatha's Chapel

Cliff

Poplar

Cave Entrance

Castel a Mar

Cliffs

Goddess Temple Cave

Benito's Climb

Prologue
Autumn, 1538 A.D.

ROME

Eneko Lopez was not the sort of man to let mere discomfort of the body come between him and his God. Or between him and the work he believed God intended him to do. The Basque ignored exhaustion and hunger. He existed on inner fires anyway, and the fires of his spirit burned hot and bright. Some of that showed in the eagle eyes looking intently at the chalice on the altar. The low-burned candles and the fact that several of the other priests had fainted from exhaustion, cold or hunger, bore mute testimony to the fact that the ceremony had gone on for many hours. Without looking away from the chalice upon which their energies were focused, Eneko could pick up the voices of his companions, still joined in prayer. There was Diego's baritone; Father Pierre's deeper bass; Francis's gravelly Frankish; the voices of a brotherhood united in faith against the darkness.

At last the wine in the chalice stirred. The surface became misty, and an image began to form. Craggy-edged, foam-fringed. A mountain . . .

The air in the chapel became scented with myrtle and lemon-blossom. Then came a sound, the wistful, ethereal notes of panpipes. There was something inhuman about that playing, although Eneko could not precisely put his finger on it. It was a melancholy tune, poignant, *old*; music of rocks and streams, music that seemed as old as the mountains themselves.

There was a thump. Yet another priest in the invocation circle had fallen, and the circle was broken again.

So was the vision. Eneko sighed, and began to lead the others in the dismissal of the wards.

"My knees are numb," said Father Francis, rubbing them. "The floors in Roman chapels are somehow harder than the ones in Aquitaine ever were."

"Or Venetian floors," said Pierre, shaking his head. "Only your knees numb? I think I am without blood or warmth from the chest down."

"We came close," Eneko said glumly. "I still have no idea where the vision is pointing to, though."

Father Pierre rubbed his cold hands. "You are certain this is where Chernobog is turning his attentions next?"

"Certain as can be, under the circumstances. Chernobog—or some other demonic creature. Great magical forces leave such traces."

"But where is it?" asked Diego, rubbing his back wearily. "Somewhere in the Mediterranean, an island, that much is clear. Probably in the vicinity of Greece or the Balkans. But *which*? There are a multitude."

Eneko shrugged. "I don't know. But it is an old place, full of crude and elemental powers, a repository of great strength, and . . ."

"And what?"

"And it does not love us," Eneko said, with a kind of grim certainty.

"It did not feel evil," commented Francis. "I would have thought an ally of Chernobog must be corrupted and polluted by the blackness."

"Francis, the enemy of my enemy is not always my friend, even if we have common cause."

"We should ally, Eneko," said Francis firmly. "Or at least not waste our strength against each other. After all, we face a common enemy."

Eneko shrugged again. "Perhaps. But it is not always that simple or that wise. Well, let us talk to the Grand Metropolitan and tell him what little we know."

VILNA

Count Kazimierz Mindaug, chief adviser and counselor to Grand Duke Jagiellon of Lithuania, scratched himself. Lice were one of the smaller hazards and discomforts of his position. To be honest, he scarcely noticed them.

The Grand Duke tended to make other problems pale into insignificance.

"If a direct attack on Venice is out of the question now, given our recent defeat there," he said, calmly, "then why don't we just hamstring them? We can paralyze their trade. The Mediterranean can still be ours. We can still draw the enemy into a war on a second front."

The terrible scar on Jagiellon's forehead pulsed; it looked like an ugly, purple worm half-embedded in his skin. A throbbing worm. "The Holy Roman Emperor looks for our hand in everything now, since the disaster in Venice. Charles Fredrik would ally openly with the accursed Venetians. Their combined fleets would crush our own, even in the Black Sea."

Count Mindaug nodded his head. "True. But what if our hand was not shown? What if those who at least appear to oppose us, took action against Venice and her interests?"

The Grand Duke's inhuman eyes glowed for just a moment, as the idea caught his interest. Then he shook his head. "The Emperor will still see our hand in anything."

Count Mindaug smiled, revealing filed teeth. "Of course he will. But he cannot act against his allies. He cannot be seen to be partisan, not in a matter that appears to be a mere squabble between Venice and her commercial rivals, especially when those rivals are parties with whom the Empire has either a treaty or a very uneasy relationship."

Jagiellon raised his heavy brows. "Ah. Aquitaine," he said. "I have hopes of the Norse; my plans move apace there. But it will take a little while before their fleets ravage the north. But Aquitaine, even with Genoa's assistance, cannot bottle up the Venetian fleet."

Mindaug flashed those filed teeth again. "But they could blockade the pillars of Hercules. And if the Aragonese join them, and perhaps the Barbary pirates too . . . they will easily prevent the Venetian Atlantic fleet from returning. And let us not forget that you now hold Byzantium's emperor in thrall."

Jagiellon shook his head. "It is not thralldom yet. Let us just say we know of certain vices which even the

Greeks will not tolerate. We wield a certain amount of influence, yes."

"Enough to send him to attempt to regain some of his lost territory?" asked Mindaug, shrewdly.

After a moment, Jagiellon nodded. "Probably. The Golden Horn or Negroponte?"

Mindaug smiled, shark-like. "Neither, my Lord. Well, not directly. If Byzantium reduces the ability of the Venetian fleet to extract vengeance on Constantinople, and on their shipping, then the Golden Horn, Negroponte, and even Zante are theirs for the taking. Even the jewel, Crete. But while the Venetians have the freedom of the Mediterranean, Alexius dares not seize Venetian property. And one island is the key to the Adriatic. To bottling the Venetians into a little corner. Corfu. The Byzantines attack and capture Corfu in alliance with Emeric of Hungary. Corfu is the key to the Adriatic. With it captured . . . Venice's traders die."

The scar on Jagiellon's head pulsed again. "Corfu," he mused, speaking the syllables slowly. "But Emeric is not a thrall of mine, not yet. He seeks to challenge me. I will devour him, in time."

Jagiellon's metal eyes looked pointedly at the count. "And anyone else who tries to become my rival, rather than my ally."

Cold sweat beaded under Count Mindaug's heavy robes. Of course he had ambitions. To be part of this court you had to have them. It was a dog-eat-dog environment. But he knew just how well Grand Duke Jagiellon defended his position. He knew—or at least he thought he knew—just what Jagiellon had ventured into, and what had happened to him.

Kazimierz Mindaug was no mean sorcerer himself. You had to be to survive in the quest for power in Lithuania. He had experimented with dangerous rites—very dangerous—but there were some things he had held back from. Jagiellon, he guessed, had not. A demon now lurked behind those metallic, all-black eyes. The arrogant prince who had thought to summon and use Chernobog was now the demon's slave. The prey had swallowed the predator.

The Count cleared his throat, trying to ease the nervousness. "Our spies have reported that Emeric has been on secret expeditions down in the southern Balkans, beginning in the spring. It is a certainty that he must be looking at expansion there. A judicious hint or two to the Byzantines, and he would not even smell our hand. Corfu would offer him a safe staging post for attacks on the hinterland."

The Count smiled nastily. "After all, the Balkans can distract Charles Fredrik as well as that mess of principalities called Italy. He would be obliged to stop Emeric of Hungary. And if the Hungarians clash with the Holy Roman Empire over Corfu . . . both of our enemies may be weakened, while we remain strong."

Jagiellon smiled. It was not a pleasant sight. There were several rotten stumps in among the huge Lithuanian's teeth. "And Valdosta may be sent there. The younger one if not the elder. I do not allow a quest for vengeance to impede my plans; only a fool concentrates on a personal vendetta when larger affairs are unresolved. But this time I could perhaps combine both. Good. I will send my new errand-boy to Constantinople."

He clapped his meaty hands. A frightened-looking slave appeared almost instantly. "Have the new man sent to me. See that horses are made ready. Captain Tcherklas must also be called. He is to accompany my servant to Odessa. The servant will need five hundred ducats, and will require suitable clothes for the imperial court in Constantinople."

The slave bowed and left at a run. He could not answer. He had no tongue any more. Jagiellon allowed his servants to retain only those portions of themselves as were useful.

"Corfu. It was a powerful place of an old faith, once," said Jagiellon speculatively.

The Count said nothing. That was wisdom. His own plotting was subtle, and the less he even thought about it . . .

The demon Chernobog could pick up thoughts. And if he was correct, then what the Black Brain knew, Jagiellon knew also. And vice versa, of course. There was a chance that events might favor his progress and his ambitions, but if they did not, he needed to keep his hands clean.

Relatively.

"Still, those days are long gone now." Jagiellon nodded to the count. "We will take these steps. We will find old shrines. The stones will have some power. We will rededicate them to our ends."

The slave returned, escorting a blond and once handsome man. Now Caesare Aldanto was gaunt. His fine golden hair hung limp about his face, matted with filth and vomit. He had plainly, by the smell, soiled himself, not just once, but often. And, by those empty eyes, this matter was of no concern to him.

Jagiellon did not seem to notice the smell, as he gave detailed, precise instructions. Caesare was to take himself to Constantinople. Letters of introduction and certain tokens of the emperor's latest pastime, were to be presented to the Emperor Alexius VI. The tokens fetched by the tongueless servant were of such a nature as to make even Mindaug blanch for a moment. Caesare did not even look discomfited when he was told to participate if the emperor so desired. He didn't even blink.

"And you'd better have him cleaned up," said Count Mindaug, when Jagiellon had finished. "He'll be noticed, else, and I doubt he'd get as far as the Greek emperor's flunkies in the condition he's in now, much less the emperor himself. He stinks."

The solid black eyes that now filled Jagiellon's sockets stared at the count. "He does?"

Jagiellon turned to Caesare. "You will see to that also, then."

Caesare nodded. Like his walk, his nod had a slightly jerky, controlled-puppet air about it. But just for a moment a madness showed in those blank eyes, a desperate, sad madness. Then that, too, was gone.

Jagiellon waved dismissively. "Go. See that Emperor Alexius engages in talks on military action with Emeric. Corfu must fall." He turned to the tongueless slave. "Has my new shaman arrived?"

The slave shook his head, fearfully. He was very efficient. Well-educated. Once he had been a prince.

"Very well," Jagiellon rumbled, only a little displeased. "Bring him to me when he appears. And see to this one. Make him fit for an emperor's company."

Count Mindaug scratched again as the servant nodded and hurried out. Lice were a small price to pay for power.

ROME

"I've gotten word from the Grand Metropolitan," the Emperor began abruptly, the moment Baron Trolliger sat down in Charles Fredrik's small audience chamber. The chamber was even smaller than the one the Holy Roman Emperor preferred in his palace in Mainz. Here in Rome, which he was visiting incognito, the Emperor had rented a minor and secluded mansion for the duration of his stay.

The servant had ushered Trolliger to a comfortable divan positioned at an angle to the Emperor's own chair. A goblet of wine had been poured for the baron, and was resting on a small table next to him. The Emperor had a goblet in hand already, but Trolliger saw that it was as yet untouched.

"Something is stirring in the Greek isles, or the Balkans," Charles Fredrik continued. "Something dark and foul. So, at least, he's being told by Eneko Lopez. By itself, the Metropolitan might think that was simply Lopez's well-known zeal at work—but his own scryers seem to agree."

"Jagiellon?"

The Emperor's heavy shoulders moved in a shrug. "Impossible to tell. Jagiellon is a likelihood, of course. Any time something dark and foul begins to move, the Grand Duke of Lithuania is probably involved. But he'll be licking his wounds still, I'd think, after the hammering he took in Venice recently—and there's always the King of Hungary to consider."

Baron Trolliger took a sip of his wine; then, rubbed his lips with the back of his hand. When the hand moved away, a slight sneer remained.

"Young Emeric? He's a puppy. A vile and vicious one, to be sure, but a puppy nonetheless. The kind of arrogant too-smart-for-his-own-good king who'll always make overly complex plans that come apart at the seams. And then his subordinates will be blamed for it, which allows the twit to come up with a new grandiose scheme."

"Get blamed—and pay the price," agreed Charles Fredrik. "Still, I think you're dismissing Emeric too lightly. Don't forget that he's got his aunt lurking in the shadows."

Trolliger's sneer shifted into a dark scowl. "'Aunt'? I think she's his great-great-aunt, actually. If she's that young. There is something purely unnatural about that woman's lifespan—and her youthful beauty, if all reports are to be believed."

"That's my point. Elizabeth, Countess Bartholdy, traffics with very dark powers. Perhaps even the darkest. Do not underestimate her, Hans."

Trolliger inclined his head. "True enough. Still, Your Majesty, I don't see what we can do at the moment. Not with such vague information to go on."

"Neither do I. I simply wanted to alert you, because . . ."

His voice trailed off, and Trolliger winced.

"Venice again," he muttered. "I'd hoped to return with you to Mainz."

Charles Fredrik smiled sympathetically. "The Italians aren't *that* bad, Hans." A bit hastily—before the baron could respond with the inevitable: *yes, they are!*—the Emperor added: "The wine's excellent, and so is the climate, as long as you stay out of the malarial areas. And I think you'd do better to set up in Ferrara, anyway."

That mollified Trolliger, a bit. "Ferrara. Ah. Well, yes. Enrico Dell'este is almost as level-headed as a German, so long as he leaves aside any insane Italian vendettas."

The Emperor shrugged. "How many vendettas could he still be nursing? Now that he's handed Sforza the worst defeat in his career, and has his two grandsons back?"

"True enough. And I agree that Ferrara would make a better place from which I could observe whatever developments take place. Venice! That city is a conspirator's madhouse. At least the Duke of Ferrara will see to it that my identity remains a secret."

Trolliger made a last attempt to evade the prospect of miserable months spent in Italy. "Still, perhaps Manfred—"

But the Emperor was already shaking his head, smiling at the baron's effort. "Not a chance, Hans. You know I need to send Manfred and Erik off to deal with this Swedish mess. Besides, what I need here in Italy, for the moment, is an *observer.*"

The baron grimaced. He could hardly argue the point, after all. The notion that rambunctious young Prince Manfred—even restrained by his keeper Erik Hakkonsen—would ever simply act as an "observer" was . . .

Ludicrous.

"I hate Italy," he muttered. "I'd hate it even if it wasn't inhabited by Italians."

KINGDOM OF HUNGARY, NEAR THE CARPATHIAN MOUNTAINS

Elizabeth, Countess Bartholdy, laughed musically. She looked like a woman who would have a musical laugh; in fact, she looked like a woman who never did, or had, anything without grace, charm, and beauty. Yet somehow, underneath all that beauty, there was . . . something else. Something old, something hungry, something that occasionally looked out of her eyes, and when it did, whoever was facing its regard generally was not seen again.

"My dear Crocell! Jagiellon, or to give it its true name, Chernobog, is an expansionist. And, compared to the power into whose territory I will inveigle him, a young upstart." She smiled, wisely, a little slyly. "Corfu is one of the old magic places. Very old, very wise, very—other."

The man standing next to her took his eyes away from the thing in the glass jar. "A risky game you're playing, Elizabeth. Chernobog is mighty, and the powers on Corfu are, as you say, very old." His middle-aged face creased into a slight smile. "'Very old' often means 'weary'—even for such as me. Those ancient powers may not be enough to snare him. The demon's power is nothing to sneer at. And then what?"

She dimpled, exactly like a maiden who had just been given a lapdog puppy. "Corfu is a terrible place for any *foreigner* to try to practice magic."

Crocell's gaze came back to the thing moving restlessly in the jar. "Hence . . . this. Yes, I can see the logic. It must have been quite a struggle, to get two disparate elementals to breed."

"Indeed it was." She grimaced at the memory, as well as the thing in the jar. "Nor is their offspring here any great pleasure to have around. But when the time comes, it will serve the purpose."

Crocell gave a nod with just enough bow in it to satisfactorily acknowledge her skill. "You will use your nephew as the tool, I assume."

"Emeric is made for the purpose. My great-great-nephew is such a smart boy—and such a careless one."

Crocell shook his head, smiling again, and began walking with a stiff-legged gait toward the entry to the bathhouse. "I leave you to your machinations, Elizabeth. If nothing else, it's always a pleasure for us to watch you at work."

Countess Bartholdy followed. "Are any of you betting in my favor yet?"

Crocell's laugh was low and harsh. "Of course not. Though I will say the odds are improving. Still . . ." He paused at the entryway and looked back, examining her. "No one has ever succeeded in cheating him out of a soul, Elizabeth. Not once, in millennia, though many have tried."

Her dimples appeared again. "I will do it. Watch and see."

Crocell shrugged. "No, you will not. But it hardly matters to me, after all. And now, Countess, if I may be of service?"

He stepped aside and allowed the countess to precede him into the bathhouse.

"Yes, Crocell—and I do thank you again for offering

your assistance. I'm having a bit of trouble extracting all of the blood. The veins and arteries empty well enough, but I think . . ."

Her face tight with concentration, Elizabeth studied the corpse of the virgin suspended over the bath. The bath was now half-full with red liquid. A few drops of blood were still dripping off the chin, oozing there from the great gash in the young girl's throat. "I think there's still quite a bit more resting in the internal organs. The liver, especially."

Hearing a sharp sound, she swiveled her head. "Do be a bit careful, would you? Those tiles are expensive."

"Sorry," murmured Crocell, staring down at the flooring he'd cracked. His flesh was denser and heavier than iron, and he always walked clumsily, wearing boots that might look, on close inspection, to be just a bit odd in shape. They were—more so on the inside than the outside. The feet in those boots were not human.

Crocell was helpful, as he always was dealing with such matters. He was the greatest apothecary and alchemist among the Servants, and always enjoyed the intellectual challenge of practicing his craft.

He left, then, laughing when Elizabeth offered to share the bath.

His expression did not match the laugh, however, nor the words that followed. "I have no need for it, Countess, as you well know. I am already immortal."

The last words were said a bit sadly. Long ago, Crocell had paid the price Elizabeth Bartholdy hoped to avoid.

After her bath, the countess retired to her study, with a bowl of the blood—waste not, want not, she always said. There was still another use for it, after all, a use that the bath would actually facilitate. The blood was now as much Elizabeth's as the former owner's, thanks to the magical law of contagion.

She poured it into a flat, shallow basin of black glass, and carefully added the dark liquid from two vials she removed from a rank of others on the shelves. Then she held her hands, palms down, outstretched over the surface of the basin. What she whispered would be familiar to any other magician, so long as he (or she) was not from some tradition outside of the Western Empire. All except for the last name, which would have sent some screaming for her head.

Rather insular of them, she thought.

A mist spread over the surface of the dark liquid. It rose from nothing, but swiftly sank into the surface of the blood. The liquid began to glow from within with a sullen red light. And there, after a moment, came the image of her conspirator.

Count Mindaug's face was creased with worry. "This is dangerous, Elizabeth."

The countess laughed at him. "Don't be silly. Jagiellon is practically a deaf-mute in such matters; he acknowledges no power but his own except as something to devour. He won't overhear us. Besides, I'll be brief. I received a letter from my nephew yesterday. He's clearly decided to launch his project."

Mindaug shook his head. "The idiot."

"Well, yes." Elizabeth's laugh, as always, was silvery. "What else is family good for?"

Mindaug grunted. He was hardly the one to argue the point, since his own fortune had come largely from his two brothers and three sisters. None of whom had lived more than two months after coming into their inheritance.

"He's still an idiot. I'd no more venture onto Corfu than I would . . . well." Politely, he refrained from naming the place where the Hungarian countess would most likely be making her permanent domicile, sooner or later. Elizabeth appreciated the delicacy, although she would dispute the conclusion. "However, it's good for us. I'll keep steering Jagiellon as best I can."

"Splendid. All we have to do for the moment, then, is allow others to stumble forward." Politely, she refrained from commenting on the way Mindaug was scratching himself.

THE ALBANIAN COAST

It was a bitter morning. The wind whipped small flurries of snow around the hooves of the magnificent black horse. The rider seemed unaware of the chill, his entire attention focused instead on the distant prospect. From up here, he could see the dark Ionian gulf and the narrow strip of water that separated the green island from the bleak Balkan mountains. Over here, winter was arriving. Over there, it would still be a good few more weeks before the first signs of it began to show.

The rider's eyes narrowed as he studied the crescent of island, taking in every detail from Mount Pantocrator to Corfu Bay.

The shepherd-guide looked warily up at the rider. The rider was paying a lot of money for the shepherd's services. The shepherd was still wondering if he was going to live to collect.

Abruptly the tall rider turned on his guide. "When your tribes raid across there, which way do they follow?"

The shepherd held up his hands. "Lord, we are only poor shepherds, peaceful people."

"Don't lie to me," said the rider.

The shepherd looked uneasily across at the sleeping island. Memories, unpleasant memories, of certain reprisals came back to him. Of a woman he'd once thought to possess . . .

"It is true, Lord. It is not wise to attack the Corfiotes. There are many witches. And their men fight. The Venetians, too, come and burn our villages."

"Fight!" the tall rider snorted. "If things develop as I expect they will in Venice, they'll have to learn to fight or be crushed. Well, I have seen what I have come to see. And now, you will take me to Iskander Beg."

The shepherd shied, his swarthy face paling. "I do not know who you are talking about, lord."

"I have warned you once, do not lie to me. I warn

you again. I will not warn you a third time." It was said with a grim certainty. "Take me to Iskander Beg."

The shepherd looked down at the stony earth. At the dry grass where he knew his body might rest in a few moments. "No, King Emeric. *You* can only kill me. Iskander Beg . . ." He left the sentence hanging. "I will not take you to the Lord of the Mountains. He knows you are here. If he wants to see you, he will see you."

The King of Hungary showed no surprise that the shepherd had known who he was secretly escorting. After all, the thin-browed, broken-nosed face was well known—and feared. Yes, he was a murderous killer. That in itself was nothing unusual in these mountains. But Emeric was also rumored to be a man-witch. That was why this guide had agreed to lead him, Emeric was sure, not simply the money. Emeric would leave these mountains alive.

The King of Hungary turned his horse. "He can choose. He will see me soon enough anyway. He can see me now, or see me later, on my terms."

The shepherd shrugged. "I can show you the way back now."

CORFU

Across, on the green island, in a rugged glen, the stream cascaded laughingly amid the mossy rocks. In front of the grotto's opening, the piper played a melody on the simple shepherd's pipe. It was a tune as old as the mountain, and only just a little younger than the sea. Poignant and bittersweet, it echoed among the rocks and around the tiny glade between the trees. The sweet young grass was bruised by the dancing of many feet. And among the tufts were sharp-cut little hoof-marks, alongside the barefoot human prints.

Far below a shepherd whistled for his dogs. The piper did not pause in her playing to draw the hood of her cloak over the small horns set among the dark ringlets.

This was a holy place. Holy, ancient and enchanted. Neither the shepherd nor his dogs would come up here. Here the old religion and old powers still held sway. The power here was like the olive roots in the mountain groves: just because they were gnarled and ancient did not mean they were weak.

Or friendly.

PART I
Autumn, 1538 A.D.

Chapter 1

Benito Valdosta, latterly a gentleman of the *Case Vecchie* of Venice, walked along a narrow alleyway in the most dubious part of Cannaregio, quite a long time after midnight. Benito sauntered in the shadows, just hoping someone would make his day. Women! Women, as every man on earth knew, were the source of all the damned trouble in the world. And then some extra, he thought bitterly.

No one obliged him. Even in the clothes of the *Case Vecchie*, walking where no sane *Case Vecchie* gentleman would go, the watchers—he could feel them, if not see them—knew who he was. These days he had a reputation, totally out of keeping with his age or size. Well, he would find a tavern. Not Barducci's. Too many memories there.

And then, in the shape of two sailors, some relief came in sight. They were, in their clumsy fashion, trying to box him in.

He let them.

The one with the cudgel tossed it from hand to hand. A mistake, Benito knew. It meant, as Caesare had taught him, in what seemed a different world, that for a few instants you were not actually holding the weapon. The cudgel-wielder obviously hadn't been taught this. He was amazingly stupid, part of Benito's mind thought. When he spoke to his companion with the knife, he actually looked away from the victim!

21

"Well, Spiro. Venice takes away . . . and she gives back to us. With interest." He laughed coarsely.

Benito judged that the one with the knife was the more dangerous of the two, if the smaller. He showed signs of a recent beating-up, sporting a black eye and torn cloak. "Yeah. I suppose so. Give us your money, rich kid. Hand it over, and you won't get hurt."

Amateurs, thought Benito, wryly. Came in on the last tide. Got drunk. Maybe got rolled. Maybe just ran out of money and got thrown out of some tavern. Still at least half-drunk. Benito cringed, stepping back, to make sure neither could get behind him. "Please sirs, you're not going hurt me?"

"Just give us your money," repeated the knife-man, "and get out of here. This is no part of town for—what do they call noblemen around here?—yeah, a *Case Vecchie.*"

"I think I might just take that lucco, too," said the cudgel wielder. He was big man. An oarsman by the looks of his muscles.

"If . . . if I give you all my money, and my lucco too, will you let me go?" whined Benito, letting a quaver into his voice, still cringing.

"Yeah," said the knife-man, relaxing, dropping the point slightly.

Cudgel smiled viciously. "Well, I think you need a few bruises to take home to mummy, and maybe a cut on that pretty face." As he said this, cudgel-man had stepped in closer, still tossing the cudgel hand-to-hand and now getting in the knife-wielder's way.

From behind the cudgel-wielder, Benito heard the knifeman say: "Brusco, he's only a kid. Take his money and leave him alone." Brusco wasn't listening.

Cringing means your limbs are bent. You're into a fighter's crouch with a moment's change of attitude. Benito didn't bother to aim. He just hit the arm of the hand that was about to catch the cudgel. Grabbing cloth, as the cudgel went flying harmlessly, Benito pushed the sailor over his outstretched foot. As the former-cudgel-wielder fell, Benito stepped forward, planting a boot firmly in the thug's solar plexus. His rapier was suddenly in his right hand, and the *main gauche* in his left. Finest Ferrara steel gleamed in the gray dawn-light. Fierce exultation leapt inside him, as he moved in for the kill. Already the moves, long practiced, were in mind. Engage. Thrust. He had the reach. Turn and kill the other one before he could get to his feet.

And then, as he saw the look of terror on the sailor's face, the battle-joy went away. Her words came back to him. "I won't marry a wolf."

He settled for hitting the knife, hard, just at the base of the blade, with the rapier. It did precisely what cheap knives will do, given that, to save metal, the tang into the hilt is usually much thinner than the blade. It snapped.

The sailor looked briefly at the hilt in his hand, and prepared himself to die. "I didn't plan to hurt you," he said, hoarsely, his eyes now fixed on the two unwavering blades facing him.

Benito flicked a glance at the other man, who was up on one elbow, feeling for his cudgel. Safety, prudence and Caesare said: "Kill them both, fast. Dead men are no threat. Desperate men are." Her words came back to him again: "Are you the son of the wolf or the fox?"

"I know you weren't," said Benito. "That's why you're still alive. But if your friend moves a muscle, that's going to change."

The sailor looked at his companion. "Then you'd better kill me, milord," he sighed. "That Brusco has no brains at all. He got us into this mess in the first place."

Benito stepped over to where the brainless Brusco was busy proving his lack of intelligence, by trying to get to his feet. A slash of the rapier severed the man's belt. By the piggy squeal Benito's judgement must have been a touch off.

"Stay down, Brusco," said the other sailor, urgently. "The *Case Vecchie*'ll kill you. Milord, he's still half-drunk. We . . . our ship left us. Winter's coming and berths are few now. We thought . . . some eating money . . ."

Benito snorted in exasperation, feeling as if he were fifty instead of seventeen. "Come on. Both of you. Up on your feet, you. Use both hands to keep those trousers up . . . Brusco. Now. In front of me. Quick march. You're no more than a pair of damned virgins in a brothel, in this part of town! You're not cut out for a life of crime, either of you. You're not local or you'd never have been so stupid. Where are you from?"

"Liapádhes. Kérkira . . . Corfu," the former knifeman said. He jerked a thumb at his companion, who was staggering along, holding up his trousers. "Brusco's from Bari. Down south."

Benito prodded the former cudgel-wielder with his rapier. "They must breed them big and dumb down there."

"I'm bleeding," said Brusco, sulkily.

They'd arrived at the canalside by this time. Benito flicked the complaining Brusco's shoulder with his rapier so the man turned around. So did his companion.

"Bleeding. Ha. You're lucky, Brusco, that I didn't cut your damn-fool balls off before you sired any dumb kids. Now listen to me, sailor from Bari. You get yourself out of Venice and don't come back. If you do, you'll be lucky if the canalers cut your throat before I find you. Swim or sell your shirt. But get onto the mainland and don't come back. Go." They both turned. Benito put out his rapier and halted the smaller man, the one with the black eye, who had once bought a cheap knife. "Stay."

The man looked wary, glancing at the canal.

Benito shook his head. "Don't be as much of a fool as the idiot from Bari. If I'd wanted to kill you, I'd have done it back there. Anyway, a couple of mouthfuls of that water is more likely to kill you than any sword-stroke.

"Here." Benito reached into his pouch, took out some silver pennies, and handed them to the would-be thief. "Get yourself some breakfast. Go that way along the fondamenta, and you're in a better part of town. And then get yourself along to the Dorma shipyards. Tell Alberto on the gate that Benito sent you. Tell him you're looking for a berth and that I said you'd do."

The Corfiote seaman looked at the money in his palm. Then he shook his head, unbelieving. "Why are you doing this?" he asked quietly. "I thought you'd hand us over to the nightwatch. I was looking for a chance to run."

"I needed a fight," said Benito, shrugging. "And I

needed to sort out some things in my head. You obliged. I owe you. Now, I've got to find a gondola. You've straightened out my mind a bit, and there's a girl I've got say good-bye to. I was going to go drinking, if I couldn't find a fight."

The sailor shook his head again, and then smiled. "If it's all the same to you, milord, next time you're in need of a fight, I'm not going to be around. I thought I was going to be killed back there. One minute you were a scared kid. Then—you were somebody else. When I looked in your eyes . . . for a minute I thought I was dead."

Benito took a deep breath. "You very nearly were," he said quietly.

The sailor nodded. "A risk a thief takes. It's not something I've tried before, or I'm in a hurry to try again. And your girl should be very sorry you're leaving. Any chance I'd be shipping out with you, Milord?"

To his surprise Benito realized the man wanted him to be on the vessel. That was admiration in his voice. "I'm not shipping out." He waved at a dark, sleek gondola out on the Grand Canal. "She is. And as far as I can see she's not a bit sorry," he added, bitterly.

The gondolier had responded to his wave, and the vessel was just about at the canalside. Benito vaulted down into it, with athletic ease. "Bacino San Marco," he said, taking his seat.

"Morning, Valdosta. Or are you too important to greet us these days?"

Benito looked up. "Oh, hell. Sorry, Theobaldo. My mind was somewhere else."

The gondolier shrugged. "It's too late, boy. She's married and he's a fine man. Besides, she is one of us and you're one of them. It would never have worked."

Benito was not in the least surprised that the canaler knew all about his private life. He'd lived next to these canals himself for far too long not to know that the real lifeblood of Venice was not the water in her canals or the trade of her far-flung colonies, but gossip. When you and your brother are real, romantic heroes, nobles hidden in slums, who come into their own while saving the city in its hour of need . . . When your patron is the new Doge . . .

Well, suddenly everyone knows you. To be fair, on the canals, most of them had known his brother Marco anyway. Marco was pretty well regarded as the local saint, for his work in healing the poor and sick of the canals. He, Benito, had a fairly well-deserved reputation for being a thief and trouble, and a pack follower of the assassin Caesare Aldanto, until almost the last. He'd redeemed himself in the fighting, to be sure. Fighting was one of the few things he was good at, thanks in part to the treacherous Caesare, and thanks in part to his father's blood—neither of which most people regarded as good things.

Benito sighed. His skills: fighting, carousing and climbing buildings. None of the three seemed to fit him for the aristocratic mold Petro Dorma wanted to cram him into.

His half-brother Marco, on the other hand, was a gentleman born. Fitting into the *Case Vecchie* mold was easy enough for him, so long as he could go on with his beloved medical studies and seeing Katerina Montescue. Besides, ever since Benito's brother and the Lion of Venice had shared a body, Marco was . . . different. He was still the brother Benito knew and loved. But he'd always been the thinker. Benito was a doer, not a thinker. Marco was no longer unsure of himself, and now it was Benito's turn to be. It was something Benito had never been before.

"I know, Theobaldo. I messed up good, huh? But I grew up as a bridge-brat. I'm still learning this *Case Vecchie* stuff, and, to tell the truth, I don't like it much."

The gondolier sculled easily, moving the boat along the limpid water of the canal, under the Rialto bridge. A few bankers' clerks were already setting up their masters' stalls. "We always reckoned you were born to be hanged," he said. "That brother of yours is too good for this world, but you! Anyway, you're not going to make trouble for Maria and Umberto, are you? Because if you are, I'm going to pitch you into the canal here. You and that fancy sword of yours."

Benito knew he was good with that fancy sword, so long as he was on dry land. He also knew what Maria had taught him: Never mess with a boatman in his own boat. The gondolier had spent forty years staying on his feet in this vessel. Benito was a landsman, even if he'd grown up canalside.

Besides, Benito had no intention of causing trouble. Umberto *was* a fine man, even if he was twenty-five years older than Maria. And never mind the gondolieri—Maria would pitch him into the water herself if he tried anything. She was certainly strong enough and quite capable of doing it.

"I'm just going to say 'good-bye,'" he said quietly. "And good luck. She deserves some."

He withdrew into a brown study, thinking back to that time of poverty he'd spent living with Maria and Caesare, when both of them, in their different ways—Maria as Caesare's lover and he as Caesare's young protégé—had thought Caesare Aldanto was some kind of demigod on earth. Until, in one night and day, Aldanto's evil nature had surfaced and Benito and Maria had wound up becoming lovers themselves. A night which was still, for all the horror of it, Benito's most precious memory.

Benito realized now with crystal clarity, looking back, how he'd been shaped by those times. His blood, if you were shaped by blood, was terrifying enough. His mother was an undutiful daughter of Duke Enrico Dell'este. The Old Fox, they called him. Lord of Ferrara, Modena, Este, Regio nell' Emilia, and, since Milan and Verona's defeat a month back, of several more Po valley towns. Dell'este was supposed to be the leading strategist of the age. A man feared and respected. A nobleman.

But Benito's father was worse. Carlo Sforza, the Wolf of the North. A man feared. The most powerful and deadly soldier-of-fortune of the day, Italy's most notorious *condottiere*. Undefeated, until the debacle at the Palatine forts on the Po during the battle for Venice last month, when the Old Fox had bloodied the Wolf. Bloodied the Wolf, but not killed him. Benito still had his father's broken sword in the cupboard at the *Casa* Dorma.

They all expected him to be like one or the other

of these men. And maybe, in time he might be. But he knew very little of either of them, or of their very different worlds. He'd learned how to live, and how to behave, mostly from two women street-thieves, until he and Marco had tied up with Caesare. Like it or not, Benito had to admit he'd modeled himself on Caesare Aldanto. The man had been something of a hero to both of them. Caesare and Maria had been the center of their world for some very crucial years.

Maria. If there was ever going to be a reason why Benito didn't turn out as much of a *pizza da merde* as Caesare had turned out to be, she would probably be it. Deep inside him it ached. Her values were hard, clear, loyal and true. And she'd turned him down to marry a caulker. Here he was, protégé of the man who was the new Doge . . . hurting because some canal-woman had spurned his offer of marriage.

Deep down, he was also worried that she was dead right to have done so. He'd nearly killed those two stupid sailors, just because he was in a foul mood and looking for excitement to distract him. Caesare would have done the same, but would not have stopped short. So, according to rumor, would Carlo Sforza. As for the Old Fox—well, stories painted him as a good friend and a bad enemy, but a cautious and wily man. A cautious and wily man might well have done as Benito had.

Or perhaps, not.

But the Old Fox, Maria—or a younger, less arrogant Benito—would never have gotten into that position in the first place. He sighed. Maybe part of it was that he was so short. One of the other things he owed to growing up a thief, living under bridges and in secret in other people's attics. With no money, but lots of enthusiasm. More enthusiasm and conviction that things would come right, than food, sometimes. Food had been hard to come by for a few years. He was growing broader now. But he'd never be as tall as his brother. Marco had done his basic growing before hard times hit the two of them. Besides, the Dell'este were not tall. The tall willowy shape was that of the Valdosta family.

"You going to sit there all day?" asked the gondolier, interrupting his musing. "Or are you going to get out?"

Startled, Benito stood up and reached for the mooring-pole.

"You can pay me, Valdosta," said Theodoro, dryly.

Flushing, Benito did. Generously. After all, money was the one thing he had plenty of now.

Benito was not surprised to find Katerina Montescue on the quay-side. And if Kat was going to be there, his brother was almost inevitably going to be, too.

Marco and Kat eyed him with considerable wariness as he came up. "You shouldn't be here!" hissed Kat.

Benito held up his hands, pacifically. "I'm not going to cause any trouble."

"You *should* have caused trouble," said Kat crossly, "before she did this. It's too late now."

Benito nodded, and swallowed to clear the lump in his throat. "I know. Now all I can do is . . . not make trouble. So I'm just going to say good-bye to an old friend."

The spitting-tabby glow in Kat's eyes died. She patted his arm, awkwardly. "Maybe it is for the best. I mean, she seems happy enough."

Benito looked over to where Maria Garavelli—no, not Garavelli any more; Verrier, now—was talking to two older women. She seemed, if not happy, at least to be her usual abrasive self.

"Don't be crazy!" she was saying. "The boat's worth twice that. Put it up on blocks in Tomaso's yard if you won't use it."

Benito missed half of the reply. Something about ". . . when you come back."

Maria shook her head emphatically. "I'm not coming back."

Benito winced at that certainty.

Maria caught sight of him, then. Immediately, she turned and strode over to him, her dark eyes flashing.

"What are you doing here, 'Nito?" There was challenge in her voice, challenge, and deep down, anger. If there was anything else there, he didn't want to know about it.

Benito shrugged. "I heard an old friend was leaving Venice. She did a lot toward raising me. I came to say good-bye, good luck, and a safe journey. And I hope—I mean, I *really* hope—she's happy."

For a moment she said nothing. Then: "Good-bye, Benito." It was said very quietly, with just a flicker of pain. She turned her back on him and walked away.

Benito had spent his life knowing exactly what to do next. For once, he didn't. So he walked blindly off into the piazza, leaving Maria to embark with her new husband on the ship outbound for Istria.

Chapter 2

The roll of the ship on its way to Istria was comforting, something familiar in an increasingly unfamiliar world. Maria needed that comfort now, as she lay sleepless. For the first time in her life she wasn't going to be living in a city. That worried her, more than she liked to admit, but it worried her a lot less than the life stirring inside her did.

Beside her, Umberto snored. She'd get used to that, she supposed, eventually. At least the snoring made him different from Caesare. And Benito, for that matter.

Benito had upset her; the baby had kicked just when he'd said good-bye. She'd swear it was his—it was so damned restless, just like him. But it would be a long time before she forgot the look on his face, there on the quay-side. Not for the first time, Maria wondered if she'd made a mistake. Still, she'd made her decisions, made her bed, as the old ones said, and now she must lie in it. Benito just reminded her too much of Caesare. Caesare had hurt her, worse than she'd ever been hurt in her life, and in ways she was probably never going to get over.

Whatever else, she wasn't going to have that happen to her again. Umberto wasn't an exciting man, true, and hadn't been even in his youth. But Maria had known him since she was a little girl. Umberto Verrier was as decent as they came and as reliable as the seasons.

She sighed. It was good fortune that Umberto had gotten this post as chief forester for a district in Istria. The post usually went to one of the master-carpenters from the Arsenal, which the caulkers technically were, but normally it went to one of the more prestigious guilds, not to the poor-relation caulkers. She suspected the hand of Petro Dorma in that appointment. His family had huge estates in Istria, and besides, the Doge had influence everywhere in Venice. But she was grateful, even if all it meant was that the Doge was trying to get Benito Valdosta, of the *Casa Vecchie* Valdosta, away from the canals and a certain boat-girl who might try to exercise a hold over him. It would take her away from Venice before her pregnancy began to show.

Now all she had to do was bear with the interminable voyage, an alien new life, and try to love the husband she had bound herself to. He was a good man, Umberto. He deserved at least that she try, try as hard as she ever had in all her life.

The voyage wound up not being as long or as uncomfortable as she had feared it would be. But once the tarette had dropped them at the tiny harbor at Rovini, the enormity of the change in her life really struck her. She had not been on the dock for more than a minute before she was aware, deep in her gut, that Venetian-held Istria was . . . different.

All her life had been formed around the bustle of Venice, around an existence that centered on people and water. She stood on the dock with a bundle of her personal belongings beside her, as Umberto looked for the forester who was to meet them, and fought down a sudden surge of fear.

Fortunately, the forester was also looking for them, and his arrival pushed the fear aside in favor of more immediate and practical concerns. There was the usual confused comedy over boxes and chests. Eventually, Umberto and the other man got it sorted out while Maria stood by, trying not to feel impatient because *she* would have had it dealt with in two minutes. The effort to control her often-brusque temperament steadied Maria—the brusque temperament itself, even more so. Whatever else Maria had to worry about in the future, her own practical competence was not one of them.

The foresters had arranged for a small caretta to transport the new chief forester and his bride up to his home in the forests and the hills. Bouncing up the muddy track beyond the olives and the bare fields, they moved into the fringes of forested land. For the first time in her life, Maria found herself out of sight or scent of the sea.

The forest smelled. A damp, rich, mushroomy smell, that probably, under other circumstances, would have been pleasant. At least it wasn't the sewage-stink of the canals in high summer. But it wasn't familiar, either, it wasn't anything she was expecting, and it was strong. That, or pregnancy, or just the bouncing of the cart, made her feel sick.

But when they got to the house Maria was so astounded that she forgot her nausea.

It was made of *wood*, like a rich man's home! Wood was saved for things that could float, and bring you profit, not used for houses. And it was big. Set apart from the cluster of foresters' huts, it was a real *house*. She could not imagine how they could afford it.

The house was new, so it must have been built by the man Umberto was replacing. "How did he afford such a place?"

Umberto looked sour. "The admirals at the Arsenal discovered three weeks back that he, and five of the foresters, were in a very convenient arrangement with the *Lazzari*, the timber buyers from Trieste. That is why the post was vacant—and probably why I got it. They didn't want anyone who might still have a hand in the arrangement to come in and start it up all over again, which meant delving deep into the guild to find a replacement. As deep as the caulkers, even."

He sighed. "The nice part is that the house comes with the post. But I will have a mountain of paperwork to do and I doubt if the oxcart with our clothes and furnishings will be here until dusk. I'm sorry, Maria. I'll have to get stuck in straight away. Even when the oxcart gets here, the house will have to wait until I have time to arrange things. We have bedding at least, Rossi assures me, but the house is otherwise bare inside."

It was a crisp, and for a miracle, dry autumn day. The hills with their leaf-bare stands of oak and larch called to her. The thought of getting off of this carriage and onto her feet called even more. She'd walk up to the ridge where the dark pines stood like the raised hackles of some huge cat.

"I'll explore around," she said, not caring a pin whether or not there was a chair to sit on or plates to eat off. Hadn't she done without those things before? Well, she could again. "I need to walk. To get some air."

"Very well. But please don't go out of sight of the house. These wild places are dangerous. Rossi has been telling of bears and boar . . ." He trailed off, looking miserably at the house.

Personally, Maria thought Rossi's tales improbable even for the wilds of the fabled east. The half-Slovene was having fun seeing how many stories he could get his new boss to swallow, most likely. But she nodded, since she wouldn't contradict him in front of Rossi. Bad thing, for a boss to be shown up in front of his underlings by a girl-wife, before he'd even met most of those underlings.

Umberto wasn't quite finished. "Just remember, you're, um . . ." He flushed. "In a delicate condition."

Maria nodded again. Poor Umberto. She'd been brutally frank before accepting his proposal: She'd told him straight out that she was pregnant. He'd gone puce, but he'd also managed to say that it wouldn't matter to him. That was quite something from anyone.

Still, Umberto struggled to talk about the pregnancy. It had begun to dawn on Maria that it wasn't the mysterious father so much as the fact that, so far as Umberto was concerned, this was an area men didn't refer to. Ever. Babies just happened, and he would much prefer that things stayed that way, thank you.

Maria walked out past the house, looking about her with wonder. She had never in her life seen trees so tall or so—untamed. Beneath her feet, the springy turf felt very different from dockside boards and stone quays, and the cool air was dry. Wondrously dry. In Venice, the air was thick enough to wring out like a dishrag. The loneliness out here was compelling, and pulled her farther under the trees. In short order, she'd very rapidly broken the injunction about going out of sight of the houses. Rossi's stories and Umberto's concern aside, the hills seemed as unthreatening as a kitten.

And she was in a phase of pregnancy where she just seemed to have too much energy. She was over most of the morning sickness now, and although she'd been told she would become heavy and uncomfortable soon, she still felt strong, not needing to be pampered and cosseted.

Still . . . there was maybe less room in her lungs than there used to be. She sat herself down on a pile of leaves with a neat rock backrest just short of the ridge. The rock was sun-warmed, and she'd walked a long way. A canaler's strength, she realized after a moment, really didn't lie in the legs. She'd just rest a while. Just a little in the sun, the warm sun . . .

She woke with a start—though, out of habit, not moving, not even to open her eyes. Voices, strange voices; near, but not near enough to see her, obviously. She recognized the one: Rossi, the forester who had brought the caretta to collect 'them.

"—see any problems. The old man they've sent up doesn't look like he'll understand what is going on, Torfini." Rossi chuckled. "I reckon after the wolf, bear and boar stories I told the man and that young woman of his, the two of them will stay barricaded in the house for the next two years, never mind the next two months."

"Even so. I'm sure it was Rudolpho and Marco who somehow got word to the admirals at the Arsenal. I don't want those two to hook onto the fact that we still have timber to move out. Oak that well curved is much in demand."

"So who is buying ship ribs now? Constantinople?"

The other man snorted. "For heaven's sake! I don't care. It's all money."

"Good money, and I want mine, Torfini." There was a threat in that voice that made Maria press herself into the rock.

"You'll get it, all right. Just keep everyone away from the Mello ridges for a couple of weeks."

"I'll find you if I don't get it."

"You'll get yours."

Maria waited a good long while after they'd left; the last thing she wanted was for either of those two *pizza de merde* to guess she'd overheard them. In fact her descent was more alarming than she'd anticipated, for darkness had come on much quicker than she'd expected. It was twilight when she got down to the cottages, which were already twinkling with firelight.

Umberto was standing outside their house, with the door wide open, beside himself. "Where have you been? I have been so worried! I've got the men out looking for you. There are saw pits . . ."

She patted his cheek, and tried to make him really *look* at her. "I'm fine. I just walked farther than I meant to. Then I stopped for a rest, and fell asleep. But Umberto, never mind all that now! I found out something very important."

He wasn't listening. "You must be more careful, Maria! This isn't the canals of Venice. It is dangerous out here. You hear me? Dangerous! Rossi told me that before the Old Chief Forester left—"

She tried mightily to keep from snapping at him. She wasn't a child! This wasn't about a new flower or a wild hare she'd seen!

"Umberto, Rossi is a *liar*. He was trying to keep us indoors. And if the old Chief Forester's name was Torfini, then he hasn't gone far. He was up on that ridge over there talking to Rossi. I *heard* them."

He wasn't even listening. He led her indoors, patting her. "You're in a . . . a delicate condition, Maria. You must rest. I'll get someone to look after you."

Suddenly she was too tired to fight for him anymore. Maybe if a man told him what was going on, he might actually listen to it. "Very well. I'll rest. If you go out and get two of your men in here, Rudolpho and Marco."

"You really must be more careful Maria . . ."

In this, at least, she would be firm. "Rudolpho and Marco, Umberto. Now. And then I'll rest and be good."

Chapter 3

Grand Duke Jagiellon looked at his new shaman with a strange glow in his inhuman eyes. Count Mindaug was sure he understood the thoughts moving in that now-demonic brain: This particular shaman's skin would offer more eating than the last. It was very wrinkled, and the tattoos would give it an interesting color and flavor.

The face, especially, was heavily tattooed. The shaman wore a coat of reindeer hide, the shoulders of which were covered in feathers and the back with small brass bells. He carried a *quodba*, a magic drum, so large that it seemed to dwarf the wrinkled old man; the drumhead had also been tattooed. There was no expression on the old face. Only the eyes, narrow and slightly up-tilted, showed any signs of trepidation. They darted about, taking in details, faintly shadowed with unnamed and secret thoughts.

Count Mindaug detected the battle of wills going on between the huge, meaty Grand Duke and the scrawny old man. Not a word was said, but the air itself shivered as if with heat.

Eventually the old shoulders slumped. "The *haltija* is too strong." He bowed to the Grand Duke. "Master."

"Remember that," Jagiellon said coldly. "But you are stronger than my last shamans."

The shaman said nothing. He waited.

Jagiellon turned to Count Mindaug. "This one is not Karelian. Why has he come?"

Pacifically, Mindaug held out his hands with their perfectly manicured and sharpened nails. "I sent emissaries into the north seeking out their most powerful. Your new shaman, the one from Karelen, killed himself some days back. This one is from Kandalaksha."

The shaman nodded. "I am master of many words of power. Many sea words. Many water words. Some forest words. I kill small Karelian. He challenged my power, but I too strong for him." His Lithuanian was good, if accented.

This was talk Jagiellon understood. "You will give me that strength. All of it. And you will only kill at my express command." The dark eyes flared. "There will be plenty of opportunity."

"Who do I go kill?"

The big hands carved a shape in the air. A vision appeared, of a tall, willowy boy. "This one. Marco Valdosta is his name. See him. Taste his magic. He is weak in skill but deep in power."

The shaman's drum seemed to shiver. But other than the faint throbbing that came from it there was no sound or movement for some time. Eventually the shaman shook his head. "Not one. Is two. One human, very strong but no skill. And one big but not human. You no kill this one."

This did not, to Mindaug's surprise, anger his master. Not visibly, anyway. The purple scar on Jagiellon's forehead pulsed briefly. "The nonhuman one is limited to a place. If the human comes out of that, you can kill him."

The shaman nodded. "Eat his *haltija*. He strong, but not skilled yet."

"Good." A gesture and the vision was dispelled. "Now, this one." Again a shape formed in the air. Reddish hair. An aquiline nose, a single line of eyebrow, and eyes that burned. "Eneko Lopez, this one's name."

The drum-skin shivered. And then, with a sound like tearing cloth, split.

The shaman averted his face, making a warning-sign. "Make it go, master!" he said urgently. "He will see us, too."

The vision disappeared. The shaman shook himself, like

a dog ridding water. "Too skilled, master. Not so strong as the last two, but very skilled. And much *haltija*. Much strength to that soul! More than the skill or power."

Jagiellon nodded. "Then we will work through intermediaries. There are powers in the shadow-world that are mighty—at least within their geographical area. And we can misdirect. He must be watched. Watched from a distance."

"Yes, master." The shaman bowed. "I have two watchers at my call. Birds can see a great distance."

"They are not magical creatures?" asked Jagiellon. "He will be aware of magical watchers."

The shaman flicked his fingers against the drum, scowling and muttering. The skin began to knit itself. As soon as it was entire, he began to drum a steady, demanding beat. Count Mindaug could see his lips moving, but despite listening intently he could not make out the words.

Two birds battered at the window. Jagiellon motioned to the Count to open it. The Count pulled open the window and then had to duck as two enormous goshawks streaked past his head to land on the shaman's now outstretched arms. Beneath his reindeer-hide robe the shaman wore heavy leather vambraces of what could only be the thickest bullhide. And well he did so—those powerful talons would have pierced anything less right through.

Like most nobles, Mindaug had flown falcons. There was something wrong with these birds. Those eyes were red insanity. Goshawks were always a little mad, but these two . . .

It was said that a goshawk with a threatened nest would attack anything short of an elephant. Mindaug had the distinct impression that these two would not hesitate at the elephant, with or without a nest under threat. Most birds of prey killed only enough to feed on; goshawks and their kin sometimes went into killing frenzies if the opportunity presented itself. Mindaug sensed that this pair would create the opportunity if one didn't already exist.

"Feel them, master. Feel them with your power."

Jagiellon looked hard at the birds. "Hmm. It is there. But very, very light. Just a hold."

"Just their names, master. But I can see through their eyes."

Jagiellon turned to the count. "You served me well with this one, Mindaug. I am pleased."

The Count bowed, his fingernails digging into his palms. The shaman was a very valuable tool to give up to his master. But the Count had one thing that the Grand Duke did not have.

He had the shaman's own name of power.

Mindaug wasn't too sure how he'd use that, yet. But treachery was, after all, the core value of his world. His researches into magical creatures had stretched a wide net away from the Polish-Lithuanian power base that was his master's realm. He'd looked far, far back. What he'd found was this old one. The shaman was not entirely human any more himself.

But then, in the Ionian islands was something far, far older; quiescent, but far from dead. Jagiellon knew it had been a powerful place once, but actually he knew very little that was verifiable about the island once referred to as Nausicaa, an island which was settled before Etruscans came to the Venetian lagoon. Mindaug wondered if this was, at long last, the moment that the Grand Duke had overreached himself.

Chapter 4

It was bitterly cold down here in the water chapel below St. Raphaella. Marco felt it, even through the thick coat and fur collar. Brother Mascoli still wore his simple light-colored habit. The fringe of gray hair about his ears was, if anything, thinner than it had been when Marco first met him. Old people were usually touched more by the cold than the young, but the priest's faith seemed to keep him warm.

Warmer than Marco, anyway. He shivered.

"You are afraid, Marco," said the Hypatian Sibling gently. "Don't be. God's will is God's will."

"I know. But I still question the rightness of what I am doing. I do it for someone I love especially and dearly. This is not just a deed done out of love for my fellow man, or to serve a greater cause." Marco shook his head. "Kat and her grandfather must have been praying for the return of her father for years, and if it is God's will that he not return, so be it. All I want to do is find out where he is. If at least they *knew* what had happened to him, and where he is—or was—it might give them . . . not comfort, exactly, but . . ."

He groped after the concept that he wanted, but he might have known that a Sibling would know very well what he was getting at.

"I understand," Brother Mascoli said, soothingly. "Remember, Marco, there is nothing *un*Christian about asking creatures that are not human for their help, just as it is not unChristian to help them when they come to us for healing." He smiled. "Of course, no evil creature would ever approach us for help; their very natures would prevent them coming anywhere near here. And since you helped to heal one undine, all of the unhuman creatures are kindly inclined to you."

Mascoli put a hand on Marco's shoulder. "If a stranger had asked this of you, you would have tried?"

Marco nodded.

Mascoli smiled. "It is not right to deny the same help to those one loves dearly. That, too, would be a sin. He who judges these things knows the intents of the innermost heart, and He is not fooled by the shallow and their pretences. In the presence of men it may sometimes be wise not to show favor to an especially loved one. In the presence of God . . . well, He knows already. And since He is Love incarnate, He will always look kindly upon a deed done out of unselfish love."

It didn't seem quite so cold down here any more. Marco took a deep breath, and began to ask the blessing of the four great archangels.

The warded corners glowed. Heaven would forfend any attempt to venture evil here. Remembering Brother Mascoli's instructions, he intoned, *In nomine Patri, et Filii, et Spiritus Sancti, fiat pace.*

Standing now within the veil of light lying weightlessly on the chapel walls, Marco dipped the wine cup into the cold, murky canal water. Discipline and concentration were called for, here. Marco held the wine cup until the water was mirror-still.

He began scrying, building up an image in his mind, calling by their true names, the triton Androcles and his mate Althea.

The images and response came quickly. *Wait. We come.*

An image of winter waves curling and foam-lines danced across the wine cup . . .

And a brief moment of a circular suckerlike mouth full of long needle-sharp teeth. And a terrible roaring.

The wards flared to an incandescent brightness, briefly, and there was a sense that *something* had impacted against them. Hard.

The tall candles were now merely burning wicks in a dripping pool of wax.

Marco nearly dropped the wine cup. He turned to Brother Mascoli. "What happened?" he asked, afraid and angry at the same time. "What was *that*?"

The Hypatian Sibling was already kneeling, ignoring the fact that the stones were wet. "Join me," he said hastily. "We need to strengthen the wards. *Now.*"

One thing Marco had learned: when a magician said "now" in *that* tone of voice, it was no time to ask questions.

"What happened? Are Androcles and Althea all right?" Marco asked as soon as Brother Mascoli had finished leading the invocation. Marco's heart was in his mouth.

"Describe exactly what you saw," the Sibling said, his usual calm considerably thinner.

Marco did.

Brother Mascoli nodded. "Yes." He let out a gusty sigh. "In my opinion, your merfolk are probably all right. In fact, they're probably completely unaware that anything happened. *They* were not the target of what you encountered."

He blinked. "They weren't?"

Brother Mascoli shook his head, and looked very grave indeed. "It is clear to me, Marco, that we need to work on your focus, and your defenses. You are very vulnerable when you are scrying like that, and I fear that this time only your bond with the Lion saved you. Part of you was outside the wards—and your ability stretches the window of vision. It is rare that one person can do that sort of scrying alone and unaided. As a consequence, you can see much more than, say, I can. Unfortunately, it also means you are then visible to anything lurking, waiting for the sign of your magic. You are at your most vulnerable under such circumstances."

"And something attacked me."

The information that he, and not the merfolk, had been the object of an attack made him feel a moment of relief. At least he had not been the cause of two innocents getting in harm's way.

Brother Mascoli made the sign of the cross. "Something is definitely out there," he said quietly. "Something that dares not venture within the ancient boundaries of our current Venice, but knows what Marco Valdosta's mage-work feels like. Something that is so evil that the wards were called on to guard your very soul."

Marco's relief evaporated, and he felt as if he had been doused in iced water. And now that he came to think about it . . .

There'd been something very recognizable about that image, a feeling that he'd met it when they'd fought Chernobog's minions. He could almost *taste* the magic, foul beyond measure and polluted, yet with an edge of seductive sweetness—seductive, at least, if you were not aware that it was the sweetness of corruption.

"But . . . I thought the Lion had defeated the evil that attacked Venice?" he whispered.

Brother Mascoli was the gentlest and kindest of all the men that Marco knew. Right now he did not look gentle. "We have won *a* battle," he said quietly, sighing. "A battle, not the war. We need to go on being vigilant. And we need to remember that in this war it is love and care that are our weapons, as much as swords or magics. Our foe can match us sword for sword, magic for magic. But love and care are ours and ours alone. Our enemy cannot give those. They would destroy him if he tried."

It was Marco's turn to sigh; he had given so much already, and now that things were settling down for him, he had hoped for a respite. "I'm just so sick of fighting. I thought . . . I thought we could give peace a try."

The Sibling shook his head. "I am not a man of arms. But it is no use simply calling for peace when our foe takes our desire for it to be an opportunity to conquer brutally without meeting any resistance. We need swords, aye, and magic, beside the love and care. You and I and the Hypatian Order want to serve the latter. But we need the former, also. We need to support them."

The still canal water, greenish in the pale light, was

suddenly ringed. The mermaid and the triton popped up.

The triton's voice boomed in the brick-walled water-chapel. "Greetings, Mage Marco. We had a sudden squall there. Very strange."

"You are unhurt?"

Marco's anxiety plainly struck the two of them as very funny. "Storms are to us what a fresh breeze is to you humans," said Androcles.

"That was no natural squall," said Brother Mascoli, quietly. "Marco is right to be anxious about you. That was caused by some magic."

"Weather magic is hard and expensive on the user," said Althea, her mercurial expression going from mischievous to somber in an instant.

Mascoli looked grim. "The squall was little more than an accidental slap of some great force's tail. Be careful, beloved ones. It was magic of the blackest, and powerful."

The two looked doubtful, and their tails beat the water behind them, in slow, measured waves of their fins. "Well," said the triton Androcles, "it wasn't trying to stop us reaching you with the news you asked us for, Marco. The truth is: We have next to none. If this friend's father is dead . . . he lies on land. But we will widen our search, and there are friends of fresh water, like the undines, that we can call upon the wide world over."

The mermaid, whose aquamarine eyes sparkled with mischief again, had wrapped her long, wet blond hair several times around her upper torso, creating an effective "garment" to cover her unclothed breasts. Her companion, the triton, blond-bearded and long-haired, looked exactly like the creatures that adorned the borders of tapestries and the basins of fountains all over Venice. Like the mermaid he had a fish's tail; unlike her, he also had a fish's dorsal fin adorning his backbone.

"Faugh! Magus Marco, how you humans can live among such filthy waters I cannot imagine!" The triton somehow managed to grin and grimace at the same time.

"Because we aren't very bright?" Marco replied, cautiously. That seemed to be the correct answer, for Althea joined in the triton's chuckles.

"Well, I cannot fault you overmuch for doing what we ourselves do," Androcles admitted. "You know, I have a friend Antonio, a netman. He drinks nothing but *grappa* and I asked him why he rotted his gut with the stuff. And do you know what he said?"

Marco shook his head.

"He said: 'What am I to drink? *Water?* After what *you* people and every fish in the sea *do* in it?'" The triton roared with laughter, which echoed in the brick-walled water-chapel and drowned out every other sound.

"If he is there, in the sea, we will find him eventually," said the mermaid, smiling with confidence. Her teeth, unlike those of undines, were white, pearly, and exactly like human teeth. Althea was very pretty indeed; Marco wondered idly if at some point his artist-friend Rafael de Tomaso would be interested in having her pose for him.

"We can follow the source of a single drop of blood in the water for leagues; it will take time, a year perhaps, but we will find him. And when we do find him? What would you have us do?"

Marco thought about the horror of Kat being presented with a body half-eaten by fish and crabs, or a skeleton—but then thought of the value of having *something* to weep over, *something* to bury, even if it wasn't much.

"Please," he said. "Can you bring him home?"

"We will, if he lies under the sea," the triton promised. Then, with a flick of tails, they were gone.

After they'd left, Marco and Brother Mascoli found themselves standing and gazing into the water. Marco wasn't certain what to think; perhaps at some level he had been so certain that Kat's father was dead and drowned that he had anticipated a quick answer to the question he had posed to the merfolk some weeks earlier.

At length Mascoli shook himself. "Come, Marco. Let us go upstairs and get a little warmer. No news is good news, I suppose."

Marco shook his head slowly. "It may be. But he could be dead on land. Or he could be a prisoner somewhere, or ill, or somehow lost his memory. It's the not knowing that is so terrible for Kat."

"Well, perhaps. But where there is life there is also hope, young man." Brother Mascoli seemed to regain his calm; he took Marco by the elbow and led him upstairs. "And I must find someone who is more skilled in combative magic to instruct you in how to ward yourself. It is a shame that Eneko Lopez is not still here in Venice. He is a harsh man, but he is on his way to becoming one of the greatest of Christian mages."

Brother Mascoli smiled wryly. "He has a belief in shared strength. That the brethren of Christ should unite, giving the powers of light a strength as of an army—while evil power stands as a tower alone, relying only on itself. Yet many of the Strega rituals are those of a bonding of power, so perhaps Father Lopez is mistaken in his ideas."

Marco pursed his lips. Sharing himself with the Lion had broadened his outlook somewhat from the one which he'd held once. "Maybe the Strega are not evil."

Mascoli laughed softly. "I might believe you. And truly, that is the opinion of most Hypatians. But you should always keep in mind when dealing with him that Eneko Lopez is not always as flexible in his ideas."

Chapter 5

Looking out from the palace on the summit of the terraced plateau of Buda, Emeric could see all the way to the Danube. He preferred the nearer view, however. Just outside the palace he had two new pole-ornaments. The one on the left writhed slightly; the chill air of late autumn had the interesting property of prolonging the futile struggle for life—in high summer heat and winter's cold his ornaments had a tendency to expire much too quickly.

The King of Hungary would not tolerate nationalism, or too much in the way of religious fervor. His kingdom's people were a mixture of Slovenes, Croats, Slavs, Magyar, Slovaks, Walachs and a half a dozen other minorities, not to mention several different religions. That didn't matter. They were, first and foremost, *his*. Impalement of those who sought to undermine that, in the interest of their insular little people, was an effective message.

His kingdom stretched from the edge of Istria to the Carpathians. Now he wanted the southern Balkans. To the west, was the Holy Roman Empire. To the east, the Ilkhan Mongols. To the north, the Grand Duke of Lithuania. Only the south offered softness, but unfortunately there were the hill-tribes between him and the Byzantines.

He wished that one of those pole-ornaments could be the infamous Iskander Beg. The Illyrian would pay that price one of these days, if Emeric could winkle him out of those mountains. The Hungarian heavy cavalry were at a disadvantage there, in the broken, steep country. Emeric hated the mountains. If he could flatten all the damned mountains in the world he could ride all of his enemies down, from the Holy Roman Emperor to the Grand Duke.

And now those idiots in Constantinople were going to give him his target on a platter; help him to bypass Iskander Beg and his hill-tribes. He smiled grimly, sat back on the golden throne, amid the tapestry-hung splendor of his reception room—he loved this display of wealth and grandeur—and let his eyes linger on the two victims outside the huge mullioned windows.

That view might unbalance the greasy Byzantine.

The servant was still waiting for orders, too used to his master's little ways to turn so much as a hair at the display outside the windows. Emeric raised a finger, and the servant snapped to attention. "Send the Byzantine emissary, Count Dimetos, up to me. Those accompanying him, also."

The servant bowed, and whisked himself out the door.

The Byzantine had been left to kick his heels for several hours. That did no harm, but little good either. He'd be used to that. Emissaries were often left in cold or overheated antechambers for hours, or even days at a time. A couple of would-be traitors on display on the top of sharpened poles would be somewhat more effective at impressing him.

"Count Dimetos, Imperial Emissary of Alexius VI," announced the majordomo from the arched doorway, "and his advisors."

Normally, Emeric discarded the hangers-on to any supplicant who came to seek a royal audience. They tended to bolster the confidence of the supplicant, an undesirable state of affairs. But the Byzantine Count had been nearly imperturbable last time, and very hard to read. Perhaps Emeric would get more from the escort's expressions.

They filed in. The effects of seeing the impaled men just outside of the windows were most satisfactory. On three of the five, anyway. Count Dimetos calmly looked away. The fifth man, the blond one—unusual, that hair color, in a Byzantine—didn't even blink or give the dying men a second glance. He bowed, along with the Count. Two of the others forgot to bow and had to be prodded to it.

Emeric's curiosity and caution were aroused immediately by the indifferent one. There was something very odd about that blond man. It made Emeric suspicious.

But he had no intention of revealing anything. Instead, Emeric nodded slightly, barely acknowledging the respectful bows.

"Well. Count Dimetos, you have taken some time to get back to me."

The emissary held out his palms. "My apologies, King Emeric. Travel is slow at this time of year. But for a few small details, about which I am sure we can reach a speedy agreement, I bring happy news."

Emeric was careful to look unimpressed. "I'm not some Turkish-bazaar merchant, Count. I do not bargain."

Actually, Emeric *was* impressed. The counterdemands he'd made a few months earlier when the Byzantines had first approached him with an offer for a secret alliance against Venice had been extreme:

Forty galleys, full crews, thirty carracks capable of carrying at least two hundred men each, and five hundred thousand ducats to cover the cost of the campaign. *And* Zante and Crete. Nothing less, and all that in exchange for simply seizing Corfu from the Venetians—which the Hungarians would keep, not the Greeks—so that the Byzantine Empire could finally be rid of the untaxed and commercially aggressive Venetian enclave in Constantinople.

To call it an "equal exchange" would be like calling an elephant a mouse. Yet, to Emeric's surprise, the Byzantines were apparently willing to settle on his terms.

It all seemed opportune, much too opportune. If Alexius came up with the money, Emeric would know that it was indeed too good to be true. There was only one place Alexius could still raise that kind of money: by making a secret alliance with Lithuania.

Emeric suppressed a vicious smile. If Grand Duke Jagiellon wanted to give him money and ships to do exactly what he had already intended to do, so be it. Emeric couldn't see Jagiellon's exact plan yet, but his target was plainly the Venetian Republic. That was also fine. Emeric wanted Venice and its holdings, too, eventually, but he would take things one step at a time. Corfu, first. That would cripple the Venetians and allow him to turn on the Byzantines. Before that weak fool Alexius knew what was happening, Emeric would have Negroponte, and then . . .

The hell with merely holding the Golden Horn as the Venetians did. Constantinople itself would do. And Alexius himself—Jagiellon also, it seemed—would provide him with the wherewithal to do so.

Now he did smile, but pleasantly, and his voice was smooth and urbane. "However, please continue, Count Dimetos. I do not object to some small adjustment of the terms. Not necessarily."

"Just details to be arranged, not really adjustments," said the emissary, fluttering his hands. "The agreement we spoke of the last time was not entirely complete."

He's nervous, thought Emeric, incredulously. *The Greek is* nervous.

What did it take to make someone like Dimetos nervous? Dimetos's quick flicker of a glance at the expressionless blond man answered that question.

Emeric leaned forward. "Introduce me to your companions, Count."

The Count bowed. He indicated the tallest man of his party. "Your Majesty, this is Admiral Lord Nikomos of Volos. He is our naval expert. This is General Alexiou. He is, as you might gather, a military man. Mavilis here has come to support me with any financial . . . details."

Emeric raised his eyebrows. "That is one detail about which there will be no discussion." He pointed to the blond man, who looked back at him with dead eyes. "And who is this?"

"Ah . . . An advisor to the emperor," the emissary stated uncomfortably. *Decidedly* uncomfortably. "Milord Aldanto, is his name."

Emeric nodded with feigned disinterest, and yawned, his voice at variance to the curiosity sparked by Dimetos's reaction. "An Italian name. Interesting. Where are you from, Aldanto?

"Milano." There was a toneless quality to the voice that matched the man's stony expression. Toneless? *Rather say, lifeless.*

Emeric simply raised his eyebrows again, and turned back to the emissary. "Well, Count. Perhaps you should explain these little details that you believe require—what did you call it?—'completion,' I believe."

There was a slight beading of sweat on the Count's face. "Well. The galleys—"

The admiral interrupted. "We just don't have that many ships to spare, King Emeric. It would leave us with too few for—"

"If I had wished you to speak, Admiral, I would have told you so," Emeric said curtly. "I need those vessels. Mine are not a seagoing people. I have enlisted what I can, but we are talking of blockades, escorts and transports. I can move men overland as far as the mouth of the Narenta. The rest will have to be achieved by sea. If you don't provide those transports, then the assault is a waste of time. The Narenta pirates have been brought into my fold for this task. Backed up by the galleys of Byzantium, you should be able to deal with any Venetian vessels. Provided we time this right, that's the key."

He studied the pole ornaments for a moment. The one on the left had now apparently died also. Pity. Emeric had hoped, idly, that he wouldn't be too preoccupied to observe the last moments.

"We must allow the Eastern and Western convoys to pass," he continued, looking back at the Byzantine envoys. "The commander of the Corfu garrison will send a request for replacement stores by coaster afterward. At that point we attack. If we fail to take the fortress and the island, we will have some months to lay siege before the Venetian ships can return."

"The emperor Alexius has arranged that neither fleet will be returning," said the blond-haired man expressionlessly.

Emeric had not asked for *him* to speak, either, but he let that pass. Instead, he snorted. "The last time that was tried it failed."

"This time it will not fail." The man made that statement with the same certainty with which he might have said, *The sun will rise tomorrow*. Which was . . . also interesting.

Emeric shook his head. "I don't gamble on my campaigns. Certainly not based on empty promises." His tone made clear his opinion of the spendthrift and debauched young Alexius.

"We do not make empty promises." There was such a cold certainty in that voice! Who *was* this fellow, that he could make such pledges on behalf of Alexius?

Emeric dismissed that with a wave. "We will calculate as if you are not that sure. First, let us settle the important question: money."

An unpleasant conviction was growing in his mind about this blond man. He would have to check with the Countess Elizabeth Bartholdy, his principal advisor in magical matters. Despite his reputation, fiercely cultivated, Emeric was little more than a hedge-wizard compared to her.

He was now almost sure that the money was coming from Jagiellon. That did not worry him. Money was not a potential threat, nor a potential spy. Gold had no loyalty, and was never a traitor or an assassin.

What he hadn't expected, and didn't like at all, was dealing with Jagiellon almost face-to-face, as it were. He suspected the blond man was little more than a talking puppet. The name Aldanto rang a bell. He would have to investigate the matter further. Emeric didn't want this—*thing*—in his kingdom for one moment longer, if it was what he thought it was. Talking puppets could become doorways.

"The emperor wants to negotiate-er-payment in tranches," the little money-man stuttered. "P-part as and when the work is f-finished. So to speak."

Emeric shook his head. Alexius thought he had best put a brake on the Hungarian advance, did he? Withhold the money if the Hungarians moved into Epirus . . .

Ha! "No. I can't see the vessels up front. So I'll see the money. Otherwise I might find myself caught like a rat in a trap, without your ships."

"But . . ."

The blond man interrupted. "You will have the money within the month."

Emeric's eyes narrowed. He was fairly certain now he was right. So this was the face of the enemy across the northern Carpathians.

Odd, in a way. He knew this kind of possession was possible, but it took demonic power. And that demonic power too often ended up devouring the user. Emeric himself dealt with a power below . . .

But very, very cautiously. Well, he would need magicians for this project anyway. He would consult with Elizabeth; she had a long memory, and longer experience. She even frightened him a little. How could a woman that old look as if she were barely twenty?

She was truly beautiful, too, with the sort of allure that literally held men enthralled. And she used that beauty like the weapon that it was; ruthlessly and accurately. It was, fortunately for Emeric, the kind of beauty that he could close his mind to.

In the craggy and cliff-hung little valleys on the north end of the enchanted island, the night-wind was full of the clatter-clatter of little goaty feet on the limestone and the hollow trilling of reed pipes. The shepherd huddled down under his sheepskins in his little lean-to. It was a full moon out there. This was when all good men stayed indoors.

Kallikazori still walked on the high, barren hillsides on these holy nights. And a man might turn over to find his wife was not beside him. If he was a wise man, he went back to sleep and said nothing at all about it to her in the morning. If he was a fool, he might beat her for being half-asleep the next day. But a man who wanted children, fertile fields and fertile flocks would keep his tongue and hands still. A wise man knew that here on Corfu, the old ones still walked and still wielded their powers.

A wiser man stilled his mind to the fact, prayed to the saints, and pretended he saw and heard nothing.

The wisest of all . . .

The wisest of all found a way to pray to the saints by day—and something else by night. After all, the Holy Word said, *Thou shalt not have other gods* before *Me.* It said nothing at all about having other gods in reserve.

PART II
Winter, 1538 A.D.

Chapter 6

Eberhard of Brunswick waited patiently in the antechamber. He looked upwards and across toward the tall, narrow windows of the throne room, and then back at the empty throne. Weak winter sunlight patterned down through the windows and onto the mosaic-tiled floor of the throne room. The mosaic, a religious scene showing Christ feeding the multitudes, had been commissioned by the present Emperor's father, at tremendous expense. Personally, Eberhard thought the byzantine splendor did not fit well with the Gothic style of Mainz. The workers had been recruited—also at great expense—by the Venetians, all the way from Constantinople. Charles Fredrik's father, nearing the end of his life, had been convinced that the pious work would help to ease his path to heaven.

If God had the taste of a Byzantine, maybe it had. Eberhard grimaced. He had been close to the old Emperor. If Emperor Walther had lived to see the work finished, Eberhard had a feeling that the old flagstones might just have been put down again, on top of the mosaic.

He sighed. Charles Fredrik would be here, no doubt, shortly. In the meanwhile it would have been nice to have something other than these damn tiles to look at. It was damnably cold for an old man. He paced, to warm himself and distract his attention from the mosaic.

When Charles Fredrik finally arrived, with his aide Baron Trolliger, Eberhard of Brunswick began to wonder if he would be arranging for more Byzantine craftsmen to smooth this Emperor's path to heaven. Charles Fredrik looked tired. He looked more than tired: he looked worn. And he looked worried.

Still, his expression lightened when he saw Eberhard. He raised the old counselor up. "I see they have not even brought you a glass of wine to fight off the chill." He shook his head disapprovingly and gestured to one of the footmen. "Hippocras, for my Lord of Brunswick, and for us."

A few minutes later the three of them were seated in a small, warm side-parlor. An apple-wood fire burned merrily in the grate. That, and a goblet of rich, spiced hippocras had helped fight off Eberhard's chill and had lightened the Emperor's expression, even given some color to his cheeks. Charles Fredrik still looked twenty years older and much closer to the grave than he should. Eberhard knew that the wounds he had received in a youthful campaign still troubled one of the Emperor's lungs. Winters were always hard for him.

"Still no news from my nephew Manfred," said Charles Fredrik heavily.

"The roads and passes are snowed closed," said Baron Trolliger. "There is no reason to get too worried, Your Majesty. The Norse are honorable about their oaths."

Charles Fredrik shook his head. "I trust those petty pagan kinglets not at all, the so-called Christian ones not much more. I've sent a messenger through to Francesca in Copenhagen."

Baron Trolliger touched his head. "That woman . . ."

"Has secured us more cooperation with the Danes in two months than you did in five years, Hans Trolliger," said Charles Fredrik, almost snapping the words. "If I had twenty more like her, I could afford to die without worrying about the succession. As it is—well, at least Hakkonsen is with Manfred. Between Erik and Mam'zelle de Chevreuse, they keep one of my heirs on a reasonably even keel."

Baron Trolliger nearly choked. "That affair in Venice nearly had him killed! I still say we should have hanged every last one of those damned Servants of the Trinity."

Charles Fredrik smiled grimly. "If we'd hanged as much as one, the entire Pauline church would have been in an uproar. Instead *they've* excommunicated a few obvious bad eggs and we must put up with and isolate the rest. As for Francesca and Erik, I still say they kept Manfred on a reasonably even keel in very dangerous waters. Without either of them, he would have definitely been killed. Erik has made a warrior out of him, and Francesca has done even more. She's made him think. She might have led him by his testicles to that point, but she actually made him *think*. To my certain knowledge, that's something no one else ever succeeded at doing. The Venetian affair has done a great deal for one of my heirs. Besides, I enjoyed my visit to Venice and to Rome, even if you didn't, Hans."

Baron Trolliger looked as if he might choke. "The visit was bad enough. The months you made me stay there afterward . . ."

Eberhard of Brunswick chuckled. "Well, Your Majesty, at least Prince Conrad hasn't caused you as much trouble, even if he hasn't provided you with as much entertainment. What is Manfred doing in Norway, anyway? Winter in Scandinavia is not something I'd ever want go through again. I did it with your father in Småland back in '22, when we went in to bail the Danes out. Far as I was concerned, the pagans deserved the place."

To an extent, Charles Fredrik agreed with his advisor, though it was hardly politic to say so.

"In winter, it can be bleak. Nice enough in summer," said the Emperor, mildly. Eberhard of Brunswick had been one of his father's closest friends and the old *Ritter* was now one of Charles Fredrik's most trusted emissaries. He'd spent the better part of the last year in Ireland, with the Celtic Ard Ri, representing the States General and the Holy Roman Emperor to the League of Armagh.

Now he was home. Charles Fredrik knew the old man had delighted in the thought of seeing his grandchildren again. The *Ritter* had dropped some hints in his correspondence that he'd like to retire to his estates.

The Emperor bit his lip. The old man deserved retirement, had more than earned it, but men of his caliber were rare. Very rare. In point of fact, there was no one skilled and canny enough to replace him.

He'd have to send the silver-haired warrior out again. But not somewhere cold and wet this time; that was the least he could do.

"It's still part and parcel of the same business, Eberhard. Well, the aftermath of it. The Danes are content to hold the coastal lands, but the chapters of Knights of the Holy Trinity that my father established there after the '22 campaign are still pushing deeper into pagan lands. They stir things up, and the pagan tribes tend to take it out on the Danish settlers. The Knights are building little empires out there. At this point, they're a law unto themselves."

Eberhard snorted. "Rein them in, Emperor. Rein them in hard. We need the coast to keep the pagan bastards from raiding our shipping on the Baltic, but the hinterland . . . not worth the price in blood the Empire will pay for some bar-sinister *Ritter* to get himself an estate."

The Emperor nodded. "That's what Manfred had gone to do. Last I heard it was in hand, but then this business in Norway cropped up, and he went off to sort that out. We haven't heard from him in over a month."

"It is near midwinter, Your Majesty," pointed out Baron Trolliger.

"I know. That treaty is supposed to be ratified on midwinter's eve. He'd have sent me word . . ."

The Emperor rubbed his eyes, tiredly. "I know, Hans, the passes in Norway are closed. But I've had the Servants of the Trinity try to contact him by magical means, also. Nothing."

To Eberhard, he said in explanation: "He's gone to Telemark. One of those little kingdoms on the Norwegian side of the Skagerrak. Dirt poor, rotten with raiders and pirates because the land can't feed all of them. We concluded a treaty with King Olaf two years ago. He's dead, and his son Vortenbras has taken the throne, and so the treaty needs to be ratified again. Since Vortenbras is pagan, the oath must be sworn in the temple on Odin's ring at the midwinter festival. Only the ring's been stolen. Manfred and Erik and two of our best diviners have gone to see if they can find it. No word from them. All I can find out is that it's snowing heavily in the north."

The old *Ritter* looked as if even the thought of a trip into snowy Scandinavia was enough to make him break out in chilblains. Nevertheless, he said calmly, "Do you want me to go, Your Majesty?"

The Emperor leaned over and patted the age-spotted, sinewy hand. "No. I've sent a message to a woman who will see to it. The same Francesca de Chevreuse of whom"—here he gave Trolliger a sly glance—"Hans disapproves. But no matter what Hans thinks of her capability, I have confidence in her over any other possible agent in this case."

Trolliger shuddered. "She's capable enough. Her methods . . ."

"Work," said the Emperor. "Even you find her attractive, Hans. Men will tell an attractive, intelligent woman things they won't tell us; they'll *do* things for her they would not consider doing for us for any amount of money. They'll go to great lengths to help her."

"They reduce us to the level of Aquitaine, Your Majesty," said the baron, sulkily.

The Emperor pulled a wry face. "Which is why our officials fail so dismally when we have to deal with the Aquitaine. I'm almost tempted to send you to Francesca for lessons, Hans."

Charles Fredrik saw the look of trepidation on the old *Ritter*'s face. He smiled reassuringly at the older man. "Not you, Eberhard. You would enjoy her intellect and company, though, I can assure you of that. Baron Trolliger here finds her physically threatening—or her breasts, anyway. He fears they will cast a fascination over him and, like Samson, leave him helpless to resist the lady's whims."

Eberhard of Brunswick shook his head. "It is not the company of an intelligent woman that I fear, Your Majesty. It is rather that I am concerned that you'll send me to Aquitaine. I was hoping to spend some time in Swabia with my family." He touched his silver hair. "I'm not getting any younger, Your Majesty. Especially for Aquitaine, you need younger men. "

The Emperor gave a small snort of wry laughter. "The last thing I need in Aquitaine is *younger* men, Eberhard. But relax, I am not going to send you there. However, I'm afraid I can't let you go home to pasture either. Men like you are too few on the ground. The Holy Roman Empire still needs you. *I* still need you."

The older *Ritter* shrugged. "Well, I just hope it's somewhere warm this time, Your Majesty. This winter seems colder than last winter. Or maybe I'm just older. At least Mainz is not as damp as Ireland was."

Charles Fredrik allowed the corners of his mouth to ease into a smile. "Would the Holy Land be warm enough and dry enough for you?"

"A pilgrimage for my soul has always been one my desires," said the old *Ritter* quietly. Eberhard of Brunswick was one of the best and most reliable of officials in the States General. He was an adept politician and diplomat, but at the core, he was a pious man. His soul might need cleansing of what he'd done for the Empire, but not for himself, Charles Fredrik knew.

"It's more for my soul than yours, old friend," the Emperor said equally quietly. "I don't know how many more of these winters I can take, either." He smiled wryly. "No mosaics this time though, Eberhard. Perhaps some churches in places that need them. I haven't lived your life and I have a feeling I'll need a good many prayers to get me away from hellfire, as well as a pilgrimage to Jerusalem. But I can't go; you will have to go for me."

He lifted a heavy eyebrow. "Of course there are some small tasks you can do for the Holy Roman Empire while you're there. And along the way."

Eberhard nodded. He understood politics thoroughly enough to know precisely whom, in that part of the world, a "small task" might be directed towards. "The Ilkhan?"

Charles Fredrik nodded. "We've had tentative feelers from them. Baron Trolliger had a long discussion with a visiting Jew from Damascus, during the months he remained behind in Italy. The man was there strictly on family business, of course, but—as they often do—the

Mongols were using the Jewish merchant as an informal emissary."

The Ilkhan Mongol Empire stretched from Egypt to the Black Sea and no one really knew just how far into the Asian hinterland. The Ilkhan were themselves pagan, but had no qualms about their subject peoples worshiping gods of their choice. Christians, Muslims, Jews—many religions—all prospered in the Mongol realm. They enforced a degree of tolerance that the fiery Christian Metropolitan of Alexandria might find irksome, but it did make things peaceful in their dominions.

Eberhard's eyes narrowed. "They won't like that in Alexandria."

The Emperor shrugged. "Politics and war make for strange bedfellows, Eberhard. And it all comes down to Grand Duke Jagiellon trying to flank me, or force me to fight on two fronts, and the Holy Roman Empire trying to flank him. The Grand Duke is building up quite a fleet in Odessa. Then, too, there's this: The news Hans brings back from his long stay in Italy leaves me concerned that the Hungarians are up to no good, either."

The *Ritter* nodded. "The Ilkhan could at least bottle them up in the Black Sea. But surely Emperor Alexius VI can do that just as well from Constantinople?"

Baron Trolliger coughed. "We have a treaty with him, yes. But we've had word that a few ships—which are definitely *not* from Odessa—have been discharging visitors, who have gone on to visit the Imperial palace."

The old *Ritter* nodded slowly. "I see. That would indeed leave our flank wide open. Very well, Your Majesty, when do I leave?"

"Not until spring, Eberhard," said the Emperor. "Even if you left today, getting passage to Acre or Ascalon before spring would be impossible. You can have a few winter months to spend cooped up with your grandchildren. By the time spring comes, even the muddy road will probably look appealing."

Eberhard smiled. "There is some merit in what you say, Your Majesty. The last time I was home my daughter's youngest was teething. Yes, by spring it may even be good to be on the road without children."

Charles Fredrik coughed. "Well. Not strictly without. He's a bit old to be called a child, these days. But he is one of my heirs."

A look of horror came across the old statesman's face. "Not Manfred? Sire, I'm an old man!"

The Emperor nodded, ruefully. "It's a symbol of great trust, Eberhard of Brunswick. I am feeling my age, and my wound troubles me. I may not survive another winter and such a trip will take the boy a long way from the intriguers of court. If I die, the succession must be a simple matter of Conrad being the only candidate at hand. Not that I have the least fears about Manfred wanting the throne, but that has never stopped factions in the past. On the other hand, if by any evil chance Conrad and I are killed—as happened to the Emperor Maximilian and his son—I want Manfred safe and ready, where no one can get to him easily. Besides, you're the leading statesman of my Empire. I want him to learn from you. If there is time I'll send the boy to Ferrara to Duke Enrico Dell'este to see if he can learn strategy and tactics from the Old Fox, but statecraft needs to come first. And you'll find he's improved a great deal. Circumstances, Erik and Francesca have made him grow up a great deal."

But all the old man said was "Manfred!" with a face full of woe.

The messenger bearing dispatches from the Emperor to Francesca de Chevreuse only took ten days, and that was by spending imperial gold like water. A brief thaw and then a vicious freeze had made the roads full of iron-hard ridges and ruts . . . which was still better than fetlock-deep mud.

Francesca looked at the imperial seal—and the scrawl. Well, the Imperial tutors probably hadn't beaten him for untidiness.

She grimaced. One had to wonder what vagaries of imperial policy had stemmed from some terrified official doing his best to interpret this handwriting. It really was difficult. Looking carefully, though, she could see that was in part due to a definite tremor in the hand of the writer. Perhaps the rumors about the Emperor's health had some substance after all.

Francesca looked out over Copenhagen and the Sound. The water was gray, bleak, wind-chopped. She'd been out earlier, wearing her beautiful sable coat and muff. Her new venture into vertical diplomacy instead of the horizontal kind still required appearances. Even though, as the prince's leman, she was strictly off-limits, men could be just as foolish when flirting as they could in bed. More so, sometimes; in bed, they weren't trying to impress a woman with their brains.

So she needed to look as good, if not more so, than she had as one of the most sought-after courtesans in Venice. That, alas, meant keeping up with her rigorous exercise regime. The air had been biting cold and full of the dusty smell of coming snow.

Just the time for a little venture into the Norse wilderness. Ah, well. What the Emperor wanted . . .

The Emperor would get. Besides, she was a little worried herself about the lack of communication from Manfred.

She sat down at her writing desk and sharpened her quill. Then, in a hand that was both beautiful and legible, penned several letters. She shook the sand off them, and tinkled a delicate glass-and-silver bell. Poor little Heinrich could go out in the cold and deliver these.

Chapter 7

Winter in the Republic of Venice was not as bleak as winter in the Holy Roman Empire. It was still wet and cold, which made repair work a little more difficult than at other times.

This fact was relevant. The *Casa* Montescue was busy getting a facelift. True, the great house of Montescue was technically bankrupt twice over, but that was a good reason to do it now. "If we don't do it," said Lodovico Montescue calmly to his granddaughter Katerina, "everyone will think we are down to our last ducat."

Kat shook her head at him, smiling. "But Grandpapa, we *are* down to our last ducat!" She couldn't bring herself to be hugely worried about it. Come financial ruin or any other disaster, she had Marco. And it seemed, now that the feud between Valdosta and Montescue was finally healed, that Lodovico Montescue, once the *Colleganza*-genius of Venice, had found his verve once again.

He chucked her chin. "*Cara mia*, if we have the place looking too shabby, then we'll have our creditors on our necks. Watch. We start spending money, they'll back off. We've got political connections, even if not business. Something will turn up."

She shook her head and sighed at him, but without the despair that had plagued her, waking and sleeping, for so many years. "All that worries me is where the money to pay for this lot is going to come from."

"If need be, we'll borrow it," he said, making Kat raise her eyes. "But watch. Things will begin to right themselves." He stretched out his big, liver-spotted hands and looked at the slightly bulbous knuckles. "Marco has not come yet?"

"He said he'd be here by the terce bell." Kat felt the warmth of knowing this lift her.

"Good." Lodovico nodded his satisfaction. "I want him to work on these old hands again. I'll swear that boy of yours has magic in his fingers, never mind his skills as a doctor."

"He is going to be great physician!" said Kat defensively, trying very hard not to think about the *other* things that he was. Magician, for one. Vehicle for—something else—for another.

Lodovico chuckled. "I don't disagree with you, girl. I'm becoming very fond of the boy myself. How is the annulment of that marriage of his going?"

Kat made a face; this was the one shadow on her days, for she and Marco could not wed until he had been rid of the wife-in-name-only he had taken out of a misplaced sense of honor and obligation to his benefactor, his wife's brother Petro Dorma. "Slowly. That Angelina! One moment it's a nunnery, and becoming a saint . . ."

Lodovico snorted with laughter. "Saint Puttana. I'll believe all the girls in the House of the Red Cat turned Siblings first."

Kat grinned, in spite of herself. "You shouldn't use language like that in front of me, Grandpapa. Anyway, one minute she's all set on being a saint and a martyr. The next she's screaming at poor Petro that he wants to lock her away."

"And if you didn't hate her guts you might almost feel sorry for her," said her grandfather, still amused.

Kat shook her head at him. "She was, and is, a spoiled, selfish brat. And stupid on top of it. She got herself pregnant and got poor Marco to claim it was his to save her face, and *then* tried to run away with her lover anyway! And she's still trying to manipulate things in her own favor, no matter what that does to people around her. And yes, I sometimes hate her. But at least I haven't taken out an assassination contract on her head."

Lodovico acknowledged the hit with a wry smile. "I was wrong that time. And Marco and Benito lived through it. Besides, if she delays any more with this annulment I wouldn't bet on you not doing just the same."

They were in a small salon just off the front hall, and thus the pounding of the great Lion-headed knocker was easily audible.

Lodovico chuckled. "He's eager, this young man of yours. Early, too."

A faint frown creased Kat's brow. That was a very forceful knocking. She'd come down to wait for Marco often enough to know he used the knocker tentatively. Maybe . . . bad news. Or good news, finally, about the annulment of his marriage to Angelina. She hastened out into the hallway.

White-haired old Giuseppe had not announced the visitor, because he was gaping at the two of them. They were . . . enormous. They loomed over Giuseppe in the way that the Church of Saint Hypatia Hagia Sophia loomed over the square outside it. Giuseppe and Kat would have been terrified, had the two blond giants not looked like two very lost little boys, crushing fur hats in their hands, hoping for a welcome.

"Pardon," said one, in Italian so atrocious that only familiarity with Erik Hakkonsen's accent enabled Kat to understand him. "But is this the dwelling of the family Montescue?"

"It is," said Kat, blinking at him. It wasn't just the accents of these—boys?—that was outlandish. It was every inch of them, clad as they were in garments like nothing she had ever seen before. Oh, in part, they resembled some sort of Norselander or Icelander; Venice saw enough of those coming in and out of their ports. But not all their garments were fur and homespun woolen. They also rejoiced in leather leggings with fringes of a kind that no Icelander had ever boasted, and there were beads and feathers braided into their hair, which was shaven on the sides, but long everywhere else. And in sheaths at their sides, each of them wore a weapon that Kat recognized. Erik Hakkonsen favored that kind of little axe or hatchet—a *tomahawk*, it was called.

"Ah, good." The speaker's face cleared. "And is the clan chieftain here? Chief-Lodi-Ludo—"

"Blessed Jesu, boy, don't mangle my name further!" Lodovico growled, as he limped into the hallway. "I am Lodovico Montescue, of *Casa* Montescue. Who the devil are you?"

Both boys drew themselves up with immense dignity.

"Gulta and Bjarni Thordarson, at your service," the speaker said, and both bowed. "Sent we were, by Clan Thordarson, a trade alliance to make. From Vinland we come, for that purpose." A corded oiled-sailcloth bundle was at the man's feet, and he used the hatchet to slice open the flax cords binding it. It opened, spilling out fine woven cloth, dyed in rich hues. Not wool; something finer, Kat thought. The weaving was done in geometric patterns like nothing she had ever seen, and when the boy bent down and pulled up a corner and handed it to her, she stroked it. And the touch—

"Grandpapa!" she cried involuntarily. "It is as soft as silk, but silk made into wool!"

"It is alpaca," said the one who had not yet spoken, diffidently. "And this is cotton."

He bent and pulled out a snowy white piece and held it to her for her inspection. She touched it as well—cotton she knew. The Egyptian and Indian cloth was shockingly expensive, so much so that only the wealthy could afford the gauzes and cambrics made from it. This was certainly cotton.

"We have these, and other things. Furs, spices. We wish a trade alliance with Clan Montescue to make," the first boy said proudly. "Carlo had said—"

At first, Kat wasn't sure she heard him correctly. "Pardon—*who*?" she managed.

The boy knitted his brows in puzzlement. "You know him not? Carlo, of Clan Montescue? Is he not here? But he had said—"

And that was when all hell broke loose.

❖   ❖   ❖

Marco walked in at just that moment, which complicated matters further. Kat was weeping, Lodovico shaking the poor Vinlander boy in a way that would have made his teeth rattle had he not been as big as he was, and yelling at the top of his lungs, while the other boy looked utterly bewildered. Somehow Marco managed to separate Lodovico from his victim, get them all herded into a quiet room, and (relatively) calmed down.

With Marco's prompting—while Kat clung numbly to his hand—the boys managed to piece together part, at least, of what had happened to her father.

His vessel had been taken by pirates, who had, in turn, sold him to some strange Vinlander tribe in the south of the continent. He had escaped, or been rescued, by some other tribe—the boys were rather vague as to which, or how it had happened—and they in their turn had traded him up the coast until he came into the hands of the Thordarsons.

Now, they had had to pay a great deal for Carlo Montescue, and by their custom and law, he apparently discovered that he couldn't just find a ship and come home. No, he had to earn his freedom; until then, he was what they called a "thrall." Not exactly a slave, but certainly not free, and branded as such by the iron ring around his neck. The boys were very matter-of-fact about it, and although Kat could have wept even harder with vexation, the part of her that was a Venetian trader to the core could see their point.

At any rate, it soon was proved that Carlo was going to earn his freedom in record time, for exactly that reason. Records. Record-keeping and accounting, at which, apparently, the Vinlanders were shockingly bad.

Lodovico grunted at that. "So not all that cursing I did when he was a boy was entirely wasted."

Evidently not. "Our clan-folk have holdings down on the valley of the Mother of Rivers, as well as trading posts at Where-Waters-Meet upon the eastern coast," the first boy—Gulta, that was—said proudly. "Carlo made our profits to rise like a swan in flight! It was he who said that a trading mission to Europe and Venice and perhaps the silk houses of Constantinople might pay a very rich dividend. And we sent him home to await us and prepare the way, while we gathered goods and chose who to go."

"But he never arrived." The loss in her grandfather's face made Kat gulp down her own tears. If she began crying, he might not be able to hold himself together.

It was a crumb of comfort that the boys looked stricken, too. "We sent him home!" Gulta half-protested, as if he thought they doubted him.

Lodovico managed to reach out and pat the boy on the hand. "We believe you, lad," he replied, his voice cracking a little. "But a great deal can happen between Vinland and Venice."

They were all thinking it. *Including shipwreck.*

All but Marco, it seemed, who stuck out his chin stubbornly. "Not shipwreck," he said firmly. "I can promise you that. Whatever has delayed him, it isn't that. And until I hear otherwise, I will be sure it is only that—delay."

It wasn't sane, it wasn't rational, but Kat took heart from his surety—and so did her grandfather, who sat up straighter and nodded.

"By Saint Raphaella, Valdosta, you shame me," he said. "If you, a stranger to our family, can have such faith, how am I to doubt? Right enough. My son has survived so much else, how can he *not* return home to us?"

"Exactly so, sir," Marco agreed, giving Kat's hand a squeeze.

Now Lodovico turned to the Vinlanders. "And that being so, young sirs, please: Let us hear your plans, and how *Casa* Montescue means to figure into them."

To anyone but a Venetian, that statement would have seemed callous in the extreme. Here, Lodovico's son had literally been raised from the dead, only to vanish again, and he was discussing trade alliances?

But Kat knew, and Marco surely knew, that this was perhaps the bravest thing that her grandfather could have done. There was nothing, or next to nothing, any of them could do to help Carlo, wherever he was. And this trade agreement was her father's hard-won legacy to the House of Montescue. Should they now throw it away because he had vanished again? That would be like taking gold he had sacrificed to send them, and flinging it into the canals and starving, setting his sacrifice at naught because he was not there himself.

No! She and her grandfather would trust to God and her father's eminent good sense and cleverness, and fight to preserve what he had given them.

Lying in bed, late that night, Kat realized her father's ambitions were going to cost a great deal. Yes, the profits from trade in Vinland goods, particularly this cotton, could be very, very lucrative. Egyptian and Indian cottons were only for the very rich. Cotton was as expensive, or more so, than silk, because picking the seeds out was such a laborious process. Either the Vinlanders had some process to remove the seeds or labor must be dirt cheap over there. Still, however it was done their prices would bring the fabric within reach of the merely well-to-do. But it would require offices and warehouses in either Flanders or Denmark or Ireland to meet up with the Norse-Celtic Atlantic trade ships. The family her father had tied in with were of Icelandic stock. The Icelanders tended to run a Denmark-Vinland journey. It was not a good route for serious volumes of merchandise. It was too slow, with too many overland expenses and tolls and tariffs. Yes, from a port somewhere on the Atlantic coast, they could and would sell to northern Europe. But the east and markets on the Mediterranean would be best served by meeting the Venetian Atlantic trading convoy and selling out of Venice. But that meant warehouses. Local agents. And money. Lots of money.

Are we in the fire, still? she wondered, before she drifted off to sleep, *or have we at least climbed back into the frying pan?*

Chapter 8

Svanhild Thordardatter was not a maiden easily intimidated; she had faced, in her time, bears, catamounts, blizzards that piled snow to the rooftree, drunken and aggressive *skraelings* who had gotten more *aqavit* than they should have, and *skraeling* war-bands. She could make a wilderness camp, milk a cow, goat, or sheep, cook a meal without a single implement but a knife, and read an Icelandic saga like a *skald*. She could hunt, fish, and ride as well as her brothers, besides having all of the usual skills of a well-bred maiden. She had, during the rough crossing, climbed into the rigging in her leather *skraeling* trews to help alongside her brothers.

She had not only been willing to go with them, she had been eager. Valkyrie-like she might well be, but like the storied Brunnhilde, she had her soft side. She wanted a husband, children, and a home of her own. But the only way she was going to get one was to find a husband who *wasn't* somehow related to her.

Impossible in Vinland. Well, perhaps not *impossible*, but difficult. The only unmarried men who were not somehow tied into the Thordarson clan were thralls (her mother would have died), *skraelings* (actually, not unacceptable, but she didn't really want to set up housekeeping in a bark lodge or a skin tent), or trolls. Trolls, at least, so far as she was concerned. Nasty, fat, obnoxious, hairy, smelly, uncouth, elderly *trolls*.

So for both Svanhild and her mother, this trade expedition was heaven-sent. For her mother, it would be an opportunity for Gulta and Bjarni to find their sister a fine, unattached nobleman, and if this furthered their trade alliances, all the better. For Svanhild, well, if unattached young men were so thick on the ground as all that back in the Mother Countries, *she* would make sure that any noblemen that the boys presented to her were young and handsome. Or at the least, not trolls.

She had strode confidently off the ship once it reached the harbor in Venice—and then, for the first time in her life, discovered something that intimidated her as bears, catamounts, and blizzards had never been able to do.

The women of Venice.

In the Piazza San Marco she encountered the women of Venice, and, though Gulta and Bjarni were deaf and dumb to such nuances, knew that although she might be considered to be one of the prettiest maidens in Vinland, here she was . . .

A troll.

The women of Venice were tiny, dainty, slim-waisted and small-breasted. Their perfumed hair was either dark as a raven's wing, or a becoming honey-colored shade. They did not stride, they glided. They did not wear leather and fur and homespun in tunics and trews, nor aprons and plain dresses; they wore elegant gowns of silk and brocade, velvet and linen, embroidered and trimmed with laces and ribbons. Their hands were soft and white; their complexions pale and faintly blushed. Svanhild towered over them; with her sun-browned face and brassy-gold hair, she looked like a huge, cheap trinket among a box full of dainty, gold-set jewels. Or a cow among a herd of deer, a goose swimming with swans. And she knew it, and *they* knew it; she saw it in their eyes, in the amused side-glances they bestowed on her.

No young man, noble or otherwise, would look at *her* with anything other than amused contempt.

In the time it took to walk from the ship to the lodgings her brothers had arranged for her, she had read this lesson in a thousand eyes, a thousand veiled smirks, a thousand smothered laughs behind their backs. Gulta and

Bjarni were indeed oblivious to it all, excited as children at Christmastide by the newness and the bustle. So she put up a good front for them, marching with head high and cheeks burning with shame, pretending that she did not notice what was going on, either.

But she did, and it didn't stop at the door of the lodging, either.

Even the servants here looked at her in that scornful way, until she was afraid to leave her room, lest she meet with their sneers and arch glances. And it quickly became clear that Venice had more people in a single one of its many districts than there were in entire cities in Vinland . . . so finding Carlo and Clan Montescue was *not* going to be the simple matter of appearing on the docks and calling out the name.

While Bjarni and Gulta searched the city for someone who could take them to Clan Montescue, she hid in her room, took comfort in what luxuries the boys found for her—food, primarily, which was of *immense* comfort, since food did not have sneers or scornful eyes—and felt despair creeping over her. And wondered if—just perhaps—Carlo Montescue, plausible fellow that he was, had somehow tricked them. That his clan was not the leader of trade that he had said. That he did not even *have* a clan. That she and Gulta and Bjarni had come here on a fool's errand, and she the most foolish of all . . .

Then her brothers finally returned after days of searching, with the news that Clan Montescue had been found, that it *was* as great as Carlo had claimed, that although Carlo had unaccountably vanished between Vinland and Venice, the ancient Clan Chief Lodovico had welcomed them and their plans with every bit of warmth and enthusiasm they could have hoped for. Which was all the more gratifying, since the resurrection and second banishment of the old man's son had been a heavy blow to him.

But then came a heavy and horrid blow to Svanhild, delivered lovingly out of the mouths of her own dear brothers.

"And we are to come to dinner with them, this night, and sit in honor at their table!" crowed Bjarni. "*Now* we will be sought for, and taken seriously! In fact, we are to come to their table most nights, and feast with them, and they will introduce us to all of the great clan chiefs of the city!"

"This will be your chance, Sister," Gulta said, in a kindly voice, as she felt the blood draining from her face. "For surely there will be many young men there. Ah, but I must warn you, do not cast those blue eyes upon the one called Marco Valdosta, for he is spoken for by the daughter of Clan Montescue."

"The daughter is clever as well," Bjarni tossed off, casually. "Well read, and canny, and of an age with you. You must cultivate her; the old one dotes upon her, and it is clear that she has great influence upon him."

The bare thought made her stomach turn over.

Oblivious as ever, the boys tramped off noisily with more of the samples of the trade goods that they had brought. In a sick panic, Svanhild looked over her best gowns, then sat down, and ate an entire basket of pastries. And in food, found what little comfort there was to be had.

If she ate like this all the time, marveled Kat, the svelte Svanhild would be the size of a barn by the time she was fifty. Unless she was one of those people who just never got fat. Looking sidelong out of her eyes at the Vinlander, Kat decided this probably wasn't the case. Svanhild had a perfect northern complexion, creamy-white with blossoming roses in her cheeks, but there was already a hint of a second chin. Well, thought Kat, uncharitably and just a touch enviously, most men would be far too distracted by the magnificent and well-exposed frontage to notice that.

Kat wondered what conversational gambit to try next. Her grandfather was deep in animated conversation about hunting with their male guests, Svanhild's brothers Gulta and Bjarni. They were as blond as their sister, and considerably larger, not that Svanhild was any midget. They were partners in her father's enterprise. It behoved her, as a good Venetian hostess, to talk to the womenfolk. Only . . .

What did one say to someone who answered your

comments with "Ja" or "Nu" and continued to eat as if there were a famine coming?

"Do you like Venetian food?" asked Kat, watching Svanhild mopping the last droplets of *mostarda di cremona* on her platter with a slab of *ciabatta*. The piece of *prosciutto*-stuffed capon breast was long gone.

Svanhild smiled. "Nu."

Kat was about to give up when Svanhild at last volunteered something: "I like more cream, ja."

"Oh. We don't use cream much in Venice. There are not many cows on the islands."

Svanhild swallowed the last mouthful. "Not many young men either, nu?"

Kat couldn't tell if that was relief or if the beautiful Svanhild was upset by the lack. "Well, a lot of the young *Case Vecchie* usually go off to the trading posts of the Republic. They say Venice lives on the patience of her women. A lot of the men are at sea or away sometimes for years. Even those who are married."

"I am supposed to make a marriage. Mama sent me with my brothers to Europe for that purpose."

It was said so blandly that Kat still had no idea whether she was in favor of the idea or not. "Er. Any suitors?"

Svanhild shrugged. "None that are noble enough for Mama, ja. Mama wants a nobleman for me."

"Do you like any of them?

"Nu." A pause. "Are there desserts?"

Chapter 9

Manfred and his fellow-confrere Erik Hakkonsen made as much noise invading Francesca's *boudoir* (or what passed for a *boudoir,* here in the frozen and barbaric Northlands) as a small army.

Then again, between the two of them, they *were* a small army. The Danish escort who had been cooling their heels here every day, awaiting their return, looked quite alarmed at their appearance, and Francesca didn't think that was entirely because of how battered they were.

She was pleased to see them, though. Charles Fredrik would be even more pleased.

The one thing that this room had was privacy, even if it was cold enough that she could see her breath except when she was right on top of the fire. And a lot of furs. Most of which were piled on top and around her in a kind of luxurious nest that Francesca was loath to leave—which was why she hadn't leapt to her feet to greet the Emperor's secondary heir as she probably should have.

Still, Manfred was not the kind to stand on ceremony. Neither was Erik.

Instead, Francesca looked up tolerantly at the two men, who were very much worse for wear than they had been when she last saw them. Then wrinkled her fine-boned nose. "You stink. And that's a thick lip and pair of black eyes you have there, Erik. How did you get those?"

They were unshaven and filthy, and she shuddered to think of how many fleas Manfred alone was providing a haven for. She was not exaggerating when she told them that they stank. In fact, they reeked: of sweat, of rancid grease, and something musky and animal. Clearly, they had come straight here the moment they arrived within the walls of the fortress-*cum*-palace complex.

Whatever had detained them had been physically hazardous, it seemed. She could well believe it. The Norwegian town of Telemark was some considerable distance inland from the sea. The countryside was steep, cold, snowy—which was to say, so far as Francesca was concerned, barbarous in all respects. She'd been born and raised in the Aquitaine and spent most of her adult life on the sunny coasts of the Mediterranean.

Erik looked balefully at her. "I'd rather not talk about it."

Manfred guffawed. "I'll tell you . . . for a consideration, darling."

"No, you won't," said Erik immediately.

Somehow, Francesca doubted she'd be getting that story. "Well, I've brought a fair number of sleighs here at your royal uncle's command." She gestured at the well-armed but nervous looking Danes. "The Emperor wants you back in Mainz immediately. Is your business here done?"

Manfred grimaced. "It is, although we had to agree to slightly modified terms. Give us a few moments to bid a farewell to Queen Signy and her—ah—consort, and we can get the hell out of Norway. It's a nice country. For bears."

"They're welcome to it," said Erik, feeling his nose gingerly.

Francesca nodded. "I saw some of the Norsemen dragging a bear carcass, earlier. A big brute."

Both knights laughed, and she wondered why. Did it have anything to do with Erik's black eyes? Or something else?

"You can say that again," said Manfred. "Where do you think we'll find the queen and that Turk of hers, Erik?"

Erik gestured at the hall behind them. "Back in her rooms in the palace by now, I should think," he said.

Francesca stuck an enquiring nose out of her sables. "I thought this kingdom was ruled by a King Vortenbras?" She didn't just *think* that. It had been—but apparently *had* was the operative term. Getting to the bottom of this was imperative enough to tempt her out of her furs.

Erik laughed. "Not any more. You might say that's what we've been involved in, although most of the time it just felt like we were trying to stay alive. Come on, Manfred. We'll not introduce Francesca to the queen. There are enough clever women in this world without getting two of them together. And the knights will be as glad to go as we are. Time they got back to Sweden, anyway."

Francesca snuggled her toes down against the still-warm brick at her feet. "From that I conclude, the knights feel even one clever woman is too many." But she had no real desire herself to emerge from her warm cocoon to meet this other clever woman. The Norse hall might be warm, but going there would mean moving out of this nest.

Still.

Before we leave, anyway. Nothing official. But if she's clever, she'll already know about me.

Just what did go on up there, anyway?

She couldn't help but notice that neither Manfred nor the icy Erik showed any signs of romantic attachment to this woman. That was a bit of a relief, since that would be a complication they didn't need. She wondered, briefly, just what a Turk was doing here, with a Norse queen.

But there'd be time for the story, somewhere warmer. Say . . . Italy. Or even . . . as she'd been thinking lately, Alexandria. She'd had several very interesting discussions with a Danish scholar about that city. And that fit in very nicely with the Emperor's plans.

After all, she was, first and foremost, the Emperor's servant, and she never, ever, forgot it. She couldn't afford to. And neither, if he was wise, could Manfred.

"Jerusalem!" Manfred nearly fell off the bed in shock. It was, especially for these parts, a very luxurious bed. It was certainly one he was very glad to be in, after all he'd been through, especially since it contained Francesca. "You're not serious, dear!"

"Do go on with your massage, Manfred," said Francesca languorously, turning slightly, and giving him a view of her magnificent breasts. He felt his blood heating up a little more; just as well, considering how cold he'd been over the past several weeks. He'd been wondering if he would *ever* feel warm again.

"I will say that the one good thing about all that drilling and training that Erik insists on is that it gives you very strong hands. You're the only man I have ever met with strong enough hands to give me a really relaxing massage." She twinkled at him. "And you do want me relaxed, don't you, dear? It gives me such a lot of energy."

Manfred went back to his task, but his mind was not distracted from her comment. "What's this about my going to Jerusalem for Charles Fredrik?"

Francesca ran a hand down his hairy, naked thigh. Nerves he'd thought frozen numb for the duration became most delightfully alive again. "Forget that I said it, darling. It just slipped out."

Manfred raised his eyes to heaven. But like a terrier onto a rat, he stuck to his questions. Rather admirably, he thought, considering the distractions. "Why Jerusalem, Francesca? I mean, it has got to be an improvement on Norway at this time of year, but—well, I thought I'd be involved in setting the Knots to rights. I'm only a confrere for another year and there's still a lot to do."

"I think you've started the ball rolling," she said playfully . . . nearly distracting the terrier. Not quite, but nearly. "Never make the mistake of thinking others cannot do the job, if not quite as you would, possibly just as well."

He grinned. "They don't have my hands, darling, or Erik to make theirs as strong. Now tell: There's more to this isn't there? Politics?"

Francesca gave him a look of deepest innocence, from under half-lowered lashes, spoiled only by a throaty chuckle. "How could you suspect that! The Emperor is an old man. He feels his age. He would like, for the sake of his soul, to undertake a pilgrimage to Jerusalem himself. But the Emperor's health . . ."

"Besides his dislike of leaving Mainz."

"Tch. Don't interrupt while I am betraying confidences, Manfred dear." She tapped his lips with one long finger. "His health and the running of an empire do not allow him to take the six months or a year necessary to go to Jerusalem. But as age creeps up on him he would like to prepare his soul for the inevitable. As would any man above a certain age."

Manfred snorted. "The Ilkhan do keep a substantial presence in Jerusalem," he stated, and was rewarded by her sly little grin, which told him he had struck dead in the black.

Well. Politics, then. Not his favorite task, but *he* wouldn't be the one engaged in it. He wasn't nearly crafty enough to deal with the Mongols. The Swedes and Danes were about at his level; if he hadn't had Francesca, the Italians would have had him raw, on toast. Even with her help, they nearly had, anyway.

"Who is going to accompany me? Trolliger? Or Brunswick?"

Francesca rolled over, exposing a front draped only in the sheerest bits of lace and silk, certainly not designed to conceal. "Eberhard of Brunswick. But I do believe your uncle *does* want to make his peace with God, and that he *is* feeling his age. And let's not talk boring business *right* now . . . unless you want to, of course?" She cocked her head slightly, lowering her long lashes, and ran an elegant finger down his torso. Reviving still more nerves.

"Argh!" He sighed, as a gloomy thought occurred to him. "I don't want to leave you for a year, Francesca."

Not that there wouldn't be plenty of distractions in the sophisticated and ancient (as well as holy) city of Jerusalem, not to mention the other delightful metropolises along the way. But they wouldn't be Francesca.

She pulled him closer and began to do very distracting things indeed. "Who said anything about leaving me behind?"

"You want to come with me?" He was startled enough to be distracted from her distraction. "But—"

Why had he thought she'd want to be left behind? Why had he thought that his uncle would *allow* her to remain behind? She was, after all, first and foremost, the Emperor's trusted servant, and he would be wise never to forget that.

Still. She was also Francesca. "That's wonderful!"

"Well, it is warmer there, is it not?"

It was only later, much later, on the verge of sleep, that it occurred to Manfred that Francesca did not betray confidences, and she didn't let things slip out. He'd been very skillfully manipulated. Very skillfully indeed.

Well, it had been more fun than being told. And even if he doubted that Charles Fredrik really needed any praying for another ten years, Jerusalem would still be interesting—and much more pleasant to visit with Francesca for company.

And if she was the Emperor's trusted servant, well, so was he. She was wise enough to remember that, even when he was distracted. Wise enough for both of them.

The thought gave him immense comfort.

Chapter 10

"Kat says I should have a talk with you," said Marco, plainly uncomfortable.

Benito put his hands on his hips. He could read the signs. *Big brother time*, he thought silently.

He wished Marco would pick some other time for it. He wasn't exactly hung-over . . . just . . . blurry.

"What is it?" he snarled. Marco frowned, ever so faintly.

All right, so it was a sulky tone. He didn't need lectures from Marco, and even less from Kat. Butter wouldn't melt in her mouth these days—but she'd been a night-bird, a smuggler, once, moving very gray cargoes of magical supplies. And, unless Benito misread the signs, by the *vacant-space-to-let* smile his brother wore these days, she hadn't waited for the marriage banns to share Marco's bed.

Right now, Marco was not going to listen to a litany of Kat's past sins. "Kat's worried about you, Benito. And so am I."

Benito could tell by the set of Marco's shoulders that his older brother wasn't enjoying this. He also knew Marco well enough to know that when Marco had decided that something must be done, it would be done. Still, Benito didn't enjoy this sort of thing either, and he was damned if he'd make it too easy for Marco.

"Well, stop worrying, Marco. I'm grown up enough to

look after myself. I'm the one who usually ends up look-ing after you, remember. Or do I need to remind you of your little escapade with the love letters to Angelina, that got you into such a mess in the Jesolo marshes?"

Marco winced. "That was then. I'm older and wiser now."

Benito cocked an ear. Upstairs somewhere he could hear Angelina's shrill voice, berating a servant for some-thing. Despite the fact that she was supposedly staying in one of the Dorma villas on the mainland, Angelina was forever finding some excuse to come back to Venice, to the *Casa* Dorma. "And heaven knows you've paid for it, Marco. What news on the annulment?" Perhaps he could head Marco off the lecture on his way of life.

Marco looked gloomy. "She's balking about which convent and which Order again. I really don't think she wants to go to one. I feel sorry for her. She's not really suited to a contemplative life." But Marco was obviously determined not to lose track. "But I want to talk about you, not my troubles. You can't go on like this, Benito."

Privately Benito thought Angelina would be better suited to a brothel than a cloister, but saying that would offend Marco. Marco was a sympathetic soul; Benito didn't like to offend him unnecessarily. He was very fond of his brother.

It would also probably also offend Petro Dorma, who was the Doge and their protector as well as Angelina's brother. Petro was not a sympathetic soul, or wise to offend, although these days Benito was often tempted. Anything to get out of here. "Like what, Brother?"

Marco shrugged helplessly. "The parties. The women. The drunkenness. The fights."

Benito shrugged in return. "The way I live my life is no concern of yours, Marco. Or of Kat's. Leave me alone."

Marco responded by putting an arm over Benito's shoulders. "You've got to get over her, Brother. She had a right to make her own choices. Maria wasn't ever the kind of person you could force to do anything."

Benito shrugged off the arm. "She's just a woman. Like all other women."

Marco stepped back, and this time he had more than a mere suggestion of a frown. "Benito, that's got to be about the dumbest thing you have ever said, and you've said some really . . ."

"Ahem." The servant at the doorway coughed. "Milor'. Milord Dorma wants to see you in his office. Immediately."

He left the two brothers, still glaring at each other. "Who did he mean?" said Benito finally.

"Probably you," said Marco curtly. "Kat and I are not the only ones to hear about your stupid escapades. Especially last night's stunt. Well, I'd better come along and put in a good word for you."

Benito tried to remember the details of last night. Truth to tell, he couldn't. He wondered what the hell he had done; he certainly wasn't prepared to ask Marco!

"I don't need your help," he said, sullenly, setting off up the passage. When Petro issued this sort of summons, nobody, but nobody, actually dawdled. It was a bit of a mystery to Benito. The head of the *Casa* Dorma was plumpish, balding and good-natured, so how come everybody jumped when he said "frog"?

"I'm coming anyway," said Marco, his long strides easily catching up with his shorter brother. "We Valdosta stick together. Besides, he may want me, not you."

"Ha." But it was mildly said. The Valdosta brothers did stick together; for many years they'd had no one and nothing else. Marco's loyalty touched him as nothing else, and when they walked into Petro Dorma's office, and Benito saw Angelina already there, looking ready for a five-star tantrum, he realized his brother might actually be the one who needed help, this time. Petro had been calling for Marco after all.

The Doge looked at him with a mixture of irritation and surprise. "What are you doing here, Benito? Aren't you are supposed to be at dancing classes or something?"

Best to dodge that one. He was in fact supposed to be at an elocution and poetry class that Dorma's mother insisted he take "to get rid of that working-class accent." Neither poetry nor dandified dottori from the Accademia, nor a desire to speak like the *Case Vecchie* motivated him. Besides, he'd been sleeping off last night.

"Came to support Marco," he said stoutly. "He's my brother, after all, and Grandfather said I was to look after him."

That was true enough, and when your grandfather was Duke Enrico Dell'este, one of Venice's greatest allies . . . it carried influence. Even if Benito had not spent much time with the old man since he'd been eight years old.

"Humph. Stay then. Even though this really has nothing to do with you." Dorma tapped the inlaid desk in front of him. "This is a document of the annulment of your marriage from the Grand Metropolitan in Rome. You will both sign it now. Angelina, I have arranged for you to take up the novitiate in the Carmelite sisterhood with the Cloister of Santa Lucia Della Monte outside Verona. Your escort will leave with you before Terce bell."

He said it like he meant it. He said it in a way that Petro Dorma, Angelina's indulgent brother, had never spoken before. Benito blinked.

"What!" squawked Angelina, rage flying banners in her cheeks. "I won't!"

"You agreed to," said Petro, calmly but implacably.

I'd keep my mouth shut if I were you, Angelina, Benito thought warily. *Or he might send you to some Pauline sisterhood in Sweden.*

Angelina pinched her lips. "I've changed my mind. I don't want to be a nun. And certainly not in the backcountry!"

"I don't want Angelina to do something that she doesn't want to, either," said Marco, though his eyes spoke volumes of despair.

Benito raised his eyes. That idiot brother of his! His own marriage and happiness in the balance, and he worried about this selfish, spoiled brat.

Petro turned to face Marco and Benito. "Marco, this is no longer a matter of what you or Angelina want; it is a matter of pledges and honor, the honor of the Dormas and the honor of the Dell'este. I have promised your grandfather that I will see you married, with all due pomp and ceremony, in the Doge's palace, within three months. This is not an option—not for you, not for Angelina."

Marco blinked, and Petro turned to Benito. "Benito, see that he signs that paper. You invoked your grandfather's name. See that his will is done."

"He can sign anything he pleases," snapped Angelina. "I'm not going to. I'd rather stay in town as the Doge's sister. Marco might be worth absolutely nothing as a husband, but he's *mine*. I've decided."

Petro stood up. He was not very tall. He was definitely plump. He still dominated the room.

He picked up a scroll of parchment from the desk, and handed it to her. "Sworn affidavits about your participation in the black lotos trade."

Angelina's blossoming cheeks went white. "It's . . . it's not true!" She tried to tear the parchment in two. The vellum resisted.

"The *Signori di Notte* and the Council of Ten also have copies." Petro said grimly. He picked up a second scroll. "This is a warrant for your arrest."

Benito, watching his brother, saw Marco take a deep breath. With deliberate intent Benito stamped on his brother's toes. Hard. Having got Marco's attention he shook his head, fiercely.

Angelina began to produce the beginnings of tears. She wept, as Benito had reason to know, very prettily. There was an artful hint of a sob in her voice. "You wouldn't dare let them do this to me. You control the *Signori di Notte* and the Council. Besides, mother won't let you."

Petro Dorma shook his head. "I would prefer you to go to a convent, far from here. Verona is not as far off as I'd like, the truth to tell. I have been considering Spain, but I cannot be seen to be partisan. The people of Venice will accept your exile or your imprisonment and nod and forgive me as a slightly foolish brother; they won't accept my condoning your actions. And you forget, our mother was addicted to that same drug."

Marco was not going to listen to Benito. "Petro . . ."

The head of the house Dorma turned on him. "Stay out of this, Valdosta. She's my sister, and only your wife by my insistence, to give the baby legitimacy. Besides, I have agreed with Duke Enrico to send you off to Ferrara, today, under armed guard, if you don't do this my way. Now, Angelina, sign this."

Tears abandoned as a weapon that no longer served, cheeks white with anger, Angelina Valdosta stepped forward, snatched up a quill, and signed.

"Good," said Petro. "You have until terce. I suggest you spend the time saying farewell to our mother. I'd say you should spend it with your child, but I know you have not been into her nursery since you arrived in Venice three days ago."

"I didn't *want* her!" snapped the beauty.

Petro Dorma smiled wryly. "We do. So we will keep her. Good-bye, Angelina." He stepped out from behind his desk, his arms beginning to reach for her.

She evaded them. "I hate you."

Marco stepped forward too. "Angelina . . ."

"And you too! You're so boring!" She turned on her heel and stormed out.

Marco turned to follow, but Benito grabbed his sleeve. Petro took the other. "I'm sorry, Marco," said the head of *Casa* Dorma, with more sympathy than Benito had expected. He had to wonder if Petro wished he'd had Marco as a brother rather than Angelina as a sister. "Stay. There are still things I need to say, and I need your signature on that document before Angelina can go to that convent."

"I don't think I should sign," said Marco, seriously. "I made my promises."

Petro shook his head. Benito noticed that there was a tear trickling down the man's face. "I love her very much, Marco. She'll always be my little sister. We spoiled her after Papa's death, Mother and I, and perhaps that is why things turned out this way. But there are two reasons, both compelling, why this is the best thing for her. First, she has been experimenting with black lotos herself. She's been spending time over at the estate of a sister of Count Badoero. The Council of Ten have spies watching it. The Badoero house suffered what should have been punitive financial losses when their attack on Venice failed, yet there is money and lavish entertainment at Contessa Mirafioro's estate again. Badoero himself is dead, but the trade he set up in that narcotic continues, and my sister is in the thick of it."

Marco's mouth opened, then closed again. He looked as if he'd like to deny it; he also looked as though he knew that he couldn't.

Petro rubbed his eyes with a weary hand. "Angelina was drawn into the wild set the contessa cultivates. She is implicated in bringing some of the drug here, to Venice. We both know how addictive lotos is; the sisters are healers, and specifically are skilled in the rehabilitation of addicts. It really is the best thing we can do for her. Besides, there is a large force of Schiopettieri going to raid the Mirafioro estate soon. I really don't want her taken, or possibly injured. There's only so much that even I can keep quiet."

Marco bit his lip. "I can't believe she'd use the stuff— after your mother, and the difficulty we've had weaning her off it. I should think anyone with two eyes in her head would know better."

Petro shook his head. "It does seem insane, doesn't it? But Angelina always believed she was special, different from other people. Superior, maybe, and immune to their problems—despite her pregnancy proving that there was one thing she wasn't immune to. Besides, it is a popular myth among those who buy and sell the stuff that the addictiveness is totally exaggerated, and she was always readier to believe the people she wished to emulate than she was to believe people who love her."

He turned to his desk again and picked up another document. "There is another reason. Angelina has her ear to the network of gossips and rumor. I wanted her away in isolation before news of this one reached her ears."

The document bore the seal of Ferrara. "Word from your grandfather. Caesare Aldanto has been seen in Constantinople."

Benito went cold, and quite sober. *Trust the devil to save his own.* "I'm going to Constantinople, then," said Benito. "I've got unfinished business there."

Petro shook his head, and once again, it was in that implacable manner that warned of dire and inescapable consequences if his will was ignored.

"You are not, and for two reasons. First, after Caesare had seen the Emperor Alexius, he reembarked on a ship. Bound, most likely, for Odessa. So he is no longer in Constantinople for you to find. And for a second reason, both the Council of Ten and your grandfather have placed considerable prices on his head. We have more competent assassins in our pay than you would be. And in this case we will not hesitate to use them."

Benito looked mulish. "I know his ways. How he operates. They don't."

"That may be true," said Petro calmly. "But he is not where you can find him now, and what is more, even if you could, there is no reason to believe that he is not . . . contaminated. *Think*, Benito. There are only two sorts of power that could have saved him from his fate—and of the two, it was not likely to be the angels. Furthermore, where he has gone to, you are at a huge disadvantage. The Grand Duchy of Lithuania would eat you alive, Benito."

"What has this got to do with Angelina?" asked Marco.

Petro raised his eyebrows. "We know how Aldanto works. How he uses women and . . ." he looked pointedly at the two boys, "intermediaries. Angelina still claims he was wrongfully accused, and refuses to accept he was in any way responsible for the attack on the Republic. Just by being part of *Casa* Dorma, she is privy to a great deal of information that the enemies of Venice would appreciate. I love my sister, and no matter what she is and has become, I will continue to love her, but I know her weaknesses now. And I love and have a duty to the People and the Republic of Venice, too. What I am doing here is the best for both of them."

Marco bit his lip. And then he stepped up to the desk, took up the quill, dabbed it in the ink and signed. "I'll go up and try to see her now. I still feel she's getting a very poor choice in all of this," he said, sadness tingeing his voice.

Benito raised his eyes to heaven again. He loved Marco dearly, but . . . Here Marco had just received the freedom to marry the girl of his dreams, had his mistakes corrected, and he was worrying about the cause of those troubles. No doubt he'd be worrying about Aldanto next.

Well, if Caesare Aldanto ever came within Benito's reach, Benito would make sure his former idol was very dead. They'd been used, and the worst was they'd been grateful to be used by the traitor and murderer. And he owed Aldanto for Maria's account too. He turned to follow his brother.

Petro put a heavy hand on his shoulder. "I want to talk to you, too, Benito. Seeing as you're here."

He led Benito to the mullioned windows of his study. They could see out along the quays, busy with canal boats and lighters, to the forest of masts of the ships at anchor in the Bacino San Marco. Benito knew it was the merchant-prince's favorite view. But instead Petro pointed to the quay-side, to a solitary man lying in squalor against a bollard. "I know that man. He used to be good boatswain. Made a pretty penny or two out of various *Colleganzas*. He should be comfortable, well-off and happy."

"So?" Benito replied, though he had a good idea what was coming. "Sir," he added belatedly.

Petro sighed. "He can't find a job, even when ships are desperate for crew. If he doesn't drink, he shakes and hallucinates. He'll do absolutely anything for another glass of wine. He doesn't care how bad the wine is. Just so long as it is wine. We don't like to admit it, but too much wine can be as bad as black lotos. It just takes a bit longer. Are you going to turn out like that old soak? Because it can happen to you too. Like my sister, you are not immune. You're behaving just like her at the moment."

Nothing Petro could have chosen to say would have made more of an impression than that last line. For the second time that day, Benito felt something hit him with a distinct sense of shock, hit him in a way that made him grow very cold for a moment. Finally Benito shook his head.

Petro patted the shoulder. "Good. Because I don't think you'd fit into a monastery any better than Angelina is going to enjoy that convent."

"I'd drive 'em all mad. Sir."

Dorma managed a smile. "I'm far more inclined to send you out to factor in one of Dorma's trading posts Outremer, now that spring is coming, than keep you here or send you to a monastery. I've told mother that I'm wasting my time trying to make you into a *Case Vecchie* gentleman. Besides, I think the Valdosta and the *Casa* Dorma would lose something of value if they tried to cut and polish you. It's like trying to make a stiletto out of a perfectly good battleaxe."

"More like a rapier out of a cabbage," said Benito gloomily. "But the truth to tell, Petro, I really want to get out of here. I don't care where to, but out of Venice. And out of this 'education.' It doesn't suit me and I don't suit it."

Petro sat himself down again. "Very well. After your brother's wedding. And only if you learn to pull in your horns a bit. I've no objection to some wild oats, but it was only your status as my ward, and something of a hero in the last attack on Venice, that kept you out of jail last night. And you know Venice; there's only so long that you can trade on that before they start treating you exactly as you deserve."

Benito nodded. He really had to find out just what he'd done last night. "I've always had a fancy for Negroponte."

Petro gave a snort of laughter. "Benito, you are to subtle maneuvering what a randy stallion is to subtle seduction. If you asked for Golden Horn, Petro might smell a rat, eh? But Negroponte . . . is close enough to Constantinople? Not a chance, Benito. Not a chance."

Benito grinned, in spite of feeling somewhere in the bottom of his stomach that his world was not right, and probably never would be again. "It works on other people, Petro."

The head of the *Casa* Dorma smiled back. He looked younger. Nicer. Less like the Doge.

"But not on me. Now go and try to stay out of trouble. And pretend to be learning to be a good young *Case Vecchie* for my mother's sake. She has enough to bear with Angelina being taken away. You can speak like a gentleman when you wish to. Do so."

PART III
February, 1539 A.D.

Chapter 11

The forests of Istria were dripping and bleak. The mists seemed to hang heavy and cold around the trees. That matched Maria's mood fairly well. She was big bellied and uncomfortable. What she really wanted was someone to have a good fight with. A good fling-plates-and-break-things fight. In that respect her husband Umberto was hopeless. For starters he was always off marking trees or accompanying the foresters. The life out here didn't suit him, but he was a fiercely conscientious man. He'd far rather have been in the dockyards in the Arsenal back in Venice. This however, was where he had been sent. And after the affair with the previous chief forester he did his best to keep going out with the tree patrols.

At least he had listened to her—or if he hadn't done so consciously, some of her insistence that he look into the peccadilloes of those under him had unearthed the culprits still running the timber-scam.

She tried not to be too irritated with him, even so. He insisted on thinking of it purely in terms of "timber being sent away from Venice" rather than "timber being sold to the enemies of Venice." Sometimes, his focus was so narrow, so parochial, it made her want to scream. And never mind that not all that long ago, her focus had been entirely on running her cargoes and not enquiring too closely about where they were from, or where they were going, on being dazzled by a pair of blue eyes and not asking what was going on in the head that housed them.

Well, that had changed. If only Umberto had learned the same lesson.

At least he was on to the cheaters now, and he was off every day, trying to match his city strides with the long paces that the foresters took, and sneezing a lot.

She envied him, envied his long hikes through the forest, envied that *he* got out of the house every day, into the open, beyond the four confining walls. To her surprise she'd found that the openness, space and silences felt welcoming. Umberto complained of missing the people and the sounds of the city. She enjoyed their absence.

In the first day here, she had learned all that, despite the fact that things had been quite chaotic. To get out, under those old, quiet trees, had been a pleasure she would never have anticipated. So far as *she* was concerned, all that had happened was that she'd had a lovely walk and solved half the timber problems—and, yes, gotten a little lost and gotten home a little late, but that was hardly anything to worry about.

Umberto'd almost had the baby for her, to judge by the performance he had given when she came back at last. And unfortunately, she was no longer the sole arbiter of what she did; she was a wife now, and half of a couple, and it behooved her not to send her husband into a state of panic. The result—with her "delicate condition" in mind, was being confined to the house and yard with an elderly forester's widow as a combination between house-servant and guard.

Not that she was in any real sense a prisoner. No, she was just confined by chains of care and Umberto's ideas of how it all should be, and the proper arrangement of the universe. Women had their place. It was a pampered and protected one—well, as pampered as a caulker's wife ever got, anyway. It didn't include being out on the canals at midnight, running gray-cargo, nor traipsing about the woods like a forester.

It all chafed at Maria's soul. She was used to her independence. She was used to defining for herself what she would and wouldn't do. And if her mother had plied her own boat until the very day of Maria's own birth, why should she now be stuck within four walls, tending to the housework as if she hadn't a care except that the floor be clean enough?

For that matter, her world was *so* much wider now! The last year—no one who had lived through what she had could be unchanged. She'd come up against challenges she would never have dreamed of, and beaten them, and if she'd chosen to marry rather than try to raise a baby on her own, well, it was for the baby's sake.

She certainly wouldn't have done it for her own sake. So she'd taken the husband that she thought would best love her baby, no matter who the father was. And now, she found herself powerless to fight the trammels of Umberto's gentle care. She didn't even know how to start dealing with his hurt expressions when she didn't fit in with his expectations.

How did you fight this? She really could use a good screaming fight.

Issie, the black-clad forester's widow who was supposed to help her, tugged at her arm. "Why don't you sit down, dearie, and rest your feet. You'll get little enough rest when the baby is born."

Maria looked out into the black, bare trees, ignoring Issie. Umberto was out there now, trying to select good timbers for masts and keels, when what he knew about was cladding. The caulkers back in Venice were undoubtedly going to be grateful for the improvement in the quality of deck planking. Maria was, however, sure that he'd be getting more letters of complaint from the masters of the carpenters' guild. At least he got regular letters from Venice. It was more than she ever did.

She sighed. It wasn't as if reading came that easily. True, she'd spent more time working on it since they arrived here. But there weren't many people back home who could write in the first place. She only ever seemed to get letters from Kat. Letters full of Marco. Letters from a life she'd chosen to leave behind, to try to forget. Benito was always carefully not mentioned.

The second reason Maria found it difficult to pick a good fight with Umberto was straight guilt. He'd married her, loved her enough to take what fellow Venetians would have called "spoiled goods." She had taken his offer, not because she felt any deep affection for the balding, slightly worried looking gray-haired man, but because she needed a father for the child. She had grown up without that social protection, and she would not inflict it on her baby. Lately, she'd come to realize that Umberto's affections had been transferred to her from his love of her mother.

Her mother! Well, she should have expected that. Even as a tiny child, she had known that Umberto followed her mother with his eyes every single time she was anywhere around the docks where the caulkers worked. The older man had plainly been crazy about her. He had even called Maria by her name a couple of times by accident. How could she start a good fight with someone who was still in love with her dead mother?

At least she wasn't in love with Umberto herself. If this was hard, trying to rival the memory of her dead mother and win over someone *she* loved would be even harder.

Maria sighed again. She leaned heavily on the broom, and some of the birch twigs cracked. Outside the chief forester's house the rain fell in heavy sheets. Once upon a time all she'd wanted was a house that was warm and dry. Now she was almost tempted to go out in the rain. It hadn't melted her in all those years of sculling her gondola through the wet winter canals of Venice.

Housekeeping, cooking and preparing baby clothes did not fill up the day, let alone her mind. True, being warm was good and so was being well fed. But being cooped up, being a good wife, even a good pregnant wife, was going to drive her crazy, even if the final stages of this pregnancy were beginning to leave her feeling permanently exhausted.

"Really, why don't you have a little rest, dear," clucked Issie again.

Maria swept irritably. She'd been just about ready to do that. Now she wouldn't.

The jingle of a horse's harness was a welcome distraction. Ignoring the rain, ignoring Issie's squawks of alarm,

Maria ran out to the messenger, who was wearing wet Venetian Republic livery. It must be something important to bring the man out here in this weather. The messengers of the Republic were supposed to conduct their business with the utmost dispatch, true. But out here, this far from the authorities in Venice, that meant "when it wasn't raining." The forests of Istria were vital to the shipbuilding in the Arsenal, but they were also a long way from the messengers' *capi* back in Venice.

She was drenched the moment she stepped foot outside the door, of course, and she didn't give a damn, of course. This wasn't the canal; she wasn't the same Maria who hadn't but two dry skirts to her name. There were several warm outfits inside that house that she could change right back into when she got inside. Issie could spread this one on chairs in front of the fire—it would give the old cow something to do.

Maria struggled with the buckle on the wet leather pouch, ignoring the shivering messenger who was trying to tether his horse with numb fingers. "Can you help me?" he asked finally.

Maria looked up from her task with annoyance. "Take yourself and your horse into the stable, you fool. Are you not bright enough to get in out of the rain?"

A smothered snort from the messenger suddenly drew her attention to the fact that *she* was apparently not bright enough to get in out of the rain.

She got the pouch off the saddle, and retreated into the house.

Issie, clucking like a wet hen, handed her a rough towel. Maria had no time for it now. The fussing about while she was trying to get to the message in the pouch would drive her insane. "Go get the messenger a drink," she snapped. "He's wet through. I'm just a little damp."

Issie sniffed irritably. "He's not pregnant." But she went anyway. The pouch buckle finally surrendered to a superior will. There was only one wax-sealed missive inside. The seal was that of the House Dorma, the Doge's house, and not the familiar crest of the Montescue. It was addressed to her . . . and not to the chief forester of Istria.

Oh blessed Jesu—

Maria tore at it with trembling fingers.

No one would send a special messenger to the wife of a forester unless it was horrible news. The worst of all possible news.

No one from Dorma would send me news by a special messenger. It must be from Marco. It could only mean Benito had been killed. . . . Why hadn't she . . .

Inside was Kat's familiar handwriting. It started with the words: *Glad news!*

Maria sat down with a thump on a hard oak settle, and composed herself with a deep breath. She patted her bulging stomach to still the flutters just under the skin. "If Katerina only knew how close she came to causing your premature birth, child," she muttered, blinking to clear her eyes before reading further.

I've got Marco to use the Dorma seal so this will get to you as soon as possible, wrote Kat. *Fantastic, wonderful things have happened!*

That seal could indeed achieve great things. It had nearly achieved an early baby, thought Maria wryly. She read on, learning of the Vinlanders who would restore the fortunes of Montescue, of the annulment of Marco's marriage to Angelina, and Angelina's hasty internment in the Cloister at Santa Lucia Della Monte outside Verona. It seemed that this had been a very busy week.

She tried not to think how busy *she* would have been, had she been there, how in the thick of it all. She'd be poling Kat about, of course, and maybe helping her a little with the Vinlanders. And she wouldn't be getting the news of the wedding plans at second-hand like this.

Petro Dorma insists it is to be a great state function. Marco and I have had to agree. On conditions: First, I want you to come and support me on that day. Second, Francesca de Chevreuse will be returning to Venice. She is to be my other matron of honor. Dorma says he will make arrangements for you and Umberto to return to Venice for the occasion. She had to read that twice, and then a third time, before it began to make sense.

And when it did, Maria could only laugh helplessly. The flower of the House Montescue and the heir of the

House Valdosta, grandson of the Duke of Ferrara . . . with a caulker's wife and one of Venice's most famous courtesans as her attendants to the altar.

Well, she could hardly refuse. Kat, after all, had come to her low-key caulker's wedding in the same role. But it would mean returning to Venice. Returning—she looked at the date of the wedding—returning with a three-week-old baby, if everything ran to time.

The back door banged, and her head came up. If it was Issie—

A sneeze. Not Issie; Umberto. He came through to the front parlor. Maria took in the wet-plastered gray hair and the faint bluish tinge to her man's lips. He smiled caressingly at her, and a wave of affection swept through her. Her man might have his faults and his rigidities, but he was a good one. People might become exasperated with Umberto Verrier, but you couldn't really dislike him; he was too mild a soul to engender anything so active as dislike. And he was such a good husband. A conscientious one, at least.

He was shivering slightly, and she beckoned to him, smiling. "Umberto! Come over to the fire, before ice forms on your poor nose."

He did, holding his thin hands out to crackling flames. "There is a message from Venice? One of the foresters said he saw a messenger in the Doge's livery coming across."

She'd pulled a chair up for him by this time, handed him the towel Issie had been trying to press on her. "It was for me, dear. A letter from Katerina Montescue, the lady who was my maid of honor at our wedding. She is to marry Marco Valdosta, you know, the Doge-elect's ward, in a great state ceremony in the early spring. It's all finally been sorted out, and settled at last."

Umberto looked at her wonderingly. "I have never understood how you came to know such a one. The *Casa* Montescue! She is a great lady."

I don't dare tell you how I know Kat, thought Maria. It was no tale to chance spreading about among all these foresters, especially as Issie had come in with a goblet of hot, spiced, honeyed wine, her lined face alive with curiosity. She'd have it all over Istria before tomorrow night. *The new chief forester's wife! Blessed Jesu, she's worse than we could have thought! A smuggler! Poling her own canal boat! And no better than she should be, no doubt!*

Well, the wine might be just an excuse to find out what was happening, but Maria was grateful. Umberto was in need of it. "There was more to it than just telling me that the wedding has been set, or she wouldn't have needed a messenger. She has asked that we—you and I—go back to Venice for the wedding. She has arranged with Petro Dorma to make it possible."

Umberto sipped some of the hot wine. "Well, it would be nice . . . I have been thinking how I would like to go to town. It would be very good to see people again, perhaps to ask if I might take a post closer to the city. But . . . what about the . . ." He hesitated, "the baby?"

Maria patted her stomach. "Baby should be born by then. It had better be. Katerina has asked me to be one of her matrons of honor."

The goblet crashed to the floor. Neither Issie nor Umberto seemed to notice.

Chapter 12

"You're not that old," protested Manfred for the fifth time.

The Emperor smiled wryly. "Thank you. Nevertheless, I still want you to do it. You will pray for my soul in Jerusalem. It needs it, believe me. And it wouldn't do you any harm to do some thinking about your own mortality."

Erik looked at the emperor's nephew. Manfred was trying to keep a straight face. He glanced at Charles Fredrik, and realized that the Emperor understood the humor in this too. Erik could see the similarity between the two men in the facial lines. Of course Manfred was bigger, and had a darker Celtic complexion, but the family likeness was definitely there—and went deeper than appearances. He could readily believe, looking at the Emperor, that there were some sins worth praying about.

Charles Fredrik shook his head ruefully. "When I was your age I didn't believe in my own mortality either. Just do it, Manfred. Humor me. I'm an old man. I know that both in Venice and now in Norway, the chances of you being killed or injured were remarkably good. Neither luck nor Erik is going to stop everything. So I'm putting in a formal request to the Abbot-General of the Knights of the Holy Trinity to furnish you with an escort of knights. He has already acceded to my 'request' that you go on a pilgrimage to the Holy Land for me, while you are still

in the holy order. I don't think he will refuse this either.
You will be invested, both of you, as knight-proctors and
given discretionary command over the Knights assigned to
accompany you. To assist you I'm sending my old friend
and mentor, Eberhard of Brunswick, with you."

Manfred rolled his eyes. "To instruct me in statecraft
no doubt, Uncle. This pilgrimage is going to be a real
penance after all."

The Emperor covered a smile with his hand. "Yes.
Poor Eberhard is expecting to find it that, for a certainty.
Now, Francesca, stay with me a while. I would like to
talk to you without that young idiot interrupting me. Go
on, you two. I'll want to talk to you as well, Erik. But
not tonight, I think."

Erik and Manfred had little choice but to leave.
Francesca waved as she walked over to stand beside
the Emperor.

"Did you see that!" said Manfred fuming. "One minute
he's dying and wanting me to pray for his soul, the next
he's stealing my girl!"

"She's scarcely a girl," said Erik, latching onto the one
safe point in the entire argument.

The disapproving look brought a grin to Manfred.
"Among the things I can promise you, she definitely
isn't a boy. Or have you forgotten a certain night in a
certain brothel? Francesca says you're the biggest stiff
thing she's ever had between her legs. Your whole body
was rigid . . . with shock."

Erik fumbled for something to say, and failed. The
memory of the first time they'd met Francesca, fleeing
from an ambush, still embarrassed him. They'd been
ambushed in a brothel in which she was employed at
the time, and she'd agreed to hide them—by using the
expedient device of hiding them in plain sight, engaged
in the sort of activity anyone would expect to see in a
brothel. Erik himself, mortified, had faked his part of
the thing. Manfred . . . had not.

Which was perhaps why Manfred reveled in the
memory. "It's old age, that's your problem. Memory's
going first. Never mind, I'll get Francesca to refresh

the picture. Just some millefiori beads as I recall, all she was wearing."

"Manfred! You know that's not what I meant." Erik wondered just how he should deal with this. "Have you no morals at all? I meant she's a woman, not a girl."

Manfred snorted. "Only you Icelanders seem to worry about it."

"Vinlanders take it even more seriously. It's just not respectful!"

Manfred went off into a guffaw. "Well, that's something, considering her former profession."

Erik found himself blushing; as usual, confused by what his response should be to the former whore, then courtesan, now a prince's mistress. His conservative upbringing said he should treat her with disdain. Yet . . .

Francesca, he knew from experience, lived by a rigid moral code too. It just had a totally different set of rules about sex.

He decided to take refuge in something he *was* familiar and comfortable with. "Come. You're getting fat, Manfred. Let's go down to the jousting yard."

"Erik, it's snowing out there. Besides, I know you just want to take it out on me."

There was some truth to that, even if, as the years went by, "taking it out" on Manfred was getting a great deal harder to do. But at the new rapier-work Erik still had the edge, and always would have. He was just faster than Manfred could ever be. "Then we will find a *salle* big enough for some more fencing practice. Come. I have the quilted jackets in my quarters."

"I'd rather go drinking," protested Manfred.

Erik threw him against the wall with a rolling hip-lock.

Francesca looked severely at the Emperor. "Using me to tease your nephew is not kind."

Charles Fredrik smiled. "It's one of the few pleasures left to an old man." The smile widened. "And by now Erik will have talked him into some training and will administer some bruises, which his disrespect deserves."

"You are a very bad old man," she said, shaking her head at the most powerful man in Europe.

The first time she'd met the Emperor she'd been quaking inside. But when all was said and done, he was also a man. Men, she understood. This one, for all his power, was a good man. And behind the smiles she read genuine worry.

"He's turning out well, you know. But he is still very young."

"And very jealous. If I were twenty years younger he'd have reason to be. Now tell me, Francesca. What do you intend to do now? I am sending Manfred to Jerusalem. But I have a place for you here in Mainz. You've served me well in Denmark, much though Trolliger disapproves of your methods! Mind you, I don't think he realizes that your methods are—"

"More refined than in Venice. And not horizontal in the least." She smiled tolerantly. "Wait until his spies are done reporting to him—or until he finishes reading those reports he's already gotten. I believe he will be astonished that I have become a veritable pillar of respectability."

"Good," the Emperor replied, and sounded as if he meant it. "I gathered that already; unlike Trolliger, I read the entire reports from my spies—and his, by the way—not just the parts I deem are pertinent at the time."

"Well, I may not be Caesar's wife," she said thoughtfully, with a long look through her lashes at the Emperor, "but—"

"But you must still be above reproach, as my nephew's paramour," Charles Fredrik agreed with her. "Though a bit of banter between the two of us, in private, is harmless enough."

"And in public," she twinkled, "I find finance to be the most fascinating possible topic for discussion."

He chuckled, as she had known he would.

Francesca licked the corner her mouth. Slowly and catlike. "So, whatever could he find to disapprove of in finance?" she asked, innocently, looking at him through lowered lashes.

She was rewarded with the Emperor's laughter . . . which went off into coughing. It took a while to subside, and now he looked older. Gray and tired, though still able to muster a smile.

"Don't make me laugh, please!" he said breathlessly. "It's a pity. I find little to laugh at these days. No wonder the Danes were so willing to help you. You must have had them wrapped around your littlest finger. But what do you intend to do now? Because I would like to ask that you accompany Manfred. Not for the reasons *he'd* like, lucky young dog, but for my own interests. And yours, for that matter. I pay well, as you know."

Francesca chose her words carefully. She was aware just how dangerous these waters were. She knew she was tolerated as the *mistress* to the Emperor's second-in-line heir. But more than that? No.

"I was planning on accompanying Manfred. Not, I'm afraid, for the reasons he thinks. But the truth is that Mainz is not my sort of town. And I fancy seeing the east. Alexandria tempts me."

"Alexandria!" She was surprised by the enthusiasm in the Emperor's voice. "What a place! I went there, you know, as a young prince." He sighed. "A paradise of a town for a young man. But there is more to it. A place of intellect, too. More than anywhere else in the world, as I know it. I regret, in my old age, that I didn't explore that aspect more."

"I would wager you didn't regret it then!"

"True. But I'll have to tell you about it some other time. Right now I want to talk to you about Eberhard of Brunswick's mission."

"To the Ilkhan."

The Emperor shook his head. "If I didn't know you better, I'd have you burned for witchcraft."

She shrugged. "It is quite obvious."

The Emperor shook his head again. "I just hope that Grand Duke Jagiellon is not as intelligent and devious-minded as you are."

"If he isn't, he's bound to have someone who is," she said.

The Emperor looked thoughtful. "Not necessarily. The plots and machinations of Jagiellon are not constructed as you or I would construct them. You've given a lot of thought to western politics. Turn your mind now to the east. There is a factor at work there you must not forget: Power in the Grand Duchy of Lithuania is wrested by strength and cunning, not just by hereditary right or, as in Venice, by election."

He held up a hand. "Yes, I know. There are intrigues and schemes here, also. But this is the playing of puppies compared to the fight for pack-dominance there. Jagiellon dares not allow anyone into his trust. He must always act, to some extent, alone. Even his closest advisor, Count Mindaug, will pull him down if he can, and thus is not privy to the innermost workings and plans and secrets. That would require trust and a loyalty born of love, not fear. Those are as alien to Jagiellon as his kind of absolute enslavement is to us. He gains their loyalty by robbing them of their will and their self. Our most trusted people can betray us . . . his cannot. But his cannot think or act independently, either. Those Jagiellon allows free thought to must be kept weaker, and ignorant. We don't have that problem, although we do need to fear treachery. We must place our trust carefully."

Francesca looked at the Emperor in some surprise. "Maybe it really is a pity that you spent so much time in the pleasure-palaces in Alexandria."

The Emperor gave a small snort. "Not nearly as much as you might think. I learned a great deal about things that my tutors hadn't mentioned, while I was there. But a fool and his empire are soon parted. Alexius VI of Byzantium is busy proving that. And while I, or Conrad, or even Manfred might not be the best person for the job . . . as my father said to me, when I protested that I didn't really want to be Emperor, better those who have been trained for it but don't want it, than someone who just wants it. A man who wants this kind of power, does not want the responsibility that goes with it." He shrugged. "Nobody would."

Francesca's smile was small, tight, and sympathetic. "I think most of them would just choose to ignore the responsibilities. I think the Holy Roman Empire has been fortunate in its Emperor."

"To my sorrow, no. One of the reasons that I want Manfred to pray for my soul is that I know I have failed sometimes, Francesca. Too often," he said quietly, shaking his head. "And thanks be to the hard lessons I got from Erik's father that I can acknowledge this responsibility. You know, I once said something stupid and arrogant about some peasants. Hakkon explained that if they'd said the same about me, they'd have died. And, as I couldn't learn if I was dead, he'd simply made me wish I was dead. It gave me an insight the imperial heir had previously lacked."

He paused, lost in reflections. Francesca waited, patiently. "Now, to return to the Ilkhan. I think we can benefit each other. Of course Eberhard of Brunswick will be doing the actual negotiation but I would like you to be able to . . . shall we say, 'smooth things over' if there are difficulties." He smiled. "This means I will have to trust you, which Jagiellon would not."

Francesca shook her head. "So: You will have to trust me, which Jagiellon would not. But, Your Majesty, neither, by the sounds of it, would Emeric of Hungary trust me. He is, by all accounts, a man who would match your image of the Grand Duke. And he is closer, too. Why do you focus on the Grand Duke?"

Charles Fredrik sighed. "It is ill fortune to have two such men on the thrones of powerful neighboring lands. But Emeric is not threatening us at the moment." The Emperor smiled grimly. "I have reliable information that he is turning his attention to the southern Balkans. Being involved in a war down there would be, for him, what being involved in the wars of Italian principalities would be for us. There is an Illyrian chieftain down there who is giving him considerable pause."

"What!?" Manfred shook his head. "You want me to take a couple of hundred knights with me? That's an army, Uncle! That's ridiculous. *You* managed fine in Italy—with just Erik and me escorting you."

The Emperor shook his head. "I enjoyed that. But we were traveling incognito, Manfred. I am afraid that part of the point of this exercise is to travel in the full glare of public view. Even two hundred men-at-arms may not be enough."

Manfred thumped a meaty fist on the table. "When I went to Sweden I had seventy! And for all the use they were, I might as well have had none!"

The Emperor glared at him. "You were within my realms and supposedly protected by my hand. The fact that you went off into Norway, to Telemark, with just on half of that, when I had clearly and expressly told you to 'take a sufficient escort' just proves to me that I have to dictate how many men escort you. *And* I hear from the master of the chapter house at Lödöse that it was only on his insistence that you even took that many with you. Accept it, Manfred. I've heard the story from Erik. Your days of being the young, happy-go-lucky knight are over. Even in the Knights of the Holy Trinity, where you were supposedly anonymous and protected, you were a target. They tried to kill you, Manfred, as a way of getting at me. The day is fast approaching when they'll try to kill you just because of who *you* are. You won't always have Erik there. Besides, you need some command experience. The men I'm going to have sent with you are older, tough, solid veterans. You'll be younger than almost all of them. Less experienced. You'll spend half your life commanding men with the advantage over you of age and experience. Learn how to do it now, when you don't have to do it in combat."

Manfred groaned. "Bad enough that I've got to put up with old Eberhard's moralizing and carping. Now you're saddling me with a bunch of graybeards who are going to spend the entire journey, to and from Jerusalem, complaining about their rheumatism and grumbling how things aren't like they used to be when they were young."

The Emperor snorted. "You will treat Eberhard of Brunswick with respect, Manfred. Learn from him. He is a statesman and a truly skilled negotiator. One of the best. I've always thought that if he hadn't been born a noble he'd have been the richest horse-trader in the Empire. He's a valuable man, probably worth as much to the Empire as you are. If you don't treat him with respect I will curtail your personal allowance—which I imagine you and Francesca would find difficult. And as for the quality of the men I'm sending with you: I took Erik Hakkonsen's advice. I have asked the Knights of the Holy Trinity to send me a knight by the name of Von Gherens. Erik suggested I get him to select the men who will accompany you."

Manfred brightened. "Well, that's not so bad. Von Gherens can drink."

The Emperor shook his head and laughed. "Manfred! What are we going to do with you? I keep hoping Francesca and Erik have worked miracles and then you give me that sort of comment."

Manfred grinned. "Well, I have made some inroads in teaching Erik to drink! He still does it badly, though. And I've failed with Francesca entirely. Teaching her to drink properly, that is. I've had successes in other important areas, of course."

The Emperor shook his head again, helplessly.

"And I'm looking forward to visiting Venice again. Some fine red wines those Italians produce."

"I hope Erik beats you," grumbled the Emperor. "And I'm going to have a word with Francesca too."

"So long as you keep to talking," said Manfred, warily.

Chapter 13

Eneko Lopez stared impassively at the face of the Grand Metropolitan. He did not allow the thoughts roiling in his mind to show. He hoped not, anyway.

"You obviously made quite an impression on Emperor Charles Fredrik, Father Lopez," said the frail, pale—and powerful—man sitting on the throne before him. The Grand Metropolitan held up a scroll, almost as if it were a scepter.

The Grand Metropolitan had a reputation for vacillation; however, he was still the most powerful figure in the Church. And Eneko was never certain how much of that vacillation was because of the Holy Father's nature, and how much was because, in the end, when one kept from making up one's mind, things tended to sort themselves out without forcing one to take a stand.

"I found the Holy Roman Emperor to be a pleasant-enough companion on the road here," said Eneko dryly. "A not overly pious man, though."

The Grand Metropolitan gave a reedy chuckle. "It appears that he, on the other hand, did find you to be one. It is a signal honor of sorts. And, quite honestly, not a request easily denied."

"God is omnipresent," said Eneko stiffly. "He can be addressed as well from Mainz as from Jerusalem."

The Grand Metropolitan gave another reedy chuckle. "A viewpoint that I am sad that I will not be able to hear you express to the Metropolitan of Jerusalem. None the less, it is the express desire of the Emperor of the most powerful Christian state that you should go to Jerusalem to pray for his soul, as he, as the bastion stone of the Christian Empire, cannot leave his duty to millions of other Christian souls merely to indulge the desire of his old age."

Eneko stood in silence.

"He is a powerful friend of the Holy Church, Father Lopez," said the old man, mildly.

Eneko sighed. "I know. But, Your Holiness, I had hoped . . . The order I wish to found. The Emperor seemed quite well disposed to the idea."

The Grand Metropolitan scowled slightly. "More so than I have been. Your problem, Father Eneko, is that you have been a valuable tool for the church in your present role. I need an agent of your caliber. I am less sure that the church needs yet another religious order to create more schisms and infighting. But the Emperor is indeed well-disposed toward your scheme; he goes as far as to suggest a name. He seems to think a Petrine-based order devoted to holy magic in the active and combative sense would act as a counterweight to the Servants of the Holy Trinity. He also thinks that Father Eneko Lopez of the Basque country would be a good man to head such an order. I must read you his words."

The old man cleared his throat, unfurled the parchment and held the scroll at full arm's stretch. Then, began reading from it in a slight sing-song:

"'I find myself in agreement with your proposal that the Hypatian order should open some chapter houses in Swabia, Brunswick and Prussia. Details may be thrashed out between our intermediaries, but I would be happy to see as many as twenty of these established in the Empire's central provinces. However, one does not use a shovel to do a sword's work and vice versa. I am of the opinion that the order of Saint Hypatia in particular and the Church in general have lost some of the militant purpose Chrysostom imbued it with. It has become very gentle, and as a result, we are seeing enemies springing up who do not scruple to use the darkest of magics against us. The Empire and the Holy Church need a force not lacking in some of the gentleness of the Hypatian Order, but with the steel to meet the spiritual and supernatural evils of the northern darkness which threaten the mother Church.' "

The Grand Metropolitan paused and peered at Eneko over the top of the parchment. "He then proposes you heading such an order. But I read further: 'However, I feel Father Lopez would still benefit from some broadening of his viewpoints before he takes up this challenge. Therefore my request that he undertakes this pilgrimage to Jerusalem can serve a double purpose. As one of the most pious men I have met, he can pray for my soul, which I fear stands in sore need of such intervention. Visiting the birthplace of our faith and then proceeding to the cradle of our learning, Alexandria, will also broaden his outlook. Besides, such an order as he envisages will need to consult the Great Library at Alexandria extensively, as it remains the greatest source and storehouse of arcane knowledge, both Christian and non-Christian, in Christendom. And if Alexandria cannot broaden his outlook, then nothing can. Even the brothels there are an education.' "

Eneko felt himself redden. The Grand Metropolitan was plainly amused by his embarrassment. "I think the Emperor's assessment is very acute," he said with a wry smile. "Both of your piety and your need for a broader perspective."

Eneko took a deep breath. "I have always wanted to undertake the pilgrimage to Jerusalem, Your Holiness," he said, seriously. "And the second pilgrimage to the heart and birthplace of the Order of Saint Hypatia. But the responsibility of another man's soul—any man's soul, never mind the Holy Roman Emperor's—is too much for me."

The Grand Metropolitan nodded. "Only Christ could carry such a weight," he said gently. "But all that is asked of us is to do as much we can and He has ever promised us that He will help us to bear the rest. You may choose some companions—say, three—to help you. I feel Emperor Charles Fredrik would agree that such broadening of the structure that you envisage will be better if it has a wider foundation, as it were. Now, my son. I have other interviews. Come, take my blessing and get along with you. You and your companions will travel as humble pilgrims to Jerusalem, and thence to Alexandria. I have prayed on this and I feel you guided to this path."

It was said with a quiet certainty and deep humility.

It was also a firm, unarguable dismissal.

"When you travel with a small army you have to behave as if you are traveling with a small army," muttered Manfred irritably. "We should break this lot up into ten parcels of twenty knights, and fit into inns rather than overflowing villages."

The grizzled and facially scarred Von Gherens smiled. "A good idea, eh, Falkenberg? We ride with the first twenty and Prince Manfred rides with the last twenty. Then *he* can apologize for all the damage and pay the peasants, and put up with short rations because we've eaten all the food, and drunk all the beer."

Falkenberg, who was riding on the other side of Manfred, was also a veteran, though younger than Von Gherens. And like Von Gherens, Manfred had discovered, able to drink his weight in ale without showing any sign of it. The Knights of the Holy Trinity—the "Knots" in popular slang—were supposed to be a religious order, sworn to abstinence from the worldly trappings of wealth. In practice, Manfred discovered, that meant they ate and drank well . . .

When someone else was paying.

Manfred was finding that being in an out-of-combat command—especially when you have a reputation as a tearaway yourself—was a lot more difficult than he'd thought. In a way a misery-guts like Sachs was almost called for. The presence of someone who'd put some fear and sobriety into this lot would keep the reckoning down. The Emperor had given Manfred what he had considered to be an ample supply of gold for the trip. At this rate they might—possibly—get to Ascalon. He'd have to sell them off as mercenaries to get back.

Falkenberg looked at Manfred with amusement.

"Sounds very good. It would make a change from the way it is now."

The problem was that both of them had been in Venice with Manfred and Erik, when they had striven against Chernobog. The two of them, Von Gherens particularly, had been the catalysts who'd broken up the fight in San Zan Degola when Erik had refused to hand over the young woman who had claimed sanctuary there to Abbot Sachs. Von Gherens had been at the final destruction of Chernobog's Vessel and had been terribly burned there.

They both liked Manfred; he knew that. They were from northeastern frontier families, from the borderlands of the Empire where the battle between good and evil was stark and frequent. There was no doubting the toughness or the piety of either man. There was also no doubting their ability to soak up food and drink when it was available. They treated their young commander with a sort of jocular respect . . . and then did precisely what they intended to do. No doubt about it, in a fight they'd be what they were—superb soldiers, disciplined and ordered. So how come they traveled at exactly the pace they intended to travel, despite Manfred's desire to pick the pace?

Manfred was left feeling he was being tested. He wished he could do with the troop what Erik did, in the daily drill session the Icelander put them through. They jumped when Erik Hakkonsen said "frog." There was always that sort of distance between Erik and the rest of the human race, and the barrier seemed to work in Erik's favor. No one, not even old Notke—who was fifty-five if he was a day—treated Erik as an equal.

That evening in the smoky room in one of the three crowded inns at Brixen, Manfred turned to Erik and Eberhard and sighed. "What the hell do I have to do to get the Knights moving? I wanted to be through to Bozen by now. At this rate, we're going to take twice as long as I'd intend to get through to Venice."

Eberhard looked at him with a frosty eye. "I was Knight of the Trinity with your grandfather. I had a commander like you once. Good fighter. Lousy commander when we weren't fighting."

Manfred had never really thought of the old man as a having once been a mere rank-and-file knight, but always as a prosy and disapproving important old man. "So, Milord of Brunswick," he said, in as serious a manner as he had ever donned. "What should I do? Lecture them on diplomacy?"

"Break a few heads," said Erik, looking up from his platter. "You are too young and too popular."

Eberhard shook his head. "That might work for you, Erik. You will lead troops. You already do that well. But Manfred is such a babe-in-arms, he still needs *them* to teach him. He will lead armies, not troops. And what he needs to learn is that you cannot lead armies on your own. You need to delegate."

Manfred stared at him in astonishment. *That* was a solution that didn't sound like a good idea. On the other hand, Eberhard . . . had experience. "Delegate to whom? I mean, wouldn't they just think I was trying to avoid responsibility?"

Eberhard gave his wintry smile. "This is statecraft, which your uncle wished me to instruct you in. I thought it was a waste of time but if you can see that there is a problem, well—perhaps you might learn something after all." He cleared his throat. "It is often a good idea to pick on the worst sources of your troubles—and make them responsible. If they fail, then you must display very clearly that you have not abrogated your responsibilities, by taking action against them, personally. But I don't suppose you'll have either the intelligence or maturity to take my advice."

Despite himself, Manfred knew that his face showed what he'd have been likely to do if the old man were not nearly seventy. Instead he clenched his fists and walked off.

"Francesca, he's going to drive me mad," said Manfred later in their chamber. "He treats me as if I were stupid and ten years old."

Francesca traced his deltoid with a delicate finger. "He's a very bad old man, to tease you so. But I think he wants to make sure he's got your attention."

"You think he's doing it on purpose?" demanded Manfred incredulously.

Francesca smiled catlike. "He is one of the leading diplomats and statesmen of the age, Manfred, dear. He's playing you like a lute."

Manfred did not like the idea of being manipulated by anyone, much less Eberhard. "The old bastard!"

Francesca shook her head in admonition. "I'm sure he's only doing it to oblige Charles Fredrik."

Manfred snorted. "Two can play his game. I won't rise to his bait. Tomorrow morning I'm going to call Falkenberg and Von Gherens. Make those two carry the can. Falkenberg can do the damned accounting. That'll stop him eating and drinking for a few minutes, which should save us a few pennies anyway."

"Good. Then maybe we can get moving a little faster. I had letters while I was in Mainz from Katerina. I said I would do my best to be there for her wedding, even if I cannot accede to her request to be a maid of honor." Francesca smiled wryly. "But I wouldn't mind being a trifle early to help with the organization."

"Von Gherens will have to make them trot," said Manfred languorously, leaning toward the caressing fingers.

Chapter 14

The woman didn't stop screaming. She'd gone beyond the edge of fear and into raw hysteria.

None of the three people in the room appeared to even notice, any more than slaughterhouse workers might notice a bellowing steer. Jagiellon simply continued to whet the cleaver.

Caesare Aldanto stood like a blond puppet that someone had propped against a wall. The position his arms were in was not quite natural and would have caused any normal man to alter it before more than a moment had passed. Aldanto stood as still as a log. His empty blue eyes stared unblinking at the altar. The shaman simply continued to rub the drum-skin, and walk in a widdershins circle, producing a low murmur of sound that seemed to slice through the screaming.

The cut, when it came, did not stop the screaming. That brutal chop was not intended to. This rite derived much of its power from the suffering of the victim. The *quodba* drum now was a fluttering, weakening, fast heartbeat, perfectly matching that of the woman. In the old face, the shaman's eyes burned with a fierce intensity. Sweat dripped from his forehead although the room was cold. Jagiellon showed no such signs of strain.

Neither did Caesare, who had come forward now to kneel, holding the stone-cut bowl into which the woman's femoral artery pumped.

Jagiellon scryed for his foes in a dark magic built on blood, pain, and defilement.

There was a price, a terrible price for this clear vision, and not just from the victim. But the Black Brain did not care. That part of Jagiellon was long dead anyway. And this was no new ritual being enacted for the first time.

In the blood that now pumped feebly into the bowl, Jagiellon saw Eneko Lopez, and a band of companions. Saw the canals of Venice, and a canal boat with what could only be a bridal couple. Abruptly that opaqued. Only a Leonine winged shadow remained.

The blood bowl cleared, showing a new vision. Eneko Lopez again, face uplifted, at peace, standing on the place which is called Golgotha.

There was a high, thin, sound that pierced the brain like a white-hot needle.

The bowl shattered. Blood erupted out of it, as if something had exploded within the depths of the bowl, splattering everything and everyone within the magic circle.

The woman's screams, which had grown weaker and weaker, were stilled. Cut off abruptly.

Silence, heavy and chill, hung over the scene for a moment. No one moved.

And then the shaman coughed, breaking the stasis.

Neither Caesare nor Jagiellon appeared concerned about being showered in fresh blood, but *something* had plainly affected them. There were sweat beads on both foreheads, mingling with the splattered blood. Caesare's eyes were wild and mad, not dead as they had been moments before.

"Very powerful place. Very powerful man," grunted the shaman, fastidiously cleaning his drum.

"I know where he is going," growled Jagiellon. "The forces of light marshal against us. A pilgrimage. And he intends to go via Venice. Somehow this ties with the wedding of the other one. Marco Valdosta. That joining must be stopped. Or at least I must stop Lopez reaching the marshes where the Lion holds sway."

The shaman nodded and rubbed his shoulder, wincing as he did so, as if the shoulder was deeply bruised. "Lion is very strong. Even if the young one is still unskilled, he is strong."

"I do not like failure. You will keep watch around the Lion's borderland." Jagiellon cleaned the cleaver on the victim's hair. "We will consult with Count Mindaug. He has been studying the magics of the West. He thinks I am unaware of this. Maybe he will know of some trap we can set."

The shaman nodded, and the Count was sent for, as servants cleared the mess away, moving with swift and fearful silence. As well they might: Any one of them might be next, if they drew attention to themselves. Until today, the dead woman had been a chambermaid.

The Count did indeed have an answer. A stray fact plucked out of a grimoire from the Ravenna region, from the southern margin of the sequence of lagoons and floodlands that had once stretched all the way from there to Grado in the north. Just off the southern margin of the ancient marshlands lay a grove of oak trees. The local people would go nowhere near the place. Local legend said a terrible rite had raised something there, something so evil that everyone for miles around found a reason to avoid the spot. It was a lonely and not very fertile area anyway, full of mosquitoes and malarial fevers. It lay not far from the causeway that led to Ravenna, and then onwards along the coast toward Venice.

"I will open the way," said Jagiellon. "Take a form to travel on land. See what, if anything, lies in this place."

The shaman nodded and stripped off his jacket with a tinkling of brass bells. The old body that lay underneath the leather was also tattooed. And considering the age of that lined face, the shaman's body was in remarkably good shape. Scrawny, yes; but sinewy tough under the tattoos.

The old man blurred into a feral-looking dog with yellow mangy fur, and yellow eyes, and yellower teeth. The dog slipped into the tunnel that Jagiellon had made.

Some hours later the shaman returned. "Some old beast

of *kaos* make nest there. There are old magics which let it survive. It is very strong but nearly mindless. It exists just to feed, master."

Jagiellon's cold eyes seemed to glow. "Ideal."

"It cannot leave that place, master. It would die."

"No matter," said Jagiellon. "We will lead the priest and his companions to the beast, before they can reach the marshes. If it fails to kill them, it may at least drive them back. I want him away from Venice, and Marco Valdosta. There is something about that meeting that I do not like the feel of. Your birds will continue to watch and follow when Lopez moves."

First babies, the wise old midwives all said, were hard. Hard on the mother, hard on themselves. Issie evidently agreed with the wise old midwives of canalside, for the closer came the day that Maria was due, the more horrifying became the tales the old woman dragged out of her memory. Tales of birth-struggles that lasted for a week; of every possible complication; of girls that died and babies that died; of both that died together. And she had the unmitigated gall to bring in all the other foresters' wives to regale Maria with still more tales of birth-horrors, until Maria wondered why so many of them had gone through the ordeal not once, but six or eight times.

Maria had cause to thank all the saints together that Umberto was never around to listen to these stories, or if he was around when Issie began one of her tales, he was so used to ignoring her that he really didn't hear what she was saying.

As for Maria—well, Issie had been one of the people who had tried to frighten her with stories of ferocious wild beasts in the forest. The wild beasts had been no more ferocious than the occasional hare or deer, and by this time, Maria was disinclined to believe any of Issie's tales.

That didn't mean she wasn't prepared for a hard go; but her own mother had given birth and gone out to deliver a load the next day. Maria knew that *she* came of tough stock. She wasn't expecting much trouble, really.

She *still* wasn't expecting much trouble when the first

pangs started, and the water broke—though *that* was a shock—and Issie chased Umberto out.

But then the real pains began. And after the first hour, Maria was vowing—between groans—that the next man who touched her with sex on his mind was going to draw back a bloody stump.

After the third hour, she knew that it wasn't going to be the stump of his *hand*.

After the fifth hour, when the pains were continuous, wave after wave after wave, and her throat was hoarse, she couldn't think of anything but the pain.

There were women milling about everywhere, praying out loud—what were *they* doing there? She hadn't asked them to come! The air was hot and stifling, her hair and bedgown were absolutely plastered to her with sweat, and someone was burning some vile herb in the fireplace. And all she could do was bite on the rope they'd given her, and tear at the bedclothes and it went on and on and on—

And that was when *she* swept into the room.

She was a tall shape in a dark, draped dress, and all the praying women fell silent as she raked the room with eyes that gleamed in the firelight.

"Out," she said. And the women, the horrible, useless women, fled before her like chickens before a falcon, cackling in panic.

She flung the windows wide, threw something on the fire that chased the stink out with the scent of fir and rosemary, and came to the side of the bed.

She leaned over Maria, and the silver pentacle gleaming at her throat told Maria everything she needed to know.

"Strega," she gasped. But in recognition, not condemnation. After all, none of those women and all of their calling on saints and angels had helped her.

"Exactly so." The woman smiled, and placed a hand on Maria's forehead; then, sketched a sign in the air and murmured some words.

Suddenly, Maria was . . . there, but not there. Detached from her body and all the pain and the mess. Floating within her own head, dreamily watching, as the Strega helped her out of the bed and got her to walk, then rest, then walk again, a little. She was *there*, but she did not care, except in the most detached possible way. Her body strained and hurt, but *she* did not.

Issie's friends all huddled fearfully at the door, and the Strega cast them glances of contempt from time to time, but said nothing. "I should have come to you before," she murmured in Maria's ear, "But I did not know your time was near. Did you think that we would leave one who was a friend to us alone with a flock of chattering monkeys in her time? No."

Then she made Maria squat on a peculiar stool, and there was a moment when Maria was *back* in herself, fully, and shouting, and then the baby dropped into the woman's hands in three, hard heaves.

Maria went back into the dreamy state, and the woman got her into bed again and put her little girl in her arms, and with an imperious gesture, allowed the silly chickens back in again. And *they* cleaned the room, and Maria, and made everything pretty so that poor Umberto would not be horrified, and she stayed awake only long enough to look into her daughter's eyes and fall in love—and smile vaguely at her husband in reassurance when he came in.

The last thing she saw was the Strega woman, whose name she never learned, sketching a sign of blessing in the air and leaving as mysteriously as she had come.

In the night, the cliffs loomed dark and threatening. The air was still cold, the wind blowing from Albania. Here, in the craggy folds of the mountains, winter still held firm. And threading her way through the darkness came a woman. She disappeared into the cliff. A little later a second woman came threading her way along the narrow path. Later a third. And then, two more. Deep within the caves the chanting began.

Georgio Steplakis was a hill shepherd. He had thirty sheep, and twenty-two goats, and a hut in the hills. He could hear the chanting. He had absolutely no inclination to leave his pallet. Rumor among the shepherds was that the women shed all their clothes for the dancing in the glades.

Georgio had reason to know the truth of this story. He'd been curious enough, and not superstitious enough, to try for a closer look when he was younger. You could be really stupid when you were sixteen or so. He hadn't believed in the naiads either. Well, he'd learned. The rite was as old as these hills and before people had chanted and danced, the nonhumans had.

And it was a women thing. Men who intruded would regret it. Georgio sighed in remembrance. Sometimes it was worth doing something you knew you would regret. She had been very beautiful.

Her hair was silvered and as fine as the finest silken threads. If she'd been standing, the tresses would have reached down to her knees. She lay in the glade, naked but for that hair. Her skin was very, very white, as white as almond-milk. It was also very, very old. The breasts were wrinkled and empty. They sprawled sideways across her chest. The chest did not move. Her eyes, wide open and sightless, stared at the sky. Half of a peeled almond was still clutched in her wrinkled hand.

When the women who had come to tend the altar found her thus, a low moan went up. There was sadness. And there was fear.

Who would take the half-almond from the worn stone altar when the winter came?

The cold lord must have his bride. There would be no fertility without it.

They buried her with honor and according to the ancient tradition, in a fetal position, half-almond still in the old hand. She was buried with the others, beneath the dancing glade.

Once the glade had been much lower than it was now, and the grass had grown less green.

Over the spot she was buried the grass would grow greener. The earth here lay many cubits deep. And it had all come from the same source. Many, many burials over long years.

Many brides.

PART IV
March, 1539 A.D.

Chapter 15

A shadow passed over the road in front of their mules; Lopez noticed that his mule flattened its ears at it. He looked up, and did not like what he saw. Those were blunt-winged hawks, not soarers.

Goshawks, he thought. What were goshawks doing here? In his former life, Encko had flown hawks against game, as every young nobleman did. Goshawks were used in forested lands, not open plains, because they could not soar aloft on thermal currents as the long-winged falcons or broad-winged buzzards could. So why were those two up there, laboring away?

"Do you see those two hawks up there, Francis?"

The priest squinted. "Well, I can see two birds, Eneko. They're very high. Could be hawks, I suppose."

Eneko frowned. "This is the third day I've noticed them. Sometimes one, sometimes both."

Francis shrugged. "Well, there are always birds up there. Why do you think they're the same ones? We've done a fair number of leagues every day, Eneko, since we left Rome. We're already nearing Venice."

Lopez had actually opened his mouth to explain, when abruptly, explanations became superfluous.

Darkness fell on them as if someone had just clapped a giant kettle over the road. Flames leapt and roared in the sudden darkness, blocking the road ahead of them. The mules were terrified, bucking and cavorting as if

there were caltrops under their saddles and venomous
snakes under their feet.

Only sheer determination had kept Eneko in the
saddle. Father Diego had been less lucky; but Eneko
had dragged him up across the saddlebow like a very
ungainly sack of grain.

"It is an illusion," shouted Francis over the wheezing and
braying of the mules, and the near-curses of the riders.

Father Francis had refused to ride anyway, so he had,
perhaps, the advantage of not trying to control a mount.
But as Eneko managed to get his beast under a little
more control, he could see the flames, too. This was one
of the most difficult kinds of sending, a kind of vision
from afar. Thus, too, it was difficult to combat. The foe
was not proximal. It was no use to attack the vision, they
had to reach the sender.

And to make something of this magnitude required
truly unearthly strength. Abruptly Eneko realized, as he
struggled with the wild-eyed mule, that there could only
be one purpose in this exercise: To delay and thwart them
on this, the first leg of their pilgrimage. Something wanted
to prevent them going on, or at least to hold them up.
Perhaps whatever or whoever this was—and it reeked
of Chernobog—wanted them to band together and try
to pursue and find it. What it didn't want was for them
to continue on their way. Ergo: they must.

"Francis!" he shouted. "A cloth!"

Francis might not care to ride, but he at least knew
what Eneko was calling for and why. There was no reason
to use magic to settle the mules. It would be a waste of
effort and less effective than a scarf, anyway.

He unknotted and pulled off the sash he wore in place
of a belt or a rope about his robes and whipped it over
the head and eyes of the nearest mule, which happened
to be Eneko's. Once the mule's eyes were covered, it
stopped bucking, and stood, shivering all over. That gave
Eneko the leisure to rummage in his pack and pull out
the cloth that had lately been home to bread and cheese.
Francis gave the next mule the same treatment, and the
next, until all of them were blindfolded and no longer
fighting to escape the illusory dangers.

The only inconvenience was that now they all had to dismount and lead their mounts, as well as the pack animals. And the mules were balky, obstinate about going forward when they could not see. Mulish, in a word. But they were no longer terrified, which meant that they were no longer an actual hazard to their riders.

The four pilgrims advanced slowly, leading their mounts. All four of them were chanting—not magic, as such, but prayers; which were probably just as effective as sacred magic in this situation. In Eneko's case, given their proximity to Venice, he elected to pray to Saint Mark.

Now they waded through sights and sounds that were nauseating, rather than frightening. Chernobog had plainly realized that it no longer served to terrify the mules. Instead, it flung alternate visions of sacrifice and torture at them. Then, when that failed, sybaritic scenes and succubi.

"Something together, perhaps, Eneko?" Francis muttered, as Eneko paused for a breath.

Eneko nodded, and led the pilgrims in the chanting of psalms. At last the way seemed to be clearing ahead. They were on a well-paved causeway across a swampland of slime-covered pools and reed patches. The relief almost beguiled them. But as Eneko was about to step forward, something whistled off to his left flank. An inhuman whistle; the kind that actually makes your eardrums vibrate.

Despite his resolve, Eneko looked—and saw an undine, rising half out of the water. She was wreathed in long green hair with magnificent bare breasts, much like the other temptations and apparitions.

Only . . . she was thumbing her nose at him. Sticking her tongue out. The gesture was so unlike the horror or the seduction of the other visions that had confronted them that Eneko realized immediately this was no illusion.

As if to reinforce the impression, the undine blew a raspberry at them. Then, beckoned. Eneko felt his brows draw together.

"Follow it," he commanded. And he stepped off the causeway into what appeared to be waist-deep water.

"We should stick to the path, Eneko," said Father

Pierre worriedly. "Swamps are treacherous. And why do want to follow this illusion?"

For an answer Eneko pointed at his feet. "Because she isn't an illusion, Pierre. My feet are not wet."

"You look to be about waist deep!"

"It is the water that is an illusion. We are already lost. The horrors and visions were just a distraction while Chernobog or his minions tried to trap us more subtly. That undine is not an illusion. It is real."

"Nonhumans can be treacherous," Pierre warned.

Eneko stepped forward boldly. "Not more than Chernobog. And if I judge this correctly, she is the emissary of an ally of ours. An alliance of convenience, in which not much love is lost between the allies, but the common foe is worse."

There was, he thought, no point in mentioning that he thought this undine had come directly from Marco Valdosta, who had inherited his Strega predecessor's adherents. That would complicate matters altogether too much at the moment.

They walked slowly toward the undine, who smiled, showing altogether too many sharklike teeth. Father Diego glanced back, perhaps feeling doubtful, and yelped.

"My God!" he shouted, his voice rising a great deal. "Look!"

Eneko turned with the others to see what it was that had Diego so shocked. Behind them the illusion was dissolving. Ahead lay a far more dilapidated looking causeway. They were just on the edge of the reed-brake around some swampy pools. Behind them the ground was in fact higher. Higher and lashing with something that hissed unpleasantly, with distinctly reptilian tones.

The darkness lifted; the sun, long obscured, came out and cast reflections onto the still pools. And Eneko felt a warm breeze . . . and thought, perhaps, that he saw a reflection of something gold in the water.

"The Lion," said Pierre.

Eneko nodded. "Our guide has deserted us, but I think we no longer need her."

The breeze swayed the reed-brake. *Indeed*, it seemed to say.

Father Francis shook his head. "I feel we are in the presence of some powerful magic. You and Pierre seem to understand what is happening."

Eneko led his mule forward. "Chernobog made an effort to turn us before we could reach a place where he holds no sway. When the ruse failed . . . it tried to kill us, by luring us away from the safe paths and deeper into the swamp and the bogs, where something cruel and bloody lurks. But we are now in the lagoons and marshes of an ancient neutral power. One which is bound to a Christian soul."

"The Lion of Saint Mark," said Pierre. "The Winged Lion of Venice."

Father Francis looked troubled. "Why would one of the neutrals aid us?"

The undine stuck her head out of the water. "The Lion bids you a grudging welcome to his marshes. He sends messages to Eneko Lopez. By the inner flames that must be you, man. The Lion bids you come in haste. He needs you for a bonding. And he says that you should remember that although your God allows you free will, he too has plans. And that one such as he guides many threads."

The undine slipped back under the water. Then she popped her head up again. "Oh. Sorry about the nose-thumbing and the raspberry. But the Lion says the one thing Chernobog cannot understand nor feign is humor." She pointed. "The path is over there. Stick to it."

Lopez remained thoughtfully looking out at the horizon for a long time after she had gone. Francis, meanwhile, had taken the blinders off all the mules. Finally Pierre nudged him, and he started.

"What's wrong, Eneko?" the priest asked.

"It strikes me that this was a singularly ineffective attack, compared to what we have faced from Chernobog before this." Lopez turned to look into the faces of his companions.

"Well . . ." Pierre began, then nodded. "You know, you're right. But we did weaken him considerably, and this may be all he can mount."

"We weakened his instrument, Pierre," Francis pointed

out. "We never touched Chernobog himself. He can always get new instruments."

"My thought exactly," Lopez replied, with a frown. "So why this halfhearted try at stopping us?"

"Because we aren't as important as we think we are?" Pierre replied.

"Your humility is appreciated, Pierre, but—" He thought a moment. "But Chernobog would assign an importance to us out of all proportion to how we actually rate in the Lord's grand scheme," Lopez said firmly. "We *hurt* him. We hurt his mortal vessel, physically, and we hurt his pride—and pride, as you well know, Brothers, is highly cherished among the dark ones. No, I think there must be another answer."

"He's dividing his attention?" Pierre hazarded into the silence.

Eneko nodded. "I think it must be. He is confined to a mortal vessel, and has limitations imposed by that confinement. At the moment, something is occupying his attention that is far more important to him than we are."

Francis snorted. "Well, I, for one, am going to consider that a blessing!" He turned and strode off up the road, leaving the rest to follow.

But it was Pierre who voiced precisely what was troubling Lopez, as he nudged his mule with his heels, and sent it after Francis.

"If there is something more important to Chernobog than we are, what *is* it?" he asked aloud. "Why haven't we heard anything about it, and why haven't the Grand Metropolitan's seers gotten any hint of it?"

"Why, indeed?" asked Lopez, and sent his mule after Pierre's. "Whatever it is, I fear it will come from a direction that none of us can anticipate."

Chapter 16

"She's beautiful! Oh, she's so cute!" Kat peered into the crib at the baby.

Maria yawned. "She's asleep. That is beautiful enough for me right now."

"She's so tiny! Oh, look at those little fingers."

Maria snorted, but fondly. "You should hear her yell. There's nothing tiny about her lungs. She yelled almost the whole way here to Venice, on the ship. Then I took her to see Umberto's sister to talk about the christening, and the baby screamed at her. You're lucky. Umberto's sister didn't seem to think much of being bellowed at. I thought she'd refuse to be a godmother, and Umberto particularly wanted her to be."

"*I* insist on being one of her godmothers," said Kat loyally. "And whether he likes it or not, Marco is being the godfather."

Maria smiled. "You're not losing any time putting your foot down, are you?"

Kat smiled back. "Start as you mean to go on. When and where will the ceremony be? At the Chapel at St. Hypatia di Hagia Sophia?"

"We haven't arranged it yet. Father Pasquari, the priest who married us, has died since. But we just need a small place. There'll only be a few friends."

"I'll talk to Marco," said Kat firmly. "We have a wedding to arrange. Let him arrange this. He's very good friends with Brother Mascoli of St. Raphaella."

Maria smiled. "That's a canalers' church. He's a good man, is old Mascoli."

The more she thought about it, the better she liked the idea. Small, intimate, and none of her friends would feel uncomfortable, as they might in St. Hypatia's.

"Marco will arrange it."

Petro Dorma blew across his steepled fingers.

"Of course a desire to please the Holy Roman Emperor must be a major factor. But . . . well. I'd have to clear a couple of great galleys. It's not just the entourage, Manfred, it's the horses, and at such short notice. The merchants are going to howl. The Republic of Venice is not like the Empire. The *Case Vecchie* are all engaged in the trade. I wish you were prepared to take carracks instead."

When Manfred and Erik and Eberhard had been admitted to the Doge's private working chambers earlier, he'd been delighted to see them. "You've arrived in Venice just in time for Marco and Kat's wedding!"

Now that they were asking to hire vessels to transport them to the Holy Land . . . he looked as if he'd just drunk a large draft of vinegar.

"The Outremer convoy leaves in less than three weeks. Even deck-space is bespoke."

From the corner of the room a stocky young man spoke up. "What about the four galleys that are in the Arsenal, Petro? The ones that are going to Cyprus? They should be finished by the end of March."

Manfred recognized the lad; it was the hooligan who had taken part in the raid on the *Casa* Dandelo slavers, which Manfred and Erik had participated in. The one who'd been in jail for supposedly killing the priest. Manfred had been properly introduced to young Benito Valdosta as Dorma's ward after Venice had been rescued, but now, suddenly, the connection made itself clear. Then he'd been dressed like a beggar-brat. Now he was dressed as a Venetian noble. But a twist of expression as he'd looked at Manfred had let him place the face.

Petro nodded. "It's an idea." He turned back to Manfred. "Would you consider remaining on in Venice for a week or two after the wedding? You would arrive in Ascalon just as quickly, as the vessels wouldn't accompany the convoy. The convoy stops for two or three days at each port to allow for trade. You'd be spared all of that, as well as all of the mess and confusion of herding pilgrims on and off again at each port. And with your two hundred men aboard, they'd be well-armed."

Manfred nodded. "That sounds fair. What do you say, Eberhard?"

The white-haired statesman looked thoughtful. "A personal convoy of brand-new ships will look as if the Empire and Venice enjoy a very cozy relationship. Rome may not like that. Constantinople may not either."

Manfred grinned. "We're expecting to have the Grand Metropolitan's very own delegation along, in the shape of Eneko Lopez and his companions, according to a letter I have from my uncle. And as for Alexius, well, let him worry. The news is he may be a shaky ally at best. A good idea to fill his mind with doubts. In fact—on the whole, I think it would not be a bad idea at all for Alexius to think the Empire and Venice are on better than mere speaking terms."

Eberhard looked speculatively at Manfred. "I detect Francesca de Chevreuse's hand here."

Manfred did his best to look affronted. "I can think of ideas too, you know."

The statesman shook his snowy head. "Explain to him, my Lord Dorma, that a wise politician always tells the truth. If one day it is necessary for you to lie, no one doubts your veracity."

Manfred snorted. "The truth seems pretty rare in politics, Eberhard."

"That," said Eberhard, grimly, "is because there are very, very few wise politicians. If you must play at politics, play by my rules."

But Petro had picked up on another point. "Francesca!" he said with unalloyed pleasure. "You have brought her with you?"

Manfred nodded, warily. There was a little too much enthusiasm in the way Petro had reacted to Francesca's name. And he began to remember a few things from their last sojourn here. How Francesca had made it very clear to him that their liaison was not going to be an exclusive one. That she had several clients. And once, to comfort him, she had said lightly that one of them was balding and big-nosed . . .

He found himself eyeing Petro Dorma's balding head and lumpy nose with new understanding. "Yes, we have," he said curtly, trying to keep hostility out of his tone. "But understand this: She is strictly off limits to anything but polite social calls, Dorma. Even if you are the Doge of Venice."

Petro smiled, not at all discomfited. "Ah, well. My loss is your gain. But Francesca's conversation is a jewel even more rare than her magnificent body."

Manfred coughed. "Hmm. Well, we are going to be staying at the Imperial embassy. Francesca's already gone to see Katerina Montescue. But she will be in this evening."

Petro bowed. "I will come and make a call. And I don't mind if Rome and Alexius of Byzantium see it as Venice wishing to cozy up to the Holy Roman Empire."

"I'll send you a messenger when she gets in," said Manfred. "No. Wait. A better idea. We'll take young Benito with us. Trusty native guide, y'know. Well. Native, anyway. And then I can send him back without exciting comments about a messenger running between the two of us."

Petro looked at Benito, who was grinning like a horse-collar. "Why do I feel this is a bad idea, Prince? Well, I can hardly refuse. Off you go, Benito."

Looking at Benito's eyes, alive with devilry, Manfred himself actually wondered briefly if this was a good idea. Then he dismissed the piece of caution with the contempt it deserved. What trouble could this young *Case Vecchie* cause that he, Manfred, hadn't had Erik rescue him from a dozen times already?

Surely none.

"Well, there is a font, yes," said Marco, thinking. "But it is a very small and very poor church."

"Maria likes the idea."

"I'll talk to Brother Mascoli, then. I don't think he'd

mind, and his Hypatian ordination allows him to do this. I've hardly seen you for days with all this arranging. Come with me. Mascoli is a nice man."

So he and Kat went down to St. Raphaella, taking simple joy in just being in each other's company.

Brother Mascoli didn't mind. In fact, he was delighted. "Sometimes people seem to forget that St. Raphaella also does the work of an ordinary church. It will be a pleasure to christen this child."

His eyes moistened. "The child is healthy? Well? So many of those that I christen here . . . their mothers just wish to make sure that at least their souls are safe, since we cannot help their bodies."

"Marco has been to see them," said Kat. "He says the child is strong and healthy."

Mascoli smiled. "Well, that assessment is good enough for me. We can do it whenever suits the parents."

"Brother, Mascoli—" Marco hesitated; then, as the little priest cocked his head to the side, he went on. "Brother Mascoli, would it be out of order to ask the water-people to come add a blessing of their own? Just in case, you know? Umberto's family doesn't all approve of this marriage."

He decided he had better not say anything about the fact that the baby had been, well, "early." Brother Mascoli knew the dates of the wedding and the birth, and he was fully capable of adding for himself.

Brother Mascoli blinked. But to Marco's relief, he answered with no hesitation. "I think that would be an excellent idea. Would you care to ask, or shall I?"

"Would you?" he replied, with relief. "If I ask, they might feel, well, obligated. If you do, and they'd rather not, there'll be no hard feelings."

"Consider it done."

"What was all that about?" Kat asked, as they left the chapel and stepped into her family's little gondola.

"Call it . . . a little something extra," he replied. "Maria's always made her living on the water, and they're likely to be in and out of boats all their lives. I just thought it would be a good thing to get the baby a little extra blessing." He left it at that, and Kat evidently forgot all about it, for she said nothing else.

The next morning they gathered outside the church. Maria had underestimated her popularity, and the grapevine among Venice's waterways. There must have been at least thirty people. Brother Mascoli, clad as usual in his faded, light-colored robes, but with a special surplice for the occasion, smiled and let them all crowd in.

"Your friends said they would be happy to help you, Marco," he whispered, as Marco and Kat took their places beside the altar rail. And that was all he really had time to say, for the crowd parted for Maria and Umberto to come to the fore at that moment.

The only person missing was Umberto's disapproving sister. They were already inside the chapel, voices upraised, when both Marco and Kat realized that Maria was looking around frantically for her.

"What's wrong?" whispered Marco.

"The other godmother," whispered Kat. "She isn't here. Can't you do something, Marco?"

Marco drew his breath in. And felt a deep roaring within him of anger and determination. Umberto's sister didn't have to take her disapproval of the marriage out on an innocent child!

He *almost* said something, when he suddenly knew that he wouldn't have to. It would be all right.

Brother Mascoli took the baby into his arms. The baby girl didn't scream at him. "She is a beautiful, healthy child, my daughter," he said. "Now, who is going to stand as the godparents to this child?"

"We are." Kat and Marco stepped forward. There was a hiss of approval from the crowd of canalers and Arsenalotti. Marco had treated enough of their children, many of them here in this very chapel, and they all knew that he and Kat had played very large roles in the salvation of Venice less than a year ago.

"And the other . . ."

The presence light on the altar flared, burning with a peculiar greenness. From behind the statue of Saint Raphaella a voice came. *"I do."*

It wasn't, as many of the stunned audience concluded, the voice of the saint herself. Marco recognized it. That was the voice of the undine, Juliette.

She plainly had the ability to cast a glamour on her appearance. She came out from behind the statue. To Marco she looked her green-haired, green-toothed self. He could even see the line of the scar. But to the others in the chapel, she obviously didn't look quite like that. Marco wondered if they could see the pool of water she stood in.

Brother Mascoli smiled. "She is a lucky little girl to have such godparents." He took the oil and anointed the baby's head, and the water, which Juliette contrived to touch. Marco was aware of the green glow to it.

Baby Alessia, in her delicate white shawl, was angelic throughout the ceremony. Juliette took the baby into her arms. *"She will never drown. And if her mother is not there to care for her, she just has to touch running water to call me or my kin to help."* She spoke quietly, so that only those at the altar could hear her.

Maria sighed happily, when the ceremony was over and the crowd had left the chapel, looking at her daughter who had lapsed back into sleep. "Thank you both. I . . . I so desperately want Alessia to have what I didn't. I must find that other woman who stepped in for Umberto's sister and thank her, too. I really thought . . ."

Marco smiled reaching a finger to caress the baby's cheek. "You won't find her, Maria. But your daughter has a fairy-godmother."

"What?" Maria looked at him as if she thought he had gone mad.

"That was an undine," said Marco, calmly. "One of the water spirits of Venice."

"What!" Now her mouth dropped open with shock.

"She gave Alessia a powerful blessing too. Your little girl will never drown, and can call on the water-sprites for help."

"But . . . she looked just like an ordinary woman." Fortunately, Maria had far too much trafficking with the Strega in her past to be offended by the notion that a pagan creature, inhuman to boot, had just become the godmother of her child.

For an answer, Marco pointed to the pool of water on the floor, and the wet prints leading behind the statue of Saint Raphaella. "There's a water-door and a water-chapel through there. It is a consecrated place, too."

Maria shook her head and stared at the footprints. "I don't think I am going to tell Umberto about this."

Marco patted her shoulder "I don't think he'd understand and it would cause complications. Besides," he continued, feeling a laugh rising in his chest, "given the glamour that she used to make herself look human, I wonder if Umberto would believe you anyway. He'd probably think you'd just been seeing things!"

"Well, this is certainly an unexpected honor, Signor Lopez," said Petro Dorma, bowing. "You are the second great visitor I've had today."

"My companions and I are simple men of God, Milord Dorma," reproached Eneko.

"Traveling with a letter that bears the seal of the Grand Metropolitan in Rome? Not exactly 'simple,' I'd say. However that may be, you will do me the honor of staying here, I hope? Rooms will be made available for you."

"We'd be pleased to. But we do not intend to stay very long. We want to find a passage to the Holy Land."

Petro Dorma allowed himself a small smile. "Well, unlike Manfred of Brittany, you haven't walked in here and asked *me* to do so for you. He was here doing that not two hours ago. And—of course!—space for a couple of hundred knights, and—of course!—their horses. Emperor Charles Fredrik doesn't mind asking the impossible."

"The Emperor is here?"

Petro shook his head. "No, just Manfred, Erik, *Ritter* Eberhard of Brunswick—and an old friend, Francesca de Chevreuse. Oh, yes—and two hundred of those steel-clad Teutons. On their way to Jerusalem on a pilgrimage. Manfred needs one, I should think."

Eneko Lopez smiled. "I will talk to Prince Manfred.

I suspect our journey is for the same purpose. Perhaps he'll have space for a few priests among his knights."

"He seemed to assume you would be joining them, in fact," said Petro. "Or, at least, he said so in our conversation. However, I'll pass on a message that you are desirous of seeing him, as I'll be seeing the fascinating Francesca this evening. And, speaking as the person who organized his ships, he does have space. Now, not to make too fine a point of it, Signor, but you and your companions appear to be generously splattered with marsh mud. I'm sure you'd all appreciate an opportunity to get clean, put on some fresh raiment, and then join us for our evening meal."

Father Pierre laughed. "You mean, Milord Dorma, we smell like a swamp, and you'd prefer us to come to dinner without the bouquet?"

"Well, I wouldn't have put it quite like that," said Petro Dorma, tinkling a small bell. "But . . . yes."

"We're lucky we just smell of swamp," said Father Francis, looking across the piazza to the column where the winged Lion of Saint Mark gleamed in the late afternoon sun.

A factotum arrived, bowed. "You called, milord?"

"Alberto, take these good men and see them to the rooms reserved for our guests. Arrange hot water, baths, and fresh clothes, and the cleaning of their present clothes. See them comfortable and happy, please."

The factotum bowed again. "If you will follow me, sirs."

Chapter 17

It was easier, Kat had learned, to say *yes* than to plan a wedding.

The momentous day when Marco's marriage was annulled and she had been able to actually say "yes" had been a wonderful one. The trouble then began immediately, although she had not realized it until the next day.

But the next day . . .

She awakened, remembered with a rush *everything* that had happened, but most importantly, that *she was going to marry Marco*! Accordingly, she had plotted her way through a wonderful bath, perfumed and luxurious, that Madelena set up for her before the fire, as soon as she had finished breaking her fast.

A small wedding, she had planned. *Just the grandfathers, Benito, Maria—perhaps a few guests. At St. Hypatia di Hagia Sophia. . . . Dare I ask Francesca?*

She would certainly ask Father Lopez to officiate.

As the day progressed Kat had gotten the sinking realization—sinking like a stone anchor at sea—that the "small private wedding" she'd been planning was going to be a matter of public—very public—celebration. And she would have very little to say in the matter.

There was no question of *where*—the basilica. The *Basilica di San Marco.* With the banquet to follow at the Doge's palace, of course. Nor any question of who would be invited—everyone. Those not important enough for a place inside would be crowding the *Piazza di San Marco.* She had stopped worrying about who would pay for all of this once she got to that point. This was no longer a wedding, it was a state occasion, and the state would absorb it. The state would also absorb the feast for the common folk, which she insisted on.

"My *friends* will be out there!" she had said stubbornly. "So unless you wish to have the ambassadors sharing their tables with Arsenalotti . . ."

Petro Dorma had gotten her point immediately. There would be a feast with enough to stuff every man, woman, and child in Venice until they were sick.

On one other thing she put her foot down. "My attendants will be Maria Garavelli, and Francesca de Chevreuse," she said to Dorma, flatly, when he presented her with a list of suitable bridal attendants. "*Just* Maria and Francesca. No one else."

She fixed him with her best glare, the one that had usually cowed her most dangerous customers back in the days she'd been smuggling in order to keep *Casa* Montescue financially afloat. *A canal-girl and a whore. But also the woman who got you the Arsenalotti and the woman who kept the Knots on your side.*

Dorma, caught in that glare, folded. "Maria Garavelli . . . Verrier," he agreed, swallowing. "That will please the Arsenalotti a great deal, certainly. And Francesca de Chevreuse has the good will of the Emperor Charles Fredrik."

He did not ask her if she could render up the canal-girl in an acceptable guise; he had wisely left her alone to deal with the piles and piles of paper this behemoth of a celebration had already begun to generate.

Benito, of course, would be one of Marco's attendants. She didn't know who the others would be, but it wouldn't surprise her to discover one would be his friend Rafael. Two more . . . interesting choices.

But at least this way, none of the Case Vecchi *can be offended, because we won't have chosen any of them. Or if they are offended, they can all be offended equally.*

❖   ❖   ❖

There had never been any question of what dress she would wear. "Your grandmother's," her grandfather had said with pride and a tear in his eye. There was no choice, really. The dress would reflect *Casa* Montescue, and that dress was, perhaps, the only piece of clothing in the entire house that reflected the fortune that had been in possession of the *old* House of Montescue.

She had gone to the storeroom with no doubt in her mind that one thing, at least, would be as it had been in those happier times. After all, hadn't she rummaged out her mother's old gowns to remake for Francesca, and hadn't they been as sound as a bell? The gown she'd found to remake into Maria's attendant's dress had been a glory of scarlet brocade, still, despite all these years.

So the ruin that met her eyes when she opened the chest that contained her grandmother's wedding gown came as a total shock.

Silk had discolored, rotted in some places; the brocade was tarnished, the bullion dulled and blackened, the pearls—

She burst into tears, there on her knees beside the chest in the storehouse, and that was how Francesca had found her.

Francesca had taken one look at the contents of the chest and gathered her into her arms to let her sob, rocking her a little, and making hushing sounds while she stroked Kat's hair.

The last person to hold me like this was mother . . .

"Here, now," Francesca murmured. "This isn't as bad as you think."

"But it's *ruined!*" Kat wailed.

"Not . . . quite." Francesca took her chin in one hand and tilted her face to look up. "First, I don't think this is as bad as it looks. And second—" Her eyes twinkled, and Kat gulped down her sobs and sniffled "I've been casting about for a gift that you won't already have three dozen of. Unless you really, truly, desire *another* incomparably, grandiosely hideous silver saltcellar?"

Kat shuddered. "A twenty-third? None of which I dare have melted down?"

Francesca's silvery laugh startled a moth up out of the chest. "You clothed me—now allow me to clothe *you*. Madame Louise has, as you may have noticed, a very accomplished suite of seamstresses working for her. She still is very obliged to me."

"I had noticed," Kat said, a little embarrassed by the envy she felt for the wonderfully, flatteringly fashionable gown that Francesca wore—and for the air with which Francesca wore it. Next to the former courtesan, she felt as ungainly as a calf.

"Just close up the chest and we'll have it taken down to the gondola. I just came to thank you for the invitation to be your attendant, and to explain that it would be better for a certain party if I declined it."

Francesca's raised eyebrow and one finger tapping a ring with an elaborate crest gave Kat the hint.

"Oh. *Oh.*" She sighed. "Oh, bilgewater. I suppose it wouldn't be a good idea, would it? Your—friend—"

"Shouldn't be too publicly associated with me," Francesca agreed cheerfully. "Now, if you still want to name someone who will provide everything I can without the shock value . . ."

She shook her head.

"Never mind, then. Let's get this down to my gondola, and we'll salvage every scrap that we can from it—and what can't be salvaged, we'll replace. *We*," she added, again with that significant tap on her ring, and Kat found herself having to stifle a slightly hysterical giggle at the idea that Manfred of Brittany was going to find himself paying for the dress of a lady he barely knew and had not the slightest chance of finagling into his bed.

It was the both of them, she and Marco together, who approached the last possibly difficult bit of the wedding plans that deviated from Petro Dorma's orchestrations.

Marco tapped on the door, at precisely the time of their carefully made appointment. One no longer sought the quarters of Eneko Lopez unannounced, not now that he was openly the Grand Metropolitan's representative and quartered in the palace of the Doge.

"Come in," came the harsh voice. "I assume it is you, Marco Valdosta."

Marco pushed open the door. Lopez sat at a desk where he had been writing. He pushed his work away, and raised an eyebrow when he saw that Kat was with him. "I had wondered if you felt the need of spiritual counsel," he said dryly.

"Actually, we had a favor to ask of you," Kat said, hesitantly. "The Patriarch is conducting the Nuptial Mass, of course, but . . ."

She couldn't get the words out; Marco squeezed her hand and supplied them. "We'd like you to be the officiating priest for the marriage."

Kat saw the imperturbable Eneko Lopez at a complete loss for words, at least for a moment or two.

"I . . . would be very pleased," he said at last. "In fact, quite honored. But *why*? Why me?"

"For a great many reasons," Kat said. "But it just seemed to us that—as a priest, as the kind of priest you are, you have to do so many things that are so difficult, so dangerous—and no one ever asks you to do anything that is, well, pleasant." She hesitated; corrected herself. "Joyful."

Then she added, very softly: "We don't think you have nearly enough joy in your life. And you can't do without it, you know. It reminds you *why* you have to face the bad parts."

For a moment, she wondered if she'd insulted him. Then amazingly, the grim, stern, rather frightening Eneko Lopez reached up and wiped the merest glitter of a tear from his eye.

"Thank you," he said simply. "I would be delighted."

The Church of St. Hypatia di Hagia Sophia was silent, that silence that speaks of emptiness. For a moment, Kat wondered if she'd come too early. Still, it was supposed to be the night before her wedding day. There would be much to do, if she did go ahead and marry Marco. Part of her, the part that was pragmatic, the part that most people saw, said that she was being ridiculous. At this point, the thing had a momentum of its own, and would carry her along whether or not she wanted it to. But as Patriarch Michael had said, humans were creatures of spirit as well as mundane flesh. And her spirit was troubled. It was always here that she came when she needed to sort that out.

Ah. Yes, there was a solitary Sibling in her white robes. Kat walked to the counseling booth, sat down and waited. A few moments later a female voice said: "Peace be with you, my child. How may I counsel you?"

Kat sighed. "By telling me I'm being stupid, probably. I am supposed to marry tomorrow."

The dress is ready. It fits like a second skin, and where Francesca found all the bits on no notice at all, I will never know. I look like a queen in it, and Maria looks like a princess in hers. The feasting has already begun, the Basilica is full of candles and flowers and priests. Everything is in place for tomorrow. Only I—only I am suddenly afraid!

"And? Do you love this man?"

"More than anything on earth."

"Is there any reason why you should not be married, daughter?

"No." Kat twisted her hands. "The Patriarch himself has sanctioned the marriage."

"I see. Does your husband-to-be abuse you?"

"*Marco?* He's the gentlest soul in Venice! The kindest, softest, bravest . . ."

"Then what *is* the problem, daughter? Is it sexual . . ." The woman hesitated, an element of doubt in her voice. The Siblings were all sworn to chastity and celibacy. Perhaps her counselor felt she might be out of her depth here.

"No. It's . . . It's nothing like that. It's spiritual, if anything."

"Ah. Marriage is a holy institution sanctified by our Lord himself. It is intended to be a union of bodies, minds and spirits."

Kat took a deep breath. "The man I am going to . . . supposed to . . . marry, is possessed. Sort of. Um. Part of him is a pagan magical creature. I am a Christian."

There was a silence. "I think, Katerina Montescue,

that it would be easier if we went out into the church and I used those murals you sometimes sit and admire to advise you."

"You know who I am?"

There was a gentle snort of laughter from the other side of the scrim. "Katerina, all Venice knows who you are, now. But I have seen you come to this church for many years. I knew exactly who you were when I sat with Eneko Lopez and listened to you tell of your problems with the smuggling of supplies for the Strega. I listened with some amusement when you put him in his place with questions about Dottore Marina. Then, as now, I listened under the seal of counsel. I did not betray you then. I will not betray you now, just because I step outside of the booth."

Kat went out, to find the Sibling waiting for her. "Come. Let us go to the Chrysostom murals. They are not your favorites, but they make my point well."

They walked down until they stood below the first mural. The golden preacher was portrayed as a gaunt man with the eyes of a hawk. His painted gaze was unrelenting. They seemed to stare through her.

"He reminds me of Signor Lopez," said Kat, quietly.

The Sibling nodded. "I think they were cut of the same cloth. He was, like Eneko, a very intense man. And very charismatic. Not always right, however, nor always wise. Narrow-minded and even outright bigoted at times. Yet, with him our Hypatia formed one of the most influential alliances in the history of the Church. It was the meeting of those two great minds that set the course of the Christian Church from thenceforth, and put an end to—well, ameliorated, at least—what had become an increasingly entrenched tradition of schismatic dogmatism and heresy-hunting."

She paused for a moment. "I will not attempt, here and now, to explain the theological complexities of the matter. In the millennium that has gone by since, their tradition has become known as 'Petrine,' just as that of Saint Augustine has been called 'Pauline.' But, as is so often true, the names obscure as much as they reveal. Both creeds within the church are more like umbrellas than fences. Do not forget that if Sachs was a Pauline, so was the courageous young prince who broke the back of Chernobog's monster—and his companion Erik belongs to the Gaelic creed, which has its own history and doctrines altogether."

Her mouth grew a little tight. "Nor should you think for a moment that simply because a man calls himself a 'Petrine' that he is not capable of the vilest sins and crimes."

The Sibling pointed to the next panel, which showed the two, back-to-back. "There you see Hypatia writing, developing the philosophy, and Chrysostom, brilliant orator that he was, expounding it. He provided most of the driving force, she—when necessary, which it often was—provided the diplomacy. Because of that alliance, Hypatia and Chrysostom were able to formalize a doctrine of compassion and acceptance that emphasized wisdom and learning. But—"

She chuckled. "Not without a multitude of clashes, and even more in the way of compromises. And both of them left their own traditions, which are somewhat distinct. I represent one, Father Eneko Lopez another. The Church needs both, you know."

The Sibling turned away from her contemplation of murals. "All of this is the basis of the core tenet of the Hypatian order within the Petrine wing of the church. Which, since you choose to come to this church, I assume you are in sympathy with. Saint Hypatia gave to us that *all* men and women of good will, ultimately worship the same God, no matter what form they attempt to place on the unknowable. Whether they are Christian, Jew, Parsee or Hindu, Strega, Muslim, or even outright pagans."

"And what has this to do with my marrying Marco?"

"You would hardly say he was *not* a man of good will?"

"Of course not."

"And the Lion of Saint Mark? The Guardian of Venice? We of the Hypatian order know it well. Would you agree that it is a creature of good will, of love?

Sudden tears filled Kat's eyes. "It loves this place,

these marshes and its people . . . I see. Yes. Thank you. Thank you."

"It is a pleasure." The Sibling patted her gently. "I foresee yet another union, a meeting of minds and spirits."

Kat laughed, a slightly watery sound. "Marco can do the diplomacy."

In the end, the thing did have its own momentum, and Kat and Marco were carried, not along with it, but riding atop it.

It began with a pair of processions of gondolas that carried her and Maria from *Casa* Montescue, and Marco and Benito from *Casa* Dorma, to meet at the Piazza San Marco and disgorge their contents in front of the waiting crowds.

Kat, veiled from head to toe with the finest of silk gauze, saw everything through a sort of fog. The veil was white, but the overgown of her dress was as blue as the Med on a sunny day, and so stiff with bullion and pearls it could easily have stood by itself. The flower-crown that surmounted it surrounded her in a second mist of the perfume of roses and lily of the valley.

Kat had a sudden image of herself, from two years before, leaping into the canal to avoid a Schiopettieri sweep—wearing *this* outfit. She'd have gone down like an anchor! Not even quick-thinking Benito could have saved her.

The image almost caused her to burst into open laughter. As it was, she couldn't help but continue the procession with her face wearing a grin which, she suspected, was quite unsuitable for the solemnity of the occasion.

Fortunately, there were plenty of things to distract her. They were met by two sets of minstrels, who serenaded them with love songs as they made their way in twin processions to the basilica. And the mobs of Venice, who could be so unruly when they chose, parted like the Red Sea for them without a murmur—and kept their chatter and cheering down to where she could *hear* the minstrels telling her of the delights awaiting her.

Marco's procession arrived at the basilica first, of course.

He was supposed to await her at the altar, so she took her time, trying to move like Francesca, with a willowy, gliding walk that would make her seem to slide along without having any feet. She was very conscious of the Lion on his pedestal as she passed him; *was* this something more than a statue? She thought she felt his golden gaze on her, warm and benevolent, as she passed by.

She had thought it would take forever to cross the piazza. It seemed to take no time at all. She had thought she would feel pressed in by all the people; instead, she felt as if she floated on their goodwill.

The minstrels left them at the porch of the basilica, and from within came the sweet voices of children, singing. She held up her head, and saw the path to Marco lying straight ahead of her, and if she did not fly up it, it was through no fault of hers.

She went through the Nuptial Mass as in a dream, hands that wanted to reach for his clasped demurely in front of her. But finally, finally, came the moment when Eneko Lopez stepped forward with his sober black robes enlivened by a blue stole, and she and Marco rose from their places, and he raised the veil with shaking hands and put it tenderly over her head and they knelt together, hands joined at last beneath Eneko Lopez's, for the blessing.

And it was at that moment, when she thought that her heart could not hold another drop of happiness, that a faintly glowing paw of golden mist placed itself atop the hand of the priest.

You will be happy, little sister. It was not a wish, it was a prophecy. And her heart rose, singing.

Chapter 18

Manfred whistled softly. "Holy Mother! See that blonde, Erik? The original paps of Anu, I swear."

Erik determinedly did not look up from the table. Ogling all the available—and, for that matter, all the unavailable—women of the world was Manfred's specialty, not his. "It is impolite to stare, Manfred. Women don't like it."

Manfred snorted. "Then why do they wear clothes like that? Anyway, Erik, you've got have a look. I'll swear she is one of those Viking Valkyries come to fetch you after all."

Despite all his best intentions, Erik did look.

And was trapped. There were occasional blond heads in Venice. A few Lombards, and travelers from further afield. But this woman was a true Scandinavian blonde, her great cascade of hair straight and fine and so pale as to be almost white. Her face, too, spoke of the northlands: the skin milk-white with blossomed cheeks, high cheekbones. And, as Manfred had pointed out, she had a magnificent figure. Despite himself Erik caught his breath and stared.

Manfred laughed coarsely. "It *is* impolite to stare at her tits, isn't it, Erik? You want me to organize a meeting for you? A quiet little alcove somewhere. I'll distract the bodyguards. And in this case, my friend, they really are *body*guards."

Erik realized that he'd been so taken up with looking at the Scandinavian woman that he hadn't noticed the two men accompanying her. Once he did, it was very clear to him why the blond woman was not being mobbed by cisebeos. Looking at the two of them, Erik was wary himself. They were as blond as the woman, even taller, and much wider. And they had beards, something she lacked.

Still . . . she was a magnificent, queenly figure. "Who is she?"

Manfred took a pull from his goblet. "I only know half the women in Venice, Erik. I'll have to find young Benito. He knows the other half."

Erik shrugged. "Wouldn't do me much good. See the furs she's wearing? And the jewelry, and the escorts. That is a very wealthy noblewoman."

"The wildest kind, believe me," said Manfred.

He stood up. "Anyway. Francesca asked that I come up to speak with the happy couple. She's scheming away for my uncle, I suspect. Wasting her time. Marco is a nice boy even if butter won't melt in his mouth, but there's steel in him that not all of Francesca's wiles will turn. Y'know one of my father's *duniwassals* back at Carnac caught me stealing arrows from the war-stores to go duck shooting with, when I was about eleven. I was the duke's son, and I wasn't really worried. He fetched me such a clip around my ear I thought it might come out of the other side of my head. I squalled blue murder, and threatened to go to my father about him."

Manfred pulled a wry face. "I still remember what he said: 'I don't care if you go and talk to the Ard Ri himself, boy. Siege stores are my duty. I keep them frae pilfering by anybody, even your father hisself. Now run along and tell him.' The old devil was as unlike young Marco as possible, but the two are cut from the same cloth in one way. They know what they believe is right and you can't turn them from that."

Erik nodded, his eyes still following the blond woman. "Besides, if what Francesca tells us is true—and after what happened here I have no reason to doubt it—he is at least in part possessed by the Lion of Saint Mark." Dryly: "That's quite a creature to try to talk into something."

Manfred snorted. "I don't think the Lion half is as easily distracted by Kat's figure." He turned and walked off.

Erik made no move to go with Manfred. After the prince was out of sight, he got up and found his way across to the three Scandinavians.

"*Goddag*," he greeted.

He wasn't surprised at the Vinlander twang when one of the men turned and greeted him in return. "Icelander! What are you doing here?"

He was the slightly larger of the two men, who were obviously brothers, as well as the older. A smile on his face—matching that on the other man and the woman, also—now displaced the wary reserve that Erik had seen characterizing the Vinlanders' response to the Venetian pomp.

Awkward questions first, dealt with as he had been instructed to do when he first took on Manfred as his charge. The role of the Hakkonsen family in imperial affairs was not something discussed. Few if any people in Iceland had any idea that Clann Harald, to which Erik's family belonged, did loyal service to the imperial house of the Holy Roman Empire. It was best so, Erik's father had always said.

"I am just passing through," said Erik calmly. "And yourselves? My name, by the way is Hakkonsen . . . Erik. Eirikur, actually, but I've grown accustomed to using the Danish version. These continentals have less trouble with it."

Hakkonsen was an honorable patronymic, as was Harald as a clan designation. Erik's own father was well known, in Iceland, and there were always some of the clan in the Althing. True, Clann Harald was not rich; in fact, wealth seemed to avoid them. His father's own holding at Bakkaflói was a place of stark beauty but little else. Still, it was a name that was well respected.

The Vinlander obviously recognized the name. The smile grew, considerably. "Bjarni Thordarson, at your service. This is my brother Gulta and our little sister Svanhild. We're setting up a trading house for Vinland goods. We have a Venetian factor and partner." The big Vinlander gestured. "This is his daughter's wedding."

"An honor to meet you all." Erik's smile might just have been a fraction brighter for Svanhild, but he thought he'd done well keeping it under control. "So, here you are invited to a Venetian function, and you don't know anyone, and your host is buried in having his daughter married. Uncomfortable."

"And it is quite an affair," said Gulta, looking at the laden tables, the richly dressed people. "As an Icelander you must find all of this ostentation odd."

Erik smiled, remembering his first Venetian banquet. The ostentation had been overwhelming, yes, but it had been less so than the magical murder of the monk. "It was quite a shock, yes, but I've gotten used to it. Why don't we find a few glasses of wine and somewhere quiet to sit and talk? It has been five years since I went to Vinland. Where is your clan based?"

If he could find a quiet spot Manfred might actually not come and join them. Under the circumstances Erik thought he'd prefer that. Manfred had far more than his share of female attention anyway.

Something about what he'd said had made Svanhild smile upon him. Erik found himself hoping Manfred would stay away a *long* while. She was stunning.

Fortunately, her brothers seemed to approve. "The Thordarsons are a trading house," said Bjarni. "We have our headquarters at Cahokia in the Mississippi valley, deep in the interior, but we have factors on the coast also. And I agree. It has done us no harm to be seen at this gathering as guests of the Doge's ward's wedding, but I'm tired of all these people staring at my sister and none of them having the manners to come and speak to us."

Erik reflected silently that he'd nearly been amongst them.

"I don't mind," Svanhild said. But there was an undertone of faint unhappiness that told Erik that she minded a great deal. "After all, they don't know us, either. We must be odd to them."

We look like polar bears in a room full of lap-spaniels, said her tone.

"Well, if there isn't any business that you need to be doing, why don't we get out of the crush," Erik said, but said it to her. "I like these people, but I have to say that they must be the most obtuse lot I've ever seen. Nothing can be said or done directly, and they use occasions like this one to chatter around and around subjects they've already made their minds up about."

The older brother heaved a sigh of relief. "So I'm not the only one who thinks that!"

"I think I know where there will be a quiet room. Or quieter, anyway." Erik caught a passing page by the elbow, and gave him instructions. "Just follow me."

One thing that his previous visits had done was to give him a good grasp of the geography of the Doge's palace, and what was more, let him know what rooms were likely to be closed off to the general invitees. The little chamber off to the side of the council chamber, for instance. It was too small to be useful in a great gathering, and there was no comfortable furniture for assignations.

Not that something like that would stop Manfred . . . But, fortunately, Manfred wasn't there.

"Oh . . ." Svanhild said, as he closed the door behind the three Vinlanders. She looked around at the rather somber room with no hints of gilding or the usual Venetian opulence anywhere, only cold stone and dark wood and grim portraits of former Doges. "I thought all of the palace was red and gold."

"Not everywhere." Erik didn't tell her that this particular chamber was used for interviews with the spies—and sometimes, interrogations. At least they were interrogations that didn't require a trip to less salubrious quarters, the kind equipped with pincers and tongs and ropes and hot irons.

"Here." He purloined Petro's comfortable chair from behind the formidable desk for Svanhild, and offered the other, uncompromising pieces to her brothers. He sat on the desk, just as the page returned with wine and more refreshments.

"So, tell me why you're here, and about your clan holding in Vinland!" he said with enthusiasm. "It's been too long since I heard anyone speaking my own tongue."

Svanhild simply lit up at that invitation. If he was

any judge, she was desperately homesick, and, if she'd been able, would have flung herself on the first ship going west. The brothers were full of enthusiasm for their mission and what they expected to accomplish in Venice, but Svanhild wanted to talk about home. About little things—how she missed being able to hunt, how horribly crowded this place felt to her.

"Just like a gigantic ship!" she said, which actually was an excellent observation, seeing how hemmed about Venice was by water. He asked her, in between declamations by her brothers, if she had seen much of the city, and she said "no" in a tone that suggested to him that she didn't want to. "There are so many people," she elaborated. "Too many. As many just in the inn in which we live as there are in all of our holding!"

Eventually, her brothers announced that they had stayed away from the celebration too long. There was, after all, *business* to be tended to.

"And the Venetians feel the same, you know." Erik escorted them out the door and back toward the party. "They discuss business everywhere, in church, even at funerals! I thought I would never get used to them, or their ways, but I can tell you that underneath it all, they're people who are no different from anywhere else. You'll find you've got plenty in common with them after all."

But Svanhild cast him a glance that told him that in this much, at least, she was in total disagreement with him.

Manfred sat down with thump next to Erik, who was sitting in an alcove staring at a wine goblet. "I never thought I'd see the day when I'd have to come looking for you, instead of the other way around," said Manfred cheerfully. "Two hours it's taken me to find you—at least! To think of what I could have gotten up to a few years back, if you'd been like this then."

Erik looked up, his eyes bleak. "Manfred, I think I'm in love."

The young prince grinned. "Don't worry. I'll get Von Gherens to give you some advice on how to do it. I think you'd prefer it from him rather than from me or Francesca."

Erik's voice was icy. "Shut up or I'll break your head. It's not like that."

Manfred was silent for a few moments. "Who?" he asked, in a quiet, serious voice. This wasn't like Erik; this could be serious. Erik usually shied away like a nervous horse from women. Francesca and Manfred had been discussing a hypothetical future partner for his mentor not a week back. What had she said? *When Erik falls he'll fall hard.*

That wasn't a problem. Manfred's opinion of what constituted a suitable girl for Erik, on the other hand, *was* a problem. She'd have to pass the Manfred test of approval. And for Erik, Manfred set very high standards.

"Svanhild Thordardottar." Erik sighed. "Such a beautiful name. And she moves like a swan too."

Manfred felt real alarm. He started looking around. He needed Francesca. "Who?"

"You're right. She is like a Valkyrie," said Erik, dreamily. "A true shield-maiden. Not one of those girls who needs ten servants just to get dressed in the morning. And such a sweet nature, too—getting stared at and snubbed, and not a complaint out of her about it."

Manfred stared at his friend, mentor and bodyguard. "You mean the one with the big pair of—of—bodyguards? The blond one?"

Erik nodded at him, scowling a bit. "You watch what you say about her."

"I wouldn't dream of uttering a wrong word," said Manfred, quite truthfully. Erik was ferocious enough on the training fields even when he wasn't mad about anything.

Erik sighed. "Not that it really matters. I think *I* must have said the wrong thing. We were getting on so well. She wanted to know all about Mainz. Next thing they got up and left. Polite, but . . . closing me out."

"Oh." Manfred tried hard to keep the relief out of his voice, because of the hurt in Erik's. "Well, I'm heading out of here. This affair is beginning to drag."

Erik stood up with a sigh. "Yes. I could use my bed, I suppose."

Manfred—given the circumstances—didn't point out

that it hadn't been his bed he was seeking. Or at least, not his own. And right now Erik wasn't picking up the undercurrent of Manfred's words as he usually did. In fact, he actually wandered off to his own quarters without making sure that Manfred was coming with him, which suited Manfred right down to the bone.

Erik was welcome to a quiet night. Manfred had other plans; the hellion Benito would either be along presently, or Manfred would go find him.

Manfred snorted with amusement at that thought. It was a shock to find himself doing Erik's usual job of slowing a tearaway down. Francesca was waist deep smiling on, and politicking with, old admirers. Manfred found being around while she dealt with them set his teeth on edge. So the last set of plans he'd made with the rascal were that they were off to a place Benito had found—good Sicilian music and some dancers that, according to young Benito, could make the tassels on their boobs do amazing things.

Manfred finally got tired of waiting for Benito to find him, and traced Benito down at the wine-butts. "Let's go, tearaway. I find myself consumed with curiosity about these tassels."

The boy swayed gently as he stood up. He was already half-drunk. Manfred was mildly surprised. The last week Benito had escorted him to choice taverns and nightspots but the boy seemed to have some degree of caution about wine. What was it that he'd said? *I don't want to end up as a lush.*"

It had seemed to Manfred then that he was more inclined to drink enough to get up to devilry and stop there, than to go on to the fall-down stage. Odd. Distinctly odd. But none of his business, when all was said and done.

"Time to find the girls," Benito said, and his speech was clear enough. "There's no one here worth bothering about."

Chapter 19

The evening was wearing on and Maria found herself exhausted. Now that the ceremony was over, and the banqueting begun, Maria had settled into having a tedious time. She'd been seated among the guests of honor, among the gilt and brightness, and had been very uncomfortable. And kept her mouth shut. Yes, she loved Kat, and she certainly had wanted to be with her for her wedding. Marco, the bridge-brat she'd seen grow up, had a special place in her heart, too.

But . . . That was Marco and Kat. Marco Valdosta and Katerina Montescue, in their magnificent finery, surrounded by *Case Vecchie*, were more like jeweled butterflies than real people. And, as with Caesare, she'd been painfully aware of her lower-class origins every time she opened her mouth.

Benito had been seated as far as possible from her and Umberto. He'd tried to catch her eye, once; she'd looked down. Umberto had also been plainly uncomfortable among all those people who ordinarily he would only see at a distance; and a far distance, at that. Now that the guests were mingling, he'd hastily gone off to join his fellow guildsmen. She looked across to where he stood with several men, all gray haired, and all at this stage very jovial. Umberto looked happy, for the first time in ages.

Maria decided she'd had enough. Out in the piazza

there'd be real music and singing. Real talk, about things she knew, not her trying to keep her mouth shut. She got up; Alessia was in a room just off the banqueting hall with a dry nurse, and by the feel of it Alessia could use some feeding.

She walked across the crowded room to Umberto, moving carefully on the slippery marble, pausing every other step to keep from jostling someone who was probably important. It took an age to go thirty feet. He was laughing when she reached him, and greeted her with a smile that spoke of both care and happiness. "Ah, Maria! It is so good to be back in Venice again. Nice to be away from rude nature."

She smiled back. She couldn't exactly tell him that she was finding the smell of the canals hard to live with. "Yes. But I must go to the baby, husband." He'd like that, being called *husband* with respect in her voice, and showing herself a good wife and a dutiful mother. It would make him feel good, in front of the other masters.

"She must be fed, and then I think I'll take her to our lodgings. It has been a long day, and I confess I'm tired."

He took her arm. "I'll come along to assist you home. A woman needs an escort on a night like this."

Irritation flared. This being a good little wife was not something she did well. This was Venice. *Her* Venice! She'd sculled a vessel around it alone since she was fourteen.

She shook his arm off, but did it gently, so it didn't seem as if she was rejecting his help. "I still need to feed Alessia, and then probably to change her." That would put him off, quickly enough. "It will take a while. Then the nurse can accompany me. She can do something to earn the wage that Katerina has paid her, and we'll take a gondola. You stay, please. You're enjoying yourself, and I don't want to spoil that for you. You won't see the other masters for a long time again."

"You're sure?" He was plainly tempted, but he was dutiful. A solicitous hand touched her elbow.

"Absolutely. Enjoy yourself." She kissed him on the cheek and went to find Alessia.

She found the salon easily enough. By ear. Alessia was bellowing. The dry nurse was nowhere to be seen. There were, however, five or six empty goblets, one of which lay on its side in a pool of spilled wine. Wine stained the satin of the chair that had been provided for the nurse. And Alessia was demanding instant attention. Hastily Maria struggled with her lacing and quelled the bellows, rage building inside her that she had to tamp down, lest it affect Alessia's feeding.

She'd just fed, winded, and changed Alessia when the nurse returned with a goblet in her hand, slightly unsteady on her feet.

Maria put Alessia down. Carefully. Only then did she round on the slut who'd deserted her baby. "Where the hell have you been?" she demanded, anger putting an edge to her voice that only a drunk could have ignored.

The nurse, it seemed, was just such a drunk, and beamed at her. "Just went to get a glass of wine, dearie. The poppet was sleeping beautifully."

Fury passing all ability to use mere words seized Maria. She grabbed the woman and shook her like a rag doll. "You . . . you *puttana*," she hissed into the wine-laden breath. The woman swayed. "You're drunk. You left my baby, all alone. Anything could have happened. Anything!"

The nurse wrested herself away, clumsily, and looked down her nose at Maria, her face reddening with more than just wine. "You're nothing but a canaler, even dressed up like that. Why should I sit here with your misbegotten brat?" she spat. "You begrudge me a glass of wine . . ."

Maria stepped forward, pulled back her arm, and slapped the woman hard. And hard again. The nurse's head jerked back and her cheeks each had a scarlet handprint on them, but Maria wasn't done. She seized the woman by the front of her gown, and threw her at the seat. It cracked as the dry nurse fell onto it, her eyes wide, her mouth falling open with shock. It didn't break—quite—but Maria knew with satisfaction that it was damaged. The dry nurse was going to have to answer to one of the Doge's upper-servants for it.

"I might be a canaler," she hissed, "but I'm worth

three of *you*. At least I always did what I was paid to do, honestly."

Maria snatched up Alessia and stormed out; out into the crowd, out past the crowd, too angry to even hear if anyone was trying to hail her. She was still so angry she wasn't really thinking, just walking, once she'd got past the revelers. But when she got out of the palace and past the fires in the piazza, the night air was cool. It helped to cool her temper and her anger, too. After a while she paused and took stock of where she was.

With a sense of surprise rather than shock, she saw that she was on one of the walkways bordering the canals, and must be more than halfway to their lodgings. She'd walked farther than she'd intended in this dress. The hem and the petticoat hems would need washing.

Her feet, crammed into shoes that were too narrow for her, complained. One of the disadvantages of marrying Umberto had been that she had to wear shoes all the time. His position, he said, demanded it. Well, her canaler feet demanded space. She kicked the shoes off, then struggled to pick them up, with Alessia fast asleep in one arm. She gritted her teeth, as she realized that the shoes were meant for dancing in ballrooms, not striding along canalside. The pretty doeskin would be ruined.

She sighed irritably; there was little point in spending money on a gondola now. Anyway, the gondolas would be as thick as flies down at the Piazza San Marco, and few and far between anywhere else. She might as well walk the rest of the way, cross the Rialto bridge and go to the apartment. Not more than a few hundred cubits now.

Besides, she'd been walking and poling for most of her life—her own two legs were good enough. She was just a canaler, after all; canal-born and canal-bred, and the day she couldn't make it anywhere in Venice on her own feet, they might as well start building her coffin. So she walked on quietly. With half of Venice already drunk on the Doge's wine, and the other half trying to get to that state, there probably wasn't a bullyboy or a pickpocket anywhere nearer than Naples. She'd be more than safe enough tonight.

❖   ❖   ❖

The riot and rumpus met her just short of the Rialto bridge.

Schiopettieri. A lot of them. The professional soldiers who served Venice for a police force had two struggling figures in their midst, yelling and fighting like young bulls. Maria stepped up onto a mounting block, partly to avoid the press of Schiopettieri, partly to see what was going on.

She looked across the heads—and straight into Benito's eyes. As their eyes locked, he stopped, and a look of absolute horror transfigured his face.

That was the opportunity that the Schioppies needed. They piled onto him. Maria caught a brief glimpse of Benito, upended over someone's shoulder. He wasn't wearing any trousers. Or small-clothes.

Maria, with Alessia in her arms, stood transfixed, watching the tide of Schiopettieri bear Benito and his large companion away. The large companion seemed content to be restrained. All the fighting had obviously come from Benito.

The tide passed, and moved on, away from her, and Maria stepped down off the block, and walked on.

For a brief moment she'd nearly waded into that crowd of Schioppies to help Benito. Then Alessia had stirred against her, and how could she interfere in a drunken brawl with a baby in her arms? She couldn't exactly have put Alessia down. Benito had gotten himself into that trouble, whatever it was. Benito would just have to get himself out of it. It wasn't *her* job to rescue him anymore.

If it ever had been.

This close to midnight, even when there was a great wedding on at the Doge's palace, with feasting in the Piazza San Marco, the stall-lined wooden Rialto bridge ought to be quiet.

It wasn't. There were several groups of people, mostly local women, gossiping eagerly about what had just happened.

One of the women, her eyes bright with excitement in the lamplight that the Republic provided to make bridges and *sotoportegos* safer, turned to Maria as

Maria tried to get past her. "Did you hear? Did you see? Isn't that younger Valdosta a scandal!" Her voice was full of glee.

Maria could not restrain her curiosity. "No, I wasn't there. I'd just come from the celebration. What happened? What did he do?"

She did restrain the "this time" she'd been about to add.

The woman pointed at one of the crossbeams that held chains that supported the center bridge section. "He was up there."

Well, Benito climbed things. He always had been like a little shaved ape. "What was he doing?" she asked warily.

The woman shook her head—then told her. "Scandalous! In a public place like that!"

Maria felt herself redden. "You mean he was . . ."

An older woman, looking out of her half-shuttered window, snorted. "Well, he was so drunk, that it'd be better to say he was *trying* to. Good thing for her the girl is a dancer."

"The Doge will have to make an example of him!" pronounced the first woman; half-primly and half-gleefully. "The last time—"

"And the other man?" asked Maria hastily.

"Oh, he was just singing some bawdy song and cheering. He only got involved when the Schioppies got here. He's as strong as an ox."

Maria walked on. To think that that was Benito. Her Benito.

No. Not hers. Never hers. And not her problem.

So she told herself. And maybe if she told herself often enough, she might believe it.

And pigs might fly.

Erik stared balefully at Manfred, and pointed a finger through the bars. "You are quite safe and I am going to leave you here. I have searched this stupid town for hours now. I thought you'd gone to bed, and suddenly I'm dragged out of my blankets and sent on a hunt that I should have known was going to end here." He glared, and an unrepentant Manfred glared back, then dropped his eyes and closed his hands around his head, looking very much the worse for wear. "I am going back to tell Francesca that waking me up was a waste of everybody's time, and that she should go back to sleep. I am going back to sleep. Back to my bed that I should never have left for a drunken oaf. I am going to leave you here, locked up like a common felon until this town goes back to normal business. After the wedding, that should maybe happen by Vespers bell."

Manfred held his head. "Don't shout, whatever you do. The jailor says I'll only be up for disturbing the peace and creating a nuisance. Just leave me some money for the fine and I'll get myself home. But find out what they've done with the kid, Erik. Dorma is unlikely to forgive me if I've let him get into serious trouble."

That was a change, Manfred thinking about someone else's woes rather than his own. Erik sighed and shook his head. "Just what did you do? Just what did *he* do? That boy must be the first person I've met who is worse than you are, Manfred."

"Uh. I don't think I'll tell you about all of it. But the first part involved some fellow bear-baiting. Benito took against the bear's master. The bear . . . Bears can swim, can't they?"

Erik put his hand over his eyes. "Why did I ask?"

"Well, when Benito set the bear after the Schiopettieri . . ." Manfred continued, and paused when Erik groaned.

"He set the bear—against the Schioppies! *Why* did he sent a bear against the Schioppies? Don't answer that," he added hastily, as Manfred opened his mouth. "It was a rhetorical question."

Manfred raised his eyebrows and managed a hurt expression. "It was very funny at the time, Erik. The tavern did get busted up a bit, but the girl seemed to like that . . ."

Oh, God. Erik shook his head. "I'll go and see Petro Dorma, and get it sorted out," he promised.

"Oh, good."

"But not immediately. In no small part because Benito

is getting exactly what he was asking for. It will be after
I have told Francesca that you are where you deserve
to be."

Chapter 20

Manfred was more than a little nervous about this interview. The hangover had barely subsided. He had not even been back to the embassy to change—and after last night, these were not the clothes of a gentleman any more. Besides, he had a definite feeling that the Doge was not going to be very pleased to hear what Manfred had gotten up to with his young ward. Even if Manfred was here on an official imperial visit and was a noble of a great foreign power.

He was therefore both surprised and pleased to see that Petro was smiling, albeit slightly, when he entered the room. "Ah, Prince Manfred. I apologize for my people arresting you," said Petro urbanely. "They didn't realize who you were."

"And I didn't see fit to inform them." Manfred had the feeling that the more honest he was about all of this, the better off he'd be. "Less embarrassment all the way around. I've paid the fines. I'm afraid I gave your clerk a false name for his records."

"Wise," Dorma said, quite as if he had expected something of the sort. "But I still must apologize. Normally my agents would keep an eye on visiting dignitaries, and keep them out of trouble. Or at least out of jail."

"Should have left him there," grumbled Erik, glaring at Manfred. A glare like that should have qualified as an offensive weapon.

Manfred felt sheepish, and very much inclined to encourage just about any other thread of discussion, especially if it involved going home to bed. But there was the question of young Benito. "Um. About Benito . . ."

He was surprised to see the Doge go off into helpless laughter. Eventually, though, Petro stopped and shook his head.

"I am going to have the Justices come down on him like a ton of bricks, if only to stop every other damned young blade in Venice from doing the same thing—or trying, anyway. I doubt very much if they'd succeed. The boy has managed to make himself a legend, from the canals to the palace. The whole city is talking about it this morning, and there are bets on whether or not he actually did what he was trying to do. Just one thing I do want to know: Where on earth did he get a woman willing to go up there with him?"

Manfred felt his ears glowing as Erik stared at him. "She . . . uh . . . she's an acrobat at that place where they have the Alexandrine dancers. The stomach-dancers. Although there is a lot more to it than just the stomach," he amended weakly.

Petro put his head in his hands. His shoulders still shook. "And the bear?"

"We didn't really mean that to happen," he pled. "It just did. The poor thing really was being mistreated."

Petro sat back in his throne and closed his eyes for a moment, the corners of his mouth still twitching. "Prince Manfred. Erik. What do you think I should do with the boy?"

"Give him to me," growled Erik. "I'll take him away from Venice and sort him out. And right now I need someone to beat, besides Manfred."

Petro Dorma blinked, gave them both a penetrating look, and smiled broadly. "You know, I think I might just take you up on that. I was going to send him out to Corfu as my factor for a year or two, anyway. You two can take him along with you. If you don't mind that is, Prince Manfred?"

Manfred nodded. "Of course not." With a wry smile he asked. "How much trouble can one boy be?"

Petro snorted. "In the case of this one, plenty. I will arrange this with the chief Justice. He keeps a straight face better than I do. I, of course, am far too angry to even see him. He has damaged the reputation of our fair city and the *Casa* Dorma. *And* his brother. *And* he's quite spoiled the dignity of his brother's wedding."

"But hasn't he?" asked Erik, seeming rather puzzled by Dorma's good humor.

Dorma smiled. "Please, Erik! This is a port city. It's not quite as decadent as Aquitaine, but we are not Icelandic puritans here. The Venetians are shocked, yes, of course. Venetians *love* being shocked. It is a wonderful story and will grow into the most improbable legend. And Benito will acquire a reputation twice as large as it is already. I must send Benito out of town before he is forced, by a desire to live up to the legend, to do something even more crazy."

Erik shook his head. "You Venetians are *all* crazy."

Petro laughed, and shook his head. "There is something in what you say. Now tell me, Manfred, Benito's um, partner in crime. Do I have to get her out of prison too?"

"Who? Lolita? No, she took off like a scalded cat, Petro. Laughing like a mad thing." Manfred remembered that quite clearly. Her little bare rear was just as luscious as the front.

Petro raised an eyebrow, but said only: "Good. I would hate to think Benito had gotten someone other than himself into trouble."

Manfred snorted. "In this case your worry is wasted effort."

"Nevertheless," said the Doge, with an attempt at seriousness. "I feel I should investigate these dancers. It sounds like a lively spot."

"That young hellion would find a lively spot in a Shetland town," grumbled Erik. "And if he couldn't find one, he'd make one."

Benito was in trouble, and knew it. More trouble than he'd ever been in before.

He'd never been in this room before; this was where they took people who had done things that were just short of murder or robbery, a darkly somber room that left no doubt in the prisoner's mind that he had trespassed on at least five of the Ten Commandments. There was pretty little doubt that everybody was still nearly incandescently angry with him. The chief Justice had not so much as cracked a smile when the affair with the bear had been related to him by the bear's former owner. By the time it had got to the challenge on the Rialto bridge . . .

Well, he sounded like God Himself, thundering out the Law.

"The Rialto bridge is one of the most important landmarks of our fair city! Your drunken and licentious behavior has brought shame onto us. I gather only your drunkenness has saved you from the more serious charge of public fornication."

The chief Justice had eyes that could pierce a fellow like a pair of stilettos. "That you should do this on the occasion of your brother's matrimony!—and as a ward of our Doge!—simply makes your lewd behavior and other offences more heinous still."

The Justice paused. He seemed to be waiting for Benito to say something.

"Yes, milord," he said, faintly.

The floodgates opened again. "This is not the first time you have been in trouble in this court. I see the record indicates you have been fined for brawling here before. I therefore sentence you to a fine of one hundred ducats, and the owner of the bear is to be recompensed for the loss of his animal. And you, Benito Valdosta, are hereby given a choice. Remain imprisoned here for a year. Or be exiled from the City of Venice for a period of five years."

Benito swallowed; this was serious. Really serious, this time. One hundred ducats! That was a year's earnings for a gentleman-at-arms. More money than he had. Dorma had paid him an allowance, but he had a feeling that would not be available any more.

All right; he'd pawn everything he had. Somehow he'd take care of the fine. But he was damned if he'd turn tail and run away into exile; he'd messed up, he'd take it like a man. "I'll take the impri—"

But he was interrupted.

"Pardon, Milord Justice! If I might be permitted to speak?"

It was the one and only member of the public who hadn't just come to gawk at Venice's latest scandal: Marco. Benito wished like hell he hadn't come.

The chief Justice nodded approvingly. "Permission is granted, Milord Marco Valdosta."

"No!" protested Benito. *Damn it, Marco, you can't get me out of this one!*

The Justice looked sternly at him. "Silence. Or I will have you silenced, Benito Valdosta."

Marco cleared his throat. "Your Honor. As Benito, my brother, is the ward of the Doge, no special consideration can be shown to him."

The Justice nodded gravely. "Well said. Indeed, I have a message here from Petro Dorma, instructing me that Benito Valdosta is to be treated in the same way that any other citizen of Venice would be treated."

Marco nodded. "Nonetheless, I would like to appeal on the basis of his youth and the fact he grew up without the guidance of good parents, as an orphan, and that in the fight to save Venice last fall he fought and led with great courage. Many here can testify to that. Perhaps some part of this—ah, incident—is due to a nature that requires an outlet, and there has been nothing of the sort to purge him of his excess of spirits."

There was a murmur of approval. The Justice, however, was shaking his head. Marco hurried on. "I do not appeal for the sentence to be reduced. I just ask that the option of imprisonment be removed. Your Honor, many of Venice's wildest young blades have gone out to the outposts of our empire and served well, and faithfully, and returned as upright and respectable citizens. I do not think Benito would be improved by a year in the dungeons. I think he might learn if sent elsewhere."

Benito felt his mouth dropping open, and snapped it closed.

The Justice nodded, the look he bestowed on Marco the very image of benevolence. "I find this a reasonable plea, Marco Valdosta."

He turned back to Benito, and God On High was back.

"Very well, Benito Valdosta, the option of imprisonment is withdrawn. You are exiled from Venice for five years. You will remain in custody until a passage is arranged for you out of the city."

Marco stepped forward. He tapped a pouch, which jingled. "Your honor, I have here monies to pay the reparations and the fines for Benito Valdosta.

The Justice pointed. "The clerk will see to it."

And Benito, his leg irons clanking, was led out. Marco did not even look at him.

On the whole, that was probably not a bad thing.

He did come down to the cell, later. "Petro would have added twenty lashes to the sentence," he said grimly, the first words out of his mouth. Not: *Are you all right,* or: *We were worried about you.*

Benito shrugged. "I'm sorry, Brother. The evening started in fun. It just got out of hand."

"Several people, including Prince Manfred, have said that you were simply looking for trouble," said Marco, who could have passed, at this moment, for one of the chief Justice's prize pupils. He was doing a very good imitation of God on High, himself. "Petro's had some of his spies keeping an eye on you. You pitched one of them into the Rio San Felice. You're lucky that was not another charge you faced, by the way."

But then, suddenly, the whole stern image collapsed, as his brother added, plaintively, "Petro says you've been so much better the last while. And then this."

Benito shrugged his shoulders sulkily. He wasn't going to justify himself to Marco. He wasn't sure he could justify himself to himself. And he sure as hell wasn't going to let Marco know just how wretched he'd felt when he'd seen Maria with the baby in her arms, and she wouldn't even look at him.

Marco sighed. "I haven't even had a chance to tell you yet, but Kat and I stood as godparents to Maria's daughter."

Benito felt truly as if the wind had been kicked out of him. But he had to know—he was as starved for some word, any word, as a swampy was for a decent meal.

"Is she all right? I mean with having the baby and all."
In a very small voice: "She wouldn't even speak to me,
Marco."

Marco looked at his younger brother with a compassion
that hurt almost as much as Maria's silence. "So that was
what it was all about, was it?"

Benito said nothing. What could he say? He couldn't
deny it, but he sure as hell wasn't going to admit it.

Marco shook his head. "She's fine. Seems happy enough,
Benito. The baby is fine, too." But then, he smiled, that
purely Marco smile, with a touch of mischief. "She's got
something unusual though. She has an undine as one of
her godmothers."

That caught Benito off guard. "What?" he said, not
sure he'd heard right.

"Umberto's sister was supposed to be one of the godmothers, only she didn't approve of Umberto's marriage.
You know she always kept house for him. I suppose she
must have thought that no one was good enough for him,
but she absolutely hates Maria. So, at the last minute,
she didn't show up. The Lion in me . . . I think the Lion
must have guessed she might do something like that. I
asked if the water-people would add their blessing, and
the priest said he'd see about it. Well, I think the Lion
sent an undine to take her place."

So that was the reason for the mischief. Benito could
hardly believe it. Marco, doing something just for the
reason of giving someone who deserved it their come-
uppance!

"All things considered, since they're going to be around
water all their lives, you could hardly ask for a more
useful godmother," Marco pointed out with just a touch
of glee. "That little girl will never drown."

Benito tried to imagine the scene, and failed. "I wish
I could have been there."

Marco looked at him hard, and raised an eyebrow.
"And who would that have pleased or helped, Benito?
Nobody would ask you to be a godfather."

Benito shrugged. "I just feel . . . Oh, I don't know. I
just feel I owe her some help." He sighed. "She saw me
that night, you know."

"So I have heard," said Marco dryly. "She told Kat."
He paused, as if he was considering something, then
evidently made up his mind about it.

"They're shipping out for Corfu in a couple of hours.
You'll have your chance to help her, if you can manage
to stay out of trouble long enough to do anything useful.
You're going there too. It's a small place. You'll probably
see her every day."

Benito's mouth fell open in horror. And worst of all,
the horror was so mixed with a thrill of delight that he
couldn't tell where one started and the other ended.

"What?" he squawked. "I can't! I'd rather go to *prison*,
Marco." He gripped the bars, pleading. "Go and talk to
Petro. Tell him about this."

All right; he had to admit it. He *had* to. It was the
only thing that might save him. "Seeing her is what sent
me over the edge. Please, Marco! I'll go anywhere else,
but I can't go there!"

Marco nodded. "I thought so. I'll ask him." He sighed.
"But don't get your hopes up. He was pretty grim about
this, and had made up his mind. And anyway, there aren't
a lot of places you can go, now."

The Terce bell had rung before he returned. "I'm
sorry, Benito. Petro says: 'If he can't learn to behave like
a gentleman, then let him take the consequences. He'll
have plenty of opportunity.'"

"No—" Benito whimpered. "You didn't tell him? Didn't
you tell him about Maria?"

Marco sighed. "I told him everything, including how
you felt about the christening, and how seeing Maria at
the wedding just made you crazy. He said you'd have
plenty of chances to help Maria in Corfu. He said you
could offer to be a dry nurse, since the one Maria had
was unsatisfactory."

Benito groaned, and dropped his head in his hands.

Chapter 21

The great carracks and the smaller tarettes in the Bacino San Marco twitched and jerked at anchor, responding to the winds, the short chop on the water and the loads being swung on board from the lighters. The fleet would proceed slowly to Outremer, hopping from Lissa, Corfu, Zante, Candia, Negroponte and points east as far as distant Trebizond. The loading would proceed for another week yet, but already many of the ships had to stay in deeper water. Weddings and celebrations were fine things in their way and at the proper time, but the ships must sail soon. So finery and jollification were best put in the past, to be talked about later. Now Venice hummed with industry. Spring was here, the time for trade was at hand, and the ships were outbound.

Over at the quay-side the great galleys bound for Flanders were at the point of final deck-cargo. They would not proceed slowly, navigating out through the Pillars of Hercules, and then across stormy Biscay; with such a voyage ahead, there was no spare time to waste. Their stops were few, but they would pause at Corfu—the last safe port, for a final refit at the Little Arsenal there. The trip to Corfu was a good "sea-trial," revealing problems, especially with new ships.

And in Corfu, the ship would discharge a new assistant foreman for the Little Arsenal: Umberto Verrier.

Maria knew that the new posting was, in a way, her

own fault. If she hadn't led to Umberto's men capturing Torfini and Rossi in those first few days ... Well, Umberto wouldn't have acquired a reputation for sorting out problems, quickly and efficiently. The more senior guilds at the Arsenal were, on the whole, not pleased with his wood-selection abilities. On the other hand, they were satisfied that he could fix problems, and the Little Arsenal apparently had plenty. So, Umberto had his new posting. It was farther from Venice, but, as he said, it was in a real town. Maria wasn't as happy as he was about that part, but at least it would be back beside the sea.

It was one thing to be married to Umberto. It was quite another to be married to Umberto and feeling as if she was going to have to be responsible for his success, while at the same time allowing him to bask in the illusion that his success was due entirely to his own effort. And it was a third to do so while caring for a baby. . . .

Two babies. Umberto is as much a child as the little one.

But that was unfair. He was a *good* man. He cared for her.

He cares for what he thinks you are.

He loved the baby. And that insidious voice in her head could say nothing about that.

She had thought that she was going be able to settle down, and now they were moving again. On yet another ship, so Umberto would be ill again. Two babies to tend, in the close confines of a ship. Another set of new people to meet and deal with, another strange place to try to make into a home. Harder, this time. She could not count on a fortuitous accident to show her what she needed to know. And she already knew that although Umberto was good enough at dealing with honest men, he was lost when it came to those who were less than honest.

She had only traded one set of problems for another, in marrying the man. But he cared for her, and would do his best for her even if it killed him. It was up to her to see that it didn't. If she could not love him, she certainly owed him.

Maria stood on the quay, watching the corded trunks and canvas bundles being loaded, as little Alessia nestled into her arms and nuzzled. Maria looked down at her child, and sighed.

"To think a year ago I hadn't even been beyond the fringes of the lagoon . . ." she said, half to herself. "And now here you are, daughter, off to another distant place."

Beside her, Kat gazed at the ships, and her eyes were still luminous with happiness. Maria thought that she had never seen a more contented person, and yet she knew that Kat was not blind to Marco's faults. Nor, for that matter, was Marco blind to hers. They had both known exactly what they were getting into, and yet they were two of the happiest people Maria had ever known.

How very different, Maria thought forlornly, *from the way I felt after my wedding.*

"I wish you weren't going," Kat said with a sigh. "Or I wish we were going along with you. I'd like to visit Corfu." Alessia stirred and Kat reached for her. "Let me hold her a little. It may be years before I see her again."

Maria handed the baby over. She watched with some amusement at how awkwardly and carefully Kat took the child. Just on three weeks ago, she'd been just as tentative.

"When I left for Istria, I was never coming back, Kat. Never ever. Now here I am again. Things change. Who knows? Petro Dorma might get so sick of Marco that he'll ship you both off to Corfu."

Kat shook her head. "Marco is as much part of Venice now as the canals."

Involuntarily, Maria glanced across the thronged piazza behind them to the tall pillar where the bronze statue stood. "Or as the Lion of Saint Mark."

Kat nodded. "The Lion is Venice after all, and Marco is the Lion, too. He *can't* leave, Maria."

Alessia twitched, gave a tentative whimper, and then burst into full bellow. Kat rocked frantically, an expression of raw panic on her face. "What's wrong, my cherub? There, there . . . Help, Maria! What is wrong? I didn't do anything to her. What do I do now?"

Maria found laughter a welcome gift. "By the smell, I think she's probably done something to herself. Don't worry, that's not what's making her cry. It doesn't seem to worry her."

Kat hastily held out Alessia at full arm's stretch, as if she were a precious piece of porcelain suddenly found to harbor a poisonous spider. Maria did not reach for Alessia. "I'll show you what do about it," she said cheerfully.

Kat searched frantically for rescue. "Ah. Er . . . I see Papa's Vinlander partners are here. I'd—I'd better go and speak to them. I'll come back and see you in just a moment." She thrust the bellowing Alessia at her mother, and bolted.

Maria, familiar now with all the less pleasant aspects of babies, took Alessia off to change, glancing as she went at the tall, large, blond contingent that Kat was greeting. And there, hastening down the quay-side from the Doge's palace, was Marco. Probably been to see Benito. Benito's face, when he'd seen her, had been quite a study.

She scowled as she thought about it. If Umberto was one sort of child, Benito was another—a brat, a bridge-brat, destined to hang, no doubt. But Venice would not forget that latest exploit of his in a hurry. Being Venice, it would embrace it as quite a favorite story.

Eneko Lopez was on a high balcony of the Doge's palace, his eagle eyes looking out over the Jesolo marshes when Marco finally tracked him down. The stern visage cracked into a smile on seeing Marco. "And how is wedded bliss, Marco Valdosta?

Marco felt himself blush. "Um. Blissful, thank you, señor."

This reply lightened the stern visage further. "It is intended to be, you know. That is why Christ sanctified the institution of marriage with his first miracle." He pointed out toward the sky. "Tell me: what is happening up there?"

Marco peered into the blue. "I'd say that a bird . . . or a pair of birds, rather, are being mobbed by seagulls. The gulls around here can be quite territorial, and there are thousands of them."

The part of him that was the Lion stirred. *And so am I*, it said within him. *They do not belong here.*

Of course, Eneko Lopez could not hear that voice, and Marco did not feel easy enough to explain. But he knew, now, why the gulls were attacking the hawks. The gulls were as much part of the lagoon as the water was, and the hawks were the eyes of the Lion's ancient enemy. The Lion would blind that enemy, if he could—and if he could not, he would at least deny him the use of those eyes over Venice.

Eneko nodded. "A pair of what I should guess were goshawks, although I am not an expert on birds. Are such things common over Venice?"

"Well, I've seen hawks in the reed-brakes and *barene* close to the fringes of the marsh, but not really out here," Marco temporized. "They don't belong here. The gulls will see them off."

The gulls will kill them if they can.

"I have seen two hawks in the sky rather often of late. They appear to be hawks, at least," said Eneko. "I have attempted to scry them. Birds are difficult to connect with, and raptors most particularly difficult. They think mostly of hunting and killing, and not a great deal else."

Well, this was the opening Marco had rather wondered how to make. "But if you were scrying and it turned out they were not hawks . . . wouldn't you be very vulnerable?" He took a deep breath. "Brother Mascoli said I should ask you for help with magical defenses for protection against evil."

He felt the eagle gaze again. "Mascoli is a good man. But he sees only good in everything. If he thought you should consult me on this, I must conclude that something particularly evil happened. Tell me about it."

So Marco explained.

Eneko Lopez's eyes narrowed when he came to the part about the undines and San Raphaella. "I was aware of this. I was also aware that the undines that live in the Lagoon have a great deal to do with the Strega mages. In particular with the late Luciano Marina." Something about the way he said it filled in the word "unlamented" before "late."

Marco nodded, but innate honesty forced him to defend Chiano. The Strega mage might have intended to kill him to save Venice—but . . . he'd also saved Marco's life before that. And been a friend when a terrified boy needed one.

And it was entirely possible—

Probable, chuckled the voice in his head.

—that the knife had been intended for some other purpose in the ceremony.

Bloodletting does not mean killing. Some ceremonies require the spilling of a token of blood, given freely. Ask your black-robed friend. He knows.

"Luciano was a good man, even if he was not a Christian," Marco said with more firmness. "And he helped the undines and they liked him, yes. Brother Mascoli said it was not wrong to aid nonhumans. No evil creature would come to the sanctified water, and no evil creature would ask help."

"We differ in levels of trust and points of theology," said Eneko, dryly. "But continue. I accept that *you* are a Christian soul, even if you are bonded to a creature about which I am less certain." He smiled. "And I do *not* mean your wife, whose Christianity I know well enough from the counseling booth of St. Hypatia. She gave me a lesson in honesty, once, when I was her counselor."

Marco took a deep breath. "Well, according to Brother Mascoli, it was only the strength of that 'other' that saved me. I got the fright of my life, señor. It was like being thistle-down slapped around by a maelstrom, just for an instant. The ward candles nearly burned up completely in that instant. Whatever it was, it was waiting out there for me when I went looking for the triton. It was . . . lying in ambush, so to speak, waiting to kill me."

Eneko pursed his lips. "The power of the Lion is very much tied to the area of the old marshes is it not?"

Marco nodded.

"And you were scrying outside of this area, and you were attacked."

Marco nodded again.

Eneko stood in thought, his heavy brows hooding his eyes. "I conclude that Chernobog still retains an interest in you. I cannot see why any other creature of power should take such a risk with a mage. You see, as much as you are vulnerable, so is your attacker. I should imagine that Chernobog uses an intermediary or a lesser servant, rather than direct intervention. Still, that servant is likely to be one who is himself—or herself—very powerful and dangerous. There are defenses. The first one however, is 'stay home.' Without you the Lion of Saint Mark would be somewhat less effective, am I correct?"

"Well, in times of crisis one of the four families must direct the Lion's power," agreed Marco.

"And if I am correct, all that remains are three Montescues and two Valdostas of the old blood?"

Marco bit his lip. "Well, Benito . . . He's my half-brother, Sir. We had different fathers."

Eneko nodded. "That is easy enough to guess without even seeing him, just to judge by his behavior. So: In fact it is only yourself and the three Montescues, one of whom is away, and one of whom is very elderly. This is a good reason to want you dead. And it is a good reason for you to keep scrying as the aspect of mage-practice you use only in dire emergency. However, I will teach you to attack when you are attacked, and how to best defend yourself—if you will agree to restrain your scrying to matters that are vital to your survival."

Marco nodded. "If you will extend that to 'what is vital to the survival of Venice,' then I will. You see, the Lion is Venice, in a way. So by defending it I defend myself, too."

"A fair caveat," agreed Eneko. He took Marco by the elbow and turned back to the chamber. "Come. Let us go inside. The gulls appear to have driven the hawks away. Gulls are less formidable than hawks, but gulls are certainly more numerous."

Marco watched with interest as Eneko Lopez laid out a few very simple objects. Four ward-candles, which he placed in each corner of the room, a silver mirror, and, of all odd things, a sharp needle stuck in a cork. With the mirror on a low table between them, Lopez invoked the four wards as Marco had learned to do, and set up the circle of protection around them. It was all done very quickly, neatly and efficiently.

"Now, your first and best protection when you attempt

to scry when you do not know if something is watching for you, is to arrange so that you are not noticed."

"But how do I do that?" Marco asked.

"By finding some other thing that is in the area, and concealing 'yourself' within it. Those gulls, for instance. Scry for one of those gulls over the Lagoon just now."

Obediently, Marco bent over the mirror, and easily called one of the gulls into its silver surface, which was silver no longer, but reflected the blue sky and white clouds.

"Very good. Now move in closer," Eneko instructed.

In the mirror, and in his mind, the gull loomed nearer, nearer, until he was looking directly into its black, bright eye.

"Closer."

He couldn't imagine how he could do that, but then that familiar warmth inside him gave him a nudge—

And now, he looked down on the Lagoon, felt the wind in his feathers, adjusted the tilt of his wing for better lift in a thermal—

Good, said a voice from very far away, as he went very still and quiet. *Now, don't actually do anything. Just sit, and watch, and when another gull comes near, make that same jump to it.*

It wasn't long before a second gull joined the first, and the two locked gazes long enough for Marco to make that "jump."

Practice this for a while. Move from gull to gull. But don't try to interfere in what they do. Just observe.

It was a little—a very little—like being the Lion. The gulls didn't have much on their minds but food and flying. He made the jump into four more gulls, when Eneko's voice came back.

Now think about flying toward the piazza and landing on one of the piers.

But the gull didn't want to do that; he felt the resistance.

You could make him, but that would make you noticed. At the moment, unless a magician was aware that you were riding this particular gull, there is no way that you would be detected. This is how you can scry and not be

*seen. So, find another bird and see if you can jump to
one that will do what you ask.*

It took two more birds, not one, before he found
one that felt that landing on the pier would be a good
thing. This was a big, strong bird who often managed
to snatch food from lesser gulls down there. With a tilt
of its wings, it made a dizzying plunge down toward the
water, skimmed along the surface, and made a graceful
landing on the stone.

*Good. Now reverse how you got to the first gull. Pull
back. See the gull in the mirror—*

And before the voice was done, Marco was looking into
the eye of a fine, bright-eyed gull, then watching it strut
nonchalantly along the stone walkway of the piazza. . . .

He was startled to see that Eneko Lopez had his
left hand firmly in the grasp of Eneko's own, with the
needle poised over it, as the mirror went to ordinary
silver again.

"Excuse me, Father, but what are you doing?"

"A precaution," Eneko replied, immediately letting go
of his hand. "In case you got lost in the gull's thoughts.
A sharp reminder to your spirit that it still has a proper
human body would swiftly recall you back."

"It would?" Marco was impressed by that; he could
think of any number of ways that he could practice
this trick with Kat's help, if this was the safeguard he
needed to take.

"Oh, yes, indeed." Eneko smiled. "How are you feeling?"

"Um . . . tired." He was, suddenly. But he knew why,
now; this leaping about from gull to gull was something
that had all come out of his own reserves. "Can I draw
on some other power to do this, next time?"

"Only at the risk of being noticed," Eneko warned.
"You will make the gull look different to another mage
if you start drawing on more power. Just as, if another
mage was to try to scry the bird you were riding, he
would notice you unless you take care to be very still
and not draw attention to yourself."

"But could I scry, say, a bird over Cremona, and ride
it?" he hazarded.

"Yes," Lopez said. "But if there was anything watching for you, it would find you. Your risk would be less, once you began riding the bird, but it would still be there."

Marco nodded. "But what about defending myself?" he asked, quietly.

"That will be the next lesson; I want you first to learn how to make yourself so inconspicuous when riding a bird or a beast that a mage will have to be very skilled to find you." Eneko softened his stern look with a little smile. "After all, the very best defense is not to need to defend yourself at all."

Chapter 22

The ships made their way, cautiously, under oars, the leadsman calling depths as ship by ship the first great spring fleet rowed around the sand-spit at the end of the Lido. In the deeper water of the Adriatic, something watched.

If the shaman had been in his own white sea he could have named many of the denizens of the cold deep and sunk all of the vessels above. Here the massive eellike creature that was his sea-form was restricted to watching. He was eighteen cubits long, but that was still not large enough to take on ships. As always his body-shape dictated his appetites. Ships were full of food that would be nice to suck dry.

He flicked his powerful tail, and began swimming southward. Best to see if the other fleet and army was well hidden.

This water was too warm. And the monk seals weren't worth eating.

The galley had a number of its berths taken by the Vinlanders that Kat had rushed over to see. Maria had watched them for a few days now, and she was fairly certain that the two men who looked like a pair of giant warriors were really nothing much more than boys, not much older than she was. They were very happy to be at sea, and she had the feeling that although they probably were quite fond of

their sister, they were also just a little tired of having her
fastened to them all the time. Back in Venice, no doubt,
they'd been able to get out and about on their own, but
here, they were forced into each others' company with no
chance for privacy.

Maria came out to put the wicker crib on the deck.
Other than the helmsman, the poop deck was empty
except for the blond woman—who was dripping tears
over the stern of the ship. It looked to Maria as if she
might join them, to splash into the water amid the kitchen
peelings the cook had just tossed there.

Maria bit her lip. She'd better go over and see what
the matter was. After all, the Vinlanders were Kat's
grandfather's business partners. And Alessia, looking like a
particularly plump and pretty cherub, was fast asleep.

Maria walked over, quietly, moving easily with the
rolling of the ship.

"What's wrong?" The Vinlander woman nearly fell
overboard.

The woman sniffed, hastily scuffed a sleeve across her
eyes, and turned to Maria with a fake smile plastered over
a face that still had tear-streaks running down the cheeks.
"Nothing. I thank you," she said. "I am well. Truly."

She looked as if she was going to dissolve into tears
in the very next moment.

*Fine. You and I are the only two women on this ship,
young lady. And we're going to the same place. I think
we had better be friends.*

One thing she had noticed about the Vinlanders was
that they seemed to be very direct, in a way that suited
Maria's canaler sensibilities. So she decided to be direct,
herself.

"No, you aren't well," She put an arm over the blonde's
big shoulders. "I'm not blind," she continued, feeling a
hundred years older than this poor young thing. "You can
tell me what's wrong. I'm a friend of Kat's."

That earned her a look of puzzlement from the woman.
"Katerina Montescue. I mean Katerina Valdosta."

"Ah. Ja." The girl sniffed again, and bit her lip—but
a tear escaped anyway. "You were with the bride. In the
beautiful crimson dress—you are the bride's friend, ja?

Such a pretty girl, and such a fine husband. I did not recognize you in those clothes."

It was plain this meant a huge leap in status to the Vinlander, and thus in acceptability as a confidante. "You know them well, then?"

"Kat's my best friend," Maria said, and was a little surprised to realize that it was true. "And her husband is very, very good to my people in Venice." Any more would be too complicated to explain at one sitting. Maybe later.

"I know that your—" she searched her memory for the word that Erik used "—your clan is going to be trading partners with Kat's family, and I know that Kat wouldn't want to see you so unhappy if there was anything she could do to help. So, can I help?"

"I cannot see how," the girl replied mournfully.

"Well, why don't you just *tell* me about it?" Maria said, reasonably. "That can't do any harm, and it's better than crying here all alone over the turnip peelings."

The girl's face worked for a moment, as if she was trying to hold herself back, but it all came out in a rush, anyway. "I am so unhappy!" she wailed softly, in tones of such anguish that they imparted a sense of heartbreak to the banal words. "I will never see him again!"

For one, sharp-edged moment, Maria was tempted to join her in her tears, for the words called Benito's stricken face up in her own memory. *I will never see him again—*

But she was older than this poor child—in experience, if not years—and she held onto her composure.

The moment passed. Maria patted the blond woman's arm awkwardly. What the hell did you say to a cry of pain like that? She settled for: "There, there . . ."

Even this provoked another flood of sobbing. "He was such a nice man. The nicest we have met here in all Europe. And so tall, too." How could something that sounded so silly also sound as if the girl had lost her first and only true love?

Tall? Well, that counted out Benito. "Didn't he, I mean, couldn't you . . . ?" Maria floundered. She really didn't know how to deal with this. "What happened? Why won't you see him again?"

"I did not want to go. But Bjarni said Mama would never allow it. I know Mama would not be happy. But his eyes are such a beautiful blue-gray. And his chin is so . . . so square-cut and manly." She sniffed; and then, obviously overcome by the vision she'd conjured up, began to cry again.

"I cannot sleep for thinking about him!" she sobbed.

From the tone of her voice, that was nothing less than the truth, and a great deal less than she felt.

"Why won't your mama approve?" Maria ventured, cautiously. "Is he married or something?"

The woman mournfully shook her head. "Erik is not married. But he is just a lowly bodyguard. *We* are the Thordarsons. We are one of the wealthiest families in Vinland. I cannot just marry a *Nithing*. Mama wants me to marry a man of position. That would help the family. But . . . but he was so wonderful."

She began to hiccup, and Maria patted her back. *Good Lord. How long has she been crying like this? Hours? Days?*

She knew all too well what the girl felt like. She'd been there—before she learned just what a scum-bred bastard Caesare Aldanto was.

Cogs began to turn in Maria's head, though. And if this Erik was the Erik *she* knew, he certainly wasn't a scum-bred bastard. "Who was he guarding?" she asked.

The Vinlander girl shrugged, as if anyone other than Erik was of no importance at all, and pulled a handkerchief out of her sleeve. By the sodden look of it, she had been crying for hours. "I do not know. A guard is a guard."

Maria bit her lip again. "You don't know the rest of his name do you? Erik what?"

"Hakkonsen. It is a good family . . ."

Maria almost choked. *Just a bodyguard!* "Ah. Well. Have you heard of Prince Manfred?"

Svanhild nodded. "Of course. The heir to the Emperor. The son of the Duke of Brittany. He was at the wedding." Her tone turned bitter. "It is very good for business, these connections that Katerina brings to the Thordarsons, ja."

"Well, he's actually not *the* heir. That's his cousin, Conrad. Manfred's next in line after him. That makes him the third most important person in the Holy Roman Empire, which is the most powerful state in Europe. Maybe in the whole world."

"Ja," the girl said, indifferently. "And also the Duke of Brittany has great standing in the League of Armagh. He is a very important man. If only my Erik could have such friends—" She began to sob again.

Maria shook the woman's shoulders, just a little, although it was like trying to shake one of those Teutonic warriors that had come into Venice among the Knots. Mostly, she was trying not to laugh.

"Listen to me! Erik Hakkonsen is Prince Manfred of Brittany's personal bodyguard and master-at-arms. Only bodyguard is the wrong word to use to describe him. It's more like—"

She scrambled for some phrase that might describe what Erik did besides "keeper." Or maybe, "nursemaid." *And if Benito only had someone like that to knock some sense into him—*

"He's a sort of teacher, or companion, and—well, he keeps Manfred from getting into too much trouble. Being a bodyguard is just a small part of it. Kat's friend tells me they are really much more like friends. What he certainly *isn't* is a—" Again she searched her memory for what the girl had said. "—a *Nithing*. I suspect if you asked Manfred, he would say that Erik is very important to him."

The sobs stopped, abruptly, and the blond woman stood up from the stern rail, a look of fierce delight on her face. "Really?" she breathed, hope replacing the despair in her sea-blue eyes so quickly that Maria's breath caught.

Maria nodded firmly. "Really."

The blonde hugged Maria. "Svanhild Thordardottar is forever in your debt!" she said thickly. "I must now go and turn this ship."

Maria didn't try to tell her that you can't alter the course of a great galley in the Venetian Western convoy, not short of being the *Bora*-wind in person. But, by the looks of it, Svanhild would have a damned good try. Bless her heart, the girl had a good steel spine to her, when she wasn't sobbing in heartbreak!

Well, the captain had survived Alessia's bellows. He'd survive Svanhild.

The next day Svanhild and her two brothers sought Maria out, where she, Alessia and Umberto sat in the lee of the mound of deck-cargo. There was a bright, steely look in Svanhild's eye. "The captain says you and your husband are going to Corfu," she said.

Maria nodded.

"Do you know how often the ships sail back to Venice from this port?" demanded Svanhild. "And can you recommend to us a good vessel and captain? Not like this stupid captain! We even offered to buy his ship. He said it was the state's ship, not his to sell. What kind of captain doesn't own his own ship? At least, as a partner."

Umberto stared at them, openmouthed. Then he shook his head.

Maria was just as dumbfounded as he was. *Buy* a Venetian great galley? She couldn't even begin to guess how much that would take, even if one were for sale!

"We don't know Corfu," Umberto stammered.

"We've never been there," explained Maria, sitting Alessia up and rubbing her back. The baby rewarded her with a milky belch.

Svanhild deflated a little. "Oh. We thought . . ."

But some of Francesca's gossip had come back to Maria, and she'd been saving it for the next time she saw the girl. "But Svanhild, you don't *want* to go back to Venice! Erik and Prince Manfred are coming along somewhere behind us. They're going to the Holy Land."

One of Svanhild's brothers looked speculative and asked: "This ship will also stop in Corfu?"

Umberto nodded. "Almost all of our ships do."

The big Vinlander patted his sister. "There, Hildi—you see! It is good that we did not turn the ship! We can just wait for them."

"They won't be more than a few days behind us," Umberto offered helpfully. "A pair of weeks, at the very most."

"But—if they go to the Holy Land—" Svanhild began, desperately.

"Then maybe . . ." the boy replied, manfully, "maybe we need to see about the trade opportunities in the Holy Land too. Sven and Olaf can go to set up the warehouse in Bruges and then go back across to the family and tell them we will be delayed."

Svanhild burst into tears again, but they were tears of relief, as her brothers seemed to recognize. And she nodded, smiling around the tears. She had, Maria thought, a lovely smile. She only hoped that Erik was going to be receptive to it. Or, Manfred or no Manfred, Svanhild's brothers might just break him in half.

High on the hillside overlooking the sea, the King of Hungary watched, unmoving. Out on the white-flecked Adriatic, the Venetian convoy sailed past. He counted ships. Sixteen great galleys, carrying a small volume of valuable cargo. Pilgrims, too—rich ones. High quality furs from as far afield as Vinland. Bullion. Amber. Twenty-three round ships of varying size laden with salt, fish, timber. Strange that Venice should export timber, but really, Venice was just a clearing house. The produce of Europe was funneled through it. Half a dozen minor galliots, carrying anything from pilgrims to arms. A lot of Ferrara steel went to the east.

He would have loved to seize that convoy, just as he would have loved to seize the convoy of ships that had overwintered in Outremer. But it would not be wise to make the attempt, even with the help of Genoa or Aragon, or even the Barbary corsairs. The eastern fleet of the Republic was not a target to take lightly. Not at sea. Where land bombards and fortifications could be brought into play, as Alexius could manage in the Bosporus, it might be worthwhile.

The Atlantic fleet had been smaller, but it was all great galleys, so it had more men, and was far faster. Emeric had been in no hurry to tackle that either. Not even outbound for Flanders, laden with the rich goods of the east. He'd get it all, if he just waited. The Greek galleys were no match for this number of Venetian ships, but later, when traffic was down to occasional vessels, they and the Dalmatian pirates out of the Narenta could seize anything that came through the Straits of Otranto.

His bodyguards shivered in the bitter northeasterly wind. If it would quicken to a gale he might yet have some of the loot on those ships. But alas, the *Bora* was not forthcoming. He must look into weather-magic some day.

When the last ship had begun its upwind tack he turned to go. His bodyguards knew their master well enough not to utter a word. They rode over the ridgeline; below lay the huge sprawl of their camp. Nearly fifteen thousand men waited there, among them four thousand of his precious Magyar heavy cavalry.

It was a measure of the king's command that not one single fire burned. The Narenta pirates were too afraid of the Venetians to light a fire. The Hungarian forces, however, were more afraid of their king. From Croat light cavalry, to Slav pikemen, every last soul of them knew: *You freeze to death before you light a fire, if Emeric so commands.*

Three of his officers rode up to meet him, looking wary. The set of their shoulders altered, the king noticed, as he smiled his grim smile. He was pleased; a good general was valuable, but they must fear him. Good generals could become threats otherwise.

He nodded to their bows. "The Atlantic Fleet will have left Corfu. Another week, if our informants are correct, and the eastern fleet will be on its way. Then, within two days, I want us at sea. Nine days from now we must be on our way to Corfu. We need to strike fast and hard."

"My cavalry are ready, Your Majesty," said Count Ladislas.

"I'm still waiting on the siege cannon," said the artillery commander. "Even with double teams of oxen we keep getting stuck in the mountains, Your Majesty. The mud is over the axletrees in places."

Another thing Emeric's officers learned, and quickly, was not to lie to him. The man was scared but honest. Emeric knew the value of tolerating failure, up to a point.

Besides, he'd come over those roads himself and wasn't surprised, nor did he blame the officer. This early in spring—which hadn't arrived in the mountains yet—the roads were just mud or still waist-deep in snow.

He waved dismissively. "If we have to move without them, we will. If we have to lay siege, then we'll have time to ship them in."

The relief on the officer's face was amusing, but best not to let it go too far. "Two weeks. *Mova ik*, or I'll have your head."

He noted that the Croat cavalry captain was looking even more tense.

He waited. The man simply couldn't take it after a minute's silence. "Your Majesty. The scouts you ordered sent out south . . . seven of them have not come back. One squad."

The king nodded. "Find them. You'll find their bodies or their mounts. Then, when you've found what became of them, find the nearest village and crucify all the men. Make the women watch."

Emeric raised a forefinger. "You have eight days."

PART V
April, 1539 A.D.

Chapter 23

Emeric erased the circle and the pentacle scratched in a section of his pavilion where he'd pulled back the carpets to expose the naked soil. Then he eliminated all other traces of the ritual he'd followed to reach the chief of his spies on Corfu, cleaned himself, and put the carpets back in place. The work had to be done carefully, since he was only guided by the light of a few candles. Night had long since fallen.

As always, Emeric was irritated by having to do such menial labor himself, instead of ordering a servant. But, he dared not do otherwise. Even the King of Hungary—even a king suspected by his subjects to be a man-witch—could not afford to have anyone observe him at such times. Not, at least, anyone knowledgeable in such matters, and it was always difficult to tell who might be.

Several features of those rituals were satanic in nature, not simple witchcraft. Hungary was, after all, a predominantly Christian country—and those portions that were not Christian were mostly Muslim. His polyglot subjects would tolerate a great deal, true, but not open trafficking with *that* prince.

Emeric didn't particularly fear rebellion, as such. His army was quite capable of crushing any combination of peasants or townsmen, as it had demonstrated several times over the past years. The problem lay with the army itself. None of Emeric's officers was burdened with any great moral sentiments. Still, the open use of satanic rituals would, if nothing else, give an ambitious general the handle to organize and lead a military overthrow of the Hungarian dynasty.

Emeric did not follow all of his aunt's advice. But he had never failed to observe Countess Bartholdy's strictures on this score: *Keep it secret, from all except those you trust. And trust only those you can control.*

Finally done, he soothed his irritation by ordering wine and cuffing the servant who brought it. He finished the goblet, ordered another, and cuffed the servant again.

Throughout, it never occurred to him—as it had never occurred to him before—to wonder why his aunt had given him those secrets in the first place, starting when he was a boy of six. To wonder why she had violated, seemingly, her own rule.

Like his master, Petros Fianelli erased all the symbols and signs of the ritual himself. In his case, not in the luxury of a king's pavilion but in the squalor of a basement owned by one who appeared to be a simple seller of secondhand goods in Kérkira, the chief town of Corfu. Which, indeed, Fianelli was—even if most of his income came from the criminal ring he operated on the island, as well as the subsidy he received from the King of Hungary.

There was only one way to perform these rituals on Corfu: to create the symbols in fire. Each one was created on a special platen made of obsidian, filled with oily cotton, fed from a reservoir of defiled holy oil. When the oil was lit, the symbol burned in the element that Corfu could not counter, the Devil's own. But the platens had to be carefully hidden when he was done. If anyone found them, it would be awkward. If anyone who understood what they were for ever found them, the consequences would be dire.

That done, he took the taper and mounted the stairs to the kitchen. It was a large kitchen, centered around a large table. Little cooking was actually done in the kitchen, these days, since Fianelli had quietly murdered his last woman a few months earlier after she'd become tiresome. Had her murdered, rather, by two of his three bully boys. Fianelli hadn't wanted to risk it himself, given his own short and pudgy stature. She'd been a large woman, full-hipped as well as big-breasted, with the shoulders of the Scuolo-born washerwoman she'd been before Fianelli made her his concubine.

No loss. She'd been a poor cook, and Fianelli preferred to dine in public eateries anyway. Besides, it made it easier to use the kitchen for its real purpose, which was to serve as the headquarters for his various criminal enterprises.

His three enforcers were already sitting at the table, lounging back in their chairs and enjoying the bottle of grappa he'd opened for them before going down to the basement.

"All right, it's on." He pulled out a chair and sat down himself. Zanari poured him a glass of grappa. "I just got the word."

None of the three enforcers asked him how he'd "gotten the word," or from whom. In truth, they didn't care. A large part of the reason they obeyed Fianelli, despite his unprepossessing appearance, was that they all considered him a veritable wizard when it came to knowing the right things and the right people.

Paulo Saluzzo grimaced. "Treason's a dangerous business."

"The more danger, the more profit," grunted Fianelli. "Besides, what do you care who rules Corfu?"

"I'm from Florence, by way of Naples. I couldn't care less whether this island is run by Venetians or Greeks or Hungarians—or manticores or unicorns, for that matter. So long as we get our cut."

"We'll get it, and then some."

"What's next?" asked Zanari.

Fianelli considered, for a moment. "The Casarini bitch, I think. If you want to betray a town under siege, you've got to have an inside link with the big shots. She can get it, we can't."

The third enforcer, hitherto slouched in his chair, sat up straighter. Smiling slightly, he emitted a soft whistle. He'd seen Bianca Casarini in the streets, from time to time.

Fianelli scowled at him. "Forget her good looks, Papeti. Just *forget* it."

The enforcer frowned, obviously a bit puzzled. Fianelli normally didn't care in the least what his men did with women. He hadn't even cared, knowing full well that Papeti and Zanari would have raped his discarded woman before they cut her throat and sank her in the sea.

"Casarini's dangerous. Never mind the details. Just take my word for it. This is strictly business."

The enforcer shrugged. But since the gesture was one of acceptance, not indifference, Fianelli let it go. He wasn't planning on using Papeti as his intermediary with Bianca Casarini anyway. Casarini lived in one of the better parts of the Citadel. The Venetian elite wouldn't tolerate someone moving in their quarters who looked like a thug, especially a Greek one. Of his three enforcers, Saluzzo was the only one who could carry off the needed pose in that area. There were traces left of the Florentine bravo he'd been, in an earlier life.

"This'll be your job, Paulo."

"I don't know where she lives. Only seen her in the streets and cafés a few times."

"You don't need to know where she lives, for the moment. Just approach her on the street tomorrow. She'll be passing by the corner where the dock-road crosses the road to the inner wall gates; you know—where Dendrago's old bake-house used to be."

"How do I know she'll be there?" There was a whining undertone in Saluzzo's voice. Like any such man, he hated to work—and, for him, spending a day lounging about waiting for someone to show up who might not constituted "work."

"Don't worry about it. She'll be there."

Fianelli spoke with confidence. He'd taken the time, after receiving his instructions from Emeric, to use the magical symbols and rituals to speak to Casarini herself.

That very moment, Bianca Casarini finished the same— very close, at least—satanic procedures. In her case, in the luxurious room her aunt and uncle had provided for her in their house in Kérkira after her arrival on the island the year before.

The face of her mistress appeared, hovering like a ghost above the bowl.

"They have approached me, mistress, as you predicted."

Countess Bartholdy smiled cheerfully. "Surely you didn't doubt me?"

This was dangerous territory. "Surely not, mistress," Bianca said quickly.

"Do as they say, then," Elizabeth commanded. She cocked her head a little, studying the woman who had become, over the past few years, something very close to her slave. Bartholdy's quick mind had detected the slight traces of discomfiture.

"Surely the fact that some of it will be unpleasant—even worse, undignified—does not bother you?"

Again, dangerous territory. "Surely not, mistress."

The countess's beautiful face became just a bit taut; harsh, even, insofar as that term could ever be applied to it. "Immortality has its price, Bianca Casarini. Many prices, rather. Cavorting about with whomever I require you to cavort with and copulating with animals—even real ones—is one of the least. So do as they tell you. I need to remain informed at all times concerning the progress of their treachery, once the siege begins. My own plans require precise timing."

She did not explain what those plans were, and Bianca did not ask. Did not even think of asking, in fact. By now, she was well trained.

"Yes, mistress."

Bianca was able to say the last rather easily. Her own mind was quick as well, and she'd already realized that she could shift the worst of the work onto another's shoulders. Several others, in fact. In the year since she'd been living on Corfu, she'd ingratiated herself into the social circles of the Venetian aristocrats and the Greek Libri d'Oro. With the skills she'd learned from Countess Bartholdy, she'd been able to detect which of them possessed inner demons and vices. The ones which were most obvious, at least.

She'd start with Sophia Tomaselli, she decided, when the time came. The wife of the captain-general would be . . .

Easy. Like leading a pig to a trough.

After the image of Bartholdy vanished and she'd erased the symbols, Bianca laughed aloud. *Leading a slut to an orgy, more like.*

Casarini was beautiful herself, if not to the extent that Bartholdy was. But, unlike the countess, a sneer distorted her features badly. So, from long practice, she suppressed the expression. That was a bit difficult, thinking about the wife of Captain-General Tomaselli.

After a bit of practice, Sophia wouldn't care if her partners were pigs in a trough.

That sour thought was suppressed even more firmly than the sneer had been. The day would come, Bianca knew, when she'd have to undergo the rituals of bestialism herself. Immortality had its prices. But there was no reason to dwell on any of them beforehand.

The last work in erasing the traces of the rituals was on her, now. Bianca made no attempt to keep the distaste from showing on her face. A simple expression of distaste, unlike an outright sneer, was expected on the face of a noblewoman. Which she was not, in actual fact, but had long since mastered the art of appearing to be. She'd even successfully—and easily—fooled her "relatives" into thinking she was their niece.

She brought the bowl to her lips. It wasn't the taste that bothered her. Blood was blood. The problem was that there was so *much* of it that had to be drunk. She was normally a light eater, and drank little beyond an occasional glass of watered wine.

But it had to be done, so she got on with it. She comforted herself with the thought that at least she hadn't had to drink the niece's blood. There had been no rituals necessary, in that work. The silk scarf Bianca had used to strangle the girl had left no messy traces at all.

It was odd, really. Elizabeth Bartholdy discovered herself, these days, often coming to visit the monster in the glass jar. True, she'd created the thing, and she usually enjoyed studying her handiwork. But the unnatural elemental fetus she'd brought into being was unpleasant to look upon. Even worse, perhaps, was the aura of malevolence that emanated so strongly from the trapped monster as to permeate the entire chamber where she kept it.

Nonetheless, she came, almost every day. The creature was the blade she'd created for a masterstroke. And if the stroke succeeded . . .

Moved by a sudden thought, she left the chamber in the dungeons and made her way through the castle to her special bathing room. Once there, she studied the obsidian bathtub, gleaming with the sheen of oil in the light. It had taken a year to get it carved and polished, and she had gone through several craftsmen, not to mention blocks of volcanic glass, before one had managed to complete the task without shattering the tub. Now she regarded it as a carpenter might measure a cabinet.

I'll need a bigger one. Better order the work started on it now. This will be no dainty little virgin. Chernobog's blood will slop over in buckets, each drop worth more than diamonds.

Chapter 24

Maria looked around the whitewashed empty house. It was made mostly of stone, with plaster over the stone, and a floor of flagstones. The windows were small, but they had glass in them, in wooden frames that could be opened. It wasn't much, not compared to the wooden home in Istria. The few other houses here were crowded around like quizzy neighbors. It was, on a small scale, reminiscent of Cannaregio.

The house is a big improvement on Benito's little place in Cannaregio though, she thought, a smile tugging at her lips. You could be happy in all sorts of places, if you tried. Still, from what the porters had said, any house here on Corfu was a symbol of status. From what Maria could see, there wasn't much to build with except rock, and that had to be quarried from the main island itself. There were only a handful of houses up here between the two fortification-topped hills of the small island that formed the Citadel, Corfu's great fortress. The two hills were in a straight line running out to sea. Hence the fortress on the seaward side was called the Castel *a mar;* the one on the landward side, the Castel *a terra.*

The town of Kérkira itself—Corfu's largest—was on the main island, separated from the Citadel by a shallow channel perhaps sixty yards wide at its narrowest dimension. The town and the Citadel were connected by a causeway and a bridge. Most of the other staff of the outpost lived between the outer and inner curtain-walls of the Citadel, or in the barracks built into the walls of the fortifications. Only a few, most of them high officials and their families, lived in one of the castles on the hilltops.

She pushed open the shutters, looking out over the Citadel at the bright waters, across to the brown smudge they told her was Albania. The spring sunshine licked in at her, along with the tang of salt in the breeze off the sea. Awash with a sudden need for affection Maria turned to the wicker crib, and lifted Alessia into her arms and hugged her. Alessia was sleepy, full and warm. The baby made the small groaning sound that Maria had learned meant contentment and seemed to snuggle into her.

Maria stood there rocking her, loving her. "'Lessi. It's a home. And it's near the sea. It's peaceful . . . and you'll always have a mama."

Umberto came in and smiled at the Madonna-like scene when Maria turned at his footstep.

"How is the most beautiful, chubbiest baby on this island doing?" he asked cheerfully. Umberto's attitude toward babies, now that Alessia was born, was far more relaxed. He was as proud of the baby as any father could have been. Admittedly he still didn't look comfortable holding her, but he did delight in her.

Maria smiled at him, her good mood spilling over onto everything around her. "She's fine."

Umberto smiled back. "The house is good enough?" he asked, cautiously. "It is not as big as in Istria."

"It's wonderful." That was an exaggeration, but so what? At the moment it felt a minor one. "The whole place feels welcoming."

"Good." Umberto was plainly relieved. "They'll be bringing our boxes and things up from the ship presently. Can you come with me to be introduced to the captain-general? Then I must get down to the Little Arsenal." He shook his head. "It is in a sorry state. The old foreman is . . . well, old."

They walked along the narrow lane up to the gray stone fortress on the hilltop. It was cool here, inside the thick walls. A guard, a bit more sloppily dressed than any Venetian Schiopettieri or one of the Doge's Swiss mercenaries, led them up to the captain-general's office. The door was open, and the voices of those inside it were quite clear to anyone approaching.

"We don't have accommodation for visitors, Signorina," snapped a sharp voice from inside. "I can't help it if you think that Kérkira's taverns are too low-class for you. Rent a house."

"We have been trying to, ja."

Maria recognized Svanhild's distinctive voice and accent. She sounded tired.

"Everything decent they want a year's lease on. We should only be here for days," rumbled a deeper, similarly accented voice.

That must be one of Svanhild's brothers, thought Maria.

"Usually they hire for either the summer or winter, to fit in with the convoys," explained the sharp voice. Definitely a Venetian, probably the captain-general himself, thought Maria. *Oh, dear.* Umberto would have to work under him and he did not sound like an easy man. "You should be able to negotiate a six month lease."

"But we only want it for a few days until the eastbound convoy comes!" said the Svanhild voice, unhappily.

Maria peered into the room. It was Svanhild indeed, and both of her large brothers. And a comparatively small, dark man at a large untidy desk. The room was generously proportioned but it looked overfull of irritated Vinlanders.

The man at the desk sighed, snatched a piece of parchment from his desk, and scrawled something on it. "Here. Count Dentico has an estate outside of the town. He has a second villa some miles away. Perhaps he would be prepared to lease it to you for such a period. Perhaps there will be rooms enough for your escort. I do not know. Now please, I have business to attend to." He pointed to the door. "You can hire horses and a local guide at the *taverna* just across the Spianada. Good-bye."

Svanhild and her brothers emerged. The statuesque blonde blinked to see Maria and Umberto. "What are you doing here?" she asked, though her surprised tone made it very clear that she was not being rude.

"We have come to see the captain-general," said Maria. "My husband will be working here."

Svanhild sniffed and rubbed her hot forehead, leaving a little smudge. "He is not a very helpful man," she said unhappily, and walked off, following her brothers.

The military commander of Corfu stood up and limped across to the doorway. He looked at Umberto and Maria, and glared magnificently. "This is not an inn. Or an employment office."

Umberto looked more than a little terrified. "My name is Verrier. I have been sent from Venice. I am to be a foreman . . ."

The glaring eyes cleared. "Ah. You must the man they've sent to deal with the Little Arsenal. We've had some problems with the local labor and the guilds." The captain-general bowed to Maria. "This beautiful lady must be your wife. I am Captain-General Nico Tomaselli. For my sins the Council has stationed me here.

"Come in," he added, in a more pleasant tone of voice, as he walked back to his desk. "You must tell me how I can serve you. My people were supposed to see you in to your home and invite you to come up to see me. The Little Arsenal is the heart of this outpost of the empire."

Maria scowled at him, behind his back, then quickly smoothed her expression into something more pleasant. She was always wary with people who handed out the flattery too liberally, especially when she'd seen the same person ready to backhand those he disliked or looked down upon. But at least he was not letting his anger with Svanhild wash onto Umberto. Though poor Svanhild could hardly know that the conditions she had found in Venice would not hold in Corfu.

Umberto bowed. "Umberto Verrier. I am a master-craftsman in the Guild of Caulkers. I had heard there were problems, I mean, I had been told that there were some difficulties that needed smoothing out. Could you tell me more?"

The captain-general shrugged. "It's quite simple, really.

The local men, whom we employ as laborers in the repair-yard, are an undisciplined bunch. They'll do any job. The journeymen complain they're encroaching. The locals say that as they can't be apprenticed, why should they obey 'prentice rules? They all drink too much and get into fights about it."

Umberto, who was a slight man, looked alarmed. "In the shipyard? But guild rules . . ."

The captain-general blew out through his teeth. "We're a long way from the guild halls of Venice, signor. If you throw one of these guildsmen out, it may be six months before you can replace him. The Greek labor *should* be easy, but the honest truth is they don't much like working here. The Venetians say they're lazy. But the truth is that they're an independent lot, Greeks. Live on past glories and expect to be treated as if they were all sons of Ulysses. Or Odysseus, as they'll insist he should be called."

Tomaselli's practiced glare was back, this time aimed at the open window and the town beyond. "I can guarantee you won't be there for more than a week before you have at least one of the Greeks calling you an uncivilized Italian upstart. There's always trouble. We've got a fair number of Illyrians from the mainland as a result. And they fight with the Greeks, too." He shrugged. "As I said: There's always trouble. You'll need a firm hand. Part of the problem is that they work frantically for about six weeks a year. The rest of the time there really isn't enough work for half of them. But to keep a skilled force we've got to employ them all year round."

Umberto had the look of a man who, in the attempt to avoid a dog turd, had stepped into a scorpion pit instead.

The town fanned out from the Citadel, on the main body of the island. Maria crossed the causeway and walked south, toward the quay-side. She had asked for directions to the market areas and got several vague pointers in this direction. It made sense: This was where the ships came in; this was where the traders would congregate. As she got closer she realized she could have just followed her nose.

The stalls along the pavements were full of things that were both familiar and fascinatingly different. Barrows piled high with crocks of olives, bunches of dried fish, boxes of filberts, trays of fried cuttlefish, mounds of cheeses . . . jostled with racks of embroidered jackets and starched white fichus. Next was what was plainly a baker, with the enticing smells of fresh bread and a display of strange, sticky-looking confectionary. Maria went into the narrow little shop and up to the counter, where a little dark-eyed woman studied her with undisguised curiosity. In a smallish town like this, the shopkeepers probably knew most of their customers.

The little women bobbed. "And how may I help you, Kyria?"

"Kyria? What does that mean?" she asked, tilting her head to one side.

The shopkeeper smiled at her curious and friendly tone. "You are new to Corfu. It is a polite greeting. It means 'milady.' How do you like our town? Are you just here with the fleet or do you stay on in Corfu?"

A woman bustled in, wearing an elegant walking dress, with her hair dressed up on combs in the height of last year's Venetian fashion. She paused briefly beside Maria, waiting for her to cede her place. Then, when Maria didn't move, shoved her aside. "Make way for your betters, woman!" she snapped.

Maria had never taken very kindly to being pushed around, and this woman had bumped Alessia into wakefulness. Maria had broad shoulders and strong arms from sculling a gondola.

"I'll have three dozen of those—"

The woman found her orders cut off abruptly by a strong arm, pulling her backwards.

"I was here first. You can wait your turn."

The woman's jaw dropped. She caught it; pinched her lips, took a deep breath, and emitted a screeching: "*Do you know who I am?* You—you—" She looked at Maria's fairly plain, unfashionable garb. "You Corfiote *puttana!*"

Maria put Alessia down, carefully. "I don't care who you are. But if you like I can throw you into the harbor to cool off. With luck, your head will go underwater and spare me from having to stare anymore at what the elderly maiden aunts of the *Case Vecchie* were wearing last year."

The last part of the statement made the woman's eyes bulge. She looked uncommonly like one of those fancy poodles that had become the latest fashion among the *Case Vecchie* of Venice. Her eye-bulge was more fashionable than her hairstyle. "You—you— *How dare you?* I'll tell my husband of your insolence!"

"Do. Then I can toss him into the harbor, too," said Maria, advancing on the woman. "He's clearly not doing his duty in beating you often enough to curb that tongue of yours."

The woman retreated, tripping over her petticoats in her haste. "You haven't heard the last of this, you Corfiote cow!"

Maria turned back and retrieved Alessia, who was going into full wail. It took her a short while to soothe her down.

The little woman shook her head incredulously. "Kyria, do you know who that was?"

Maria shook her head, her temper cooling. "No. Who?"

"That is the wife of the captain-general! Sophia Tomaselli!"

Maria said something very indelicate.

The little woman just about fell apart laughing and trying to restrain herself. "They say that's what she was before the marriage."

Maria gritted her teeth. She'd better tell Umberto about this. It was not a very promising start to their stay in Corfu. She bought some fresh bread and headed back to the house.

Umberto's gloomy expression got deeper when she told him about it. "More troubles. I'm getting somewhere with the senior journeymen. I am not winning with the Corfiotes or the other masters. Oh, well. We must expect things to take time. There is a reception and dinner tonight for the new people sent out by the Senate. We will have to attend."

❖   ❖   ❖

Maria had done certain small adaptations to the dress she had worn for Kat's wedding. She only had five dresses—though that was more than she would have ever dreamed of owning once, more than most ordinary women would ever own. This one, however, was special. Francesca with her impeccable eye had picked out the fabric from among all of the gowns that had once graced Kat's mother. Francesca's dressmaker had remade it, knowing it would adorn one of the ladies who would get an enormous amount of attention at the wedding.

The dressmaker had wanted to be absolutely certain of two things: First, that the dress would fill every aspirant of fashion in the *Case Vecchie* with a desire to own it. And, second, that the owner would love the dress so much that she would send all those who asked about it to Madame Therasé.

And, indeed, the dressmaker had succeeded beyond her expectations, even among the haut monde of Venice. By the standards that prevailed in little out-of-the-way Corfu . . .

The wine-red gown would excite envy to a fever pitch. The red velvet, with a pattern woven into it of high and low pile, was the sort of stuff that would never go out of style and was appallingly expensive. The low, square neckline and the flattened bosom were of the very latest style, as was the natural waistline, rather than the line that came just under the bosom. As was proper in a married woman, the undergown, of the finest linen, covered most of her exposed chest, right up to the collarbone, and it was pulled through the myriad small slashings in the sleeves, which were faced with scarlet silk.

The sleeves themselves were enormous, like a couple of hams. Maria often thought that she could probably smuggle most of what her old pole-boat used to carry in those sleeves. They ended in tight cuffs, though, which would make getting anything into them rather impractical. The beautiful pillow-lace that finished the sleeves of the undergown showed at the cuffs, and trimmed the edge of the undergown's neckline. The bodice of the overgown was sewn with tiny seed pearls in a latticework pattern, a pattern that was repeated on the sleeves.

The captain-general's wife had worn a gown with a high waist, and no slashings in the sleeves at all. And while her gown for this festivity would probably be of more opulent materials, Maria doubted that it would be of more recent date.

Jewelry . . . well, she only had two pieces. They'd not pass a jeweler's eye. But the three ropes of "pearls" of glass and fish-scale would stand up to any lesser scrutiny. Francesca had seen to that, and if anyone knew jewelry, it was a courtesan. And there were earrings to match.

Maria felt some pride when she looked at herself in the mirror. She gave a vixenish grin at the elegant woman with her dark, lustrous hair done up "a la didon" as Francesca had showed her. She was sorry that Caesare couldn't see her like this. Then she'd have been able to spit in his face and laugh at him. He'd always played her origins against her in a nasty game designed to keep her feeling at once utterly inferior to him and at the same time terribly grateful that he deigned to honor her with his attentions. She could see that now, with the benefit of looking back from a distance, and from the positively old age of nineteen.

She bit her lips to redden them, make them fuller, and used just a touch of belladonna around her eyes to make the pupils widen. Umberto's sharp intake of breath when he saw her brought a smile to her face.

She took his arm, and allowed him to reverently escort her to the reception, feeling a wave of warmth for her husband. Yes, granted, Umberto was unimaginative, often even stodgy—in bed as well as everywhere else—with not a trace of Caesare's golden charm or Benito's wit and bravura. And so what? He was conscientious, considerate, kindly; scrupulously responsible in his family duties; and, in his own sometimes fussy and always respectable way, he doted on her. That was its own treasure, after all, which she would repay in full with loyalty and affection.

Maria did not love Umberto, not really; but, slowly and steadily, she was growing very fond of the man.

The captain-general and his wife stood beside the elderly podesta and his wife to welcome the guests. Maria managed to keep an absolute deadpan face when she was introduced. Sophia Tomaselli did not. The captain general's wife saw the face first. And then . . . just as she was about to explode, took in the elegant hairstyling and the dress. Maria smiled vaguely at her as if she'd never seen the now ashen-faced woman in her life before.

It got worse. The podesta's wife was frail and white haired. She smiled at Maria with genuine warmth, instead of the *Case Vecchie*-greeting-the-lowly-Scuolo attitude that the captain-general and his wife adopted.

"My dear Maria! Welcome to Corfu. I have had a letter from the Doge's ward about you, begging my kindness to a dear friend. Marco tells me you are a close friend of his wife's, who was of the *Casa* Montescue."

The little white-haired woman twinkled at her husband, making light of a friendship between one of the Scuolo and a *Case Vecchie longi* house like Montescue. "My dear Alexio stole me away from that scamp Lodovico Montescue. Lodovico was a terrible tearaway when I was young. The scandal of the town! But very charming. I remember him with great fondness. Have you met him?"

"I . . . Yes, I know him, milady. He is a grand old man, gallant as anyone half his age. He can still be very charming."

The podesta's wife laughed and patted Maria's arm. "I am delighted to hear it. We must have a talk later. I can't wait to hear what that old rogue has been up to."

"I look forward to it, milady," said Maria with trepidation. How would she cope with *Case Vecchie* gossip? It was bad enough keeping her mouth shut, in case her tongue betrayed her origins in a crowd, where everyone simply said polite nothings. Back then—several lifetimes ago it seemed—she'd dreamed of being fine enough to be a *Case Vecchie* wife for the aristocratic Caesare. Well, a master-craftsman's wife stood far lower on the social scale, but it was still a long step from "canal-woman." A one-on-one conversation would be hell. But for Umberto's sake she'd had to try.

Maria couldn't help flicking a glance at the captain-general and his wife. Sophia Tomaselli's face was white under her makeup, and two red spots burned in her cheeks. Maria didn't need to look at her fulminating eyes to know that she'd acquired an enemy for life. Aside from their confrontation . . . now, thanks to Marco's well-meaning attempt to smooth her path, the woman also knew that Maria and Umberto had powerful political connections. If Maria knew anything about that kind of woman, the captain-general's wife wouldn't let that stop her. She'd just honey her spite in public—and plot, scheme and gossip in private. And doubtless nag that husband of hers. He, poor man, obviously knew his wife's expressions well. He was already looking nervous.

Then, Maria realized she'd done more than merely make the captain-general's wife look like she was wearing her mother's unaltered gown, which someone like Sophia Tomaselli would consider an insult of the first water.

Umberto smiled at her. "Phillipo here tells me you have quite stolen Signora Tomaselli's thunder, my dear. She is used to being the center of attention; everyone in our community considered her to be the most beautiful lady on the island. Tonight there are far more people looking at you. You cast her into the shade."

He meant it well, but Maria was hard-pressed not to groan. All it needed was that! She looked across the hall to where Sophia was saying something to two other women. They both suddenly glanced at her. And hastily looked away.

Chapter 25

She stood at the head of the stone breakwater, her long blond hair streaming like a banner in the wind. Farther back along the breakwater, Maria could see the inevitable brothers were lounging against some crates, along with four or five of their Vinlander escort. To the north the galleys of the Outremer-bound Venetian convoy cut the bright water under full sail.

Maria suppressed a chuckle. Svanhild was making absolutely certain that the first thing that Erik saw was going to be her. The dockyard tarts were also on the quay-side, but Svanhild was making damn sure she got her hooks set before the island's hookers did.

But that wasn't really fair, Maria knew. She was thinking like a canaler. The Vinlander woman wouldn't see it that way; her heart might know what she was really doing, but her head would be telling her that she only wanted to get the first possible sight of the convoy and of Erik.

Maria left off watching the convoy coming in. They were still under sail; they'd have to drop their sails and come in to port under oars. Maria hoped Svanhild felt like a good long stand, because she was going to be on her feet there for a while.

But Maria couldn't wait about; she had food to prepare. The one thing that Corfu had going for it was the presence in the market of even better fish than were available in Venice. She'd bought some small octopus this morning. Umberto loved them, and he was having a rough enough time at work for Maria to wish to improve his day just a little. Umberto was used to working within the framework of rigid guild discipline, where a master-craftsman said something and was obeyed, instantly and precisely. Here, away from Venice . . . what was needed was a sharp clout from the Master before the 'prentices would stop their pretense of immobility.

The small house was redolent with the scent of *zuppa con popli*, and Umberto was still sitting with a glass of white wine, the frown-lines easing around his eyes and forehead, when someone knocked at the door.

Maria went to it, angry. "Can't you even leave the master to eat his meal in peace!" she yelled. The Little Arsenal would work day and night now until the fleet left, and she expected it to be yet another problem for Umberto's attention.

But, when she flung the door open, she saw it wasn't someone from the shipyard. Instead it was a very woebe-gone looking Svanhild and her brothers and their men. The narrow roadway seemed very full of large Vinlanders.

Maria was taken entirely aback. "Oh! I . . . I thought it was someone for my husband from the shipyard. I'm so sorry."

"Erik is not on the ships!" By the reddened eyes Svanhild had already been crying. The poor woman-child seemed to spend her life crying.

"Oh." That seemed a very inadequate thing to say. Maria knew the Vinlanders had almost certainly extended their stay in Europe for a whole season on the basis of what she'd told them about Erik's plans. The only reason they were here at all was because of what she'd said about the convoys stopping at Corfu.

"I know Prince Manfred is definitely going to the Holy Land," she protested. "Katerina told me herself! And she got that from . . . uh, from Mademoiselle de Chevreuse. She's, ah, a close friend of the prince."

"None of them are on the convoy," Svanhild repeated, half-wailing. "I've lost him!"

"I believe I can help you, my lady," said Umberto diffidently, from the table where he had hastily risen to his feet. "Prince Manfred and his Knights of the Holy Trinity are coming with four special great galleys that have been built for service off Cyprus. I heard from the admiral of the Outremer fleet that they were doing final outfitting in the Arsenal the day his fleet left. He says they should not be more than a week behind the Outremer convoy." Gloomily, he added: "The Little Arsenal will be sore pressed to fix those vessels as well, if we haven't got the Outremer fleet out by then."

It was like the sun coming out on Svanhild's face again, and it looked as if she would gladly have flung herself at Umberto and kissed him, if it hadn't been so improper to do so. So Maria did just that for her. He was a good man.

Far enough away from the house not to be spotted in the darkness, two women studied the figure standing in the doorway talking to the enormous and crude Vinlanders. Sophia Tomaselli's expression was tight and pinched with anger; that of her friend Bianca Casarini, simply cool and calculating.

Maria Verrier's face was illuminated fairly well by the lamps inside her house. After a moment, Bianca turned away and began walking slowly toward the Castel *a terra*.

"I'll recognize her, Sophia, whenever I see her again. Let me give the matter some thought."

"You should have seen her earlier!" hissed Tomaselli. "The slut! She must have spread her legs for half the *Case Vecchie* to afford a dress like that—her, a *scuolo*'s wife!"

"Umberto Verrier is not exactly a *scuolo*," murmured Bianca. "Yes, he started as a simple guildsman, but he occupies a considerably more prestigious position these days."

She glanced at Sophia's face, which was momentarily well-lit by a lamp in a taverna they were walking past. "Be careful, Sophia," she said softly. "Whatever her past, Maria Verrier is well-connected now. Better than you are, to be honest, and—"

Her eyes slid down to Sophia's midriff. "Please take no offense, but she's also got a child."

As Bianca expected—the Tomaselli woman was *so* predictable—that drew an angry glare. But even Sophia had enough sense to understand the point. A married woman with a child, in provincial Corfu even more than in Venice, had a certain aura of respectability that a childless wife like Sophia didn't. Especially when the wife in question had now been married for several years, to a man as generally disliked as Captain-General Nico Tomaselli—and was herself detested by almost everyone except her cronies. Over time, quietly, snickering remarks had spread, speculating either on Sophia's frigidity or her husband Nico's impotence—neither of which enhanced her status at all.

They walked on in silence for a bit. Diffidently, Bianca cleared her throat. "Querini has been no help, I take it?"

Sophia's scowl was heavy enough to spot even in the sliver of moonlight. "That pig! Bad enough he ruts like one, but he doesn't even manage the job."

"Ah. His lovemaking does leave a lot to be desired, in the way of finesse. I admit I rather enjoy his energy myself. But then——" She issued a soft laugh. "I've been taking precautions to make sure I *don't* get pregnant. Unlike you, I have no convenient husband to assume he's the father."

Again, they walked on in silence for a time; and, again, Bianca cleared her throat. "I have another lover who might do the trick—two, actually—but . . ."

Hearing the pause, Sophia seemed to shrivel a bit. "You think it's me, Bianca? Tell me the truth."

Casarini kept the surge of triumph from showing. Hard, that. She truly enjoyed snaring her prey.

"I hate to say it, but . . . it could be, yes. Crude he may be, but Querini's certainly not impotent—and I know of at least two bastards he's sired."

Sophia Tomaselli seemed to shrivel still further. Bianca watched, sidelong, gauging the moment.

"I might be able to help, there," she added. "I know someone who's . . . well. A Strega mage, I think. Or . . . something else, but similar."

Sophia made a face. Bianca laughed softly again. "No, no, Sophia, not what you think. Ha! Aldo Morando's no shriveled up crone, that's for sure. Quite a handsome devil, actually. In fact, I've been considering . . . well. The point is, he's an accomplished apothecary and knows a number of magics."

"Have you . . ."

"I certainly wasn't trying to get pregnant! My problem was the opposite, actually. If Morando's as good at fertility as he was at abortion, you'll be fine."

They were now near the entrance to the Castel *a terra,* where the Tomasellis lived. Bianca drew to a halt. "So, do you want me to set you up with him?"

Sophia didn't hesitate. "Yes," she hissed. "If I could get that problem taken care of—" She glanced over her shoulder, back the way they'd come, her eyes narrow. "That bitch!"

Bianca issued her soft, friendly laugh again, and placed a hand on Tomaselli's shoulder. "One thing at a time, Sophia. I'll give some—*ha.*" She broke off, as if struck by a sudden thought.

"What is it?"

"It just occurred to me that Morando might well be of help on that problem, also. Apothecaries and magic-workers—good ones, anyway, which he is—often know . . . You know. Poisons. Hexes. Curses."

The words seemed to fill Sophia Tomaselli's figure, removing any trace of hunched shoulders. "*Yes.* Set it up for me with this Morando, Bianca."

Bianca nodded and began to turn away, headed toward her own domicile in a less prestigious part of the Citadel. But Sophia stopped her with a sudden hug. "You're such a good friend!"

That was a bit startling. It was the first time Sophia had ever expressed any affection for Bianca beyond the gossipy and sniping camaraderie of two women of like temperament. Their friendship was close, after all these months that Bianca had spent cultivating it, but only in the sense that two spiteful conspirators were intimate with each other. There had never been any warmth in the thing before.

Immediately, Bianca returned the embrace. Rather fiercely, in fact. Partly, to maintain the pose—but mostly to disguise the sheer thrill from showing. She *loved* that moment when the trap was sprung.

"Well?" asked Morando, closing the door behind her and giving Bianca his well-practiced arching eyebrow. Morando, Bianca knew, thought the expression gave him a certain enticingly satanic air.

It did, in fact. Studying him for a moment, Bianca decided to let him finally seduce her. That would help snare him as well; all the more so because a man of Morando's type invariably thought of himself as the conqueror. Of all prey, predators were the easiest.

Besides, Bianca was tired of Querini's clumsy love-making herself. She'd only initiated the affair and continued it in order to tangle Sophia Tomaselli in her web. Morando would probably make a pleasant change. If nothing else, he'd be too suave to grunt.

"Well?" he repeated.

"It's done. She should be coming here before much longer."

Morando waved at the table where an open bottle waited. And two glasses. Not all *that* suave, alas.

So be it. Bianca had had worse, and would have much worse in the future. Gracefully, she slid into one of the chairs and allowed Morando to fill her a glass. Before it was half-finished, she'd accepted his invitation to tour his establishment.

It proved to be quite a bit more impressive than she'd expected. Later, after Morando fell asleep, she slid out of the bed and tiptoed into the hallway. There, she paused for a moment, listening carefully to be sure that she hadn't awakened Morando. Fortunately, he snored, though not as badly as Querini.

Yes, he was sleeping soundly. Bianca made her way to the flagstone in the floor that was actually a trapdoor. Prying it up slowly and carefully, making sure to remain silent, she peered down into the darkness. All she could see in the dim light were a few steep wooden stairs.

She rose and padded, still nude, to the door to the bedroom. After listening for a moment longer to Morando's snores, she decided he was a heavy enough sleeper to risk further investigation. She went to the kitchen and picked up the oil lamp burning there. With it in hand, she returned to the trapdoor and went quickly down the steps. She left the flagstone pried up, rather than closing it behind her. That was a bit risky, perhaps, but less risky than finding herself unable to lift it when she wanted to emerge. The damn thing was *heavy*.

Once she was down in the cellar, she spent little time examining what was obvious. Morando had already shown it to her, in the tour he'd given her earlier. She'd had a hard time to keep from laughing, then, and now found herself smiling sarcastically. Morando had been quite proud of his "secret magical lair," dropping a number of hints that he was even skirting the edges of satanic rituals. But to someone like Bianca Casarini, for whom those rituals were a reality and had been for several years, Morando's fakery was obvious. The man was a charlatan, pure and simple. Somewhere along the line—perhaps in Milan, in the days when Casarini had first met him as they each plied their separate swindles—he'd learned just enough of the trappings to be able to put on a reasonably good show. Good, at least, to anyone who didn't know the truth.

She wasn't interested in any of that. The only reason she examined the "satanic altar" at all was to check for a secret passageway. There was none, as she'd expected. That would be too obvious.

There *had* to be a bolthole somewhere. Morando would not overlook something that basic. The man might be a charlatan when it came to magic, but Aldo Morando was a genuine professional when it came to his real trade. Trades, rather, since Morando was many things: procurer, swindler, narcotics peddler, seller of information. Anything, really, that was outside the law and involved no muscular effort other than copulation. When Bianca had discovered him on the island a month or so after she arrived herself, she'd practically crowed with glee. He'd make the perfect instrument for her plans. Countess Elizabeth Bartholdy's plans, rather. Working through Morando, Bianca could manipulate both Sophia Tomaselli and King Emeric's agent on the island, Fianelli.

Eventually, she found the bolthole. It was hidden, not by cleverness, but by the crude expedient of size. An entire wall in a very small side chamber in the cellar could be swung aside. Not easily or quickly, though. At least Morando kept the hinges well oiled.

Bianca frowned. Morando was getting careless. He'd been on Corfu too long, two years longer than Casarini herself, and it was evident that he'd picked up some of the slack nature of Corfu's society. In Milan, he'd have made sure to have a bolthole he could get through in a hurry. Duke Visconti's agents were ferociously shrewd as well as ferociously brutal.

So be it. Bianca Casarini had no intention of finding herself trapped in that cellar, after all. She'd mainly wanted to find the secret escape route to see if she could get *in*, not *out*. The countess wanted the coming siege protracted long enough to force her nephew Emeric to come to her for help. Eventually, however, the Hungarians would overwhelm the city—Bianca's orders were to delay Emeric's victory, not prevent it. And when that day came, she wanted to be well out of the rapine and carnage that was sure to follow. It had occurred to her, when Morando gave her his tour earlier, that the cellar would make the ideal place to hide during the sack of Kérkira.

She'd have to make sure that Morando was out of the way by then, of course. But Bianca was not particularly concerned about that. Most likely, in the long months of the approaching siege, Morando would outsmart himself and get arrested by the island's Venetian authorities. If not, Bianca herself would see to his removal, when the time came.

After, with considerable effort, prying the wall open wide enough to slip through, Bianca used the oil lamp to guide her down the narrow passageway beyond. She had to stoop, bent almost double, to make her way through it. The tunnel—it could hardly be called a "corridor"—looked to be ancient in its construction. It had probably been built when the stone building was first erected, centuries earlier.

It wasn't long. Some twenty yards down, after a single sharp bend, Sophia found herself in front of a grating looking out onto an alley. The grating was old too, the iron coated in rust. From the outside, to anyone passing by in the narrow and—she had no doubt, though she couldn't really see it in the dim light thrown by the oil lamp—filthy, garbage-strewn alleyway, the grating would attract no notice at all. A town as old as Kérkira had a multitude of such architectural oddities.

Inspecting with her fingers, she discovered that, here also, Morando had taken care to oil the hinges on the inside of the grating. He hadn't grown *that* careless. When and if the time came, the grating could be opened—where most such would be rusted shut.

So. All that remained was to examine the latch. It was a simple bolt on the inside—her side—of the grating, tucked out of sight of anyone in the alley. She experimented a bit and satisfied herself that she could reach through the grating and pry it open, when the time came.

A good night's work. Now moving quickly, Bianca retraced her steps and, soon enough, was silently lowering the flagstone over the secret entrance to the cellar. She returned the oil lamp to the kitchen; then, made a quick inspection of her body to make sure there were no tell-tale traces of her activities. Beyond cleaning the soles of her feet and wiping her hands on a rag, there was nothing. Bianca, unlike Morando, had not grown careless with the passage of time.

She returned to the bedroom and eased her way back into the bed. Morando grunted faintly, as her weight depressed the mattress, but didn't wake up.

Bianca started to sneer, in the darkness. Sloppy oaf! But she removed the expression almost instantly. First, reminding herself that she had a powerful motive for always remaining careful which Morando lacked—her quest for immortality. And, secondly, reminding herself that too many sneers would eventually disfigure her face. Eternity was . . . forever.

Chapter 26

Benito was frog-marched onto the galley, still with leg irons on. The Justices were making absolutely sure he didn't escape, he thought grumpily.

As if he'd want to while he was still here in Venice! He'd spent a number of days in prison, any one of which was a day too many. It had brought home to him just how valuable being able to do things really was—especially being able to come and to go at times of your own choosing. Reluctantly, Benito came to acknowledge that maybe Marco knew him better than he knew himself. Staring at those walls for a solid year would indeed have driven him crazy. And if the food wasn't quite as bad as the swill the *Casa* Dandelo had fed their slaves, it was pretty close. Even the water was vile. Wine was a vain dream.

So: He kept his head down, he kept his mouth shut, and he behaved himself, irons and all.

It was only when he saw Erik Hakkonsen, with Manfred, staring down at him that he realized they'd played yet another trick on him.

Erik had the keys to his manacles. They dangled loosely, but obviously, from his left hand. "I have been given the duration of the voyage to Corfu to drill some sense into you," said Erik coldly. "I have nine days, perhaps, so we will start right now. You will address me as 'Sir.' You will speak only when you are spoken to. And if you aren't quick enough to do as you are told I will beat you."

"What the hell am I doing on board ship with you?" Bonito blurted, more in surprise than anger.

He got a sharp slap about the ear from Erik. "Have you already forgotten what I have told you? *Sir*. Speak when you are spoken to. Do everything as fast as your flesh will allow."

Benito found himself fiery mad clear through to the core. Why the hell should he put up with this? It wasn't as if he'd been alone in his carousing. Manfred had been there too. He stuck his chin out. "Make me."

In later years he would say that this proved the wise proposition that stupidity provides its own punishment. Erik proceeded, coldly and methodically, to prove that yes, he *could* make Benito do what he was told to do. Or, at least, regret that he had failed to do it.

As he lay against the bulkhead later, groaning, he looked up when Manfred leaned over. The prince's grin was cheerful, but sympathetic. "Best just do it, Benito-boy. Erik is mad with both of us for partying when he thought I was tucked up in my little bed. What's even worse, he's crossed in love. He's in the vilest temper I've ever seen him. Most of the knights are creeping around on tiptoes. Me too."

Benito heard Erik's ominous voice. "Manfred, I think it is time that you and I had a little more drill together."

Manfred's big shoulders shook with suppressed laughter. "Not again, Erik! You beat up Benito for a while, that should do. You've got all the way to Jerusalem to take it out on me. And my ribs are still sore from yesterday."

Erik's face loomed over him, his chill eyes back on Benito. "Up," he said. "You aren't nearly as damaged as you think you are. And once you've warmed up properly, most of your bruises will stop hurting."

Benito was engaged in Erik's idea of warming-up exercises, which he suspected would have him dead on the deck, when relief in the shape of Marco and Kat arrived to bid him farewell. And, to his surprise, Petro Dorma was with them.

Petro had brought with him Benito's rapier, *main gauche*, and also several porters with the rest of Benito's clothing. "You sail within the hour, and it may be some years, five perhaps, before I see you again. I have taken one liberty. I have given to your grandfather the broken sword that was in the armoire in your room. The duke requested it. He says he will have it reforged, since one day you may wish to give it back to Sforza. In which case, he says, it will be more useful if has a point with which you can drive it home. I will have it sent to you."

Somehow that polite civility made it all worse. "Thank you. And Petro . . ."

"Yes?"

"I'm really sorry I made all this trouble. It's just . . ."

Petro smiled. "That is behind us. You understand that as the Doge I have to be seen to be fair, dispensing justice, rewards and punishments, with an impartial hand. Even to my wards; perhaps *especially* to my wards. Now. Go well. Enjoy Corfu. Report to my senior factor there."

"Couldn't I go somewhere else?" begged Benito. *"Please?"*

"No." Petro shook his head emphatically. "You will just have to learn to live with her there, too. I suggest you go and see her, make your peace. If, after a year or two I hear good reports from my factor, you will be transferred elsewhere to learn more of how the Dorma business is conducted. Now, farewell, Godspeed, and try to stay out of trouble, boy."

Benito swallowed. "I'll do my best, Petro."

The farewell to Marco was harder. He wouldn't be seeing his brother for years. They'd never been apart for more than a month. Even when Marco was hiding out in the Jesolo marshes, at least Benito had always known where he could try to find him if he needed to. Now it would be a long time before they saw each other again. "Good-bye, Marco. I'm sorry I've been such a fool."

Marco was as gracious as Petro, and more understanding, perhaps. After all, he'd done stupid things for love, too. "We've both done that, Benito. Please take care. I

know you usually ended up looking after me, but I won't
be there to help. Remember to write to us."

"I will," said Benito gruffly. "Kat, I hope I didn't spoil
your special day for you. You know . . . I wish you both
to be very, very happy."

Kat smiled radiantly at him. "I don't think anyone could
have spoiled the day for us, Benito. And we didn't even
know about your adventure, anyway, until after lunch
the next day." She blushed rosily and looked sidelong at
Marco. "We didn't get out of bed until then."

Benito reevaluated his brother's enjoyment of premari-
tal favors. "Beds are better than bridges," he said with
perfect sincerity.

"Benito!" They shook their heads at him in tandem. His
brother sighed and smiled. "You're impossible, Benito."

Kat grinned. "But if he wasn't . . . well, we might never
have met properly, Marco. And he did sort out our misunderstanding, dearest. We'll have to forgive him."

Marco hugged his brother. "I'm going to miss you,
Benito."

"Yeah. Likewise."

Kat hugged him too. "Listen. Try to be understanding
about Maria? Give her and little Alessia my love when
you see them."

"I will do. I promise."

The capitano of the galley came up and bowed respectfully to Marco. "We'll need to be getting underway, Milord
Valdosta," he said.

So Kat and Marco went. The ship cast off, and the
rowers began edging her out into the lagoon, toward the
sea. Benito watched and waved.

And then Erik bellowed in his ear.

By the time Benito collapsed into sleep that night
he was: first, sore in places he hadn't even known he
had muscles; second, awake to the realization that Erik
was possibly an even better swordsman than Caesare
had been.

Benito was a lot of things, but a fool he was not. Not
about learning combat skills anyway. Erik had had him in a
quilted jacket, practicing with a blunt-edged, round-pointed

rapier until he could barely keep the point up. Then Erik had pulled up a grizzled old knight, who was at least as broad as he was high. "Semmens's weapon of choice is the axe or the morningstar. He will drill you for an hour. You're not really big enough for those weapons, but knowing how they work will help you to stay alive when people armed with either are trying to kill you."

Then, when it seemed things could get no worse . . . Eneko Lopez came up on deck. "I have been asked by Petro Dorma to see to your spiritual welfare. This task is probably beyond me, but I will do my best."

He did, with an incisive tongue. When he finally left, Benito realized that having his brother's superb memory would have been more useful at this point than an ability to climb buildings. He also knew a great deal more than he had about Saint Hypatia, Saint Simon, and aspects of ecclesiastical magic he'd never even considered before. Magic was more complex and more frightening than he'd realized. He wished Marco wasn't involved in it.

Then more drill. Then Erik produced a stocky, bow-legged knight with the characteristic blue-speckled facial powder burns of a bombardier. The bombardier had a peculiarly high voice, totally out of keeping with his "pet": a small cannon, chased, ornate and heavy.

"Erik Hakkonsen has told me that the best way to your mind is to drub it into your hinder end with the flat of a sword. However I am prepared to give your mind a chance. If it fails, I will assist it with this cleansing rod. If you are lucky, I will only beat you with it."

By the time the day ended, Benito was only too glad to collapse into an exhausted sleep. To think he'd once dreamed of being one of these Knights!

The great eellike creature burrowed into the ooze and lay as still as if its physical movement could betray it to that which sailed above. The adversary's presence and magic burned like a balefire on an overcast moonless night to the shaman's perceptions. He lay still and tried not to even think. If he could sense the adversary . . . then surely the mage could feel him?

For weeks now, his hawks had watched the roads away from the great marshes. He had driven them into it at first. He had nearly lost both birds doing that. Not only had the ancient lord of that place detected his hold, and sent his creatures to harry the hawks, but it had also attacked and somehow weakened the bonds that the shaman used to control them. The shaman found his creatures far less biddable now. They would turn and hunt, even when he commanded them to follow. And they would not go out over the open sea. It was contrary to their natures, but that had not stopped them obeying him before. They were becoming wilder, more their own, less his.

Above him the ships sailed on. At last he felt safe. As soon as he was sure this was the case he called: Master, open the way.

Not with his voice, of course; this shape didn't have a voice.

The answer came immediately; a kind of hole in the real world opened before him, with a shimmering green-black curtain across the mouth of it that kept off the seawater. Not a round hole, though; more a kind of rift, an outline that changed constantly, warping and writhing like a living thing.

The great eel-shaped creature swam through the twisty contorted gap between the real and the spirit world. The passage, too, twisted and writhed from moment to moment. But the monster was well shaped for negotiating it.

He fell out of the passage onto the floor of the palace, where Jagiellon waited. The shaman shook himself back into a shape that could speak, taking care that the shape was prostrate on the floor before he tried to utter a word. One could not be too servile with Jagiellon.

He bowed his head right down onto the stone. "Master. The adversary is at sea. He sails south from Venice." Only when the report was given did he look up.

The black eyes glowed. "I fear he must somehow have gotten wind of my plans for Corfu. The old shrines there must be far more powerful places than I had realized. They must be found, and the rites of blood enacted there. And if possible we must destroy Eneko Lopez. Sink him beneath the waves before he gets to Corfu. Where are the Byzantines and Emeric?"

"Master, Emeric's galleys are already at sea. His army should be landing on Corfu by morning. The rest of his fleet is still to the north of the island."

"I am aware. My slave Aldanto is with them. Emeric plans to blockade the straits of Otranto. It will be difficult to do this effectively. But maybe his blockading fleet, and those that come with the rest of his troops, can be used to kill Eneko Lopez. That could be worth more than Corfu itself, in the long run."

Jagiellon's eyes flared. "You will return. Keep a watch over my adversary. I will use the slave Aldanto to direct forces against them. There are several of the galliots with the transport fleet of carracks. Between you and the slave they can be directed to contact the blockading galliots. We will direct them like a pincer on Eneko Lopez."

The priestess in the cave was old. The magics drew more from her each year. Soon she must find another acolyte to serve the great Goddess. Someone who could chant the ancient words, and who could instruct the women in the rites. It was no small responsibility.

And there must be a new bride for Him. Of course, ideally, the two should be one and the same. But that happened very rarely; not for many centuries now.

She sighed. Well, spring was here. And, though men might war and burn, the earth and the women of the island would bring forth new life.

Chapter 27

The outcomes of great ventures often hinge on small things. In this case it hinged on a southerly wind, and the price crates of cuttlefish were fetching at the fish-market at Kérkira. A few copper pennies increase in price had formed the basis of Taki Temperades' decision. The best time to catch cuttlefish, in these parts, was the twilight and the predawn, and the best place was the bay of Vlores some ninety miles north of Corfu.

The southerly wind had delayed Emeric's carracks. The galleys were forced to anchor in the bay of Vlores and wait.

Captain Taki left Corfu with four crewmen, some cheap wine, a lot of cuttlefish jigs and a sail-full of southerly wind in the late afternoon. The moon was full and the run simple. The wine was bad, but not that bad. The wind was dropping toward early morning. Taki was pleased by that. It meant it would swing to the north by dawn.

Taki's ratty little fishing boat rounded Cape Gjuhezes. The Corfiote skipper looked at the town of vessels lying there, in the sea-mist.

"Bloody Illyrian sons of bitches!" slurred the captain. He'd had quite a lot of that wine. "Stealing my fishing . . ." He shook his fist at the multitude of ships.

Spiro looked up from where he'd been busy with his horsehair lines. "Well, the cuttlefish must be as thick as flies on horseshit for so many vessels."

They sailed silently toward the ships, ghosting in on the last breaths of the wind. It had been dying and turning to westerly anyway or there would have been no wind here at all. The moon was nearly down. On one of the ships a horse snorted. Someone said something to someone else. Across the water the voice carried clearly. It wasn't Greek. Or Italian Frankish.

"Turn, Taki. Turn now," whispered Spiro. His eyes were wide, taking in the size of the vessels they were now nearly between. "Those aren't fishing boats."

Taki didn't need telling. He swung the rudder hard across. The sail flapped lazily. "Pull it down!" he whispered urgently. "I'll get the others up. We start rowing, quietly." Taki wasn't drunk any more. Just scared.

As quietly as they could, expecting yells behind them at any moment, the fishermen eased themselves out past the cape, out of direct sight. Taki slumped against the tiller. "Saint Spirodon preserve us! That's the last time I drink that terrible *Kakotrigi* of Yani's. We nearly sailed into them! Let's get that sail up and get out of here!"

"Who the hell are they?" asked Kosti, the youngest of the fishermen, hauling on the coarse rope to pull the single patched sail up again.

"Byzantine-style galleys," said Spiro, also hauling, for once not being sarcastic.

"And Narenta galliots," added Taki, shortly. Like Spiro and most of the islanders, Taki had done a stint or two as crew on Venetian ships. It was hard work, but the money was good, if you could hang onto it. He knew a pirate galliot's looks from close up. That was why he'd come home and become a fisherman. A fishing boat was such a poor target, with so little loot, most pirates wouldn't bother. Mostly, as a fisherman, you didn't go hungry, and the wine—so long as you didn't set your standards too high—was cheap on Corfu.

"But horses!" exclaimed Kosti. "And what did that person say? It wasn't Greek."

"I don't know. I reckon it was trouble, though. And that's our catch gone," said Taki, sourly.

❖   ❖   ❖

Up on the headland a Serb guard stamped his feet in the cold. The bay behind him was shrouded in sea-mist. But what was that out there on the dark water? It could be a sail. He squinted at it for a while and then went off to call the guard commander. Make it that son of a bitch's decision whether to wake someone else.

Emeric stared at the shivering Serbs, guard and commander. "A small vessel. Why didn't you report it earlier? Where had it come from?"

"Y-Your Majesty." The guard pointed out of the tent mouth. "The mist. I just saw it. I called Micholovich . . ."

The man looked like he was going to soil himself. But what he'd said was true; no one could see far in this. And the man had at least reported it.

Most likely a coaster or a fishing boat, Emeric decided. As likely as not the mist had hidden the fleet, too. There was not much use in sending a galley. If the mist was this thick at sea they'd never find it. But it was a sign: Waiting would not do. Sooner or later vessels would find them, and he wanted to strike an unguarded target. One more day, and carracks or no carracks, they'd launch the attack.

By the next day when the story got home to Kérkira, it had grown somewhat. By afternoon, the story was all over the streets of the town. By sunset, the commander of the garrison had Captain Taki Temperades in his office.

Taki had a good memory—at least when fueled by fear. He remembered fairly closely the foreign words he'd heard, even if he hadn't understood them. And the garrison commander had been stationed in Istria. Commander Leopoldo knew a little Hungarian. Enough to recognize one swear-word.

The detachment on Corfu was a relatively small one, doing little more than policing work. Nine hundred men, some mercenaries, some Venetian marines. Fifty cavalrymen, nominally under the command of Captain-General Tomaselli. In practice, Leopoldo saw to the day-to-day running of most things, not just the garrison itself. This was Gino Leopoldo's first command post and he was determined to do well. Rumor had it that this could be Tomaselli's last command, and he might be able to replace him.

The commander had the *Capi* of the Cavalry in his office, before the sweating fisherman was going to be allowed to depart.

The cavalryman was skeptical. "I don't know, Captain. These Greeks exaggerate. Probably one vessel with a horse on her."

Taki wrung his hat. "Your honor. It was a lot of ships. I don't count too well, your honor. But Narenta galliots I know. And Greek imperial ships. My cousin Dimitri did service on one. I went to see him when he was stationed at Levkas. I saw them in Constantinople, too."

"And there is no way he makes up Hungarian blasphemy," said Leopoldo. "I want some men stationed on the slopes of Pantocrator. I don't know if this man was seeing things, I don't know if they're coming here, but I'm not taking a chance. We have to start preparing for siege."

He pulled a face. "I'll have to go and talk to the captain-general and the podesta. If people are going to be called into the Citadel, he has to authorize it."

"And stationing my men on the mountain? It's a waste of time. You should talk to Tomaselli about that."

The young commander looked at him in absolute silence. Eventually the *capi* said: "All right, then. It'll be done. But it is a waste of time."

Commander Leopoldo looked at Taki. "And you stay here before you chase the prices up in the market."

Taki leaned against the wall. "I think you're too late. The *capi* may not believe me, but the peasants do. You'll find the peasants are driving their flocks up into the hills, and sending their wives and children up, too."

The garrison commander snorted. "You stay in that corner."

The table, King Emeric thought, reflected his genius. There, molded in damp sand, was a reasonable scale model of Corfu and the Albanian coast. He'd studied the island from the Albanian shore. He'd assessed it from the sea-side nearly two months prior to that.

"It will be a three-pronged attack," said the king, pointing to his model. "Count Ladislas, you will disembark with your men, three hundred of your finest, here on the western side of the island directly in line with Corfu-town—Kérkira, as the Greeks call it. You will proceed with as much speed as you can overland. Seize a few locals for guides. Make sure that they give no warning. You should arrive at Kérkira about dawn. They have a habit of opening the gates at that time to allow inside the women of the town who work in the fortress. If possible you are simply to occupy the fortress. Admiral Volos, you will be in charge of the galley fleet coming around from the south. Should my flag be flying over the fortress, you will have a holiday."

There was polite laughter. "See that you enter the strait between the mainland and the island at dawn. Not before. If we have not taken the fortress, your men are to land and join the assault. The few cannon we have already will be landed with you." He turned on the chieftain of the Narenta pirates. "Chief Rappalli. You and yours will sail through the strait from the north. You are going to carry the Croats. Set them ashore to the north of the town. You will then take up the positions assigned to you in the North Channel. Sink any vessels attempting to flee the island. I warn you. If I find your men ashore, looting, while boats flee and spread the word . . ." Emeric drew his finger across his throat.

"Now. We are undermanned for this. The carracks with the bulk of our men have not yet been sighted. The forty-eight-pound siege cannon are still coming, behind them. If we need to put the island under siege . . . well, the men and the cannon will be here. But in this, speed and surprise are our allies. We still outnumber the garrison five to one. If my Magyar cavalry can strike at the fort as it opens at dawn . . . we're in."

Taki had sat quietly in the corner of Garrison Commander Leopoldo's office. It was a big, dim room. Officers and officials had come and gone. The scruffy Greek fisherman went on sitting in his corner. It was cool and comfortable. It was only when the garrison commander was finally ready to call it a night that Taki cleared his throat and asked, "Can I go home now?"

The commander had started in surprise. "I forgot you were here," he said gruffly. "Yes, get along with you. You've heard all sorts of things you shouldn't have. On the other hand, I don't suppose it makes much difference."

So Taki had found his way to his cottage on the western shore late, and, for a change, sober. He'd done a fair amount of thinking, sitting there in the corner. Early the next morning he'd gone around to the houses of his crew.

"I'm not going fishing anywhere," grumbled Kosti. "We might meet those galleys. I thought I'd go and visit some relations in the mountains."

"We're not going fishing," said Taki. "We're just making sure that we've got a boat to go fishing in, when all of this is over. Now get up. We'll need Spiro and my cousin Yani."

"Yani?" Kosti asked curiously stirring himself into an upright position. "What do you want him for?"

"He's got a dinghy," said Taki shortly. "We'll need it to get home."

Kosti pulled his shirt on. He pointed up the hill. "He's off burying his wine. I think it can only improve that last vintage."

Taki snorted. "I wouldn't bother putting it underground myself."

Kosti chuckled. "Spiro offered to drink it all for him. He reckoned it would end up in the ground that way, anyway."

Taki shook his head. "Spiro would drink anything."

Kosti laughed. "That's what he says about you, skipper."

"It is, is it? Well, I'll go and wake him up," said Taki. "I went to bed sober last night. I hope he's got a sore head on him this morning. You go and see if you can find Yani. Ask him to pick us up on the place we collect firewood from."

Together they sailed the old boat out to a little rocky islet off-shore. The current side of the islet was piled high with driftwood and debris from the winter storms. Taki made a habit of coming out here in the summer every year when it had dried out nicely, to load up with firewood.

"You reckon they're definitely coming?" Spiro asked, holding his head. "I don't feel like doing a whole lot of heavy labor for nothing. The last time I felt like this I was in Venice. I got beaten up and nearly killed by a *Case Vecchie* kid who turned out to be a lot tougher than he looked. This time it was just the wine."

Taki shrugged. "Where else could they be going? Once this is done I'm going to spend a few days up in the hills. Once they get over their looting and burning we can come back and get the old boat in the water again. They'll want fish, whoever wins."

Using some logs as rollers, they began to haul the fishing boat up onto the islet.

"Do you think the Venetians stand a chance?" asked Kosti.

Taki shrugged again. "What difference does it make to us? Or any fisherman or peasant?"

Spiro grimaced. "According to my grandfather, they're not the worst landlords."

"But they're not Greeks," said Kosti. "At least it would be a Greek island again."

Spiro grunted with effort, and the boat moved up some more. "You should hear what sorts of taxes some of my mother's people on Ithaca pay. So little they have to eat roots and bark to pretend they're being starved."

"Uh-huh. Is that the people you said were no better than—"

"Shut up, Kosti!" said Taki, hastily. Young Kosti still hadn't learned that it was all very well for a man to insult his own relatives, but you'd better not do it for him. Even if he had said it to you earlier. "Let's cover the old scow up with this driftwood. I want it to look like it's all part of it."

"That shouldn't be hard," said Kosti.

Taki gritted his teeth and set about stepping the mast. Kosti really had better learn to watch that mouth of his. Spiro was as sarcastic as a man could be, but somehow you always knew that he was joking.

Yani came along in his dingy at about midday. "Hurry up, Taki. I've still got some wine to move out."

With the four of them in the dingy, water had been slopping over the gunwales. Still, they made it back to the shore without throwing Kosti overboard. Then Yani and Taki loaded a few limestone boulders into the boat, took the dinghy back out into the cove Taki launched out of. Having firmly anchored it with some rocks in a net-bag . . .

They sank it.

Yani knew his cousin well enough not to doubt what he'd seen off the Albanian coast. And Taki was ready to bet there were a good few carefully sunken boats around the island. A sunken boat couldn't be burned, smashed, or stolen. With a bit of patience and a few oxen—or even enough donkeys or just strong backs— it could be hauled out again.

Maria put the platter of grilled fish on the table in front of Umberto. "The prices in the marketplace today are just unbelievable. I wanted some chestnut-flour to make castagnaccio. Apparently, never mind chestnut-flour, there is no flour to be had at all. What's going on, Umberto?"

The gray-haired man rubbed his eyes tiredly. "There's a rumor about that there is a fleet of ships up the coast. Of course everyone believes they'll come here. It's probably nothing more than a bunch of pirates. They'll not trouble Venetian shipping or Venetian possessions. Put off buying for a few days. The prices will come back down. And maybe I'll be able to get those idle fools in the boatyard to stop begging for news and doing some work instead," he finished irritably.

"There's no truth in it?" she asked, rocking Alessia's cradle with a foot.

He shook his head. "I doubt it. Some fisherman came in with the story. The man's a notorious drunkard, to hear the locals tell of it. You'd probably find the ships were pink and crewed by worms if anyone bothered to question him properly."

Maria nodded. And resolved to go and buy what she

could. As a canaler, rather than a guildsman, she had a lot more faith in what fishermen claimed to have seen. She'd already bought basic household supplies in the first days, being pleasantly surprised by the low prices here, this far from Venice, of things like olive oil, honey and wine. She'd been unable to resist the bargain of a huge crock of olive oil. She had ample flour for a month . . . Salt fish had still been available . . . dried figs. They'd get used, eventually.

"I did think we might buy a goat. There is a pen in the back yard. And a chicken coop. I've never kept these things, but the goat would be useful for milk and cheese. Chickens lay eggs."

Umberto nodded. "So long as you don't spend too much on them."

"Very well. I'll see what I can find. Will you be back for lunch?"

Umberto shook his head. "No. I'll take something with me. There is a sea of paperwork to catch up on." He sighed. "This is not an easy task. The yard is an unhappy place, full of fighting. And the Greeks and the guildsmen are all as lazy as can be. My predecessor made up for lack of method by ordering huge stocks of everything. So: I have several years worth of stock of cladding timber, some keel and mast timbers we'll likely never use and enough pitch to caulk the entire Venetian fleet—but no brass nails, and barely a handful of tow."

When he had finished his breakfast and gone back to work, Maria took her largest basket and Alessia, and walked. There was no point in heading for the market, not when she was looking for living things instead of foodstuffs. But this was not such a big place that she couldn't reach a peasant cottage outside town.

After an hour's walk, Maria was less convinced she'd find what she was after. By the deserted status of the peasant houses, *they* certainly believed there was trouble coming. She was now away from the coast, and she could see the scallops of azure bay, and Kérkira, white in the morning sunshine. The air was already thick and warm and full of the scent of the fine-leaved shrubs by the roadside. Bees buzzed lazily while collecting their bounty from the flowers. Except for the empty cottages, stripped of everything moveable, it would have been hard to believe there was anything that could go wrong in this Eden.

Eventually she found a man and his wife struggling to remove an iron bedstead from a cottage. There were a couple of hens in the yard.

"Good day."

"Day to you too, kyria."

Maria was startled. *Kyria?* Lady? She'd dressed in an old dress, a relic of her days as a canaler. Then she realized that she spoke Venetian-accented Frankish, not Greek. The Venetians had been here for more than a hundred years and all the islanders she'd met could certainly understand the language. But Maria had rapidly gathered that there was a strong divide between even the lowliest Venetians and the local people. Among the women of the garrison this seemed to be even more of an issue. Greeks were servants! And one had to keep them in their place. You didn't speak to them. You gave them orders. Besides . . . she wore shoes. That set one apart from peasant women.

Maria set the basket and Alessia down, and took a hand with the bedstead. It was obviously the poor cottage's pride and joy, and the most treasured piece of furniture. A bed and the bedclothes were the one thing that the rent-collectors could not seize for debt, so they were usually the finest piece of furniture in the peasant houses, she'd been told.

The man and his wife nearly dropped it when Maria came to help. Their jaws certainly dropped.

The doorway had two broad buttresses outside. Inside, the door to the room that they were trying to take the bedstead out of was at such an angle that the bedstead just couldn't do the corner without hitting the strut. After a few moments of struggle Maria asked: "How did it get in?"

The man shrugged. "I do not know, lady. My grandfather put it in before I was born. There was only one room then."

Maria's patience was exhausted. Besides, she'd walked

a long way carrying a baby on a hot morning. She took charge. There were some advantages to being a lordly foreigner. The peasant wouldn't have taken such instructions from his wife. "Put the end down. It'll have to stand on end to get it out."

At an angle, stood on end and scraping the white-washed clay, the bedstead came through.

The peasants grinned. "Lady, you are clever. And strong too," said the man admiringly. "Where do you come from?"

"Venice."

The peasant shook his head. "Can't be. Eh, Eleni? The women who come to the garrison and villas, they all are weak."

The wife nodded. "Anastasia is in service at Villa Foiri. She says the woman cannot even pick up a dish for herself."

Maria laughed. "They aren't weak, just lazy. Too lazy to do for themselves what they can pay someone else to do!"

This provoked laughter from both. "Why, lady, they say *we* are the lazy ones!"

Alessia stirred, and Maria went to her. The peasant wife looked longingly and adoringly at the baby. "She is so beautiful, lady."

Maria wondered why people always said babies were beautiful. She loved Alessia more than anything, but she wouldn't have called her baby "beautiful." Plump, yes. Soft and tiny, yes. Adorable, yes. "She is very lovely when she's asleep."

The peasant was plainly keeping out of this women's talk. "Eleni, why don't you bring us some of that young white wine and some food. It has been hot work, but now, thanks to the lady, the worst job is over."

Eleni nodded. "Sit, lady." She motioned to the bedstead. Her husband had already taken up the important task of supporting a tree, by sitting against it in the shade.

"I'll give you a hand," Maria offered. "I was brought up to know my way about a kitchen, never mind what the others do."

They went into the cool, dim cottage. The kitchen was

around the back, actually a separate little room—the only light coming either from the hole in the roof or the door. The only "furnishing" was a hearth a few inches high, and a few small soot-blackened shelves. By comparison, Maria realized her little home was a palace.

The young peasant woman had plainly decided that such a person could be trusted with the innermost secrets of the heart. Questions about pregnancy and birthing followed as she took bread, olives and cheese, and a clay jug of wine from places in her kitchen and loaded these onto a board.

"I think I am pregnant," she confided in a whisper. "I have not . . . Yani and I have been married for three years and I have had no children. But this year I have been to the mountains. To the holy place for the dancing." She giggled. "It was very cold without my clothes on. But I will be blessed this year." She touched Alessia with a gentle hand.

She seemed to assume Maria knew what she was talking about.

They went outside, and woke her husband. The wine was cool and crisp, the bread crusty. The olives, wrinkled, tiny and black, were flavored with some rosemary. They ate in silence. Peasant table manners were simple: Talk and food did not go together. Maria smiled. Back in the days she'd been trying to learn to be more ladylike to please Caesare, one of the hardest things she'd had to try to master was the idea of eating and talking at the same time. It gave you indigestion. It was pleasant to slip back into the business of taking food seriously and talking later.

But when the eating was done, then it was time for talk and for business.

Maria found herself learning a great deal about the fleet that had been spotted at the bay of Vlores. She also found herself walking back to Corfu town leading a kid that did not wish to be led, and with a dozen fresh eggs, a crock of olives and some cheese. And with two disgruntled-looking brown chickens in her basket, their feet tied with twine and attached to the wicker.

Chapter 28

On the slopes of Mount Pantocrator, two bored mercenary cavalrymen were preparing a late dinner of a skinny fowl that some peasant was going to be very upset about in the morning. Spatchcocked and grilling over the flames, it had more of their attention than the sea-watch their not very impressed *capi* had ordered them to keep. They had every intent of finishing their chicken and some young wine, and sleeping beside the embers of the olive-wood fire. Gurnošec was a Slovene, and his companion from Lombardy. Their loyalty to the Venetian Republic was purely financial.

Still, when the one got up from the fire and wandered into the dark a bit to relieve himself of some of that young wine . . . he did glance at the moonlit sea. He nearly wet his boots.

"Chicken looks about done, Gurni," said his companion, from the fireside.

"Forget the sodding chicken! We'd better get to our horses." His tone of voice told his Lombard companion that this was no joke. The man stood up and came away from the fire.

"What is it?"

The Slovene pointed at the sea. "This wasn't the stupidest idea that Commander Leopoldo ever had after all."

The chicken, untended, burned. The cavalrymen riding through the dark olives had other things on their minds.

Was a real war worth what they were being paid? And would it be possible to go somewhere healthier? Both of them now saw, with crystal clarity, the folly of taking service which involved being posted on an island.

The bells were ringing in Kérkira three hours later. The sound carried a long way. Up in the hills, other church bells took up the chime. The sound carried across the water.

Count Ladislas ground his teeth. "Well, so much for surprise," he said grimly.

His second in command patted his horse's flank. "They'll be expecting attack from the sea. If we can cross the causeway-bridge we'll still be in. We'll take them."

Count Ladislas said nothing. But that in itself was a condemnation.

They landed at a fishing harbor on the western coast—nothing more than a beach with a few boats pulled up. The island hills loomed dark beyond. The moon was down, and ripping a local or two out of their beds ought to have been easy. But Count Ladislas soon realized that they'd been watched. The doors were still swinging in some of the little whitewashed houses as they rode past. Finding a guide was not going to be that easy, after all.

However, there was a track leading inland. And it was a distance of not more than two or three leagues to the Venetian fortress on the other side of the island. The Magyar cavalry rode off on the heavy horses, up through the olive groves, vineyards and fields. It was very dark, and the track—for it could hardly be called a road—was quite indistinct.

Two or three leagues can be a very long way in the dark. Especially when She who watched over the island did not love invaders.

The hills and Mediterranean scrub on them were a good enough grazing place for goats. They'd found the goats, but not the goatherd. Just a dead-end valley. In the darkness, the scrub oak and myrtle bushes were sweet-scented. Pleasant for a ramble, the place was hell for an officer in a hurry. They found two peasant farms and huts, but no peasants. Dawn eventually found them on a hilltop a good league from the eastern shore, and a league too far to the north.

By the smoke puffs, the Croats had already entered the town of Kérkira and were now attempting to assault the fortified Citadel. The Citadel was most definitely closed up and was most definitely returning fire on the Croats. The Venetian fortress, as Ladislas could now see, was going to be no pushover. It was on an islet just to seaward of the town. The wooden causeway he and his men had been intended to take by speed was reduced to a few smoking piles on the far shore.

So much for rushing it. The burning houses in the town, outside the walls, showed the Croats had been busy. It was unlikely they'd done much to the fortified Citadel though. All they'd achieved was to get shot at.

Count Ladislas sighed. King Emeric was not going to be pleased. He never was when his plans went awry, which they frequently did because he was inclined to excessively complex ones. The failure of his plans was always blamed on the errors of his officers when they went wrong, and attributed to his genius when they went right—despite the fact that success, as often as not, meant that some officer had disobeyed.

Still, they'd better get down there.

Taki leaned back against the big granite boulder and looked at the Hungarian cavalrymen. Saint Spirodon! Those horses were big! He and old Georgio had had quite a night up here with the devils. Of course they hadn't really been chasing after them or even Georgio's goats—as they discovered when they abandoned the goats. It had just seemed as if they were being followed.

They'd choose a place no sane man would go—if he wasn't chasing you—and the horsemen would come around the bend. They'd covered a good three leagues in the last few hours and these crazy soldiers must have ridden a lot more.

He watched in relief as the three hundred horsemen set off for the Viros road. Kérkira was burning down there. He looked gloomily at the scene, at the backs of the Hungarians, then at the black smoke from what had been a sweet taverna once. He wasn't surprised to see other Corfiote heads popping up from the underbrush of another hillside. They wouldn't be able to stay up here forever, but until the worst excesses were over, a lot of the peasantry would stay in the hills. It was still not summer, still cold at night, but at least it wasn't winter. And maybe She would provide. You never knew.

There really was nothing worth destroying out here. The town of Kérkira outside the walls of the Venetian fortress was ruined or burning. Out of range of the arquebusiers on the walls, the Croats and Hungarians milled about ineffectually. By the screams, some of them had managed to find a woman. Or maybe not; a man with his privates blown off screamed like a woman, sometimes. Riderless horses roamed, wild-eyed. The air was full of gunpowder, smoke and shouts. Occasional cannon fire from the walls increased the carnage, and the invaders, without cannon, were unable to even return fire.

Count Ladislas knew by then that it was a complete fiasco. The fort and its cannon could defend the harbor very effectively. The buildings the Croats had been firing indiscriminately belonged not to the Venetians, but to the locals. They provided at least some rudimentary cover from the cannon fire . . . So the Croats were burning them. Wonderful.

True, the fortress was in reality designed to defend from attack by sea. The larger cannon would be there. But, no doubt, they could be moved. Ladislas couldn't really see how the situation could get any worse.

And then, looking back down the slope he realized it could—at least on a personal scale. That was one of the king's messengers. And by the way he was riding, His Majesty wanted someone in a hurry. With a terrible, sinking feeling in his gut, Count Ladislas realized that Emeric's messenger was looking for him.

Emeric of Hungary believed in personal comfort. He'd come close to the fighting, but not close enough to risk actual combat. Still, he'd been close enough on his hillside, outside his hastily erected palatial tent, to have seen Count Ladislas and his precious Magyar cavalry arrive too late. He watched them discharge their wheel-lock pistols ineffectually at the fortress wall across the empty kill-zone.

The narrow streets of Kérkira were no place for a cavalry charge. Emeric, instead of watching the victory he'd expected, had seen his plan totally unravel.

As Count Ladislas had known, someone was going to suffer for this and he had a feeling it would be himself. The king stood outside the tent. Count Ladislas dismounted and gave his great war-horse, seventeen hands at the shoulder and his pride and joy, a last pat. He hoped they'd find a good master for him.

He knelt before the king. There were little livid spots of fury on Emeric's sallow cheeks.

"You incompetent, bungling fool!" A quirt slashed at the count's face. He did his best not to flinch, as the blood began trickling down his cheek. "Where have your men been? Why did you come after the attack? Are you a coward, Ladislas? I don't tolerate cowards. Or incompetents!"

Count Ladislas knew the truth would serve him badly. "Sire. The peasant we took as a guide was there simply to betray us. He led us into an ambush the Venetian scum had prepared for us. Your heavy cavalry flattened them, Sire. But they knew we were coming. Someone must have betrayed us!"

The Count played on the king's passion for heavy cavalry and his belief that they could ride anything down. It was not a hard belief to feed. The Count believed in it himself. He also played on Emeric's belief that treachery lay everywhere.

For a brief moment, Count Ladislas thought it had been enough. Emeric's cruel eyes narrowed. Then he shook his head. "The peasant you found just happened to lead you into an ambush? Ha." The quirt lashed at the other cheek viciously. "Where is this peasant?"

No use looking to see how many of your troops the cannon were taking down when you charged. Straight ahead and devil take the hindmost. Scarred cheeks were a small price to pay for his life. "Sire. I ran him through myself. The village was deserted, except for this one man. He was hiding, but not well. He ran out of a building my men entered. He claimed he'd come down secretly after the others had left to steal some wine."

Emeric stared at him. Then shook his head. "Truth or not, I'll have to make an example. You love that horse, don't you?"

The Count had held back the cold sweat with difficulty. Now he felt the sweat pouring out. "Sire . . ." he croaked. "That horse is great bloodstock. Some of the finest bloodstock we've bred. Don't kill him, Sire. Kill me."

Emeric reached out his hands and put them on the count's shoulders. "I'm not going to kill your horse. It is far too valuable. You, on the other hand, Count Ladislas, are not. Your horse is going to kill you."

The king's brows flared satanically. "You've heard I am a man-witch? You've heard that I derive my strength from the pain of my victims?"

That wasn't all the Count had heard. "S-sire, please."

The king smiled, like a kill-mad weasel. Agony washed through the count, flowing from those hands. "It is true. All of it."

The Magyar officers stood in a silent circle. The corral that had been hastily knocked together contained their former commanding officer. And a horse he'd trained to follow him like a dog.

Count Ladislas had been a brutally efficient officer, but he'd loved that horse. Now, his eyes, fixed on the once beloved steed, were full of terror. The king reached out his hands and touched the horse. The animal screamed like a woman, reared and backed away. The king stepped out through the gate.

The horse was . . . shivering. Its eyes rolled, and its lips peeled back. It turned, then, its mad eyes suddenly fixed on the count. He tried to climb the corral, but the Magyar flung him back at the king's command. He scrambled to his feet in front of the advancing horse.

The horse lunged forward to bite and lash out with

his iron-clad hooves. Ladislas dived, but the war-horse was faster. A hoof caught him and flung him into the rails. Blood flew. The Count was a tough and a strong man, though. He grabbed at his horse's mane and vaulted onto its back.

The great horse went berserk. It dropped and rolled; kicking epileptically.

It took a while to kill the count. But eventually the horse stood, head hung low. And in a bloody ruin lay the remains of the Magyar commanding officer.

Emeric walked into the corral. The horse backed off. Emeric spat on the corpse and turned to the silent audience of Magyar cavalrymen. "Learn. If I order you to be at a place at a certain time—you will be there."

Towards midday King Emeric gathered his commanders on the hilltop overlooking Kérkira. Smoke and ruins surrounded the island fortress called the Citadel, but it was undamaged. "We have a handful of four-pounders. Not enough to make a dent on their walls. We have, however, an effective sea blockade in place. We have, even if the Greeks fail to stop the returning convoys, some months to reduce their defenses."

He pointed to a savagely scarred man. "You, General Krovoko, are going to remain here. You're in charge of the assault on the Citadel. You'll have cannon shortly, even if I have to go back to the Narenta mouth myself to find Dragorvich, the rest of troops, and the rest of my cannon. In which case, heads will roll."

He pointed to the Greek admiral and the chieftain who headed the fleet of Narenta pirate galliots. "You will arrange the blockade. I will have one ship captain's head for any vessel that escapes. On the other hand, the loot is yours—except for one fifth, which is mine. You will arrange how it is divided, Admiral. I leave it in your hands. Make me satisfied with the arrangements."

He turned to the second in command of the three hundred Magyar cavalry. "You are promoted into Count Ladislas' shoes. See that you fill them better than he did, Commander Hegedes. The cavalry will be of little use in this siege phase. See the locals are suitably cowed. Strip the Venetian estates. One fifth for Hungary. Two fifths for the besiegers . . . on success. Two fifths for the cavalry. When you've done that, let these Corfiotes know who their new masters are."

"Sire, it will be done to perfection," Hegedes stated crisply. "You'll be proud of us."

"I'd better be," said Emeric. "You've seen what happens to those who fail me."

As she held Alessia close, Maria listened to the thunder of the cannon. A pall of smoke hung over the city outside the walls, the fresh morning breeze bringing the smell of gunpowder and burning. War might sometimes be the stuff of song and full of dreams of glory for men. But a part of her knew without any telling that for women and children, wars were hell.

And sieges were usually worse.

She looked through opened shutters at the small walled courtyard. The goat-kid was eating the grass that straggled through the paving stones, ignoring the patch of grass farther back. The chickens were pecking about. Cannon fire hadn't put them off laying. It was still a pitifully small extra ration toward the siege she knew would come. It might be five or six months before some relief came to the fortress. Maybe longer.

The raiders had timed this well: The Venetian convoys were gone until autumn. Occasional vessels would have come past, little tarettes trading up the coast. But it could easily take two or three weeks before the news even got to Venice—if the invaders weren't sinking every vessel they could find. If they were, then it would take longer. Except . . . there were the vessels that Prince Manfred, Erik and the Knights were traveling to the Holy Land in. Great galleys, if she remembered rightly. They should get away, surely?

The thought of these vessels brought Svanhild to mind. Lord! She was out there somewhere, in an unprotected villa. Maria bit her lip. What could she do about it? A prayer maybe.

Smelling the smoke, Maria's thoughts turned to the

peasants she'd been with only yesterday. Would they have managed to hide from the raiders?

A mangy, vicious-looking yellow dog hanging around the edges of the crowd snarled at a cavalryman who had made a move to kick it. The cavalryman picked up a stone and the dog slunk off into a gully. But the shaman had heard and seen enough. He walked away toward the water's edge to assume his other form. The sea attack on his Master's adversary needed orchestration. He was becoming quite casual about following the adversary-mage now. The mage did not seem to be able to detect him. That was very odd, but quite welcome. And foolish.

Chapter 29

"The other guild foremen and assistant-foremen have got to go and see the captain-general," said Umberto unhappily. "He has sent for us."

"I hope it isn't his wife complaining about the chickens," said Maria. "But you'd think he'd have other things on his mind."

"It is a great pity that you should have fought with her, Maria. She seems to wield a lot of influence here."

"I'm sorry, Umberto. It just happened. She's a vindictive bitch." Sophia Tomaselli had found small ways to needle at the Verrier family already.

"It's a shame she hasn't got any children to occupy her time," mused Umberto, looking at his wife rocking Alessia.

"They certainly occupy enough of it!" said Maria, dealing with a milky belch. "Wave good-bye, 'Lessi." Maria assisted a fat little hand. The baby gurgled and Umberto managed to leave with a smile.

He was back a little before the terce bell, frowning. "The commander wants to draft our men in as soldiers. He says the boatyard is sitting idle while the siege is on, and he hasn't enough men to guard his walls."

"It makes sense, I suppose," said Maria. "If the Citadel falls we'll all be in the soup. What happens to you, Umberto?"

The master-caulker shrugged. "He says he will brevet

us as officers, but that's not the point, Maria. He simply can't do this. The guildsmen will refuse."

She blinked; she could remember all too clearly the fighting in the streets and canals of Venice, and calling out the Arsenalotti. Why wouldn't they help now? "But why not? I mean, if the Hungarians get in they'll butcher half of the people at least."

Umberto shook his head. "The Arsenalotti are already part of the military reserve—but of the Arsenal, not of Corfu. He is not our commander. We are part of the Militia, to do Militia duties when we are not at work. To assist local authorities at any time in dealing with fires, disasters, and in dealing with immediate military threat. It is very clearly stated in the deeds of the guilds. It is one of the oldest privileges. We are not soldiers under his control. And it is not within the right of the captain-general to terminate our employment. Even the podesta cannot do that. Such an order can only come from the full Senate in Venice."

Umberto pulled a wry face. "The guildsmen here are hazy about their duties. But their knowledge of their privileges is crystal clear. They're absolutely insistent on the maintenance of the same. I wish they felt the same way about their duties." He sighed. "I'm afraid their hardness of attitude has made the commander equally awkward. We'll be doing shifts of guard work, every night."

It was a peaceful and beautiful spot, if a little isolated, reflected Svanhild from where she sat on an outcrop just above the villa. The villa was perched above a little fertile valley of patchwork fields, olive groves and some salt-pans beside the bay. She sat plaiting sedge-stems and looking out across the sea. Of course the ships would not come from along the western coastline, but anyway. She reached for more sedges. She'd never been able to keep her hands still.

As she did this she noticed a column of white dust coming down the winding roadway that lead to the villa. Could it be news? Bjarni had ridden over to Corfu town earlier. The Greek servants had been full of some story the day before yesterday about an invasion. Then, yesterday, none of them had come to work. Today Bjarni had insisted on riding to the town, despite the fact that they'd offered the port officials handsome bribes to send them word if any ships were expected. And they'd been very reliable with the last fleet.

She got up and began walking down toward the villa. She could see the rider's blond head by now. Bjarni was flogging that poor horse. And it wasn't really up to his weight in the first place.

"To arms, all of you!" she heard him bellow.

By the time she got to the house, the Vinlanders were strapping on bucklers and breastplates.

"What is happening?" she demanded.

"Corfu town is under siege," he said, wrestling with a recalcitrant breastplate strap. "And there are bands of marauders out looting and burning the great houses."

"Who?" She tugged the strap through for him.

"How do I know? All these continentals look the same to me. All I know is that the one group I saw had red sashes on, and horsehair plumes on their helmets. There's a bunch of them not half a league hence and I think they saw me."

He turned to one of the men. "Olaf, go up onto that little knoll behind the house. Give Sven a wave if you see them coming. Gjuki, open that front door. There are not more than twenty of them. We'll give them a welcome. I want men with arquebuses hidden at the upper-story windows."

He pointed to the dark-haired Kari. Kari's mother had been an Osage tribeswoman, tall, strong, and handsome— no mean hand with a bow and a knife herself—and she'd raised her boys in many of the tribal ways. Kari and his brothers had been trouble all the way across to Europe, and through it. Now they would come into their own.

"Kari, you take your brothers out by the outside wall. I want this place looking open, deserted. Svanhild, you go back up to the knoll with Olaf."

Svanhild nodded. She also took a bow with her, and a belt-knife she hadn't worn since she'd left the holding on the Mississippi.

The marauding horsemen had indeed spotted Bjarni.

They came on at a ground-eating canter, riding huge, magnificent horses. There were in fact only eighteen of them and they were loot and captive hungry. So far they'd met no resistance, and they needed to beat the Croats to as many more villas as they could find.

They yelled in delight and eagerness, seeing the villa with its open front door. It was plainly a wealthy nobleman's residence. The looting of Venetian villas had so far been a very profitable business indeed. Much wealth flowed into the Venetian Republic up the Adriatic, and not a little of it stayed here in this colony. Corfu was fertile, and had a good climate, and all the trade passed through it.

The doorway was fortunately too low or they might have ridden into the house itself. Instead they scrambled from their mounts in their haste for loot, yelling like banshees. The first eight were in through the door when Svanhild heard Bjarni yell: "Fire!"

There were six arquebusiers at the upper windows, all veterans of Vinland campaigns. All of them could shoot, and shoot well. Kari and his three brothers leapt over the wall and pulled down the only Magyar knight who hadn't dismounted or been shot. They attacked the last of the knights who was on foot outside, before hurtling into the fray inside the house.

From the knoll Svanhild could hear the boom of a wheel-lock pistol and clash of metal, mixed with screams.

She saw, briefly, someone emerge at a run from the front doorway and leap for a horse. It was a well-trained animal, and the rider was a great horseman. Almost flat on the horse's neck the rider clung, and spurred it to a gallop.

Svanhild took careful aim.

The horse ran on. But the rider lay dead, sprawled on the track, a feathered shaft between his shoulder blades.

Bjarni came striding out of the house. "Get the horse!" he bellowed.

Svanhild loosed. But neither aim nor heart was in it. She loved horses and this one was a beauty.

"God rot it, Hildi!" said Bjarni furiously. "Now they'll

have a riderless horse coming back to tell them that someone is killing these useless *nithings*. Come back to the house. Hrolf has a cut that needs tending. And we need to gather food and gear. We can't stay here."

He brightened perceptibly, when she came up to him. "At least we have got some nice horseflesh out of it. And Gjuki hit one of them on the head—we can find out just what is going on here." Bjarni cracked his knuckles explosively. "He is going to be telling us. Or I'll pull his ears off and force-feed them to him."

It wouldn't be ears he'd be pulling off, if he left the work to Kari. The *skraelings* had some gruesome means of getting information out of captives.

"Where are we going to go, Bjarni?" asked Svanhild, hastily scrambling down to him.

The huge blond Vinlander shrugged his shoulders. "Let's see what the prisoner tells us. We can base our decision on that. But I suspect we'll have to hide out in the mountains to the north."

Unfortunately, the domicile from which Fianelli ran his operations had been built right against the fortifications. The walls of Fianelli's kitchen rattled every time the Citadel's cannons fired. So, at least, it seemed to Bianca.

"You get used to it," grunted Fianelli. He raised the bottle, offering her some more, but she declined with a little wave of her hand. Bianca Casarini didn't have a good head for wine, so she never drank more than a glass at a time. Half a glass, when she was in the presence of men such as Fianelli and his goons.

Fianelli set down the bottle, after refilling his own glass. "Been through it before," he said. "Twice."

Bianca frowned. Fianelli was only in his mid-forties. "Corfu hasn't been attacked in—"

"Not here. Someplace else."

He provided no details, and Bianca decided not to ask. She wasn't afraid of Fianelli, but she was cautious around him. A man like that . . . it didn't pay to press questions. Bianca didn't know what had happened to the woman he'd once been keeping as a bedmate. But she did know that the woman had disappeared a few weeks after she got bold enough to start nagging at Fianelli.

"Nagging," at least, as Fianelli would consider it. The criminal chief's definition had a pretty low entry bar.

So, best not to ask any questions not directly relevant to the work at hand. Bianca leaned forward in her chair a bit.

"I think I've got the man you want. And the way to trap him."

Fianelli cocked an eyebrow. "Can't be just some common soldier you're playing with."

Bianca suppressed a spike of anger. *I don't copulate with common soldiers, you—!*

But she suppressed the reaction. First, because while she didn't sleep with common soldiers—not lately, at least—she was in no position to be finicky about her bed partners. Second, because the moment was too delicate for anger to be muddling her. Third, because a part of her was enjoying the vengeful twist in the game. Querini really was an oaf.

"He's a cavalry captain. Querini's his name. Alfredo Querini."

One of the three men who were also lounging around the huge table grunted. Bianca thought his name was Zanari. "I know him. A bit, not well."

"What's the hook?" asked Fianelli.

"He likes to gamble. And he's not good at it, even in the best of times. Give it a few months—" Bianca let the rest of the sentence trail off. She'd been in a siege once herself, but saw no reason to let Fianelli know.

"Sieges get boring, true enough," mused Fianelli. "And since before too long everybody's on rations, there's always a lot of loose money around. Idle hands and idle money, so there always starts to be a lot of gambling."

He squinted a little, looking at Bianca. The expression was not exactly suspicious, but . . . close. "I don't run the kind of gambling establishments that a cavalry captain would frequent."

"No, but you can make contact with someone who does. Count Dentico and his sons."

Fianelli's suspicions rose closer to the surface. "Why

not you? You're closer to those Libri d'Oro circles than
I am."

This was the tricky moment. Fianelli was right, of
course. In the year she'd been on Corfu, Casarini had
made it a point to cultivate good relations with a number
of the Greek aristocrats on the island. The "Libri d'Oro,"
they were called, after the "golden book" in which the
Venetian masters of Corfu had recorded the names
of those Corfiote families who were given preferential
treatment.

The truth was that Bianca could easily introduce
Querini to the Denticos. She knew all of them, after all.
But Bianca was determined to keep herself at least one
step removed from the treasonous links she was creating. Fianelli, like almost all criminals she'd ever known,
tended to look at the world solely through his own eyes.
He thought of what *he* would do, giving little more than
cursory attention to what the authorities would do other
than the obvious. Understandable enough, given the generally crude and sloppy methods of police work followed
in most Italian or Greek cities.

Sloppy and crude when it came to simple *criminal*
activity, that is. When it came to treason, those same
authorities—given the history of Italy and the Greek
territories—were far more energetic and astute. Bianca
was pretty sure that Fianelli's activities in the past had
steered clear of politics, though, so he wouldn't really
understand the difference.

But she did. Sooner or later, there was a good chance
the Venetian rulers of Corfu would detect treachery at
work. They were almost bound to, even with a captain-
general as incompetent as Nico Tomaselli. First, because
anyone with any experience knew that treason was the
single most acute danger to a fortress under siege, so
they'd be looking for it. Second, because in this instance
Bianca would also be undermining the traitors as well as
the authorities. Her mistress Elizabeth Bartholdy wanted
Corfu to fall to Emeric, true; but not quickly.

Fortunately, Bianca had prepared for the moment. She
squirmed a bit in her chair, doing her best to let a trace
of an embarrassed flush enter her skin. "I can't," she mur-

mured. "Count Dentico—his son Flavio too, well . . . Let's just say we're not on good terms, any longer."

Fianelli smiled thinly. One of his thugs smiled broadly. Papeti, his name was. He had the annoying habit of openly ogling Bianca, she'd noticed. She was sure that her veiled suggestion that she'd had sexual relations with both the Count and his oldest son would make the man even more aggressive toward her in the future. Probably to the point of becoming a real problem, in fact.

But the future could take of itself. Bianca Casarini was not worried about her ability to handle a common thug. Countess Bartholdy was still withholding many secrets from her, but she'd given Bianca a great deal of other training.

Her ploy did the trick. Fianelli leaned back in his chair, visibly more relaxed. She was not surprised. Another characteristic of criminals was their ready willingness to believe the worst of people. "The worst," as they saw it—and they had a very limited imagination.

In point of fact, while Bianca knew the Denticos, she'd been careful to keep a distance from the family once she'd assessed them fully. Early on, she'd decided they would be the easiest among the Libri d'Oro to lure into treason, when the time came. For one thing, they were fairly open about their pro-Byzantine inclinations; for another, they were almost blatantly corrupt. But that had become apparent so quickly that she'd seen no reason to develop intimate relations with either the Count or his sons. She never lacked for bed partners, after all, and she wanted no obvious links between herself and those whom she was fairly sure would eventually be executed.

"All right," Fianelli said. He cocked his head a little, glancing to the man who seemed to be the chief of his little squad of enforcers. That was the Florentine, Saluzzo.

"See to it, Paulo. Since Zanari already knows Querini, he can start that side of it. Put on your best Italian manners and start cultivating the Denticos."

Saluzzo nodded. He murmured something in addition, but Bianca didn't catch the words. The kitchen was rattling again.

"I hate sieges," grumbled Fianelli, finishing his glass

and reaching for the bottle. "Good for business, sure—but risky."

Bianca wondered what arrangements Fianelli had made with his master, King Emeric, to see to his own safety once the Hungarian troops finally breached the walls and poured into the Citadel. She was sure they were quite good arrangements. Fianelli was too experienced a criminal to be careless about something like that.

She was even more sure that Fianelli's arrangements would be meaningless, when the time came. Fianelli was accustomed to dealing with criminals and corrupt officials. He simply had no idea what the King of Hungary was like. Emeric took as much pleasure in betraying his own, once they were useless to him, as he did in betraying his enemies.

More, actually, Bianca suspected. She did herself, after all. Bartholdy had trained both of them well. The difference between Emeric and Bianca was that Emeric was too egotistical to realize that, sooner or later, his great-great-aunt would have the pleasure of betraying him. Bianca, on the other hand, had no illusions that eventually the countess would betray her as well.

Try to, rather. Bianca Casarini's skill and strength were growing constantly. Someday . . .

She shook her head slightly. The future was the future, and now was now. The kitchen walls seemed to be rattling again.

"I'm on duty tonight on the Vidos wall," apologized Umberto. "I've volunteered for the fourth vigil. If I take it, then none of my underlings can complain."

Maria wondered how many of the men doing militia duty had a small, restive child in their homes. But she said nothing. Just: "Wake me. I'll prepare some frittata. Jemma and Rosa have been laying well."

"Those hens are a blessing. The goat, however—it has eaten one of my gloves," said Umberto crossly.

Maria shook her head. "I see why they are used as a symbol of Satan. The beast seems possessed by an eating-devil."

"Well, if she doesn't take care we'll dine on her," said Umberto.

Even if she does, we probably will, Maria thought, but did not say.

Chapter 30

"Up. Drill time."

Benito groaned, but after nine days of Erik's discipline he knew better than to argue. The wind had been blowing steadily from west-southwest since yesterday morning and they weren't making good speed. It looked like this purgatory would continue for at least two more days.

Oh, well. It was only purgatory, not hell. Besides, he'd realized the truth in what Manfred had said: Erik was savagely unhappy about some woman. Benito had exorcized his own demons in this respect with strong drink, wild antics, and occasional fights. Erik dealt with it by a regimen of training that would make mere war gods weak at the knees. He pushed Benito. He pushed Manfred. He pushed various of the Knights of the Holy Trinity. Most of all, Erik pushed himself.

Personally, Benito thought his own method of dealing with the decisions of those irrational creatures was easier, if not better. It wasn't something he was going to point out to the Icelander, however. Erik shared the inclination to an occasional fight, and Benito had realized by this time that you really, really, *really* didn't want to fight with Erik. Benito understood now how the Corfiote seaman who had tried to rob him must have felt when he had seen his intended victim turn, and realized that what he faced was an unleashed wolf.

Benito kept quiet, as quiet as ever he had in his

life, maybe quieter. Manfred, however, was allowed to complain. So long as he actually did exactly what Erik demanded, of course.

Just now, it was dark, and Erik was toeing them both in the ribs.

"It's before dawn, you Icelandic madman," grumbled Manfred, in a voice like millstones grinding gravel. "This is a time for sleeping. For snuggling down next to a warm, cuddlesome woman. Just because you can't, don't take it out on me."

The fulminating look that Erik gave Manfred promised that in fact the Icelander would take it out on him, which suited Benito just fine. However, on this particular occasion both of them were saved from being Erik's frustration-release by a yell from the masthead.

"Sail ahead! Blessed Jesu—lots of sails!"

Within a few minutes, the knights were all awake and on deck. The capitano peered nervously forward from a perch on the bow. Erik joined him with Benito and Manfred in close attendance. "There's a lot of them," he said unhappily. "No reason for a fleet that size to be here, my lords, except for trouble. There'll be cannon on them too."

He shook his head. "We'll have to turn and run, my lords—"

"No. We won't," said Erik grimly, pointing to the northeast, behind them. Now that the gray dawn was breaking they could see a fan of other smaller vessels, under oars, stroking toward them.

The capitano turned, looked, and blanched. His lips moved silently as he counted. "Twenty-two galliots. No, twenty-three. Pirates, by the looks of them. That's the biggest fleet of galliots that I've heard of since my grandfather's day, when Admiral Gradineri broke their power off Otok Brac and burned their lairs on the Narenta."

"They don't seem to have stayed broken," said Manfred dryly.

The capitano shook his head. "They're like rats, milord. You can never find all the holes. What are we going to do? We're trapped between them."

"Run with the wind and fight our way out of whatever trouble catches us," said Manfred.

"No." Benito hadn't meant to say anything, but the words just came out of him without thinking. He couldn't believe that neither the capitano nor Manfred nor Erik could see it—but it was so obvious. Maybe it was all that time on the rooftops as a boy, but he could see the battle in his mind's eye as if on a map.

"Look at the pattern! The galliots are aiming to cut us off. Look at them! They're not rowing toward us at all. They're heading toward where we'll be if we turn and run. I'd guess we were spotted from the shore yesterday and this was planned between them. Those carracks there are bearing down on us with the wind. The galliots only have to burn our sails and stop the oarsmen from getting a good stroke with a peppering of arrows, and the carracks and their cannon will catch up with us. We need to drop the sails and bull straight into the wind."

Erik's eyes narrowed. "We'll evade those carracks. They can't quarter close enough to the wind for that. But the galliots are smaller, lighter and faster. They'll catch us."

Benito smiled savagely, seeing it all unfold in his mind. "They'll have to row a good dogleg to do it. And then they can face our cannon. We don't outgun all those round ships, but we do those little things." Then he looked at Erik and said, "Uh. Sir."

Erik snorted. "That was for training. Speak if you have sense to speak, and it certainly sounds to me like you do."

Someone clapped. It was Eberhard of Brunswick. "Well, he is speaking it now. That is the Old Fox's grandson talking. That is thinking. Real strategy."

Manfred nodded. "Give the orders, Captain. And make signal to the other vessels." He turned to the knights. "Right gentlemen. Below and arm yourselves! Into armor. They won't be expecting fifty knights on each of these ships."

Erik held up a restraining hand. "Wait. Those galliots—the rowers fight too?"

The capitano nodded. "Yes. One or two of them might

have small cannon, but they rely on boarding vessels and hand-to-hand fighting."

"Good." Erik turned to Manfred. "I don't think we should have the knights don armor yet. If we give those galliots a long chase . . . They'll be good and exhausted by the time they do catch us." For the first time since he'd come aboard, Erik gave Benito an encouraging smile. "Or what do you say, young Benito?"

Benito nodded, looking inwards at the map in his mind. "Yes. If we can keep up the chase for long enough we can turn again and quarter on the wind. We'll be upwind of the carracks. The galliots will change course, to cut the corner . . . But that'll mean that they have to keep rowing while we can rest on the oars."

Manfred bellowed, "No armor, gentlemen. Not yet. You'll all be taking a turn at the oars."

The grumble at this order was stilled by Falkenberg, who swatted an already gauntleted hand against his breastplate. "You heard the prince! Those of you already in armor, strip it off."

"Falkenberg!" yelled Manfred.

"Sir!"

"I'll want a roster of what order the knights and squires will row in. I want them to spell the rowers but not exhaust themselves. Set it up for me."

In the meanwhile, the capitano had sailors on the rigging, with orders flying. A sailor on the poop deck was making signals to the other vessels. As the sails came down, four steersmen swung the great rudder hard over. Oars came out and the steady drumbeat began.

"The carracks are resetting their sails," said Erik, squinting across the water. The vessels were, Benito judged, still more than a league away.

"Won't matter. They can't sail close enough to the wind."

Eberhard of Brunswick looked thoughtfully at Benito. "Just how do you judge this? I know from speaking to your grandfather that you are not a sailor. You've never been outside of Venice before."

Benito shook his head. "I . . . I can *see* it, milord. In my head. I know how close to the wind the galliots can sail. We've done that for the last two days. The capitano said to Erik—yesterday—that he was lucky this wasn't a round ship. They cannot get enough points to the wind." Benito shrugged and held up his hands helplessly. "It's a like a picture in my head from a high rooftop. I can see where people are going. I can see where they *can* go."

The *Ritter* nodded. "I knew your Grandfather well. I was based in Milano some twenty years back and he and I met on a number of occasions. Once, when he had delivered a crushing defeat against the odds to Phillipo Maria of Milano in some minor border dispute, I asked just how he did it. He described something similar. Only he spoke of it in chess terms."

Chess had been one of few things Benito had discovered in his life as *Case Vecchie* that was more enjoyable than the way he'd lived as a messenger and thief. "It is a great game, Milord."

Eberhard smiled wryly. "When this is over, you must give me a game. And if you desire a true challenge, that man is the master." He pointed to Eneko Lopez.

The cleric looked away from the sea, raising his eyebrows. "It is a challenging game. But the only man *I* know who sees a battle like a map is Carlo Sforza." He looked very penetratingly at Benito. Someone had obviously been telling family secrets.

Benito said nothing. So Eneko continued. "It is your birthright, boy. A God-given gift. See you use it wisely in his service." Eneko Lopez straightened up. "I will go below. Francis, Pierre, Diego and I will see if any protective magics may be worked."

"Better if you could blast them all to ash," grumbled Eberhard. "The pagans I fought in Småland had a magician who could do that, until someone put an arrow through his eye."

Eneko shook his head. "It is not fitting to destroy human souls, for thus is evil magic defined. In wars among Christian men, it is common for kings to claim God is on their side, but that is vainglory. God is on the side of those whose souls need him. God decides on rights and wrongs of a cause, not kings, and our magic will be as sand in the wind if we try to use it to attack. But evil magics—ah, now those *are* best countered by ecclesiastical power." He turned and went below decks.

Eberhard snorted. "He said much the same thing to the Emperor, can you believe it? He's a stiff-necked man, that one." He looked wryly at Benito. "I don't think you got much else from Carlo Sforza, boy. You should be grateful for that skill—from both your father and your mother's side. Yes, I know, too, Benito. Half the world does."

Benito felt his face grow hot as he flushed, and he thought of Maria, and what she had said. "They keep expecting me to be like one or the other of them. I'm not! I'm myself."

The elderly *Ritter* tugged at his white moustache. "Some of us struggle to live up to the reputation bequeathed to us by our blood. Others struggle to rise above that reputation. It can be done, boy. But we are shaped by it. It's whether we allow it to rule us or whether we direct it. That stiff-necked priest is right. You have a gift. Use it well. Use it as Benito Valdosta would use it, not the Wolf of the North—nor, even, the Duke of Ferrara."

Falkenberg came up to the deck and spared him having to answer. "Milord of Brunswick, here is the roster for the rowers. Prince Manfred asks that you control this matter. He says it will take true statesmanship."

The old *Ritter* smiled ruefully. "I detect Francesca's hand. I'm supposed to be training him and instead he's manipulating me." He took the list. "Well, you don't have a monk's fist, Falkenberg. What's this? I see Manfred's name heads this list."

"Erik said it would set a good example, milord. He said all chieftains take a hand at portage, and therefore Manfred could do some rowing. Manfred swore at him."

The *Ritter* raised his eyes to heaven. "Well, I daresay if nothing else that will make it impossible for any other knight to claim rowing is beneath his dignity. Very well. Young Valdosta, I suggest you divest yourself of any extra clothing. Rowing is hot work, I've been told. You're also in the first shift."

❖　　❖　　❖

Manfred had had Von Gherens assign places to all of the passengers. Von Gherens had arrived at "where to put everyone" by the simple expedient of counting an equal number into each cabin. Under their vow, all of the knights of the militant order were officially equal regardless of former station, or present rank. So knight-proctors had ended up in broom cupboards, while several squires had the third best stateroom.

Except, of course, for Manfred and Francesca's cabin. Francesca had smiled at Von Gherens. They had the very best stateroom.

Eneko, Diego, Francis and Pierre, on the other hand, had nothing but some floor space—if they all exhaled at the same time.

The others were waiting for Eneko. They'd plainly anticipated what he would try to do: Scry to see if this was some part of a larger evil. Eneko knew the dangers here at sea. The alignment of the consecrated area wouldn't stay aligned.

The candles were prepared. The incense was in the censer. Diego was taking a bottle of water out of his pack.

Weaving the sevenfold circle in this confined space took care. But one thing Eneko had learned: Magic required precision. There was no room for mistakes.

"In nomine Patri, et Filii, et Spiritus Sancti, fiat lux."

Enclosed in the magical curtain of light the four joined hands and began the ritual of searching.

This was not simple scrying; in scrying, one knew where one wanted to look, but not necessarily what one wanted to look for. Here, they knew, not only where, but (in general), *what*. This might be nothing more than the ongoing battles of Venice against pirates, or pirates and some greater enemy—but Lopez did not think so. Here they had one of the possible heirs to the Emperor *and* one of Chernobog's great enemies—more than that, really, in the form of Erik Hakkonsen and the four priests. These fleets, this alliance, might be what the Black Brain had been focusing on when it had let them go so lightly, back in the Jesolo swamps. This, then, might well be what Lopez had feared. And if it was, then there would certainly be an agent of the Black Brain somewhere nearby.

That was what they were looking for.

Each of them undertook the invocation to one of the four archangels of the compass; this was no time for mere wards. But not without a moment of thought.

"You, Pierre, or me in the North?" he asked of the others. They all knew which creatures were the most likely to be under Chernobog's sway.

Pierre considered it. "Perhaps six months ago I was your superior in combative magic, Eneko," he said, soberly. "But I think you have surpassed me. I will take the East, though, which is—"

"Another source of trouble. Very well." This would mean that Pierre would begin the invocations, and Eneko would end. Pierre faced outward, raised his hands, and began to intone the prayer to request the presence of the Archangel Gabriel in their work.

The fact that, instead of a simple ward-pillar, they got something that was a towering blue flame, vaguely man-shaped, was not comforting. And yet, in a way, it was. They now knew, for certain, that this was what they had been expecting, dreading, waiting for. It had begun.

When it was Eneko's turn to invoke the Archangel Uriel, he had barely intoned the first sentence of the prayer when his ward roared up, in brilliant gold flame. Nevertheless, he completed the prayer, ending with a bow of thanks.

It was Francis, as the representative of the West, who blessed the chalice of wine that they would use as their mirror—though it was not the standard shape of a chalice, being more of a footed bowl to provide a satisfactory surface to use as a mirror.

They exchanged glances; Pierre looked fierce, Diego somber, Francis resigned. Eneko did not know what he looked like; his face just felt stiff. They focused their concentration on the chalice of blessed wine, and began the first careful probes for the taint of evil. Since there was no "earth" as such, and not much chance that even the Black Brain's creature could force a spirit of fire out over so much water, Eneko joined with Francis to search the waters, and Pedro with Pierre to survey the air.

They expected that the creature would be subtle. It wasn't.

Eneko felt the nausea, the icy chill, and the shock of encountering naked, unshielded Evil. The result was near instantaneous. The wine seethed and began to boil. The light curtain pulsed, as if sheet lightnings striated within it. And the North ward was filled with the sound of great angelic wings.

All four of them reeled; Eneko was the first to recover. Perhaps Pierre was right; perhaps he had grown in skill! But this was no time for pride, though the confidence that the fleeting realization gave him was a bulwark under his feet.

They were now no longer within the bowels of the ship. They, and their circle, wards and all, were . . . elsewhere. Not quite out of the world, but not in it, either. It was a place of swirling darkness, green and black flame, and sickly, polluted clouds.

Moving sinuously through it, looming over them, was—something. Serpentine, but it was no serpent. Black and green, with a mouth of needle-sharp, needle-thin teeth, long as stilettos and twice as lethal, piggy little eyes, and a strange, spiny crest. It confronted them.

No. It confronted Lopez. It focused on him, and drew back to strike.

"That which cannot abide the name of Christ, begone!"

Eneko Lopez drew strength from his companions, strength from his faith, and from the Archangel of the North to strike at the thing.

Perhaps it had not expected the blow, for it did not move out of the way. Perhaps it had expected that they would be paralyzed with fear. It neither dodged, nor did it invoke shields. The blow, a sharp lance of golden light modeled on the archangel's own weapon, pierced the thing's hide. It opened its maw in a silent scream.

Then, huge, slimy and vastly strong, the creature bled and fled, and they whirled away out of that not-world and were back in the belly of the ship. There was nothing left but the faintly glowing ward-circle, the overturned chalice, four thin Ward-candles, and a puddle of blood on the floor just outside the circle. The blood was black and stank.

"Well, now we know that it is more than just a conflict between commercial rivals," said Eneko, grimly. "The eel-thing smelled of the far north. That is confirmed by the Archangel of the North's intervention. I perceive the hand of Chernobog."

"But Eneko, there was more to it than that. It knew you—and feared you. The target of all these ships is nothing other than . . . you. We must pray and summon intercession," said Francis.

"And that was no eel," added Diego.

Eneko raised his eyebrow. "It was human, once. But it looked like an eel to me."

"It was a lamprey," said Diego, with certainty. "A hagfish."

"But it was enormous!" said Pierre

Diego shrugged. "It is very old. Fish don't stop growing as long as they are alive."

"Lampreys are parasites, aren't they?" Trust Pierre's basic curiosity to get him sidetracked.

"They can be. They like to feed off living flesh." And trust Diego to follow him down that diversion.

Francis cleared his throat. "In all of that . . . was I the only one to hear the panpipes? Further off but still distinctly."

"Panpipes?" mused Eneko. "As we heard in the scrying in Rome?"

"Yes."

Eneko shook his head. "No, I did not hear them, but I'd guess you were right. This is another attempt to either kill us or to lead us from the course again. And that course leads to the place where there is already some old power. Elemental, crude, and which does not love us. We know now where Chernobog and his minions focus their attention: Corfu.

"Brothers," Eneko said, carefully, "I believe that the Lord will not be averse to the judicious use of magic in the material plane. After all, if this galley is captured or sunk—"

Pierre grinned mirthlessly. "It will be, after all, purely in self-defense."

"Purely," Eneko assured him. The wards flared, as if in agreement.

Chapter 31

"Benito was right," said Erik, up on the poop deck after a spell at the oars. "The carracks will pass to leeward of our stern."

"They might be in cannon-shot for a short time," said the bombardier, "depending on what cannon they have on board."

"That would depend on who they are. Genovese most likely."

Erik squinted into the distance. "The pennant on that lead vessel is a black horse in flames."

Eberhard of Brunswick drew a breath between his teeth. "Emeric of Hungary! Our spies reported he was massing troops. But it was assumed that they were for his campaign against Iskander Beg. Where does he get a fleet from?"

"And where is he going with it?" asked Francesca, from where she stood under the canopy.

The old statesman narrowed his eyes and nodded. "A good point. Helmsman."

"Yes, milord."

"Do you see anything that gives you any idea whose ships those are?"

The helmsman, the sort of man who looked as if he'd been at sea on the very first hollowed log, and had only come ashore briefly since, nodded. "Aye. Not Genovese, Sir. Byzantine. You can tell by the way they rig the foresail."

The old *Ritter* turned a grim face to Francesca. "Alexius has allied himself with Emeric of Hungary."

Francesca frowned. "The only possible reason I can see for that is to attack Venetian properties."

"I can see that Alexius might want to do that, but he's too weak to go on military adventures against Venice. Also, it puts Emeric at his throat instead of Venice—which if anything is worse. I must admit I can't see why Emeric would attack Venice's colonies by sea, instead of Venetian holdings nearer home. To come overland through Fruili would make more sense."

Francesca nodded. "There will be a reason that is less than obvious. From what I've heard, the reason could be that Alexius is too weak-witted to see what he's doing."

Eberhard snorted. "I don't know if you're joking, Francesca. But you are being too accurate. And now I think it is time for a change of rowers. These men have nearly learned what they should be doing. Therefore it is time to change." He walked over to fore-rail and began calling the next group of knights and squires to oar-duty.

It was midmorning before the knights were actually called to leave the oars and don armor. The round ships were well astern, by then. They'd turned and were attempting to take a tack that would bring them closer. The galliots, having started in a tight group, were now trailing out in a long arc. The knights had made strong if inept rowers, although they'd been getting better with practice. However, what this had meant was that the great galleys had kept going under oars for nearly three hours now, and the actual rowers—the Venetians who were professional at it—were still reasonably fresh.

The enemy galliots were close now. The great galleys' sails were hoisted and they began to run with the wind. Now the galliot crews thought they would reach their prey, and their oarsmen began putting extra effort into their stroke.

Manfred came up on deck. "If we can keep this up for another half an hour, we won't even have to kill them. The beggars must be half-dead already."

Erik, ascending the companionway behind him, smiled

wolfishly. "And the fools have not had the sense to regroup."

The capitano shrugged. "They're pirates, Milord. They fight for loot. The best loot goes to the first ships."

Manfred felt the handle of his great sword. "So does the best dying. All right, Erik. You too, young Benito, seeing as you seem to have developed a genius for this sort of thing, how do we deal with them?"

Benito blushed and got up to leave. "I've only really been in the battle in Venice. And to tell you the truth that was all just hand-to-hand skirmishes. Our battle plan went to pieces after the first few heartbeats."

"He knows the difference between strategy and tactics anyway," said Erik dryly. "Stay and learn, youngster. You're not too bad when you're not out causing trouble." Erik pointed at the galliots. "They still outnumber us. If they want loot—let's give them some. Casks of wine will do for a start. Half empty ones so they'll float. Some of them will start on the jetsam. And that will break the followers up."

"Well, at least you want to start on the half-empty ones," grumbled Manfred. "And what else?"

"Tenderize them well with cannon when they get close. Keep the knights down until they're trying to board."

"And keep lots of casks and buckets of water on hand for the sails," said the capitano gloomily.

"Fine horse-flesh" grunted Bjarni. "Like to take them home."

Svanhild could only agree. She was having some difficulty riding, as the saddles were nasty, heavy things, and not the simple pads that the *skraelings* used and had taught her to use. But the horses themselves were magnificent. The horses at home had been bred, for the most part, from chunky little Icelandic ponies, with the occasional importation of something larger or more exotic, or the odd Spanish barb taken from the infrequent Spaniard expeditions come looking for gold and finding death. These, on the other hand, were bred for war, not packing. Steady, patient, big, and strong. And smarter than they looked. Rather like her brothers.

They rode northward along the high ground, keeping away from the smoke plumes, heading for the mountains.

They did see some local peasants doing the same. They scattered the moment they saw the horses, leaving their goods and fleeing. "Real fighters," said Gjuki, disdainfully. Svanhild kept her own council; the peasants they saw were armed with next to nothing, and certainly not mounted. How could they even hope to accomplish anything by standing and fighting? Except to get killed, of course.

"Why are they running away?" wondered Olaf, looking at the disappearing backs. "We could use some guides and we mean them no harm."

"Don't be more stupid than you have to be," snapped Bjarni at the lanky *duniwassal*. "We're riding cavalry chargers, and we are plainly foreigners. How many blond heads have you seen here?"

"Oh. I hadn't thought of that."

"Your trouble is you seldom think."

"It's going to make finding shelter difficult."

Bjarni swore. "*Fandens osse!* I hadn't thought of that."

Svanhild bit her lip. Suddenly, that nasty little inn, overrun with bugs and rodents, where she'd have had to share a bed with six other women she didn't even know, didn't seem so bad. "We'll manage, Bjarni," she said, stoutly. "We'll find something."

The riderless horse joined up with another troop of Magyar cavalry. The officer in charge of this detachment of looters looked at it carefully. And felt his heart sink. It had once belonged to Hegedes—the commander who had promised King Emeric he'd be proud of the looting campaign. That everything would go well. It looked as if he had been wrong. It also looked as if he wouldn't be around to take the blame.

The cannon roared, kicking back against the restraining ropes. "Venetian gunners aren't worth shit," said the high-voiced Knight bombardier, with dispassionate professionalism. He moved in, shouting instructions, cuffing heads.

The next shot hit the second of the galliots.

The stern cannon, bearing now on the closest galliot, began firing.

The nearest galliots' crews rowed frantically, pulling hard to close, to get near to the galleys so that the cannons could not be depressed enough.

Some fifteen of the galliots were close enough to pose a threat. Others were so far back that either they would never catch up or they knew they would arrive far too late for the looting; their crews had already stopped trying.

The gunners were now working as fast as the Knight's bombardier could drive them. And that wasn't going to be fast enough. The first galliots were already too close. Already burning, pitch-soaked arrows were being fired at the sails. Sailors scrambled with buckets of water.

The arquebuses began firing in volley from the great galley. Despite this, there were wild-eyed men standing up on the bows of the first galliot, grappling irons in hand.

Then the pirates weren't there anymore. They might have been safe from ship's cannon, but the bombardier had his own little two-pound cannon loaded with fragments of steel and ready for them. To Benito it looked as if some giant blade had abruptly scythed through the crew of that galliot.

But the second vessel was already coming. Plainly they had decided to concentrate their attack on this ship. The bombardier could not reload in time for that one. One of the Venetian gunners grabbed a cutlass.

"Put that down you fool!" yelled the bombardier. "Reload! There are still other ships behind this one. You sink those and we only have this one to deal with."

The knights still waited silently behind the rampart of crates and boxes. The raiders targeted the bow—as far from the poop deck as possible. Grappling irons came along with a bunch of yelling, gleeful, loot-hungry boarders.

Then the knights stood up behind the rampart, and the yowl that went up from the mob of boarders was no longer one of glee. Even in the wilds of Dalmatia they knew the armor of the Knights of the Holy Trinity.

To get to the knights they'd have to mount the rampart. The Narenta pirates were unarmored. They had boarding axes, a miscellany of swords and knives, and occasional pistols. The steel-clad knights with their broadswords were backed up by Venetian sailors with pistols and arquebuses. Manfred had positioned two further sets of ramparts up on the poop deck.

Benito had elected himself an exposed but potentially death-dealing position. The great galley carried four grenadiers, and an ample supply of black powder grenades. Out on the end of a wildly swaying main-mast spar, with a bag of grenades and a slow-match, he could pick his targets. So long as he could cling to the spar with his legs, he could virtually drop grenades into the attacking vessels.

"You'll be partly hidden by the bell of the mainsail, Benito," Manfred had said seriously, when Benito had suggested taking this position. "But you'll also be a good target. The canvas and the spar are no protection at all against arrows or gunfire. Also, if they succeed in firing the mainsail, you'll be fried. You work to my orders. Don't draw attention to yourself. Wait until the melee starts. No one will be looking straight up while they're fighting. Then you see if you can drop something directly into the attackers' boats.

"But not before—have you got that?" Manfred demanded, jabbing a forefinger—to the first joint, it felt like—into his chest.

"Yes, sir."

Erik snorted. "You can quit that right now. I don't know how well you'll fight in actual combat. But I do know you can climb things."

Manfred grinned. "Yes. I've seen him do it. Don't take company up there, hear."

Benito held his tongue. He'd never live that one down. But he was still thinking about it, despite the coming battle, when he reached the spar end.

He had a bird's eye view of the boarders from up here. He also realized the one fault with his idea: The sway out here was wildly magnified. He clung, lit, and threw.

Only he hadn't factored in the roll. To his horror, he saw that the grenade was going to hit the great galley, not the galliot alongside. He gritted his teeth and restrained himself from closing his eyes.

It hit the rail, and bounced harmlessly into the water.

He lit again, as fighting raged below him. Waited for the roll . . . realized how short the fuse was and hastily flung the grenade as far as he could, not worrying about where he threw it, just wanting to get it *away*.

It exploded in the air between two galliots. Not if he'd tried for a twelvemonth could Benito have used a single grenade so effectively. The explosion sent steel shards flying at those who remained on both galliots.

Lighting the third grenade took immense determination. Especially as a couple of shots were now being directed at him. But he knew when on the roll to light and throw now. It landed in one of the galliots. A brief shower of sparks . . .

And it failed to go off. He waited on the roll to light another. A shot burned across his shoulder, sending the slow-match spiraling downwards. He was left with a newly lit grenade in one hand and another four in his bag.

He did something incredibly dumb, but the bullet graze had both frightened him and given him a rush of pure insane strength. He dropped the lit grenade into the bag; then, in a smooth movement, drew his *main gauche* and slashed the strap with the other hand.

He flung the entire bag. It splintered into the storm-decking on the prow of the latest galliot to join the fray; and, a moment later, erupted and blew a smoking hole in the bow at the waterline. The little vessel started to go down almost immediately.

Benito began edging his way backward along the mainsail spar. His shoulder was oozing blood and didn't seem to want to take any strain. Out here he'd get shot again for sure. And there wasn't anything more he could do up on the mainmast spar, anyway. Looking down he saw it was still going to be a vicious fight. They'd sunk some galliots and simply outrun others. But because all of the little vessels were concentrated on this one, the knights on board were badly outnumbered. They outclassed the pirates, to be sure. But sooner or later the mainsail would go down, more vessels would catch up, and eventually the carracks would get here.

As he thought all that, he saw a little sortie of pirates had indeed managed to get up to where the mainsail was tied. Benito saw one of the band slash at the port-side mainsail rope. As the saber struck the rope the man was thrown back in a great gout of sparks. The cable was undamaged but the pirates who had fought their way up to the sail were shrieking and diving over the side of the galley, not caring whether they hit water or their own ships.

Of course the shrieking wasn't in Frankish, but Benito was still sure he guessed what it was: "Witchcraft!" What had been a determined assault rapidly turned to a frantic attempt to reach their boats.

Clinging to the ratlines, Benito noticed the mast was actually thrumming, and the mainsail was now cracking with the strain. It was hard to say where the wind was coming from but it was certainly driving the galley forwards. The sail was glowing a bright royal purple. The other galliots, which had been closing, were now beginning to fall back. By the boom of the cannon they were back in cannon-range.

Benito just went on climbing down the mainmast rigging, struggling to do so with one arm not working properly. By the time he got low enough to jump down, the fight was turning into a rout, with pirates jumping into the sea rather than remain on board an accursed vessel.

Superstition can be a wonderful thing when it is someone else's problem.

Chapter 32

Manfred winced. "That's sore, you know."

"Why are men so brave about battles and so scared of having their wounds tended?" asked Francesca, calmly cleaning the bullet graze on Manfred's side. "I thought armor was supposed to protect you from this sort of thing?"

"Ow! It's less than perfect against firearms. Pretty fair against swords or magical efforts."

"And what is effective against firearms?" she asked, sprinkling on basilicum powder.

"Getting out of the way. Or a nice thick earth rampart. Even stone can be shattered by big enough cannon. But earth absorbs it."

"I'll get you to carry one, next time," she said, beginning to wrap a bandage around his ribs. "I would hate to have had to explain to your uncle what had happened to you, and if anyone's big enough and strong enough to carry around his own rampart, it's you."

The last was not said in an entirely admiring tone of voice. Francesca had spent a number of hours under that weight of bone and muscle—and Manfred did not always remember to support himself on his elbows.

She finished pinning the bandage with a cabochon-encrusted broach. "It's all I have in the way of pins, other than hair pins—which would certainly stab you." She kissed him. "There. You'll do. Now, tell me, where do we go from here?"

"Eneko Lopez says we go to Corfu. Some of the surviving pirates talked. They say Emeric of Hungary has invaded the island and the Citadel is under siege. They also say we have no chance of getting back to Venice, or even across to Italy. There are some fifteen galleys between us and the mouth of the Narenta. And more galliots. Onward is a risky proposition, too. There is a fleet in the straits of Otranto."

"So: They intend to keep Venice bottled up?"

Manfred shook his head. "The capitano thinks that's a ridiculous idea. The Venetian convoys would punch holes through any other sea force trying to block the Adriatic."

Francesca was silent for a while. "I think I must go and talk to Eberhard. At sea, the Venetians have mastery of the Mediterranean. But Alexius controls the Bosporus and the Dardanelles. And if the Outremer convoy has already sailed for Trebizond, then he can prevent their return. If they hold Corfu—well, the straits of Otranto are only twenty-five leagues across. They can harry shipping even if they cannot stop it."

"Well, maybe." Manfred shrugged. And winced, for he'd momentarily forgotten his wound. "I'm no naval expert. But bickering between Venice and the Byzantines is nothing new. Venice's trading privileges and possessions, like Corfu, Zante and Negroponte have driven a succession of Byzantine emperors to try and redress matters. It doesn't happen. Imperial Greek naval power is no match for the Venetians. And the depth of the Byzantine Empire's money pouch is far shallower than Venice's. This time Alexius has gotten Hungary in to be his muscle. I suspect his muscle may end up eating him. But if it gets to that point the Empire will distract Emeric. We really don't want a powerful Hungarian empire all the way through the Balkans and Greece. We also don't involve ourselves in petty fights between our allies."

But Francesca had other news that she had not thought relevant until this moment. "I think it may be more complicated than that, not to mention nastier. According to Petro Dorma, Alexius VI has recently been entertaining a visitor, who possibly came from Odessa. An old friend of Erik's: Caesare Aldanto."

Manfred grinned, showing his square teeth. "The pretty blond who set him up to be arrested—or more likely killed—in the brothel? You'd better not tell Erik that or he'll want to go chasing straight to Constantinople."

"Aldanto already left there, a shade ahead of the Duke of Ferrara's best assassins, I gather." Francesca frowned and tapped an elegant finger against her lips as she tried to recall everything else the Doge had told her. "Dorma hinted that the Council of Ten has put an unprecedented price on Aldanto's head, too. But, Manfred, the reason I must talk to Eberhard is that this cooperation between Jagiellon, Alexius, and Emeric puts a very different slant on the Holy Roman Empire's desire to remain uninvolved. Alexius may want Venetian possessions. Emeric may want Byzantium. But Jagiellon wants only one thing—a route into the underbelly of the Empire."

Manfred grunted. "I guess we'll just have to stop him succeeding. Corfu is a large island, if I recall one of my more boring tutors. Surely there is more than one fortress?"

Francesca smiled in spite of herself. "You didn't pay attention, so you rely on the fact that I did. Of course." She waggled a finger at him. "You'd better start learning to pay attention! Someday you'll be somewhere where I'm not, and you'll curse yourself for not having the information when and where you need it."

He grinned sheepishly; she delivered a frown, then gave him what she knew. "There is only one real fortress. There are a number of small fortified towns, and villas, built to withstand attacks, but nothing that will stand up to modern siege weapons except the Citadel at Kérkira. The fortress there is on an islet, and the actual rock makes part of the ramparts. The Byzantines and then the Venetians have improved on what nature had already made fairly good."

Manfred assumed the impassive oxlike expression that Francesca had learned indicated deep thought. "I think we need to hold a council of war," he said eventually. "I don't know enough of Venice's affairs, their military strength on Corfu, the ability of the Venetians to withstand a serious siege or what our best course of action is. I have to think for the Holy Roman Empire, not Venice or Eneko Lopez. I think I will go and call Eberhard, Eneko, Erik, Benito—if they've finished with his wound—and Falkenberg. It's a pity Von Gherens is on the other vessel."

"I'd also ask the capitano to join you, if he's gotten over having a divine gale push his ship. He was still gibbering, according to Falkenberg."

"I'll ungibber him." Manfred cracked his knuckles. "He's been at sea in the service of the Venetian Republic for forty-five years, man and boy, as he has repeatedly informed me. A man of his experience shouldn't let a little of what Father Lopez assures us is ecclesiastically sanctified magic worry him."

Manfred looked regretfully at Francesca's lush form. "I know it seems a pity but maybe you'd better put some more clothes on." He looked appreciatively at the outfit. "I haven't seen that one before. Why were you wearing it when we were going to be attacked?"

"Practicality, dear."

He looked puzzled. "It doesn't look very practical . . . except for one thing, Francesca."

"My legs are not enveloped in clinging petticoats. And we fight with what we have. I know full well when men's bollocks start thinking, their brains stop. If I put on breeches and took up a sword, even one of these attackers little brother's could kill me. But if the best of warriors is intent on undoing his breeches . . . well, I have two knives. There are certain other features about this outfit that are less obvious than knives, too."

She did not add that, if the fight was lost, dressed in this fashion she'd almost certainly be booty for the captain. Manfred would possibly not understand that sometimes the things one did to survive were not pleasant. And she had a great deal of practice in that vein.

Manfred took a deep breath. "You'd probably get raped."

Ah, my dear, tell me something I don't know. Francesca gave a wry smile. "A nun's habit and a wimple wouldn't stop that, Manfred. Now, you go and get the others and I shall get changed."

He looked admiringly at the diaphanous outfit, which was intended to hint at, rather than reveal, what was underneath. "I admit the need, because I want your input at the council. But it does seem a waste of time."

"Dressing is never a waste of time, Manfred dear, because undressing someone again is part of the pleasure. I shall dress and contribute what I can to your councils. Then later you can help me undress and contribute something to me as well," she said, lowering her lashes.

"And now I'm supposed to concentrate on military matters," grumbled Manfred.

Eneko Lopez looked gray with exhaustion. The capitano looked as if his eyes were still about to start out of their sockets. He chose a position as far away from Eneko as possible. The others looked battered in various degrees, too, noted Eberhard—except for the old duke's grandson, Benito. Benito had a bandaged shoulder, but it didn't seem to have slowed him down much. He looked like one of those fused grenades he'd tossed so effectively. His eyes reminded Eberhard of a sparking and sputtering wick, as if he were alternating between wild excitement and exhaustion.

Eberhard was an old man and a politician now, but he'd been a soldier once: *This one loved danger*. You had to watch that kind. They took chances. And they took others with them into their danger.

Privately, Eberhard was pleased by the way Manfred had handled the battle. Manfred would serve the Holy Roman Empire well, with some more experience; very well indeed. Eberhard noted he was able to take advice. That was rare, especially when combined with an ability to act decisively and effectively, and even rarer when combined with the ability to lead. Advice seekers often wanted others to make decisions, not merely advise, or else they merely wanted their own opinions confirmed, and didn't listen when advice ran counter to it.

This meeting, too, showed a maturity that he'd not expected. Merely calling them together like this proved that he was thinking past the successful escape.

Of course, Eberhard wouldn't tell the young prince

that. But Manfred had come a long way from the spoiled brat he'd had the displeasure of meeting when he'd been in Mainz some years before.

"I suppose the crucial issue is how well this Venetian fortress at Kérkira will withstand the siege. Basically it is the only fleet-size anchorage around."

The capitano made a wry face. "It could withstand nearly any siege . . . if it were well enough supplied, and had enough men, milord. But last time I was there the garrison commander was complaining bitterly about how few men he had."

"Commanders always complain about that," said Falkenberg. "The Venetians couldn't have taken and certainly couldn't hold the island without enough men."

But Francesca was already shaking her head. There was another one whose still waters ran deep, thought Eberhard. The old diplomat had a good idea that Manfred had learned as much at the white hands of Francesca as at the calloused ones of Erik Hakkonsen. Probably more, in fact.

"It wasn't *taken*," she said. "The Corfiotes invited the protection of the Venetian Empire, more than a hundred years ago, because they were having a lot of trouble with Illyrian raiders. The Venetians sorted that out with superior sea power very quickly and easily. They set up a feudal system of puppet local Greek aristocrats—the *Libri d'Oro*, as they're called. Things have gone a little less smoothly lately and—correct me if I am wrong, Capitano—the captain-general has little more than a policing force, to make sure taxes are paid and Venice's rules obeyed."

The capitano nodded. "They're mostly mercenaries. Dregs, signorina. I'd guess at less than a thousand on the whole island. The barracks are almost empty and several of the buildings haven't been used for some time. There are a couple of other castles—Vidos in Corfu bay, for instance. But a lot of the places have just got a local *capi* and a few men. All right for dealing with petty crime.

"And the mercenaries!" he spat. "Pah. They're not worth much as soldiers, ones who would take a job like that. There's no fighting, so there is no opportunity for extra profits, bonuses or loot. But you won't get killed either. Lazy and stupid—and maybe cowards."

"Locally recruited?" asked Erik.

"Not so as I'd noticed, milord," said the capitano. "If I remember right, I heard tell that the present Byzantine Emperor's father sent agents across to Corfu and stirred things up. Told them that they're Greeks, not Venetians; that Byzantium regards them as its own, and that they would be rewarded with Venetian-held positions and estates if they got rid of Venice. It's true the Corfiotes begged the Venetians to annex Corfu and protect it but . . . as is the way of things, the best jobs went to appointees of the Senate sent out from Venice. The Venetians have taken over a lot of estates. The local Greek nobility has a bit of an attitude about Venetians. As if they didn't want us in the first place! The Corfiotes are quick enough to take our money, though."

Francesca raised a perfect eyebrow. "And of course the Venetians are as innocent as lambs and do nothing to exacerbate the situation," she said dryly.

The capitano laughed coarsely. "Except treat the locals like shit. Sorry, signorina, pardon my language. Too much time at sea and not enough talking with ladies."

"I forgive you, Capitano." She looked at Manfred pointedly. "I'm used to occasional lapses."

Eneko Lopez yawned. "Forgive me too, but I am very, very weary. This discussion is all very well, but I must get to Corfu. If Chernobog seeks to prevent it . . . then there is a reason. Even if the Citadel stands or falls, I must get to the island."

He regarded all of them broodingly. "That fleet was sent with one end in mind: to sink us rather than to allow any of us to reach there. That may have been because of me and my brothers, or because of the large number of armed knights on this convoy, or because of—who we carry." He blinked, slowly. "However, I do know this much. Before we reached Venice a similar attempt was made to stop me and my brothers. I must conclude that this was no coincidence, and that Chernobog wishes to keep us, specifically, from reaching Corfu. I don't know why Chernobog is doing this, but there must be some far-reaching reason he has scryed. He does not play for small stakes. The Holy Roman Empire or even Christianity may be threatened. You can put Diego, Pierre, Francis and me off on a beach on the north end of the island."

Erik cleared his throat. "Aren't you forgetting some- thing, Señor Lopez?"

Eneko blinked at him. "Quite possibly, Erik. The magic we worked was draining. I am exhausted and not thinking at my best. What is it?"

"They tracked you here. Chernobog tracked you previ- ously, too. He can sense your movements, and now you tell me that you wish to land on an island occupied by his allies." Erik was not normally inclined to irony, but Eberhard sensed the tone now. "You are a great mage, señor. But an arrow or sword can kill you as well as it can kill me, especially if you are exhausted, as you are now. And unless you and your brothers have learned something new about turning invisible, I think this is not the wisest of plans."

"I've seen that on the northern frontier," rumbled Falkenberg. "Mages can fight great magics, but when all is said and done they need ordinary men and ordinary steel to guard them against purely physical threats. I've seen a pagan mage that could blast men to ash chopped down, unresisting, because knights with cold iron and the holy cross attacked while he dueled magically."

Eneko blinked again. "Still, I must go," he said tiredly. "Danger or no danger. Forgive me. I cannot even think now. But I see my duty clear."

Eberhard patted him on the shoulder. "Go and rest, Eneko Lopez. You are no use to us or your duty when you're exhausted. Leave it to us ordinary soldiers to get you into the Citadel. You'll be protected there, and on Corfu. Will that do?"

Eneko stood up. "I believe it will. But we will pray for guidance."

"When you wake up," said Erik, with rough kindness. "Go and sleep now."

The cleric nodded and stumbled out, leaning a hand against the wall.

When he'd gone, Erik shook his head. "You may

have just offered to do the impossible, *Ritter* Eberhard. Or volunteered us to do the impossible. We only have two hundred knights. Even with the ship crews and the squires, we muster perhaps twice that. Breaking the siege is more than we can achieve. Emeric must have at least . . . say ten thousand men there, and his siege cannon will prevent any access by water—even if we fought our way through his fleet."

"We lost two knights and five damn-fool glory-hungry squires, in that last effort. Some injuries, too. Gunpowder should never have been invented," grumbled Falkenberg.

Eberhard smiled dryly. "While the prince was being bandaged and you and Erik were seeing to the men, I saw to questioning one of the pirates. It helped that Knights of the Holy Trinity have something of an *unholy* reputation, and that he'd just seen some very terrifying magic. We didn't even have to resort to torture. The man was a mere sailor, but he had a very good notion of just how many ships were employed in the attack on Corfu. Most of them, most of the troops and most of the cannon, are still behind us: To wit, that fleet of carracks we avoided. So right now there are, at a guess, no more than three or four thousand troops investing the Citadel at Kérkira. Actually, there will be fewer than that, as many are out ravaging Corfu's countryside. If we can reenforce the Citadel, then it can hold until Venice and the Empire will send more forces to break the siege."

Manfred grunted. "We'd need to send word to get them here. Maybe send one of these vessels running for Bari, and send messengers overland to Venice?"

Eberhard was dubious. "The sailor seemed to think more vessels were on their way from Constantinople."

"Even so, it seems a fair idea," said Erik. "Split up. Squeeze all the knights onto one vessel. Land as much force as possible on the western coast of Corfu. Storm the besiegers and hope that someone has the brains to let us into the Citadel before Emeric's troops can regroup."

"Er," said Benito, tentatively. "Why don't we just sail up to the Citadel?"

Manfred made a face. "Siege cannon would smash

the ships to kindling . . . Wait a bit. There are no siege cannon!"

"According to our pirate informant, anyway," said Eberhard.

"We'd hear and see the cannon duel from a good league off if it is happening. It'd be a risky enterprise, nonetheless. We'd have to sail into the strait between Corfu and the mainland at night. There are bound to be patrols."

"It might succeed for sheer audacity."

Benito had been looking thoughtful throughout all of this. "It is not as risky, milord, as all that. The moon is down from about three in the morning. We can come in under oars from the south. If we need to, we can turn and run with the wind. And it has to be the last thing they'd expect us to do."

"Aren't you forgetting something?" asked Erik. "Somehow, something is tracking Eneko Lopez."

Benito shrugged. "It still has to marshal its ground, or, in this case water, forces. Look at the trap we have just escaped. It's as likely to follow us at sea as to intercept us coming into Corfu."

Erik still wasn't convinced. "The other problem is that even if there are no siege cannon, the Venetians are as likely to sink us with their own cannon. In the dark they'll be watching for sneak attacks."

"We could unfurl the pennants," Benito countered. "They're unlikely to fire on the Lion of Saint Mark."

"Not in the dark," Erik pointed out.

Manfred brought his hand down. "Gentlemen. Francesca. We've got at least a day's sailing, before we have to decide. I suggest we eat and rest. I will think about the various ideas and reach a decision. But now I need to concentrate on the various contributions possible."

Eberhard wondered why Francesca smothered a smile.

Chapter 33

Manfred had had them bring four of the knight-proctors and the captain over from the *Dolphin, Swordfish* and *San Raphael* to the *San Nicolò*. The captain's cabin was rather crowded; Manfred wondered if he ought to ask them to breathe in shifts.

"Right. First, the bad news. We are being followed: Galliots under sail have been spotted from the masthead. That was why we changed course in the dark last night. A different sail was spotted this morning. They are spread out and looking for us. Second, more bad news. Corfu, our next port of call, is under siege, by the Byzantines and Emeric of Hungary. I have it from Eneko Lopez that making sure Corfu does not fall into the hands of these foes of Venice is vital to the future of the Church. Eberhard of Brunswick says it is also vital to the future of the Holy Roman Empire. Obviously, it's also vital to the Republic of Venice, a state with which we are on friendly terms if not formally allied."

Manfred looked at his audience, which wasn't difficult, since half of it was looming over him and the table, and the other half was crushed in against him. "So. We need to reinforce the garrison at Corfu. We also need to get a message back to Venice and to Emperor Charles Fredrik about what is happening here. We have four vessels, two hundred knights, and fair number of sailors. We need to achieve both of these objectives. We need to split

297

into three parties: one ship to run on, one to attempt to dodge back—and two ships to attempt to relieve the Citadel at Corfu, or at least to add men to its garrison. We'll make landfall on one of the Diapondia islands. I will be taking the knights and what sailors and food can be spared to Corfu. Capitanos Selvi, Bortaliscono, and Da Castres—of your vessels, one must come with us. It may be sunk, and I can't promise anything, not even safety. One of you must run for the open water of the Mediterranean and sail on to Rome."

His expression was grim. "You'll face interception, interference, and you won't be any safer than we are. If you get through, messengers can be dispatched from there to Venice and Mainz. Eneko Lopez will provide letters to the Grand Metropolitan of Rome. I will provide letters under the seal of the Empire for our embassy there. The other ship will attempt to return by sea to Venice. I'll do a note for Petro Dorma, but the captain can give the story best in his own words."

He cleared his throat. "All of these ventures are fraught with risk. There are vessels pursuing us. There are supposed to be Byzantine vessels on a blockade ahead."

"Prince Manfred, how do you intend to relieve the siege?" asked Captain Da Castres. "Surely the vessels with the knights on them can off-load you at some small fishing harbor or something. Then we can sail as a convoy. That will be a great deal safer."

Manfred smiled wryly. Captain Da Castres had an exaggerated notion of safety, if he thought four ships were going to be any safer than two. "The key to defending Corfu's citadel is actually getting the knights, and as many sailors as possible, *into* the Citadel. We—on horseback—could possibly take the besiegers by surprise. Hope that someone inside opens the gates and that the causeway bridge is intact. We and our squires, all mounted, could undertake that. If fortune favored us, if we took the enemy by complete surprise, if the cannon from the Citadel didn't simply fire on us . . . we could get maybe half of the knights into the Citadel. With no extra supplies and none of the crews of the ships. We could add maybe a hundred and fifty men to the defense."

He shrugged. "Not a great help, but some. However, we know the besiegers have several thousand men—but no cannon." Manfred pointed. "Benito Valdosta there . . . You all know the boy, you all know his bloodline."

Benito looked furiously at Manfred. Manfred knew why. For Benito, his bloodline—at least that on his father's side—was not something he boasted of. Manfred was *using* that reputation.

Manfred gave him a quelling look—*Damn right I am.* He would use anything he could get his hands on right now—and went right on. "He came up with the plan that got us out of the pirates' grip. Now he's come up with another idea, the only way I can see that will deliver an extra five hundred men to the citadel, as well as whatever supplies can be loaded into the vessels. When he put the idea forward, I thought he was mad. I've pondered on it all night. Talked to Capitano Douro here. We can indeed sail to the Citadel itself, by night. But once they're in, the ships won't be leaving."

"And assuming you succeed in the madness of sailing by night, through the fleet of the enemy, the guns in the Citadel will sink you," said the oldest of the captains, Selvi. "It has to be the most harebrained idea I have ever heard. Ah, Prince Manfred."

Manfred now knew which skipper to send onward. That one. He shared a look with Benito, who gave him a slight nod.

"Milord Valdosta. Do you think it will work?" asked Da Castres, ignoring the older man.

Benito nodded more vigorously. "I can't see a better way, Captain. There are some things in our favor. I have thought about it long and hard, believe me. We know from the interrogation of our prisoners that only eight or so vessels remain at anchor out of cannon-shot in the bay. The northern entry is guarded by Narenta galliots. The south is blockaded by some of these eight vessels. The rest of their fleet is out in the straits of Otranto. More ships are probably due from Constantinople, and if we're going to do anything, we need to do it before they get here."

He pointed at the sky. The low cabin deck, rather. "For

a second thing, the moon is down from early morning. We can approach under muffled oars. Capitano Douro here has found a Corfiote serving among the oarsmen. This man swears he can navigate safely to Kérkira under those conditions. The enemy will have less confidence in unfamiliar waters, in the dark. Finally, the guns of the Citadel will not fire on the Lion of Saint Mark. Eneko Lopez and his companions say they can work a holy magic which blazons the banners as brightly as if in broad daylight. We'll never get a better chance to get more men and supplies into the Citadel with the fewest losses."

Manfred patted Benito's shoulder, proprietarily. "There you have it, Capitano Selvi. Besides, we'll have our trumpeters on the foredeck, sounding the battle hymn of the Knights of the Holy Trinity. There are few soldiers anywhere who would not recognize that. Finally, this is not a matter for discussion."

He hardened his tone, straightened his back, and tried to sound as much like his uncle as possible. "This is what I have decided. This is what will be done. All of the vessels will take the parts I assign to them. All I have called you together for is to finalize details. To decide which vessel will have the honor of joining in our attempt to assist the Citadel."

"I am captain of my ship," said Selvi stiffly, "and responsible to the Republic of Venice for her safety."

Von Gherens stood up and put his hand on his sword. "Captain, I am a soldier of Christ. I am sworn by a holy oath to serve the Church. *Señor* Lopez is a direct emissary of the Grand Metropolitan. I've been in combat with him. I have never met a man who serves Christ as well and with as much integrity as Eneko Lopez. He has said that the Church needs our aid. If I have to chop your head off and sail your boat myself to get there, I'll do it."

Benito looked at Von Gherens, and Manfred watched sudden realization dawning in his eyes. Well, not surprising; he hadn't lived with Von Gherens the way Manfred had. Benito had never really understood the bluff, hearty knight. There was a core of deep piety under that hard-drinking exterior. If Von Gherens truly believed in the rightness of his deeds, it would take a cannonball to stop him. That could be a problem, when his ideas were wrong—but when they were right, there was nothing short of an armored elephant that it would be better to have on your side.

The captain also plainly realized he'd misjudged. "It's a ship, not a b-boat," he stuttered. "I—of course, I'll do my best to assist. But—"

"I'll volunteer to take my ship to Corfu," said the plump Da Castres. He smiled, revealing skewed teeth, yellowed like a mule's. "I'm more afraid of that knight than I am of either the Senate or the enemy. Besides, my wife says I'm too fat. A siege will be just the thing. And if it lasts long enough, maybe absence will make her heart grow fonder."

"I'll explain that to her when I get back to Venice," said the lean, dapper Bortaliscono. "Are there any other little services you'd like me to render? While I'm there, you know."

Da Castres shook a fist at him, grinning.

Bortaliscono bowed mockingly to his fellow captain, and turned to Manfred. "I'll need those letters before this evening, Prince Manfred. As soon as it is dark we'll sheer off westward. The farther south we go, the more I'll have to beat back. I'll want to head for the Italian coastline, and creep up it."

Manfred nodded. "We'll need to bring the ships together, and transfer the knights, horses and food. I think we should be prepared to split up this evening. Selvi, it looks like you're going on to Rome."

"It's the course I should have chosen anyway, Prince Manfred," said the captain sourly . . . but not too loudly.

Manfred ignored him. "It will still be dangerous. But it could also be the crucial route. A message from there to Flanders could beat the Atlantic convoy. They'll have to return posthaste. I suspect the Outremer convoy will be out of contention, stuck in the Black Sea."

"And the enemy will know that," Da Castres pointed out. "They can count. If there are only two of our ships in the harbor—and you can be sure they have spies everywhere—then they'll know that the other two are running back for help."

He smiled nastily as Selvi looked a little green. Manfred went below to write the letters.

Benito was left scowling, trying to think if there was any obvious hole in the plan that had now been laid squarely at his door. He was scowling, too, at Manfred's reference to his parentage.

"I think that went off rather well," said Francesca to him, smiling. "So why do you look so unhappy, Benito?"

As if he was going to tell her. "Oh. Nothing."

She looked quizzically at him. "It was that reference to your blood, wasn't it?"

"It's not exactly my favorite point of public knowledge," he said grumpily.

She patted him on the arm. "Benito, it *is* public knowledge. And Manfred needed to mention the fact that you are descended from not one, but *two* of the greatest strategists of the age to prevent any doubt."

"That doesn't mean I inherited anything from either of them," he pointed out, still irritated. But his irritation was fading fast. It was impossible to stay out-of-temper around Francesca, particularly when she was exerting herself to be charming. Maybe she was a little old for him, but . . . on the other hand, older women were . . . He forced his mind away from that line of thought.

Francesca nodded. "Benito, whether or not you have inherited your strategic sense, nevertheless, you *have* it—and if it's suggested that you inherited it from the Fox and the Wolf both, people will accept it as genius and be willing to act on it instead of thinking you're just an impudent boy."

Benito sighed. Well, that much, he could accept. "But Manfred's a commander—"

"Manfred is neither a seaman nor a Venetian. He isn't even Italian. Had this scheme been put forward as his idea, the seamen might have refused. They trust you and they trust that reputation."

"Von Gherens could have severed a few heads," said Benito, though he didn't really mean it. Well, maybe he did.

She shook her head. "Manfred, and especially Erik,

are well aware that it would not have helped. You can threaten a weak-kneed captain that way, but not entire crews. Knights are not seamen. If the seamen thought what was being proposed was suicide—a hundred Von Gherens wouldn't have stopped them. Da Castres, Bortaliscono, and Douro are not cowards, even if Capitano Selvi is."

"I suppose so. But tell him I wish he hadn't done it."

Francesca dimpled. "He knows that. Just because Manfred is big, people think he doesn't notice things. Besides . . ." She pecked Benito on the cheek. "It wasn't his idea. I told him to do it. I apologize. I wouldn't have done it if I hadn't thought it necessary. But I think you let it worry you too much."

"Being illegitimate is not important, is it?" he asked sourly.

She raised an eyebrow. "Was it important when you were staying alive by your wits on the canals of Venice?"

He shrugged. "Not really, I suppose. Half the canalside brats and bridge boys didn't know who their fathers were."

"So it was one of the *Case Vecchie* who mocked you about it?"

"Caesare did," admitted Benito. "Back after I went to live at *Casa* Dorma."

Francesca gave a little snort of laughter. "And you are letting the opinion of such a one as *Caesare* worry you? A liar, a spy, a breaker of every oath he ever made, who was for sale to anyone who had the money? He was a bigger whore than ever I was—at least I always keep my promises."

Benito acknowledged a hit. "I hadn't thought of it that way."

She smiled. "It's all right, Benito. You may be of the bloodline of the strategists of the age, but I am a woman and therefore infinitely more perceptive. And now I'd better go and correct Manfred's spelling. For someone of royal blood he is near to illiterate. Mind, you should see his uncle Charles Fredrik's handwriting! The Emperor normally has a scribe, but anything he considers confidential or really important he insists on writing himself."

As she left, Eberhard of Brunswick came across from the other side of the table, and clapped him on the shoulder. "I hope this complicated plan of yours works, boy. I don't actually like complicated plans. Too much can go wrong when the actual fighting starts."

Benito nodded. "I don't like plans where things have to be well coordinated or rely on something else happening right or exactly on time either. Um. In my misspent youth, milord, I was involved with a thief who worked like that. It got him killed. Caesare Aldanto also liked multifaceted, multipronged plans." Benito cleared his throat. "I admired him, milord. I did understand that often his plans only worked because *he* was very good at what he was doing, and he changed his plans as he went along. He also didn't mind who else got killed or hurt, as long as he was all right."

The old man smiled wryly. "I've dealt with commanders like that when I was a soldier. I've dealt with kings and chieftains like that, as a statesman. If they must go down they'll pull everyone and everything down with them, but they'll sacrifice anyone and anything to keep from going down themselves."

"Well, yes. Except most complicated plans rely on other people. And if the word gets around they can't rely on you, your reputation is ruined. People need to know they can trust you to be where you said you'd be, and do what you said you'd do, before they'll even consider taking part in complicated plans."

"Which is why you wish to be seen as reliable?"

Benito blinked. "Actually, I hadn't thought of that. What I meant is: These people don't really know me. So this plan doesn't rely on other people. It might be crazy . . . but it is dead simple, really. It doesn't rely on others having done something. It's just a simple sequence of events."

Eberhard laughed. "Events that just wouldn't occur to most commanders."

Benito smirked. "I've found plans work best when the enemy isn't expecting them."

Chapter 34

Swimming silent and deep and as far behind the ships as he dared, while still keeping some kind of trace on them, the great hagfish followed. The encounter with the adversary had been terrifying—all the more so because the adversary had been not only supported by his companions but linked to them, in a way that was as alien to the shaman as mother-love. To link together thus was to open your mind and will totally to your companions. The shaman would never do that voluntarily. He could think of no one he would dare trust like that.

He soon realized that the vessels above and ahead of him had diverged. Hagfish can pick up blood and other scents in a part per million. The darkness above was no cloak at all to the chemical-sensitive barbels around his mouth.

For a moment he dithered, before deciding. Make it his master's problem. His master's slave Aldanto had virtual control of all of the Byzantine ships, and by virtue of exploiting ignorance, control over the galliots. The captains of those little vessels were superstitiously terrified of Aldanto. He could direct pursuit of the other ships. The shaman could tell the master where they were heading.

A little later, after this was done, the shaman returned, determined to follow and if possible arrange an attack on the two vessels heading for Corfu. The adversary was in one of them.

❖   ❖   ❖

Father Francis frowned, bracing himself against the bulkhead while the vessel lurched. "Much of this plan relies on the enemy not being forewarned. But, Eneko, if we are being followed by some magical creature, and it was able to direct those fleets to attack, will it not warn the besiegers?"

Eneko nodded; he was tired, and he had rather not do this now—but there was certainly no time to wait. "So we shall have to try to drive it away."

Diego stretched. "Bah. So we have to deal with that *thing* again! You know, Eneko, I think I can still taste the slime. Well, soonest done, quickest mended. When will we try it?"

"Before the ships turn to make the tack back toward Corfu. It may conclude that we plan to make landfall. That is well and good. If it is in contact with the land-troops, let them patrol there while we attempt to reach the Citadel." He stood. "Brothers, let us cast the circle and call the wards. I believe that we will have much the same aid this time as the last. Perhaps, forewarned, we will make better use of it."

Perhaps, he thought, *This time the surprise will be on our side.*

Two hours later the shaman had retreated with desperate haste to deep water, and was begging the master to open up a passage. Jagiellon answered, with the same twisting passage through the spirit-world, but it seemed an eternity to the shaman. He fled up it, and was spewed out onto the stone floor in a heap, gracelessly.

The hagfish transformed into its human form, and the shaman started screaming. His wrinkled skin was blistered, with long, raised lash-marks. Even transposition could not heal them.

Jagiellon allowed him to scream for some few moments, before commanding: "Be still."

The shaman had little choice but to obey despite wanting to scream, and scream, and never stop screaming. It had not been a sword nor a lance that met him this time, but a great fiery form that had *dragged* him into some neutral part of the spirit-realm, and lashed him with a many-tailed whip while he frantically tried to crawl away. He had not gotten in a single blow of his own. He'd barely managed to escape.

"Eat skin," commanded Jagiellon. "Come. I go to eat some myself."

The shaman picked up his *quodba* drum with blistered fingers. He could not help noticing that the skin of his one-time foe, now the drumhead, was singing. Vibrating just faintly all by itself.

Benito, a Corfiote seaman, Capitano Douro and Erik stood in the captain's cabin, peering at a chart of the island. "If they have patrols out, it will be here, milord," said the seaman, pointing. "Between Kavos and the mainland. It is only, oh, maybe three leagues across the strait there."

"They'll have lookouts on both sides, I presume?" asked Erik, studying the chart.

The seaman shook his head fiercely. "Not on the mainland! The Lord of the Mountains would never allow that."

"The Lord of the Mountains?"

"Iskander Beg. He is chief of the Illyrians over there. He is a very bad man." The Corfiote shuddered.

"So there will be a watch on the Corfiote shore," mused Erik. "But probably just a ship at anchor well off the other shore."

"Do ships sail this strait at night?" asked Benito.

The sailor managed to look shifty, evasive and shocked, all at the same time. "Oh, no! It is dangerous. It is not allowed. The podesta has ordered—strictly—that there is to be no shipping in the straits at night."

"But you just happen to know how to sail it," said Benito, dryly.

The sailor shrugged. "Fishermen do it. There are some fish best caught at night."

"Ah. Fish which would pay taxes if they were landed by daylight? You needn't worry my friend," chuckled Benito. "I'm not a tax collector. In fact a good friend, a very, very good friend of mine, used to be involved in smuggling stuff into Venice. Someone all of us here know, in fact, except maybe the capitano, and I wouldn't be too certain about that."

The sailor looked hastily at the Venetian captain, and said nothing.

Benito looked at the captain too. "Capitano Douro. Unless I'm a lot stupider than I think I am . . . you've got some goods you weren't planning to pay taxes on when the ship reached Ascalon?"

The captain looked startled. "Well . . ."

"I'm not planning on telling anyone," said Benito. "And this ship won't be getting to Ascalon. I just wish to reassure our guide."

The captain nodded. "A matter of some amber . . . just a few small, choice pieces."

The seaman looked at Benito, shook his head and chuckled. "You're too sharp for one so young, milord. Yes. We'd bring cargo in and land it right on the wharf in Kérkira. I've been up the strait in the dark more times than I can count. There are a few places you need to avoid. This time of year the current runs strong. The worst piece will be the last bit. We need to approach close to the mole. Farther east, we'll rip her guts out. But as I said to the skipper: I can get us in."

The captain grunted. "Not as well as you could if we had a load of taxable cargo on board," he countered, but he did so with a smile.

The oars were bound in sacking. Men sharpened weapons. The gunners prepared the cannons, though they were not to be used, except as a last resort. Armor was readied but not donned. If they got through the screen of guard boats, then the armor would be hastily put on. Boarders and armor did not go together, and they might have to board a guard ship.

It was an awkward combination of circumstances. The moon, a hazy object often hidden behind gathering clouds, was slipping beneath the horizon. It was going to be as black as the inside of a cat out there. If they came upon a guard boat suddenly, the knights would act as boarders—no firearms, just swords and murderous haste. A single shot fired would mean retreat, and landfall elsewhere.

After that, if they were spotted they'd run for shore and try to beach the vessel. The knights had already planned to smash out the cladding timbers between the ship's ribs and swim their horses to shore. Once again armor was likely to drown both the knight and the horse. So, for that it would be helmets and shields only. But in the final attempt to reach the Citadel, they aimed to bring the ships to rest on the shingle just off the northern side of the islet. Sea access to this was between the islet and castle on Vidos and the Corfu Citadel itself.

The biggest difficulty was going to be keeping two silent, darkened vessels in touch with each other. They had one steersman, and two ships. A long line between the two helped. A man on the bow of the second ship kept a coil of this line in his hand, keeping the line tight without allowing it to pull. He had to feel whether it was pulling away to any direction or if the front vessel was slowing or speeding up. A second man in the bow of the second ship was ready to listen to softly made gull cries. One for port, two for starboard. Gulls shouldn't be calling in the small hours of the night, but Benito's ingenuity deserted him on this one. At least it wouldn't sound as unnatural as voices.

By the time they reached the southern channel it was so dark that all that could be seen was a shape of deeper darkness where the landmasses lay. Well . . . except for the cheerful lanterns that burned on the four equidistantly placed watch vessels.

How nice of them to show Benito where they were!

It was all Benito could do to stop himself laughing helplessly. They slipped through relatively close to the lantern-lit vessels, just in case the enemy had put unlit vessels between.

In the tense darkness, Manfred snorted. "We're past. Let's give a rousing cheer to celebrate."

"There are more hurdles," said Benito. "Listen. You can hear the cannon fire."

They could. A distant deadly rumble. The steersman

pointed. "Those lights are Lefkimi. We're passing Lefkimi point now."

"How long is it going to take us to get to Kérkira?" whispered Erik.

The man looked at the sky. "If we get the sail up now, we should be within hailing distance just before dawn." Benito caught the flash of teeth. "Or within cannon shot. I hope those priests can come up with the magic they promised, milord, or the Venetians' own fort and Vidos castle will blow us apart."

"They're very powerful Christian mages, those priests," replied Erik stiffly.

The Corfiote didn't seem especially impressed. "I've no faith in priest's magic. On Corfu we have some real, old magics. Scary things, but powerful, sirs, maybe more powerful than anything you've ever seen."

"Eneko Lopez is one of the most scary men in the world. And he is not going to let us down." Benito spoke quietly, with a faith he hoped he felt.

"I reckon we'll get a chance to see if that is true. If he fails we're shit. Fish-shit, soon enough," said the steersman with morbid humor.

On the main deck the seamen were raising the carefully blackened mainsail. Under oars it had been tricky to keep the two vessels running in tandem. Under sail it would be virtually impossible. The second vessel would just have to do its best with a helmsman following the dark patch that was the sail of the lead vessel. They still had a good few leagues to go before the final dash.

"There's a small vessel ahead! Also running without lanterns. Running away from us."

"Smuggler?"

"Must be. We've made someone shit themselves." The seaman grinned.

Manfred came up on deck. "What was that?"

"Smuggler-ship. Avoiding taxes," said Benito knowledgeably.

Manfred half-choked. "And just who is collecting taxes right now, Benito?"

"Oh, hell! Do you think it was a watch-boat? We'd better run for shore."

"No," said Erik decisively. "If it was a watch vessel, someone would have fired off a signal. What you saw there was a sign that things are pretty bad on the island. That 'smuggler' will have a human cargo. He's taking refugees away, not bringing illegal goods in."

"I've got three sisters and a brother in Achilleon," said their steersman, quietly. "I wonder what's happening to them."

"It's to be hoped that your brother was also involved with the *night fishing*, sailor," said the captain, dryly. "Emeric of Hungary has a vile reputation for how he allows his soldiers to treat conquered citizens."

There was a chuckle. "Spiro is my older brother. That's how I came to be involved in the first place."

Chapter 35

There was just a hint of lightness in the sky. Dawn was still a little while off, but morning was definitely stirring in the bed of night. "You can see the Citadel against the sky. It seems pretty quiet now," said the Corfiote steersman.

"Well, maybe we can sneak in," said Benito. "I hope so. If we have to use the priests . . . The minute those banners are visible, the gunners on the ships that are sure to be lying just out of range will open fire on us."

"Uh-huh." Falkenberg grunted his agreement. "That's a sure sign that the Hungarians haven't gotten their cannon yet. When the cannon get here, they'll pound those walls night and day. But the Venetians in the Citadel will be watching for a sneak assault by sea. According to our captain there are places men could be landed outside the walls. If men could get inside the fortifications they could spike the cannon and nothing could hold off the assault."

"Er. Not from what I can gather," said Benito, diffidently. Falkenberg had, after all, been at a dozen sieges as opposed to his none—hard to believe in a man that relatively young, but still . . . Falkenberg was a veteran of the northeastern frontier of the Empire, where he'd been born and raised. "There are three walls. An outer curtain wall, the inner wall and then the two castles on the hilltops."

"A wonderful place for a holiday," said Falkenberg, dryly. "Great defenses are more than just three walls, Benito. They're enough men—with good morale—enough ammunition, and enough food and water. Perhaps most important of all, a loyal and determined population supporting them, with no traitors. And even if you've got those, there's a lot to designing walls so that they work effectively. Making walls that can stand endless cannon fire is simply not possible. Entrenchments are more effective."

He went on to give Benito a concise study of siege-craft. "I've been years in the learning of this stuff, and before that, I had the best teacher in the world. It occurred to him that he should pass it on to me before I had to spend thirty years relearning it. I think maybe I'll start passing it on to you, just in case. You never know. You might be able to make some use of it."

Benito was sharp enough to understand the unsaid. Falkenberg thought most of them would die. And he approved of Benito Valdosta and wanted to pass his knowledge on.

It might be spring, but it was still bitterly cold here on the outer curtain wall in the small hours of the morning. Especially after crawling out of a warm bed, from beside a warm wife. True, the warm wife had gotten up as well, and had given him some food and a small flask of wine. Maria had her moments, but generally she was a gem.

Privately, Umberto acknowledged that his advancement was largely due to her, and her connections. He'd entered the marriage with a lot of qualms, but had come to treasure it more than anything he'd ever had in his life.

Still, Maria was back in that warm bed now, and he was out on this cold tower. By the grumbling from the other Arsenalotti, they were feeling equally miserable about the situation. While staying within the law—just barely—of Venice and guild alike, Captain-General Tomaselli was doing his best to make sure that they felt the misery of thwarting him.

Umberto stamped his feet. They were frozen already. He would dress more warmly next time.

He stared into the night. Just what would he do if a Hungarian or a Croat stuck his head up over the parapet right now? Panic, probably. He'd been a craftsman all his life, not a soldier, and had spent a lifetime holding tools in his hands rather than weapons . . . The arquebus felt as unfamiliar as the issue rapier.

Suddenly the darkness was lit by a bright golden blazon out on sea. And then a second. "Sound the Alarum!" yelled someone. "To the guns! To the guns!"

There was a boom and a flash from out in the dark strait. And, virtually a heartbeat later, an answering shot from the walls. Umberto ducked instinctively. He looked seaward again and saw clearly: The lateen foresail and the pennants of two vessels out there were glowing with a golden winged lion that outshone the darkness.

"Hold your fire!" he yelled. "Hold your fire! It's the Lion of Saint Mark!" His voice, he found, was being chorused by many others.

And then, echoing above the pitter-pitter of arquebus-fire from the shore—ineffective at this range—came the bright, glad sound of trumpets. It was the battle hymn of the Knights of the Holy Trinity, and it struck fear into the hearts of their foes. Umberto recognized it, and was deeply grateful he'd never faced it as a foe. Looking at the light from the glowing emblem of Venice he could see that it was gleaming off spiky helmets and armor. The captured shore was now a mass of hastily running figures. The enemy hadn't expected a night attack, and certainly not here, at the main point of their own assault.

"San Marco! San Marco!"

The men on the walls yelled and cheered. There was another flash as yet another one of the Byzantine or Dalmatian pirate ships fired a cannon. The ship was plainly in pursuit of the two galleys that were flying pennants with the strange glowing winged lions. The vessels looked like typical great galleys in the dim light from the pennants.

"Bring the guns to bear on those who follow!" Umberto shouted the words without thinking about whether or not he had the authority to give orders to the bombardiers. He might not be familiar with weapons—certainly not cannons—but he'd been a foreman by the time he was thirty. Commanding men in practical tasks was now second nature to him.

Already, he saw, there was cannon fire from Vidos.

"I hope to God they're firing on the pursuit!" The two galleys with their golden winged lion pennants streaming were now within cannon shot of both fortresses.

The Venetians' fire, seeking for targets in the darkness, might have been hampered by the lack of visibility—but luck, or the winged lion, was certainly with one of the gunners. Sudden fire flared out on the dark water behind the two galleys. Perhaps a ball had struck a banked stove and scattered embers into a smashed powder keg.

Whatever the cause, there was now a vessel on fire out on the water, and it wasn't either of the two flying the Lion. And the sky was definitely lighter. Umberto could see that the great-galley crews must be stroking as if their very lives depended on it. Which, in fact, they did. The blazoned winged lions, so clearly visible, made them easy targets. The cannon fire from the Citadel and Vidos would discourage pursuit, but they'd still be within cannon-shot of other vessels. But they were firing their own stern-cannon now. If they were in range, so, too, were their foes.

Along the shore, the trenches were flash-speckled with the muzzle-flash of arquebuses. If they planned to make landfall there, they'd do it in the face of stiff opposition. But it looked to Umberto as if the vessels were bearing down directly on the Citadel. The usual anchorage behind the berm-breakwater would be directly under small-arms fire from the shore.

Behind him, Umberto heard horsemen. The captain-general and the bulk of his cavalry were coming down at a hasty trot. Umberto saw that many of the troopers were still trying to buckle themselves into their breastplates. People, too, were streaming out of the houses behind the curtain-walls, heading for the wall.

"Direct your fire on the trenches! Keep the buggers' heads down!" bellowed an officer. "The galleys are going to make a landing here beneath the wall."

Umberto found himself holding his breath. There was

a strip of shingly beach below the wall on this side of the berm. On the sea-side. The berm would provide some shelter and the ships would be at least three hundred and fifty yards from the enemy-held shore. That was well and good—but was the water deep enough, close in enough to allow the vessels to beach?

Umberto was a ship-builder. He doubted it. And moreover, the gate that had been used for workers to get access from the Citadel to the port was at least a hundred and fifty yards closer. The storehouses of the Little Arsenal lay just inside that gate.

He hastened over to Leopoldo, the garrison commander. "Milord. Permission to take some Arsenalotti down to the port gate. We can push some heavy balks of timber onto the beach for them to shelter behind."

Leopoldo peered at him. "Umberto Verrier. Go to it. Here, Sergeant. Go with him to provide my authority to the gate." He turned to one of his captains. "I'll want all the fire we can muster from the northeast tower. See to it, Domenico."

Umberto hurried down, calling to various people as he ran. He wasn't much of a fighter, maybe, but he could handle timber. And he loved ships—not sailing in them, the ships themselves. The thought of those ships ripping their bottoms out was not a pleasant one.

Maria had slipped back into sleep after Umberto left, but the sound of the cannons woke her.

It sounded serious; she got up, and listened harder.

It *was* serious. Had the Hungarian king got his cannons onto the island, then? Was this the moment they'd all been dreading for days? If so—

If so, then every able body would be needed on the walls!

There was no way she could leave Alessia, and she had a horrible feeling she might need both hands, so she tied the baby to her back in a large shawl. Then she took up the wheel-lock pistol that Kat had given her, when they'd gone out in search of Marco, in what seemed a lifetime ago. She also took the largest cleaver in her kitchen on her way to the door.

As soon as she was outside, she headed for the wall. She had no doubts as to what her fate would be, and that of Alessia, if the Hungarians breached the walls. If nothing else she could fling rocks. You didn't have to be a soldier to fling rocks down on those below.

She went pelting down the hill, along with several hundred others, all showing signs of hasty dressing and of seizing the first arms that came to hand: here a rolling pin, there an arquebus, or a boar-spear, or a bread-peel. Half the citizens of the Citadel seemed to be running to the outer curtain-wall.

Then, she heard the cheers. *"San Marco! San Marco!"*

That didn't sound as if things were going badly. In fact, it sounded more like a welcome than a call-to-arms. And it was coming, not from the landward side, but the seaward side. Her headlong run slowed slightly; she looked out into the darkness, peering at where the shouts were coming from. For a brief moment she thought she was seeing things. The Winged Lion of Venice was coming across the sea! And it was as golden as the sun itself.

Then she realized it was just an image of the winged lion glowing from lateen sails and pennant flags. There must be a couple of vessels out there. Corfu wasn't being attacked, it was being reinforced! She went to join the throng on the wall, to join the cheering now, rather than the defense.

The two vessels, now easily visible in the growing light, looked as if they were racing each other for the shore. They were rowing toward the sheltered water of the L-shaped berm—except that they didn't seem intent on getting into it, which would have put them right up against the enemy-held shore. Instead, they were heading for the seaward side of the berm.

She saw the lead vessel shudder, and heard the snap of oars as the vessel hit some underwater obstruction. She could make out a stick-figure frantically waving at the other vessel from the poop. The other vessel bore hard to seaward. The first vessel was still edging forward—she was barely thirty yards from shore—but obviously leaking and sinking. The silence from the wall was now profound.

People were hardly breathing. Cannon still roared from the landward wall, but here it was still.

The second ship passed over the obstacle and, with a sugary crunch they could hear from the wall, slid to a halt. It was still in the water, but not very deep water.

Men began pouring off it, jumping into the shallows on the eastern side of the vessel, with the ship between them and the firing from the trenches on the mainland of Corfu. Then part of the cladding timbers were smashed out of the side and knights, waist-deep, began hauling horses out of the hole in the hull of the ship.

By now, it was obvious the other vessel was not going to get much farther. Water was over head deep, to judge by the men swimming ashore. To her shock, Maria recognized the stocky figure who emerged, dripping, from the sea.

Benito Valdosta yelled up at the watchers. "Hands to these ropes, all of you. Move!"

She was even more shocked when she recognized the emotion surging through her.

"Don't be stupid!" she snarled at herself, joining the little mob racing to help with the ropes.

Chapter 36

Benito was nearly thrown overboard when they struck the rock. He knew straight away they were in trouble. The galley had a draft of one and a half fathoms, when she was this heavily laden. They were relying on hitting the shore at speed to beach the vessel so that the men could emerge without swimming. Now they'd lost their momentum and she was holed. The ship would ride deeper than her one and a half fathoms. The sailors could easily manage the twenty yards to shore . . . if they could swim. The knights in heavy armor had not a chance.

"Get them to strip their armor!" yelled Benito.

"Takes too long!" bellowed Manfred, above the bedlam of screaming horses and shouting men.

"Get a rope to the shore!" commanded the captain.

Benito took the end of a light line. "Get the anchor rope on the other end!" he shouted, and dived overboard.

On the beach, he saw he'd arrived in the shallows just ahead of the Corfiote steersman who also had a rope.

"Hands to these ropes, all of you. Move!" he commanded.

Maria saw how the port gate had opened farther up the shore toward the Hungarian trenches. Great balks of timber were being thrust out and now, in the shelter of these, hundreds of men and women from the Citadel were streaming to help.

319

Maria ran to join them. It was only when she was out on the shingle that it occurred to her that a woman with a baby on her back shouldn't do this. It was too late by then, though, so she ran on. By the time she got there, the men were hauling at the anchor ropes—twisted hempen lines as thick as her arm—of the galley still wallowing and sinking further out. They were using the second galley as a bulwark. And by the looks of it, the Arsenalotti who had pushed out the timber barrier were extending and raising it. Still, shots whistled overhead as, handspan by handspan, they hauled the other galley closer. Someone had unlimbered a small boat from the first galley and it was hastily paddled out the fifteen remaining yards or so, to begin bringing people in.

"Get men with shovels and start digging a trench, we need to unload!" shouted a voice Maria recognized. Erik Hakkonsen!

What a bitter irony. Svanhild was not in the Citadel but out there somewhere. Hopefully safe . . .

"What the hell are you doing out here, Maria?" Benito looked anything but pleased to see her. "And—Jesus wept!—with your baby! Get back! No, stay here! It's safer here."

"I've come to help you out of your mess!" she snapped back. "And my child goes with me. At her age she has to."

"*Merde!* Well, just stay behind the *Dolphin*. At this range they're not going to get a bullet right through her." He ran out, regardless of his own safety, getting into deeper water. "Come on! She's only neck deep on a short knight. Let's have what people we can off and then we'll haul her a bit further in. Another five yards and we'll get the horses out."

Maria saw Francesca and Eneko Lopez and some other clerics coming ashore in the small boat. She waved, but they didn't notice her. Well, there'd be time for greetings if they survived all this.

A group of very brave Magyar cavalrymen, or perhaps just very stupid ones, had swum their horses across the channel between the Citadel and Corfu Island. The cannon and gunfire from above had had a devastating effect on what had been perhaps four hundred men who had set out to cross the gap. Now the remainder had won the sand strip and were charging down it.

A handful of arquebusiers had taken up position behind the balks of timber. The gate swung hastily shut behind them . . . but there was timber in the way. It could not be closed. What had started out as a glorious rescue mission was fast turning into a fiasco.

And then Maria realized that Knights of the Holy Trinity were already swinging themselves into the saddle. Perhaps only thirty of them were ready to mount, but they were up and riding, broadswords out, hurtling toward the oncoming Hungarians. When the Hungarians had begun their charge they'd outnumbered the Knights by five to one. By the time they clashed, however, those odds had been viciously reduced. The wall on their right was lined with people—some soldiers, firing, but the rest just men and women throwing whatever they had in their hands. Even cobblestones.

The Knights were still outnumbered three to one. But these were the Knights of the Holy Trinity, perhaps Europe's finest. They hit the Hungarians on a narrow strip of beach, too narrow for either side to ride more than eight abreast. For the swim across, the Magyar knights had reduced the weight of their armor to breastplates. They were very much at a disadvantage compared to the Knights in full armor.

Even as the first handful of Knights charged, more Knights were mounting, yelling and swearing at the Venetian sailors in their way. The sailors, too, were running to the timber-balk barrier with arquebuses, pistols and cutlasses.

If the Magyars could have carried their charge to the open gate, it would have been a different story. Speed had lent them some protection from those on the wall. But now, stopped and completely defenseless against the attack from above, they were being annihilated. And the second galley was now discharging more wet, angry Knights.

"Let them handle that!" roared a bull-like voice. Manfred strode through the small waves, and grabbed the anchor rope. "Haul! On the count of three!"

Manfred had both the voice and the presence for command, so more men rushed to seize the ropes. The ship however was filling up, settling, heavier. Much heavier. Maria, who was now hauling the water for their little house daily, knew just how much water weighed.

"One, two, three! *Heave*."

The vessel moved sluggishly. It wallowed like a drunken cow.

"And again! One, two, *three*."

Out beyond the ships, the Magyars were being reduced to bloody fragments. Maria promptly dismissed them from her mind, and went back to something she *could* do something about.

The rope snapped. Manfred's first heroic impression made on the Corfu garrison was of himself sprawling on his backside in the shallows, legs in the air. The roar of general laughter was inevitable, if hardly kind to his dignity. Because only one rope was now hauling the boat it slewed sideways a bit, till the prow touched the stern of the other vessel. "I wouldn't have put my nose there!" said one wag.

Erik had returned to the scene. "Up, all of you. The ships must be unloaded." He, too, had the presence of command. Those who had been hauling on the first rope, if they could not find space on the second, fell into a line heaving bags and boxes and unidentifiable bits into the fortress.

Maria found herself sharing a burden, carrying in a grain bag with another garrison woman. The woman looked at her with the liveliest of curiosity. "You look terribly ordinary after the stories I'd heard."

"What stories?" asked Maria warily. "What have you heard from whom?"

"I had it from Rosalba Benelli, who heard it from her maid, whose sister is one of the poor girls who work for Sophia Tomaselli's friend Melina, that Milady Verrier had been seen in an alley in Kérkira with your dress up and two sailors." She snickered, clearly not in the least inclined to believe it—not now, at least.

Maria snorted. "She's talking about her own daydreams. I'm a respectable married woman. Besides, when would

I have time? I do the work of my household myself, and thank you. I don't need twenty little girls to do it for me."

She felt slightly guilty saying that, since Alessia wasn't Umberto's child. But she owed it to Alessia—Umberto too, for that matter—to kill any such rumors.

The woman, slightly plump and with a distinct twinkle in her expressive eyes, clicked her tongue. "Tch! And there I was going to ask how you managed two." She rolled her eyes. "I can't even manage my Alberto. He keeps falling asleep, especially now they're doing these guard shifts."

Maria grinned. "I think we women should complain to the captain-general."

The woman at the other end of the sack snorted. "And have randy Tomaselli offer to help out? No, thank you very much!"

Maria's mouth twitched. "Maybe we should suggest to dear Sofia that he needs a little . . ."

The other woman began giggling. "What? That would be beneath her dignity. Besides it would spoil her makeup."

"Only she if she smiled, which seems unlikely," Maria said, thoughtfully, as they tramped over shingle that slipped and rattled under their feet. "Or maybe she doesn't just plaster her face . . . does she have to do the whole body?"

The plumpish woman looked as if she was going to fall over and drop the sack. "Oh, Lord and Saints! If she could hear you . . ."

She went off into shrieks of laughter. They reached the gate and the pile of food bags just as Maria was beginning to think the woman would kill herself laughing. They dumped the bag. And the woman hugged Maria. "You can't know how nice it is to hear someone being malicious about Milady Sophia Tomaselli for a change. My name is Stella Mavroukis. I don't care if we've been told by 'her ladyship' not to talk to you."

"Maria Verrier. I'm married to . . ."

Stella grinned wickedly. "We know *all* about Umberto. I even know what you send him for lunches. That's the trouble with Corfu. Small community. Not much to do but gossip. But it used to be fun back before 'her ladyship' got here. Come on, let's fetch another sack."

By the time they got back with the next sack, Maria knew the names, ages, childhood diseases and mischief of all five of Stella's brood, as well as several intimate details about her Alberto that Maria was sure would never allow her to meet Alberto without blushing, or at least laughing. She also knew that Alberto was a "Greek" Venetian, son of one of the many craftsmen that the Republic of Venice had seduced into her state with offers of citizenship, money and employment.

Also, of course, they'd torn Sophia Tomaselli's character, appearance and morals to shreds, very pleasurably.

Benito staggered under his load. Falkenberg in full armor was no lightweight. He was also not helping much.

They'd been up on the beach, where the battle-hardened knight had just gotten his precious horse to shore. He'd clapped Benito on the shoulder. "Well. We made it. Although this last bit has turned into a horse's—"

Then a stray ball hit him. It was one of those flukes that happened. It had hit his visor, which had shattered. The knight had fallen slowly . . . so slowly that Benito had been able to catch him.

Now they staggered toward the fortress. Benito no longer thought of strategy or tactics, just of getting the bleeding man to help, and off this beach. A Venetian came and took the other side of Falkenberg and together they staggered to the gate, while the firefight raged and the knights ripped the Magyar heavy cavalry to pieces. Falkenberg was now totally unconscious and lolling between them.

"What happened?" panted the Venetian. With a little sense of shock, Benito realized it was Umberto Verrier. The man who had married Maria.

"He was hit in the face by a ball." They were inside the gates by now.

"Let's put him down. See if we can stop the bleeding."

They laid Falkenberg down on the cobbles and Benito bent over his face, feeling sick. If only Marco was here!

"My God. What a mess." Fragments of steel had torn into the eye and right side of Falkenberg's face and head. The inside of the helmet was a mess of blood and flesh-shreds. It was still bleeding. "What the hell do we do?" he asked the older man.

For an answer, Umberto had already run over to two other men. He brought them over to the knight, with a couple of broad slats. "These men are from the hospital. They'll take him up there. The chirurgeons will help him."

"Will he live?" whispered Benito.

"Too early to tell," said one of the hospitalers critically. "But we'll have him on these planks and up there in two shakes of a lamb's tail. If you'll get out of the way, sir."

Hastily, Benito complied.

Meanwhile, Umberto called to two of the men who were struggling to push the timber further out so that the gate could be closed.

"The timber at the bottom is not going to move, Alberto! There's too much weight on it."

"So what do we do?" asked the other. "We need to be able to close this gate."

Umberto took a critical look. "They're still using it as a shelter. Let's move what we can on the top. It's only two or three of the lower balks that should be a problem. Maybe if we can get a lever of some sort to them."

Benito found himself manhandling huge pieces of keel and strut timber, when Maria came past. She was so busy talking to another woman that she didn't notice her husband, or Benito.

Working side-by-side with Verrier, Benito was finally coming to accept, not simply acknowledge, the truth of what everyone had always said about Umberto. He was a quiet, good man who loved his craft. And he was, by the looks of it, very good at it. Benito had met Umberto once or twice over the years, briefly, if not socially; a bridge-brat went everywhere and saw everything. He knew him to look at if not to talk to. But everybody always said the man was a solid fellow.

Working with him, Benito had to concede that they were right. He'd prepared himself to find reasons to dislike Umberto. Now he found that it was impossible.

And it stuck in his craw. And he hated that it stuck in his craw. Did life always have to be such a confusing mess?

Benito left organizing the off-loading of the galleys and the orderly retreat from the beach to Manfred. He concentrated instead on helping to lever the pile of timber a little further out, while Umberto organized ropes on each timber so that they could be snaked back over the wall. Umberto was a typical Venetian in that way. Not wasteful.

Benito was rewarded, when, a little while later, he saw Maria, still walking with her friend, still talking, stop abruptly and gawp at the two of them, working next to each other.

Chapter 37

"I can't deny I'm very glad to see reinforcements, Prince Manfred. I've been wishing I had some way of getting word to Venice."

Captain-General Tomaselli limped over to a cabinet on the wall, hauled out a metal flask and a tray of Venetian glassware, and limped back to his table. "Try this, gentlemen. I think we all need something a great deal stronger than wine. It's from the mainland. They distill it from plums, I believe." He poured the clear liquid into glasses and motioned that they should help themselves. He took one of the glasses.

"Is a lady permitted to try some too?" asked Francesca.

"Of course. Of course!" The flustered Venetian handed her a glass. "Unless you would prefer some wine? This stuff is frightfully strong."

Francesca lowered her lashes. "I think, milord, after the morning we've had, I'd better have some strong drink." She tossed it back without any sign of discomfort.

That was more than could be said for Erik. He choked and spluttered. Even Manfred went a little red. Benito sipped the clear liquid cautiously. It burned his throat and all the way down to his gut. Only Von Gherens managed to drink it with anything like Francesca's aplomb.

The captain-general stared at her with respect, for the first time seeing something beyond her cleavage. "Saints

alive!" He shook his head. "I can't drink the stuff like
that. Did you enjoy it?"

Francesca smiled and nodded her head.

The captain-general sat down, shaking his own. "Well.
Back to the matter in hand. The podesta has offered the
officers—and you, of course, Prince Manfred—quarters
in the Castel *a mar*. Your escort also. We can quarter
all your other men and horses here, at the Castel *a
terra*." He sighed, softly. "Truth to tell, we could hold
several hundred more men. There was no perceived
threat here and we're badly undermanned. Four thousand
men would be an optimum number for this fortress. I
had twelve hundred under my command, but that is
on the whole island. Only nine hundred and fifty odd
are here."

"Where are the rest?" asked Manfred.

"About a hundred and seventy are on Vidos—that
small islet out there. The rest were stationed in various
towns and villages. Still, this siege can't hold. There are
relatively few men out there, and they don't appear to
have any siege pieces."

Manfred looked grim. "The guns and a lot more men
are on their way, I'm afraid. You're in for the long haul.
How are you for food and water?"

"There are a couple of springs on the Citadel, and we
have reservoirs here in the castle. The reservoirs are full,
and this soon after winter, the springs are strong. As for
food . . . we're not so well-off. Winter is over, but with
the fleets coming and going, we're used to reprovisioning
wheat, particularly on the autumn convoy. So we're about
half way. Good for eight months at the very least. Arms
are the one thing we have plenty of."

"Well, even rocks will do when it comes to defending
walls," said Erik. "Rocks and enough people is what we
need. And we have enough rocks, even if we could use
more people."

"We brought you a good supply of knights and some
extra citizens," said Von Gherens with a smile. "How are
the Corfiotes outside the walls being treated?"

The captain-general blinked. "We've seen a lot of
fires. Could be Venetian villas burning. Could be some

peasant villages. We've seen some atrocities from the walls. Why, sir?"

"One of the things I've seen over and over again on the northeastern frontier: where the peasantry resent the hand of their overlords, we push forward easily enough. Emeric of Hungary is renowned to be a harsh man, a firm believer in the lash and the knout. I know my friend Falkenberg was involved in some fighting down in Bohemia—against Emeric's father—before the Emperor concluded the Peace of Brno. He said it was like a knife through butter. The peasants were fawning on the Prussians as if they were saints. Showed them all the Hungarian defenses, traps and so on. Found them food and fodder and guided them. And tore their former masters apart when they had the chance. It's different up in Sweden. There the tribesmen, even the Karls, resist us to the last man. Belike if your men out there stir up trouble it'll be more than Emeric can do to hold this island."

One of the captain-general's officers sniffed disdainfully. "I hardly think that will apply here. The Greeks are degenerate. Can't work, can't fight. All they can do is talk about ancient glory."

The plump captain of the *Dolphin* snorted. "I've had Corfiotes in my crew. They're good oarsmen. Better than Dalmatians, better than Venetians even. Seems to me you've got a local problem with them." He turned to Benito. "And how is *Ritter* Falkenberg, by the way, Milord Valdosta?"

"The chirurgeon says he will probably live. But he's lost an eye."

"I was across there, too," said Von Gherens, shaking his head. "His face is a mess, and he looks like he's been cupped fifteen times. But he's alive and has his wits. He said he got hit on the only soft spot in a head that's as solid as a rock. He also said the last thing he remembers is you lugging him in, boy."

"The landing wasn't the success I had hoped it would be," admitted Benito glumly.

"Hell's teeth, boy, it's a damn sight better than we'd have done any other way!" snapped Von Gherens. "We lost three men and we have three more with serious injuries. If we'd tried to charge our way in . . . we'd have considered ten times that light. War means casualties."

"Yes—but—"

Von Gherens slapped his breastplate with a mailed hand. "But me no buts! Our comrades get hurt. Our friends die. Falkenberg is a knight who swore an oath to serve the Church and to defend the weak. He'd be the first man to tell you to stop puling and start planning. Because what we are doing—at risk to ourselves—is what we have sworn to do. The West relies on us. It is a risk we take with pride. It is an oath we honor. Even when some soft southern burgher mutters about us, we know the reason he sleeps soft and comfortable, why his wife is able to complain about the price of cabbages as her most serious problem and why his children dare to throw dung and yell 'Knot' when we pass. It's because we are what we are. For all our faults we stand for law and light."

He smiled, and his tone softened. "A good plan is one that keeps our casualties light and costs our enemy dear. Keep making them, Benito Valdosta."

Manfred cleared his throat. "And that brings us to discussing the defenses of this place. With all respect, Captain-General, we have veterans of a dozen sieges here. We offer you our expertise as well as our arms."

"Your arms are appreciated," the captain-general said stiffly. "But this is a Venetian fortification, under Venetian command."

Manfred opened his mouth to speak and Francesca kicked him.

Von Gherens unfortunately wasn't in kicking range. He snorted. "You're undermanned, underprovisioned, and badly organized. You—"

"That will do, Von Gherens!" barked Eberhard, in a tone so stern it made even Manfred blink. "I apologize, Captain-General. The *Ritter* spoke out of turn."

"And we appreciate your hospitality and especially this drink," added Francesca throatily, holding out an empty glass. "But is it already being rationed?

The captain-general lost his train of angry thought and gawped, as she poured charm on him. "My apologies, signora! Of course not. Allow me." He poured out another.

After a moment's hesitation, Von Gherens put out his glass. "I spoke hastily there, Captain-General. Apologies."

"Accepted," said the captain-general stiffly. He limped forward and filled the knight's glass. "Anyone else?"

Benito watched Francesca calmly empty the glass into the purse hanging from her chatelaine, while the Venetian officer's attention was on Von Gherens.

"Perhaps later," she said, putting down the glass. "Right now I am dying to put off these salty clothes and have a wash." She fluttered her eyelashes at him.

Erik nodded. "Yes. The armor, especially the joints, must be cleaned and oiled. The salt water does it no good."

Von Gherens groaned. "That was the worst aspect of your plan, Benito."

The captain-general rang a bell. "I'll have one of my men show you to your chambers."

Francesca smiled at him. "Thank you, Captain-General Tomaselli. You are too kind."

"You may call me Nico, signora," he said bowing over her hand and kissing it.

Benito felt rather than heard the low rumble from Manfred. He also caught Francesca's wink to the prince, while the Venetian officer's head was down.

"Well, it's a nice bed," said Manfred, testing it. Naturally enough the bed complained. "But I don't know if it was worth you nearly seducing that Venetian ass for."

"A good bed is past price, darling," said Francesca, carefully emptying her purse. She looked at it sadly. "You will have to get me a new one, Manfred. I think the leather will be quite ruined by that vile drink."

"I thought you liked it?" said Manfred, with an evil grin. "You nodded when fancy-pants asked you. I saw you."

"I had to nod. I couldn't speak. I'm afraid the disgusting stuff may have ruined my vocal cords forever. Besides, if I had opened my mouth I might have been sick." She sniffed cautiously at the reticule. "*Bleh*. Even if it doesn't ruin the leather I refuse to live with the smell."

"And there I thought you'd finally learned to drink." Manfred shook his head sadly. "I'll admit the stuff was strong enough to make me pause. He might run a lousy garrison but he certainly has a drink that would put hair on your chest."

"I certainly hope not!" said Francesca. "But it was all part of the show, Manfred."

Manfred stood up and reached for her laces. "I better check about the hair," he teased. "What do you mean? 'Part of the show'? I hope you don't mean the hair . . ."

She lifted his hands aside, kissed them and said: "Later, when you don't smell of oil and old iron and fish and seaweed. What I mean by 'part of the show' was that it was our little captain-general's attempt to show how tough he was. Think of it. This is a backwater of Venetian defense. It's a major point in their resupply and trade routes, but for a commanding officer—well, it's not a place Venice expected to be attacked."

"A junior posting."

"More like a backwater posting. He's not so young." She patted Manfred's broad shoulder. "Now, think. You are a given such a posting—a good trade spot but militarily a sign of being relegated to someplace where you can't do any damage. And suddenly—a siege! He hasn't done too badly, really. From what we've been told, had he been a totally arrogant ass like that fool who told us Greeks were no good, the fortress would have fallen to Emeric's sneak attack. Instead . . . someone did some preparation, saved the citadel, and saved a good many lives outside. It doesn't look as if he's doing too badly, so far, all things considered. Venice will be proud of him, that's what he's thinking. And then . . . in come a couple of hundred of the Empire's greatest knights, in the most dramatic style, poking a stick in the eye of the enemy. Led by a prince of the blood who offers to assist him in conducting the defenses."

Manfred swallowed. "It was well meant, Francesca."

"I know," she said, gently. "But then I'm not a thin-skinned minor noble with a dying military career. And I nearly ruined my toes kicking you. I wish I could have kicked Von Gherens too."

Manfred grinned. "He'd have asked why you were kicking him."

Chapter 38

Benito was assigned a room in the Castel *a mar*. After washing, he found himself in no state to sleep. So he set out to do what he had been told to on arriving in Corfu: reporting to the Dorma Factor.

Asking directions, Benito set out, got himself thoroughly lost and eventually found his way to the man's residence. He was not at home. So Benito left a message and walked across to the hospital to see how Falkenberg was doing.

"You can't see him," said the monk. "He's finally asleep. He's in pain, young man. Sleep, even assisted by laudanum, is the best thing for him."

"Tell him . . . I'll come back later. Is he going to be all right?"

The monk shrugged. "If he doesn't get secondary infections. We've prayed over him. We've used such skills as we have. We have used a fragment of the blessed Saint Landry's hand."

Benito wished, desperately, that his brother were here. But all he could do was thank the monk and leave.

He stood outside on the street, looked about, and bit his lip. Finally, with a feeling in his stomach as if he'd been kicked there by Von Gherens, asked a passerby: "Where can I find the home of Umberto Verrier?"

The man shrugged. "Never heard of him."

"He's a master caulker. Just come out from Venice."

"Try the store-yards down at the outer northeastern gate."

So Benito passed out through the inner curtain wall, and on down to the store-yard. Given the way his day had been going so far, he was not surprised to find that Umberto had taken a belated breakfast and was now back at home, which was inside the curtain wall.

"Look for the last house before the road to St. Agatha's. Between the hills. He's got a goat in his yard. You can usually hear it. It leans over the wall and bleats at passers by. They feed it. Only man I know with a watch-goat," said the Corfiote laborer, grinning. "It's got a weakness for Kourabiedies."

Benito knew exactly which house the man was talking about then. He'd passed it on his way to look for the Dorma factor, and again while walking to the hospital. He sighed. It had been that sort of day.

"What's wrong?" enquired the burly laborer.

"Nothing much. I've just walked down from virtually next door. Anyway, thanks."

The man grinned, showing missing teeth. "You're welcome. I saw you coming in from the ship this morning. And working with old Umberto. He's not a bad soul, for a Venetian."

So Benito walked back up. He found the house. The goat leaned over the wall and bleated at him. Taking a deep breath, he walked up to the door and knocked.

Maria opened the door, baby on arm. "Benito! What are you doing here?"

"You know this young fellow?" asked Umberto, smiling and getting up from the table. "He gave me a lot of help this morning. Come in, young man. We never got formally introduced. I know your face from Venice. This is my wife, Maria . . . but you already seem to know that?"

Benito bowed. "Maria was very good to me while I was growing up. I'm Benito Valdosta."

"Marco Valdosta's brother?" Umberto looked faintly awed. "The ward of the Doge?"

"And more trouble than he's worth," said Maria. It wasn't exactly welcoming . . . but at least she wasn't yelling at him.

Benito held out his hands pacifically. "I'm trying to reform. Really. Back when Maria met Marco and me, we were both bridge-brats and always in trouble."

Maria snorted. "You were. Marco wasn't. He was a trainee saint even then."

Benito grinned. "Even when he ran off into the Jesolo, after writing love-letters to Angelina Dorma?"

Maria shook her head, a reluctant shadow of a smile coming to her face. "He was a young idiot. He grew up."

"Oh, I agree. About the saint part *and* the idiot part, which he never grew out of. I still love him dearly." He sighed. "And if this wasn't such a hideous situation, I'd wish he was here now."

Maria smiled properly now. "He and Kat are both idiots—at least by your standards, Benito—but I also love both of them very dearly. They're our Alessia's godparents, you know."

"I know," said Benito. "She couldn't ask for better ones."

Umberto beamed on both of them. "Well, why don't you come in and have a glass of wine with us, you being by the way of things a sort of god-uncle to my daughter. Then you can tell us what we can do for you. You have a place to stay?"

Benito had to swallow hastily. He nodded, looking around.

Maria and Umberto's little home was small, Spartan, and lovingly tended, from the simple tablecloth to the little wicker cradle in the corner. Umberto certainly hadn't been able to smother Maria Garavelli in worldly goods. But he'd given her what she'd needed: a home, stability, and a reliable father for her baby. Someone who wouldn't go doing crazy things that might get him killed.

"I have a place to stay, thank you. I just came to pass on Kat's messages. She sends her love to you and to little Alessia. She said I must tell you to write. I also came to offer my help if there was anything useful I could do for you . . ." he finished lamely. It didn't seem like a very good reason for seeking someone out. He looked at the baby and Maria, standing Madonna-like. "She looks well-fed."

"At least you didn't say she looks beautiful like everyone else does," said Maria, tartly. "Here. Hold this well-fed baby while I get the wine." She passed the plump bundle over.

Benito found himself with a soft, milky-breathed baby in his arms. After the initial shock, it didn't feel too bad.

The habited woman on her knees tending the flowers outside the Hypatian Order chapel looked up as Eneko Lopez and Father Pierre approached. "And how can I help you, my sons?" she asked pleasantly.

"We're looking for a Sibling Eleni," explained Pierre.

The Sibling got up, dusting her knees. She had the ageless sort of face, ornamented by bright brown eyes, that Eneko tended to associate with Hypatian Siblings. There was something about the cloistered life that kept age at a distance.

"That is me. Actually, there is only me here. How may I help you?"

Eneko nodded. "It's rather a long story, Sibling, but we have here a letter from the Grand Metropolitan of Rome. We were on our way to Jerusalem, before our ship was diverted here."

The nun smiled. It was clear then, as fine lines appeared around her mouth and eyes, that she was, if not old, certainly no longer young. "If it is a long story, let us go into the chapel. God doesn't mind listening out here, but it is cooler for us there."

She nodded politely at Eneko. "Your reputation and description go before you, *Señor* Lopez. I'm afraid I don't know you," she said to the priest accompaning him.

"Father Pierre," he said simply, smiling.

"Ah." She said nothing else until they were within the tiny chapel, and seated on some stools she brought from the back of the building. "Well, now, how may the Hypatian Order on Corfu serve you? You've come to heathen parts, I'm afraid." She shook her head, but with more fondness than irritation. "The locals attend church faithfully, but I know for a certain fact that many of them continue their worship of a pagan deity. A bloodthirsty goddess of some sort, I suppose. That is, I suppose she is bloodthirsty, because the men seem to hold her in some fear. The women—well, they keep their secrets to themselves."

She sighed. "It's all nonsense, of course, but they are happy in their nonsense, and we try to educate them slowly. The island is simply stiff with such superstitions."

"You would not mind, Sibling, if we enact the ritual of the veil of divine privacy?" Eneko shook himself. "I've just seen two birds of prey high in the sky. I know there is a war on and the hawks and eagles come to feast . . . but I'll swear I've seen those birds following us since we left Rome."

The Sibling spread her hands wide. "You may do as you wish, Father Lopez. You know the Hypatian Order believes strongly in the appropriate use of Christian magic whenever needful."

The chapel was built with a careful alignment to the four cardinal directions. Statues of the archangels Michael, Gabriel, Raphael and Uriel stood on plinths in their corners. Eneko and Pierre set about raising the wards. Soon the distant sounds of the Citadel were shut off inside the veil. It was with a feeling of relief that they returned to their stools.

"We have had scryings both of great deeds and portents of magical conflict here, Sibling," Eneko said, certain now that nothing could overlook him. "Evil in the shape of Chernobog, and an ancient power that we could not identify."

The small Sibling started. "Here? Here on little Corfu? Oh, no, Father Eneko! Nothing ever happens here. The locals talk about magical Corfu, but it is small magics, if there are any at all. Superstitions and mutterings about the Goddess, but never have I seen a sign of great pagan power. There are a few Jews who may be involved. A Strega charm-seller or two. Virtually every hamlet has its so-called wise-woman, who might dabble in birthing spells . . . but that is it."

She shook her head emphatically. "Unless it is something the Hungarian invaders have brought with them, not something from here."

"Hmm. Might we try a scrying?" As an afterthought, Eneko added: "And also a contact spell. If there is any chance of contacting him, Brother Mascoli of St. Raphaella in Venice could pass word to the Venetians about the siege, and perhaps get it relieved."

"Of course, the chapel is yours, Father! I wish I could help you, but I fear that I myself am very unskilled in such matters." The Sibling smiled, but wistfully. "You know that the Order welcomes those with many skills—and there never seemed to be a need for a magician here, so they sent me. I'm better with small children and gardens than I am with great magic. A little magic to make my herbs grow, a soothing spell for a colicky child, that sort of thing. I do not believe these will be of service to you now."

"On the other hand, I could not soothe a child," Lopez felt impelled to tell her. "In fact, I rather think I would give it nightmares. The Lord welcomes all who serve, Sibling."

But a few minutes later, when concentrating on Brother Mascoli's image, Eneko Lopez discovered that now the greater magics were beyond him, too. It was a shock—like reaching for something you knew was there, only it wasn't. Or waking up to find that someone had amputated a hand.

"Look at the archangel Uriel," whispered Pierre, round-eyed.

Eneko turned, slowly, to look. What he was looking at . . . just wasn't there. The golden glow, haloing the statue, summoned by the invocation, was gone. There *was* no Ward of the North.

"We enacted the veil ritual without any difficulty."

"A power great enough to attack an archangel . . ." He took a deep breath and tried to steady himself. "No wonder our scrying didn't work!"

Pierre shook his head. "It's not so much 'attack,' as 'nullify.' It just isn't there."

Eneko Lopez stared at the statue of Uriel. "It can't be the creature of Chernobog; we sent that scuttling. And the archangels were potent enough against him, anyway. Why the keeper of the creatures of the Earth?"

❖   ❖   ❖

Maria watched sidelong to see how Benito took Alessia, waiting to be amused at his awkwardness. To her surprise, there was none. He didn't, as Kat had, hold Alessia as if she was made of fragile porcelain. He didn't, as Umberto did, seem to have a problem knowing what to hold. He took and held her as if it was the most natural of things. He supported her head . . . without being told. And he looked oddly pleased. Not something most men looked when handed a baby.

Maria went into the kitchen, drew a jug of wine, and . . . sighed. At times like this, Benito—

She shook her head firmly, snatched up three wine cups and returned to the outer room.

Benito was rocking Alessia with a peculiar smile on his face. After Maria put down the wine and cups, Benito handed Alessia back to her mother.

"You know, that's the first time I've ever held a baby. They're heavier than they look." He sat down and took the cup of wine that Umberto poured out. "Thank you."

Maria smiled wryly. "And noisier, too. You know, Benito, there *is* something you could do for me. I've been trying to think how to get a message to him since I saw him this morning. Do you know Erik Hakkonsen? Prince Manfred of Brittany's companion? Sort of a bodyguard?"

Benito grinned wryly. "You might say so. He's beaten me, drilled me till I fell over, and made my life a misery for the last ten days or so."

"Oh," she said, sounding disappointed, but with a twinkle in her eye. "Well, then you're probably not the right person to tell him that a Vinlander girl called Svanhild, who was on the ship with us, has waited on Corfu to see him. Her and her two brothers. A whole crew of them, in fact."

Benito jumped to his feet, almost spilling the wine, grinning. "I'll go and find him right away. He's been like a bear with a sore tooth because of this woman—if it is the right woman. Svanhild, you say she's called? I'll go and ask. Where is she?"

Maria lost the twinkle, and sobered. "That's the bad part. She's outside the walls, somewhere on the island.

I forget the name of the count whose villa they were staying in. Oh, wait—yes, Dentico, I think it is."

He stared at her in shock. "Out there? But why aren't they inside? I mean, I thought all the people would have been called into . . ."

Umberto shook his head. "Nobody was called in. See, some of the townspeople and Venetians who got wind of it just happened to be here. The call has to go out from the captain-general. The commander readied the citadel, but when he asked Tomaselli if the cavalry should go out and escort the people in, the captain-general refused permission."

Benito swallowed. "So they're out there—with the enemy burning, raping and looting. And you want me to tell Erik?"

She nodded.

Benito took a deep breath. "Well. I thought he was bad before. But I have a feeling that this is going to be worse. She definitely wanted to see Erik?"

The corners of her mouth went further down. "They waited here on Corfu, getting off the Atlantic convoy, just so that she could see him. She was on the breakwater-head waiting when the Outremer fleet came in because she thought he'd be on it."

"She was in tears because he wasn't on it," added Umberto.

"Oh. Like that, is it?" said Benito. "I got the impression that she'd given him the push."

Maria sighed. "It was a bit of a bit of a misunderstanding. Tell him to come and see me and I'll explain."

Benito swallowed the last of his wine. "In that case, I'd better see if I can find him. Today's been my day for not finding people easily. Thank you for the wine."

Umberto smiled. "It is our pleasure. Come again."

Benito gave a wary look at Maria. "I will . . . If I may?"

Maria snorted. "If you stay out of trouble. Which probably means 'no' in your case."

Benito grinned. "I'll do my best. But I think you've just landed me in it with Erik. Anyway, *ciao*. Good-bye, Alessia." He waved to the baby.

❖   ❖   ❖

Benito walked out and set off in search of Erik, full of mixed feelings. Yes, it hurt seeing Maria, listening to her acerbic tongue. But still, he found himself curiously at peace. He had always regarded babies as good things for other people, something to be personally avoided at all costs. But his heart had gone out to Maria's child. He must think of ways to help her. To help Maria . . . and Umberto for that matter.

The search for Erik was like the rest of his day—a roundabout. Erik was not in his quarters. He was not with the knights who were assembling under Von Gherens's tongue lash. Von Gherens told Benito to try Manfred and Francesca's rooms. It was where, had Benito thought about it, he should have gone in the first place.

He knocked with some trepidation on the door. Manfred, Benito had noticed, was cavalier about the privacy of others, but protective of his own.

The door opened. Manfred grinned down at him. "Ah, Benito. So have you run to earth all the taverns in this place, and maybe some exotic dancers?"

Benito shook his head. "I can't run anything to earth in this place. Besides, I'm trying to stay out of trouble."

Manfred laughed and opened the door wider. "That'll be a shock to the world! A first time, I should think. Come in and have a drink. Francesca won't. She enjoyed the captain-general's liquor so much that she won't touch ordinary armor-polish like mine. And Erik is so crossed in love that I'm keeping him off the drink."

"Um. Is Erik here?"

Manfred nodded. "He is, indeed. In his personal cloud of gloom worrying about the Atlantic convoy and not this siege. Why? Are you in need of some drill?"

Benito hesitated, then realized that *not* telling Erik— immediately—would put him in worse trouble than anything. "I need to talk to him," he said firmly.

"Talk to me, then," said Erik from the corner.

"I thought . . . a private word."

Erik sighed. "I haven't any advice to give you, Benito."

Erik plainly wasn't going to make this easy. "Well, I wasn't really looking for advice. I just heard about a girl called Svanhild—"

Erik crossed the room in a single lunge, picking Benito up by the shirt front. With one hand. "I have enough of this from Manfred. You leave her name out of it. You leave her out of it! Do you hear me?" He put Benito down with a thump against the wall, glaring at him.

"She's looking for you," said Benito, in a kind of undignified squeak. He had the satisfaction of seeing Erik totally rocked on his heels.

"What? Where?" demanded the Icelander. The look of hope in Erik's eyes took away the satisfaction.

Benito took a careful step away. "Erik . . . it's bad news. She's here on Corfu. But she's outside the walls."

Erik sat down. His blue-gray eyes bored into Benito.

But it was Manfred who spoke. "Where do you get this from, Benito? This no subject for your practical jokes." His voice, bantering earlier, was now deadly serious.

Benito held up his hands. "No joke, I swear, I got it straight from Maria and Umberto, who specifically told me to tell you. It's true. Someone called Svanhild from Vinland, who was on the Atlantic convoy, stopped here so that she could wait and see Erik. Specifically. Maria said she had two brothers with her and a number of other Vinlanders. Only they stayed in a villa outside town. Nobody warned them about the siege."

Erik's eyes were still boring into him. It was at times like this that Benito understood exactly why the Holy Roman Emperors relied on Clann Harald for their closest bodyguards. Erik Hakkonsen practically shrieked: *Deadly!*

"Maria, you know . . ." Benito half-babbled. "Er . . . Katerina's bridesmaid—at the wedding!—was on the ship with her. Svanhild, that is. She asked me—Maria, that is—to tell Erik, I swear it. And her husband Umberto confirmed it."

Erik got up, took a deep breath, and gave himself a little shake. "Benito, I owe you an apology."

Benito shrugged and grinned. And paid back the

scores of an entire week of training. "It's nothing. No one expects logic of a man in love."

Then he lost his smile. "I'm sorry that I had to tell you she's out there. You can see fires up and down the length of the Island."

Erik swallowed. "Has she got her bodyguard, her brothers and their hearthmen, still with her?"

Benito shrugged again. "I don't know. I've told you literally all I've heard. Maria said you should come and talk to her about it."

The rangy Icelander put a hand on Benito's shoulder. "Will you take me to her? Please? Now?"

Benito nodded; he'd expected as much. Probably Maria had, too, if Svanhild had been as irrational about this as Erik was.

But if the girl had a pile of brothers and whatnot with her that were like Erik—well, maybe she, and they, were all right. In fact, maybe he was going to feel a little sorry for the invaders.

Manfred turned to Francesca. "I think we'd better tag along as well."

Francesca stood up. "Yes, I'd like to see Maria anyway. I never really got to know her." She raised an eyebrow at Benito. "This is 'your' Maria, isn't it? The one you got into trouble over?"

Benito reddened. "I've got over that now. Umberto Verrier is a very decent man. Gives her what I didn't."

Francesca smiled. "If you can come to terms with that, you've grown up more than most men ever do. Come, Manfred. Erik wants to go."

Manfred took her arm. "Do we need horses?"

Benito shook his head. Horses were one of the aspects of being "promoted" to the *Case Vecchie* that he really could do without. Living in Venice he'd not been on the back of one until he was fifteen. And then he hadn't stayed there for very long. "It's close. Five minutes' walk."

Francesca looked down at her little pearl-fringed Venetian leather shoes and grimaced. "Oh, well. I have ruined the purse that matched them already. Let's go."

Erik was already halfway down the hall, forgetting that it was Benito who would have to show them where to go.

And as they walked, he was constantly having to check his long strides for the rest of them to catch up.

Benito didn't like this at all. It was fairly likely the Icelander's sweetheart had fallen prey to King Emeric of Hungary's forces. Erik was like a loose cannon with a lit wick on a crowded deck. When—if—he found out she'd been hurt or was dead, someone was going to pay in blood.

Probably Captain-General Nico Tomaselli.

Chapter 39

Maria decided that skirting Svanhild's reason for considering her true love ineligible was probably wise. Erik didn't seem to care anyway. All he wanted to do was to get out there and find out if she was all right.

"So you say her brothers and their party stayed with her?"

Maria nodded. "Two of them went on, saying they were going to return to Vinland. But the other fifteen or so stayed with her. Her two brothers included."

Erik shook his head, angrily. "I don't understand why she didn't stay here. The podesta has lots of space up at the Castel *a mar*. He told me that it is quite usual for important or high-ranking travelers to be their guests."

Maria made a face. "Um. She had a clash with the captain-general . . . and instead of sending them to see the podesta, he gave them directions to Count Dentico's villa. They had been trying to find place for a party of sixteen in the town. But Kérkira's tavernas, um, weren't good enough. Apparently."

"The Thordarsons are very wealthy. A powerful family in western trade," said Erik. "Svanhild would expect everything of the best. In a taverna, she would have to share a bed with other women, strangers."

Maria blinked. *Well, of course*, she almost said aloud. After all, what else? You put up in a taverna, you were going to have to share the accommodations with other travelers. That went without saying. Didn't it?

Erik seemed to read her thoughts; but, a bit to her surprise, he didn't react angrily or defensively. He simply shook his head, smiling a little.

"You're not telling me all of what she said, I'm sure, because you think I'd be offended at the thought she found me unsuitable until she learned about Manfred. But I understand her, Maria, and you don't. Well enough, anyway. Vinland's not really that different from Iceland. I lived there myself, you know, for three years."

Maria had forgotten that about him, if she'd ever known. But it explained Erik's skill with that peculiar Vinlander weapon called a *tomahawk,* and with the *skraeling* style of wrestling.

"She's from a very wealthy family," Erik explained softly, "but has no experience with towns and cities. Sent by her family, I'm sure, to find a proper husband. A girl who's known few strange men of any kind—and those, men whose customs she understands. Vinlanders or *skraelings*, who, at least in some ways, aren't all that different."

Manfred was staring at Erik oddly. "You understood all this about her? Then why . . ." He winced.

Erik shook his head. "Clann Harald is true to its oath to the imperial family. Always. I could explain nothing to her, even though it was obvious to me that—"

He waved his hand, curtly. "Ah, never mind. The point here, Maria, is that she's probably never shared a room, much less a bed, with any female she didn't know. She's never been away from home before, and I'm sure in all of the places she's stayed so far, they fell over themselves to give her a room to herself. Here, it's so crowded, not all the money even the Thordarsons have could buy a private room in a taverna."

He sighed. "And her brothers, naturally—you have no idea how protective such men can be, in matters like this—would not have dreamed of asking her to do something so outlandish."

"Well, they did seem to have plenty of money. I suppose you look at things differently when you have that kind of money," Maria said.

Erik nodded, glumly. "She's as far above me as the earth is above the moon."

"Oh, nonsense!" muttered Manfred.

"Oh, nonsense!" Maria snapped the words, like a whip. "She was blubbering about you on the ship. The moment she found out your status was suitable—however those odd Vinlanders calculate such things—she stopped blubbering and tried to *buy* the damn ship to turn it around. I couldn't believe it! Then, when that didn't work, she got off here in order to wait for you. She was down on the dock, every day, watching for the galleys to come in. And her brothers didn't seem in the least unhappy about her interest, either!

"If that helps any," Maria ended, a bit lamely, her voice now less sure of itself. It had just dawned on her that, under the present circumstances, the girl might as well have been on the moon . . . if not further away.

The same realization seemed to have come to Erik as well. He was subdued, now, punctilious in thanks and farewells, but not really there.

Maria watched them go, feeling obscurely sorry for him. The last time she had seen anyone that mad for someone, it had been Kat for Marco . . . Or maybe Benito . . .

She pushed *that* thought away, firmly.

Poor Erik! She felt savage for a moment. And this was all Captain Tomaselli's fault!

Well, if—or when—Erik discovered Svanhild had been hurt, or worse—

Umberto would be getting a promotion again, probably. Could someone be promoted from the Arsenal into the captain-general's job? Eh, it probably wouldn't matter; if the captain-general was dead at the hands of Erik Hakkonsen, and the siege was still on, the captain-general would be whomever the governor said it was, and the governor and his wife both liked Umberto.

Maria closed her eyes, and recalled to herself those huge brothers, and equally huge followers. Maria had never seen Erik Hakkonsen fight herself, but both Kat and Benito had described to her the Icelander's ferocious ability in combat. If these Northlanders were all like that—

Maybe Umberto wouldn't be getting that promotion after all. She hoped so. In fact, she prayed so.

They trudged back up the hill. Now it was no effort to keep pace with the Icelander, which was a pity. An idea was brewing in Benito's head, but he wanted to talk to Manfred about it first.

When they got up to the Castel *a mar*, Erik finally obliged him. Manfred suggested a spot of rapier practice.

Erik shook his head. "I think I want to spend some time alone, Manfred. I've much to think about."

"I'll give you a bout, Manfred," said Benito, as Manfred stared open-mouthed at Erik.

Erik nodded. "You go and give the boy a lesson or two. I'll be in my room, if you need me."

He turned then to Benito. "I am in your debt. I have used you very hard over the last while. Forgive me."

" 'S nothing. I understand," said Benito awkwardly. He'd rather have Erik chewing him out than being like this.

Erik nodded and went into his room.

"Well, let's get the quilted jackets and the buttoned rapiers," said Manfred, far too heartily. "They're with my gear."

When they got to Manfred's chambers, Francesca said, firmly, "Your swordplay will have to wait, Benito. I need to talk to Manfred."

Benito grinned. "So do I. And the truth to tell, all I feel like doing is falling asleep once I'm done talking. I didn't sleep at all last night. The last thing on my mind is rapier practice."

Manfred grimaced. "Except it is *never* the last thing on Erik's mind. I'm worried about him. Up till a couple of weeks ago I'd have thought he'd rather fence than make love to a woman. Cut line, Benito. Talk quickly. I need to discuss this with Francesca."

Benito cleared his throat. "Well . . . I thought . . . A siege, especially with that captain-general in charge, I'm not going to see a lot of action."

He looked pensively at Manfred. The prince had folded

his arms across his massive chest, and was now looking at Benito in the totally expressionless, ox-dumb manner that Benito recognized, by now, as a sign of Manfred in deep thought.

"So I thought . . . Well, I can't do a lot of good here. Maybe I should go to where I can—out there. I'm pretty sure I could swim with the current, using a float of some kind, and come out clear of the troops tonight. I could probably even have them lower a small boat over the walls on the seaward side. Then I could do what Von Gherens was hinting at: raise the peasantry against the Hungarians. And I could also find out what has happened to Erik's girl. It's not likely to be anything good. But he's going to be torn up until he knows."

Manfred's eyes narrowed slightly. "I'll think about it. The captain-general won't approve."

Benito shrugged. "I don't think I really give a damn. But I do need your help to signal back what I find out about the girl."

"I'll think about it," said Manfred. "I'll come and talk to you later. Now go and get that sleep you need. I need to talk to Francesca."

Francesca pointed to a seat. "Actually, I think Benito had better stay. And *no*, Manfred, you are *not* going out there with Benito."

Manfred shook his head. "How the hell did you guess?" To Benito, plaintively: "The woman's a witch, I swear it."

Francesca smiled knowingly. "Your face doesn't give anything away. But I know just how your mind works. The minute you said you'd go and talk to Benito later, I knew just what you were planning. And quite simply: *No*. You can't do it. You, with your rank and the Knights at your command, are the only person who can effectively influence the defense of this Citadel. The captain-general will lose it to the enemy. He's done well enough so far, but he'll swiftly be out of his depth. You are the only one here who outranks him, and you, of everyone, are the only one here who can command the Knights to lock him in a room, if necessary, and take over command. Given how his own men have reacted to his commands,

I do not think you will find a great deal of opposition if you are forced to that action."

She glanced at Benito. "And there is one thing that needs doing a lot more than raising the island's countryside—its rather *little* countryside—against the Hungarians. That is getting news to Venice. In time the news, garbled and distorted, will trickle overland. But unless the two ships that did not take part in this landing manage to get to Rome or Venice—and I doubt they will, now that I've seen the effort Emeric's put into this—help will be many months in coming. It could take a month or two, if the blockade is effective, before the Venetians even realize there *is* a blockade. We'll get you a small boat, a few seamen, and you should go across to Illyria."

"Forget it." Manfred shook his head. "Francesca, I'm barely a mouse to your elephant as far as your knowledge of politics is concerned. But I do have some military acumen, you know."

He grinned. "Even if Erik won't admit it. Look, assuming Benito got across all right, his chances of crossing the Balkans alive are nonexistent. Darling, why do you think a nonmaritime power like Hungary is transporting its troops and weapons by sea? The answer is pretty obvious even to the nonmilitary mind. Emeric is coming by sea because even with an army of tens of thousands he probably couldn't get through the Balkans. There's a fiercely independent Illyrian chief over there named Iskander Beg who is welding the tribes into a nation. And one thing that all those tribes do is kill people who try to pass through their territory. Do you imagine I'd have paid Dorma a fortune for the hire of these four vessels to transport horses if I could have sent them overland? We could have sailed in one vessel, and met them at Constantinople. However, crossing over the Adriatic and going via Rugosa down the old Roman Road to Constantinople is out of the question these days."

Francesca raised a perfect eyebrow. "What was it that Eberhard said to you the other day: 'If all politicians had to be soldiers first, they wouldn't ask soldiers to do the impossible.'"

Manfred shrugged. "He does make good points, occasionally."

Francesca laughed deliciously. "The poor old man. Every time he's getting to approve of you, you do the next rash thing, according to him. But as it happens I don't agree with him."

"Miracle of miracles." Manfred grinned. "Why not? For once he is simply making sense."

"Because it would make for monolithic thinking. All solutions would be militarily influenced, and military men don't always understand how civilians work, either. Anyway, forget Benito for a moment. You, too, Benito. Let's get back to what should be done for Erik."

Manfred, flopped into a chair, making it groan in protest. "I was all for Erik getting over her. Quite honestly, Benito, you and that ex-girlfriend of yours have stirred up something I had hoped would blow over."

Francesca had come to stand behind Manfred. She rubbed his shoulders. Benito couldn't help but notice how small her hands seemed on them. "I don't think it is going to happen quite as you'd like, Manfred dear," she said slowly. "He's a very intense man. A serious one. He is torn between his duty to you and his . . . shall we call it . . . infatuation, with this woman."

"He's stuck here. Fortunately, as far as I'm concerned! Can't we get him another girl to chase? I am not convinced *she's* good enough for *him*. I set high standards for Erik."

Francesca shook her head and smiled. "Manfred, you know as well as I do that that might work for you, but it won't work for Erik. In your company, he has been trailed past more attractive ladies than most men would see in three lifetimes."

Manfred grunted. "And half them wanted that clean-cut face of his. And he didn't notice them at all. No, I suppose you're right, as usual, but the point is that he's still stuck here. She's probably dead by now, anyway."

Francesca patted him. "Too little sleep, that's what it is. Manfred, Erik is an Icelander. He probably has spent more time in small boats than he has on horseback. That means he's as capable of getting out of here as Benito. He is staying here out of loyalty to you and tearing himself apart in the process. Worst of all, for him, is the uncertainty. Erik is one of the most effective warriors alive. He's used to taking initiative. Right now loyalty means he can't."

Manfred flicked himself onto his feet. From reclining to standing in an instant. Benito realized again just how strong the prince was. Not simply strong, as an ox might be, but phenomenally athletic as well.

"Well. No point in that! I'm as safe here as a man can be with three thick walls and a moat around him. Well, sea channel and a small ocean—better yet. Erik should get out there, set his mind at rest and either bring this charmer home or bury her."

Francesca sighed. "For an example of why only ex-soldiers should take part in politics, you've just failed, Manfred. You regard this place as militarily secure?"

Manfred nodded, cheerfully. "It would do better with twice or three times the garrison. With six thousand men you'd be able to hold this place against virtually any force, as long as the food and water held out. But it is not too bad, actually. According to Captain-General Tomaselli, with his forces, our men, the ship crews and the militia we have maybe two thousand men. The food stocks should last that number a couple of years with rationing."

"And yet," said Francesca, "there are at least eleven thousand souls here in this Citadel. Aside from children, that is. Does something not strike you as odd?"

Manfred made a face. "Uh. These guys have four wives each? No wonder they look so dozy. How did you get this figure, Francesca?"

Francesca laughed. "Dozy indeed! I asked the podesta's secretary, Meletios Loukaris. He's a very efficient little Greek. The local eminences fled to the Citadel when the warning came on the night before the attack. Most of them are Corfiotes, the local gentry, people of the *Libri d'Oro* who live in town and have estates in the country. The Citadel refused to allow in arbitrary locals, but in addition to these, some people had chits signed by the podesta. There are nearly six thousand of them. The captain-general is not well pleased with this."

Benito blinked. "You mean he wanted to leave them outside? But . . . this is supposed to be a Venetian protectorate!"

"True," said Francesca, in an absolutely level voice that conveyed as much by its evenness as her normally expressive tones did. "Unfortunately, the Senate did not vote the captain-general a budget to allow siege provisions for the people of Kérkira. Or so my little Greek informant told me."

Manfred bit his knuckle. "Are you telling me this ass is planning not to feed them? They outnumber his troops, oh, nine to one, and he's not going to *feed* them?"

"Fortunately the podesta prevailed on him that this would be foolish. They'll be issued a ration. Smaller than the Venetians, of course. There is no love lost between the locally stationed Venetians and the Greeks."

Manfred shook his head. "How do you find all this out so quickly, Francesca? Here we are sitting on a powder keg waving slow-matches and I thought it was quite safe!"

She smiled demurely. "It is because I am just a woman, and not a soldier."

"You're not ever going to let me forget that, are you?" grumbled Manfred. Insofar as a man could grumble while grinning.

She chucked him under the chin. "No. But I am also not going to let you forget that many more fortresses fall by treachery than by strength of arms. And this fortress, with its divided populace, is probably in more danger than most."

Manfred's eyes narrowed. "It sounds like the captain-general is going to have to go. That could be difficult."

"It's difficult from more than one direction. The Corfiotes themselves reciprocate the feelings the Venetians have about them. They won't cooperate unless their lives are in direct danger." Francesca smiled gleefully. "To think I thought I would be bored during this siege! Manfred, between Eberhard and myself, we will manage the captain-general and keep an eye on the locals. The actual commander of the garrison is quite young, but a better soldier, apparently. Relax. Erik wouldn't be any good at this sort of thing anyway. He might as well go and look for his Svanhild."

She looked consideringly at Benito. "*You*, however, would probably be very useful here, because—"

She broke off, cocking her head a little. "What is happening out there?"

They went out, following the people who were streaming to see what the commotion was about.

The strait was full of sails. Emeric's cannon and the rest of his army had arrived.

Chapter 40

Capitano Da Castres pointed out something else, glumly, quietly: a hulk under tow. "My dapper friend Bortaliscono won't be going to comfort my wife after all."

Benito realized the implication of the burned and battered remains of the great galley. Those messages would not be getting back to Venice by sea. Of course, there was still a chance that the other vessel might have escaped and headed for Rome. But Benito had his doubts of Capitano Selvi, who, if he had managed to evade the blockade, was probably halfway to the Arabic emirates or the Khanates by now.

He turned to Manfred. "If Erik is going to go . . . this means he has to go tonight."

Manfred nodded. "True. By nightfall, Emeric's men will already be getting those cannon into action. By tomorrow night, they will keep up the bombardment. Sneaking out thereafter will be nigh impossible. I'll go and talk to him."

"Also, I think I'd better go with him."

Manfred shook his head. "Francesca wants you here."

Benito took a deep breath, and began his plea. He knew he would have a very limited time to convince Manfred of what he needed to do before it was too late to do it.

"I believe I can get a message back to Venice, Manfred. Francesca is capable of all of her schemes without a little guy like me. I'd rather stay and fight. I'd rather go out with Erik and organize guerillas. But I believe my duty to Venice, to Petro Dorma, is to get back to Venice. Magicians can send word to the fleets, warning them. Venice itself can prepare to relieve Corfu. I believe I've got an idea of how it could be done, without going through the Balkans."

Francesca nodded and smiled. "If you could do that, it would be worth more to us than your skills in fraternizing with lowlifes would be."

"Ha. How come I can't do the fraternizing with lowlifes while Erik is away?" protested Manfred, assuming an expression of hurt. "I've got years of experience!"

Francesca smiled. "Because as a leadership figure we need the people, all the people, to look up to you."

"Spoilsport!" muttered Manfred. "Mind you, Benito mentioned an option I hadn't even thought of: Eneko Lopez." Manfred grinned. "Maybe we can keep your low-life fraternizer here after all. If the clerics can send magical word, the taverns of the Citadel will not have to lose such a valued customer."

Eneko Lopez shook his head tiredly. "No. Magically we are hamstrung. We have tried, repeatedly, together and separately, to invoke the guardian archangels of the cardinal points. One simply does not respond. The angels did . . . once, for a minor magic. Since then we have failed."

Eneko sighed and rubbed his eyes. "I do not know what magical knowledge you have, but this is fundamental. We *must* operate behind our protections. As well for a knight to go into battle having forgotten to armor himself. Still, we ventured on a harmless minor spell to see what would happen. A blessing on the flowers around the church. Magic has a feel to it, Manfred. This was like wading through thigh-deep mud. There is something here, about this place . . . not so much opposition to us, as a simple resistance. In the end, the magic we worked was words. Merely words, nearly without substance."

"Chernobog?" asked Manfred, thinking of the terrible powers they had defeated in Venice. "Or something like that?"

Eneko shook his head, a puzzled frown on his face. "No. I have encountered various nonhuman powers. Chernobog . . . This is as unlike that as is possible. The Black Brain is a violent and malevolent force. It is unlike the Lion of Etruria, too. That has a personality, a shape. This seems amorphous, unfocused—almost as if it had lost its focus, somehow. But one thing is certain: It, too, is our enemy, if only because it does not love us at all." He sighed. "It must however have human agents. We'll try to find those. But I wish I could contact Rome. There are magic-workers in the service of the Grand Metropolitan who are as far beyond my brothers and me as we are beyond a charm-seller."

Benito had never been entirely at ease with the intense cleric, which, considering how they had met, was not surprising. "I'm thinking of trying to get a smuggler or a fishing boat to drop me across on the Italian shore, Father Eneko. I'll make my way overland to Venice. Do you want me to try and deliver any messages?"

Eneko's dour expression lifted. "I will prepare letters. Perhaps . . ."

"I don't think I want anything in writing," Benito interrupted. "I'm going to have to go as a fisherman or a common sailor. I don't want to get searched and have embarrassing things turn up. Dorma will believe me without such evidence."

Eneko nodded. "Yes. I quite see that." He exhaled through his teeth. "Unfortunately, the Grand Metropolitan might respond to something written in my fist, whereas a traveling youngster like yourself is just not going to get an interview with the Grand Metropolitan."

He smiled wryly. "It is difficult enough for high potentates to do so. I think the best possible thing would be for you to proceed straight to Venice. There you could speak to Siblings Mascoli of St. Raphaella or Evangelina of St. Hypatia di Hagia Sophia. Your brother can establish your credentials with the former and Katerina with the latter." Eneko raised the bar of eyebrow again. "I don't think they'd recognize you from your regular visits for counseling."

Manfred's shoulders shook. "If you want messages to

the tap-man at Barducci's . . . that's a priest and a chapel more likely to recognize him."

Eneko cracked a wan smile at this. "This is probably the case of the pot calling the kettle black, Prince."

Manfred shrugged. "Meaning no offense, but the way I see it the average barman has the experience of life to make him a better counselor than the average oblate who has grown into a cloistered monk. Anyway, what do you want Benito to tell these priests? I want him to get some rest before this next stunt of his."

Eneko nodded as Benito yawned copiously. "He should be at his sharpest for such a venture, and he doesn't look it."

"A couple of hours and I'll be fine." Benito yawned again. "I've just got to track down that Corfiote seaman that guided me onto a rock, coming in."

"I'll see to that," said Manfred firmly. "You are heading for bed. Alone, too. Get along with you."

When Manfred spoke like that, one went. So Benito went. Even the thought of the coming venture couldn't keep him awake.

Far above in the blue, two hawks circled.

Bjarni knocked Kari's arm up hastily. The shot ricocheted off the limestone rocks, and Svanhild winced. Thank goodness Bjarni had more sense than the rest of them, or they'd soon be fighting both the locals and the invaders. And the locals knew this area like the rabbits in the rocks did.

"What the hell do you think you are doing, you idiot!"

"But chief, he threw a rock at us!" protested the young Vinlander.

"Of course he threw a rock at us, you mindless fool! And now we'll be lucky if the locals don't shoot at us. You shoot at the Hungarians. They already shoot back. The kids throwing rocks we wave at and shout 'friend, friend!' "

"And when they throw more rocks?" growled Gulta, wiping the blood off his face. "The little devil hit me."

"Duck faster next time," Bjarni said flatly. "If a kid

with a rock can hit you, you aren't paying near enough attention to what's going on. You can't hit anything with wheel-lock pistols anyway, more than a few paces off. And there's no way to use an arquebus on horseback."

But Bjarni's orders were unnecessary. Word must have run up the valleys ahead of them. Nobody threw rocks. And there was nobody they could shout "friend, friend" at either. Locals seeing them ran.

"Maybe we should ride one of them down," suggested Kari. "We could explain afterwards."

Bjarni snorted. "You should be thinking of this as if it were the plains around Cahokia and you were a foreigner chasing your mother's people. This is their place. Their rocks and paths. Ten to one they'd get away from you here. And if they did that, then the fat would really be in the fire. No, we'll find a spot to fort up and sit tight until things settle down. They'll come to us in time."

They rode on. Toward evening they came to a gorge. Kari pointed. "You won't let me shoot rock-throwers. Can I shoot us some dinner instead?"

Bjarni looked up. "Sure. I never was that fond of goats anyway."

Kari missed again. Twice. In the end, laughing, Svanhild used her bow to kill the goat.

Meanwhile, scouting ahead, Gulta had found them a cave. "They use part of it for penning goats. There's another section where we can sleep. It isn't luxury accommodation, but it is better than the houses in the burned-out villages we've passed. At least, the cave's still got a roof. There's a lot of cloud about, too. It looks like it could come on to rain."

"Is it defensible?" Svanhild asked. Other considerations no longer applied.

Bjarni shrugged. "Is anything?"

Manfred knocked on Erik's door. There was no reply. He knocked again, waited, and then was about to turn his heel and leave when Erik said: "Come in."

Erik was seated in a chair by the window staring out. He turned to see just who had come to disturb him, with a look that said it would be the worse for them. "Oh. Manfred. I thought it would be some servant or orderly or something. I've had a chambermaid and a page come looking for you, all in the last hour."

"I've come to talk to you about this Svanhild."

Erik sighed. "Yes. I'm sorry, Manfred. I've let myself be distracted from my task. It's just . . . I wish . . . Well, I can't. I'll try to put it aside. My oath comes first."

Manfred grinned, hiding emotions far from humor. "Besides, as a confrere Knight of the Holy Trinity you are supposed to be celibate and not think such things. Listen, I have talked it over with Francesca and young Benito." Manfred chose his words now with extreme care. "You are sworn by clan-oath to be my personal hearthman. To guard me and also prepare me for the possibility that I might become heir to the throne of Charles Fredrik. To keep me alive. To take appropriate long-term steps to make sure this happens."

Erik nodded, dully. It was a matter of note on his mental state that he did not snap that he knew all of this. "Yes. That is my duty."

"If my bodyguard—you, that is—arrived with a severe chill or was injured—I'd send him to bed until he was well enough to be effective. I'd use another bodyguard if he insisted." Manfred waited for a response.

"I would insist, if I was sick." Erik did not even look indignant.

"Who would you nominate?"

Erik shrugged. "Von Gherens, I suppose. Or Falkenberg, had he not been injured."

Manfred nodded. "I will have both of them. Falkenberg, if he recovers. Because you *are* sick. I'm sending you off to get cured. Benito, a Corfiote seaman and you are taking a small boat out tonight. You will go and see if this sweetheart of yours is alive. Come back when you're well."

Erik gaped at him. And then closed his mouth and shook his head. "I can't do that."

Manfred had come prepared for that. "Your responsibilities go beyond those of some simple day-to-day bodyguard, Erik. You're responsible for my long-term safety. How would you best ensure that?"

"Putting you in a padded cell and feeding you through the keyhole," said Erik, still staring at him.

"Be serious, will you? Besides, Uncle Charles Fredrik said I'm supposed to go to Jerusalem. How would I do that in a cell? The answer is breaking this siege. And the answer to that is getting word back to Venice. And that's exactly what I want Benito to do. But without you he'll probably fail."

Was Erik following all this? It was impossible to tell from that poleaxed look on his face. "Look, his plan relies on sneaking out of here in a small boat lowered from the seaward walls. But the rest of Emeric's troops and cannon have arrived. You can bet Emeric has shore patrols aplenty out now, especially after last night. The boy's a fighter, but he's not in your league. And he doesn't have your experience of small craft. He's Venetian, but a city-dwelling landsman, really."

Now, finally, he was getting a reaction out of Erik; the Icelander nodded, slightly. Manfred went in for the kill.

"But the crunch is that he's got to move overland by night to a fishing port, well away from here. The boy can move around a city like a ghost. But I don't think he's ever been outside a city. He'll get killed for sure if you don't go along with him. Once you've got him safe—you can give your time to hunting for Svanhild." Manfred paused. "But Erik . . . my friend, you do know what usually happens to beautiful young women when an army invades."

Erik nodded. "Yes. She may be dead, or she may be raped and enslaved. But . . . I have to know." He sighed. "I'm sorry. I can't accept your logic. What you say about Benito and a message to Venice makes excellent sense, even if you are using it as an excuse. But I can't desert my post."

"Oh, for heaven's sake!" Manfred sat down on the bed. It complained. Beds generally complained when Manfred sat on them. "I didn't want to do this. I've lugged this around since Venice."

Manfred hauled a letter out of his pouch. It was plainly much traveled. He unfolded it. "Here. Come and have a look at this. Uncle Charles Fredrik sent it to me when things started to unravel in Venice."

Erik came over. The letter dangled half of the seal of the Holy Roman Empire. The sprawling spidery handwriting was unmistakably that of the Holy Roman Emperor himself.

"Read from the top of this paragraph," commanded Manfred.

Erik did.

Manfred, The most valuable coin the House of Hohenstauffen has is loyalty. The house has no coin of a larger denomination than the loyalty of Clann Harald. The reason is simple: they owe their loyalty not to the Empire, or the Emperor. They owe it to us. The Hohenstauffen. The Clann have repaid their debt to the Hohenstauffen many hundreds of times over. Yet they still answer the call. Why, nephew? First, it is because they're raised and bred to it. They're a very honorable house, even by the standards of a very honorable society. But that is the lesser of the reasons. The reason is that they are our friends—because we are as loyal to them as they are to us. Always remember that. An Imperial house has very few true friends. They are more valuable to us than to ordinary folk for that reason. In every generation the time has always come when we, the Hohenstauffen, must put that friendship, that loyalty to our friends, above all other obligations. Do not fail me in this, Manfred. When the time comes, you will place Erik's interests above your own. I order this. Do not fail me or our house.

"I'm not going to fail him," said Manfred grimly. "You *will* be on that boat this evening. This is not a matter of duty, Erik. It is a matter of friendship. I won't see you dying by inches in front of my eyes with your heart somewhere over those walls."

Erik stood up, came to stand before Manfred and put his hands on Manfred's shoulders. "Thank you," he said, gruffly. "I was . . . not happy when the summons came for me to come to Mainz to serve. Willing, because it is our sworn duty. But not happy. Our regard for the Empire isn't high in Iceland, or Vinland either for that matter. My father said something to me then that I didn't understand at the time. He said: *You will find it is not service.*"

Manfred felt those powerful long-fingered hands squeeze his shoulders. "I understand now. You have been a friend for some time now. I just hadn't understood. If I have sons . . . I will send them to learn this, too. The Clann Harald are loyal to their oath. They are also loyal to friends. *Linn gu Linn.*"

The emotion in that voice told Manfred that his uncle had been perfectly right. Manfred also knew that buying loyalty wasn't his reason for doing this.

Manfred stood up, and put an arm around Erik. He felt emotion thickening his throat and voice, and didn't try to stop it. "Wouldn't have mattered a bugger what Uncle Charles Fredrik said anyway. You need to go. You're going. I've made up my mind."

Erik took a deep breath. "Very well. Under certain conditions, which you will swear to me. First, Von Gherens will become your constant bodyguard. Second, you will not leave this fortress, unless I return or the siege is lifted. You will not make it a repetition of the affair of the Red Cat. You will *not* come after me. Promise me this."

Manfred was intensely grateful that Erik had not been there when Francesca had explained just how insecure the Citadel really was. "If there is a sally, I must lead the knights, Erik. You know that yourself. And this is a siege—God knows what will happen if Emeric breaks through. But within those limits . . . I'll swear. My Oath on it."

"If there is a sally. But don't stretch it." Erik took a deep breath. "Manfred, I didn't think you understood what it meant to be in love with someone. Thank you. Thank you from the bottom of my heart."

That didn't make Manfred feel much better about Svanhild. But all he said was: "Well, let's go and organize a small boat and see if we can find that Corfiote sailor who doesn't know the draft of a great galley."

Chapter 41

Sitting under a tasseled awning in front of his tented pavilion, King Emeric regarded the Citadel in the growing dusk. Oxen had proved more of a problem than he'd anticipated. The islanders seemed to rely heavily on donkeys. Unfortunately, the heavy forty-eight-pound bombards really needed teams of oxen to move them. And the cannon of the Citadel and the island of Vidos commanded the deep-water landings for some distance. The carracks had too deep a draft to bring them in the way that those bedamned galleys had run up the beach. The bigger guns were too heavy and too unwieldy to unload onto lighters and bring in. They needed a dock, a quay next to which the ships could tie up.

Unfortunately, the nearest spot they'd been able to find was the village of Patara, nearly a league away. Emeric had had his cavalry scouring the countryside for oxen, or even mules, to move the guns. And now to make matters worse, it looked like rain. He was scowling ferociously when the senior Byzantine captain of the seven carracks that had just come in from Constantinople arrived. The Greek saluted smartly.

"Well, Captain?"

"Sire, the Venetian Outremer Convoy had arrived in Negroponte before we left. They should be on their way to the Golden Horn by now, except for the vessels heading for the Holy Land."

"While that is good news, I wanted to know if you'd brought the supplies Alexius agreed to provide. And why you are late?"

The captain bowed. "Contrary winds, Sire. And this morning we met, engaged and captured a Venetian great galley. I have her captain and most of her crew prisoner."

The captain cleared his throat. "They were carrying certain dispatches addressed to the Doge, the Grand Metropolitan and the Holy Roman Emperor. The captain, one Bernardo Selvi, pleaded for his life, saying he could give you valuable information. He has agreed to cooperate fully with us. I have promised him his life in return, Sire. He told me he was part of a charter for Prince Manfred of Brittany, and some two hundred Knights of the Holy Trinity, going to Jerusalem. They were on board their four vessels when they were attacked by a combined fleet of Dalmatian pirates and carracks bearing your banner. He said the others plan a night landing, perhaps at the very Citadel itself."

"Your news comes a little too late, Captain," Emeric said grimly. "Nonetheless I will see the prisoner and the letters he was transporting. Have them sent up to me."

The Byzantine saluted crisply again. "At once, Sire. And where and when shall I have my men land the food supplies?"

Emeric smiled his thin-lipped, crooked, and utterly humorless smile. "Vessels are discharging about a league away at a village called Patara. See the goods get handed over to my quartermaster there, see you don't get in the way of my cannon being off-loaded, and see I get the prisoner and his letters very, very fast."

"Sire!" The Byzantine saluted and left at a half-run.

Emeric, for the first time since the galleys had arrived that morning, felt something akin to pleasure. He enjoyed seeing Byzantines run. And the fact that the Holy Roman Empire's best troops were here purely by accident, caught up in this because they were on their way to Jerusalem, was excellent news. He must tell his spymasters to stop searching for the leak in his security.

Four men-at-arms from the Byzantine vessels and a

prisoner, shackled neck-and-legs, arrived shortly thereafter. The prisoner was an elderly, slightly stooped man with a wattled chin. He fell on his knees before Emeric. "Spare me, Your Majesty. Spare me, I beg you," he wept.

Emeric stood up, put his hands on either side of the man's head, and forced him to look him in the eyes. He hardly needed to do anything; the Venetian was already crying with fear. Still, there was more to exerting his power than simply the need to cow.

"But of course, my dear chap. Provided you tell me what I need to know."

He blinked, and released a spell. A bolt of searing pain shook the captive. His back arched and he fell over backwards. The Venetian captain lay there on the ground gibbering, whimpering and crying. Emeric ignored him and held out his hand to the escorts. "The letters."

Hastily one of the men fumbled open a leather message pouch and handed the king the three letters. Two were sealed with the Imperial seal of the Holy Roman Empire, and addressed to Emperor Charles Fredrik and Doge Petro Dorma, respectively. The other was addressed to the Grand Metropolitan in Rome. Emeric walked to his desk, a particularly fine ivory-inlaid escritoire, pulled a stiletto out of a drawer and carefully cut the seal away. He walked closer to a multi-wicked lamp and read the letter, his smile growing more feral all the while. A prince of the Empire, no less—now, within Hungary's fist.

The king turned back to the Venetian captain still kneeling on the floor. "You will explain the purpose of this voyage. You will also tell me about this prince, or I will give you more pain. If you do well, I will reward you with my mercy."

When Selvi had done, Emeric called to his guards. "Take him out there and crucify him next to that fool who brought me news of the lost troop."

"You promised me mercy!" screamed the captain.

Emeric shrugged. "I lied."

Sophia Tomaselli looked nervously about. Despite the hooded cloak and the lateness of the hour, she really didn't want to be found here. The address, given to her in the strictest confidence by Bianca Casarini, was not a part of the Citadel she'd ever visited before. The poorer houses down inside the outer curtain wall were not in a place she would have admitted knowing even existed.

But she'd try anything. Now, especially, with her husband Nico's status likely to rise because of the siege.

Anything. She'd already tried at least twenty potions. All that they had done was to make her sick. She'd tried everything from saints' bones to amulets that made her clothing smell faintly of dead rat. She'd even, on Bianca's advice, tried a different man. She snorted at the thought. The young cavalry commander Querini thought he was the world's greatest lover. His breath smelled of onions. Then there'd been the long, nervous wait, to find her courses ran as normally as ever. And now she had to put up with a stream of lewd suggestions from the fool Querini.

She knocked on the dingy door, glancing hastily around to see if there was anyone in sight. The street was deserted, as far as she could see anyway. She knocked again, slightly harder.

The door swung open. At first glance the man standing there was not very impressive. She'd expected robes, not ordinary clothes. He was tall and stooped, and framed against the light his hair was sleeked and perfectly ordered. The most occult thing about him was a rather neat beard. "S . . . signor Morando?"

He nodded, cocked his head inquiringly, and said in a voice which was just faintly sibilant. "You have the advantage of me. Who are you and why have you come here?"

"S . . . signorina Casarini said you might be able to help . . ."

Bianca Casarini's name acted like a magical talisman. The man beamed. "Come in, signora." He ushered her forward respectfully, closed the door behind her. "And how may I help you, signora? Potions to draw a lover? To inflame passions? Perhaps to deal with some unfortunate consequences?" He rubbed his long hands.

"I want something to assist fertility. Not quack potions."

He looked at her thoughtfully, but didn't say anything.

"Please!" she said. "I'm desperate. I can pay well."

"There are certain rituals. You understand, they are frowned on by the Church?"

She laughed bitterly. "The Church hasn't exactly helped me so far. And they're a lot richer for not helping."

He nodded slowly. "Very well. Wait here. There are certain preparations I must make."

By the time he returned he looked far more like her idea of a practitioner of the black arts, right down to the robe. His eyebrows flared satanically and his beard and mustachios were now waxed to sharp points.

"Come," he said. "The sacrificial chamber is prepared. You must now be prepared. I must blindfold you."

Part of Sophia filled with fear at the idea of "sacrifice." But there was a guilty fascination too.

Stepping out into the cold street, Sophia wasn't too sure what time it was. Her head was still mazed from the liquid in that chalice—or perhaps from the smoke in that room. She would have to wash her hair to get rid of the smell of it. Next time . . . and she felt the compulsion to admit there would be a next time—she must make sure she was dressed in something easier to remove. She would have to undress herself until the symbols he'd painted on her washed off. She could feel them. They seemed to have a heat of their own.

She stumbled. It was very dark, and a fine rain had begun to fall. She put out a hand to keep in contact with the wall. She heard the sound of footsteps. A number of people. She shrank back against the buildings, until they passed. At least six men. One, even in the darkness, loomed huge. They were carrying something between them, and they didn't notice her.

After they were well gone, Sophia continued hastily on her way home. Whatever those men were up to it was bound to be no good. But there was no way she could report it, without implicating herself. Thank heavens for Bianca's wild ways. She had told Sophia which guards were susceptible to bribes.

✧   ✧   ✧

Sitting back in a comfortable chair, the black robes thankfully tossed off, and a glass of ouzo in hand, Aldo Morando grinned sharkishly. He'd hooked a big one tonight. A very big one. Did the wife of the captain-general think, honestly think, he wouldn't recognize her? Even if his accomplice Bianca Casarini hadn't told him she'd be coming, he'd have recognized Sophia Tomaselli.

Morando had been many things in a long and varied career. Pimp. Spy. Procurer. Seller of "saints'" relics. Seller of shares in *Colleganzas* that were remarkably lacking in substance. And latterly . . . magician.

He would never have believed the number of wealthy idiots just dying to pay over good money for some wicked thrills. Particularly women with too much money and too much time on their hands. With husbands who had long sought mistresses, or were much away. Of course things could get a bit hot with the Church, and with injured husbands, from time to time, which was why he had been obliged to leave the Italian mainland. Corfu, he had been sure, would be far enough away. He'd been dismayed, at first, seeing Bianca Casarini here, but she was proving to be a remarkably good accomplice for him.

He put down his glass and gazed cheerfully at the stack of ducats on the table. Besides that, Sophia Tomaselli would be a mine of information. Very valuable information in the right hands, and he knew where to find those hands. To think he'd been angry about the siege. Well, he was now sure that he wouldn't go hungry, and the opportunity for pleasure as well as profit—she wanted to get pregnant, after all, and she wasn't bad-looking—was considerable.

A tall graveyard poplar grew flush against the cliff that was topped by the old Byzantine fortress. The cliff beside it was too high and too steep to make the tree any threat to the integrity of the fortress. The tree itself was, in the fashion of the plant, densely packed with small branches. Attempting to climb it would have been folly, anyway: The thin branches would cascade the climber down again.

About twenty-five cubits up, the branches masked a narrow gash of an opening into the cliffs. If you ascended the ladder, and then walked back along it, the cave widened considerably into a labyrinth of passages. Once, many years ago, these would have acted as one of the defenses of this place. Now you just had to follow the most worn path in the stone. It had taken the passage of many feet over many long years to wear away the stone, to round and smooth the steps. The sacred chamber was lit by a small oil lamp. Right now all was silent except for the steady slow trickle and splash of the fountain that fed the holy pool between the two altars, the great Goddess's altar and the smaller, darker one.

The white half-almond lay on the black stone. Waiting, for someone to come and take it up, and all that it represented. Behind the larger altar, half-hidden in the shadows, was the image of the Goddess Herself. It towered over the altar and it was old, old—older, some said, than the island itself. It did not look anything like the graceful statues of the great Grecian sculptors from the island's glory days. It was not even anything like those earlier images, stiff and rigid, with fixed, staring eyes and jutting breasts like twin mountain peaks. No, this was more like a pile of boulders, round-headed and faceless, with the merest suggestion of hair and of arms and legs, and enormous, sagging breasts and belly, the hallmark of fertility and plenty. And there was, if you looked at Her long enough, the suggestion of a faint haze of gold about her, and the feeling that She was looking back at you, out of her eyeless face.

The two women came in, one sweeping the old, dried leaves before her, the other strewing the new leaves. When the chamber was prepared, the two acolytes went to lower the ladder. Few would come tonight, for it was raining so hard that it would be difficult to come and go undetected. Here, in the middle of the Venetians, there were few devotees anyway. But this was the second oldest temple on the island, a place where the life-flame had been kindled many thousands of years ago. The temple had always had at least a holy mother and three or four devotees.

The priestess had not expected a group larger than three or four. But as she stepped out of the shadows she saw that tonight, despite the rain, there was an unfamiliar face, a comfortably middle-aged woman.

The priestess saw with a twinge of disappointment that the newcomer was beyond child-bearing age, unfortunately. Months had passed, and there was still no one willing to take up the almond. The rains had come, the crops—if the invaders left anything of them—would be no worse than usual, but this could not last forever.

Not for the first time, the priestess wondered how much of this was because of the Christians and their priests. For centuries, She and they had lived, if not in harmony, at least not in conflict. But just after the death of the last bride, the priestess had sensed that there was something inimical to the Goddess that was searching for the source of Her power.

Shortly after that, the attacks began. And shortly after *that* the four stranger-priests had arrived, and the two hawks that were the eyes for the hostile power. Was it coincidence? It hardly seemed possible, and that was especially so once the priestess had learned that these four priests, and their leader in particular, were closely linked with the Grand Metropolitan of Rome.

True, they had close ties to the Hypatian Order, which, unlike the Servants of the Trinity, were not known for the persecution of those who were pagan. In fact, it had been the Hypatian Siblings that had dwelled here quietly for so very long. But this particular priest had a reputation for militancy that was not typical of the Order. And directly after arriving here, he had attempted to work magic.

She had put a stop to that, needless to say. No one worked magic upon this island without Her approval. But how long could that hold? Great and evil powers were being bent against Her, to usurp Her Power, and without a bride, the Cold God could not defend Her.

The priestess drew her thoughts back to the ceremony, and the new woman who had come. After purification and the rituals she must speak with her. But now the withered bay leaves swept up from the floor must be fed to the life-flame.

The women repeated the old, old words. "Out of death there is new life."

It was, as the priestess suspected, someone from outside the walls. She had known this would come; to an extent, she was only surprised that it had taken this long. The captain-general was not, by nature, a cruel man, but he was a foolish one to think that he could demand the labor and allegiance of the populace and not assume the responsibility for them.

And attempting to close the gates against those who deserved shelter here was nothing but an exercise in futility, as the presence of this woman showed.

"My brother is with the boatyard. The sea took my Yani three years ago. My daughters are married. My sons are at sea," the woman said, simply. "My brother is here. The captain-general refused to allow the men to bring their families. But the men brought us in anyway, by the boatyard gate. There are several of the timber-sheds that are not in use, and now that the Hungarians are outside the walls there is nothing happening in the Little Arsenal anyway. It is crowded, but it is safer than outside." She sighed. "Why does the Goddess allow these *Xenos* to trample our soil?"

"Men's business, my daughter. We do not make war, and they do not make children. Invaders come and go, but the Goddess remains."

She did not speak aloud the question that was in her own mind.

. . . *for how long?*

Caesare Aldanto walked past the man who had been crucified upside-down outside King Emeric's tent as if he wasn't there.

Emeric was sprawled in his gilded and gemstone-encrusted throne. Aldanto bowed mechanically. "You wished to see me?"

Emeric stared at the blond man. He stood up, and put his hands on Aldanto's throat. "You interfered with the admiral of my carracks and sent them north in pursuit of four vessels. You interfered and used my name to direct the Dalmatians in an attack on the same vessels. We lost a number of the galliots. According to my admiral you have only captured one of the Venetian vessels. Why should I allow you to live?"

Emeric allowed the pain to flow from his hands into his intended victim. But Caesare Aldanto didn't scream and writhe. He didn't even blink. He answered in the same calm voice that he'd used earlier.

"Because I had credible information that they were coming to the relief of Corfu. The ships had Knights of the Holy Trinity on board, including, according to our captives, Prince Manfred of Brittany. I considered that you would wish them sunk rather than at large on Corfu. There were also a number of powerful and dangerous magicians on board. We were not aware of that. That is why three of the ships escaped."

Emeric was somewhat shaken by the lack of response from the blond Milanese man; it took him aback, and left him thinking madly down directions he would rather not have gone. There could be little doubt now—Aldanto was indeed a puppet-man. He stepped back. Always before, he'd known his power stood between him and any threat of a knife-wielding assassin. With this man . . . he was potentially in his enemy's grasp. He had no doubt at all that Grand Duke Jagiellon was indeed his enemy, even if their purposes ran in the same direction for now.

Or could this be a trap?

Then logic reasserted itself. Jagiellon's man would hardly have risked his position and Emeric's displeasure if Jagiellon did not desperately wish the Knights to be sunk at sea.

"I was not told about the prisoners," said Emeric, moderating his tone by a degree or two. "Why have they not been brought to me?"

Aldanto shrugged. "Ask your admiral. But in truth only a handful of seamen were captured. The captain elected to remain with his vessel and blow her magazine up when she was boarded. The captives were taken from one of her small boats. The charges failed to sink her, but there were considerable losses among our boarders."

PART VI
May, 1539 A.D.

Chapter 42

"It strikes me very much as a conspiracy," said Eberhard. "I agree with your assessment, Francesca, but of course it is still likely to place us in very bad favor with the governor—the podesta, as they call him—and the captain-general, if and when the messages get through."

Manfred shrugged. "What they don't know, their hearts won't grieve over. Besides, Francesca has already cleared it with the governor."

Francesca looked innocent. Too innocent, Benito thought. "He's an old dear, but quite ineffectual. The conduct of war or siege is officially the military's business. However, I did ask him if the prince might be allowed to send messages to the Emperor. He said it was hardly something he could refuse permission for, but that it was of course impossible at the moment. I smiled and thanked him."

"Well, I suppose if the messenger happened to go via Venice, you could hardly blame him for telling the authorities about the situation here," said Eberhard with a perfectly straight face. "How are your preparations going, by the way?"

Manfred grimaced a little. "Well, the early morning detail guarding the outer wall was easy enough to organize. Our men are tired but still wish to do their part in the defense of the Citadel. The boat . . . well, that's the reason I suggested to Francesca we might have to go to the captain-general. I've tried to find one to buy, without making a great to-do about it. But this isn't Venice, you know. Most of the boats in the Citadel belong to the shipyard. Of course there were lots of fishing boats out in the town. But they're rather far out of reach."

Francesca tilted her head to the side. "And I said, you and Benito should perhaps go and talk to Maria and her husband."

Benito shook his head. "Maria would give us a shipyard vessel in the blink of an eye. But Umberto—well, he's a good fellow, but he's a rules and regulations sort of man."

"He might still know someone with a boat to sell." She looked consideringly at Erik and Benito. "I think we need to think about your appearances, also. You can't go like that."

Benito caught on immediately. "I look as if I could possibly be a local. But Erik wouldn't pass in the dark. We'll need hair dye and old clothes."

"Something to stain Erik's skin too," said Francesca, looking pointedly at both hair and skin.

"I'm not planning to go passing as a local," said Erik, a little stiffly. "I'll stick to the hills and forest patches. These Hungarians won't even see me. I might blacken my face for the night-work. . . ."

Francesca smiled. "She'll still love you even if you're dark-haired, Erik. And never mind the Hungarians. It's the locals who will run from a blond-haired man, and you will need them if you are to find her, I suspect. We've got a map of how to get to Count Dentico's villa, but they might easily have moved out. You'll have to get directions from the locals. It won't help that you can't speak Greek and will frighten every local silly."

Erik shook his head. "How do you cope with her always being right, Manfred? I have a little classical Greek, but the language has changed."

"Get used to it," said Manfred with a grin. "It's usually easier to say they are right even if they're patently wrong." He ducked hastily.

Francesca just raised an eyebrow.

"That is a real danger signal," said Manfred. "It means

it's being saved up. I'm just trying to further his education, Francesca."

"I'll just save that up, too," she said, with a thin smile. "Now, let's go down and talk to Umberto and Maria. There will be people selling things here in the Citadel, and Maria will know where."

Von Gherens looked speculatively at Benito. "The other thing you'll need to get him is a knife. He can't carry a Ferrara *main gauche* that would cost a fisherman five years' earnings, and a rapier's right out."

Benito gritted his teeth. Changing out of *Case Vecchie* clothes was something he was actually looking forward to, although he knew his feet would find being shoeless a painful experience. Going without his rapier and his beautifully balanced dagger would be a lot harder. He didn't feel dressed without at least the *main gauche*. But Von Gherens was right; he knew that from his time as a bridge-brat. One look at his *main gauche*, and even an idiot would know he wasn't what he was supposed to be.

Erik grinned. "And I suppose you'd like me to leave my new hatchet behind too? It's not a patch on my Vinland one, but the swordsmith at Mainz didn't seem to understand me clearly enough."

The scar-faced old Prussian *Ritter* sniffed "I think he probably thought you wanted it for chopping firewood, not having seen you use that barbaric thing. The Hungarians probably won't recognize it either. Until it's too late."

Erik nodded. "I can relieve them of anything else I need. And I think I've got a knife for you, Benito, in with my gear. It's better than any cheap local blade, anyway. I'll dig it out for you. It's a Shetland islander's knife. It's very plain. Could pass for a fisherman's tool, but it's good steel and well balanced."

"I'd have to get permission before selling you a boat," said Umberto, worriedly.

"Do you know of anyone who has one to sell?" asked Erik delicately.

Umberto shook his head. Then put up a finger. "It's not strictly a boat . . . but one of the Corfiotes who does some work for the Little Arsenal has his coracle stored down at the shipyard. He'd probably sell, right now. I don't see him using it for a while."

Maria, however, seemed enthusiastic about the project. "And clothes and dye for Erik's hair . . . Well, there is Fianelli. He sells secondhand goods. I wouldn't look too hard at where they came from, 'Nito, but that won't be any shock to you. He's got some quack medicines and stuff too. I wouldn't be surprised to find some dye there. I'll go along if you like. And green walnuts will do for skin color."

She looked at Benito. "You came to wish me farewell and Godspeed. You're doing the kind of mad thing you like doing best. I'll wish you the same. At least you're doing it for a good cause and not your usual damnfool reasons."

Benito grinned. "And you and Umberto take care too, especially of my god-niece."

Maria scowled fiercely at him.

Fianelli had what Benito was looking for. After he left, Benito muttered to himself: "Good thing Erik didn't come along with me. That man practically stinks of foulness. If he knew an obvious non-islander was trying to leave the Citadel, he'd try to sell the information. Me, he just thinks I'm seeking a disguise for an assignation."

That was, in fact, exactly what Fianelli thought. It never occurred to him to warn his master Emeric that an escape was being planned from the Citadel. Within a day, he'd forgotten all about the sale. Fianelli sold a lot of stuff.

Unfortunately, it didn't occur to Benito to warn anyone about Fianelli, either. Benito had run into a lot of foul men in his short life, after all. And while he'd learned a lot about sieges from Falkenberg, he really hadn't fully absorbed yet one of Francesca's lessons: *More fortresses fall by treachery than by strength of arms.*

By midnight it had started to rain. A scruffy, tousle-haired, barefoot young man and a tall, dark-haired, plain-clad, and very dark-faced man were standing in front of Francesca for inspection. "Your hair's too clean, Benito. Remember you've got Manfred's seal there."

Manfred grinned. "He's the scruffiest personal letter I ever sent."

Benito grinned in reply. "You had to drop the sealing-wax on my ear, didn't you? Black wax is hotter than red."

Francesca had a close look at the tangle of black curls around Benito's ear. "It certainly isn't easy to find. Won't Count Von Stemitz be a trifle surprised? Give him my best regards by the way, when you see him."

Hiding coin had been a bigger problem. Benito had some ten ducats in smallish change. Too much would attract suspicion. Too little and he wouldn't be able to afford to live, never mind travel. He had a battered pin in his scarf, which might possibly once have been silver, and looked like plated brass from which the plating was rubbing off. No one would look too hard at such a tawdry thing. Except . . . The cheap stones that had been in it had been replaced with two good rubies, mounted in so hard you would have to break the thing to get them out, and had a liberal coating of dirt reapplied. It looked like rubbish. Benito wouldn't have bothered to steal it himself when he'd been a bridge-brat. The stones, cleaned up, would fetch a good thirty ducats each, even from a fence.

Benito was barefoot. In a ragged waist-sash, he carried a plain knife with a small brass guard and a cord-bound handle.

In all, Benito looked the part. Erik didn't. His face shape was just wrong. Too angular; his hair was too straight and too fine; and his eye color was a sure giveaway.

Francesca shook her head. "I think this is a lost cause. Maybe we could curl his hair . . ."

"I could break his nose for him," offered Von Gherens, feeling his own skew organ set in his burn-scarred face. "Always makes a man look different, that."

"Thank you," said Erik, putting his hand protectively over his threatened nose. "You are well suited to body-guarding Manfred."

"I think you should just wear this woolen hat," said Francesca decisively. "And keep away from people if you can. Claim a passing sailor got you on your mother. That could account for the looks."

Erik smiled. Now that he was actually going to look for Svanhild, he seemed imperturbable; strangely at peace and at ease. "Why, thank you, too, Francesca."

Manfred grunted. "It's barely a cockleshell, Erik. If the wind comes up you'll be swamped in moments."

Benito agreed with Manfred, but they'd had some trouble finding a boat, quietly.

Erik didn't seem perturbed, however. At the moment nothing seemed to perturb Erik. The Corfiote seaman had refused, even for a considerable bribe, to guide them out. His first experience of being under fire, and the new troops arriving in the carracks, had frightened the bravado out of him. When he'd refused, Erik had just shrugged, asked a few questions, and proceeded as planned. The arrival of several more ships from the south at sundown hadn't worried him. Even the skin and withy coracle, normally used to hold a caulker working around a larger vessel, was fine by him.

"It's light enough to lower down the wall, Manfred. And the sea out there is not the Atlantic."

"Still looks like a cockleshell. And I wish you had your armor on."

Erik chuckled. "Von Gherens, this is what you'll have to deal with. One minute, I'm going to capsize. The next I should wear armor so I can drown when I do capsize. Stop worrying, Manfred. Next thing you'll want me to take a horse in the cockleshell, and wood for the signal fires."

"He's just jealous because he doesn't want to sit inside a fortress under siege while you're out there," said the older *Ritter*. "And don't worry, Hakkonsen. We'll keep him here."

"You're not savvy enough to be let out on your own," grumbled Manfred.

Erik smiled, a flash of teeth in the darkness. "I'm not dealing with the political infighting in Mainz, or tavern or brothel brawls, Manfred. I'll be fine out there. There's a lot of wild country; I cut my teeth in wilderness like this. You worry about Benito. He doesn't know how to move in it. Now let us go. I want to get moving while we still have a chance to get out without detection."

The rock wall was wet with the rain, feeling greasy underfoot. Manfred, along with several knights who were on guard on the outer wall, lowered Benito down first. From their daytime scouting Benito knew there was a little sill down there, just before the water. He felt for it on the rain-slick rock with his feet. Once he was down, Benito whistled up, and freed the rope. The ledge was less than a cubit wide. It sloped toward the sea and it was rounded. Benito was used to the pan-tiles of Venice, but this was even slipperier; it was like being on icy roof-tiles.

Erik nearly landed in the water as a result. His feet scrabbled for a purchase, and Benito put a steadying hand on his arm. "You're supposed to be looking after me," he hissed, as Erik cursed softly. "Anyway the rain should make it easy enough to paddle out of here."

The coracle came down next and it nearly had both of them off the ledge. And of course it was farther to the water than they'd realized from above. You couldn't just jump into a hide-and-wicker boat, either. Still, with care and patience they managed to board; each of them took a paddle, and they set off onto the dark water.

Maria stood back in the shadows, rain dripping from an eave above her. She didn't really know why she'd slipped out so late at night. She couldn't absolutely guarantee that Alessia would stay asleep—although she'd timed her feeds very carefully for this. Umberto wouldn't wake for anything short of the last trump. She'd wanted to say "good-bye, good luck, and don't be an idiot" to Benito, but there wasn't an opportunity. All she could do was watch him and the dark shape that was Erik go over the wall.

He hadn't even known she was there. She turned and walked back into the dark, feeling a little frightened, and very depressed. This might be the last time she ever saw him, and she hadn't really seen him at all. She wanted to let him know—

—what?

Maybe it was better this way. She had Umberto, who was good for her, and good to her, and she hoped she was being good to him. Benito could never be other than what he was, and it would do no good for him to know what she still felt.

She must have gotten a bit lost in the streets as she was lost in her own thoughts, for when she looked up she realized that she was not where she thought she was.

She took her bearings by the bulk of nearby buildings. There was St. Agatha, the Hypatian chapel, and she knew then that she had gone a little too far. Just as she was about to turn back, she caught sight of a flicker of light.

Someone was coming.

She leaned back against the wall, feeling a shock of apprehension, the kind of thing she used to feel back in Venice when she prowled the canals at night, waiting to be caught in her smuggling by the Schioppies.

But it was only two women talking quietly in Greek. Maria's Greek was still limited. The only word she could catch sounded like "Goddess." It was an odd time to be out, and an odd coincidence to see people. Well, less of a coincidence than all that. If anyone was going to go down to the houses inside the outer curtain wall this was the only road they could follow. Perhaps these were the wives of Arsenal workers or militia, or even guards, back from bringing them something to eat. After the women had gone by Maria proceeded back on her way, crept into the house, and bolted the door quietly. She slipped out of her wet things, rubbed her hair dry and left the wet clothes in the kitchen. Then, crept quietly up the stairs. She stopped and checked on Alessia, and slid into bed next to Umberto.

But sleep was a long time coming.

Chapter 43

Out on the sea in the darkness, Benito was getting a first-hand lesson in the difference between paying a gondolier to transport you, or telling sailors where you wanted to go, and rowing yourself.

The first pointed difference was that you actually had to paddle. He was a lot less experienced than Erik, and the coracle was round, which meant they were spending a lot of time spinning slowly. The second difference was that in his previous experience Benito had simply told those in control of the boat his destination, and made finding it their problem. Now it was his and Erik's problem.

The rain obscured them from enemy watchers, which was a good thing. The trouble was it obscured everything, including possible landmarks.

At this rate, thought Benito, *we might just end up in Albania after all.*

And they hadn't guessed about the wind or the current or even the chop on the water either. They might just end up *swimming* to Albania . . . if they didn't end up swimming round and round in circles.

"I think we're going south," whispered Erik.

"I thought we planning on going north?"

Erik grunted. "In this thing we just go where the sea takes us. Bail for a bit."

So Benito bailed; it made more sense than having him try to paddle. It seemed the sea outside the coracle was keen to get into it as fast as possible. It came aboard in enthusiastic splashes that soon had Benito wet to the skin. Here he was, cheek-by-jowl in a giant bowl with Erik Hakkonsen, and he might as well have been alone on the water. Erik was as silent as a dead man, he couldn't see anything, and Benito was so cold he couldn't feel anything either.

The whisper came out of the dark again, at his ear, and he jumped. "There's a headland, I think. Help me paddle."

Gradually the headland loomed up out of the rain. Benito's feet were now ankle-deep in the water in the bottom of the coracle.

It proved to be an islet. They hauled up on it anyway. But they could vaguely make out a white building off across the water. "I think this must be Mouse Islet," said Benito quietly. "We could see it from the wall. There are some buildings on it."

"Dawn can't be that far off, Benito. Is that building we can see over there another island?"

"No. It's a monastery, I think. Just off the mainland jutting into the sea. We could go there, but there's a big inlet ahead. If we go ashore here, we'll be forced to go virtually back into Kérkira."

Erik sighed. "We'll be forced back into this bedamned tub instead, then. Come on. Let's get on with it."

They did. But it became rapidly obvious that the coracle had suffered during the landing on Mouse Islet. The water was calm here, but Benito had to keep bailing. By the time they got within sight of the further shore, it was a race between water coming in and the bailing and paddling. Of course, the more water there was in the vessel the heavier it was to row, and the slower they went, too. Benito started preparing himself to swim.

It proved unnecessary. Just.

Mind you, Benito thought, *my clothes are so wet by now that I can't really get any wetter*. Despite the exercise, Benito was shivering almost uncontrollably. At least the rain had stopped, but there was still a cold wind blowing.

"I don't think it is worth hiding that . . . bathtub," said Erik. "We won't be using it to get back, so we might as well just get away from here."

The darkness was still thick as they blundered off into it. Even Benito, used to "seeing" his way around by feel in the darkness of Venice's nighttime rooftops, found the going difficult. Man-made structures had the decency to be at predictable angles! Then his nose picked up something. A hint of wood-smoke.

"There's a fire ahead," whispered Benito.

Erik snorted. "I know. I've been trying to stalk it, with something stumbling along just behind me that makes more noise than a pair of bull-seals having a territory fight in the middle of a Venetian glass-shop. If it's local peasants, we need to ask them some directions. And if it's Hungarian soldiers, we need to avoid them if we can."

Benito shivered. "Right now I'd be happy to go and ask them if I could borrow their fire for a bit."

"Well, come along. But try to keep it quiet! If it is soldiery, we are staying out of a fight. You're too keen on fighting."

But when they got closer, and Erik worked out just what the two Croats were doing, it was he, not Benito, who rushed in to the kill. The two Croats weren't well positioned to resist.

By the time Benito got there with his Shetlander dagger in hand, Erik was already kneeling next to the woman, untying her; and a moment later, he was undoing the gag.

Her first response was to scream.

"Hush!" hissed Erik.

He might as well have tried to stop a storm with his hands. She had a proper breath now for the next hysterical scream. It was understandable. Besides being raped, she was covered in her erstwhile rapist's blood. When someone's head is more or less summarily removed by a hatchet, they bleed. A lot.

But understandable as it might be, she was probably telling everyone within a mile that there was a woman here. Even the Croats' horses were shifting nervously. Benito shoved Erik aside, hauled her up by what was left of her blouse, and slapped her. "Shut up!" he hissed. "We're rescuing you. You want others to come?"

She shut up. Erik cut her hands free. "Now we'd better run. Someone must have heard that scream."

"What about taking their horses?" asked Benito. "They're tied over there." He pointed with his chin.

Erik looked. "Good. That's the first bit of luck we've had."

The horses still had their tack on. It was plain that the two soldiers had slipped off from somewhere else for a little private pleasure. "You're lighter than I am. You take her," said Erik, pushing the staggering woman toward Benito.

"Uh. I don't ride so well, Erik."

"Oh, hell. She'd better come with me, then. Help her up behind me."

Benito did. She clung to Erik like ivy. It was just light enough now for Benito to see her huge, terrified eyes. He was then left with the difficulty of getting onto the horse himself. It kept moving every time he put a foot in the stirrup. Finally, in desperation, he jumped. He nearly went clear over the other side, but did manage to cling to the saddle. He pulled himself upright into it. He managed to find one stirrup. It was too long. This was a whole continent away from the *Haute Ecole Equestrienne* Petro Dorma had sent him to. There, he'd been surrounded by respectful grooms, docile mounts and mounting blocks.

But he had to try. Erik was already out of sight. The horse plainly knew it had a total amateur in the saddle. It was being as balky as only a horse can be, when it knows it has mastery of the rider.

There was a clatter of hooves behind him. Benito prepared to jump. Only his foot was now stuck in this damned stirrup. If he jumped he'd drag . . . He hunched in the saddle and struggled with his foot.

"Get a move on, Benito," snapped Erik. The clatter had come from him, returning to see what had happened to Benito. He slapped the rump of Benito's horse and the vile animal took off as if someone had shoved something red-hot in an unmentionable spot. With Benito swearing and clinging to the saddle, they headed upward into the rougher terrain. At least his horse was following Erik's now.

By the time they reached the ridgeline, the sun was just burning its way through the clouds. Benito had long since abandoned any pretense of "riding." He was just trying to stay on the Godforsaken animal. It took all his finely honed burglar's acrobatic skills to do so, and all his strength, too. He'd managed to get his foot free of the stirrup, at last. That meant when he fell off—not if, but when—he could try to fall clear.

When they got up to some pines on the ridge, Erik called a halt. More precisely, he pulled his horse to a halt, and Benito's horse stopped also.

Very abruptly. Benito continued for a few yards without it.

He got to his feet, to find the Icelander looking at him, his shoulders shaking with laughter. "Why didn't you say you couldn't ride at all, you crazy kid!"

"Uh. I *have* been to classes. *Case Vecchie* can all ride, but, well, I was a bridge-brat, Erik." Defensively: "I've only ridden a horse about five or six times before this, you know."

Erik snorted. "Well, you can't count this as another time. I've seen a sack of meal do a better job of it. And those things hanging down are stirrups. You are supposed to put your feet in them."

"I couldn't reach them."

Erik shook his head. "We'll shorten them now. Help this poor woman down, Benito."

Benito did. She almost fell off the horse—and then pushed away from him. "Who are you?" she asked warily, her eyes darting looking for a place to run. There was naked fear in that voice.

Benito waved his hands at her, trying to look helpful and harmless at the same time. "We're Venetians." It was easier than trying to explain. "You're safe now."

The young woman crumpled and began to cry. Then she started speaking Greek. At speed.

"Whoa." Benito squatted down beside her; it seemed

it was up to him to try to calm her down. Well, he was smaller than Erik; maybe that made him look less threatening. "We don't speak Greek," he said gently. "I can't help you if I don't understand."

"They killed Georgio!" she wailed—but softly, hardly more than a whisper. "They—they—" she dissolved into tears, and Benito patted her shoulder, thinking that trying to hold her would probably be a bad idea at this point.

She got herself under control, a lot faster than he would have thought. "What happened?" he asked. "Why did you come down out of the hills?"

She gulped for air. "See, some of the goats were missing. He thought they'd gone home. So he went down to the house. And when he didn't come back I went down to look for him. He was . . ."

Her eyes were round with the memory of things Benito didn't want to think about. "They were torturing him. Burning him to get him to tell them where he'd hidden the money." She shuddered, then said, plaintively, "We don't *have* any money. Just a few pennies. We've only been married for two months."

She began to cry again; great heaving sobs, wringing her hands together so hard that her knuckles were bone-white. Then she caught her breath. She seemed determined to tell them; to get the vileness out. "I ran in to try and help him. The one . . . the one who . . . he said: 'Here's the bitch. We'll get it out of her instead.' They cut Georgio's throat. They cut my man's throat like you would butcher a hog."

"Here." Erik had produced a small, squat bottle. "Manfred gave me some of his armor polish. Give her a drink, Benito."

Benito did. She choked, but then drank some more. The woman looked at Erik. "At least you killed them."

Erik looked decidedly uncomfortable. "Look. Is there anyone we can take you to? Somewhere safe where they'll look after you?"

She laughed bitterly. It was a horrible, tragic sound. "Safe! Safe like you Venetians sitting in your fortress. There is nowhere safe for the poor peasants. We must hide in the hills."

"So . . . there is no one we can take you to?" Erik persisted, but without much hope.

She shrugged. "I have a brother on a galley at sea. Georgio's parents are somewhere in the hills." She looked at both of them with resignation, as if she was perfectly prepared for them to abandon her.

Erik cleared his throat, and looked worriedly back down the hill. "Look. We have to get on. I've got to get to Count Dentico's villa. My . . . my . . . a lady . . . I must go and see if she's all right. But we can't just leave you here."

"I have nowhere to go," she repeated tonelessly.

Erik cocked a wary ear toward the slope. "Then you'd better come with us until we find a place for you. Benito, let's shorten those stirrups. And try holding on with your knees."

Benito shook his head. "Erik, the only thing I wasn't holding on with were my teeth. And that was only because the mane kept bouncing around when I tried to bite it."

The Greek peasant woman managed a tremulous laugh. "I can ride. My uncle was a groom for Count Di Valva. The Count wasn't there very often. Where is this place you wish to find? I can probably get you in the right direction, at least." Underneath her shock and her grief, she was recovering some hope, and only because they had not offered to abandon her.

Erik nodded. "You ride, then. Benito can cling on like a tick behind you. The estate is somewhere near a place called Giannades. Do you have any idea where that is?"

She nodded. "I haven't been there. But it is to the west of Kérkira."

She went over to the horse and shortened the stirrups quickly and efficiently; clearly she knew what she was doing. Then she hitched up her skirts in a most unladylike but very practical way, and mounted with an ease that Benito envied.

"It's best that she does something," Erik said, quietly. "She's ready to go to pieces, Benito. She's like a glass that's cracked to bits; one touch, and she'll shatter."

"I'm not surprised."

Erik sighed worriedly. "That could be what happened to my Svanhild. Come on, let's go. If you look over at Kérkira, you'll see Emeric has troops coming in by the column. That's a good few thousand men down there. We should move before they get too organized, never mind before they notice a couple of missing Croats."

Caesare Aldanto's body slept. Long, long ago Chernobog had learned this was a necessity. They died quickly if you did not allow them to rest.

Caesare lay on a cot in the tent that had been allocated to him, and twitched occasionally, as a dog might when dreaming.

Chernobog's other dog, yellow and feral, prowled the hills. The shaman had been told to look for holy places, to sniff them out so they could be rededicated.

It should have been easy. It was proving impossible. The smell of magic was easy enough to find. The trouble was . . . everywhere reeked of it. Up in the wind-tumbled sky his two aerial eyes flew hither and yon, looking for groves. Or temples. Or even standing stones.

So far, all he'd seen through their infinite detail-seeing eyes were churches. The shaman-dog shivered, thinking about those. His master could and no doubt would rededicate some of those to his purpose, but it was a dangerous process, and there was that about them which struck at him. He could, of course, strike back . . . but that could easily draw the attention of the master's adversary. And the shaman was not ready for that.

The shaman-dog stumbled and sneezed. Pollen. It seemed as if every plant on this accursed island was flowering. Like the magic of this place, the pollen was in the air everywhere.

He left the roadway in haste. Horses, and a double-span of donkeys struggling to drag a heavy cannon, were coming along it. Horses took a great aversion to this body-form. They would smell him out and chase and kick him if they could. This road was busy with troops and cannons coming along it. By evening at least a third of the guns would be in place. Already the pounding thunder was beginning. The shaman wrinkled his nose in distaste. He didn't like the smell of gunpowder either. It was a new thing. The shaman hated new things.

Chapter 44

"It's not that serious, Hildi!" Bjarni's voice was gruff, but underneath the impatience was affection, she could tell. "Just a few fragments of rock knocked off by a bullet. Head wounds always bleed like mad. Don't fuss about it. Just bandage it up so that when Kari or Gulta come back with a way out of here for us we can go. We might have to leave the horses."

"But they are such beautiful horses!" Svanhild protested, wrapping a torn section of her petticoat around her brother's head and ear. Now she was glad she had some of those travesties of Venetian gowns that her brothers had insisted she have made up. The masses of petticoats made excellent bandages. "If we leave them behind—those Magyars—"

"They won't be hurt. It's us they're after, not the horses." Bjarni managed a strained chuckle. "Actually, those brutes treat their horses better than they treat their wives. The horses will probably be better off with them."

Gulta and Kari scrambled down into the cave mouth. "There's only one other way out, like I said, Bjarni. And they've got people up there. Rolled a rock down on us."

"But there are a good few caves up there," said Gulta. "Looks like one of them is used. We could hide Svanhild up there."

Svanhild raised herself up. "I can shoot better than

most of the men. And I will stand with my clan, not hide up in some other cave. We cannot get out of this valley? Well, so what? They cannot get in, either. We have food and water. Let them sit out there."

She did not add that if her brothers and hearthmen died, and she were hiding in a cave, her best option would be to fling herself off the side of the mountain.

"And tonight we'll slip out and cut a few throats," said Kari evilly.

Bjarni regarded him with a jaundiced eye. "Well, if they can get to shoot into the cave mouth the ricochets will kill us."

"Without being able to shoot around corners they'll hard pressed to do that," pointed out Hrolf. "From the lip over there we can target anyone who comes into the valley. They can't even roll rocks onto us. And there is not enough growing here to burn properly."

Bjarni sniffed. "They don't have to. They'll smoke us out."

The villa was still standing as Erik and Benito rode toward it. Not torched, as most of the others they'd seen so far. The presence of Thalia, the peasant girl they'd rescued, had a very beneficial effect. They'd been forced to the back paths and side roads by patrols. She had actually managed to draw the hastily hiding or fleeing peasants back to them to get some directions. They would have struggled to find their way, otherwise.

Erik kicked his horse into a gallop when the villa Dentico came in sight, and rode straight up to it, as hard and as fast as he could make the horse gallop.

Benito, clinging to Thalia as she followed Erik, knew from Erik's own lectures that this was plain foolishness. He also knew stopping Erik would be beyond his ability.

Besides, Thalia was the one in control of this four-hoofed bollock-cruncher, not him. He was just trying to stay on.

Erik dismounted in a leap, and ran into the house calling "Svanhild! Svanhild!" at the top of his lungs. Alerting every single enemy within hearing distance, or lying in wait in the villa, that there was someone up here. Benito winced; he had expected nothing less.

Erik did at least have that tomahawk in his hand.

Benito dismounted with as much skill as he could muster, and pelted after Erik. "Catch his horse. And stay out here!" he shouted to Thalia. What he expected to find in there would be no sight for her. He raced into the villa with the Shetlander knife in his hand, wishing desperately for his rapier.

However, what Benito found was merely Erik, examining some bloodstains in the hallway. The blood had long since dried and gone a reddish brown, but a fair amount of it was splattered onto the whitewashed walls in various spots. There had been a lot of killing done here.

Benito swallowed. "Erik. I'm sorry."

But to his astonishment, Erik smiled at him. "It wasn't their blood. Or at least, not all their blood."

He ventured closer, and peered at the bloodstains as Erik was doing. He couldn't see how Erik could tell anything from them. "Vinlander blood is a different color?" ventured Benito.

Erik swatted his ear. From past comparative experience, Benito knew he was doing it gently. "No, you young idiot. There are no bodies. Somebody took the bodies away. I don't see that being the Hungarians, not if the bodies were Svanhild and her people. And with that many men and this much blood splashed about . . . I don't see that they'd have just captured everyone."

Well, it made sense when Erik pointed it out, if you accepted the idea that the Hungarians wouldn't take away the bodies of their victims. "So what happened?"

Erik shrugged. "How would I know? But at least they made a fight of it. They weren't caught unawares because there are no bloodstains anywhere except here."

Presumably Erik had already been everywhere but there. "So where do we go now?"

"We try to track them," said Erik, heading for the front door. "Ask anyone we can find, I suppose. It isn't going to be easy. Actually, I should say *I* try to track them. You should get up to the north coast and see if you can find a fisherman willing to transport you."

"The siege isn't going anywhere," he pointed out. "I can help you find them."

Erik shook his head. "With the numbers of men and guns that Emeric is moving in, this is going to be no light siege. And no besieged castle is that secure anyway. Days can count, Benito. Days mean lives. Lives of people like Thalia. I am a knight sworn to defend them. That doesn't mean I can let you waste time. Duty is not a narrow thing; you have yours, and I have mine. Mine is to find Svanhild if I can, then get back to Manfred with all possible speed. Yours is to make all possible speed to Venice, or at least to someone who can get help from Venice."

"I suppose so, Erik. But . . ." he began.

"Just make all possible speed to Venice. Do it, Benito."

They were outside in the courtyard by now. And Benito realized that Thalia wasn't. He tensed, heart suddenly racing . . . But there were the horses, tied up carefully.

Thalia was outside the wall, talking to a very nervous boy of twelve or thirteen. "He says the people who were staying here went north, on the horses of the raiders. He says they killed those who attacked, all of them. He says the soldiers came two days ago, and took the bodies. They've been looking for people to question. There are some of the soldiers in the next valley."

"Ask him if there was a woman with the people who got away. A woman with long blond hair."

The boy nodded. He made an unmistakable gesture with his hands. Benito had to stifle a laugh. Manfred had said she was top-heavy. "It looks like we go north together after all, Erik."

Erik nodded, and Benito had the satisfaction of seeing that it was not with reluctance. "As long as our paths run together, yes. Let us go now, before those soldiers come back. "

They rode out, heading for the mountainous north of the island. "Do you have any idea where we're going?" Benito asked Thalia, as they headed up toward the ridge through the olive grove.

"North. Up there. I have never been up there. They

say it is very different." Thalia spoke as if she was referring to a different continent instead of a few miles off. She pointed to Mount Pantocrator. "There is a very holy place up there. There is another one near Paleokastritsa where my Aunt Eleni went when she was young."

She shivered suddenly, for no apparent reason. "But that is not men's business."

More to distract her from whatever thought this had been, Benito asked: "But haven't you been up to the north? I need to find a fishing harbor to find a boat that will take me over to Italy."

She shook her head. "I have been to Kérkira. Twice!"

That made her a well-traveled woman, in her opinion. After all, Corfu-town was at least a league away. Corfiote men traveled; women didn't.

Well, war had the effect of changing things. By now Corfiote women were doing all manner of things they'd never done before.

Benito was exhausted. It hadn't been possible to ride all day, as the heroes in the stories had. For starters, it looked like Emeric's commanders were finally starting to get themselves organized. There were patrols to dodge. And they'd spotted several guard posts being set up on hilltops. Fortunately, it appeared that Erik's combat experience against the Vinland tribes and with clan feuds on Iceland had involved a great deal of just this sort of warfare.

They were moving steadily north, at least. Benito's clothes were dry, which was something he was grateful for. His belly button was meeting his backbone, his stomach was that empty, but he kept reminding himself that he'd been this hungry and more before, and hadn't died of it. And Thalia was drooping in the saddle. Maybe she hadn't paddled a leaky coracle out of a besieged fortress, but she'd had the worst day of her life.

And it wasn't showing any signs of being over; Erik was driving them relentlessly. According to several peasants he'd found and questioned, with Thalia's assistance, the northern villages had closed their gates and were holding off the marauding bands. Not that this would do them any good when the Hungarians stopped being marauding bands and started being segments of an army; but for now, they were holding their own. None of the peasants had seen the Vinlanders, but that was hardly surprising. The sound of horses' hooves was enough to send the peasantry diving for cover.

At the last guard post, Erik had left the two of them and gone on a lone sortie. He'd returned, cleaning his tomahawk fastidiously. And smiling.

"They haven't found them yet, anyway. The guard told me about what happened at Dentico villa. The Magyars are furious, but they think they're after a bunch of Venetians. They have been trying to track them for days. They've gone to the northwest. There are several villages up there that are walled and resisting."

"There is one near the coast at Paleokastritsa, where many of the women go to the shrine," volunteered Thalia.

Benito sighed. "Do you think this shrine-place is serving dinner?"

Erik reached into his sling-bag. "The guard up there had some bread that he won't be needing any more." He pulled out a flat country loaf. "He had some wine, too, but I knew you wouldn't want that."

Benito glared at him. "Erik! I'll kill you!"

Erik hauled out a clay flask, miraculously unbroken. "It killed him," he said grimly. "Fortunately there isn't enough left to kill you. I hope."

Erik had also helped himself to the guard's pike and his arquebus. The latter was filthy enough to give Erik the mutters. Still, with wine and bread in them, pressing on seemed easier. At last they saw a patch of lights.

"A town that isn't deserted. It must be one of the ones that is holding out." Erik peered through the dusk at them. "They can't last long."

"Could be a Hungarian camp," Benito observed, wearily.

"True," Erik sounded positively cheerful. "But we'll have to sneak a closer look to tell. Probably have more fleas than people in it, though."

Benito groaned. "If it is a town, and so long as it don't

fall tonight, and they've got a place for us to sleep, I'll be pleased to meet the fleas."

"Our chances of getting in tonight are nonexistent," said Erik, urging his tired horse forward. "Unless it is a Hungarian camp, of course. In which case we won't get out. It's far more likely to be a Hungarian camp."

He was wrong about the Hungarian camp. He was also wrong about the town letting them in. Refugees had been coming up the steep narrow track for a week now, most of them by night.

Benito, Thalia and Erik found themselves with several others, requesting entry to Paleokastritsa. Benito found no trouble in understanding just why it hadn't been sacked. It didn't look large enough to be worth the huge effort it would take.

"Stand against the wall. Now take all your weapons off. Once that is done you can come forward one at a time. Remember, any false moves and you'll be shot from up here."

Paleokastritsa was crowded. A place to sleep . . . well, eventually they joined some thirty others, sleeping on the church floor.

Erik was right about the fleas, though.

Chapter 45

Benito woke to the certain knowledge that he was getting soft. Sleeping on a cold stone floor might once have been luxury. After all, he was dry, and the other sleepers kept the place relatively warm. But the stone was a lot harder than what he had become used to. Erik and Thalia were already up. So he assumed, at any rate, because they weren't lying on the stone next to him.

Benito got himself up, rubbed the sleep from his eyes, bowed to the altar, and walked off to find either the others or the town fountain. He hadn't slept that deeply for many years, and he knew that if he was going to keep alive out here, he was going to have to go back to the habits of his days as an unwanted and uninvited secret tenant in people's attics. He'd have to learn to sleep with his senses keyed again, where the slightest sound would wake him. Only, he had been so tired when they first arrived, he knew he couldn't have slept lightly. Now he was just so hungry, he couldn't have slept at all.

The first familiar face he saw, also at the town's fountain, belonged to neither Erik nor Thalia. The Corfiote sailor no longer had his black eye. The sailor looked at Benito. Blinked. Looked again.

Benito hoped that this wouldn't get unpleasant. He was fairly sure he could deal with the man's inept knife-skills. What he didn't want was the trouble that would inevitably follow. He also didn't want his identity nosed about. It might not cause trouble—but there could be ears out here in the street that it shouldn't come to. Benito glanced about. There was no one in earshot, at least.

The sailor shook his head. "I'll be damned! Just what are you doing here, *Case Vecchie?*"

He didn't say it too loudly, or with any malice. Benito decided to chance friendliness. If he remembered rightly, the sailor from Bari had called him "Spiro."

"Trying not to give away that I am a *Case Vecchie*, Spiro. Do me a favor. Don't shout or call any attention to it or I might have to remind you how we last met. And I don't want to do that; I've got plenty of trouble as it is."

The man didn't really seem to have heard. Instead he was studying Benito intently. "You are him!" he said unbelievingly. "You really are him!"

"I *really* don't want everyone to know, Spiro," Benito repeated, fixing him with a stare.

The sailor grinned widely. "Safe enough with me, milord. I owe you."

Benito noticed that a couple of people were staring at them. He clapped Spiro on the shoulder, and turned the gesture into an arm around the sailor's shoulders, as if they were old friends. Which, at the moment, Benito really hoped was the case. "Let's go and find some wine. I was going to drink some of the water, but I've decided that I'm really not that thirsty."

Spiro looked skeptical. "Right now, wine in Paleokastritsa is damn near as expensive as wine in Venice. And I'm afraid I'm broke again, milord, even if I owe you a drink or two."

"For heaven's sake, call me Benito. Forget the 'milord.' And the wine is on me, and something to eat, if you can forget that fact. Venetian *Case Vecchie* are not popular right now. Out there, the Hungarians want to kill us for protecting the island. From what I can work out, the Corfiotes in here want to kill us for not protecting the island."

Spiro shrugged. "As you're buying the wine, I wouldn't dream of killing you, m . . . Benito."

"Afterwards is a different story," said Benito wryly.

Spiro chuckled. "After a few glasses of wine even the stupidest idea can sound like a good one. But I did learn that that was a really, really insanely stupid one. So what are you doing here, m . . . Benito?"

"I'll tell you about it over that cup of wine. Where do we find one?"

Spiro pointed across the square at dark doorway. "Papavanakis'. His taverna is dirty, it smells, his wife's face would curdle milk and I think he waters his wine."

Benito grinned. "So why are we drinking there?"

Spiro shrugged and grinned back. "At least what he's putting in the wine is water. And he is less of a thief than most of them."

They strolled over and went into the dim coolness out of the already bright day. Benito blinked, adjusting his eyes to the lack of direct sunlight. The taverna was clean and smelled of food and wine. Fresh bread and meaty smells, and the wine wasn't slightly used by prior customers. The pretty young woman behind the counter scowled at them. "Not you again, Spiro! Go away. Not another cup will I give you until you pay."

Spiro nodded to Benito. "See what I mean," he said mournfully. "Curdle milk, that face would."

She snorted and pretended to throw a wine cup at him. It was obviously an old joke. "Go away, Spiro. Papas will kill me if I give you any more credit."

Spiro gestured expansively. "It's all right, Anna. Beni here is paying."

The woman raised her eyebrows. "With the same coin as you pay? Or real money?"

Benito produced a silver penny.

"You shouldn't show her that much!" said Spiro. "She'll faint and we'll never see any wine. Or that food you promised me. It's been a while since I ate."

The taverna's keeper clicked her tongue. "He's impossible. How did he talk you into wasting good money on him?" She said it with perfect amiability, while filling two wine cups.

Benito realized that Spiro had addressed her in Italian Frankish . . . and that she'd replied in the same way. Plainly, by her accent and rapidity of speech, it was her

mother-tongue. He'd been keeping his own mouth shut to
play down his origins but it now seemed safe enough. "He
borrowed money from me. He's had it for a year. So now
he says I owe him interest," said Benito, earnestly.

The young woman snorted with laughter and handed
them the wine. "And you'll keep owing him interest until
the day he dies." She pointed to the tables. "Sit. I'll go
and find you some food."

They sat. Spiro took a pull at his wine cup. "More
water than wine."

It tasted pretty good to Benito. "So, what are you
doing here, Spiro. Is this home?"

The Corfiote gestured expansively. "This dump? Ha.
Liapádhes is a great metropolis. Broad streets, wonderful
tavernas. Wine like a young lion. As far from this place
as the sun is from the earth."

Benito was beginning to get the hang of Spiro by now.
"So it is just like this, is it?"

Spiro gave him a conspiratorial wink and took another
pull of his wine. "Two peas in a pod, really, except this
has got a good defensive position. It's about a mile and
half south."

"How did you get home from Venice?"

Spiro raised his cup. "A Dorma ship, thanks to you.
I was with her all the way to Constantinople. I'd have
stayed with her too, but when I got back to Corfu, on
the return trip, there was a bit of family business I had
to settle. A fellow had taken some liberties with my sister." He swallowed half the contents of his cup at a go.
"So after I had thanked him very politely, I went back to
Kérkira, but the ship had left. I couldn't come back to
Liapádhes for a while. So I took a job with a fisherman.
Taki drinks too much but he's a good skipper. Then this
lot blew up. So I thought I'd come home. Only home
seemed to be full of Hungarians. And you, Benito?"

Benito's ears had pricked up with the mention of the
fisherman. "Got sent out here to be a factor for Dorma.
And then this war blew up. Look, this fisherman friend of
yours. He wouldn't like to earn a bit of money? I really
want out of here back to the Italian mainland."

At this point, Anna the taverna keeper arrived with

two earthenware platters, fragrant steam curling up from them. "I had some of last night's *stifado* still. I've just made it hot. That one," she pointed an elbow at Spiro, "didn't eat last night. So I thought he might as well eat this morning, and you looked hungry."

Spiro looked suspiciously at the plate of pearl onion-laced stew that she put in front of him. "It hasn't got quinces in it again, has it? You know I hate quinces."

She shook her head as she wiped her hands on her apron. Then she held out a hand to Benito. "And that's why he ate three helpings."

Bénito handed over the silver. She looked at it very carefully. She was polite enough not to bite it in front of him. "It seems real enough. You want more wine with that?"

Spiro drained his cup. "Seems like a good idea. I'm not likely to get this lucky again in a hurry, and I don't see us fishing for a while yet. Which answers your question, Benito. The Dalmatian pirates sink any boat they can find. Even fishing boats."

Benito waited for the taverna keeper to walk off. "Even for a good bit of coin? Working at night?"

Spiro shrugged. "I'll ask around. My old skipper Taki would be your best bet. He's up in the hills with his cousin Georgio. He's probably so sick of the old man and his goats that he'd be ready to try anything by now. I could get word to him. Some of the boys who go out with the goats would do anything for a few coppers."

Wordlessly, Benito dug out a few copper coins and a silver penny. He held back the silver penny. "That one is for finding somebody else. A whole bunch of them. Big guys with blond hair and a blond woman with them."

Spiro stuck his hand out. "I'll have the silver too, thanks. Easiest money I've ever earned. They're in a cave in a gorge about a mile and a half east of here."

"What!" Benito started. "Are you sure?"

Spiro grinned. "Well, I was fairly sober when I heard about them. That's the trouble with being broke, you know. Do you want them alive or dead?" he asked around a mouthful of stew, still holding his hand out.

"Alive! Definitely alive!"

"Then you'd better get a move on. They stole some of Cheretis's goats and he's got all the men going out this morning. They're planning to burn them out."

Benito knocked over the chair in his haste to get up. "Come on! We must find Erik!" He hauled Spiro out of his seat.

"But I haven't finished eating! And the wine is still coming!"

"You want gold, not silver, you'll come and show us the way to this place as fast as possible." Benito hustled him along, trying to think where he'd be most likely to find Erik. The stables perhaps?

"Where are you going?" yelled the taverna keeper. "Here is your wine and your change. You haven't eaten your food!"

"We'll be back. Emergency!" yelled Benito.

Sure enough, Erik and Thalia were in the stable. Erik looked up as he and Spiro panted in. "So nice of you to bother to come and help. Finished in the taverna I saw you going into?"

"Get the tack on those horses! We've got to move, now!"

Erik didn't waste time asking questions, before starting to do that. Neither did the suddenly wide-eyed Thalia. But as he worked, Erik asked what was up.

"Your precious Svanhild is about to get roasted for goat-stealing," said Benito. "Spiro here knows where they are."

Erik didn't waste time on talk. But he worked at a pace that made lightning look as if it moved at a comparatively glacial speed. "Up." He hauled the one-time sailor onto the horse, behind him. Thalia was up and Benito struggled and scrambled behind her as they clattered for the gate. Erik nearly rode the stableman down. Benito almost fell off as the man used a pitchfork to make the horse decide to stop abruptly. "You owe—"

Benito frantically dug out some money and flung it at him. "We'll be back!" And then Thalia set off after Erik. Benito just hoped they'd catch up.

They did. The town gate was closed. "Let us out!" yelled Erik.

"Not likely. Let's see who you're running from first, foreigner," said the guard, clutching his spear.

Spiro saved the man's life. "Open up, Adoni! They're not running from anyone. They're trying to get to someone in hurry."

The guard peered. "Oh. It's you, Spiro Volagatis. Well, I guess if it gets you out of the town it's a good thing." He unbarred the gate, and they rode off down the steep, winding trail.

"Where now?" Benito heard Erik yell as they reached the foot of the trail. Benito missed the reply but they did manage to follow Erik off to the west. Then he spotted the trickle of smoke. By the way Erik was urging the horse into a gallop he'd seen it too.

The Corfiote men and boys, armed with a motley array of old arquebuses, pitchforks, spears and slings, were piling brushwood right across the mouth of the narrow gorge. Already someone had lit one edge. Benito arrived into what certainly sounded like a full-scale riot.

By the three men on the ground some of the locals had been foolish enough to try and stop Erik kicking the fire apart. But now he was under the noses of a dozen arquebuses, and there was a full-scale shouting match going on.

Thalia quelled it with a shriek and a stream of what could only be Greek vituperation. Hastily the locals began to pull the burning branches away and beat at the fire with branches of green leaves. "What did you say to them?" asked Benito.

"This is a sacred place! The holy mother is in the temple cave up there. This valley ends in some cliffs. There is no other way out."

"But they've stolen our goats!" bellowed one of the men at Erik. "They're bandits! They've been shooting goat-boys. And who the hell are you, foreigner? You knocked down my brother. I've a good mind to knock you down."

"When I come back," said Erik grimly, hauling brushwood out of the way, "you're welcome to try."

But the fire already had its teeth into the dry brush. Benito, beating at flames, got the feeling that he should somehow have gotten Erik there sooner. Already the heat was pushing at their faces and a river of smoke was funneling up the gorge.

And then there was a rumble.

Even the wet rag wrapped around her mouth couldn't stop Svanhild coughing as she tried, desperately, to calm the horses. Their eyes were wild and rolling and the animals were whickering and stamping. There was little likelihood that anyone could ride them now. The horses were already on the edge of panic.

"We'll have to leave them, Hildi," said Bjarni. "We'll have to get to the cliff and try and climb out."

"We can't! They'll die."

"If we stay much longer, we'll die."

There was a rumble and it grew darker, almost by the moment.

"Look at the stream!"

From atop the high rock Benito reached down and hauled Erik back by the collar. As the Icelander struggled to turn and throw Benito's hand off, the water flumed through, hitting Erik at about knee-height. It knocked his feet out from under him anyway. Benito clung to Erik as if he were a roof-beam four stories from the ground. If he hadn't hauled Erik back, the water-wall would have stuck the Icelander at least belly-button height. Another strong pair of hands came and grabbed Erik's arms. Between Spiro and Benito they hauled him up.

The sudden rain hissed down like arrows. A glance showed the local heroes running for shelter, bedraggled figures pelting away from the scene.

"Thanks," said Erik, as they hastened to a rock lip that offered some vague shelter. Looking at the torrent and the already decreasing rain, Erik shook his head. "What caused *that*?"

Thalia shrugged. "I told you it was a holy place. The priestesses command the magic here."

Erik shook his head again. "Whatever it was, it certainly wasn't natural. It was a clear morning a few minutes ago. Anyway, let me see if I can get up there."

Thalia took him by the arm. "I tied the horses just back there. You can probably ride up the valley now."

Erik smiled at her. "You're the practical one, Thalia. Seeing to the horses, doing all the things we forget."

The peasant woman looked serious. "Somebody has to."

But Erik had already left at a run.

Benito looked out. The rain was slacking off. It would be gone in a minute or two. The stream was already dropping. And on the blackened, burned brush a green creeper was already twining, growing as he watched.

The intervention had been magical, of that Benito was certain. He was less certain that he liked it.

Chapter 46

Svanhild peered over her brothers' shoulders as they watched by the little protruding ridge of limestone, arquebuses at the ready. The stream, which had been no more than a bare trickle so recently, was now making so much noise that they were forced to shout. But at least the smoke was gone. The rain, too, was nearly over.

"Give it a little while longer and I'll go and scout. That was the luckiest rainstorm in history," said Kari.

Bjarni raised an eyebrow. "Maybe so. But why did the stream flood *before* the rain fell?"

"It must have rained higher up in the catchment, Bjarni."

The oldest Thordarson brother shook his head. "This damned trickle hasn't got a catchment worth talking about, Kari. There is something funny going on here. I hope things haven't just got worse."

"There is someone coming up the gorge!" shouted the hearthman on guard up on the slope.

They all took cover, including Svanhild. "Pick your marks!" commanded Bjarni. "Don't open fire until I say so."

Svanhild peered anxiously toward the mouth of the gorge. Bright sunlight was shivering into scatterings of brief rainbows through the last veils of rain. The rider came in sight around the corner. His dark hair was wet and plastered about his face, but Svanhild knew those

410

facial planes instantly. Her heart hammered, and she found herself abruptly breathless.

"Svanhild!" he called, his voice echoing off the cliffs.

A shot boomed. The bullet kicked a white spurt of dust from the limestone next to the rider's head. Erik Hakkonsen whirled his horse in the direction of the firing and shook an empty fist. "You stupid Vinlander bastard! I've come to rescue you!"

Svanhild stopped only long enough to lay down her bow, and then was out and running down the slope. "Erik! Erik!"

A huge smile nearly split Erik's face in half. As she skidded to a halt on the slippery rock beside his stirrup, his face went from angry and anxious to—well . . .

Foolish. "Er. Good morning, Svanhild Thordardottar."

She stood there smiling up at him, feeling equally foolish and desperately wishing she could think of something to say. He vaulted down from the dun he was riding. She could see, though it was no help, that he too was fumbling for words. All the long and carefully thought-out speeches had gone from her head, as if she had never even considered making them. But she had to help get something started, or they would both stand there, looking, not touching, not saying anything.

"Why is your hair dark now?" was all she could think of to say.

He ran his fingers through his hair as if he had not known it was dark. "I was trying to pass as one of the locals."

Svanhild looked at him, branding his appearance into her memory, in case—well, in case. He was tall, lean and athletic; she had known that, of course, but now she was *aware* of it. His face had a hewn masculinity to it, planar and strong, and nothing detracted from the way he looked in her eyes, not even the soot on his face and the water dripping from his hair.

Then a thin sliver of reality intruded. With the high cheekbones and the straight hair, even with his skin and hair darkened, Erik looked as much like a local as a wolf looks like a bison. She had to laugh. And Erik began laughing with her. By the time that her brothers and their hearthmen joined them, they were virtually leaning on each other, helpless with laughter.

Benito heard the shot, and decided he'd come running. He was wise enough about his own horsemanship to approach on foot. He also kept his head down. Still, by the time he got to where he could see them, the Vinlanders, Erik and his sweetheart were all standing around beaming at each other.

"Well, they look really miserable."

Benito turned to see both Spiro and Thalia had followed him. Spiro was being his usual quirky self.

"Good," said Benito. "Let's go and make them more miserable and tell them they have got to get out of here. Before the villagers come back and roast them again, or roll rocks on them."

Thalia shook her head. "Not likely. The men will be hiding under their beds and hoping their wives don't find out where they decided to make a fire."

"I wouldn't tell these foreigners that in case they decide to have a roast goat to celebrate," said Spiro. "People are very touchy about their goats around Paleokastritsa. More touchy about their goats than their wives, which, if you look at the wives, makes sense. Not like the women in Liapádhes, of course."

Thalia looked at him with her mouth open, as if she wasn't entirely certain whether or not Spiro was mad.

Spiro winked at her. "Of course the goats around Liapádhes are prettier than those in Paleokastritsa, too. They have to be."

Benito walked out to the Vinlanders rather than find out any more about the local goats and goat-herds.

"Ah, Benito," Erik greeted him. "Friends, this young gentleman is the reason I'm here."

"And will be the reason we're getting out of here, Erik." Benito was getting increasingly anxious to break up the happy reunion. "The locals might come back, and besides, that fire will have told every Hungarian trooper in the area that something is going on here."

"But where will we go?" asked Svanhild, her face

passing from joyful to desperate in a single moment. "Everyone is trying to kill us."

"We'll go back to Paleokastritsa," Benito said firmly, as Spiro and Thalia picked their way toward the group. "You'll have to do some explaining about their goats. And pay for them."

The biggest of Vinlanders snorted. "Of course we will pay for their goats! We would have paid in the first place, if anyone had been willing not to run away from us. What were we supposed to do? Starve?"

"You'd better pay up generously and say you are very sorry," said Spiro. "I'll handle it for you. For a fee, of course."

One of the huge Vinlanders—they all looked alike to Benito—looked nearly apoplectic. "Apologize? But they nearly killed us. They nearly killed my sister!"

"And you did kill their goats, no 'nearly' about it," Benito retorted. Then, couldn't resist adding: "And according to Spiro, goats are a lot more appreciated around here than sisters. Come on, let's go and see if they'll let us back into Paleokastritsa. I left my breakfast and a glass of wine behind to come and rescue you from the goat-avengers. Erik is not so bad-tempered, because he was only currying horses and he was looking for you anyway."

"He was?" Svanhild gazed upon Erik with blue eyes so bright they seemed to have stars in them.

Benito smiled slyly at Erik. "Oh, yes! When he heard from Maria Verrier that you were out here, he did not even let an entire besieging army stand in his way. He left the citadel by night, over the walls with a leaking boat, braving enemy patrols and the wild sea in the torrential rain, staying neither to sleep nor rest, riding *vent a terre* until he reached the villa Dentico. All that was in his mind was the safety of his golden-haired Svanhild."

"Shut up, Benito," growled Erik, glowing dully. Under the dye, that pale skin produced a truly vibrant red color. Benito decided that the next time they were cold, he'd embarrass the Icelander; you could warm a family of five by the heat he gave off.

"But it is true!" insisted Thalia. "He saved me from the raping Croats, kyria. He killed two of them, just like that. And the sentry on the hill. He is a great fighter. He pulled at the burning wood with his bare hands and he beat back the men of Paleokastritsa and—"

"*And* let's get out of here! Please," begged Erik. "Either the Hungarians will arrive, or the locals are bound to come back."

"Or both," agreed one of the Vinlanders. "Don't want to be in the middle of that."

Soon the entire party was riding to Paleokastritsa.

The yellow dog almost howled in triumph. At last the shaman had a trace of magic that rose above the general reeking miasma of this place. He ran through the olive groves, pine forests and the macchia. He ran on past sentries and past hiding peasants. He had many miles to go.

But it had been a piece of intense and powerful sorcery, not finely crafted and precise as the names of power he used, not demon-bludgeon strong as Jagiellon used. Precisely, he thought, what Jagiellon was looking for. This magic was raw and primal, elemental—big, in the way an earthquake or a thunderstorm was big.

Dangerous, too, but that was not his problem. His problem was to find it, Jagiellon's to tame it.

He sent his hawks winging north, a part of him seeing through their eyes, eyes that could see a field mouse twitch the grass at five hundred feet. It took him quite some time to realize that the hawks were being subtly pushed away. The thermals slid them off to the west, the winds seeming to buffet against them whenever they tried to fly to one corner of the island. The hawks were becoming exhausted. Worse, they were becoming recalcitrant. Ever since he had tried to use them above Venice, the shaman had noticed that his control over the two hawks was not as it should be.

He was both angry and astonished. It was not possible! He had their true names, which made them his. His absolutely. Yet . . . he could not ignore the fact that they were rebelling. Not in great things but in small ways, in a slow and steady erosion of his control. It must be this vile place's magic.

Well, where they could not go was as good an indication of where he had to go as them actually seeing something. The yellow dog ran on, allowing the hawks to go to roost.

It was midafternoon before he reached the place. He looked at the few burned branches and the evidence of the recently flooded stream and smelled raw magic.

He tried to take a step forward, and stumbled. Grass had grown around his feet, the thin strands intertwining and binding. He kicked his way loose, then moved forward, sniffing. A dog's nose is a wondrous instrument. He could smell the horses as individuals; he could smell the people, the peasants and the others, and know who had wandered where. He could smell the women among them, two of them. He could smell . . .

Achoo! He erupted in a volley of sneezes.

All the flowers suddenly seemed intent on smothering him in their scents. He flicked his ears. A horsefly buzzed about them; then another. One bit him just below the tail on the exposed flesh. The shaman turned and snapped angrily at it, cracking it in his yellow teeth. Another bit his ear as he did so. Several more came buzzing up. One affixed itself to his nose. The shaman pawed furiously at it.

The shaman was one of the greatest and most powerful of magicians. He was proofed against many great magics.

Horseflies made him flee.

Horseflies in those numbers could make anything flee. They seemed immune to his protective spells.

Still, he knew the area in which the magics were being worked now. The master could send Aldanto. It would do the blond puppet good to be bitten by few horseflies.

"Go away or we'll shoot you," said one of the pair of guards on the wall. He brandished his arquebus in a manner that was more awkward than fierce. "You're not wanted here!"

One of the Vinlanders, the one who seemed to do all

of the talking, contrived to look sheepish and apologetic. "It was a misunderstanding, truly. We were running from the invaders, and we were starving. We have money! We want to pay for the animals."

There was a hasty consultation between the sentries. "We'll get someone to call old Cheretis. It was his goats."

The other guard peered at them more closely. "Oh. It's you again, Spiro. I thought we'd gotten rid of you. I see you're in bad company, as usual."

"But I haven't been anywhere near your sister, Adoni," said Spiro with a grin.

The guard glared at him. The other guard nearly fell over the crenellations laughing.

The goat owner, when he arrived, reminded Benito more of a sullen, bad-tempered porker than a goat. Like the ones a few people over on Guidecca had kept on the scraps in those big market-gardens over there. He had the same sparse, bristly beard and pronounced jowls.

But he was as obstinate as a goat, even if he didn't look like one. "They must be punished! Even if they pay for the goats, they must be punished!" He pleaded with the guards, in a squeaky voice. "After all, if you shoot them, I get paid for my beasts from the money they have with them. And you get the rest."

Spiro shook his head. "Don't be dafter than you have to be, you old *Malakas*. They were strangers visiting our beautiful island when the Hungarians attacked. Where is our famous Corfiote hospitality? Why are you fussing over a few miserable, scrawny goats?"

"Scrawny goats! They killed my best milker! She was the most beautiful goat on the island, hair like silk, an udder as soft as a baby's face and milk, so much milk you'd have thought she was a cow. And as for hospitality: what sort of guests kill your livestock?"

Spiro turned to the Vinlanders, Benito, Erik and Thalia. "See? I told you how they felt about their goats in Paleokastritsa!"

The laughter might have infuriated the goat-owner, but it decided the two guards that they were obviously no threat. "Have you got the money to pay the old bastard?" asked one guard.

"In gold," said Bjarni, curtly.

Not much gold came to Paleokastritsa. Even the goat-owner looked less sour. "Such fine goats as mine are worth a great amount of gold."

"Let us in and we can argue about it," grumbled Benito, "before some Hungarian troopers come along because of all that smoke. And *they* take all the gold instead."

Benito reached into his own small pouch and hauled out a silver penny. "Here, Spiro. I owe you this for information. I promised him a ducat from you, Erik."

Erik dug in his pouch. "Here are two." He handed them over with a flourish carefully visible to the gate. "I'm in your debt for finding and helping my friends."

Guards and goat-owner had developed eyes like saucers; the goat-owner's were full of greed.

Spiro looked at the coins, beaming. "I'm rich!" He walked over to the gate and pounded on it. "Let me in. I need a drink."

"You'll have to leave your swords and guns in the gatehouse," said one of the guards. "And you owe me a cup of wine, Spiro."

Spiro grinned. "I'm buying, so you might as well get yours before the money's all drunk up."

"After you send some goat-boys to look for that friend of yours," said Benito. "The fisherman."

Spiro nodded. "Sure. But I intend to be already hung over and broke before Taki Temperades gets here." Then he elbowed Benito in the ribs. "Trying to rob you was the smartest dumb thing I ever did, eh?"

At the moment, Benito was inclined to agree.

Chapter 47

In the darkness, up on the landward wall of the inner curtain, Manfred paced. Von Gherens, as a bodyguard should, paced alongside him.

"It was a mistake. I should never have let him go." Manfred stared over the cannon-flash in the darkness. Emeric's heavy guns were being maneuvered into place and the first of the forty-eight-pound bombards were already in action.

"It's early days yet," said Von Gherens. "Erik won't be easily caught. And even if the boat sank, he swims like a fish." He looked pensive. "You know, there's something very wrong about that. A good knight should have the decency to avoid learning how to swim. After all, if you're in the water with armor on, what is the point?"

Manfred ignored him. He gnawed on a knuckle, and welcomed the pain when he bit a little too deep. "He and Benito were too valuable to risk like that. What the hell was I thinking of?"

Von Gherens didn't reply. Perhaps he realized that Manfred didn't really want an answer. Presently Francesca came up to the battlement, and took him by the elbow as he stared off into the hills. Reluctantly, he turned to face her. "It's time to come down, Manfred. Perhaps tomorrow night . . ."

"Look. Look, Manfred!" Von Gherens pointed. Manfred whirled and followed the direction of his finger.

On the far hills a bonfire had blossomed, a tiny pinpoint of yellow and red. Now another. Then a third.

"You're hurting me, Manfred," said Francesca quietly.

Hastily, Manfred let go of her shoulder. "Sorry, dear." He took a deep breath, then let out a long sigh of relief. He should have known; and he should have trusted that those damned Vinlanders were as hard to kill as his Icelander. "And he's even found the girl! Come on, Francesca. Now, I really will sleep. Not even Emeric's damned guns will keep me awake."

"About time, too," grumbled Von Gherens. "Keep him under lock and key, Francesca. I'm going across to the hospital to see how Falkenberg does."

Manfred smiled. "I'm too tired and, to be honest, too relieved to gallivant tonight, Fritz. How is Falkenberg, by the way?"

"He had some fever and infection. But Father Francis, one of Eneko Lopez's companions, has been treating him. It looks like he might mend, Manfred. He swore at me this morning, at least. That was a relief after all the 'I-am-about-to-die' piety when I visited him the time before. He must think he has more time to make his peace with the Lord."

"Well, we can use another knight-proctor. I must go over and see him tomorrow morning, and get him used to the idea."

"Oh, no." Von Gherens shook his head. "When he's up, he's coming to run alternate bodyguard shifts with me. Erik ordered it. And now that we know the mad Icelander is alive out there, do you really think any of us are going to take a chance on him coming back and finding out we didn't do exactly what he said?"

Taki looked at the boy. Looked at the silver on the battered table. Looked back at the boy.

He could easily be one of Taki's usual crew. Curly black hair, olive skin, old clothes, bare feet. Short, but broad of shoulder. Taki looked at the silver again. There was quite a lot of it, but Taki could count a table-full of coins with a single glance.

Finally, deciding, he nodded and reached for it.

The youngster put his hand over the coins. "Not so fast, Captain. One quarter when I get to your boat. One quarter when I get over there. And one half when you give Erik a note I write for you when I'm safe."

Taki eyed the man called Erik. A scary one, that. Nothing would get past him—and nothing would stop him if he felt the need to do something. Except maybe death, and Taki wouldn't bet on that. "How do I know he will give me the money?"

Spiro chuckled. "Taki, take it from me, the *Case Vecchie* isn't trying to cheat you. He just doesn't trust your ugly face."

Taki did his best to look affronted. "Me? You can trust me. Ask anyone!" he bellowed, gesturing theatrically.

"Except about the freshness of his fish," said one of men in the tavern with a gap-toothed grin.

The tavern's occupants laughed.

Taki scowled and waved a fist vaguely. "You want to lose some more teeth, Adoni?"

Spiro shook his head. "He's all right, Benito. One of the best skippers on the island. Even if his fish . . ." He ducked.

Benito grinned. "I'm not that fond of fish anyway."

"Ah, but do you like cheap wine?" grinned the gap-toothed one.

"I only know one person who is fonder of it," snorted Erik. He shook his head, dubiously, studying Taki and his crew. "I think I should ration all of you. Between the lot of you, you'll end up sailing off to Vinland instead of across the Strait of Otranto."

"I sail best when I'm drunk!" insisted Taki, belligerently.

"At least he thinks he does," said Kosti.

"Has he ever tried it any other way?" asked Benito. This fishingboat's crew were beginning to give him a pleasant feeling of nostalgia for his days as a rooftop thief. They were as crazy as Valentina and Claudia had been in the early days.

Kosti shook his head. "Not so as anyone has ever noticed. But to be fair, he hasn't sunk us yet."

"Let's hope he can keep that up." Benito put the silver back in his pouch. "When and where do I see you, Captain?"

"Tomorrow night. We'll have to go and fetch the old boat, and get her round here. But there's a cove a couple of miles beyond Paleokastritsa we can lie up in. If you don't know the coast, it doesn't look like it's there at all. We should be there sometime before tomorrow, and we'll sail on the windrise after dark. Spiro can get one of the local kids to guide you over there. We've got a fishing boat to get off an island."

"And we've got to get over to the islet," said Kosti, suddenly glum. "Yani's boat is still underwater, I suppose."

The captain grinned evilly and slapped him on the back. "And guess who is going to be swimming out there."

Trudging up the hill carrying Alessia, Maria felt ill at ease about her destination. In the background she could hear Emeric of Hungary's cannon pounding away at the outer wall, reminding her that things weren't normal. But that wasn't what was making her nervous. She was going to the governor's palace in the Castel *a mar*. The Castel *a mar* was not nearly as grandiose as the Doge's palace in Venice, but it was somehow more intimidating. As imposing as it was, the Doge's palace in Venice had been the property of the people of Venice by sheer familiarity.

The guards at the gates also thought she didn't belong here.

They barred her way with their pikes. "You can't go in here, woman. His Excellency only has public audiences on Wednesdays. Come back then." The guard who spoke looked at her without much interest, his tone of voice more bored than anything else.

"I don't want to see his Excellency. I want to speak to Prince Manfred. He will see me."

The guard snorted. "And no doubt you've brought his baby with you! Go on with you, get lost."

"Maybe she's a Teutonic knight in disguise," said the other, chuckling at his own wit.

She reined in her temper, and remained polite. "Can't

you send a message to him? Tell him Maria Verrier would like to see him. Please?" She hated her own voice, so subservient—but angering them wouldn't get her anywhere.

"Hark at her!" One of the guards jerked a disdainful thumb at Maria. "'Please!' Listen, dearie. We don't run a messenger service for Scuolo women to have chats with princes. He'll send for you if he wants you."

Maria flushed with anger, and was just considering whether it would be worth the consequences of pushing her dagger through his ear when the guards suddenly jerked themselves out of the slouch and came to attention. The frail, white-haired podesta's wife was coming down.

For all the attention that Contessa Renate De Belmondo paid the guards they might as well have been statues, except one does not nod to statues. She did, however, greet Maria with every sign of pleasure.

"Maria Verrier, is it not? Have you come for our little chat? I am so sorry! I have to go across to the garrison in the Castel *a terra* right now. Would you mind coming in and waiting for me?"

Maria realized that Marco's efforts on her behalf had borne fruit after all. She did her best to curtsey, which, as she'd never been taught and she had a baby in her arms, was not a success. But Lady Renate was real quality, certainly as far as Maria was concerned, and ignored the awkwardness. Such things were only important to *Case Vecchie curti*, new money that still had to try to establish how important they were. For the Lady Renates of the world, it wasn't important how you looked—money could buy looks—it was what you were.

Lady Renate smiled. "I see you've brought your baby up, too. I wish I could see my own grandchildren. Or Lodovico Montescue trying to be a good great-grandfather, ha! Mind you, hooligans usually turn out to be very strict with their offspring . . . but it is impossible to think that he might be a great-grandfather soon."

She touched Alessia's cheek gently. "So soft! I love them when they're this age." She smiled again. "What I love most, of course, is that you can give them back when they cry!"

"Actually, milady, I came up to see Prince Manfred, about a friend. To be honest, I hadn't come to see you at all."

Lady Renate pulled a severe face, with just trace of a betraying dimple in her lined cheek. "And why not me, Hmm? Young men have, as a rule, no liking for babies. They don't know how to hold them."

Maria blushed. "I was . . . embarrassed to come and see you, milady. I'm just a *Scuolo* wife."

Lady Renate shook a finger at her. "And a friend of my old flame's granddaughter! Close enough a friend to have stood as her maid of honor at her wedding. That is an honor for anyone, for it means the *Casa* Montescue holds you in very high esteem. As ancient a house as there is in Venice. And if Lodovico thought I was good enough for him, then you must be good enough to keep me company. Come up and see me—and soon. What about Wednesday just after Terce?"

Maria settled for a half-bow rather than trying to curtsey again. "Thank you, milady. I will come."

Lady Renate laughed. "You'd better! I look forward to it. And now I must run. The women from Kérkira have come in a delegation to see the captain-general. I shall go and prevent bloodshed." She waved and walked out.

"No escort," said the one guard disapprovingly. "And not riding."

The other shrugged. "There isn't a person in Corfu who would dare hurt her, and riding makes her sore these days." He nodded to Maria. "I made a mistake. Come on, I'll take you up to the prince's quarters myself. You won't report us, will you?"

Maria tempered the sharpness of her retort with just enough amusement to let them know that she wasn't really joking. "Not this time. But next time I'll pull your bottom lip over your ears. And don't tempt me to show you how it is done. You came that close." She showed a gnat-sized gap with her fingers.

The guard chuckled. "If they had women in the army you'd make a good sergeant major. Sorry, Signora Verrier. I'll pass the word around so you don't end up stretching too many lips around here."

"You tell them to watch cheeking the *Scoulo* people," she warned him. "We've got short tempers and long memories."

The guard led her up through the castle, around enough passages and up and down enough staircases that she was thoroughly lost, before finally knocking on an ornate door.

"Who is it?" asked a woman's voice.

Maria knew that voice well enough to answer before the guard could. "It's me, Francesca. Maria."

The door opened immediately, and the guard ushered Maria and Alessia into a sybaritically appointed chamber, vanishing prudently and closing the door behind them as soon as they were well inside. Manfred was sprawled on a heavy oaken settle, grinning cheerfully.

"We don't know a whole lot," he said, without waiting for the question. "I was going to come and tell you later that Erik signaled that he was ashore and he had found his Svanhild. I imagine Benito is all right."

"He was born to be hanged," said Maria, trying to hide her relief.

Maria must have squeezed Alessia. The baby woke and objected to being treated like a bundle. Maria had the interesting experience of seeing the normally imperturbable Aquitainian woman look decidedly alarmed, as an indignant squall arose from the wrappings. "Is something wrong with her?" Francesca asked uneasily.

Maria rocked and bounced; Alessia made a few more pointed remarks about her cavalier treatment. "She's fine."

"Good." Francesca shook her head. "I'm not really maternal. I don't like babies much, I'm afraid."

Manfred grinned. "They're not infectious, Francesca." He pointed at Maria. "Come on, Maria. Advance on her. Let's see if Francesca will retreat into the bedroom to escape. I've been trying to tempt her back there all morning. I never thought of herding her."

Francesca was recovering her composure, possibly because Alessia hiccupped and decided that she had registered enough complaints for the moment. "Manfred! Babies hold no interest for me, for excellent reasons."

She began counting off on elegant fingers. "You cannot have an intelligent conversation with them. They are utterly and selfishly demanding of all of your time and energy, regardless of war, peace, or any other considerations. You—ah, never mind." She shrugged. "Not all women love babies, legends notwithstanding. I'm one of the ones who doesn't."

Manfred stood up. "I won't hold it against you. I must admit I'm not too keen on them myself. Maybe one day. But certainly not yet."

Francesca chucked him under the chin. "I can't tell you how relieved this makes me."

Maria said nothing. She knew that talking to people who didn't have children about the subject was a waste of their time and her effort. Besides, it was hardly her business to go around urging parenthood on people. She certainly couldn't see Francesca with children. And truth to tell, at one time she'd thought she would not like to have any herself.

Instead, she decided to bring up something else that had been nagging away under the worry about Benito. She'd heard about it from Umberto and now had it refreshed by Lady De Belmondo. The food rations, even though they were barely into the siege, were already causing unrest.

"I met the podesta's wife at the gate. A delegation of women from the town is going to see the captain-general. She said she was going to keep the peace." Maria looked sidelong at Francesca. "From what Kat told me, you collect information. Maybe you already know all about this, but there is a problem about food."

Francesca smiled. "I trade in gossip, yes. I did know about the food. I didn't know about the podesta's wife. There is something of distance between me and 'respectable' women. They don't like to be seen talking to me. But tell me more. I'd like a female handle on what is happening out there."

"Lady De Belmondo is . . . different. She talks to anyone, and everyone talks to her; the guards at the gate said she can go anywhere without fear. And Lodovico Montescue was one of her suitors when she was young."

"The old dog probably made up to half the women in Venice," said Manfred lazily. "If the stories I've heard are anything to judge by, he was worse than I was." He raised an eyebrow at Maria. "Worse even than Benito. Anyway, I'll leave you women to chatter. I'm going across to see Falkenberg. And then I'll go and look at what Emeric is doing in the way of siege preparations. I need to keep an eye on that."

"Not without Von Gherens," said Francesca sternly. "I promised him I wouldn't let you go out without him, and I won't let you break my promises."

Manfred grunted. "All right, I'll collect my baby-sitter. He'll be pacing the hallway anyway." He went out, blowing a kiss to Francesca.

When the door latch had clicked closed behind him, Francesca turned again to Maria. "I'm glad you brought this up. I had wanted to come and talk to you about it anyway."

She paused for a moment as if gathering her thoughts. "I need to set up a network of contacts. Manfred and the Knights worry about what Emeric's army is doing out there. I worry about what is going on in here. In the few days since the siege began, I've established that the Citadel is overripe for internal troubles, which I think are more dangerous than the external army. This food story is just one aspect. I wanted to ask for your help. This place has limits as far as access is concerned."

Maria laughed, a little bitterly. "You have no idea! You might not be considered 'respectable' by the ranking women, but there isn't a man in this place who would dare to stop you from going anywhere you wanted to. Getting in here for me was quite difficult. I scarcely dare think how the ordinary Corfiote would be treated."

"Yes. And the problems in the Citadel, I think, will mostly come from the Corfiote citizens who are excluded." Francesca frowned, then focused intently on Maria. "I need people out there who can tell me what is going on. I need a place for them to meet me, that won't attract attention. I've some gold, and some favors to offer to them."

Maria looked at her thoughtfully. "Can you get out of

here without drawing attention? Because if you can, I must introduce you to my friend Stella Mavroukis." Maria smiled. "She can talk the hind legs off two donkeys, but she knows everyone. She's been here for years, and she speaks Greek."

Francesca's eyes brightened with interest. "She sounds ideal. When can you organize this?"

"Tomorrow afternoon?" Alessia stirred in Maria's arms. "But now, I must go. Or you will get an experience of babies you won't enjoy."

Francesca was quick about showing her to the door.

Chapter 48

The rocks, in the paling predawn, were just visible by the lacing of foam around them. The wind was blowing spray off the water, leaving the descent greasy. The stony surface compared well to mossy pan-tiles in the rain, but it was steeper than any self-respecting roof would be. Benito decided the young shepherd guiding him had a great future in housebreaking, if he should need it.

Coming closer, Benito could now see that the rocks were twisted, shattered and sharp-edged, even in this poor light. That anyone would bring even a dinghy in here, let alone a thirty-five-foot lateen-rigged fishing boat, seemed like insanity. Yet, there she was, snugged up beside a huge boulder. Someone was busy attaching a bush to her mast, the only bit that stuck out above the rock.

Benito whistled. Kosti nearly ended up in the cove. He dropped the bush. "Now, see what you made me do," he said grumpily.

"How do I get across?"

"There's a ledge of rocks over there. Time it right and you won't get too wet."

Benito paid off the guide, rolled his trousers up, and walked into the surge. The water was cold, and the mussels underfoot were sharp. He walked forward cautiously, his city-born imagination putting sharks and giant octopi in the dark water. Encountering seaweed nearly had him into the deeper water with a shriek. However, he reached the fishing smack's mooring without any incidents. He pulled up onto the rock, and stepped into her. The smell nearly knocked him back ashore.

"Where is the skipper?"

"Where I'll be in a minute," said Kosti, finishing tying the bush to the masthead, just as the first rays of sunlight hit the mountain above them. "Under the sail. Asleep."

The sail had been made into a crude tent, and through the long, hot spring day, the crew slept. After an hour or so, Benito grew tired of the heat and the flies and waded back onto the shore and slept under a pine tree. He could see the open sea from here; and, waking during the day, he saw several patrolling Dalmatian galliots. But they didn't come close enough to the dangerous-looking rocks to spot the fishing boat. Even a land patrol would have to come very close to the edge of the near-vertical vegetation and crumbling limestone cliff to see her. The tough part was going to be avoiding being seen that night, once they were at sea.

The two men were overly well dressed for Paleokastritsa. They approached the table in the taverna diffidently. "Milord. We've heard a rumor that you came out of the Citadel."

Erik looked them over cautiously. The clothes, on closer inspection, had once been fine but showed signs of very hard wearing. Erik doubted that the Hungarians would have gotten around to using spies or informers . . . yet. "Why do you ask?"

The older of the two, the one with the neatly trimmed beard with hints of salt and pepper in the blackness, said grimly: "Milord, we're both Venetians who have estates here. Or, I should say, used to have. Our families have been killed and our homes burned. We want to know what is happening. We want the Republic's armies to sweep these Hungarian bastards into the sea. We've scouted along the ridgelines . . . all we can see is that the Citadel is under siege. There aren't that many men attacking."

"I just want to kill the bastards," said the younger

one, morosely, his pudgy, neat hands forming themselves into fists.

Erik pushed his chair back. "What I can tell you is that Emeric has landed many more men. As for when the Venetian Republic's relief forces will be here—"

He shrugged. "That is anyone's guess. I believe word has been sent, but whether it got through or not, I can't tell you. Of course, Emeric's Dalmatian pirates will try to stop the messages. So it may take a long time. Months at the very least."

The younger man said: "I told you so, Ambrosino. I'm going back out to kill a few of the bastards."

In Erik's assessment, the young man would probably die the first time he encountered a real soldier.

The older man patted him on the shoulder. "Forgive him, milord. He lost his wife and their newborn son. Pardon us for intruding on you."

Erik took a deep breath. If he was going to organize resistance to Hungarians, he had to start somewhere. This unlikely looking material was as good as any. The younger man was going to get himself killed anyway in his fury and grief. Let him at least put them to some use.

"Sit down." It was a command, not a request.

Both men looked at him in some surprise. So did the Vinlanders. But the two sat.

"If you go out there, you may kill a Croat or a Hungarian or two. However, if you really wish to hurt Emeric and his troops, you're going to have to be more methodical about it. Emeric has plenty more Croat troopers. But if you destroy his cannons or burn his supply dumps, then not only will you hurt him far more badly, you will save the lives of others."

The young man shook his head stubbornly. "I just want to kill the bastards."

"You'll only die quickly without achieving anything." Erik gave him a measuring look, and allowed a touch of scorn to come into it. The young man detected that scorn, and reddened. "You aren't a fighter. You aren't a soldier. You certainly aren't a mercenary, who by nature is the toughest and cruelest sort of soldier. Your fancy dueling-master won't have taught you a single thing that will work in a fight against these bastards, and what you don't know will get you killed the first time you run up against one. Is that what you want? Or would you rather make Emeric pay fifty-fold for what he's done?"

The young man was scarlet by now, but he raised his chin defiantly. "I want him to pay a hundredfold, never mind fifty-fold. But I'm not scared of dying."

"Then either learn to be," said Erik grimly, "or go somewhere else. I have no space in my troop for fool-hardy men."

"Your troop?"

Erik nodded. "I came out here for three purposes." He saw no reason to blather in public about his feelings for Svanhild, and certainly not Benito's secret mission. "Never mind the first two. The third, acting on Prince Manfred's behalf, was to recruit men and engage Emeric of Hungary's forces in . . . call it 'irregular warfare.' The kind of fighting we do in Vinland. I want to bleed Emeric white—draw off some of his forces from their attack on the Citadel, and make keeping the Citadel under siege a battle on two fronts. I want to make it as expensive as possible for him to be here, but I can't do that without men who are as interested in keeping their own skins intact as they are in killing Emeric's men. I don't need heroes, I need men who can be as cunning as foxes and hard to catch as weasels. Are you with me?"

"I am," said a firm voice from an unexpected quarter. Thalia spoke quietly but clearly. "I am. If I can save one other life, that's enough. If hurting this king will avenge my Georgio . . . then even if I am a woman I will fight. What kind of men will not?"

The plumper young man nodded, looking at Thalia in some surprise. Suddenly, with no warning, he began to cry. Deep, bitter sobs.

"He's upset," said the older man. "But he'll be an asset, milord. Giuliano's father was a master-at-arms. When he retired here, he married a local girl and they had one chick. Flavio Lozza gave his son one-on-one training from the day he could hold a sword." He smiled. "I think Flavio was secretly disappointed that the boy only wanted to grow olives and play the lute."

Lozza's son? Erik reflected that appearances could deceive. Flavio Lozza had been Giuliano Dell'Arta's instructor. Giuliano had taught both Manfred and him when they'd been in Venice with the Knights of the Holy Trinity's ill-fated tour with the Woden-casket. He had regarded Lozza as the father of rapier-work. Flavio, it would seem, had named his son for his old protégé—and this was certainly the last place Erik would have expected to see the son of Flavio Lozza.

Almost, he regretted what he'd said about "fancy sword-masters." But not quite. It was one thing to be a master of rapier-work; it was quite another to face mercenaries and Magyar horse-barbarians whose interest was in killing you quickly, not stylishly. Perhaps the plump boy wouldn't be killed that quickly. But there was a large difference between even the best-trained amateur and a battle-hardened professional soldier. "And you, signor? Have you got surprises for me too?"

The older man shrugged. "Not really. I hunt. I can ride. I know the island well."

"And you speak Greek?"

The older man shrugged. "Not as well as Giuliano. He got it from his mother, and then his wife was a local."

"And of course we will help, too," said Bjarni, slapping him on the back.

"To be direct, you are going to watch over Svanhild," said Erik, feeling uncomfortable. "Not go running around the Corfu hills in the dark. If possible I'd like to get you all a passage across to Italy or even Greece. This is not your war."

"We stand by our kin," said Bjarni, stiffly.

Erik grinned. "I'm not exactly that . . . yet."

The big Vinlander grinned back. "You haven't a chance, Erik. Hildi's made up her mind. Even if she has to chase you with a baby she'll get you."

"Bjarni!" said Svanhild, blushing. "It's a good thing Mama can't hear you." But she didn't deny it. In fact, she gave him a sidelong glance that had speculation in it.

"Maybe you can just lend Erik three or four of us. Like me," said Kari, looking eager.

"Maybe I can just pay him to take you away," growled Gulta.

They hugged the coast with great care, creeping southwards. No one who didn't know these waters intimately was going to come this close in the darkness. It was an alarming place to be sailing at some speed.

"It's coming up for a blow," said Taki ominously.

"So what do we do?"

Benito saw a flash of teeth in the darkness. "We set our nets. Then we haul them and then we run with the wind. We're fishermen from Levkas who've been blown off course. Fishermen have fish in their boats. So we're going to get ourselves some."

So, for the next two hours Benito learned to set nets. "Taki is making an extra profit out of your labor," said Spiro. "Demand wages. Or a share in the catch."

"You'd better hope it is a bad one," said Kosti. "Or we'll be here all night."

When the nets came in, twitching with silver, and Benito saw how Taki beamed in the moonlight, Benito began to realize Kosti might not have been joking.

With wooden crates full of fish they headed away from Corfu on a following wind. By that time, they all looked and smelled like fishermen, even Benito. He was no stranger to hard work, not after the way that Erik had been drilling him, but this required a whole new set of muscles and calluses. His hands were raw and cut up, and his arms and shoulders ached by the time it was over.

Taki rubbed his hands and produced the wine, passing it around to the rest of the crew. "Never let it be said nothing good comes out of a war. I've wanted to fish old Scathos' bank for years, but never dared."

"I kept wondering whether the old bastard would still come out and shoot at us," said Kosti.

Spiro took a pull at the wine. "What? Shoot at your handsome face? Scathos' daughters would kill him."

Kosti pulled the jug away from him and handed it to Benito. "I hear that's the reason he wants to kill *you*."

"Me? I'm shocked."

"Well, you or any other passing fellow. Those are wild girls of his."

"Time to shift those sails!" Taki yelled.

The boat went about and they sailed on, but the direction troubled Benito. It felt wrong. "Just where are we going?" he asked Taki eventually. "You're supposed to be running me across to the Italian shore."

Taki belched contentedly. "And I am. But we'd not get across the Straits of Otranto in the dark. Not with this wind. So we're taking a longer cut at it. Have some more wine."

He frowned. "I don't want to be drunk if we have trouble."

The captain chuckled. "What are you going to do if we do have trouble? Fight a galley's worth of men? Try and outrun them? This is a fishing boat, not a galley. There is nothing much you can do except try and look like a drunken bum of a fisherman. So have some more wine. The more like us you look and sound, the safer you are."

The day was still very young, and Antipaxos some miles to the north of them, but still in sight, when they were intercepted.

It was a Byzantine galley. Benito realized, as it raced closer, just how futile trying to run would have been. Briefly, he thought the galley was simply going to run them down. But it drew up beside them. The officer on the bow bellowed something in rapid Greek.

Benito had the unpleasant realization that his life was in the hands of a bunch of poor people he didn't know very well, who would be well rewarded for selling him out and who would be killed if they were caught harboring him. Worst of all, he didn't understand what they were saying. He resolved to learn Greek, if he got out of here alive.

With his heart pounding, his mouth dry, Spiro heard the Greek officer yell: "What are you doing out here?"

"We're fishermen," said Taki. "What do you think? We're on our way back home to Levkas. We got caught up in the blow last night and came too far north."

"Stand by to be boarded."

A dozen or so marines boarded the boat. The *Case Vecchie* did his best "I-am-a-poor-scared-fisherman" look. It wasn't hard to do the scared bit, Spiro realized. But he rapidly realized what a genius Taki had been to insist on catching fish last night. The fish, under damped sacks, were still cool and fresh—the most convincing evidence possible that this was, indeed, nothing more than a fishing boat.

The officer with the marines looked about—obviously searching for refugees, or maybe arms, supplies, valuables. There were few places anyone could hide, so it was a very cursory look. The nets, the boxes of fish, the small crew all said *fishing boat*.

"Why did you come so far north?" he demanded. "Orders went to all the villages that no one was to fish within sight of Antipaxos."

Taki cringed. "My lord. In the dark we drifted too far. We didn't mean to . . ."

The Byzantine officer hit him, sending him sprawling across the fish. "Fool. By the smell of you, I think you drank too much to celebrate the catch. It wasn't the wind that got you here, it was the wine. If we find you this far north again, we'll sink you. Do you understand?"

Taki, on his knees now, nodded furiously. "Yes, milord! It won't happen again." His voice quavered.

"It had better not." The officer pointed to two of the marines. "Here, you two. Take one of these boxes. We could use some fresh fish."

"Milord, my fish," protested Taki.

"Consider it a fine for breaking the law," said the officer. "And think how lucky you are not to have your filthy little vessel sunk."

Taki did the grovel magnificently. "Thank you, milord. But . . . can I at least have my box back? I'm a poor fisherman, milord . . ."

The officer laughed. "No."

The galley receded. The apparently hard-working crew of the fishing boat started to laugh. And laugh.

"Prissy-assed *malákas*." Taki blew a raspberry at the

departing ship and then grinned at Benito. "You're my witness, *Case Vecchie*. They boarded my ship in the Venetian Republic's waters, stole my fish and—worst of all!—stole Venetian property."

Benito looked suitably mystified. "Venetian property?"

"The fish box. It belongs to the fish market in Kérkira. It is the property of the Republic of Venice—which is what that prim little official at the fish market tells me every time I come in. Property of Venice! And he took it!"

The crew started to laugh again.

"Piracy! That's what it was," said Spiro, trying to keep a straight face, passing over a jug of wine.

Benito took a swig and nodded sagely. "We'll swear out a charge against them in front of the podesta, and let him have the ambassador summoned, for a severe reprimand and a demand for reparations."

"Especially for the valuable catch," said Kosti. "The idiots chose a box of trash fish."

"So when do we turn and run across the straits to Bari or Brindisi?" asked Benito.

Taki raised an eyebrow. "We're not going to run across the strait. There they have twenty-five lousy little leagues to patrol. But they can't patrol the whole Ionian Sea. You're in for a haul, boy. I hope you don't get seasick easily."

Emeric looked with satisfaction at the bluish haze of gunpowder smoke blowing gently across the channel. The forty-eight-pound bombards took a huge amount of powder and a long time to load, but they were his second choice for reducing and penetrating the walls of a besieged fortress. Evening was drawing in, but the bombardment would not stop for that.

His first choice was treachery. Months before the assault on Corfu, he had begun to prepare the ground for it. Far better than the captain-general, he already knew the number of Corfiote refugees within the walls of the Citadel. He knew how much food there was in their garrison's storehouse, and he was already getting daily reports from Fianelli. He knew a great deal about the likes and weaknesses of the various officers, too.

One of the things that had made Emeric so sure Corfu would be an easy conquest was the past history of the captain-general. True enough, the man was not corrupt, but he was a vain and incompetent fool. His handling of the insurrection in the Venetian enclave in Trebizond had been so bad that it had gotten him sent to a station where there would never again be a need for military action. He was a bungler, but a bungler with political connections. In the Venetian Republic, a bungler whose godfather is the Doge could go far. Unfortunately for Captain-General Tomaselli, there was a new Doge.

The garrison commander, on the other hand, was a disaster from Emeric's point of view. Commander Leopoldo would have to die. Emeric had bought several of the soldiers within the forces at the commander's disposal. Most of the troops serving the Venetian Republic were mercenaries, for sale to the highest bidder. It was just unfortunate that they did not have a mercenary commanding officer. So: Commander Leopoldo would have to be assassinated. When he was engaged in some firefight—best to do it unobtrusively.

Emeric went back into his tent and drew the circle. Scratched the pentacle and began the ritual that would allow him to speak to the chief of his spies within the Citadel. At this time of day, Fianelli would be in his cellar waiting.

PART VII
June, 1539 A.D.

Chapter 49

Francesca shook her head. "To be honest with you, Eberhard, this place is positively Venetian with intrigue. There is a strong pro-Byzantine faction, of long standing, among the Libri d'Oro. Not surprising of course, since Corfu's local aristocracy are Greeks themselves. Fortunately, they distrust Emeric of Hungary. But they long for Venice to lose power and for their own stars to be ascendant under Alexius."

Eberhard snorted. "That wastrel would be more likely to sell their precious island to pay off some of his debts. Or just to have more money to spend on his vices."

"Precisely," Francesca agreed, nodding. "But not having the knowledge that you do, *Ritter*, the pro-Byzantines here entertain some very unrealistic ideas. So far as they know, Alexius is cut from the same cloth as his father, which would make them Byzantine allies rather than vassals. And, most importantly, would put Corfiotes—or at least Greeks—back in the seats of power here. They resent the way the Venetian overlords here on the island often treat them. It's the sneering, really, not anything material. But noblemen—especially sorry, idle ones like most of these wretched Libri d'Oro—take offense easily."

"And how well placed are they to act on those unrealistic ideas?" asked Manfred, looking concerned. "I've known people to be prepared to die for some really stupid things."

"I am still compiling a list, Manfred. But so far, they have some bodyguards and some interesting working positions."

Manfred nodded, frowning. "One thing in our favor is that the Hungarians are present in such force. Nobody, not even the most self-deceiving pro-Byzantine Libri d'Oro, can believe that Emeric is going to give up this prize so easily."

Eberhard shook his head. "Self-deception is the greatest strength of such people, Manfred. Petty noblemen with neither work nor war to keep them occupied will often spend all their time wallowing in perceived insults and fantasies of retribution."

"True," said Francesca. "But Emeric's vicious reputation does work against him. So long as it does not appear that Alexius is allied with him in this venture, we may be able to keep the faction quiet. Quieter, anyway."

Manfred poured another cup of wine. "I never thought I'd be pleased to hear that Emeric was such a murderous, treacherous son of a bitch. So who else do we have stacked against us? A pro-Hungarian faction?"

"Fortunately, Emeric's reputation works for him there, too—or rather, works for us. There is, however, a Montagnard faction, that believes *you* have come to take over the island under the pretext of this war, and are very much in favor of the notion." Francesca dimpled. "Of course there are a few who also think it is true, but are opposed to the idea. And I have found evidence that someone is buying information. That suggests Emeric has some spies here in the Citadel."

Eberhard had been staring at her with more and more astonishment as she spoke, and now his mouth was actually agape. "How do you find all this out, Francesca?" he asked in disbelief.

"Among other things, Maria introduced me to the main artery of gossip in the Citadel. Sooner or later everything gets told to Stella." Francesca's smile faded, and turned to a frown. "She also told me another thing I must discuss with Eneko Lopez. She says there is a cabal of true magicians here, and they are not Christian."

Manfred chuckled. "Sleepy little seaside town, eh?"

❖   ❖   ❖

In the living quarters which Sibling Eleni had provided for them adjoining the chapel, Eneko Lopez was scowling. "There, Francis—again. Did you sense it? And you, Diego?"

Both men nodded. "Someone is using Satanic magic in this Citadel," muttered Diego. "That was fairly close, although I couldn't sense the direction."

"And *that* one! A sending ritual requires blood."

"Most Satanic rituals do, Francis." Eneko shook his head. "At least that one doesn't require human blood."

"That's not my point, Eneko. We're under siege. Soon enough, finding a goat or chicken to slaughter isn't going to be so easy."

Lopez thought about it, for a moment. "True. We should speak to Francesca. Unless I miss my guess, she'll be running the counterespionage work here before much longer. The podesta is an old man and the captain-general is . . . well. Not competent."

"So charitable, Eneko!" chuckled Francis. "I would have used a stronger expression."

Lopez smiled thinly. "Well, charity *is* a Christian virtue."

Diego didn't seem to share in the humor. "Finding a stray goat or a chicken will be getting hard. But with thousands of people packed into this place, finding a human to slaughter won't."

Eneko and Francis stared at him. Diego shrugged. "I would remind you that charity is not a Satanic virtue."

"We'd best talk to Francesca about that as well," murmured Francis. "Although . . ."

Gloomily, Lopez finished the thought. "How do you keep track of people to see if any are disappearing—when half the people in this Citadel are here illegally to begin with? Thanks to that jackass Tomaselli!"

"Charity, Eneko, charity," cautioned Francis.

"I *am* being charitable," grumbled Lopez.

"Not to jackasses."

Through the open door of the taverna in Paleokastritsa, Erik could see that the sky across the straits of Otranto was traced with clouds the color of salmon-flesh. The closer view was even more distracting to him. Neither Svanhild's profile nor the memory of salmon in the ice-fed rivers of home were helping Erik with the matter in hand: planning an irregular campaign against Emeric's forces.

"Essentially, we need two things. We need information, and we need safe bases."

"What's wrong with Paleokastritsa?"

Erik shook his head. "Its defenses are good, but not that good. It'll fall eventually, either to a determined assault or more likely to siege. There is no second way out of the town. And we think like foxes now. Foxes always need a second or third exit to their lairs. We'll rely on friendly towns and peasants for food and information—but never from the same one twice in a row, and we'll never stay in any of the settlements. If we bring the wrath of the Hungarians down on any Corfiote town, not only will we have betrayed them, we will have betrayed ourselves. We'll get no more help from the peasants."

He looked at the faces around the table; no one disagreed. "You all know what the Hungarians are going to do, every time we strike: they'll destroy the nearest village, if it shows any signs of our presence. The peasants are in hiding now, but they'll have to return to their holdings soon. Farms and crops don't wait. We need the countryside sympathetic to us and hostile to the Hungarians."

Ambrosino nodded. "It makes sense. Well, there is a spot I used to use when I was hunting. Not a village for three miles. You've got an excellent view of the surrounding countryside, there is water in the cave, and there are two ravines leading away. There'll be a bit of grazing down in the ravines, too. I thought of building a hunting-box up there, but it was just too expensive to get the materials up. There are wild boar and bears up there. Good hunting. And I've eaten worse than bear."

"We'll check it out tomorrow," said Erik. "We also need to organize proper scouting of Emeric's forces."

"We'll put you in at that fishing village," said Taki, pointing to the Italian shore. "The locals are at sea, by the looks of it, so we won't have to try and explain that we're not stealing their fish."

"As if we would," said Spiro, virtuously.

"Unless we got half the chance," snorted Kosti. "I thought we might visit a decent-size harbor and taste the local girls and meet the local wine."

"You mean meet the girls and taste the wine," corrected Taki.

Kosti shook his head, grinning. "I prefer it my way around."

Benito realized he was going to miss these fishermen. He was going to miss being at sea, where all the responsibility devolved on Taki. Now he'd have to manage for himself, and it was a long way home to Venice. He had written up the prearranged message for Erik. It would pass as a bill of fishmarket landings. The Bonito on the listing would tell Erik to hand over the money.

Benito now felt guilty. He'd done his dangerous bit. But Taki, Spiro and Kosti would have to get back through the cordon before they saw the paltry bit of silver. The only trouble was, short of the jewels—all he had was paltry bits of silver himself.

"Likely if we go to one of the big ports there'll be questions asked. We'd end up having to pay port fees!" Taki sounded as if he'd rather have his teeth drawn.

The idea seemed to horrify the others too. Spiro shook his head. "Besides, Kosti, we need to get home. There is a war over there and we've got people to look out for. Your mother. My sister—and you watch your mouth about my sister."

"Wouldn't say a word. Not while you're listening, anyway."

Spiro took a swing at him on general principles.

So Benito climbed off the boat and onto the Italian shore with no more than his clothes and the three fishermen's good wishes in his ears. After several days at sea, the ground seemed to be moving up and down.

He turned and waved. Taki's ratty old boat was already moving out to sea at a fair clip.

Benito turned his face to the shore and his more immediate problems. He was now faced with the problem of where, exactly, to go. It was midmorning, and he was outside a tiny little whitewashed fishing village near the toe of the boot that is Italy.

Originally someone, maybe Erik, had said he should ride up the coast to Venice. That was before Erik had seen him ride. Also . . .

Well, it seemed very easy when discussing it with people like Erik, who knew how to do this sort of thing. "Get to Italy and ride to Venice." The first question, in a spot like this, would be: *Ride? On what?* By the looks of the fishing settlement even a donkey would be wildly optimistic.

Maybe he should follow the course of the cowardly Capitano Selvi, and head for the Tyrrhenian sea; then, travel up the west coat of Italy. The immediate question was: Should he cut across the Calabrian Apennines—or remain along the coastline?

The mountains looked threatening. Unfamiliar. In the distance up there he could see a hilltop village—other than that, the area was forested, with the forest only being interrupted by patches of what could be vines and white rock. A lot of white rock. It all looked very big and daunting.

He saw an urchin from the fishing hamlet—calling five tiny houses a village was gross flattery—approaching cautiously. Ready to run, curiosity overwhelming obvious fear. He looked at Benito as if he expected him to sprout wings and horns or at very least large teeth.

Maybe thirty yards back were three others of still younger age, all peering, big-eyed, nervous but fascinated by this strange apparition. It didn't look like the village saw a lot of strangers. Benito waved at the kid, who was, at the outside, six years old. The older boys would be at sea, he supposed. *"Ciao,"* he said.

The kid backed off two steps; then realized Benito wasn't following and that *"Ciao"* was not really a threat. He said *"Ciao"* back, and was rewarded with a smile from Benito. And then the kid let go with such a rapid fire of local patois that Benito managed to understand one word in ten. Some of the words sounded like Greek. Spiro had said there were a fair number of Greek settlers here.

"Whoa." Benito spoke slowly and pronounced his words with care. "I want to buy food. I want to ask directions."

He still had to say it twice.

The fishwife in her peasant blacks was a little more intelligible. Slightly. She was just as curious. Benito didn't see the point in too much secrecy. "There is a blockade on the straits of Otranto. I'm from up north and I want to go home. So I scrounged a voyage over here. Where is the nearest big town? And can you spare some food for me? I can pay."

He pulled out a copper penny, guessing that even these didn't arrive too often in a place like this. The smile and the haste with which she produced some rosso wine, cipudazzi—little red onions pickled in olive oil and vinegar—and tiny spiky artichokes, told him he was dead right. She bustled off to bring him some fresh bread and some maccu, a broad bean and fennel purée; also some fresh figs. It was a repast he was sure would have been the family's main meal. Benito hoped the husband would bring home a good catch.

The peasant woman, with the children peering around her skirts, was less useful about the nearest town. "Catanzaro. It is great city! It has more than this many streets!" She held up a hand of work-calloused fingers. "But it is far. Perhaps thirty miles away, up a ravine. We go there with the dried fish every autumn for the festival of Saint Gamina. Or there is Reggio di Calabria, in the straits of Messina, but that is a huge place and so far I have never been there. My man once went there to sell fish, but he was cheated and never went back."

A town that had a reputation for cheating rural fisherman sounded good to Benito. He might at least be able to find a ship and also be able to sell a jewel in such a place—neither of which, he knew, he'd be able to do in a small rural hamlet.

"How far is this place?"

"Oh! It must be seventy miles, Your Honor."

A vast distance, almost unthinkable. Once, confined to Venice, it would have seemed so to Benito himself.

After his meal Benito set off, walking. It was slower than riding, but it seemed to be the only real option. By midafternoon he was very aware of just how soft his feet had become. He cut himself a sturdy stick, which didn't seem to help a great deal.

Leaving the fishing hamlet he'd struck a trail. It seemed unpopulated, and determined to take him away from the coastline. Eventually another track joined it, but it was equally lacking in traffic. He was beginning to wonder where he could sleep that night, when he caught sight of the hind end of a donkey, disappearing around the next bend.

Circumstances, thought Benito wryly as he hurried to catch up with the donkey, change your perspective. He'd never ever have thought he'd be glad to see the tail end of a donkey. The donkey was part of a string of seven, laden with gurgling, oil-sheen-gleaming ticklike skin-bottles. It was being led by a fellow who looked more than a little like a donkey himself. The oilman produced a thing that was somewhere between a knife and a sword, and well-supplied with rust.

"What do you want?" he demanded suspiciously. Benito repeated his story. It didn't seem to convince the oilman at all. "You stay behind me. I'm not having you tell bandits I'm coming."

"Saints! Look, any self-respecting bandit would kill you in about ten seconds. All I want is some information. And I'm not moving at less than donkey speed just to oblige you."

"Stay back or I'll make you into sliced salami!" The oil seller waved his knife about at Benito's nose.

"Look, I can pay." Benito pulled out what he'd thought was a copper. "I'm happy to pay . . ."

The oilman's eyes lit up. "Give it to me." He waved the knife at Benito.

Benito looked at his hand and realized he had silver, and not copper there. "I'll give you a copper penny for your help. I need this."

The oilman lunged. Benito used the stout stick he'd

cut to hit the man's elbow. Hard. The clumsy knife went flying. Benito grabbed him. A nasty short scuffle ensued, ending with the oilman pinioned under Benito and shrieking: *"Help! Bandits! Murder!"*

Benito swatted the oilman's ear, reflecting as he did so that Erik had taught him very well even in such a short timespan. "Shut up. You tried to rob me, you idiot. Now get up and stop yowling. I dropped my silver penny because of you. If you don't find it for me I'll kick your ass through your teeth. Now get up."

"I can't. You're sitting on me."

Benito stood up. The oilman, on his knees, looked for the silver. Fortunately it was easy to find; nervously, the oilman handed it over.

"Pick up that cheese-cutter of yours." The oilman gaped at Benito but picked up his knife.

"Now—I need know where I can sleep tonight. And does this track lead back to the coast? I want to get to Reggio di Calabria."

The oilman bowed. "Your Honor, no one goes down to the coast. Well, only a few very poor fishermen. The Barbary Coast pirates raid it, and it is full of malaria. But this track joins another track which leads to Cantonia, maybe a mile away. There is road from there you can follow on to Reggio di Calabria."

"Right. Well, I think we go on together. Otherwise you'll come to this Cantonia place claiming I've robbed you."

The oilman did his best not to look as oily as his wares. "Your Honor, I would never do that! I'm an honest man."

"The sight of my only piece of silver seemed to change that," said Benito grimly.

They walked on at donkey pace. At length they came to the walled town. The oilman held out his hand. "Give me the copper you owe me for guiding you."

"Where are the two coppers you promised me for helping you with the donkeys?" demanded Benito very loudly, for the benefit of at least a dozen local residents. "Give it to me or I will swear out a charge against you with the podesta."

"I never promised you—"

"Yes, you did! Cheat! Thief!"

The oilman gaped. "But you—?"

Benito turned to the interested locals. "This man promised me money! I have worked and now he wants to cheat me!"

One of the women sniggered. "The podesta is in Montaforte. And if you can get money out of that old skinflint without a knife against his throat, you will have managed something no one else can do." She eyed Benito speculatively. "Though there is no knowing what a handsome man could do."

"Especially with you, Bella," said one of the onlookers. She snorted and flounced her hips for Benito's benefit.

Benito threw up his hands. "I'm a peaceful man. And I was coming this way anyway. Is there a taverna where I could buy a glass of wine to get the smell of donkeys out of my nostrils?"

"I can show you the taverna," said Bella archly.

Benito shook his head ruefully, looking at her swaying walk. Certain kinds of trouble you can get rid of. Others follow you around. He'd be leaving very, very early the next morning.

Predawn found him heading, very quietly, off down the trail for Reggio di Calabria. Evening found him there. As cities went it was a small one. After the back-country Benito found it busy, bustling, and comfortingly familiar.

"And so we came to Corfu." Maria took a sip of some of the finest wine she'd ever tasted. The white-haired Contessa Renate De Belmondo, wife of the Podesta of Corfu, smiled. She was one of those people who smiled to their eyes, and the fine creases in her skin bore testimony to the fact that she smiled often.

On the lace cloth between them, on a silver salver, lay some delicate almond biscotti. Maria marveled at them. Marveled at where she was. Marveled at the fact that she had just finished telling a *Case Vecchie* lady—a *Case Vecchie Longi* lady, born, bred and raised—more about her life than she'd ever told anyone.

There was something motherly about this woman. Maria's mother hadn't been "motherly." She'd been a working woman who'd done her best to look after her daughter, but she hadn't had any time to spare for cuddling and comforting. Their lives had been hard, Maria's as well as her mother's. Maria suspected that her mother had made the decision to ensure that her daughter learned early that life was hard, and would always be.

Francesca had helped and advised Maria, but she wouldn't choose the word "motherly" to describe her either. Maria smiled to herself. Francesca ferreted out information; she manipulated, charmed, sometimes lied through her teeth, but she showed no signs of being "motherly." But the contessa . . . got you to volunteer it. If Francesca could get her, as well as Stella, to provide information . . .

There would be very little in the entire confined world that was Corfu, great and small, that she couldn't find out. But somehow Maria knew that Renate De Belmondo was the perfect listener because she wouldn't ever tell anyone what she'd heard. Most people used conversation to talk about themselves. Renate De Belmondo volunteered little; she just listened.

The conversation shifted to babies. And here the contessa did offer something about herself. "My children were all born here on Corfu. I tried earlier in Venice, oh, I tried and I tried, but it was only here that I finally got pregnant." She smiled mysteriously. "It's a very fertile place, Corfu."

Chapter 50

From the shelter of the pines high up on the slope, Erik's small force watched and waited. Erik now had seventeen men. Some Venetian settlers, some locals with grudges, and Kari and his two brothers. They were about a mile and half south of the Citadel, above the oil-store that Emeric's men had taken over as their storage depot. The huge forty-eight-pound bombards took a lot of powder and it had to be stored somewhere a safe distance from the battlefront. There were some forty Serb pikemen doing guard-shifts and ten Croat light cavalry riding patrols.

The worst of Emeric's forces, Erik suspected. Probably a punishment duty for the Croats, as most of their comrades were still looting among properties that had not yet been picked over. The cavalry patrols consisted of going to a nearby village and sifting through the ruins for anything that even looked like loot, or sleeping. The guards at the gunpowder magazine looked unseasoned, and already looked bored. They were certainly lackadaisical about the patrols around their new palisade.

Erik and Kari had crept within twenty yards. From here Erik could see facial expressions and, if he'd been able to speak Serbian, could have eavesdropped. Erik studied the guards, their positions and their camp. Then they leopard-crawled back to the pines.

Giuliano had a surprise for them there. A shepherd boy who had come upon the group had been hastily seized and persuaded they weren't going to kill him. In fact he could profit by telling them about the Hungarian magazine.

"He says there is a place at the back where the stones prevented them from digging the logs in. There are some small gaps. He has crawled in and stolen some things."

Erik sighed. "Now Kari will have to moan about how this crawling is ruining his breeches again. We'd better go and have a look-see."

Kari snorted and examined his knees, rubbing the material. "I wouldn't say no to a decent set of buckskins. These weren't meant for this work. This is almost too easy, Erik. We go in this hole, cut a few throats, and set fire to it."

Erik shook his head. "When that lot blows . . . well, I want to be at least a half-mile away and traveling. We might go in that way but we're going to have to get out fast. That means by the gate and onto a horse as quickly as possible."

King Emeric had been modeling things again. He pointed now to the model of the Citadel of Corfu; to the channel between it and the mainland. "How is the progress with the moles going, Count Dragorvich?"

The stocky count, Emeric's chief siegemaster, rubbed his chin reflectively. "If we worked on one at a time I could have one done in three weeks. But the two-pronged approach means progress is slower. Maybe five weeks? The channel is quite deep and we're under heavy bombardment. The mine is not going to work for now, Your Majesty. Water comes in as fast as we can take it out with a bucket-chain, and the diggers are not even at sea level yet. The ground is still saturated from the winter rains. Summer's only begun."

"I'll get the guns to focus on the south and north towers," said Emeric. "That's where their guns are firing onto the moles from. We'll leave off pounding the gate and the rest of the walls for a while."

An officer came hastily out of the dark and into the king's pavilion. Once there, he stood rigidly before the king. Emeric acknowledged the Magyar cavalry commander with a curt nod. "Ah. Colonel. How go things with sacking of the Venetian estates? Any resistance?"

The colonel sneered. "These Venetians are soft, Sire. There have been a few minor bits of fighting, but we've barely lost men. A couple of Croats who were where they weren't supposed to be. A checkpoint guard. But other than that, nothing much."

"You've taken appropriate retribution for these incidents, I trust?"

"Sire, the problem is: On whom? The peasants have hidden out in the hills. We've caught some, of course, but most of them just aren't there, and the men haven't left those they've caught in one piece. As for the Venetians . . . most of them have been killed anyway. So, Sire, the problem is there is no one to extract retribution from. There are few walled towns we haven't bothered with, but anything we can get to has been dealt with hard already."

Emeric pursed his lips, looking thoughtful. "I think it is time to stop using the sword on peasants, Colonel. It's time for the knout, instead. We need someone to work the land here. Pass the instruction to your men. Hunt the maquis. Round them up, put them to work. There is no need to be gentle, however. And any resistance still gets the sword. Or make an example of one of them on a sharpened stake."

"Yes, Sire."

In the darkness Erik sucked in his breath and squeezed his body forward through the gap. A ten-year-old shepherd might fit through it easily enough. A hundred-and-ninety-pound Icelander was a different matter altogether. He pushed forward.

Someone grabbed him by the hair.

"Got you, you thieving bastard," said the grabber. "Hey, boys, I've got him!"

Erik was in an awkward situation. One arm was still trapped in the gap between the two logs. His tomahawk and knife were on the wrong side of the barrier. Clawing upwards with one hand he managed to grab his assailant by the shirt front and hauled.

"Let go!"

Something smashed against Erik's ear. Suddenly the hand grasping his hair went slack. The man Erik was holding by the shirtfront flopped toward him. Pulling himself forward and rolling over, Erik saw Kari jump off the palisade, land in front of him and retrieve his knife from the man's back . . . And a guard came running up.

The guard saw Kari, his fallen companion, but not Erik. Erik snagged the newcomer's ankle as he rushed at Kari with a spear thrust that would have spitted the young Vinlander like a pigeon. The result of Erik's intervention was that he pole-vaulted on the spear to land in a crumpled heap at Kari's feet. The Vinlander leaned over and hit the guard with calculated force on the back of the head.

Erik had by this stage struggled free. "Wait!" he whispered to the others just through the hole. Grabbing a victim each, Kari and he hastily dragged them into the deep shadows.

No more guards came. So, after waiting perhaps a hundred heartbeats, Erik called the rest through.

Thalia came first. "You were supposed to stay with the horses!"

"There is work to be done," she said with a grim intensity, hands on her hips, but still holding a knife. "On Corfu, women work. I am here to do it. I've cut a pig's throat, and I don't see the difference between this filth and a pig, except that pigs are better."

Erik saw no point in a stand-up argument. Besides, as he'd learned on the Vinland frontier, a determined woman can be a lot more deadly than a reluctant male warrior.

"What happened?" whispered the plump Giuliano, after they'd popped him out of the hole like a cork from a bottle of petillant wine.

"That young shepherd wasn't as undetected as he thought," Erik whispered grimly. "The guards had set a trap for him. Fortunately they were expecting a small young thief and not for Kari to pop over the top of the palisade. Anyway, move out. They still outnumber us."

Shortly, they no longer did. It was brutal, murderous work. But, as Erik reflected, their enemies' choices were stark. Die quickly at the hands of the Corfiote guerillas, die when this magazine blew, or die slowly at Emeric's hands for failing him. The Corfiote guerillas couldn't keep prisoners, and the alternative to killing the enemy was to fail in their objective.

Erik didn't plan to fail. After this, Emeric's forces would be wary, and successes would be much more hard-won. They had to start big, because if they'd started with raids on outposts, they'd never have gotten to a big target like this.

But he didn't like killing sleeping guards either. It was too much like butchery.

The trickiest phase was the last one. The magazine was not a place anyone would want to strike a lucifer in, and they had no access to wicks. Before Erik set the long powder-trail, they took sixteen small casks of powder, one per horse, and loaded them up.

Then all but Erik left quietly. There was the barrack encampment not two hundred yards off, with sleeping Croats, and the rest of the guard detachment. One galloping horse could not be avoided, but at least there didn't have to be seventeen of them. The gate was arranged with a spike holding the bar up, and a stout cord that could be tossed over the top of the gate. Erik could pull it when he was outside and drop the bar. Even if someone heard the horse gallop past and came to investigate the palisade, they would have to climb it to get in. Hopefully, by that time the powder trail would have burned to the open cask.

Erik laid the trail of black gunpowder carefully, wishing he had a better sense of how fast the stuff burned. He was experienced enough with firearms, but this kind of work really needed a bombardier who knew exactly what he was doing.

He laid it right to the gate. Lit it. It fizzed briefly and went out. He took a deep breath, forcing himself to be calm, then went back and laid a second, more generous trail. Lit it again . . .

It burned, burned fast—fizzing and racing toward the

dark buildings. After an instant's horrified pause, a voice within him shrieked: *Go—go—go!*

The Icelander stepped out, closed the gate, his fingers shaking a little as he tugged the bar into place and pulled his horse's halter loose. Erik flung himself into the saddle and urged the horse to a gallop. He might break the horse's knees doing such a reckless thing—he might break his own neck—but this was still a lesser risk than staying around.

He heard a shout and a shot in the darkness. He just kept his head down and applied the spurs.

And then he didn't have to anymore. He just had to stay on the horse.

He certainly couldn't have heard any commands to stop.

Manfred and Von Gherens were up on the battlements of the inner curtain wall, looking out at the muzzle-flashes and campfires on the Kérkira side of the Citadel. So, for the first time since his injury, was Falkenberg.

"Two moles." Falkenberg shook his head disapprovingly. "This is Emeric interfering with his commanders again. He has the notion that he is a military genius."

"Thank God for a small mercy," said Von Gherens. "We could have someone who didn't sit on his brains out there, and then we'd be between the hammer and the anvil."

Manfred snorted. "Instead we have a commander in here who sits on his brains."

"The commander of the garrison is not too bad," said Falkenberg. "A likeable young fellow, if not very experienced. The captain-general . . ."

"That's who I was referring to," interrupted Manfred, sourly. "Do you know what he wanted to do this morning?"

"Hush," said Von Gherens, nudging Manfred.

Captain-General Tomaselli had just come up onto the battlements. He bowed to Manfred. "Prince Manfred. The guard told me you were up here." The tone was suspicious.

Manfred waved a hand in greeting. "We were having

a look at the disposition of the enemy's cannon and their camps," he said pacifically, pointing out at the muzzle flashes in the darkness.

The captain-general didn't even give it a glance. "There is not much we can do about the position of the enemy's cannon, or their camps. It seems a poor reason to be out in the night air so late. Would you like to come and take a glass of wine with my wife and me instead?"

Manfred stood on Von Gherens's foot. He wished Erik were here to stand on Falkenberg's. Besides missing Erik's company, Manfred had come to realize that the blunt-spoken Icelander was a marvel of tact compared to either of the two Prussians who guarded him now.

He was spared Falkenberg's comments by an interruption. Off to the south of the Citadel, the sky was suddenly lit up. Moments later the flash was followed by a thunderous boom that seemed to keep rolling over them.

"Holy mother of God! What was that?" The captain-general's eyes were wide.

"I think that used to be their magazine," said Von Gherens.

"Hakkonsen's work or I'm a castrato Sicilian," said Falkenberg, grinning in the moonlight. "That's no accident. That is that mad Icelander of yours, Prince Manfred."

Manfred slapped his two bodyguards on the back. "I hope you're right. Typical Erik. He's got his girl, and now he's done more to hurt Emeric's siege cannon than ten cavalry charges could achieve. I just hope he didn't blow himself to glory. Saints! That was a huge explosion."

"You know what is happening out there?" Tomaselli looked totally nonplussed.

"We've got a knight out there raising native resistance to Emeric," said Falkenberg with obvious satisfaction. "That'll be his work."

Tomaselli shook his head. "But . . . but you did not ask my permission to do so! *I* am in charge of military operations on this possession of the Republic of Venice. You cannot take these steps without advising me, Prince Manfred!"

Under his breath, Manfred swore at himself for easing his vigilance over his tongue in front of this insecure ass.

His happiness at seeing signs of Erik's handiwork had made him forget himself.

He stood on Von Gherens's foot again. "Unfortunately, the knight was landed before we were able to consult with you, Captain-General. Actually, it would have been impossible to keep him here—he has a woman out there—so we just ensured he got out as safely as he could. To tell you the truth, I thought he'd probably be still hunting her—but evidently she was somewhere safe, and now he has nothing else to occupy him."

Manfred shook his head, as if he regretted what he had to say. In reality, he was doing it to hide the shaking of his shoulders with repressed laughter. "He's a headstrong fellow, with a very powerful idea of his duty, which includes doing all in his power to oppose Emeric. I'm afraid he's taken the bit in his teeth—independent action, which I certainly didn't order—and since there is no way to get beyond the walls now, I'm unfortunately not able to communicate with him."

"What was this about a woman?"

Trust the fool to concentrate on the single irrelevant piece of information!

"He had an attachment to a Vinlander lass that was here on Corfu. We landed him early to see if he could find her."

"I think we should go back to our quarters now," grumbled Von Gherens. "I don't think you should go and drink the captain-general's wine. You've had enough already. You keep standing on my toes."

From up here, they could see all the way to the gulf, and even beyond to Epirus. The thin bronzed scythe-blade of moon rose from somewhere over mainland Greece, as Erik sat with Svanhild looking out into the star-salted heavens. Their fingers barely touched, but Erik was intensely conscious of the warmth of those fingers.

The tintinnabulation in his ears could still be from the explosion, he supposed. Then Svanhild turned her head, and smiled at him, the stars overhead reflected in her eyes, and he knew that it wasn't. It was the sound of his own heart.

❖   ❖   ❖

Francesca cocked her head sideways. "So why are two moles not better than one? It would seem logical to me. Does one never use more than one mole? I seem to recall that more than one mole was used in the siege of Acre, yes?"

Falkenberg assumed an oratorical stance. "It does depend heavily on the position, the number of forces at your disposal, and the ability of the defenders and the attackers to provide sufficient artillery cover. For instance, if the defenders cannot split their resources and you have plenty of munitions and manpower, the more moles the better. But a mole is no small task under fire. Emeric no doubt thinks he will pincer any attempt to sally from the main gate and attack or destroy his moles. Here, however—well, there are sally ports on the northern and southern sides and Emeric has relatively few men for such a siege. Making concerted use of both moles would be difficult. Once his forces are on this side of the channel they're directly below the walls. Either they must get inside those walls, fast, or they're going to be killed, easily, from the wall tops. Emeric will need to provide his troops with heavy covering fire just to get them across the mole. And for that he needs more cannon than he's got—and lighter cannon. Those forty-eight-pound bombards are so inaccurate they're as likely to kill his own men if he tries to use them for that purpose."

Falkenberg was now pacing back and forth slowly, like a lecturer. "We've been counting his lighter field pieces. He hasn't got what I would judge was enough for a worthwhile two-pronged assault. Which means he's going to have to rely on arquebus fire; which, in turn, means he'll have to build forward revetments or trenches on the Spianada—that open area in front of the fortress—and those will be under the Citadel's guns. That, in turn, will take a substantial number of his men out of the attack force, which, in turn—"

"Stop, stop!" said Francesca laughingly. "Enough. I'll never dare question Falkenberg's military assessment again."

"Even if he's wrong," said Von Gherens, sitting and

rubbing his foot, "it is easier to go ahead, do it his way, and die if need be rather than listen to him explain it all to you."

He swiveled his head, transferring the sour gaze onto Manfred. "Prince, I've met lighter carthorses than you. I understand, since you explained it me, that you want me to keep my mouth shut when you stand on my toes. But my toes would certainly prefer it if you just said 'Shut up, Von Gherens.'"

"I'll cough," said Manfred. "Or can I stand on Falkenberg's toes for you, my love?"

"He seems to have stopped, anyway."

Falkenberg rubbed the scars above the empty eye socket. "I was just getting into my stride," he grumbled. "I wish young Benito was back here. That boy had a positive talent for understanding siege-craft. Reminds me of me. I started younger than he was, you know."

"I think you were born in armor, which must have made it damned uncomfortable on your mother," Manfred replied. "Benito's riding for Venice by now, to make this siege a thing of the past."

"I hope so," said Francesca, grimly. "I think this fortress is far more likely to fall from within than from the effects of one, two or even three moles."

Chapter 51

Sophia started, when she saw the back of Nico's head above the chair. Usually her husband was in bed by now, not sitting in the salon. They slept in well-separated rooms, and he was seldom in hers, these days.

Fortunately, she'd already removed her cloak, so she quietly dropped it on the floor behind a settle—it would be difficult to explain why she'd been outside at this hour—then gave herself a quick inspection. The dress she wore was unremarkable enough. What was under it wasn't, but then she had no intent of letting him or anyone else see that. Her maids had been dismissed already. She was getting quite good at undressing without them.

"Good evening, my dear," she said casually.

The captain-general swiveled his head, looking equally surprised to see her. He had obviously been so deep in thought he had not even heard her entering the room.

Probably been thinking of something really complicated, like what he'd had for supper. Sophïa had no high opinion of Nico's brainpower. But then, what woman wants an intelligent husband anyway? A husband with money, power, prestige and prospects was more important.

Lately, she'd begun to realize that he had less of all of them than she'd thought.

He smiled rather abstractedly at her. "What are you doing up at this time of night, Sophia?"

"I might just ask you the same question, husband," she said archly, gliding toward him.

He yawned. "I've given orders that the guard are to call me when this prince goes wandering about. I don't trust him. He's undermining my authority among the men."

That won't be hard, Sophia thought sarcastically. Her trafficking with the guards who let her in and out of the fortress, unofficially and for small bribes, had given her an insight into his real prestige.

But all she said was: "And?" with an enquiring tilt of the head.

"I was called to say he was up on the inner battlements." He looked furious, in the petty way of a child. "The fellow *just happened* to be there when a huge explosion went off behind enemy lines. And he says he knew nothing about what his man there was planning. Ha!"

He rose, came over, and put his arm around her. "So what *are* you doing up, Sophia?"

Dangerous moment. The truth—

I sneaked out of the fortress to see a Satanist with whom I sacrificed a black cockerel, and then he painted fertility sigils around my nipples and vagina, before I performed certain acts on him with my mouth and then later on myself with a polished piece of vine-root in a pentacle pointed with black candles.

—was not going to be well received.

"I heard the explosion." She hadn't noticed it, but he plainly had. "I was worried, so I dressed and came looking for you."

"It's fine, dear," he said, patting her reassuringly. "Just some saboteurs attacking the Hungarians."

Best to distract him. "It's so comforting that you're in control," she murmured, leaning into him. "You're so manly!"

She felt his chest swell under her hands. "Yes, there's nothing for you to worry about." His own hands were starting to wander.

Sophia stroked his chest, calculating for a moment. Her cloak was dropped just in front of the cabinet in which the brandy decanter stood. She certainly didn't want him going that way for a nightcap!

No help for it, then. She successfully managed to lead him to her bedroom. She blew out the candles in the fancy girandole, making everything dark, since there was no way to remove the insignia now.

The painted sigils felt hot, and so did she. For the first time in at least two years, she actually enjoyed sex with her husband. Not the sex itself—Nico was as clumsy and oafish in bed as the cavalry captain Querini—but what surrounded it. The knowledge of her duplicity, her sin, inflamed her.

Afterwards, as they lay in the warm darkness, she realized she could take further advantage of the now-rare moment.

"So why are you so suspicious of this prince? He could further your career."

Her husband snorted. "He seeks to ruin it, more likely! He is close friends with Petro Dorma. You know my father was a close friend of the late Doge, and also with Ricardo Brunelli, who was seen as the Doge-in-waiting. *Casa* Dorma's ascension has been a severe blow to us. The prince controls a sizable cavalry force, but the Knights will not take orders from anyone but him. He's refused to hand them over to me."

"Refused?"

"In the politest way. But refused nonetheless. And he's meddling in the defense of the Citadel." He patted her derriere. "Anyway. Why am I boring you with all this politics, eh? Some things it is best a woman doesn't know."

"You don't trust me," she pouted, tracing patterns on his chest. The sigil Ogerda, which Master Morando had told her was the sign for control. He'd also asked her for inside news on the siege. She was determined to find out something for him.

"Of course I trust you dear, but it is quite confidential."

"You're teasing me." She started teasing him, quite a bit more physically.

"Don't stop." His voice sounded somewhat breathless.

"Only if you stop keeping all these secrets from me!"

"Very well. If you go on . . . Well, you remember the prince's bodyguard?"

"Erik Hakkonsen. Handsome, blond, worried-looking."

"As handsome as me?"

"Of course not! Go on." To encourage him, she began applying some of the new skills Morando was teaching her. Her husband gasped a little, then:

"The prince lied to me about the Icelander being landed before they came here. I remember him. And now, he has somehow left the Citadel and started a campaign in the countryside, trying to rally some of the peasants. Silly business! War should be left to regular soldiers, not mules pretending to be men. But what's even worse is that"—Tomaselli's voice grew heavy with indignation as well as passion—" he sneaked out of here without my permission. Didn't even consult me! He's out there with that snotty Vinlander woman who tried to come and stay here in the Citadel."

"Really? This Erik broke out after the siege started? A likely story. He must be in league with the Hungarians. I wouldn't be in the least surprised to find this prince in league with them too, the way he openly consorts with that woman of his. Rumor has it she was a *cortegiana*. No morals at all."

By now, her husband's mind was addled enough by what Sophia was doing not to find anything amiss in the utterly illogical conclusions his wife was advancing. Sophia filled her mouth again just to keep from laughing. Addling Nico Tomaselli's mind was not much of a challenge.

"Yes, mistress, I think all is going well."

The image of Countess Bartholdy floating over the blood-bowl frowned a little. "Make sure it doesn't go *too* well, Bianca. I want this siege to drag on and on. It'll take months of frustration before Emeric will finally be willing to come to me for help."

"I understand, mistress." Casarini hesitated. Then, decided that risking Bartholdy's immediate displeasure was less dangerous than risking eventual failure. "But it would help me—considerably—if I had some better idea of what you are specifically seeking."

The frown on the countess's face deepened. Bianca grew tense. Elizabeth Bartholdy was less concerned than Bianca herself with the way in which grimaces could, over centuries and millennia, permanently distort her face. But she was not oblivious to the problem. To see such a frown on her face was . . . frightening, to anyone who really knew her.

Thankfully, the frown eased, replaced by that silvery little laugh. "Very well. I suppose I have kept you a bit too much in the dark. You needn't concern yourself with my final goal, Bianca, but . . . Let's just say that I need to inveigle my great-great-nephew to release some magics on the island which will advance my purposes. In order for that to happen, however, he will need to leave the siege and come visit me in my castle near the Carpathians."

Immediately, Bianca understood the point. Emeric of Hungary was one of those kings who insisted on meddling with the military details of his campaigns—much to his officers' despair and, often enough, grisly punishment. It would not be easy to get him to leave the siege in order to make the long journey from Corfu to the Carpathians.

A *long* siege, then, stretching through the summer and autumn and well into the winter.

Bianca had no control, of course, over the military side of the matter. Although—

"At a certain point, mistress, it may be necessary to have Captain-General Tomaselli removed. He's such an incompetent commander that, with him in charge—constantly interfering, rather—it may be impossible to prevent Emeric from simply taking the Citadel by force, before winter comes. The defense would be far stronger if it was fully in the hands of the garrison commander, Leopoldo—especially with Prince Manfred and his Knights here. They seem to get along well with Commander Leopoldo."

Elizabeth pondered her words, for a moment. "True. But keep in mind the opposite risk. I *do* also want

Corfu to fall to my great-great-nephew, eventually." She cocked her head slightly. "You understand that if the military defense is capable enough, everything will eventually depend on treachery. Well . . . treachery combined with what I will unleash on Corfu. I will provide the magics—but will you be able, when the time comes, to provide the treason?"

This was no time for hesitation. Bianca nodded firmly. "Yes, mistress. I will."

"See to it, then." The image of the countess began to fade. Within seconds, it was gone.

For the next hour or so, after cleaning up all signs of the ritual, Bianca sat in her room simply thinking. She'd gambled, making her claim to the countess, and now she had to make good on it.

By the end, she'd reached two conclusions. One pleasant, one not.

She'd already reached the tentative conclusion anyway, once the siege began, that she'd have to have her "uncle and aunt" killed sooner or later. It was already cumbersome, the way she had to sneak around and keep her activities a secret from them. Over time, the needs of her work would be impossible to hide from people living in the same house—especially the assignations she'd have to begin with one of Fianelli's men.

That was the pleasant conclusion. Betraying those who had given you their trust was always enjoyable to Bianca—not to mention spiritually profitable. Casarini, like her mistress, hoped to cheat Satan out of her soul. But doing so required emulating the Great One in all respects. She was already doing quite well in that regard, she thought. Killing her "relatives" would enhance her progress further.

She began considering the ways to accomplish that. But then, guided by years of rigorous self-discipline, put the matter aside in order to ponder the other conclusion.

Not pleasant, that one. For some years now, sex had stopped being anything for Bianca Casarini other than a means to an end. Still . . .

Eventually, she was going to have to betray Fianelli

also. And the surest way to do that was to form a liaison
with one of Fianelli's three chief goons. Between the
pleasures of her body and the lure of taking his boss's
place, Bianca was confident she could manage it.

Paulo Saluzzo, she decided. *That won't be so bad. At
least he's Florentine and takes a bath more than once
a week.*

The next day, Bianca began both projects. At midday,
by wearing a rather provocative gown when she went to
meet Paulo Saluzzo in order to pass on further information to his boss Fianelli. Bianca was normally careful to
wear nothing but modest attire whenever she met Fianelli
or any of his goons.

Saluzzo noticed—immediately—but was suave enough
to do nothing more than give her a fairly subtle ogle, and
a leer that could charitably be called a friendly smile.

Bianca did not return the smile. Moving too quickly
would make Saluzzo suspicious. He *was* Florentine, after
all. This needed some finesse. In any event, Bianca was
in no hurry.

"And make sure you stress to Fianelli that we need
to start setting up a sacrificial lamb," she said sternly.
"That whore of the prince's—the one who calls herself 'de
Chevreuse'—she's a canny one. My informants tell me she's
already more or less running the Citadel's countertreason
work. There's no way she won't spot something, sooner
or later. When that time comes, we need to have made
sure that someone else's head goes on the block."

Saluzzo grunted. The sound was mildly sarcastic.
"Don't teach double-dealing to double-dealers, Signorina
Casarini. Fianelli's already got the man picked out, and
Zanari's starting to work on him. Nachelli's his name. He's
a small-time loan shark and rent collector. Too greedy
for his own good. We'll cut him in on just enough to
make him visible, without letting him know enough to
lead anyone to us."

Bianca had her doubts. How could you "cut someone in"
without the man knowing your own identity? But . . .

Fianelli was direct, after all, and not squeamish in
the least. Presumably, when the time came, he would

see to it that the Venetian authorities would be trying
to interrogate a corpse.

She'd leave that to Fianelli and his thugs. Bianca had
her own plans for getting rid of them, when the time
came. They'd be her sacrificial lambs, just as this Nachelli
would be theirs.

She left the hidden alley where her meetings with
Saluzzo took place. They couldn't afford to be spotted,
so the meetings were always very brief. On her way past
him, she felt Saluzzo's fingers brushing her hip. But it
was a tentative thing, more in the way of an automatic
reflex to the gown and what it suggested than anything
serious. Saluzzo was not actually stupid, and he would
understand as well as she did that there was no safe
place for them to pursue any affair. They might be able
to find a place hidden from public eyes, to be sure. But
they'd also have to keep it hidden from Fianelli—and
that would be a lot more difficult.

The knowledge would frustrate Saluzzo, and for weeks
to come. *Good*. After she arranged the killing of her
"relatives," Saluzzo would be that much more eager to
pursue Bianca, now that she had a house of her own in
which to meet him.

When she'd arrived on Corfu, the year before, Bianca
had brought several large pieces of luggage with her.
There were secret compartments in two of those valises,
where she kept her grimoires hidden along with her magical tools and ingredients. After pleading a headache to
her "aunt" and "uncle," she spent the afternoon in her
room studying the texts. By nightfall, she'd decided on
the method she would use.

It required the blood of innocents, of course—and no
mere animal blood. Not for that ritual.

Bianca rose and put away the grimoires. Then, moved to
the window in her room. Looking down, she could see the
narrow street of the Citadel which her room overlooked.
As always, these days—even in this relatively prosperous
area of the fortress, set aside for Venetians—the street
swarmed with people. Children, many of them, and most
of those beggars.

A little boy, perhaps five years old, looked up at her window and gave her a big smile. It was a beggar's smile, seeking aid from the fine lady.

Not all *that* innocent, to be sure, not with that trace of calculation which had no business on the face of a five-year-old. But . . .

He'd do. Bianca smiled back, very sweetly. Tomorrow, she'd start giving him food. Quite a bit, in fact. That ritual required fat as well as blood.

Chapter 52

First things first, Benito decided, when he arrived in Reggio di Calabria. He still had two silver pennies—he'd told that rogue of an oil trader he only had one to avoid trouble. He'd need money, but right now, immediately if not sooner, he needed food.

He found a very respectable-looking taverna next to the quay, plainly not a seaman's place, but aimed at the clerks and minor merchants who worked down there. It was a bit above his present guise, but . . . the bouquet drifting out of the doorway was pure temptation.

Benito had never been very good at resisting that kind of temptation. Or most any other, for that matter. He went in, looked around the crowded room for a seat, and finally took his place at the end of one of the benches. The clerkly type next to him gave him an opaque glance, but at least he didn't pull in the skirts of his coat.

The waiter looked rather doubtfully at Benito. "You have money?" he asked. The tone was carefully neutral. As likely as not, given the proximity to the quay, occasional sailors fresh off a ship and with their pockets full came this way.

Benito nodded. The waiter took a quick glance toward the kitchens, and then whispered to Benito: "I shouldn't say this, but my brother's a seafaring man. The prices here are sky-high. The food's good, so long as you don't touch the pork. But there is a cheaper place down the quay. The food is lousy but it's cheap."

Benito grinned at the fellow, and winked. "Well, this time I'll go with the good food with sky-high prices. Will two silver cover it and a jug of wine?" It was foolishness to spend down to the reserves, but Benito felt in need of a bit of foolishness. Finding a fence in a strange seaport was going to be a challenge.

The waiter nodded. "*Si.* I'll see you get the best," and he was scurrying off to the kitchen.

Benito had timed his arrival well. He hadn't been sitting for more than a few minutes when the locals came in. Mostly, Benito noted, middle-aged or elderly men who took the needs of the stomach seriously, by the looks of them.

The waiter appeared from the smoky kitchen sooner than Benito had expected, not that his empty stomach was going to complain. The man seemed bent on proving that, besides being a waiter in a sky-high–priced taverna, he had all the skills of a juggler. He carried a carafe of wine, a bowl of bread-rings, a platter of chargrilled baby octopus redolent of thyme and garlic with just a hint of bay leaf, a jug of extra sauce, and some olive oil and vinegar. He brought a plate of Melanzane alla finitese next, the crumbed aubergine slices bursting with hot melted cheese.

"Eat up. The cook gets upset if you aren't ready for the swordfish the minute it arrives. And do you need more wine?"

The fish, when it came, was worth suffering a fussy cook for. The succulent flesh, scented with bergamot, capers and oregano, was the kind of dish whereby gastronomes set their standards. Somehow, outside of this meal, the thoughts of finding a fence seemed far less threatening. Maybe it was the carafe of wine from the local Greco di Bianco grapes. They were a great improvement on the stuff he had drunk with Taki, Spiro and Kosti.

Feeling full, and almost somnolent, Benito parted with his silver and, as a well-deserved tip for the waiter, the rest of his coppers. He then went out looking for an alley in which to get mugged.

It seemed like a good idea at the time it had occurred to him. If he wanted to find a fence . . . ask a thief.

Finding a thief just took some bait. Benito hoped he would get a solitary operator, and that he was able to avoid getting hurt first and robbed after, not that the mugger was going to be very pleased with the state of Benito's pouch. Well, that made two of them. Benito wasn't very comfortable about its flatness himself.

A little later, someone did oblige him. Very professionally. The thief stepped out of the shadows, put an arm around Benito's neck and a knife against his kidneys. "Don't try and turn around. Just give us the pouch and you'll stay alive."

With a calm that belied his racing heart, Benito untied the pouch and held it out.

"Drop it."

"You might want to look in it before I do that."

"Why?" asked the mugger suspiciously. "What's in it?"

"Absolutely nothing. Not even a copper penny."

"Damn liar." The mugger swung him around. "You're loaded. You ate at old Forno's. Give the money belt."

Benito lifted his shirt to show skin. "There isn't one. I spent it all. Every last penny."

The mugger gaped. "Wha—"

He never got any further than that. He found he'd been neatly disarmed and now faced his own knife and Benito's Shetland blade. Benito shook his head. "Never let yourself get distracted, my friend."

The mugger showed both courage and a sense of humor. "Well, I haven't got any money either." His eyes darted, looking for escape.

Benito flipped the mugger's knife over, and held it out, hilt first, to the man. "You can have it back. I'm not interested in your money. All I want is some information. If you wanted to sell something, ah . . . with ownership claims other than yours, where would you go? Who is buying?"

The mugger took the knife warily, not sheathing it. "Di Scala. He's the only big-time buyer in town. Follow the quay to the end. There's an alley there. It's up the stairs in the third last house."

"Thanks."

The mugger shook his head. "Watch him, laddie. He's bent." Which was about the worst thing a thief could ever say about a fence.

Di Scala looked like an underfed vulture. The fence shaded his hooded eyes with a skeletally thin hand.

"It's a fake," he pronounced, shaking his head. "A good fake, but a fake. I'll give you a florin for it." He took a golden coin from his desk and pushed it toward Benito.

"It's no sale," said Benito, grimly. The ruby was worth at the very least thirty ducats, a coin whose greater purity made it more valuable than the florin.

The fence tapped his long fingers. "The sale is not up for negotiation."

The faintest of sounds made Benito realize that they were no longer alone. That finger-tapping on the desk had been more than just a mannerism.

He glanced back. The two men who had come in behind him had that heavy-set look of brutality common to all enforcers. Between the two of them, there was enough flesh to make three of Benito, with a fourth not being that far off.

One of them cracked his knuckles. "You called, boss."

The fence nodded. "This fellow will be leaving. Now. With or without his money, but without this." He held up the ruby.

Benito considered his options, which weren't good. The sleazy little room offered him no space to maneuver. And the rent-a-thugs coming to grab his elbows were distinctly better than average.

Right now, he reminded himself, his primary task was to get to Venice as fast as he possibly could. "I'll take my money," he whined, cringing. Out of the corner of his eye he saw the bully boys relaxing. Not unready to hurt and possibly maim, but not expecting any resistance. He could take them . . .

Resolutely he put the thought aside and reached gingerly for the florin. "It's not fair," he complained, hangdog, looking at the coin.

Di Scala laughed sardonically. "And how you came by the loot was, of course."

Benito hunched his shoulders still more. "It was my grandmother's."

"Yes. Very likely. Now get lost."

"I won't bring you any more stuff."

"I will sob myself to sleep tonight," sniffed Di Scala. "You aren't from round here anyway. That's enough money for you to waste on wine and whores. You're lucky I don't let the boys just drop you over the wharf with a couple of weights on your feet—and if you don't get out of here, that's just what I will do. *Get.*"

Benito got. "There's no need to push," he snarled at the thugs on the rickety stair. He was rewarded by a buffet and them grabbing his pouch. They took the florin reposed there, kicked him out to sprawl in an alley, and threw his empty pouch after him. The alley was narrow, slippery and reeking with ordure. He got up and staggered away, theatrically waving a fist at the laughing pair.

They'd have laughed less if they'd seen him round the corner and then grease up a drainage pipe. Before they were back inside, Benito was lying in the shelter of a chimney pot just behind the shady lip of an eave of a house beyond.

Watching. Without money he wasn't going anywhere anyway. He'd allowed himself to get careless. Rusty. Overconfident. He still had one jewel, but if he sold it anywhere in this town news was bound to get out, and they'd be looking for him.

Besides, he'd discovered that he had an extreme dislike of being robbed. It occurred to him, with somewhat wry amusement, that some of his own victims over the years might have felt just as angry. There was a kind of justice in it, he supposed, but he needed money to get to Venice. Corfu needed help. Maria needed that help. So did that kid of hers.

He waited and watched. A fence's busiest hours would be toward early morning—this rogue wasn't going anywhere. As the night wore on, he'd just get more careful.

Benito had no money and nothing else to do, after all. He steeled himself—as he'd done often enough above the canals of Venice, in years past—to ignore hunger, cold and tiredness. At least this time, hunger wasn't part of the equation; that excellent meal was still enough with him that his stomach was happy, but not so much as to slow him down.

Eventually, Di Scala and his two thugs appeared on the street. Moving surely and silently across the roofs, Benito trailed the fence back to Di Scala's own house. That was where the fence would keep his stash, he was sure.

The two thugs followed Di Scala into the house; then, a few minutes later, they emerged and headed off to wherever they slept themselves. As soon as they were gone, Benito came out of hiding and swung into position. Hanging like a bat from the eaves, he watched the fence through a shutter-crack in his bedroom. The man unlocked his cassone, opened up a cunningly disguised compartment in its lid and secreted some coin into it, and an item of what was probably jewelry.

Smiling to himself, Benito found a rooftop corner, rolled himself into a ball and slept. By midday he was back at his post. He watched the fence leave. As soon as darkness provided cover, Benito began slipping tiles from the roof, as quietly as possible. Then, he eased planks from the ceiling with the Shetland knife. It was proving a good, strong tool. Not exactly a Ferrara *main gauche*, but a workingman's ideal knife.

Lightly, Benito dropped into the fence's bedroom. He made no attempt to force the lock on the cassone—it would be a good one. Besides, the hidden compartment probably had a booby trap. Instead he set to work with the knife on the board making up the back edge, being careful not to move the cassone itself. That might have unpleasant consequences. There'd been a case like that back in Venice. The thief had lost his hands, his sight, and, because he was caught in the screaming aftermath, his life.

Benito was not planning to chance imitating him. He cut a neat slot through the solid wood, and then tipped the cassone. It wasn't the most effective way of getting money out, but Benito was rewarded by a succession of coins and bits and pieces. He put them all hastily into his pouch, before leaving the way he'd come. As neat a job as he'd ever done, and as well-deserved a one as he'd ever pulled, thought Benito, quietly slipping out onto the roof.

But, as Valentina had taught him—in what seemed a lifetime away—the job wasn't done until you were clean away. Benito had done his homework. Two boats carrying fresh produce for the market in Messina left long before first light from Reggio di Calabria to have the crisp wares unloaded and in the market by dawn. This morning they took an uninvited fresh thief as well as their fresh vegetables. He had the grace to get off quietly on the Messina quay-side, carry a load of carrots to the waiting wagon, and even to steal only one carrot.

It was fairly woody, but, munching at the purple root as he went in search of a taverna, Benito found it remarkably pleasant. Sweet and tasty, even. His nose led him to a panetteria where stevedores were already buying hot ciabatta, before going on to a stall where a butcher was selling liver and tripe ragout from a steaming pot, at a copper a dip of the loaf. Benito felt in his pouch. He hadn't really investigated what his loot was yet.

What his fingers encountered was round—but not money. He stepped into a noisome alley to check it out.

He had to laugh. What he'd assumed was money was valuable all right. It just wasn't currency or saleable, except by priests. He had acquired some fifteen golden Hypatian medals. Four pilgrim medals, also golden, struck in Jerusalem, engraved with the pilgrim's name, some twenty-three pieces of silver of some foreign origin—a coin he'd never seen before—and . . . a ruby.

His ruby. Well, there was *some* justice in the world.

Chapter 53

Despite his hunger and tiredness, Benito set off in search of a Hypatian chapel. He would just drop the medals in the poor box or leave them in the font or something.

He found the chapel all right. This time luck wasn't with him. He slipped in quietly, only to have a Sibling emerge from the counseling booth as he approached the font.

"Can I help you, my son?" she asked gently. "Are you in need of counseling?"

Benito took in the small, round, serious face of the woman in the pale Hypatian robe, liked the quiet calm in her eyes, and decided to chance honesty. "I've brought something that was stolen from the Church, back to it." He pulled out the golden Hypatian medals.

The Sibling looked, looked again, her eyes widening, then took a deep breath. "God be thanked! We have prayed for their return. May God forgive you for stealing them. I am so glad your conscience has made you bring them back to us."

A reasonable conclusion for her to have come to, but he decided he wasn't going to let it go. "Actually, I came upon them by accident."

The little Sibling looked sternly at him. "We are not going to prosecute you, young man. There is no need to lie to us. God knows the truth anyway."

He snorted. "Well, then, he knows I am telling the

truth. I have just come over from Reggio di Calabria on the vegetable boats. I've never been here in my life before."

She looked doubtful, but there was a crack in the doubt. After all, he didn't have the local accent.

He laughed, which put another crack in her doubt. "I'll swear to it, my hand on the Bible. Or believe what you please." He shrugged. "I suppose I did steal them, but not from the Church. I took them from a fence in Reggio di Calabria, after he'd robbed me of my own property. I got my own back, and I got these as well."

Then it occurred to him that he had yet another card to play. "And I got some other things I'd like to see go to their rightful owners. They were headed for being melted down, I guess."

He produced the Jerusalem pilgrim medals. "They're worth," he felt the weight, "oh, maybe four ducats in raw gold. But they were really important to some people. They're named, but the names don't mean much to me. Except for this one, of course."

It was engraved: *Carlo Sforza.* Benito's father. Benito had been astonished when he found it among the others.

At a guess . . . after his defeat at the hands of Duke Enrico Dell'este, the Wolf of the North must have undertaken a pilgrimage to Jerusalem. Someone had robbed his baggage. For the thief's sake, Benito hoped Sforza had never caught up with him.

The little Sibling gaped at the medals, at the name, at the scruffy young man holding them out to her.

"He'll have traveled incognito. I'd like his medal, and the others, to get back to their owners. I can offer some silver to see that it does."

Benito emptied out his pouch again, only keeping back the ruby. "All of this is stolen. All of it is too hot to handle, I suspect, because it was hidden with the medals. I've no idea who it belonged to. But I get the feeling it would be best used for the support of those who'll carry these to their owners. All I ever wanted was to get my own property back from that—" he killed the obscenity before it got to his tongue "—worm, who cheated me."

8ᴛ4

The Sibling shook her head in amazement. "God moves in mysterious ways," she said faintly.

Benito sighed. "Good lady, you've no idea just how mysteriously. And this time I can only assume He intervened directly. And now I am broke, hungry and tired. You'll excuse me, but I need to go and do something about all of these things."

The Sibling smiled; whatever doubts she'd had, they'd disappeared the moment that he turned out his pockets. "Well, it seems only right that seeing as you have brought our property back to us, we provide breakfast and a place to sleep." She raised an eyebrow with faint amusement. "The order has also offered a reward for the return of our property."

Benito's spirits lifted. "I don't suppose it's cash?"

"Well, no." The small round face dimpled. "You must know our order is sworn to poverty. But a medal, blessed by the holy Michael, our bishop, is worth having in its own right. He will be very pleased at the return of the medals. We use the sale of them to fund our charitable work. And we are sending a delegation to Rome in five months time. There is to be a convocation of the order, to discuss the new chapter houses and cloisters in Germany. We can use that opportunity to deliver the pilgrim medals to others of the order who will convey them onward to the owners."

She looked shyly at Benito. "Could I know who God's instrument was?"

Benito grinned. "Tell Sforza it comes back to him with the compliments of Benito. I think he'll know which Benito, if he thinks hard about it."

A thought occurred to him. "Sibling, I ended up retrieving your stolen property because when I wanted to change a jewel into cash, I was assumed to be a professional thief." Benito hoped he looked suitably horrified at the very idea. He stared very pointedly at her. "Actually, I have had the same reaction from other people."

The Sibling had the grace to look embarrassed. "You can speak like a nobleman born . . . but at first you sounded . . . and you look . . ."

"Scruffy. I have my reasons, Sister. They're honest

enough for Father Eneko Lopez. You have heard of him?"

"Who has not? He is already famous in the order. A stern man," she added, a bit doubtfully.

"He's that, all right. But he is also a good man. A pious man, certainly. My journey has his blessing."

It was best not to say too much, he decided. The Hypatian Sibling might be closed-mouthed and as good as one of the choir of angels—but she might say something inadvertently to the wrong person. Venice was not popular with the Kingdom of Naples. Benito didn't need to spend time in a dungeon because he'd had too loose a tongue.

"But to get a passage on a ship I need money." She looked faintly alarmed. "For safety and security I have carried my funds in the shape of jewels. They're easily hidden. And they're easily turned into money." He smiled disarmingly. "Except when you look like a thief."

The Sibling looked rather nonplussed by all of this. "I suppose you are a messenger of some sort. A carrier of secrets . . ." She also didn't look as if she entirely approved.

"I am something of the sort, yes. But just because something is secret, doesn't mean it has to be evil, Sister. This isn't. I'll swear that on your Hypatian medal if need be. It is just politics. And I need to sell a ruby. Is it possible that the Siblings could sell it for me? After all, your order must get gifts you need to dispose of sometimes."

She looked sternly at him. "I know this seems ungrateful, but I must ask. Is this jewel truly yours to dispose of?"

Benito nodded. "Yes. I swear it, as God is my witness."

She held out a hand. "Give it to me. I will give it to Brother Marteno. He was once a jeweler, before he renounced worldly things and devoted himself to serve Christ."

Against his nature, but trusting his instincts, Benito handed over the ruby. He still had one more, after all.

✧　　　✧　　　✧

The food in the Hypatian refectory was not exactly hot murseddu and steaming ciabatta—but bread, olive oil and sharp goats-milk cheese at least filled the hole where Benito had once kept his stomach. And the cell in the monastery was dry and cool, letting him sleep deep into the afternoon.

It was also not exactly where an irate fence would be sending his hirelings looking for a thief. But Benito found the bells no aid to sleep.

He was awakened by someone coming into the monk's cell they'd assigned him. For most of his life, Benito had slept lightly—a thief living on his wits in other peoples' property couldn't afford to do otherwise. It was better to sleep lightly and uneasily than to snore like a hog and be slaughtered like one. Since he'd left the Citadel, Benito's senses seemed to have honed themselves even more. But this time they'd woken him for something harmless. It was a small, large-nosed monk, bearing a chinking bag. "That was an exceptionally good stone, young man. I have some seventy-three ducats for you."

Benito reflected there were some advantages in not selling to a fence. The one disadvantage was the embarrassment of riches.

The little man cleared his throat. "Sister Genina has explained to me that you obviously don't want publicity, but we have this medal for you. It was offered as a reward, and it seems fair that you should get it."

He produced a small silver medallion. "It is supposed to have a strand of Saint Arsenius's hair in it, and it is blessed by the bishop. We cannot claim there is any miraculous great virtue attached to it, though. It may be of help to a seafarer and will protect and glow if you are exposed to evil magic."

The little man looked more than a little uncomfortable. "She, um, Sister Genina, led me to understand you'd recovered our medals in the course of getting your own property back. I realize you may not be able to do this but, well, there are certain church vessels missing too, and another four of those medals. You couldn't perhaps tell us where to look?"

Benito's youthful experience said: Betray someone to the law? Not likely.

On the other hand, the fence had already played foul, by the thieves' code. Besides, any piece of excrement that was low enough to take holy medals deserved whatever he got.

"A fence in Reggio di Calabria. His name is Di Scala. His home is up on the hill. Big place, walls with coppo tiles on top of them. He trades from upstairs on the third last house in the alley at the end of the quay. His small—ah, dubious stuff is kept in a secret compartment in the cassone in his room. I suggest you have whomever you send take an axe to open it. Those things have booby traps nine times out of ten. And I suggest the order send someone very large and well-armed. Actually, I suggest you send several someones like that. The fence has a couple of big bullies working for him, and I doubt, all things considered, that they'd respect the cloth."

The slight monk smiled. "I think not for long. Down here in the south the order is held in high esteem. The people will not allow us to be hurt."

Benito shrugged. "Make sure there are a lot of witnesses around, then. I got the feeling that this man has no respect for the Church, either."

Benito left without fanfare that afternoon and went to a respectable dealer in secondhand clothing. By the time he walked down to the Messina quay-side to hunt a dockside tavern for a passage north, he'd changed from a shag-rag sailor into a minor, but respectable trader, with a plain but serviceable rapier and the Shetland knife riding where a *main gauche* would.

The weight of the rapier was comfortingly familiar. The boots were not comforting or comfortable on feet that had gotten used to being bare again—and before that to having boots cut by the finest cobblers in Venice—but Benito had little choice but to wear them. No scruffy seaman would pay for a passage. And right now, if it meant paying for the whole vessel, he'd do it. He felt time pressing on him. He wanted to get through to Venice, and back to Corfu.

Chapter 54

It only took three cups of wine to find a caique heading up the coast in the morning as far as Livorno. And another cup and five ducats had him installed in a cabin on her. It wasn't a big cabin, but it had a hammock and a small window.

Benito was resting in the hammock, enjoying having his new boots off, with the spicy warm evening breeze blowing off the straits and in through the window. He was slept-out, so he passed the time sharpening the Shetland knife and despairing of getting a good edge on the rapier. It wasn't a bad weapon, really. It just wasn't Ferrara steel. He examined the edge in the candlelight.

Suddenly, the door to the cabin was opened so violently it was nearly thrown off its hinges. In came the cadaverous Di Scala and his two thugs. There was very little doubt they'd come with murder in mind.

Benito rolled out of the hammock, landing on his feet, catlike, with the rapier in his right and the Shetland knife in his left. The cabin was narrow and quite full of hammock. This did mean that the three were in each other's way.

"You thought you'd got away with it, didn't you, you little *pizza da merde*!" hissed the fence, closing the door behind him. "Nobody does that to me! I'm going to make an example of you. Cut your *cazzo* off and shove it down your throat, spill your guts and leave you to die slowly. Take him, boys."

Benito grabbed the hammock with a forefinger and slashed the hanging rope with the Shetland knife. The rope raveled, parted, as Di Scala's two pieces of muscle pushed their way forward, slightly cautious. They'd plainly expected him to have a knife at best, and to be the cringing little thief they'd bullied. The rapier was unexpected.

But they weren't going to let it stop them. They were professionals, after all.

Benito flung the hammock at them. It was spread by two hardwood batons and therefore the net stayed open. The two thugs both had the same hand-and-a-half guardless knives that the rascally oil merchant had had. Perhaps they were popular here in the south. The hammock tangled one of them, so Benito neatly dealt with the other.

Terminally. There was no space for a swing here, but a rapier lunge was quite as effective. The extra reach made the thug's knife an ineffectual defense.

The other freed himself of the hammock, and pulled the spreader-baton from it. It still wasn't rapier-long, but it gave him something to fend off rapier cuts and thrusts with. Benito balanced on the balls of his feet, aware that Di Scala was fumblingly trying to prime a wheel-lock pistol,

Lunge. Twist. A slash of the *main gauche*.

The remaining thug's hand-and-a-half blade skittered across the floor. Blood pulsed from the man's wrist.

Benito kicked the knife into the corner behind him, nicking his toes. The thug, his eyes huge in the candlelight, dodged back, crashing into his master.

"*Testa di cazzo!*" snarled the fence, nearly dropping the gun. He pushed the man roughly away, back toward Benito.

The wolf was at the surface now. Both of them were going to die.

And then Benito paused. The medallion he'd been given was hot against his flesh . . .

✧   ✦   ✧

He settled for neatly flicking the baton out of the hand of the surviving tough and kicking his legs out from under him. Di Scala was trying to aim the pistol, his hands now shaking so badly he could barely hold the weapon. Benito looked scornfully at him. Here was one who hired his dirty work done. Even the dead thug was worth two of him.

He jumped forward, planting both feet in the fallen thug's solar plexus. The man struggled weakly for breath.

The fence pressed against the door he'd closed, pointing the quivering pistol at Benito.

"I can put this knife through your eye," said Benito coldly. "You, on the other hand, haven't primed that thing properly. You'll be lucky if it goes off at all. It's rusty, too, so it's as likely to kill you as me. Besides, you couldn't hit a barn door from inside shaking like that."

Now the boot was truly on the other foot, and the fence knew it. "Just let me go! Please. I'll give you money."

"I've every intention of letting you go. You and your carrion. You're taking both the living and the dead one with you. But first I need to tell you something."

With a bare foot, he prodded the thug who was struggling to sit up. "This idiot, too. You may decide that being dead is easier. First, I returned those stolen Hypatian medals you had to the Church and I told them exactly where, and from whom, I got them. They want your guts for garters."

The thug looked accusingly at his master. His face was an unhealthy white and he was still struggling for breath, but he managed to gasp: "You bought 'ose?" His tone was one of unadulterated shock.

"They're just gold, you superstitious fool," snarled the fence.

The moment the fence looked at the thug, Benito stepped forward and knocked the pistol out of his hand. He used the flat of the rapier, but a couple of Di Scala's fingers were probably broken. Di Scala shrieked.

Benito held the rapier ready for the thrust. "I imagine you made sure we wouldn't be interrupted. You'd better hope we aren't, because if we are I'll kill you. Now, the other reason I wanted to speak to you was to advise a pilgrimage. Because the only place you might be safe is kneeling in the Church of the Holy Sepulcher, praying for forgiveness. I've already sent word, and his pilgrim's medal, to Carlo Sforza. I should imagine that he is going to send agents looking for you. You really don't want them to find you anywhere else, because compared to Sforza, I'm a gentle and kindly man."

"*Sforza?*" The fence stared at him as if he was mad.

"One of those medals that you bought for their gold value was stolen from the Wolf of the North." Benito grinned mirthlessly at the way all of the blood drained from the fence's face. The scum might not be afraid of the Church, but he was properly terrified now. "I think I'll leave you with the thought that gold is really worth far less than other things. Now, you'll take this dead man between you, and precede me onto the deck. I've foregone killing you, but I'm going to enjoy kicking you off this boat. I hope you can swim."

He marched them up on deck, dragging the corpse between them. "Drop that over the side."

They did. Benito's keen eyes noticed movement among the boxes and barrels on the quay-side. It could be helpers, or, more likely it could be those who'd been told to get out or get hurt. He'd give them a show, whoever it was.

He remembered what the Sibling had said, and decided, maliciously, to make life as difficult as possible for the fence from this moment on. He'd studied drama enough with Valentina to know how to declaim at volume. He filled his lungs, and began an oration for the benefit of the hidden audience.

"DI SCALA, YOU CUR! You came here TO KILL ME, but I have defeated you WITH GOD'S HELP! And you and I know that you also bought golden medallions STOLEN FROM THE CHURCH! Stolen from the Hypatian Siblings who would have used the money raised to care for the poor, to do Christ's work! See what sort of ILL-FORTUNE follows SUCH WICKEDNESS!"

Not bad, he though. Benito flicked his rapier forward, cutting the fence's pouch free. He stabbed it as it fell.

And then, using thumb and forefinger from his rapier hand, he held it, ripped it open, and showered coin into the dark water.

"My money!" squalled the fence.

Benito clucked his tongue. "Sinner. Some things are worth much more than money."

With that, he applied his foot to the skinny fence's little pot-belly, sending him over the stern-rail. The thug didn't wait. He jumped.

Benito watched them flounder to the shore. No one came out of the darkness to help them scramble, dripping, up the rocks of the quay. No one followed them as they left.

Benito looked out at the quay for a while. Then he sheathed his sword and the Shetland knife. "All right," he said, "you can come out now."

Shamefacedly, the seven-man crew came out from behind the stacked cargo where they'd been hiding, led by their captain. Benito noticed another couple of people sneaking away. It would be all over the tavernas by morning, thought Benito, knowing how these things worked.

So much for keeping his passage quiet. Still, with any luck he hadn't betrayed who he was or where he was from—or even where he was headed.

"Well, how much did he pay you?" Benito said grimly to the captain. "I should have smelled a rat. It was too easy. You weren't planning on going to Livorno, were you?"

The captain shook his head. "We only go to Naples, signor. Never been further. But word was out to agree to take you wherever you wanted to go."

Benito smiled wryly. "I'm getting old and getting soft. Well, Captain. Just how soon do we sail? Because these parts are going to be very unhealthy for a while. You might be wanted for questioning, about why you allowed a man with the Church's blessing on him to be attacked on your ship."

The captain looked about nervously. "We're not supposed to sail at night."

Benito just looked at him. Then looked at the water. You couldn't actually see a corpse there.

"However there's a good breeze," said the captain hastily. "Stilo. Cast us off, boy!"

"But, Captain . . ."

"*Don't argue, Stilo.*"

The seaman did as he was told. When he jumped back on board he asked Benito: "Is it true about the medals?"

Benito nodded. "The Siblings were going over this afternoon to fetch home the rest."

The seaman took a deep breath. "Di Scala is a big man, and he's got connections. But this time he's gone too far. You don't mess around with the Hypatians here. The people, especially the women, won't stand for it. He'd know that, if he could get a woman without paying double for her." Then he snickered. "Actually, after this, he couldn't get the worst puttana in town for the price of a prince's courtesan."

Benito pulled a face. "Besides, no matter how big a man you are . . . someone else is always bigger. There were some Jerusalem pilgrim medals, too. One of them belonged to a fellow with a reputation big enough to make even princes nervous. And when *he* finds out . . ."

He sighed. Having Carlo Sforza for a father had been the kind of thing that had made a boy wonder about himself, sometimes. He was finding that to be just as true, now that he was a young man.

"I think, Captain, you'd be very wise to stay away a long time. At least as long as the trip to Livorno is going to take you."

Chapter 55

Aldo Morando approached the secondhand merchant Fianelli with a smile. "I believe I've got some information that might be of interest to you."

"I deal in old clothing and cheap medicines," said Fianelli, disinterestedly. "Not information."

Morando wasn't fooled. Fianelli didn't want it known that he was the kingpin. His underlings did the legwork, bought and brought in the information, delivered it to the drop point, and collected their money from the same. But Fianelli was less professional than he thought he was. Morando had been a spy for Phillipo Maria once, in Milan. Now *there* was a son of a bitch who really understood underhand dealing. Fianelli was a provincial amateur by comparison.

Aldo Morando knew how the money worked, too. A lake at the top; a stream to the next tier; and drops to the actual sources. Well, that wasn't how it was going to work here. He was going straight to the lake.

"The details of who blew up the magazine out there might just be worth buying. But they'd be expensive."

"I don't know what you're talking about."

Morando raised his eyebrows. "I have a source to the captain-general's innermost secrets. For a price I can let you into them. It's as simple as that."

Fianelli shrugged. "And why would I want to know his secrets? Now do you want to buy, or just talk rubbish?"

"I'm not buying. I'm selling." Morando turned and walked out. The next move would be Fianelli's.

It wasn't long in coming.

Petros Nachelli wasn't a man whom Aldo Morando would have chosen for a go-between. A short, fat, glib little man who oozed greasiness and dishonesty in equal proportions. The Greek was a rent collector for the landed gentry of Corfu's Libri d'Oro. Cockroaches came higher on the social scale of things. Spying was a big step up for Petros.

He knocked on Aldo's door with a smile of false bonhomie on his podgy face. "Ah, my friend Morando. I received a message that you had some . . . merchandise you wished to sell. You can entrust me with it. I'll see you get the best possible price."

"I deal directly or not all, Nachelli. You can tell him that."

The smile fell away from the pudgy face. "I was informed that you were either to sell or I was to take it." He twitched his head over his shoulder, in what he apparently intended for a menacing gesture. Across the road, two of Nachelli's men were loitering. Rent collection sometimes required a beating or two.

Morando gave them no more than a glance. Fianelli's three goons were, in their own way, fairly impressive fellows. Genuine professional thugs. Nachelli's "enforcers," on the other hand, were about what you'd expect from such a lowlife. From the looks of the two scrawny fellows, they were just some relatives of the rent collector pressed into service here. Reluctant service, from the expressions on their faces. They'd be accustomed to bullying long-suffering peasants, not someone like Morando who had a somewhat scary reputation of his own. Aldo suspected that a loud *Boo!* would send them both packing.

"I think not," Morando sneered. "I have taken precautions, Nachelli. His name—Fianelli's—and the names of his three errand boys. Due to go to the podesta, the captain-general, the garrison commander and this newly arrived imperial prince, if I disappear. So go away and tell the boss I don't deal with intermediaries."

Morando smiled nastily, before closing the door. "And remember that your name is on the list now, also."

Aldo Morando was in fact delighted by one aspect of Fianelli's choice. The use of Nachelli fingered several of the Libri d'Oro families who'd been enriched by the feudal system the Venetians had imposed on the island—and were now conspiring against the Republic. A potential source of much income, for a blackmailer.

Fianelli came to see him after sundown. When he left, Morando went to the flagstone that served as a trapdoor to the "satanic cellar" and lifted it up. Bianca Casarini emerged from the stairs.

"I *still* don't understand why you didn't pass the information on to him yourself," he grumbled. "This is a bit dangerous for me, Bianca. Nachelli's just a toad, but Fianelli—crude as he may be—is something else again."

Bianca gave Morando her most seductive smile and chucked him under the chin.

"Surely you're not afraid of him? *Aldo Morando?* A veteran of *Milanese* skullduggery? Quaking at the thought of a criminal—ah, not exactly mastermind—on a dinky little island in the middle of nowhere?"

Irritably, though not forcefully, he brushed her hand aside and stumped over to the table in the kitchen. "Save the silly 'manly' stuff for someone stupid enough to fall for it, Bianca." He lowered himself into one of the chairs. "I survived Milan by not being foolhardy. So please answer the question."

Bianca came over and slid into a chair next to him. She took her time about it, to consider her answer. Morando was a charlatan, true, but it wouldn't pay to forget that he was also considerably brighter than any of the other men she was dealing with on Corfu.

She decided the truth—most of it, at least—would serve best.

"I can't afford to become too closely associated with Fianelli myself. Even more important, I can't afford to let *him* start getting the notion that I've become indispensable to him."

Morando arched a quizzical eyebrow. From long habit, he did so in a vaguely satanic manner. "Satanic," at least, as he—a charlatan and a faker—thought of the term. Bianca, as it happened, had once gotten a glimpse of the Great One, in her dealings with Countess Bartholdy. So she knew Morando's affectation was silly.

The real Satan had no eyebrows, nor could he. They would have been instantly burnt to a crisp, so close to those . . .

Not eyes. Whatever they were, they were not eyes.

She shuddered a little, remembering.

Morando misinterpreted the shiver. "Fianelli's not as bad as all *that,* Bianca." He chuckled. "I would have thought you'd want to be indispensable to him."

She shook her head. "You're misreading him. No, he's not that bad—but he is that sullen. Fianelli is the kind of man who hates anyone having a hold on him, especially a woman. If he gets sullen enough, he'll cut off his nose to spite his face. The nose, in this instance, being me."

Morando looked away, thinking for a moment. "Probably true," he mused. "He does remind me a bit of those crazy Montagnards in Milan, even if he hasn't got a speck of political loyalties. But . . . yes, he's got that somewhat maniacal feel about him."

"I don't think he's entirely sane." Confident now that she had Morando diverted down a safe track, Bianca pushed ahead. "He murdered that woman of his, you know—had her murdered, anyway—and for what? She was docile as you could ask for, and so dumb she posed no threat to him whatsoever. Didn't matter. At a certain point, she irked him a bit. Why? Who knows? Probably asked him to wipe the mud off his feet before entering the kitchen she'd just cleaned."

Morando grunted. "All right. What you intend, then, is to make sure that the information we feed him comes from both of us. You feed him stuff from the Libri d'Oro, I feed him stuff from the Venetians. And stuff which jibes with each other. That way he'll think he can play one of us off against the other. That'll please his fancy—enough, you think, that he won't start thinking of either of us as a threat to him."

"Exactly."

Again, he gave her that false-satanic eyebrow. It wasn't all fakery, though. Bianca reminded herself sharply that Morando hadn't survived Milan without being willing to shed blood himself, on occasion.

"Just make sure it isn't true, Bianca." The menace in Morando's voice was barely under the surface. "If I start thinking that you're playing me . . ."

"Don't be silly! Why would I do that?" She didn't try for offended innocence—Morando wouldn't believe that for an instant—but simple cold calculation. "This partnership is proving profitable for both of us. Besides, sooner or later—we're doing our best to make sure it happens, after all—the Hungarians are going to pour into this place. When that happens, I have every intention of being on the best possible terms with you."

She glanced at the flagstone. Morando, following her eyes, smiled. "It will make a nice hideout, won't it, until the Hungarians have sated their bloodlust?"

His eyes moved back to her, lingering for an instant on her body. "Simple lust, too, for such as you. Mind you, Bianca, I *will* expect to be entertained while we're waiting in the cellar."

She laughed huskily. "And have I ever given you grounds for complaint on that score?" Her hand reached out and began stroking his arm. "Now that you bring it up, in fact . . ."

Regretfully, he shook his head. "Can't, sorry. Not tonight. The Tomaselli slut is coming over later and she's supposed to bring a friend of hers with her." He rolled his eyes. "I need to save my energy. And other stuff."

Bianca laughed again. "What are you complaining about? Two women, naked, squirming all over you—most men would think they'd died and gone to Heaven."

Morando's face was sour. "Most men have never copulated with Sophia Tomaselli in a rut, with paint and ointments smeared all over her body and with her groaning what she thinks are words of passion. I'm coming to detest the woman." The face grew more sour still. "God only knows what her friend is like."

Discreetly, Bianca said nothing. She knew what the

friend was like, as it happened, having been the one who steered her to Sophia in the first place. Like Sophia, Ursula Monteleone had all the vices and the unpleasant personality of a *Case Vecchie* woman moldering in a provincial backwater; unlike Sophia, who was at least physically rather attractive, Ursula was almost obese and had bad breath.

"Some other time, then," she murmured seductively. That was a waste of time, with Morando. But Bianca liked to stay in practice.

At midnight, Bianca communicated with Countess Bartholdy. Unbeknownst to her, not five minutes later, Fianelli used almost exactly the same magical methods to communicate with Emeric.

Both mistress and master were pleased at the reports. Others were not.

Eneko Lopez glared out the window of the lodgings he shared with his fellow priests. There was nothing to see, in the middle of the night, except the occasional flashes of cannon fire.

Hearing footsteps enter the room, he glanced over his shoulder. It was Diego and Pierre, not to his surprise. Of the four of them, Francis was the least sensitive to evil auras.

"Yes, Diego and Pierre, I felt it also. It woke me up. Twice—and with a different flavor to each. They're using the same rituals but following slightly different procedures. We've got *two* Satanists, or packs of them, working in this place."

"Yes. But why two, I wonder? One of them will be Emeric's agent, for a certainty. Who is the other working for? It wouldn't be Chernobog. For his own reasons, the demon avoids satanic rituals as carefully as we do."

Lopez shrugged. "Hard to say. The Dark One penetrates everywhere, in this wicked world." He slapped the windowsill with exasperation. "This cursed island!"

"It does not really smell like an evil place to me, Eneko. And I am—you may recall—a rather accomplished witch-smeller."

Eneko sighed. "Yes, I know. But whether it's evil or not, there's something on Corfu that impedes all of our own magic." He clenched his fist, slowly, as a man might crush a lemon. "Were that not true, we could deal with these Satanists easily. I could sense that they are skilled enough—one, especially—but not powerful."

Diego cleared his throat. "Two things, then. The first is that we should let Francesca know what we know."

Eneko's lips quirked a bit. He could guess what the second thing was. "I agree to the first, not that I think she'll have any more success than we're having. I will not agree to the second. Not yet, at any rate."

He could hear Pierre's sigh. "So stubborn! Eneko, this island—whatever lurks on it, rather—is *not* evil. Not friendly to us either, no. But not evil. So why *not* try to form an alliance with . . ."

"With what?" Eneko demanded. "A formless, faceless something? About which we know nothing, really, except that it seems able to absorb all our magic like a sponge absorbs spilled water?"

Pierre cleared his throat again. For the first time since he and Diego had entered the chamber they all used as a common room, Eneko turned to face both of them squarely. The Basque priest's eyes were perhaps a little wider.

"Ah. You're right, actually. We *do* know something about it. It impedes earth magic, in particular."

"In particular? Perhaps—exclusively." Pierre stepped forward to join Eneko at the window. Looking out into the darkness, he frowned thoughtfully. "I admit, it's hard to prove, one way or the other. None of us can fly and—"

Cannon fire illuminated the night. "—going out on a boat is probably not a practical idea, these days."

The next evening, the prevailing northwest wind—the *maestro*, it was called—was blowing hard enough to make the poles of Emeric's great pavilion tent creak, despite their heavy burden. The assembled officers carefully did not look at the two corpses swinging from them. One of those corpses was that of a purported rebel. But the other was that of a former officer in Emeric's army, the man who'd been in charge of the magazine that had been sabotaged—and there were still vacancies on the other four poles.

"His name is Hakkonsen. Erik Hakkonsen," said Emeric coolly. His men had been running around like chickens with their heads cut off since the destruction of the magazine, trying to find out who had blown it up. It gave him great satisfaction to show them that he could do what they could not.

"He's an Icelander, a Knight of the Holy Trinity. He's Prince Manfred of Brittany's personal bodyguard, so you can assume he's an excellent swordsman. He stands about six foot two, he is lean and athletic, broad-shouldered. He had fine, blond, straight hair, but it is now probably dyed black. He's wearing a short, dark Mungo cotte, a gray homespun shirt, and tawny woolen breeches. One of my agents actually sold him the clothes. He is possibly in the company of a blond woman. I want either of them. The woman will do for bait. Him, I want his head."

A guard came running in. "Sire! Sire! The camp at Patara is on fire. I can see it burning."

Emeric and his officers rushed out. In the darkness, the arc of leaping wind-driven flames stood out clearly. Some of the flames were easily thirty feet high. In their ruddy light, even from here Emeric could see the tents and the tiny stick figures of soldiers, fighting the fire.

"Get down there!" shouted the king. "That's the new shipment. That is the horses' hay!"

Cavalry commanders, particularly, left at a sprint.

Chapter 56

The remount guards had their attention on the blaze across the inlet. Stalking them was ludicrously easy, thought Erik, even in the bright moonlight. Would have been, at least, except for the horses. Horses are a lot more wary than men. Still, if the herd guards had noticed, then they put those whickers and ear flattenings down to the fire-smoke.

Erik's five arquebusiers, their fire all directed on the guard tower, cut loose a moment too early.

The rest had to rush the last few yards, but surprise was still on their side. Erik didn't waste time on finesse. He ran one of the sentries through as the man was attempting to bring his pike to bear. A second blow felled another man. He half-turned to see how the rest were getting on.

In horror, he saw it was not going so well. One of the men was down. Thalia, thrusting wildly at another sentry, was nearly skewered. The guard had knocked her legs out from under her, even if he'd missed his pike stroke. Erik knew he'd never get there in time.

Panting, Giuliano did—but there were three sentries, all with pikes, facing a single pudgy swordsman.

And Erik was treated to a virtuoso display of blades-manship.

Erik had been worried about Giuliano. Kari told him that he'd hesitated to cut throats in the magazine-guard barracks raid. Now, however, Giuliano had suddenly become transformed from a plump youth into a whiplash-fast razor. The three, prepared, ready and with a far greater reach, proved no match at all.

Guiliano administered his last coup de grace, and gently offered Thalia a hand up, as if he was at some court function.

Meanwhile, the guard tower had fallen. Erik's men were hastily opening the sheep pens that Emeric's forces had been using for their spare horses.

"Come on!" yelled Kari, already mounted, cracking a stockman's whip he'd found somewhere. "Let's move out. Let the Hungarians chase their own horses through the maquis instead of chasing us."

It had been one thing to talk, and to hate. But Giu-liano had stuck to farming olives, wine and no livestock at all because he hated the thought of killing so much as a mouse. The magazine raid had been a moment of truth for him. When the fellow opened his eyes, so ter-rified . . .

It was perhaps fortunate that Kari had been there. Giuliano found himself replaying the blood and the hor-ror, on top of the blood and the horror of finding his gentle doe-eyed Eleni raped and murdered. He hadn't slept much since then, without a lot of wine. Before this evening he'd been seriously considering taking a pistol and ending it all. In fact it had only been their unthink-ing assumption that he would go along on this expedition that had had him here at all.

He didn't know how to tell them he didn't want any more of this . . . this killing.

And then she'd fallen. He'd been close enough to hear her scream. He'd heard what she'd been through from Hakkonsen. Obviously, it was still raw in her, too. Her voice was remarkably like Eleni's.

Something inside him had snapped. He hadn't even thought about what he was doing. Years of papa's train-ing reasserted themselves.

When he helped her to her feet she staggered. He caught her and she leaned on him briefly. He could feel her trembling and her heartbeat against him, racing, then she pushed away. "I'm sorry, master," she said, peasant-to-landowner relationships reasserting themselves. "I was just so scared."

"So was I," he said quietly.

"We'd better ride."

Most of the others had already mounted. Other guards would be coming; there was indeed no time to be feeling sorry for himself. She must have seen the helpless look on his face. "Follow me. I used to live near here."

Giuliano, riding just behind her, wondered how a peasant girl learned to master a horse like that. There were few cavalrymen in the same league.

Up in the dark maquis near a stubby, wind-twisted Aleppo pine, she stopped and dismounted.

"What is it?"

"I just wanted to collect something. This is where Georgio and I were hiding." Her voice cracked slightly.

Giuliano decided he'd better dismount too. There was a narrow crack at the foot of the pine, that she'd slipped into. Giuliano tied his horse and, with some difficulty, squeezed in after her.

She lit a rush dip, and Giuliano could see that her eyes were brimming with tears. But she walked resolutely past the bed made up so neatly on the cave floor, past the ashes of the tiny fire. Past the two cook pots, and the oil crock. She took down a bundle of spidery net that hung from a crossbar that someone had rigged. Giuliano saw she was holding her lip between her teeth and determinedly not looking left or right. Her chin quivered slightly. She came back to the crack that was the door, turned briefly, looked at the bed, and let out a single, strangled sob. Then she put the rush dip out, and without waiting or even seeming to see Giuliano, scrambled out.

He was left alone in the darkness. He swallowed and pushed into the crack and out into the night.

She was struggling to mount with the bundle. "Can I hold that for you?" he asked, quietly.

The peasant girl seemed to see him again for the first time. "Please, master. Hold it here in the middle."

It was a fibrous bundle and surprisingly heavy. "What is it?" he asked, as he handed it up to her.

"My bird-net," she replied as he mounted.

He'd seen the peasant women casting their nets into the air to catch wild birds before. A fowling-piece of any sort was simply beyond the means of the peasantry, but with nimble fingers and a few weights they could catch feathered bounty. "What for? We have money for food."

She shrugged. "I can't fight men. I could cut their throats like animals when they were asleep. But I nearly died tonight, because I don't know how to fight. But I think a man in a net will not fight well. Then I can deal with him."

He took a deep breath. "I'll teach you. I should have taught Eleni."

"Who?"

"My wife. My beautiful, gentle wife. They killed her." It seemed very necessary to tell all of it. "They raped her first. They killed my son. My baby boy. I was away at my uncle Ambrosino's estate. Eleni doesn't," he swallowed, "didn't like him. So she and little Flavio stayed home. One of the family retainers brought me word. We rode as quickly as we could but . . ."

"Georgio and I never had a child." She paused. "You Libri d'Oro joke about the peasants always trying to save money with the priest being able to do the wedding and the christening at the same time."

Giuliano felt himself redden. He'd made the comment himself. Pregnant brides were almost the norm among the peasantry on his Ropa valley estate. "Yes. But I'm not one of the Libri d'Oro. My uncle is in the Golden Book, though."

They rode in silence, heading for the rendezvous. "But you are a landowner?"

"Yes. But my father did not approve of the Golden Book."

"And you lived on the estate and not in town. Very strange." She sounded slightly more at ease. "But you Libri d'Oro don't understand. A bride must be pregnant to prove that she can be fertile. Georgio loved me enough to marry me even though I . . . didn't fall pregnant. I had very little dowry, because my father died at sea. He married me anyway. I wanted a child. I wanted one so badly for my man. But now I am glad I didn't ever have one. This is no world for a child."

There seemed to be no reply to that. Peasant marriages, indeed even most noble marriages, had at least an element of commerce about them. It had been one of the things that had made him acceptable to Eleni's family. Thalia's must have been a rare marriage.

He decided, firmly, that by the next time this young woman went out seeking repayment for what their enemy had done, she'd be very capable of getting it. Hakkonsen had said he wanted two quick, immediate successes to draw recruits—and then they'd go to ground for a few weeks, and train properly. The Hungarians would be expecting them after this. The cavalry would recapture many of the horses—those that didn't come home by themselves, anyway—but they would be hunting horses for a while. Besides, more horse-tracks would muddle tracking operations. There would be time to train her. Maybe time enough, and recruits enough, that he would be valuable again, as a trainer, even if he couldn't slit throats.

Chapter 57

Emeric tinkled a little crystal bell. An officer appeared hastily. "I want to talk to the blond-haired one. Aldanto. Have him sent to me."

The officer of the royal guard bowed and left at a brisk run.

He was back very quickly. Alone. "Sire, he has gone out. The guards saw him walk out just after dawn. He went northwards."

"Hmm. Alone? Or with one of these Byzantine rats he is supposed to be with?"

The young officer hesitated. "Sire, he had no man with him. No woman, either. But the guards tell me he was accompanied by a yellow dog. The guard said it looked more like an overgrown jackal than a dog. An ugly yellow-toothed mangy thing. His horse tried to kill it, and Aldanto stopped him."

A yellow dog . . . . The puppet-man would not have a pet. His master wouldn't allow it.

"Have the guards told about this creature. If it is seen again, have them shoot it."

After the officer left, Emeric's eyes narrowed thoughtfully. He was slowly—reluctantly—coming to the conclusion that before too long he would need to go back to Hungary and talk to his great-great-aunt, the Countess Bartoldy. His plans for Corfu were not working out as well as they should have, due to the incompetence of too many of his officers. And, what was worse, due to the delay it was becoming clear that magic would be playing more of a role in the campaign than he'd foreseen. Or wanted, even though he was a skilled sorcerer in his own right.

The problem with sorcery was that it was, ultimately, something that had no greater respect for monarchs than anyone else. That made it a risky business for someone with the name of "Emeric, King of Hungary." He hated to be beholden to his great-great-aunt any more than he needed to be, but it was just a fact that this sort of thing was Elizabeth Bartholdy's field of expertise, far more than his.

Traveling with the shaman, Aldanto was obliged to walk. No horse would tolerate the shaman within sight, and even the scent of him seemed to make them uneasy.

Being forced to walk was hard on Aldanto. It meant that muscles that had been torn by torture and forced to heal, laced with scarring, were forced into more work than they really should have had to do. He had not walked much in years before Jagiellon captured him, either. In Venice, he had traveled almost exclusively by the canals, and he had relied on someone else's muscles to propel him. His legs screamed with agony that he was not permitted to show.

Nobody was listening to his internal suffering. The puppeteer did not really understand life's prerequisites. Nor did he care. He worked his tools ruthlessly and sometimes they broke. So, driven by his master, Caesare walked on. The yellow dog walked on beside him. The shaman knew enough not to wish to go back to the place the horseflies had driven him from, and it would be Caesare who faced whatever guarded it this time.

They walked beneath the tall lianolia olives starred with tiny white flowers, past bee-busy masses of yellow broom by the dusty roadsides. Caesare trod on delicate orchid blossoms, thrust through myrtle bushes.

"The place stinks," said the shaman-dog, sneezing. "We should be there by now, surely?"

"I would have thought so. It didn't take me that long

to get back to the camp, master." The shaman looked at his paws. "We have been heading northwest for much time."

Caesare turned and looked up at the sun. He did not shield his eyes the way a normal man would. The sun was plainly heading toward rest, in the heavy hazy golden afternoon. "If this place is to the northwest, then why is the sun now on my back?"

The shaman blinked. "But . . . we have walked as straight as it is possible! I will look through the eyes of my hawks." He bent his will, using true names, names of power.

His eyes did indeed see through theirs. The ground hurtled toward him at terrific speed. The yellow dog lost its footing and sprawled—and the hawk struck the hare cleanly.

Aldanto, having stopped for the first time in many hours, fell over like a pole-axed steer.

The yellow dog staggered to its feet, calling desperately for the master to take him away. Away from the magic.

Barely five hundred yards away, Erik and Svanhild were lost in the magic. Their fingers entwined, they walked in the dell where anemones bloomed. The cicada song rose to its summer crescendo, and then as they walked closer to the holm-oaks, was stilled. An enormous orange-yellow butterfly suddenly skittered into hasty flight from the flowers in front of them.

Instinctively, Erik tensed. A tortoise stuck its head around the flower clump, regarding these invaders to its realm with a suspicious, unblinking yellow eye. Then, having correctly labeled them as moonstruck, it put its beaky face down and mumbled up a wild strawberry.

Erik found laughter and happiness, pure, easy and as sweet as the warm breeze, bubbling up within him. He picked up Svanhild in his arms and spun her round, her long golden hair flying. Round and around laughing like children together, until they fell together dizzy and still laughing, into the flowers, frightening the tortoise off his late afternoon snack. The tortoise lumbered away.

Erik held her gently now. Touched her cheek. "I love you, Svan. Will you marry me?"

For an answer, she pulled him closer.

The shaman shook himself. Spat. He behaved, for all Count Mindaug could see, just like a dog who had too closely encountered a skunk and was now trying at all costs to rid himself of even the memory, by any means.

"It too strong, master. Too strong and too . . . spread out. It has killed the slave." The shaman trickled his fingers across his drum, bringing a whisper of sound from it. It was almost as if the tattooed drum-skin sighed.

Jagiellon shook his head. "The slave just lost consciousness. I have been forgetful about feeding it."

"But master, that place." The shaman shuddered. "It eats me. I hate it. It has a dangerous magic there."

Jagiellon paused. And Mindaug hardly dared breathe. If the Grand Duke started really *thinking* about the shaman's experience, instead of being consumed by his lust for possessing Corfu's power . . .

But the dangerous moment passed. The Grand Duke shrugged heavily and said: "Yes, it is stronger than I had anticipated. Still, it seems purely defensive. And a crude sort of magic, too. Big sweeps of clumsy enchantment. Not blade-strokes of true power. We will find its cores, find them and break them to our use."

He turned to the count. "Well, Mindaug. The magic of the West is your study. What do you know of the magic of this place?"

Mindaug bowed. "Relatively little, Grand Duke. There is a mention in Angenous Pothericus of 'the rough magic of sea-girt Corcyra.' He says the place is a poor place for spell-craft. But I will search further."

"Do that."

Erik had drilled them all since early morning. He'd worked on simple, basic things: fitness, strength, how to fall. Thalia rubbed her arm reflexively. She'd always thought falling was something you could do without any lessons. But Erik believed "fall" was just the first part of "get up, fast, and unhurt." The Icelander was . . . odd.

Like all peasant women, Thalia had worked since she could walk. She'd been privately disappointed when Erik had said he was "going to get them fit first" before he taught them to fight. Getting fit was what the young master from the Ropa valley estate needed. The recruits called him *Loukoúmia*—slightly more warily, though, now that some of them had seen him use a sword.

He needed this fitness; she only needed to know which end of a sword cut, how to hold it, how to use it.

Well, Giuliano had struggled in this "fitness" regime; he was red-faced and panting. But so, to her surprise, was she. Peasants work, but they don't do so at the run. They don't waste strength. They conserve it so that they can work all day. Thalia found out that according to the Icelander's standards, she and Giuliano were equally unfit.

When he finally let them rest, Thalia sought out a patch of shade, and flopped down in it, too tired to think.

To her surprise the plump young man came over to where she lay in the shade of the myrtle bushes. He had two daggers in his hand. "I promised to teach you blade-craft," he said.

He was still red-faced and sweating. His fine linen shirt was so wet it stuck to him. And here he was wanting to teach her how to use a knife. A knife, not a sword. A knife was a tool you cut up food with. She didn't need to be taught how to use that! She shook her head. "You need to rest and I need to rest. You can show me later."

He took her arm and pulled her up. "Now. While you are tired. What you learn to do now you will do best, with least wasted effort. Trust me. My father used to do it this way, and he was the best swordmaster in Venice."

She felt the knife edge. It was razor keen. "But . . . these are sharp. Dangerous."

"Right. And those who are going to try to kill you are not going to use blunt knives. Now. Try to stab me. Not like that! Hold it like this. Now. Try again."

He was a very good and patient teacher. And, she had to acknowledge, a knife did not just have to be a tool you cut up food with. This *Loukoúmia* was plump, but he wasn't just sweet.

Erik walked across to the stream where he'd arranged to meet Svanhild. It ran through a glade quite unlike the rocky harshness where he was training the recruits of his guerrilla unit. This small oasis of fertility was green and soft and cool under the relentless sun and limitless blue skies of the Ionian islands. Svan was, as usual when she was waiting for him, plaiting things. Her long fingers moved steadily, gracefully, almost magically.

Often as not, when they were in camp, or almost anywhere else, she plaited practical things—bowstrings, the kind of twine that Thalia would knot into bird-nets, even rope. Here, she always plaited flowers.

At the moment she was making a chaplet of daisies. Not the mere simple twist that had satisfied lovers for time immemorial, but a complex thing. When she saw him she dropped it and ran to him. His arms were full of the softness and roundness of her. He led her back to where she'd been sitting, and picked up the daisy confection. "Come, darling Svan. Finish it for me."

"I'd rather hold your hand."

He smiled. For some reason, whenever he was here, all the urgency to get things done ran out of him. Well, for an hour or two—why not? "That's a persuasive argument. But I don't want to see something less than perfect on your golden hair."

She dimpled at him, finished it off with a few deft twists and presented it to him. "There."

He set it gently on her head and leaned in close to kiss her cheek. She pulled him closer, and changed what had been planned as a chaste kiss into something far more volcanic.

"I . . . ah, think we'd better stop. One of the recruits might come up this way."

She giggled. "I'm sure they're all too tired to move. Isn't that what you intended?"

Erik blushed. "Tactics," he mumbled.

From the shadows of a Judas tree, a satyr watched approvingly. This was what this place was intended for, after all.

PART VIII
July, 1539 A.D.

Chapter 58

Benito entered the city gates of Ferrara unobtrusively. Fourteen days of riding had improved his skill at staying in the saddle, if not his liking for horses.

The mare he'd bought in Livorno had been guaranteed as "quiet." The horse-seller had omitted words like "old" and "destined for glue-making, very soon." Benito, being fairly ignorant of horses, realized he'd probably been gulled. The horse-seller said the mare was very even-paced. That sounded good to Benito. He'd discovered it meant "moves at one speed—a slow walk." Still, it did carry him without his ending in a ditch. But he was very glad to abandon the beast at a hostelry near the gate and proceed on foot.

He made his way toward the castle, thinking how best to get access to his grandfather. He could simply go and ask, announcing his name. That should be enough to get him an audience at least. But for some reason he was reluctant to spread his identity around.

He was deep in thought when someone took him gently by the arm and began leading him into a shop. Benito was, by nature and background, wary. He hadn't even seen this fellow approach. The man was the definition of nondescript. Middle-aged, mousy and plainly dressed. "Good day, Milord Benito Valdosta. Step this way, will you. Come and admire the knives on display here."

Benito tensed. This man knew him. An enemy? The

Milanese and Montagnard cause had been severely dented when the assault on Venice last year failed, but they were still a power. They could be resurging. And heaven knew, they wanted Benito Valdosta's head. "Who are you?" Benito asked, forcing himself to remain calm.

"One of your grandfather's emissaries. He's away right now, by the way. In Verona. A matter of a treaty."

"With the Scaligers? But they're our enemies."

The man shrugged. Benito recognized the gesture. He had indeed seen this man before, but until he'd seen that shrug, he'd been less than certain about it. "In the politics of princes, expediency is the key. At the moment, Verona leans away from Milan—and in uncertain times like these we need allies, even unsavory ones like the Scaligers."

Benito made a show of examining a blade. "What's uncertain? I thought things had stabilized nicely after the Holy Roman Emperor let it be known that Venice was his friend in the region, if not formally an ally. Or isn't this true any more, Signor Bartelozzi?" He said it in a tone that would suggest the merits of a so-so blade being discussed.

Antimo Bartelozzi allowed him a flicker of a smile. "Not since the Holy Roman Emperor fell suddenly and very seriously ill. A problem with his heart, they say. Now, I think we will part ways and you will go to a nearby inn, just up the road a ways. The Mandoril, it's called. The food's good, and your follower can be dealt with. I'll be there to talk to you later."

Walking to the inn near the gate, Benito looked for followers. Now that he was aware of it, he spotted the fellow fairly easily. He was good to a Caesare-fit sort of level. It took him some time to spot the second one, Bartelozzi's man, who was even better at it.

Knowing Bartelozzi's reputation, Benito made no attempt to shake them off. That problem would soon be solved. He went to the Mandoril, asked for a room and some dinner. After washing up, he went down to the tavern's main room and enjoyed a solitary supper of *risotto con finocchi* and a bottle of Venegazzù from Treviso. He reveled in the pleasure of familiar, simple, northern food again.

When he returned to his room, Antimo Bartelozzi was sitting there, waiting.

"The fellow marking you is following someone out on the road to Venice. He won't be returning," said the spymaster with grim certitude. "Now. What brings you to Ferrara, Milord Benito Valdosta? Your grandfather believes you to be in Corfu."

Antimo Bartelozzi was, Benito knew, the operative his grandfather used for family business. The best and most trusted; an exemplary assassin, too.

"I'm here *because* of Corfu. The island has been invaded. I've just come from there—via Sicily and the west coast of Italy—because the Byzantines and Dalmatian pirates are blockading the Adriatic."

Although Bartelozzi was not likely to let fall any expressions that might betray his feelings or his thoughts, his eyes did narrow, just a trifle. "Byzantium has attacked Venetian possessions? Alexius must be further gone into debauchery than we had thought. But he has been having dealing with emissaries out of Odessa."

"He's allied himself with Emeric of Hungary."

Bartelozzi showed no surprise. "We have had reports of emissaries going to and fro. But we assumed that it was for mutual cooperation against Iskander Beg. The mountain chief controls quite some part of Epirus that Alexius lays nominal claim to." Bartelozzi's voice grew very dry. "The duke said that if Alexius was fool enough to prefer Emeric for a neighbor to Iskander Beg he deserved what he would undoubtedly get. Giving Emeric a foothold on Corfu is sheer insanity. But we have suspected for some time that Alexius is unwell in the head."

"Well, Emeric is there all right. You can see his pavilion from the Citadel. All gold and crimson. His Magyar are pretty recognizable too." Benito sucked his teeth. "I've been instructed to relay this to the Imperial embassy in Venice. But if there is someone I could speak to here, it might save days."

"Unfortunately *Ritter* Von Augsberg has gone with the duke to Verona. All of Italy north of Naples has been in something of a turmoil since word came that the Emperor has fallen gravely ill. For all that many people disliked him—his policies, if not the man himself—the truth is that Charles Fredrik has been a pillar of stability in Europe for decades. If he dies . . ."

Bartelozzi shook his head. "I will of course prepare a full report for your grandfather, but I think the best would be for you to proceed with all speed to Venice. In the last two weeks, Doge Dorma and the Imperial embassy appear to have had a cooling of their former warm relations. The news of Charles Fredrik's failing health has allowed all sorts of rumors to spread. We are in for some turbulent times, and the Montagnards of Milan are sensing the change. That was one of their men who followed you. I think you should travel onward to Venice somewhat more circumspectly."

Benito swallowed a sense of urgency. "I don't care how I travel, so long as it is not by horse. I was thinking of a passage on one of the Po barges. Would that be circumspect enough?"

"Passengers will be watched. But as one of the crew of a cargo vessel, excellent. You may leave it to me, milor'."

Antimo took a long bundle out from under the bed. "The duke wanted to give this to you himself. But, I think he will forgive me for doing so. He has always said that expediency is more important than sentiment, in politics." He handed Benito the bundle. "It is your father's sword. Your grandfather had Marco De Viacastan repair it. Of course, being De Viacastan, he did a bit more than that."

Of all the swordsmiths in Ferrara, the Spaniard was rated the best, by far. His blades were for generals, princes and kings—and wealthy ones, at that. "I'm honored."

Antimo smiled in his wintry fashion. "It was one of his weapons in the first place. I know your grandfather wanted to reforge it himself, but he did not let sentiment stand in the way of practicality. He gave it to the man who could do the best job of it. But he took a hand in the work, so that any virtue in the Dell'este tradition might pass to this blade. You may need it. The Wolf of the North has been south lately, to the Kingdom of Naples."

Benito savored a moment of knowing more than a man who was plainly a master of his trade. "Actually, he's been further. He went to Jerusalem. I crossed his path, in a manner of speaking." And he related the story of the pilgrim medal.

An unholy glint lit up in the spymaster's eyes. "Not for a moment will he believe you were not stalking his footsteps. Interesting. This may prove useful to us."

Benito unwrapped the hilt first. It had been refurbished with tassels of Ferrara crimson.

Antimo saw Benito fondle them. "At your grandfather's express order. When you carry this blade openly . . . he wants everyone to know you are under his hand."

The tassels were worth a great deal more than mere silk to Benito. "The Fox's colors . . . on the Wolf's sword . . ." he mused. "I've had my birth thrown at me here, Antimo."

The spymaster's smile grew more wintry still. "This sword will throw it at your enemies instead. Reputation is a weapon, and wars are won and lost on reputations. Let them see that. Let them know fear."

Benito nodded, and continued to peel away the swaddling to reveal the sheathed blade. He drew it out. The steel trapped and shivered the candlelight into the myriad oyster-shell folds in the steel. "Saints! It's beautiful."

Bartelozzi nodded, his eyes glinting with appreciation. "And deadly. There is more than just fine craftsmanship in that blade, however. It has been a-journeying on its own, you see. Your grandfather took it to Rome. He said it was time the sword of the Wolf was rededicated to more wholesome purposes. I know only that it was thrice blessed."

Benito looked at the sword, so graceful, so deadly, almost hypnotized by it. It was no dress-sword with gilt and filigree. From the sharkskin hilt to the tip, it was a weapon. Benito picked it up. The balance was perfect. It felt like an extension of his arm.

"A killer's weapon."

Antimo shrugged. "A tool. A spade can be a killer's weapon too. A sword used for ill is an evil thing, a thing of oppression. But always remember there are also evil things that need killing."

Benito grinned. "You know, Eneko Lopez said something of the sort. Why is it that people are always preaching to me? Is it something about my face?"

Antimo Bartelozzi looked long and hard at him, as unblinkingly as a cat. Eventually he nodded. "Yes."

By morning, Benito was a deck-hand on a downstream-heading barge, piled full of hides. The smell was quite enough to discourage anyone examining its crew too closely. It could have been worse, though. They passed downwind of one laden with onions.

Benito Valdosta returned to Venice without pomp or ceremony, but with a great deal of bouquet. Some of the hides were definitely not well cured. Normally one got used to a smell, and stopped noticing it, but it had been hot and the bright Italian sun had ripened this one past ignoring. Even the familiar canal reek seemed positively perfumelike after that. And the sight of Venice stirred him. How grand! How . . .

Small.

That came as a shock. He stared, calculated, examined, trying to work out what had happened. The buildings were no smaller. Nor the canals. Benito realized abruptly that what had changed was himself. He felt a pang for the old Venice. The Venice that had been his whole world.

Hopping off the barge at the Fondamenta Zattere Ponto Lungo, Benito looked about for a familiar face, especially among the gondoliers. He didn't want to waste time.

He spotted someone. Carlo Zenetti was not a man Benito knew that well, but at least he knew him. He climbed down into the gondola.

Zenetti nearly dropped his oar. "Valdosta! Benito Valdosta! Saints! What are you doing here? We all thought you'd been sent to Corfu." It was plain that however well his disguise might have worked elsewhere, here among the *popula minuti* of Venice they knew the face of their prodigal.

Benito put down the small hide roll he'd used to camouflage the sword. Doing so gave him a moment to think. The last thing he wanted to do was start a panic on the canals of Venice. And he knew the speed at which gossip ran on those canals. It wouldn't do to have the news of Corfu's invasion arrive with a clamor of people in the Piazza San Marco before he'd even gotten to see Petro.

"I'm traveling on the quiet, Carlo. Let's get out of here before someone else recognizes me. Please."

"Sure." The gondolier cast loose. "But I reckon you're chasing a lost cause," he said with a grin. "I'm sure before Vespers tonight, good men will already be locking their daughters up. Where can I take you to?"

"The Doge's palace, I suppose."

Afterwards, Benito came to regret that decision. But at the time it seemed like a sensible one. After all, he had urgent matters to attend to there. Best discharge his duty as soon as possible, before he went looking for Marco.

"So how are things in Venice?" he asked idly. Might as well pick up on the news before he was having his news demanded of him. Perhaps his war tidings had already gotten here.

It appeared not, by the gondolier's reply. "Trade's a bit slow. Plenty still coming in from the north. But nothing much recently from the Adriatic side."

Well, that was hardly surprising. He fished further. "No wars to speak of? Is the Philippo Maria of Milan finally getting to accept that the Venetian Republic is here to stay?"

"I reckon the Milanese might start one soon," said Carlo, grimly. "They're used to being dominant."

"They'll *try* again," said Benito with a grin. "And get the same again."

Benito climbed ashore at the Piazza San Marco. The great winged lion of Venice gazed sternly down from its pedestal. Benito gave the statue a fond wave, and turned to the palace with its Swiss mercenary guards.

Benito's chest swelled a bit. It had been a tough task, but he'd done it, and here he was, alive and undetected. Emeric would pay for his sneak attack on Venice. He walked up the shallow steps to the guard commander. "I need to see Doge Dorma on a matter of extreme urgency."

The guard commander was not one of the *populi minuta* of Venice. He was from a small village in the Alps. He plainly did not know this scruffy barefoot youth with a dirty face and an impudent grin. "And then you want to see the Grand Metropolitan, I suppose. Go on. Get off the stairs before I have my men throw you off. The Doge doesn't see common sailors. Not even on matters of *extreme urgency.*"

Benito sighed. "I'm in disguise, you ass. I'm Benito Valdosta. The Doge's ward."

Never call an officer an ass in front of his men, even if he is one. The man swung the butt of his pike in an arc designed to bring it into contact with Benito's crotch. Benito jumped back. Unfortunately the hide-roll under his arm slipped in the process. The contents fell to the steps.

"A concealed weapon! Seize him, boys!"

Benito found himself again in a position he was all-too-familiar with: being sat on by a number of large representatives of the forces of law and order. Knowing that resistance—normally the only enjoyable part of the exercise—would only make things worse, Benito did his best not to. Very shortly he was being led down to the cells, his Shetland knife and the reforged sword of the Wolf of the North seized for evidence.

According to the charge list, he'd been clumsily attempting to assassinate the Doge before being arrested by alert guards.

"Look. Can I just get a message either to Marco Valdosta or Petro Dorma?" pleaded Benito. "This is a misunderstanding. Corfu has been invaded."

Snorts of laughter came from the guards and jailors. "It's not a dungeon that this one will end up in. He's for the madhouse." The jailors were new, both of them. No one recognized him.

Benito realized it was hopeless. Well, he'd be hauled up in front of the Justices shortly. Then they'd laugh on the other side of their faces.

By late that afternoon, he realized that "shortly" was a word that applied to the cases of the *Case Vecchie*. For a common—and mad—felon, the period before being charged and sentenced could be a long one.

It was at the changing of the guard at nightfall that Benito thought his luck had finally changed. The new guard coming on duty took one look at him and swore. "Lord and Saint Mark! What are you doing here, Valdosta?"

Benito recognized the man as one of those who'd overseen his previous stay in the dungeons. "Thank goodness somebody recognizes me. Please tell them who I am and get me the hell out of here. I've rushed to get news here—only to find myself put in jail by these . . . people."

The day-warder looked at his relief and at the prisoner. And then back at the relief. "You know this young man?" he asked his coworker, warily.

The night-warder nodded. "He's Benito Valdosta. We had him in here just after the big Valdosta-Montescue wedding."

The day-warder took a deep breath. "You mean the one who . . . on the Rialto Bridge?"

The night-warder chuckled. "That's him. What's he up for this time?"

"Attempted assassination of the Doge. Assaulting members of the Swiss Guard."

"Saints!" The warder shook his head in amazement. "Couldn't you just have stuck to public indecency, young Valdosta?"

Benito sighed. "It's a complete misunderstanding. I asked to be taken to see the Doge, as I have important news for him. I've been traveling in disguise from Corfu. The matter is urgent so I came straight here still dressed as a seaman. And then that *testa di cazzo* of a guard commander decided I was an assassin. As if I'm going to march up to the Swiss Guards on the steps and demand to be taken to the guy I want to kill! The 'concealed weapon' they're going on about is a rapier as you might see on the hip of any *Casa Vecchie* gentleman walking into the Doge's Palace. It's my father's sword, sent by the Doge to be repaired in Ferrara. I picked it up there."

"But, signor. You claimed to have come from Corfu."

"I *did*. I came around Italy and across the Apennines, because the Adriatic is blockaded. I came through Ferrara as a result, and tried to see my grandfather. I didn't, because he is in Verona, but I got my sword. I couldn't put it on my hip, as I would normally, because a sailor wandering around with a sword would be picked up by the Schiopettieri. So instead I got thrown in jail by some officious idiots who won't even believe who I am. Now can you get me out of here?"

The warders looked at each other. And then at Benito. At last the day-warder said: "No, Signor. But we can take you to one of the Justices. He can order you freed."

Benito sighed at the bureaucratic pettiness of it all. "Well, let's do that."

"But Milord Valdosta . . . they have all gone home."

Benito closed his eyes, begging for patience. "Then get one of them back here. Please. Or at the very least send for my brother Marco. We need to start preparing to break the siege on Corfu, and every day more people will die. The Citadel is secure, but the Hungarians are raping the country."

The night-warder pulled a face. "But, signor. Your brother Marco . . . has gone to Verona."

Benito felt like pulling his hair out. "And I suppose his wife has gone too?

The jailor nodded.

"Well, can you get me one of the Justices? Please. I know. They've gone home. But this is urgent."

The night-warder nodded. "I will go and ask the chief night-warder."

He returned a little while later. "I am very sorry, signor. The chief says no. It is not in the rules."

"*Testa di cazzo!* Rules! I'll have his guts for a skipping-rope, when I get out of here," said Benito savagely. He shook the bars in frustration. And had an inspiration. "Listen. Can I at least see a priest?"

The warder nodded. "Brother Umbriel comes to see the prisoners every evening anyway."

"I need to see someone specific. Either Brother Mascoli of St. Raphaella or Sister Evangelina of St. Hypatia di Hagia Sophia."

The night-warder looked thoughtful. "You could ask Brother Umbriel. He is Hypatian."

And Benito had to content himself with that.

Brother Umbriel, when he came, proved to be willing to help. "Benito Valdosta needing to see Evangelina or Mascoli . . . on a matter of some urgency concerning Eneko Lopez." He smiled. "You certainly know how to inflame a poor Sibling's curiosity, don't you? Very well, my son. I will interrupt my work and go to old Mascoli now."

Brother Mascoli came a few minutes later. "Ah. Benito Valdosta. You are very unlike your brother! You wish to see me in connection with Eneko Lopez. I'm afraid Eneko has gone to Holy Jerusalem . . ."

"He's on Corfu. I'm afraid Brother Umbriel got the wrong end of the stick. I have messages from Eneko Lopez, too. For the Grand Metropolitan—and you."

Mascoli raised his eyebrows. "Which are?"

"What Eneko wanted me to tell you is that they have hit magical problems on Corfu, where they are besieged. He says that the archangel Uriel, the guardian of the creatures of the earth, cannot be raised. They are unable to raise wards. There appears to be some malign force preventing them from contact by scrying with other sacred magicians. He wants help from the Church. He wants help from Rome."

Mascoli gnawed his knuckle thoughtfully. "Well, these things can be confirmed. I will go now to Sister Evangelina. The Siblings will attempt to contact Eneko magically. And should we fail, we will try Rome. There are magical ways of establishing authenticity."

"Great. At least I will have succeeded in part of my mission," said Benito.

Mascoli looked at the bars. "I'm afraid I don't know if I can get you out of here, my son. I'll talk to Evangelina, and perhaps we can approach the Patriarch Michael . . ."

Benito yawned. "Don't worry about it. The Justices can spring me in the morning. I suppose there is not much that could be done tonight anyway."

Chapter 59

Odd. Unsettled. That was how Katerina would have
described this meeting in Verona. Petro had insisted that
Marco come with him, along with part of the Venetian
Council of Ten. Marco had not wanted to go, but had
been persuaded against his better judgment because of
all of the strange and contradictory rumors that were now
spreading about the likely intentions of the Holy Roman
Emperor should Charles Fredrik die. More of these were
coming out now that the meeting was in full session—and
it occurred to her that if their Great Enemy wanted to
eliminate most of the thorns in his side in one swoop,
he would have had only to arrange for a human agent to
pack the cellar of the palace in which they were meeting
with gunpowder . . .

Which might explain who was spreading all these
rumors, and why.

Fortunately, that seemed to have occurred to more
than one of their allies as well; you couldn't move without
bumping into a very alert-looking guard.

She couldn't make heads or tails of it. Some rumors
had it that Prince Manfred had open designs on Corfu,
and after that outpost, presumably Venice as well. Others claimed that he had quarreled with his uncle the
Emperor over the *Emperor's* designs on Venice. Some
said Manfred had quarreled with his cousin Conrad, the
heir presumptive, over the same thing—with half the

rumors ascribing evil designs on Venice to Manfred; the other half, to Conrad. Still others swore that nothing of the sort had happened, that, in fact, Manfred had never left Corfu and that so far as intelligence *out* of Corfu was concerned, there wasn't any.

Certainly ships were not coming from that direction, which was . . . odd.

"Tension" was not even close to describing what the atmosphere in this room was like.

And Marco was in knots. He'd told Kat yesterday that he knew there was something terribly, horribly wrong, but he was too far from the Lion to tell what it was, and too far from the Lion's protection to dare try to scry for it, either. Finally he'd gone out last night in search of the largest Hypatian establishment in Verona to ask them to find out what they could for him.

But if anything, this morning he was in worse case. Even the Old Fox had been forced to take notice.

"What's wrong? You look like you've been drinking the water out of your own canals." The tension underlying his words made the attempted jest fall flat.

Marco shook his head. "There's something wrong about all this—these rumors aren't spreading accidentally—and there's still more wrong back home—"

At just that moment, there was a commotion at the door. A burly man who looked more warrior than Hypatian Sibling shoved his way inside.

"Brother Ancetti!" Marco called, recognition and welcome in his voice, forestalling the guards who were going to shove the Sibling back outside again.

The Sibling bowed, in a curt manner. "Marco Valdosta, I have that word from Venice that you asked me for, and your instincts were correct," he said grimly. "Only this morning I have news from Sibling Mascoli, and from the Grand Metropolitan as well, and I believe it is something that everyone at this council needs to hear."

The Sibling proceeded to relate a tale that, had it not been vouched for by the most powerful Christian magician in Verona and, by his word, verified by the Grand Metropolitan's own magicians in Rome, would

have sounded more incredible than any of the tales of
Manfred of Brittany's supposed treachery.

Stunned silence greeted most of it, until the priest
came to the end—and the fact that Benito Valdosta was
at that very moment on trial for treason, and possibly
worse.

Three men rose from the table at an instant, all three
roaring the same incredulous word.

"*What?*"

It was Marco who recovered first. "Horses," he said
decisively, looking at Petro. "Fast ones."

"Can't you—"

Marco shook his head. "The Lion's powers only hold
within the boundaries of Venice. Once I reach the
boundaries—then I can call on him, but not before."

Petro nodded, though it was clear to Kat that the
Old Fox was utterly baffled. "Right, then. You and that
hideous bodyguard of yours, on my bay and Giovanni's
roan. We'll come behind you as fast as our horses can
manage."

Marco didn't waste a word, and spared not more than
a glance at Kat—not that she was going to complain,
not when Benito might find himself facing execution
before the sun set! He ran out the door, calling to his
scarred shadow, Bespi, that strange, silent man with the
haunted eyes.

And it was left to Petro and her to explain, as well
as they could, what that abbreviated conversation had
been about.

But *they* did it on the trot, because it was altogether
possible that even Marco and the Lion would not be
enough to do more than delay things until the Doge
himself arrived.

Having his identity known did move Benito's case up
the slate to head the morning list. Which was something
positive . . . Benito thought. For the first moment. Until
he saw the facial expression of the Justice assigned to the
case. It would have curdled vinegar, never mind milk.

"What are the charges?"

"It's a misunderstanding," said Benito.

The Justice turned grimly to look at him. "Speak when you're permitted to. The clerk will now read the charges."

The clerk did so. Benito had in the meantime been struggling to place the sour face in front of him. When he did, he realized that his troubles almost certainly weren't over. The man was a Capuletti. A cousin of the man he was supposed to have murdered. A house that had fallen from grace along with Ricardo Brunelli. A man, by the looks of him, who held grudges.

The Justice turned to stare at Benito. "Are you Benito Valdosta?"

Benito nodded. "Yes."

The Justice looked at his clerk. "You may prefix that list with the breaking of exile. It is a charge which carries the maximum penalty."

"But I came to bring warning . . ."

"*Silence!*" thundered the Justice. He beckoned to the two Schiopettieri. "If the prisoner speaks without my express orders again, you will silence him. And Valdosta, if you speak out of turn again, I'll have you gagged. Is that clear?"

Benito said nothing. He knew if he did he'd explode. Fury was building up in him. And, because the jailors had been convinced by now that this was all a mistake . . . they hadn't shackled him when they'd sent him up.

"I said: Is that clear?"

Benito said nothing.

"The prisoner will answer or be held in contempt of the court. Is this clear?"

Benito leaned forward, gauging the distance to the door. "If I say something you'll gag me. If I don't say anything you'll hold me in contempt. This is a farce."

"Add contempt of court to the charge list. Now. We have the prisoner's own admission that he is Benito Valdosta, a person proscribed from the city and environs of Venice. The second charge relates to an attempt to carry a concealed weapon into the Doge's palace. Is that the weapon in question?"

"It is, Your Honor," said the reedy-voiced clerk. He drew the rapier from the scabbard and placed it on the desk. "It was hidden inside a roll of cowhide, your honor."

"Doubtless he wanted to avenge himself for being banished. And now to the assault charges. Call the first witne—"

Benito jumped up onto the rails of the dock that held him, and then feinted as if to leap for the doorway. Instead he sprang out into the room, knocked aside the little clerk and seized the rapier.

And Justice Capuletti. The man gave a terrified squeak as the blade touched his throat.

"Back off or I'll kill him," said Benito to the two Schiopettieri assigned to the court.

They looked doubtfully at each other. The Swiss mercenary guard commander who had been about to be first witness intervened. "Do what he says. That man is a professional, boys. He'll kill the Justice and chop you into dogmeat if you try and rush him. And if you try to shoot him you'll as likely kill the Justice."

"Listen to the man. This sword—you all see it? It's the sword of my father, The Wolf of the North. Do you want me to prove I can use it just as well as he could? If you do, just push me. I've come a few hundred leagues, by sea, foot, and bedamned horse, and nearly been drowned, caught or killed a couple of times to bring word about the attack on Corfu. I'm not going to be stopped by some small-minded petty bureaucrat. Now, if you do things my way, we can clear up this little misunderstanding and no one needs to get hurt. Isn't that so, Justice?"

The man squirmed. "Yes. Just do what he says. You can go free Valdosta. I . . . I meant no harm. Just let me go."

"And I mean no harm either. I'll let you go just as soon as I've had my say. Now someone can go and fetch Petro Dorma. Then if it's all the same to you I'll go back into exile. I've discovered just how much I hate the pettifogging bureaucracy of this place."

One of the Schiopettieri cleared his throat nervously. "Signor Valdosta. The Doge has gone to Verona."

Benito sighed and raised his eyes briefly to heaven.

Very briefly. "Why don't we just move the whole town there? Very well . . . Is Lodovico Montescue in Venice?"

The two Schiopettieri hastily consulted. "We think so, signor. We have not heard anything about him going."

Benito grinned. Lodovico Montescue might be old, but he'd do just fine. He was influential enough to get things moving. And he and Benito saw eye to eye.

"Have him fetched. You." He pointed to one of the Schiopettieri. "Go. And don't even think of bringing anyone but Montescue back here. If you let me talk to Lodovico, no one gets hurt. If you bring a bunch of Schioppies charging in here, I'll cut this Capuletti's throat first, and then see how many more of you the sword can bring down before I die. "

Wide-eyed, the Schiopettieri nodded. And went with a degree of speed Benito was sure his plump body hadn't managed for many a year.

"Now," said Benito, looking at the tableaux of waxwork-like people in the chamber, "the Swiss gentleman with common sense, if you wouldn't mind bolting that door. I've come a long way to bring this story to Venice, and I'd hate to be interrupted while I'm telling it. Also, if something goes wrong and I get killed I'd hate to have failed to bring this warning after all this. Clerk, you will write all of this down."

The small clerk nodded hastily.

"Right. I won't bother with things you already know about, such as when we left Venice. As our ships were approaching Corfu, we were attacked by two fleets of vessels, Narenta galliots and Byzantine carracks . . ."

He led them through a brief synopsis of the landing in besieged Corfu and his escape from the citadel and his adventures on the way here.

At the end he prodded Justice Capuletti in the ribs. "I have done my best to serve the interest of the Republic. Yes, I have broken my banishment to do this. Once my warning has been heard I am willing for the Chief Justice of the Republic to pass appropriate sentence. I just wonder whether this man's actions were prompted by malice and a desire for revenge against the *Casa* Valdosta, or whether he is an agent of King Emeric's attempting to silence me. I'll leave that for the court to decide, too."

The Swiss mercenary cleared his throat. "It's something of my fault you're here, milord. I made an error of judgment. Apologies."

Benito grinned wryly. "We all make mistakes, soldier. Some of us have the balls to admit it. No hard feelings. I was fairly stupid in my approach."

The mercenary looked at the door and scratched his chin. "In my professional opinion, Signor Valdosta, we ought to put a few of these benches across the door, and you should move across to that corner, away from the direct line of fire. If you don't mind, I'll ask these lads to give me a hand." He jerked a thumb at the Schiopettieri and the clerk.

The Schiopettieri nodded. "Good idea, signor."

The clerk stood up nervously. "Signor Valdosta . . . couldn't we just end all of this now? Now that Justice Capuletti has heard the reasons he understands what you were doing and why. I certainly think we could end this unpleasantness now."

Benito turned the Justice's head by his forelock. "Well, Capuletti?"

"Ah . . . yes. Of course. Just let me go."

Benito shrugged. "Very well." He let go of the Justice's pinioned arm. The Justice staggered forward.

And ran for the door. The clerk attempted to stop him and was floored by a flailing fist. But the Schiopettieri stepped in front of the door, his weapon in hand.

"Shoot him! I'm free now! Shoot him!" shrieked the Justice.

The Schiopettieri raised his piece . . . and knocked the Justice to the floor with it.

"You better come and grab him, Signor Valdosta," said the Schiopettieri, hauling the bloody-faced Justice to his feet. "Here. Hold him in front of you. They're battering at the door."

Benito held the half-limp Justice in front of him.

At this point the upper half of the door broke.

"Back. Back off or he gets it," yelled Benito.

"Just what in the name of heaven is going on here?"

The voice was old, cracking slightly on the upper registers. But Lodovico Montescue's voice was still strong enough to stop everyone in their tracks.

Lodovico stumped forward. Reached over the gap and opened the latch. "Well, Benito Valdosta. What is going on around here? What are you doing in those clothes? Did you pawn your boots for drink?"

It was like olive oil on wind-riffled water.

"I've just brought news that Corfu is under siege. It's blockaded, so I had to travel in disguise. And I'd kill for a bottle of good Veneto Soave, never mind pawn my boots."

"Siege, eh. Who?"

"Emeric of Hungary, together with the Byzantines."

"The bastards!" He turned to the Schiopettieri officer accompanying him. "The Marangona must be rung. So must the Campanile of San Marco's bells. We're at war. Have some of your men summon all of the Council of Ten that have not accompanied the Doge to Verona. And call in the Senate."

The old man took a look at the Justice. "Well, no one's allowed to even give you a cup of Soave for killing Venetian Justices, much though some of them might like to. So you might as well let him go."

"With pleasure. All I wanted to do was tell the Republic that we are at war. This one—who is either a traitor or a fool—wanted to stop me. I haven't harmed him."

Lodovico looked at the clerk on the floor. "And that one?"

The clerk sat up, looking embarrassed. "I just thought I'd stay on the floor for a while, milord."

Lodovico snorted. "Probably a good idea with all these guns. Let's uncock those weapons, gentlemen. And Benito . . . *are* you going to let him go?"

"Certainly." Benito pushed him away.

Justice Capuletti staggered free. "Shoot him!" he shouted.

"Have you lost your mind, Justice?" snapped Lodovico, interspersing his powerful old body between Benito and the Schiopettieri. "Go and get that cut cleaned up, and have a glass of wine. You're overwrought. You'd better hope you're overwrought. If you're not, what you keep trying to do is treasonous."

He turned around calmly to face Benito, presenting his back to several half-raised firearms in a show of the bravura that had once made him the talk of Venice. "Do you mind sheathing your sword, young Benito? It causes unease."

The bells of the Campanile of San Marco began to peal, calling the people to the piazza. Benito knew that whatever happened to him now—and despite Lodovico's calm, Benito knew he was still in deep trouble—he had succeeded. Venice would go to the rescue of Corfu and Prince Manfred. He took a deep breath, allowing some of the tension to ease from his shoulders. And Maria and baby Alessia would not have to face the danger and privations of a siege. He calmly nicked his forearm—the blade must be blooded before it was put up—and put the blade back into its sheath. Then, hung that on the sash he had for a belt.

Chapter 60

Only seven of the Doge's Council of Ten were in Venice and only five were in the Doge's palace. On their way to the great chamber where the Senate met, they were accosted by a functionary, who quietly escorted them into a small salon. Council membership was secret and anonymous; it rotated every three years with different members of the *Case Vecchie* selected through a complex process to serve. Benito was not surprised to see that the five assembled were wearing carnival masks. After all, their anonymity had to be guarded.

The military questions were terse, pointed and incisive.

"Tell us what force attacks the Citadel."

"We estimate at between ten and fifteen thousand. Croat light cavalry, Magyar heavy cavalry, Slav pikemen mostly. From what we could see."

"What cannon did they have?"

Benito scratched his chin. "Well, most of the enemy cannon were not ashore and deployed when I escaped. That was how we were able to effect a landing the previous day."

"How do you assess the Citadel's state of readiness for siege?"

"Sir, it is both good and bad. Provisions seemed adequate by what the captain-general said. But the fortresses were undermanned. The Citadel has nine hundred and

531

fifty and the fortress on Vidos a further hundred and
ninety. There were very few cavalry. In the region of
fifty, perhaps. Of course, we added to that a bit."

"Well, that tallies with the known facts anyway," said
one of the men. A portly one, that Benito was almost
sure was Lodovico's friend Admiral Dourso under that
mask.

"This will still have to be thoroughly investigated,"
said another sourly. "And now, thanks to the furor you've
stirred up, Montescue, investigated in the full Senate and
not in private. They're clamoring for news in the piazza
and in the great hall."

Lodovico smiled wryly. "I've never really approved of
the secrecy of the Council of Ten's doings anyway. Best to
have this out in the open. I think there is less room for
deception there. Come, boy. Let us go and face them."

The huge hall was crowded. Benito found himself
looking at a number of expectant, worried faces. The
Venice rumor mill was already working.

"Why are the bells being rung?" demanded one elegant
Case Vecchie gentleman in the foreground. "Are we at
war?" The hubbub of questions coming from the hundred
and twenty members of the Senate—who, with all the
other functionaries of state, had multiplied amazingly—was
overwhelming. This many despite the short time? It was
frightening. There must have been at least three hundred
people there. Benito took a deep breath. It would probably be the great Council of a thousand five hundred
members next . . .

A very badly played trumpet blast stilled the crowd.

"*Quiet!*" Lodovico returned the trumpet to an indignant young herald. "Valdosta can't be heard above this
racket. First he will speak. Then I will allow questions.
At *my* discretion."

Benito cleared his throat in the hush. "First, I am
here to bring news. A Venetian possession, the Island
of Corfu, has been invaded. The Straits of Otranto have
been blockaded by Byzantine and Dalmatian vessels."

"That explains the paucity of trade," muttered one
of the senators. "We haven't had a vessel in for weeks.
There's normally a trickle of coasters at least."

"Invading our territory—"

Lodovico snatched the trumpet again and blew it discordantly. It was a sound to make brave men quail. Even being quiet was easier than listening to it again.

Benito went on. "The Citadel of Corfu is under siege. Emeric of Hungary is conducting the siege in person."

A senator at the front of the press of people raised a long arm. "Lodovico, I need to ask a question."

"Ask away, Enrico. That's the gist of Benito Valdosta's news, isn't it Benito?"

"Have Byzantines also attacked other Venetian territory? And what is the proportion of Emeric's forces as opposed to troops of the Holy Roman Empire?"

Benito was almost sure that this had been one of those questioning him a few minutes before. "I don't know about other Venetian possessions, milord. I was sent from Corfu to bring word. I traveled disguised as a fisherman—which is why I am dressed as I am now. We were intercepted by a Byzantine galley but were lucky enough to talk our way out of it. We had attempted to send two great galleys following different routes with the news, but I think we may assume that the blockade vessels captured them, as you had not heard the news from Corfu. As for troops of the Holy Roman Empire as opposed to Emeric's forces . . . Well, we think Emeric has between ten and fifteen thousand men—and he may be bringing more. We managed to land some two hundred Knights of the Holy Trinity under Prince Manfred of Brittany to add to the Citadel's garrison."

"Are you trying to tell us that Manfred of Brittany is *inside* the Corfu Citadel?"

Benito nodded, puzzled. "Yes. I traveled south with his convoy of galleys. We managed to effect a landing the day before Emeric's carracks arrived with his cannon."

The tall man raised himself up to his full height. "Valdosta. I cannot think what you thought you'd achieve with this—this—" He fumbled for words. "This complete farrago of lies!" He turned to the other senators. "My fellow Venetians. I must tell you that well-substantiated reports—"

"They're nothing but rumors, you fool!" shouted another, but the speaker plowed on:

"—have Manfred of Brittany—having left Corfu for Canea—stating how much he would like to make it a possession of the Holy Roman Empire."

It was Benito's opportunity to fumble for words "But . . . that's impossible. There is no way he could have gotten out of the siege."

The tall man looked at Benito with cold hauteur. "It has been carefully verified."

"What nonsense!" That came from the same senator who had tried to interrupt earlier. He began pushing his way to the front of the crowd. "Rumors, that's all! And there are hundreds of them, flying all over Italy ever since word came of the Emperor's illness!"

The crowd in the huge hall started buzzing with jabber. Then, at the back of the hall, someone cleared his throat. "If I may speak?"

It was an elderly voice, but carried well. The assembled crowd turned to look at the elderly Patriarch of Venice. He came forward through the crowd, slowly. He plainly had no intention of speaking from where he was. All the time he was slowly walking down to the front of the hall Benito's mind was in ferment. This tall lord . . . he thought his name might be Enrico Licosa—a *Case Vecchie* who had served in Spain, and also in Naples—was he a traitor? Had the attempt by Justice Capuletti to sentence him to death really been nothing more than bureaucratic maliciousness? Benito started looking for ways out.

The elderly Patriarch reached the front of the hall where Benito and Lodovico stood. He was old, stooped, white-haired and white-bearded. No danger, surely.

He advanced on Benito, determinedly. Benito began to wonder if he was right about the danger. Did you kick the head of the Church in Venice in the crotch if he tried to seize you?

The old man reached out both skinny arms for Benito.

And then embraced him, and placed a blessing hand on his head. "This is a specific instruction from the Grand Metropolitan in Rome himself," he said, loudly, for the benefit of the audience.

Well, thought Benito. *This reduces my chances of*

*being lynched. I'm not sure what it's all about, but it's
welcome.*

The Patriarch continued. "Know all of you that as far
as we have been able to determine the island of Corfu
is under siege with great magical forces concentrated
on it. The practitioners of sacred magic in Rome have
detected demonism at work here."

He turned to the now-gaping Enrico Licosa. "I suggest
this entire story of Prince Manfred reeks of the snares
and deceits of the Evil One."

The Senate was in a hubble-bubble of frightened
whispers now. Benito heard shreds of *"the Devil himself . . ."*

Then another man stood up. This one Benito recognized: Andrea Recchia. His son and Benito had had a
small affray consisting largely of Benito giving the handsome scion of the house a black eye and a broken nose,
and ending in considerable trouble with the law for the
Recchia boy. By the look on his face Benito could tell
he thought this was payback time.

"If you ask me, fellow senators, you need look no further for the Devil's helpers than the *Casa* Valdosta. That
man"—pointing at Benito—"has only this very morning
assaulted the core of our republic. He viciously attacked
and held hostage one of our Justices. He was banished
from our fair city, to the relief of all respectable citizens.
He has broken his exile—a clear breach of our ancient
laws! He is using this tissue of lies to benefit himself.
He hasn't come from Corfu. He has just come from the
deceivers in Ferrara. I have witnesses to prove this! No
doubt now he will come up with some plan to have the
Imperials 'liberate' Corfu."

"Recchia," said Lodovico Montescue, "is your son out
of jail yet for the bearing of false testimony under oath?
Against the *Casa* Valdosta, if I recall correctly. My fellow senators, it is normally said 'Like father, like son.'
This time it appears to be 'like son, like father,' eh? The
Casa Valdosta is one of the *Case Vecchie Longi.* One of
the oldest houses, and loyal and true to the Republic.
The *Casa* Montescue once was entrapped into doubting
them, to our cost. Let us trust to those who have stood

by us in our hour of need. Benito here fought on the barricades during the Badoero and Milanese attacks. His brother was prepared to even offer his life for our great republic. Their names are both entered on the lists of volunteers who enlisted for our defense."

The old man glared at his opponent, even shook his fist. "And where were *you*, Recchia? Where is *your* name?" To the rest of the crowd, Lodovico perorated: "Young Valdosta here was banished for the sort of wild foolishness of youth that most of you, and myself, engaged in. I could tell stories about half of you that you'd rather have forgotten, so don't tempt me. Benito went too far, and it was decided that he needed tempering that would enable him to learn the deportment and responsibilities of a man. It was for that reason he was banished, not because he is a threat to the state. But when danger threatened our Republic, the *Casa* Valdosta was again the first to answer the call. Like Ferrara. Let us not forget who our true friends are."

Recchia ignored the cheers. "That's as may be. But I have witnesses—reliable witnesses!—who saw Valdosta disembark from a Ferrarese barge yesterday. Ferrara, I remind you all—you especially, Montescue, as senility is obviously catching up on you—is to the north. And what took him from yesterday morning till now to bring this 'urgent news'?"

Benito put a hand on Lodovico's shoulder. It looked like the old man was likely to go and run Recchia through. "May I answer this? The Adriatic is blockaded. *Block-a-ded.* Think now, those of you engaged in trade: Have any ships come up from as far as the Straits of Otranto in the last three weeks? No. I was smuggled out of Corfu by fishing boat to Italy. Southern Italy. A nasty little fishing village on the coast of Southern Italy, and I was dead glad to get there at all. From Southern Italy I came up the west coast, across the Ligurian sea. I then crossed the Apennines by the best route. Which leaves me approaching the city from the north. But short of growing wings, how else was I to travel? And as for not bringing the news yesterday—that is, if you please, what I was attempting to do *when I was arrested.* And

I would have been still effectively silenced, if I had not resorted to extreme means."

Benito drew his rapier. "And if necessary to get the Republic stirred to action I'll do it again. And you've offered insult to my friend Lodovico. The Valdosta stand by Venice and by our friends. Do you want to name your seconds, sir?"

Well, that put the bull in the glass-shop. The hall erupted into a bedlam.

Or—started to.

The room was suddenly hushed by the slamming open of the great doors at the far end of the hall.

Except that "slamming" was far too mild a description for what happened.

The doors exploded inward, with the sound of a thousand bombards. Benito looked up to see a familiar figure standing there. His heart leapt to see Marco. But his soft, kindly and gentle brother could scarcely quell this lot—

But this was not his soft, gentle, kindly brother. In fact, it wasn't entirely his brother at all.

Oh, Marco was there, all right. But he was completely overshadowed by a great, hazy golden figure with widespread wings that overfilled the doorway.

And it spoke in a roar, a roar that was also words that reverberated in the chest and actually caused some of the *Case Vecchie* to drop to their knees. *"What fools are you, who threaten my City?"*

The windows and walls trembled from the force of those words. Marco strode to the front of the Senate, and with each step he took, the shape of the Lion shrank in around him until he wore the golden aura like a garment. And in nowise was that lessening of apparent size a lessening of the very real *power*.

Marco turned when he reached Benito's side, placed one hand on Benito's shoulder, and faced the gathering. The windows still shivered slightly with the force of his words.

"I have come in haste from Verona, sent by Doge Dorma as soon as we received word from our ally, Duke Enrico Dell'este, of the invasion of Corfu. We are at war and have work to do, gentlemen. You are the leaders of our Republic. Get out there and lead. The people need you."

Only Recchia stood his ground. Benito could not imagine how he could. *He* wanted to drop to his knees in front of his brother. Was the man too utterly blind and stupid to see nothing but what he wanted to see?

"The charges against Benito . . ."

"SILENCE!" Marco roared, and Recchia, at last, seemed to realize that he was in the presence of something that really did not give a damn about petty bureaucrats and petty feuds.

Marco—or the Lion—moderated his tone. Slightly. "These *charges* will be answered in a court of law and not in an open assembly. And your part in this will be questioned too, Recchia, be sure of it. *Now go!*"

It was an order, given with such force that even Benito felt compelled to obey.

Marco put an arm over his shoulder, holding him in place. As the *Case Vecchie* fled from the room, the gold aura began to fade, until it was only Marco again.

"Not you, Benito. And do you think you could put that sword away?"

Chapter 61

Marco handed Lodovico and Benito each a goblet of wine. "Bespi and my horses will be along from the border shortly. Petro, Kat and Grandfather are coming as soon as they can get to horse—and I expect that the treaty negotiations will be completed, if not within hours of my leaving, possibly in the saddle. We couldn't all leave without breaking the whole thing up, and we'd come a long way toward concluding a treaty. But when the word came about you—the siege—I knew I had to get here before someone managed to silence Benito. Or worse. Make him disappear, maybe. The moment I crossed the border and I could invoke the Lion, I did so, and I left my horses in Bespi's hands. I'm afraid—or perhaps I should say, I am glad—flying as the Lion in broad daylight is something that no one can silence; everyone in Venice knows that when the Lion flies, Venice is in danger, so besides getting here faster, it let everyone in the city know that *something* horrible has happened."

"Um," Benito said. He felt odd. Humbled. To be the center of *that*—

Marco smiled. "To be honest, all of this uncertainty since the Emperor's illness, and all of the conflicting rumors and reports, could have served us a backhanded good turn. Ferrara and Venice would have been a lot less obliging and conciliatory if they hadn't been spooked. As it is, it looks to me as if we'll get a good deal, which will improve security, benefit trade, and sideline Milan a bit further."

"Sounds good, Brother," Benito replied, trying to regain a bit of his composure. "But when I've finished drinking this, I need to get along to the Imperial embassy and show the ambassador my head."

Marco blinked. "Your head?"

Benito chuckled. "Come along and see."

Count Von Stemitz at the embassy was a very urbane and unflappable man, as a rule. But he looked a little taken aback at being told to feel in the hair behind the grubby, scruffy-looking young man's left ear. "There should be a lump there," said Benito.

"Er. Yes," said the Count rather gingerly. He'd met Benito before, briefly. Now, vouched for by Marco, whom he knew well, and Lodovico Montescue, who was a long-time friend, Von Stemitz was prepared to accept that this tousle-headed sailor was in fact the *Case Vecchie* tearaway, and normally attired somewhat differently. He was even prepared to grant that this bizarre ritual might have some deeper purpose.

Might. Benito's reputation preceded him.

"Cut it out, please," asked Benito unable to refrain from grinning. "I hope you have a sharp knife."

The grin plainly worried the count. "This is not one of your practical jokes is it, Signor Valdosta?"

"It's not my joke. If it's anyone's, it's Prince Manfred's."

Now that he was near to the end of this, Benito was beginning to feel all of it catching up to him. He was going to eat his way down the banquet table, and then sleep for a week. "And being funny is not its purpose. Believe me, I'm going to be glad not to have that lump there. A girl in Calabria tried to run her fingers through my hair and nearly pulled it out by the— Ow! You should sharpen that thing."

Count Von Stemitz stood examining the Imperial seal of the Hohenstauffen Dynasty. "I presume you are going to explain this. It is not used in jests," he said dryly.

"Oh, its purpose is earnest enough. Manfred just said

I was the scruffiest personal letter he'd ever sent. We were in a situation where actually carrying a letter would be dangerous, given the possibility of a search. So this seal is to authenticate that I have come from the prince. I must tell you that he and his men are under siege in the Citadel on Corfu. Both King Emeric of Hungary and the Byzantines are laying siege to the fortress. The prince conveys his respects to his uncle, and asks for whatever assistance might be brought to their rescue."

Lodovico chuckled. "A talking letter. These modern advances! What will they think of next, eh, Hendrik?"

The Count had to smile too. "It's a very serious matter . . . but maybe cleaner envelopes? Well, if you will excuse me, gentlemen. A letter, slightly more conventional in form perhaps, must be dispatched to Mainz with the fastest messengers. I have a fit young *Ritter* here. I am going to dispatch him, with a covering letter, to see the Emperor—or, if the Emperor is too ill, at least the Privy Council and the States General."

"Good," said Lodovico. "Because I think the biggest problem with a relief force will be ships to transport them. Venice's fleets are away. We'll need ships from further afield. Few of the other Mediterranean powers are likely to wish to help us. Perhaps they will oblige the Emperor."

Benito hadn't thought of that. And ten to one, neither had Manfred.

The Count nodded, sighing. "We will surely find that Emeric has tried to prevent others coming to your rescue. I imagine part of the Hungarian's strategy is to get Alexius VI to trap the eastern fleet in the Black Sea. The western fleet is another question. Do you think the Barbary pirates may be involved?"

Benito bit his lip. "I don't know, milord. But this I will tell you: Eneko Lopez believes Grand Duke Jagiellon is also involved in all this. And that means Lithuania and its allies. And now, if you'll excuse us, Count. You have letters to write. And we have the Arsenal to visit. They'll be working night and day until another fleet is ready."

✧　　✧　　✧

The situation at the Arsenal, Benito had to admit, was worse than he had hoped. Doge Giorgio Foscari had let the old policy of keeping a number of spare vessels in readiness, just needing to be rigged, lapse. The Senate had recently passed a new appropriation to restart the program, but it was still in its infancy. Only two extra new keels had been laid. The work had of course been proceeding on seven new great galleys to replace existing but elderly vessels, but the Arsenal simply didn't have a new fleet ready to sail. At least twenty great galleys would be needed, and three times that number of smaller galleys.

"How long?" asked Benito.

The representative of the Admiral of the Arsenal shrugged. "Six to eight months, milord. We'll start launching the smaller vessels within two, but it all takes time. We can't just throw money and resources at the problem: The limit is skilled manpower. You can't make shipwrights overnight, and they've got to sleep sometimes."

It was not what Benito had wanted to hear.

After two days Benito was rested, his saddle sores almost entirely recovered, and his appearance returned to that of a *Case Vecchie* gentleman.

By then, apparently shortly after Benito had fallen into a bed, Kat had returned from Verona, as part of the retinue of Petro Dorma. The Duke Dell'este was expected the following day.

Marco was watching Benito devour his second breakfast of the day, when Kat appeared. She melted into her husband's arms with a sigh of deep contentment, holding him as if she never wanted to part from him, even though Benito knew she couldn't have been away from him more than an hour or two.

Marco always just looked somehow more complete and at ease with Kat at his side, Benito decided. She was never waspish with him either, as she used to be with Benito. Still, she even kissed the prodigal fondly before taking a seat next to Marco.

"I supposed it's to be expected that you would find a unique reason to break your exile," she said, with a wink. "How is Maria?"

"She and Baby Alessia were fine when I last saw them. Mind you that was more than a month ago, and they're in a fortress under siege. But Umberto is looking after them." He paused. "That's a good man she married, Kat."

Now Katerina scowled at him, looking far more like the Kat that Benito remembered than the joyous Madonna-like person who was married to his brother. "You were a fool, Benito."

He grinned, though to be fair his heart wasn't in it. "I still am, Kat. But at least she's happy. Be honest, he gives her the kind of stability I can't."

She sniffed. "Stability is all very well. But you could have settled down a bit if you'd tried. Anyway. There is nothing you can do about it now. I'm supposed to tell you the Doge and your grandfather want to see you as soon as possible. They're in council with the Patriarch, Sister Evangelina, Brother Mascoli, and several other clerics that I don't know. They wanted to talk to Marco, too.

"I'm coming along," she added militantly, "just to see that they don't talk you into doing something dangerous, Marco."

"Flying with the Lion isn't really dangerous, Katerina. And we had to get someone down to Venice quickly when we heard about Benito's predicament from the Hypatians."

"Perhaps flying with the Lion is not entirely dangerous," she said sharply. "But you know very well what happened to Bespi once you left him! And if it hadn't been that you moved so fast, it might have been you who encountered that ambush, off Venetian soil where the Lion couldn't help you—"

Marco winced; Benito gaped at him, then demanded, "*What* ambush? What happened?"

"Oh," Marco replied, "Bespi ran into some—trouble."

"*Trouble?*" Kat's voice dripped sarcasm. "He was ambushed, Benito. And the only reason he's alive now is because Marco wasn't with him." She glared at him. "And the fact, I suppose, that they couldn't actually set up a good ambush, since they were expecting to catch you before you got on Venetian territory."

Bit by bit, Benito pulled it out of them. It happened right after Marco left Bespi on the road with their two horses, when he broke through a group of mercenaries who had set up an ambush on the road that showed every evidence of having been hastily set up. Wisely, rather than try to fight, he spurred his horse through them. But he hadn't gotten away without adding more scars to his considerable collection, and it was Bespi's opinion that the only reason the ambushers had broken off was that they had been confused, seeing only one man, and that man looking nothing like Marco Valdosta. He was recovering, but since the mercenaries were aided by something that Bespi had refused to describe, except as "black magic," there was no doubt that Jagiellon was involved.

"And if you had been outside the border of Venice, what then?" Kat repeated.

Benito shared Kat's distrust of these magical doings. Perhaps Marco understood and was in control of these forces, but they left Benito feeling like a weak swimmer in an undertow.

They walked across to the Doge's palace together, where the Swiss guards saluted very respectfully. It was amazing what a difference the clothes one wore made. No one even glanced at the scabbarded sword at Benito's side now. Ha! So much for the fuss about "concealed weapons." The same weapon could be carried openly without any comment by the *Case Vecchie.*

A footman led them up to a large, airy salon where Petro Dorma was in animated discussion with a number of other parts of the state machinery, and several clerics. The Doge broke off his argument to greet them. "Well, Benito. I thought I told you to stay away from trouble?" As it was said with a broad smile and general laughter, Benito knew that at least he wasn't still in Petro's bad books.

"Nonetheless, you have given us something of a legal conundrum," said the one hawk-nosed secretary. Benito recognized the voice from the Council of Ten interview. "You are still legally banished. And there are a small group saying no matter who you are and what you have done, or whatever the reason, holding a Venetian Justice hostage at sword's point is unacceptable."

"I'll face my trial and accept my sentence," said Benito stiffly, feeling irritated. "I did what had to be done, and I was the right person to do it."

"And Venice and the Church are conscious of their debt to you," said Petro. "But the form of the law must be observed."

"It's a pity you couldn't have put off arriving until tomorrow," said the secretary with a wry smile. "Your pardon was on the agenda for the Senate meeting."

Benito found this more than a little odd. He'd hardly been gone from Venice a couple of months and they wanted him back? Not very likely. "You were going to pardon me?"

Petro waved a hand, dismissively. "For reasons of state that no longer apply, since the rumors about Prince Manfred's schemes to seize Corfu proved to be untrue."

The hawk-nosed secretary cleared his throat. "Still, the item is on the agenda and must be debated. I think it would sit very ill with the commons if Benito were not pardoned now."

Dorma shrugged. "Very well. Leave it scheduled. It may help our case. Just try to stay out of trouble this time, Benito. We have scheduled the case for nine tomorrow morning, with a full bench of Justices. I'm afraid that will include Capuletti. I can't influence or be perceived to have influenced the case at all."

Benito snorted. "I did what I thought had to be done, Petro. If they want to be petty about the matter—well, so be it."

The Patriarch shook his head. "The church will certainly appeal strongly for clemency. Magical contacts have been made—considering the gravity of the situation and the involvement of the Ancient Enemy, the expenditure of magical power was reckoned worthwhile. The Hypatians in Messina give you a glowing character reference. And you have alerted the mother church to a terrible evil. Our sacred magicians are gathering to take the war to the enemy."

"Anyway," said Petro, "that is for tomorrow. Today

we just want to extract as much information from you as possible. Wring you out so that a court-case will seem a minor thing." He sighed. "It will take time to relieve the Citadel. I wish we had a fleet at hand, but this attack was carefully planned to catch us when our ships were away."

"I have a feeling they've made plans to keep our fleets away," said Benito. "This wasn't a spur-of-the-moment attack, Petro."

"No," the Doge agreed grimly. "It wasn't."

Chapter 62

The court hearing was somewhat different from Benito's previous appearances. For starters, there were many more people there. For a second, Benito's sword was not even in the same building.

Petro had insisted on that. He'd also insisted that Benito swear out a charge against Justice Capuletti for treason.

"I'm sure it was just pettiness," demurred Benito, uncomfortable at the idea. "Revenge on the Valdosta."

Petro Dorma shook his head. "You're probably right. We probably won't make the charges themselves stick. But—and this is the point of it, Benito; you're still a political innocent—the *mud* will stick."

Petro Dorma's own legal counsel stood for Benito. He started by reading the synopsis of Benito's travels as told to the clerk. "Your Honors, it was necessary to have someone who could travel disguised as a commoner, yet whose testimony would be accepted at the highest level. Someone who was also skilled with weapons and subterfuge. With respect, your honors, there wasn't much of a choice. I think you will grant that he plays the part of a scruffy common sailor to perfection, and his skills with weapons and—ah—subterfuge cannot be gainsaid."

The Justices laughed; so did the audience. Benito tried not to squirm in his seat.

"He's a troublesome young blade," confessed the counsel. "And yet, to those of us who know him, he is utterly reliable. So reliable that Prince Manfred of Brittany chose to make him his personal messenger—and that Eneko Lopez, a churchman whose moral integrity is a byword, also trusted him to bring further vital information to the Hypatians, and thus, the Grand Metropolitan."

The chief Justice nodded. "You have made your point. Continue, signor."

Counsel turned to Benito. "We have now read the synopsis of your journey as transcribed by the Clerk, Michael Di Coulo. Benito Valdosta, you have had an opportunity to hear it. Is this a faithful and accurate account of your travels and your efforts to bring word to Venice?"

Benito nodded. "Pretty much."

"You do not mention your dealings with the Hypatian church in Messina, other than to say you overnighted there."

Benito shrugged. "I accidentally recovered their property and returned it to them. It didn't seem to have much bearing on either Corfu or Venice."

Rather dramatically, the counsel brandished a sheet of paper. "Nonetheless I have here a letter from the Patriarch, thanking you for your efforts for the Church, and stating that the Church would be glad to provide witnesses proving you were of great service to them." He paused. "Your Honors, we have here a young man who has served the Republic well, and the Church also. His banishment was for acts not of treason, but simply youthful folly. The banishment was due to be considered by the Senate on this very day. It seems likely that it will be rescinded, in any event. This case, with respect, must be considered on its merits. I appeal to you to consider any transgression in the light of the service performed."

The chief Justice steepled his fingers. "Does the prisoner have anything to add to this?"

Benito shook his head. "Except to say that if there had been anyone available who could have done what I did, or have done it better, they'd have been sent. We didn't have much time to make up our minds before the

cannon were emplaced. And it is my intention to return
to Corfu as soon as I can. I may not be able to get back
into the Citadel, but I can join the irregular forces who
are harrying King Emeric's rear. I've only stayed on here
to show my respect for the law of the Republic and for
the Doge. I came to give warning. I'll leave as soon as
I am permitted to go. Unless there is need to warn or
need to stand by the Republic I won't be back."

He allowed a trace of hurt to enter his voice. "I know
when my presence is unwelcome. But the Valdosta honor
their responsibilities, their promises, and their debts. We
owe a great deal to Doge Dorma and to Venice."

The chief Justice scratched his chin. "Benito Valdosta,
it is not that this court is unaware that the Republic owes
the *Casa* Valdosta and you in particular a debt of honor,
or that we do not understand why you undertook this
mission. It is not even that Venice does not want you
back, despite the fact that, as your eloquent defender
put it, you're a troublesome young blade. The problem
that this court faces is that despite the best of intentions
your actions breached the law. And Venetian law is not
arbitrary. It applies to everyone, regardless. What we
wish to see is how we can combine Venetian law with
Venetian justice. The court can grant clemency for your
breaking of your banishment, under the circumstances.
What is difficult is your conduct within the court. We
cannot allow anyone to assault a Justice within his own
court and get away with it."

Admiral Dourso rose to his feet. "Your Honor, may
I offer the court a piece of information. The Justice to
whom you refer is not on the bench today. The reason
for his absence is that he is in fact in custody of the
Signori di Notte, charged with treason and conspiring to
aid an enemy of the Republic."

The Schiopettieri had to sound their rattles to restore
order.

"Nevertheless . . . Yes, what is it, Signor Di Coulo?"

The little clerk who had written out Benito's story
had advanced to address the Justices. "Your Honors.
To prosecute Benito Valdosta for threatening Justice
Capuletti you will need witnesses. I have to tell Your

Honors, there are none. I will however testify that Justice Capuletti gave me this black eye when he assaulted me on that day. Schiopettieri de Felts will also testify that he inflicted an injury on the Justice, who appeared to be in a violent and disturbed state. The Justice was plainly not in his right mind that day, your Honors."

The chief Justice looked severely at the little clerk. "As a clerk of this court, you must be aware that you and these others are thwarting the law."

The little man didn't quaver. "We are aiding justice, Your Honors."

At this point a messenger entered the courtroom with a note, which he took to the chief Justice. The latter peered at it. "Ah. It appears that the first charge of breaking your banishment no longer stands. The Senate has decided to lift your banishment, and override the court for what is described as reasons of state." There was disapproval written on every line of the chief Justice's face. "And they have made this retroactive from the sixth of June of this year. So this charge is thereby struck from the roll. And as it appears we have no witnesses for—"

Benito stood up. "Your Honor. I appreciate the gesture of Senate. I also appreciate the fact that the people of Venice have shown their love for the *Casa* Valdosta in their testimony . . . or lack thereof. But *I* cannot accept it. The truth is—I did return when I was banished. I must admit that I didn't even give it a thought. My period of exile is both fair and right. I came to give warning because that was more important. I'll leave as soon as I can. I transgressed the letter of the law. If you like you can put me in prison, or, as is common in times of war, put me into the military. I'm volunteering anyway. My name is already on the list on the pillar of the Winged Lion of Saint Mark. Why not put me into a military encampment—like the Arsenal—until I leave for Corfu, and my banishment can continue? As for Justice Capuletti, I admit I did threaten him with a naked blade in his own courtroom. If need be I'd have cut his throat for the people of Corfu's sake. You need no witnesses. I admit guilt. Now the Court can decide what it is going to do about it."

In the silence that followed, only one person spoke. Lodovico Montescue. "Valdosta honor!" he said, almost shouting.

Then, with satisfaction and pride: "Now, Justices of Venice, the Valdosta have challenged your honor. What is more important? The spirit of justice and the honor of the Republic for a loyal son—or the dry letter of the law?"

The Justices looked to the chief Justice. He sat with his fingers steepled looking at Benito.

One of the younger Justices suddenly spoke. "I would like to recuse myself. I cannot give impartial judgment."

The other young one—young being a relative term, thought Benito, the fellow must be about sixty—cleared his throat. "I, too, am going to recuse myself."

The chief Justice looked more than a little taken aback. "Spinosa! You cannot just abandon the law when it suits you."

"We who administer the law tend to begin to think it sacred," Justice Spinosa said, stoutly. "It isn't. Justice is. And we forget that the law we administer is by grace of the Republic, and the Republic stands by the *vox populi*. Anyone who believes the law can stand without the people and without justice, is deceiving themselves."

"Thank you for reminding me of our status *quamdiu se bene gesserit*," said the chief Justice, dourly. "It is something that few have the courage to do. Nonetheless I will continue to act as both the law and my conscience dictate."

The younger Justice shrugged. "That is what I am doing. The Law must find him guilty and sentence him."

"I think you should not stand down until we have decided what verdict we reach . . . and what sentence we will impose."

Spinosa shook his head. "I cannot do so afterwards. Thus I will do so before."

The chief Justice shrugged. "Very well. Can the rest of us withdraw?"

The remaining three judges did. And they returned very rapidly.

"Benito Valdosta," said the chief Justice. "We find you

guilty by your own admission of the charge of threatened assault with a deadly weapon on an officer of this court. However, as circumstances must alter cases, we feel that under the circumstances your actions were justified. You are free to go."

Benito looked uncharacteristically grim, especially for someone who had essentially beaten the legal system to its knees. "I'm still going to confine myself to the Arsenal. Get myself involved in getting vessels ready. The Arsenalotti have already agreed to work double shifts."

"We rather thought you would come and stay with us," said Kat.

Benito shook his head. "To be honest, it suits me to be busy. What would I do in Venice, waiting around for an expedition to Corfu? Get drunk, chase women and get into more trouble? Best to follow Erik's regimen. Go to sleep so tired I can't stand."

"Well, grandfather wants to see you," said Marco. "He's with Lodovico, so I have no doubt you'll do some of that drinking. We'll visit you, Brother. Right now, though, the Hypatians seem to need us to make another attempt to contact Father Lopez." He didn't look very happy about it.

"Lodovico can call it Valdosta honor. But you're a Dell'este by blood," said the Old Fox.

Benito grinned wryly at both of the old men. "I'm a product of place, companions and blood. I'm a Valdosta by rearing, Grandfather."

"It's a fine house, even if that brother of yours is sometimes too good for this world," said Lodovico.

The Old Fox said nothing for a while. And then sighed. "You've come out very well, considering the likes of Aldanto and the part he had in your rearing."

Benito shrugged. "The bad I learned there got canceled out by my saintly brother and Maria, not to mention that granddaughter of Lodovico's."

"What happened to this Maria?" asked the Old Fox, casually. That casualness would have fooled most people.

"She's in the Citadel on Corfu now," said Benito quickly. "Married. And with a fine daughter."

Lodovico chuckled. "She's quite a young termagant, that woman. Between my granddaughter and her they were a pair to frighten any young man into the paths of righteousness. Not that it seems to have worked on you," he added, frowning fiercely at Benito.

"Well, I've still got some time in exile to go and to learn it." Benito was determined to get Maria out of the conversation, and quickly. "I want to lean on Petro to let me go back to Corfu as soon as possible. If I can let the defenders know somehow that Venice is coming, it'll do a lot for morale."

"True. But this blockade of theirs . . ." the Old Fox said, eyeing him with speculation. "It seems too good to be natural, boy."

Benito pulled a face. "Well, maybe we also need some unnatural help. I know Marco has had some traffic with undines and tritons. I'll talk to him. But I wanted to ask your advice, grandfather, on strategies. Erik Hakkonsen is conducting the campaign using the locals. I'm going to join him if I can. Talk to me. Tell me what works."

Chapter 63

The water trickled steadily into the rock bowl. Not in all the thousands of years that the faithful had tended the shrine here in the caves in the cliff, had that spring run dry. The holy pool remained full and still and drifted with the offering of flower petals.

Tonight there were more devotees than ever. The priestess looked around. The women from the Little Arsenal, smuggled in and hidden, were here in numbers. She was not surprised. The cult was mainly Greek, these days, although—as she proved herself—it did not make objection to foreign worshipers. The great Mother considered them to be women first; nationality was a secondary and unimportant thing. In troubled times, the Goddess knew that women came back to the old religion.

The priestess noticed that the devotees were looking thin and pinched—not starving, yet, but starvation was not going to be far away. She sighed. The women and children were always the first to suffer in sieges. And the women hiding away would be, if anything, worse victims than those who were legitimately within the walls. After the rite she would move to speak to them, to see if anything could be done.

The rite soothed her, and even seemed to give some comfort and courage to the other women. Enough so that when the priestess drew one aside as the rest left, she did not even get a token resistance to her questions.

"There are two of the guards," the woman said wearily. "They found where we women were hidden and now they demand some of the men's rations and money to keep their silence. They are selling food to those who have money. They were demanding sex, too, but some of the men said they would kill them, even if it meant discovery."

The priestess frowned. "We will see what can be done. Do you know the names of these two?"

The women nodded.

On the small black altar the half almond lay, unwithered, still waiting. The priestess looked at it and sighed again. There was power there. But it was not hers. It was not anyone's . . . without a price.

Stella had come over principally to gossip, but officially to see if Maria would sell her a few eggs. They were sitting in the kitchen because it seemed the place where Stella's smaller two could do the least damage. Maria looked on Stella's younger children—who were now engaged in an exercise in seeing how far they could try everybody's patience—as an experience that would put most women off motherhood. They were both little boys, and Stella let them get away with the kind of mayhem she plainly didn't tolerate in her older daughters.

There was a furious bleating from the goat, followed by a polite knock at the door. Maria went to it. Stella peered curiously around her shoulder—and gasped to see who the visitor was.

Contessa Renate De Belmondo did turn up on her charitable missions at any place she chose. Still, she was the first lady of the island, and this was a tiny Scuolo house—not where you would expect to find her.

She smiled as brightly as if this was a *Case Vecchie* mansion, while Stella made big eyes and backed up. "Maria, my dear, may I come in?"

Maria was more than a little flustered too, but she had her pride. With Stella watching, she had little option but to behave as coolly as she could, as if she entertained the governor's wife in her kitchen every day. She made her best attempt at a curtsey. "Certainly, milady. I am very glad to see you again."

Renate De Belmondo smiled and came in. "My dear, what a gorgeous rug. Where did you find it?"

Maria felt herself glow. The woolen rug was one of the few luxuries she had bought for Umberto and herself during their stay in the forestry region of Istria. It glowed with bright peasant colors, but was also beautifully woven. "I bought it at a fair in Istria. It comes from Dalmatia somewhere. The Illyrian women make them."

"It's a beautiful piece. We get some southern Illyrian goods here, but nothing nearly so fine." The contessa allowed herself to become aware of Stella, and the two children peering around her skirts. "Good morning. Signora Mavroukis, is it not?"

Stella did her best to curtsey with two clinging children. "Milady! Do you know everybody on Corfu?"

The contessa shrugged and laughed. "No. But I try. Signora, I hate to interrupt, but I need to talk to Maria. Can you spare her to me for a little while?"

Stella was plainly dying of curiosity, but could hardly say "I'll stay and eavesdrop." So she made as polite an exit as possible while, the moment that Renate De Belmondo turned her head away, miming to Maria: *I'll talk to you later. I want to hear all about it.*

When the door was firmly shut, and Maria's curiosity also fully aflame, she still felt she had to go through the niceties. "I have some of the local spoon-sweets, milady."

"Thank you. That would be delicious. And perhaps a glass of water?" Lady De Belmondo fanned herself with her hand; somehow, it was not an affected gesture. "I'm not getting any younger, and it is so hot already for walking. By August the full heat will be with us, and I'm really not looking forward to that at all. The first rains of autumn are always such a blessing."

So Maria fetched out the spoon-sweets and cool water from the earthenware ewer in the shade around the back of the house. They talked polite nothings while the contessa sampled the Sultanína glykó. "Ah. I love the flavor the *arbaróriza*—the rose geranium—gives to the grapes. Delicate yet definite."

"You speak Greek, Milady?"

"Fluently." She nodded her head gravely. "You really have to learn it, if you are going to live here. It's one of the greatest mistakes so many of the Venetians make. If you can't talk to people you can't get along with them, or really understand them."

"I am determined to learn," Maria said decisively.

The contessa smiled. "You will find the local people happy to teach."

Finally Maria could restrain herself no longer. "Milady, why have you come to see me?"

The contessa half hid a small smile behind her hand. "Because I need your help. Your husband is fairly senior in the Little Arsenal, and I hope less set in his ways than old Grisini. I want, through you, to enlist his aid."

"I can try," said Maria doubtfully. "But the truth is, milady, Umberto is not the most flexible man in the world either. He's a good man, but he's a senior guildsman, and you don't get to be a senior guildsman without being very set in their traditions and ways."

The contessa nodded with understanding. "I have something of a problem with the wives and children of the Greek workers."

Maria made a face. "They're out there," she said, waving her hand vaguely in the direction of the rest of the island. "Their husbands must be distraught. Why did the men come in to the fortress when the siege threatened? They could have run away like the peasants did. They would have at least been together and a little safer."

Renate De Belmondo looked speculatively at Maria. And then said calmly: "They did one better. They brought the women in here. They're hiding in the sheds at the back of the Little Arsenal. There are more than sixty women and an uncertain number of children there, at least double that number. They're living on the men's rations, and a couple of the guards have found them and are exploiting the situation. According to my informant the men think the Illyrians must have informed on them. They're ready to kill the guards . . . which would be trouble. And the Illyrian workers too."

"Which would be more trouble," said Maria, grimly. "Those Illyrians are keen on using their knives, according

to Umberto." She sighed. "The trouble between the Illyrians and the Corfiotes goes way back, he says, and both
sides hold a grudge. The Corfiotes complain the Illyrians
are stealing their work, the Illyrians say the Corfiotes are
stealing their places."

"Oh, it goes back a lot further than that," chuckled
the contessa dryly. "Further than you may think. Corfu
has had waves of settlers for many thousands of years,
but the original people of the region came here when
there was no channel between here and the mainland,
just a broad marshy valley and big bay. Then the invaders
came; they were not the Illyrians . . . or even the Illyrians' forefathers, but they came from the same general
direction: Thrace. The Illyrians are merely the inheritors
of that hatred. Anyway, the point is that the hatred goes
back so far that there is no counting the years. So far
that there is a peasant belief among the women, that a
desperate priestess of the Earth mother gave herself to
be the bride of the lord of the under-earth to save her
child. It's one of those things about the magic of Corfu
I was telling you about. He moved the earth to drown
the armies and forever put the sea between the invaders
and this place."

Maria stared in puzzlement at the contessa. One minute she was telling Maria about a mess that could end in
rioting—the next telling her about some ancient myth.

"How do you know all this, milady?"

The contessa shrugged. "It's a very old story. Or do
you mean about the Greek workers' wives? People tell me
things. I don't betray confidences, but I do sometimes act.
This time I think I shall have to act. They can't remain
a secret, but if the guild supports us in this . . . Well, it
will be very difficult for the captain-general to make a
fuss. I know Nico Tomaselli. He is likely to try to expel
them, and certainly won't feed them. Now, the guild is
in control of those sheds, and the Arsenalotti are not an
inconsiderable force. Any attempt to throw the women
out could cause a riot or even a breaching of the walls,
if the Arsenalotti get involved."

"Besides, they're our own," said Maria resolutely. "You
leave this with me, milady. I'll talk to Umberto."

The Contessa smiled. She took a small crystal bottle out of the pouch hanging from her chatelaine. "You may find this helps with your . . . talk." She laughed. "Sometimes men need to be distracted before they'll listen. I find a dab of this behind my ears even these days has the power to obtain my husband's full attention."

Maria blushed. "Milady. It is not necessary."

The contessa stood up. "I know. But I think you will enjoy it."

Another thought occurred to Maria. "Milady. I . . . am friends with Francesca de Chevreuse."

Maria expected disapproval. Instead she got another little laugh. "She has all the respectable matrons of this town in a terrible state! Mostly self-righteousness tinted with envy, I think. Do tell her that her attempts at information gathering have been reported to my husband."

That was more than a little alarming. But Maria persisted. "I could get her to ask the Knights to help."

The contessa shook her head. "This really is our own affair, Maria. We should handle it."

The contessa was scarcely around the corner when Stella reappeared.

"All right," she said with a terrier look on face. "Tell all. What has she got you to do?"

Maria hadn't thought of a good story yet. "Ah. Well she wanted to ah . . . ask me to get Umberto to organize something down at the Little Arsenal. Nothing important, but she did ask me to keep it a secret. And Stella, I can't tell you and keep anything a secret. It'll be a nice surprise for her husband." Maria thought that was a good touch. The podesta was a renowned naturalist, collecting everything from butterflies to eggs. Surely Stella would assume it was a special cabinet or something.

Stella snorted. "It must be those Corfiote women hidden down in the Arsenal."

Maria gaped at her. "How—?"

Stella shrugged. "The contessa is forever helping women. So it had to be a women's problem, and if it involves Umberto and the Little Arsenal, then that must be it."

"But how did you know about it?"

"I have my sources."

Maria scowled at her. "I need to know."

Stella looked mischievous. "If you must know, Alberto found them. He went up to the top sheds to look for some missing tools a few days ago. They've got lookouts, and they hide if someone goes to the timber-stores. But Alberto took a shortcut up the wall. He's lazy, and it saved him a walk. So he came up to the upper gate very suddenly. A couple of the big porters tried to head him off, but you know Alberto, he's like pig after truffles when he gets onto something. And he speaks Greek so he gets on with the boys. So . . . because he was a friend of theirs, they put off hitting him over the head until it was too late. There was a bit of a scuffle, but my Alberto is quite solid."

He was indeed. A very large, amiable man. "And what happened then?"

"Well, you know what Alberto's like. Soft as goose grease with children. Of course he promised he wouldn't tell a soul." Stella smirked. "I had it out of him in two shakes. He's like you, Maria. A terrible liar."

"And so? Does the whole town know?"

"Not from me. It's all very well saying they shouldn't be there, but what kind of person would leave them outside the walls? The Croats and Hungarians—" She shuddered. "They're like wolves with two legs, Maria. But somebody else has found out about them. I've heard two juicy rumors about it already, as I said to Francesca."

Well, then. "I think you should take me down there to meet them. The contessa's right. This is going to blow wide open soon, and I'll need to work on Umberto about this. The *scuolo* need to stand by them."

"Most of the guildsmen don't like the Corfiotes much," said Stella doubtfully.

"But they like the *Case Vecchie* trespassing on their areas even less," Maria pointed out. "The *scuolo* are touchy about their rights and privileges. The porters and laborers at the Little Arsenal are ours. And if I can convince Umberto of this, and you get Alberto to back him up, we'll be able to sway the rest of them."

Stella pulled a wry face. "Especially if that idiot Tomaselli puts all their backs up like he usually manages to do." Her eyes lit up. "The latest malicious gossip is about Sophia, believe it or not. She's been slipping out of the fortress to come and see a lover down in the old town!"

Maria snorted. "I didn't think anyone was that desperate."

Stella giggled in a worldly-wise fashion. "Honey, there are some men that would make love to a hole in the wall. And others, like Alberto, who would just fall asleep. I'm going to ration his wine soon."

"If you take me down to meet the women hiding out in the wood-store, I'll give you a drop of this perfume to put behind your ears." Maria showed her the bottle. "It was given to me by the contessa. She guaranteed it would even wake her old man up."

Stella chuckled throatily. "If it can wake that old man up, it should be called resurrection juice, not perfume. You're on, sister."

When Maria went down to the wood-store with Stella, she was shocked by the thinness of the women, and by their obvious desperation.

"We can't go on like this, kyria," said one young girl—barely sixteen and trying to nurse a pair of twins. "I just don't have milk for them any more."

Maria took a deep breath. "We're going to sort this out. By tomorrow. Nobody should have to starve like this."

"We expected the siege to be over in a few weeks at most. When will help come from Venice?" asked an older woman bitterly. "Are we only worth keeping as expendable serfs, and not worth protecting?"

Maria looked her straight in the eye. "Venice had to be told before they could mount a rescue. And the Island is blockaded. You know that. I can tell you this much—a messenger has gone over to Italy, taking word to Venice, a clever messenger, who can get past anything."

She wondered just where Benito was, and uttered a silent prayer for his well-being. "The Republic won't fail you. And the *scuolo* won't fail you either. Your men work for us. It's up to us to care for you."

She was surprised by the hastily hushed cheers.

That evening Umberto arrived home a little late and looking worried. He didn't even notice Maria's belladonna-widened eyes at first. He was just looking gray and stooped. He took the cup of wine gratefully from her hand, then swallowed a long, appreciative draft. And then blinked at his wife. "You're looking beautiful tonight, dear. And your hair is done up in that way I like so." His nose twitched. He smiled tiredly. "I'm a lucky man. And I don't appreciate you enough. And how is our little girl tonight?"

Maria felt truly guilty. Like a complete slut. "She's fine, asleep now," she said gruffly. She decided that directness and honesty suited her better than feminine wiles. She was better at those than seduction anyway. "Umberto. I need to talk to you about the wives of the Corfiote laborers."

"They're hiding in the back sheds at the Little Arsenal," he replied conversationally.

She didn't need the belladonna to widen her eyes. Had everyone known except her?

"I'm sorry dear," he said apologetically. "That's what kept me. There was a fight between one of the Illyrians and a Corfiote—something to do with the women. I'm afraid both of them are with the hospitalers. I had to see to it."

"Oh, hell!" she said in dismay. "Will this mean fighting between the Illyrians and Corfiotes?"

He actually laughed. "Not unless they both don't recover from being hit by me with a cladding plank."

She stared, seeing a man she hadn't known hiding in Umberto's very ordinary frame.

"I had to do something," he said, uncomfortably. "The Corfiote accused the Illyrian of betraying the women to the guards. But Guildmaster Grisini asked the guard to organize more food, quietly."

"Two guards called Oliviolo and Nona."

It was Umberto's turn to gape at her. "How did you know—?"

"Because far from organizing more food, the pair of

bastards have been extorting money and food from the Corfiotes," she told him with savage satisfaction. "The Corfiotes blame the Illyrians, which is where your knife-fight came from."

Umberto shook his head. "I don't understand them. They're our people. Why didn't they come to us? The *scuolo* looks after its own."

Looking at him with a mixture of pride and love, Maria realized that the perfume probably wasn't wasted after all. And she realized that—just as old women always said—you didn't have to be *in* love with the man you married to learn to love him. "Can I get you some supper?" she asked, rubbing his shoulders.

He looked at her. Speculatively, with a shy smile. "Maybe . . . later."

Chapter 64

The end came faster and more abruptly than any of the conspirators had anticipated. And it came at a damned awkward moment for Maria.

She'd gone up to the governor's palace the day before and missed seeing the contessa. Not wishing to make herself too obvious, she'd waited until this morning. Umberto had told her last night that the two guards had been transferred on to another duty, so something must be happening.

Renate De Belmondo had been organizing. Among the things she'd organized, Maria found, when she got up to the palace, was a huge basket of foodstuffs. Maria had the muscle in her back and shoulders from years of working heavy loads in a small boat—this basket she could hardly carry. "It's too heavy, milady."

Renate De Belmondo smiled. "You'll manage. There is considerable stage-management to be done before we can bring them out of there. Those women and children need food. And there are a lot of them."

So Maria had staggered down to the sheds. They were a good place to hide, actually; their men had chosen well. Although the sheds were within the compound, they were well away from the rest of the yard—up a steep bank, where there was a winch for loading materials from the street and a chute for sending timbers down to the workshops or the ship-gate. They were used when ships were in port and kept securely locked when they weren't. At the moment there just wasn't the call for cladding or masts. Getting up there unnoticed was considerably more difficult, but as Umberto's wife she could at least get into the shipyard.

She was distributing the contents of the contessa's basket when a hoarse whisper came up the bank. "Hide!"

Maria found herself dragged hastily into a long cavity roofed with masts and stacks of timber. It was dark, hot and airless.

And also a vain effort. Captain-General Tomaselli's men knew exactly where to look; somebody had plainly told them where to go. The women, Maria included, were hauled, blinking, into the bright July sunlight.

Maria knew that the one thing she must not do was to reveal who she was. At the moment the *scuolo* could still claim injured innocence; if they found *her* here, the cat would be out of the bag. Alessia was safely with Stella, but any baby would do for camouflage; almost all of them were awakened by the rough handling and almost all of them were crying. The poor mites were mostly hungry. She "borrowed" one, hastily. If there was one thing she'd learned since Alessia's birth it was that very few men will look directly at a breast-feeding woman that is not their own. It was as near as she could come to disappearing. She also realized that the moment was more serious even than she'd thought. There were some seventy of the captain-general's soldiers—quite enough to deal with frightened women and a gaggle of children.

What the captain-general hadn't taken into account was that there were some hundred or so Corfiote porters and laborers in the Arsenal. And they weren't about to watch their wives and children being herded away without a fight. Even if they weren't soldiers, they were men in a shipyard full of edged tools.

And more than just tools. Within less than a minute, a dozen angrily shouting laborers were standing on the walls around the compound holding, one between each two of them, pots of boiling pitch.

There was something very persuasive about that boiling pitch. A few of the troopers had been behaving with a fair amount of roughness to the captives. They suddenly became positively respectful.

"What do you men think you're doing?" demanded the captain-general.

"You tell them to leave our women and children alone and no one will get hurt!"

It was a very nasty situation. On one hand, the troops were armed, and armored. They had the women and children as virtual hostages. On the other hand, armor is no defense against hot pitch. And the Corfiotes were between them and the way out of the shipyard. Something else ominous was happening beyond the Corfiotes too. The *scuolo*, being Venetian guildsmen, were all part of the Militia. So they were in the habit of bringing their weapons and breastplates to work for duties afterward—and now they were arriving, armed, in dribs and drabs. They were positioned behind the Corfiotes with their pitch and crowbars, their felling axes and knives.

One of the guildsmen pushed forward. "Don't try to stop this, Master Grisini," said the big Corfiote. "We're desperate men."

The elderly guildmaster sniffed irritably. "We've no intention of stopping you. But I warn you, Dopappas. You get one drop of that pitch on my deck-planking and I'll shove that cauldron up your ass." Maria risked a quick peep to see that her Umberto was backing old Grisini up, coming up the ramp to where the soldiers stood with their prisoners. The master wasn't a big man. The Corfiote laborer he was threatening was enormous.

But the Corfiote nodded respectfully. "Yes, Master Grisini. But they want to take our women."

Grisini sighed gustily. "I'm old. I'm tired. But I'm also aware of the *scuolo*'s rights and responsibilities."

The Corfiote blinked.

The old man walked on through the Corfiotes, Umberto following behind him.

Maria saw that some more entrants had arrived for the affair. The Contessa De Belmondo and her husband, the governor. And, peering nervously through the gate: Stella, with Alessia and several of her own children. She'd plainly gotten a message to the contessa.

"Good morning. And what is happening here?" De Belmondo enquired with gentle curiosity.

"We've found these illegal entrants hiding here, Your Excellency," said the captain-general. "These men seem set on daring to rebel against legally constituted military authority in a war zone. The penalty for that is death, as you might like to remind them."

Old Grisini bowed respectfully to the governor. "Morning, Your Excellency. We seem to have a problem here about authority. Would you please explain to the captain-general that the Little Arsenal is part of the Arsenal of *Venice*—not part of the military of Corfu. He has no authority here. We explained that to him when he tried to draft us, but he doesn't seem to understand it."

The captain-general looked frigidly at him. "In this case food and shelter intended for the island's people are being wasted on these women."

De Belmondo blinked. "Are these women and children from some other island then?"

"No, but they're not Venetian! They're locals." Tomaselli's tone added the unsaid words: *and thus beneath contempt*.

"I do not recall—as governor of this Venetian possession—anything which abrogates our responsibility for 'locals,' as you put it." The governor's voice was decidedly frosty. "In fact, I wasn't even aware of any such official category of people."

"But they're here illegally!" sputtered the captain-general.

Old Grisini snorted. "Not to make too fine a point of it—so are *you*, Tomaselli. They are in *our* building. They're the wives and children of *our* employees. We'll see to them. We'll see to their appropriate treatment."

The captain-general played his trump card. "Not with the food from the Citadel's stores. They must be put out!"

De Belmondo shook his head. "I cannot allow you to do that. And I don't think your men would be prepared to do something that would have them forever labeled as murderers of women and children. The Senate of the Republic would have my head, and yours."

This plainly hadn't struck Nico Tomaselli. "But we can't just allow them to freeload on the Citadel's stores!"

Umberto cleared his throat. "Excuse me, milords. I have an idea. If we put these women to work for the Republic, they would be entitled to a place as these men are."

The captain-general sneered. "You haven't even got work for yourselves! Besides, what can they do?"

Umberto answered instantly. "Weave sailcloth. We have flax, but the stores of sailcloth are very low."

"And what do we do with sailcloth in a siege?" grumbled Tomaselli, but you could see he was weakening.

"There is life after siege, we hope," said De Belmondo. "And if there isn't . . . well, we shall have no use for anything—never mind sailcloth."

There was no help for it. Maria came and had her name—Elena Commena, she decided—scribed in the book with the other workers' wives. Umberto nearly dropped his quill.

"But why sailcloth? The flax is intended for ropes, Umberto. It's too coarse for good sailcloth," said old Grisini. He'd virtually collapsed when the tension and need went—he was in his late seventies, and it was hard on him.

Umberto paused. Bit his lip trying to think how best to put this to the old man. "Because, master, the captain-general is right. We don't have work for ourselves. That's really the main reason there's fighting and dissatisfaction. So I have been thinking ever since the Teutonic knights arrived here under fire, that we need to be able to strike at the enemy ships. We have everything we need, except brass nails and sailcloth, to build ships ourselves."

The old man blinked at him, confused. "We can't launch ships. And without nails we can't even build them."

Umberto shrugged. "We've got iron nails by the bushel, master. And we can lower smallish craft directly over the walls."

"But what good will that do?" asked Master Grisini,

tiredly. "The enemy has some huge carracks out there. And iron nails will just rust."

"If the boats are on fire they can burn craft thirty times their size. And they won't have time for the nails to rust."

"It's a good idea," conceded the old master shipbuilder, after thinking about it for a few moments. "But how are we to convince the military of that? The captain-general would not exactly thank us for military help."

Umberto shrugged. "We will deal with that, like we did with this. When the time comes. In the meanwhile we can give the men work to do. It'll cut down on the fights."

Sophia Tomaselli lay wakeful, trapped in her husband's bed by the sleeping man's leg. She wanted out of here. Out of this boring man's bed, and away from his clumsy and drunken rutting. And "rutting" was the right word, too. She knew perfectly well he was only taking out his frustration with the world by mounting her.

As soon as she could get out of here, Sophia would make her way through the dark streets to her new interest. Now *there* was a man who could teach this husband of hers a thing or two about lovemaking. She felt herself aroused by the very thought of the shameful, exciting lust, the thrill of forbidden pleasuring. And she had some information about the plans for repulsing any attack on the inner wall. He always rewarded her well for these little snippets.

Bianca closed the lid of the chest in her room, after finishing the needed rituals to prevent decay. Fortunately, she didn't need a large chest, nor had the rituals taken much time—in both cases, because the body of the beggar boy was so small.

The corpse would keep, for the moment, under the linens. There'd be no tell-tale traces of putrefaction coming from the chest for at least a month. By then, Bianca would have Saluzzo under her control and would have him dispose of the body in some more permanent manner.

She put that problem out of her mind. Right now,

she needed to concentrate on finishing the materials needed for the ritual she'd use to have her "relatives" removed. The beggar boy's blood needed to be mixed properly with the fat she had carved from his internal organs. The very little fat, unfortunately—the beggar boy hadn't been emaciated, exactly, but he'd been scrawny. There had been a little around the liver, the intestines; not as much as she had hoped. She might have to extend it with some of her other unguents, and hope that the principles of contact and similarity would make good the deficiencies.

Gingerly, she fingered her forearm where the boy had punched her, at the end. She thought there'd be a bruise there, by the morning. Little bastard. He'd put up more of a fight than she'd expected, once he realized the arm she'd wrapped around his throat was intended to kill him rather than to hug him.

True, it hadn't been much of contest. Bianca had not yet dared begin the rituals that would eventually provide her with the superhuman strength of her mistress, Countess Bartholdy. But she was still a full-grown woman, well-fed and in good health. Against her murderous resolve, a malnourished five-year-old boy had had no chance at all. She just wished that he had been a little fatter.

She lit the brazier under the bowl containing the blood and fat, and picked up the special instruments carved from human bones. With her right hand, she began stirring slowly; while, with her left, sprinkling into the mix the other ingredients required. All the while, softly chanting the needed phrases and intonations. Some of the words had never been meant to be formed by a human mouth.

As the mixture cooked down, she saw that there was no help for it; she would have to add precious defiled and deconsecrated oils to the recipe, or there would not be enough of it for her purpose. She reached for the vials and added them carefully, drop by drop, watching for some change that would warn her that this addition had "soured" the mix.

But it didn't. In fact, as she added the precious fluids,

so difficult to come by and so very expensive, she felt the sullen power in the bowl increasing, and her lips stretched in a little smile of surprise. Well, well, well!

Last of all, she added the ingredients that had been the most difficult of all to obtain; the powdered hair of her "aunt" and "uncle," and allowed the fire to die away beneath the bowl. Finally the mixture ceased to bubble, and she now had, for all of her effort, a little puddle of a thick, black, tarry substance in the bottom of the bowl—black as tar, but not sticky. No, this stuff would be smooth and creamy to the touch, and would swiftly vanish into whatever it was combined with or rubbed on, leaving no outward trace.

And the power contained within it made her laugh aloud.

"We *must* find this monster," hissed Eneko. His hand came up and stroked a brow gone suddenly pale. "I have not sensed such a shriek of pure evil since . . ."

Diego, if anything, looked even more shaken. "At least we finally know the creature's sex. It's got to be a woman. That ritual—done that way, with a child—"

Francis and Pierre were frowning. Neither of them had the depth of knowledge regarding the Black Arts that Eneko and Diego possessed. Francis was a healer, essentially, and while Pierre's talents as a witch-smeller were superb, that was by its nature an applied rather than theoretical skill. They'd sensed the sudden blast of evil magic that had seemed, for a moment, to shake the entire island. But they'd been unable to discern the details.

"A woman?" queried Pierre. "Are you sure?"

Eneko shook his head. "Say a 'female,' rather. That *thing* is no longer human, in any sense of the term that matters."

Chapter 65

Commander Leopoldo had chosen to come and see Manfred while the knights were at morning drill, because he could do so while remaining unobtrusive. A party of men—and an officer—would come to do a stock-count at the magazine every Wednesday anyway. Leopoldo did this duty himself sometimes, so his presence while they were drilling in the courtyard was unremarkable. When the knights broke for a rest, it was simplicity itself to walk the few hundred feet under the arcade to the shade where Manfred sat with his watchdogs, and squat down so that he was virtually invisible. He was not a man given to peacocky clothes like Captain-General Tomaselli.

"Milords. I'm looking for some quiet advice. I've little siege experience and some things are worrying me."

Falkenberg grunted. "Not half as much as they worry me. And I have plenty of siege experience."

Manfred grinned at the young Venetian. "What can we help you with, Commander? Be warned. You give Falkenberg here the opening for a word on sieges and he'll give you ten thousand. And redesign your fortress. He's done so at least five times since we got here."

Gino Leopoldo smiled back, a little nervously. "The captain-general has expressly forbidden me to fraternize with you, Milord Prince. So if you don't mind keeping this quiet . . . I want to ask about those moles."

Manfred nodded. "They're creeping closer. Erik destroying

the magazine out there stopped the covering fire for nearly twelve days. But ten or twelve more days should see the south one complete. Another day, the north. And Emeric's siegemaster has men on a bucket chain on the south side of the Spianada. You can bet he has a tunnel project going. What are the plans to deal with this lot? The captain-general has decided to keep us in the dark."

The stocky young man grabbed a hank of his hair and tugged at it. He sighed. "We're planning on a sortie from the main gate. With footmen."

"I see," said Manfred, putting a restraining hand on Falkenberg. "Tell me more. Are these pikemen? Or arquebusiers? Or both?

"Arquebusiers. In a tercio. Only . . . the shingle is very narrow. No room for a tercio."

Manfred put another hand on Von Gherens's shoulder. "I see. But there are two moles. How are they to face both?"

"The first tercio will go south. The second north."

"The captain-general is certainly rewriting the science of war," said Manfred, so calmly that he thought Francesca would have been proud of him.

Falkenberg could take it no more. "No preemptive strike to destroy the moles?!"

The young Venetian shook his head.

"No flanking from the posterns?!"

Leopoldo shook his head again.

Von Gherens exploded. "Foot soldiers! Is the man insane? The minute those clumsy tercios try and get out of the gate the Magyar are going to charge from both sides. Without pikemen to allow the arquebusiers to reload they'll annihilate them! And the front gate'll be so packed with fleeing men they'll never close it!"

"Er. Yes. I know."

Manfred's eyes narrowed. "So where are the cavalry supposed to be in all this? Where are *we* supposed to be?"

Leopoldo looked, if possible, even more uncomfortable. "The captain-general wants to prove you're unnecessary. And my cavalry—and I don't have much, to begin with—is going to be kept in reserve for any street-fighting."

He shook his head ruefully at the gaping knights. "I am in charge of the Citadel garrison. But he is in charge of me. There is not a lot I can do."

Falkenberg took a deep breath. "Then I guess it is up to us."

Manfred shook his head. "Let's just remember what Erik and you two have drummed into my head: The minute the first shot is fired the best battle plan in the world comes apart. And then, of course, commanders must act on their own initiative. What can you do?"

The commander shrugged. "All I'd thought of was the cannon. The captain-general has said they're irrelevant because the fighting will be below the walls. I've got about two hundred pikemen he seems to have forgotten in his plans. . . ."

Aldo Morando sat sipping his wine, waiting for Fianelli to come. He had a few interesting snippets, for which Emeric's agent would pay well. These rich, spoiled women—especially Sophia Tomaselli—were proving very effective spies. And now that he'd convinced Sophia that she should try to seduce Prince Manfred . . .

True, Aldo would be surprised if she actually managed the feat. Sophia was attractive enough, but nothing compared to the prince's leman, Francesca de Chevreuse. Still, who knew? Some men—Morando was one of them, himself—enjoyed variety. It was worth a try. If she succeeded, Aldo would possibly gain access to information hitherto locked away. To this point, he'd been able to discover nothing about the inner workings of the Imperial contingent in the Citadel.

There was hardly any risk, after all; to Morando, at least. If Sophia was publicly rebuffed or got caught in the course of success, the whole thing would just be ascribed to her sexual appetites—which were already fairly notorious in the Citadel, even if her dimwitted husband knew nothing about it.

Morando yawned. And success would have the added advantage of distracting Sophia from *him*. Ye gods, the woman was demanding! She came to him so often that he'd finally been forced to show her the secret entrance, or else she would have surely been spotted. Truth be told, Morando preferred his sexual liaisons to be with someone like Bianca Casarini. Casual, relaxed, basically distant despite the physical intimacy.

Speaking of whom . . .

He should start considering, with Bianca, the best ways to get out of here when the place fell. They couldn't hide in the cellar forever, after all, and there was no point in being rich and dead. He knew she was no more trustful than he was of King Emeric's final intentions toward his spies and agents on Corfu. She'd proven to be an excellent partner, and he thought she might be willing to continue the partnership somewhere else.

The Aquitaine, perhaps. Bianca would like the Aquitaine.

Sophia watched until Francesca went out into the town behind the second wall. She'd gone beyond being nervous about it. After all, men were just creatures of lust, easy to manipulate. And the thought of copulating with royalty, once Morando got her to think about it seriously, was . . . exciting.

She made her way across from her suitable vantage point where she had been apparently painting a picture of the battle scene, down to the prince's chambers. She was about to knock, when the door opened. Sophia took one horrified look at the profile of the woman turning to speak to the prince and fled.

Maria Verrier was not whom she'd expected to find there, beating her to her quarry.

"She should be back soon. You must literally have missed her at the gate," said Manfred. "Anything important?"

"No. Well. It's just odd. You know, Umberto's been doing night-watches. All of the men from the Little Arsenal have. Well, he told me that they've all been taken off duties on the north wall and at the tower that guards the postern at the Little Arsenal."

"Hmm. So who's taken over?"

Maria shrugged. "And how would I know, Prince Manfred?"

She opened the door to leave. As she did so, Manfred said, "If you hear—from your side—just who is on that shift, let me know as soon as possible."

She turned back and nodded. "I will." Who was that who had turned and ran when she saw her?

Sophia's face was contorted with fury. "I want her womb to shrivel and her breasts to turn to wrinkled dried-out dugs. I want her marriage blighted. I want her baby to scream. I want her dead. She's a thorn in my flesh. You promised me the curses. Give them to me."

Aldo Morando didn't entirely follow the logic of the woman, but then, if she'd been logical she'd have been useless to him. It seemed such a slight thing. But Sophia Tomaselli was unused to even the slightest check on her. He lifted an eyebrow, as he had practiced so long in the mirror. It made him look, he thought, particularly satanic. It had the desired effect on her, anyway.

"Please, master." She petted and fawned now.

"Remember that power has a price." He meant it in money.

She didn't. "Oh, yes. Whatever you like, master."

Morando considered the problem, for a moment, before deciding to accede to Sophia's wishes. She was an attractive enough woman, after all. And if she was now willing to do anything Morando told her to . . .

That could give better returns—as good, at least—as her spying. Leaving aside her own charms, such as they were, there were plenty of men in the Citadel who would pay handsomely for spreading this one's legs—just to cuckold her husband.

To think she'd originally come to him to help with fertility! She'd lost interest in that now. He'd certainly entrapped her well. This was what real Satanists were supposed to do. Typically, those who were crazy enough to deal with the Devil were not as good at it as he was, who did what he did for a sensible god: money.

He nodded. "Very well. Come tonight at midnight. Some things like this cannot be achieved under the sun. Bring gloves."

When she'd left, Morando reflectively scratched his

beard. The belief in curses and cantrips was a strain on his imagination. A good curse token had to have one dominant feature: It had to convince the user. So Morando used some of the popularly recognized symbols. Deadly nightshade. Henbane. Pigweed. A rat skull. Some blood. And to ensure it smelled rightly vile—a sprig of parsley dipped in the privy. All tied together with entrails and a strip of parchment with a lot of garbage scrawled on it in red ink. The thing should cause a disease just by being in the house, thought Morando, inspecting the concoction with satisfaction. If the recipient found it—well, belike they would think themselves bewitched. That was usually enough to make a spell seem to work.

At midnight, with the inner room suitably lit with seven green candles, he handed it to her from under his cloak.

"You must hold it with a glove only. And you must burn the glove afterwards, saying the words *Rotas Astor Sotar Sator Araso*, seven times." He repeated the words twice, carefully, as if they really meant something. "It should be placed under the victim's bed or within the hearth ashes."

She reached a gloved hand eagerly for the bunch. "What is in it?"

"Some things which you are not ready to learn the powers of. But don't shake it. It has grave-mold from the tomb of an unbaptized infant mixed with the blood from the menses of a virgin sacrifice." He managed to say the last sentence with a completely solemn expression on his face. A bit difficult, that was.

She took it eagerly, but carefully, holding it as one might fragile porcelain, her face a candlelight-shadowed study in nastiness. Morando knew a brief inward shudder. From what he could work out the victim's main "crime" was a lack of respect for Sophia. Morando knew that he was dealing with a sick mind here. But business was business, after all.

Besides . . .

Morando had the psychological shrewdness of any successful swindler and procurer. Bianca Casarini was by nature an independent sort of creature. She might very well decide to go her separate way, after the Citadel fell and they made their escape to the mainland. If so, it would be wise to make sure that Sophia was still with him. She knew the secret entrance and would come to the cellar herself when it looked like the fortress was finally falling. He'd already, somewhat reluctantly, made the arrangements with her.

Now, thinking back, he was glad he'd done so. Sophia would have no choice but to abandon her past life and place herself under Aldo's wing. She was an attractive woman, and still young enough. The one thing about the future that was sure and certain was that a pimp could always get by.

Chapter 66

Maria habitually took Umberto something to eat and a small jug of watered wine at about Vespers bell, now that the Little Arsenal was working so late. It was amazing how purpose had transformed that place. Everyone but a few of the Illyrians seemed to be getting on fairly well.

She walked out carrying Alessia and a basket, closing the door behind her. Few people owned locks here. Maria and Umberto weren't among them. There was little enough to steal and besides the goat was turning into a terror. All she wanted was food, but then, would a thief be aware of this? The thief might of course want to steal her. . . . With each passing day the taste of meat became more of a memory.

There was of course food, even meat, to be bought. Some of it legitimately and on the open market: the produce of a few gardens; or hoarded by the wise before the event; a few fish caught over the walls that went down into the sea. Some—undoubtedly stolen from the Citadel's stores—on the black market that flourished for those who had real money. Maria and Umberto didn't number among them.

She was deep in these thoughts when the bleating of Goat—she'd never acquired a name, despite Umberto wanting to call her "Satan"—penetrated her brown study. She turned back to the house. The door was closed. But it sounded as if the goat was inside.

There was no telling what the creature would do if she'd got into the house. Maria turned and ran back as fast as a baby and a basket would allow. She unlatched the door and burst into the small living room.

Goat had someone cornered by the hearth. A cloaked woman who was thrashing away at her with a bunch of something. Maria had a moment's delay, to put the baby down, and then she sprang forward. She didn't think the intruder dangerous—half her mind was on restraining Goat.

She abruptly changed her mind. The intruder was all manic, scratching strength. Only the fact that the woman wore gloves saved Maria's eyes. Maria swung the basket. It and the strange bunch of stuff in the woman's hands landed just short of the grate. The woman grabbed desperately for the bunch. Maria lunged for her. The woman's gloved hand and forearm ended up in the hot ash as they wrestled.

The intruder might be manic, but Maria had both the weight and upper-body strength advantage on her opponent. Maria pressed her opponent's arm down against the fire grate. Was rewarded by a terrible scream, and a savage bite on her shoulder. Then, as the woman broke free, grabbing a poker, someone called: "Maria? Maria are you all right?"

Maria used the moment's distraction to grab the poker-wielding left hand, as well as the other arm. There was a frantic moment's struggle as old Mrs. Grisini—whom, to Maria, seemed half-absent from her own mind most of the time—peered at them. Then the strange hooded and masked woman wriggled her hand from the glove and tore free, bolting for the open back door.

Maria ran after, but she slipped on the spilled wine from her basket and fell, winding herself. By the time she got up, gasping, Mrs. Grisini had picked up and was comforting Alessia.

"She reminds me of my own babes. I lost all of them, you know," said the old woman in a dreamy voice, as if she had not just witnessed a savage fight.

The old lady's minder, a young Corfiote girl, hurried in. "Kyria, kyria? Where are you?" She saw the old lady with considerable relief. "Oh, thank heavens . . ."

Then she took in the rest of the scene. "What happened . . ." She looked at the bunch of strange stuff on the hearth that Goat was sniffing, screamed and pointed.

Maria nearly had her breath back now. She weakly shooed Goat off. Then, took a closer look at what had made the young Corfiote girl scream. It was pretty unappetizing, whatever it was. There was a rat skull and some hair. And some plants. Maria had grown up in Venice. She wouldn't have recognized many food plants before they'd gone to stay in Istria. But there old Issie had at least showed her some of those that were dangerous—including the deadly nightshade which she recognized in the bundle.

"A curse!" The girl crossed herself hastily. So did Maria. Old Mrs. Grisini just looked dreamily at Alessia.

Maria reached for the revolting bunch of nastiness to toss it into the hot ashes. "Don't touch," squeaked the girl. "Don't touch, kyria!"

Maria looked at the glove she was still clutching. "Makes sense. So what do I do with the damned thing, then?"

"You must take it to the Papas . . . the priests, kyria," said the girl fearfully.

Maria shook herself. "I suppose so. But how?" She didn't have so many pots that she wanted to sully any of them with the horrid bundle. Then she had an inspiration. The pot beneath the bed. It was only clay and could use replacing anyway.

The curse bunch fitted into the pot. The pot fitted into the basket. She tossed the glove in too. Poor Umberto would just have to wait for his dinner. Most of it was in the ashes anyway, and Maria didn't know what she'd find to give him instead. There wasn't too much to spare in the cupboard.

She went to old Mrs. Grisini, who reluctantly parted with Alessia and allowed the young Corfiote girl to lead her home. Maria set out once again.

She was heading for the church, at first, but then she changed her mind and headed for the small Hypatian chapel. If there was one person who knew all about magic and witchcraft it was that terrifying Eneko Lopez who

was now staying in the monks' cells behind the chapel
with his companions.

If they were there, of course. They seemed very busy
these days trying to wander around the Citadel looking
innocent . . . and failing completely. They were up to
something, Maria was sure.

Fortune favored her, this time. They weren't in their
rooms, but they were at prayer in the chapel along with
the nun whose gardens were a byword in the town.

Not knowing how to disturb them, she waited. One,
the tall dark one, noticed her. "Can we help you, signorina?"

Eneko Lopez's heavy line of dark brow drew together
as he looked at her. He nodded. "Maria Verrier. The
friend and maid of honor to Katerina Montescue. Are
you looking for us?"

Maria nodded. "Father. Uh, yes. You are an expert on
witchcraft, I think?"

Lopez smiled wryly. The others chuckled. "I have had
to deal with various forms of pagan magic. Whether that
qualifies me as an expert, I don't know. But how may
I help you?"

She opened her basket and, to everyone's surprise,
took out the very recognizable pot and pointed into it.
"I interrupted someone leaving this in my house."

Looking up and seeing the bemusement on the faces
of the monks, she realized the possible confusion. "Uh.
I just used this pot to carry it in. I didn't want to touch
it. I think it is a curse."

The priests came up and peered into the pot. "Come.
Put it in front of the altar. Let us exorcize it anyway,"
said Eneko Lopez, taking it from her. "And this other
thing in here?"

"It's a glove. The woman who was putting it in my
house lost it in the struggle. She was using gloves to
carry the thing."

Eneko's line of eyebrow raised. He went and placed
the pot in front of the altar. He and the others arranged
four candles very precisely around it, and then began to
sprinkle salt, and then water, and burn incense as they
chanted a psalm while walking around the pot.

Maria tried very earnestly to pray. Not for herself, so much, but for Alessia. Children were very vulnerable to disease. She wasn't sure, but she thought they might be especially vulnerable to black magic also.

When they'd finished, one of the priests went and fetched a pair of fine tongs—simple black iron things, but surprisingly delicate. They blessed the tongs and asked for protection on them, and then they began examining the bunch of plants and other fragments carefully. After a few minutes Eneko came over to where Maria still knelt.

"Maria." He spoke gently, and in a way she'd not expected from such a man. With understanding. "I know this is very frightening, but I have some good news for you. That revolting thing is as magical as a brick. It was someone playing a very unpleasant and particularly nasty trick. It's a complete fraud."

One of the other priests had come up too. "A fraud by a person who knew more than is good for them about black magic and its symbols, but a fraud nonetheless. The words on the strip that bind the bunch together are indeed some demon names. But two of them are misspelled and there are no words of summoning. And one of those is the demon associated with senile dementia and the others are of little relevance, either."

"But the smell . . ."

The other monks had come up by this time. "I think you put it in the right place," said one of them. "It has been dipped in night soil. Unpleasant and smelly, certainly, but quite unmagical. Of that we are certain."

"A pity," said the other. "I really thought, Diego, that at last we had a lead on these devil-worshipers."

The short dark saturnine one shook his head. "I'm afraid not."

Eneko patted Maria, reassuringly. "Although you're disappointed, I don't think Maria is."

Maria shuddered. "No. Not at all. But . . . are you sure it is harmless?"

"Absolutely certain. There is not even a trace of magic about this thing."

"The woman I interrupted didn't think so. She fought me like a mad thing. She obviously believed in it."

Eneko walked back to the pot. "You say this was her glove? A wealthy enemy, this one of yours."

Maria had come over to it, too. She looked at the glove. It was made of the finest blemish-free kid with small pearl studs. Yes. Someone wealthy beyond Maria's dreams of avarice. Someone who could afford to spend on a pair of gloves the kind of money that Maria didn't spend on clothes in a year.

She shook her head. "But who? I don't really have any enemies—not that hate me that much, surely? And I know hardly any wealthy people. Here on Corfu, at least."

"Hmm. Do you want this pot back right away? We might try divining on it if we fail in this project we're currently busy with," said Eneko. "It may not lead us any closer to the devil-worshipers we seek, but it may be a good idea to root out whatever fraud is preying on people and letting their worst natures lead them into this."

Maria looked at the pot and shuddered again. "I certainly don't want it back. Ever."

Chapter 67

Emeric smiled rapaciously, looking at the assembled cavalry. When the details of the planned sorties had reached him, he'd been unable to believe the naiveté of them. But Fianelli assured him that the information was absolutely rock solid. It came from the best of sources. Emeric had told Count Dragorvich, his siegemaster. The Count had simply stared at him and then begun laughing.

"Why not just give us the keys to the gate, Your Majesty? We're finishing the south first, so they'll face the south. Well, Sire, you wanted to use the heavy cavalry. If this is really their battle plan, here is the opportunity."

Emeric nodded. "Light skirmishers and a testudo-covered ram on foot, as the sacrificial troops. Not too many. Use some of those Slovenes. And when the gates are full of arquebusiers—a two-prong charge. And tell the gunners not to aim for the gate any more. We want it to be able to open nicely and easily."

The moles had been basically complete since the previous day. Emeric made no effort to push troops across them yet, but kept the men working on them, widening and improving them; even clearing the sheltering mole walls, making the moles into causeways, under heavy Venetian fire. Then, in the morning, the first skirmishers began pushing across, using leather shields to protect them as best as possible. With them came the testudo and ram on its clumsy wooden wheels.

Watching from the southern postern, Falkenberg scowled. "Something's wrong, Prince. Even the captain-general can't believe that in an age of black powder and cannon, someone is going to sit and pound the gate down with a ram. They're waiting for a sortie. That's why there are so few of them. They are supposed to be able to get out of the way of the heavy cavalry, when it comes."

"We just happen to be wandering around with a hundred knights in full armor near the gate. We know nothing about this," said Manfred.

"And neither does that ass. Hark! There they go."

The trumpet sounded the sortie.

"Give it three hundred heart-beats before the first volley, and ten before the charge," said Falkenberg professionally.

He might have been off by two heartbeats when a horn blew on the Spianada.

"Here come the Magyars!"

Even from half a mile across the water they could hear the thunder.

"All right," said Manfred. "Out lances, *Ritters!*"

Commander Leopoldo, on foot among his arquebusiers, watched as it began going wrong. They'd burst out of the gate, the press of men behind him. The captain-general, perched on a showy gray, rapier in hand, attempted to organize them. The few Slovenes had fled, abandoning the testudo and diving into the water. "Reloa—"

The yells and thunder of heavy cavalry, massed and waiting between Emeric's earth cannon-ramparts, drowned the rest. Coming in a thick mass, ten abreast, Hungary's finest streamed onto the mole causeways.

Leopoldo gritted his teeth . . . waiting.

Emeric's cannon were not firing—too much chance of hitting his own troops, or possibly preventing the sortie. So, until that moment had Leopoldo's gunners been holding their fire also. Now all the Citadel's guns that it was possible to bring to bear on the causeways fired in unison. Leopoldo had had help from the blue-scarred

Knot bombardier in ranging, and even in the choice of ball in those cannon.

The chainshot—intended to bring down masts, sails and rigging—hit the two Hungarian charges like sudden brick walls. One minute the Hungarians had been unstoppable.

The next . . . stopped. But the Knights had been right about their foe, Leopoldo saw. Not even that would stop them, and now the cannon would have to reload.

The pikemen on the walls poured the pitch and even managed to fling a few barrels to burst and shatter on the shingle just short of the north and south bastions.

"What are they doing!?" screamed the captain-general furiously. He waved his sword wildly at them. "Wait until they get to you, you idiots!"

But they were obviously too far off to hear that. Panicking, too. Some had even thrown a few faggots into the sticky mess. And in their panic, obviously everything else on hand—including caltrops and a number of burning brands. Leopoldo knew a moment's heart-stop when the naphtha and faggots on the south didn't catch. Pitch always was the devil to light. Then some brave soul tossed a grenade into it.

Between two fires, but still with half his men inside the gate, the captain-general yelled, "Charge!" His horse reared, and he waved his sword—a heroic figure.

And then he fell off his horse.

It's one of those things that will happen, even to the finest horseman—if a trusted sergeant has undone the belly cinch. But Leopold had no time to watch. He had a battle to deal with. He began bellowing orders.

Which did *not* include "Charge!"

The Knights of the Holy Trinity charged instead, sortieing from the northern and southern posterns. Hitting the flanks of the Magyars, they trapped some between the wall, the fire and themselves. Others they flung back onto the causeway. The Magyars had lost most of their impetus, the sheer weight of their charge that made them so unstoppable, in the cannon barrage. And then they'd had to gallop onto the thin strip of pebbles in front of the walls, and then the burning beach.

Horses—even well-trained war-horses—do not like fire. And the arquebusiers on the other side of the flames were making a very orderly retreat. Fire a rank. Step back. Within the gates, the officers had pushed the tercio apart and sent the men up onto the walls above.

The Knights of the Holy Trinity had the full two hundred and fifty yards to build their impetus. And on the narrow strip of land, superior numbers were no advantage. The Knights didn't like challengers to their position as the foremost heavy cavalry in Europe, and they inflicted a sharp lesson.

And once the causeway was packed with men dying, men fleeing, horses leaping into the water . . . they retreated at a sharp trumpet call. The near-rout was just being turning into a rally and second assault, when the reloaded cannon fired a second time. This time the targets were packed as tightly as possible. The carnage was terrible. The second charge of the Knights of the Holy Trinity was not so fast or fierce . . . but the resistance of the foe was gone.

The pride of Hungary were streaming from the causeways, and now the rout was unstoppable, even with Emeric's savage discipline.

The hastily following Venetian sappers, running up with kegs of black powder, whirling slow-matches and a prayer, had a good while in which to work, before one of Emeric's generals had the sense to push foot soldiers and Croats forward. Emeric himself had been too preoccupied shrieking threats at his cavalrymen.

The southern mole was blown apart, and only a narrow ridge remained of the northern one.

And someone had been kind enough to drag the captain-general inside.

Emeric seethed with rage, once he realized he'd stumbled into a trap. *I will crush them. I will crack them like lice. Every man, woman and child in that citadel will die.*

Despite his fury, a calm and calculating part of him was finally accepting the truth. The Citadel would not fall—not quickly enough, anyway—simply through military means. And while it might fall to treachery, treason was in the nature of things a slippery weapon.

I'll have to go back to Hungary and ask for help, damn her eyes.

"Ah . . . Your Majesty." Count Dragorvich, a clever man who always made sure that the king made all the crucial decisions—and took the credit for them, naturally—was without words this time. He just pointed.

The ricks of hay for the cavalry were on fire. Someone had obviously made the best of the distraction offered by the assault to attack their rear. Again.

"Get me the blond," Emeric hissed. *"Now."*

"You're supposed to be an advisor to the Emperor Alexius VI of Constantinople. Why are you still here?" asked Emeric, looking at the blond man.

There was a pause. "I am here to see to my master's interests."

An interesting reply, thought Emeric. *Which master?*

However, all he said was: "It is very much in your master's interests to see us win here, and win decisively and soon. So I have a task for you. There is one of these Venetians—or rather an Imperial—on the loose. He and his men are attacking our rear. Our supplies, our materiel, even our men."

King Emeric leaned forward in his throne. "I've checked on your background, Aldanto. I know who you are, my Milanese traitor and sell-sword. This is the right sort of task for you, I think. Find Erik Hakkonsen—or his woman. Find them and bring them in. Hakkonsen I will have dead, happily. If you only get the woman . . . see that she survives. If not quite as she was, but in a good enough state to be bait. In the meantime, I'm returning to Hungary to fetch more troops and enlist some very powerful support. When I come back, I want to see Hakkonsen's head."

The blond man paused and then nodded jerkily. "Hakkonsen. Yes."

"Good," said Emeric. Nastily: "That'll keep you and that yellow dog of yours busy."

❖   ❖   ❖

Chernobog did understand long-standing hatreds, for such things were meat and drink to it—and it indulged in such things itself, from time to time. It also understood the elimination of threats. Hakkonsen was the one who had put that throbbing scar on his forehead. The puppet himself hated the Icelander, for that matter, insofar as the puppet was still able to feel anything.

As for Emeric, well, Emeric did not merely nurse his grudges, he nurtured and watered them with blood, something else that Chernobog understood. So the demon would cooperate. It did not do this for Emeric, or in fear of Emeric. It did this for itself.

Compared to hunting for this place's seats of power, hunting peasants around the maquis was as easy as breathing to the shaman. He sent the hawks up, spotted a peasant and his son, and hunted them down with Caesare and his Croat escort.

"You will find these hill-fighters," said the scary-looking blond in charge of the soldiers. "You will ask other peasants until you find them. And then you will give the leader this note. You will tell him I am a Greek with the Imperial fleet—but that I am from Corfu. I am shocked by the devastation, and wish to strike back at the Hungarians. Your family has worked for mine for many years. If he comes . . . Your son is free. Do you understand?"

The boy was perhaps four years old. The Greek peasant nodded. "Yes." He paused; quavered: "Do you promise you will do nothing to hurt him?"

The blond blinked. "Of course."

The yellow dog made no promises.

"It seems worth looking into," said Erik. "It would hit Emeric where it hurts. Money and weapons we certainly need. But can we trust this Xerxes?"

"My family have worked for them for many years, sir," said the peasant, nervously wringing his hands.

Erik's heart went out to the man. To be loyal enough to go looking for people the Hungarians would kill. Still, it could be a trap. "I'll meet him. Go back to him and tell him there is a small mountain just north of Giannades. There's a shepherd's hut on the ridge. I'll meet him there at moonset. Alone. Anyone else and he'll die. You'd better come back as a hostage, too."

"Where will I find you, master?" asked the man. "I'm from down south. I don't know my way around these foreign parts."

The Corfiotes always managed to make their island sound six hundred miles long, not about forty. "Just come up this valley. Someone will see you and bring you to me."

The man nodded resignedly.

"You must let me see my little one before I will go back. You must." There was an edge of hysteria and distrust in that voice.

The one named Aldanto shrugged. "See. But not touch or speak to. He's in the hut, guarded by the dog."

The peasant walked fearfully to the entrance of the hut. That yellow dog made him very nervous. Then, peeking inside, his face relaxed. He stared a while, then turned and reset his face into a grim determination. "Very well. But you hurt him and I will kill you."

The blond smiled at him. "Just do your part."

"You will let him go unhurt?"

"I will not touch a hair on the boy's head, if you do as you're told. I swear it. And I'll reward you with ten gold ducats."

"I don't want money. Just my child."

He turned and left.

High up in the clear blue sky, two hawks turned, too.

In the shepherd's hut, the shaman studied what was left of the boy: only a scrap of chewed bone on the bloody, but once lovingly embroidered, child's waistcoat. Just enough to conjure a good seeming from the magical principals of contagion and sympathy.

The dog's long red tongue licked the yellow teeth. Even the marrow in those dainty bones had been sweet.

❖   ❖   ❖

"This is a bad place. Hawks keep chasing rabbits."

"Your control over them is weak."

"I have their names. They cannot do this," grumbled the shaman, muttering a string of words in Finno-Urgic.

The Caesare puppet shrugged. "Well, we have the general locality, we have a rendezvous. We need to plan everything carefully. It's not going to be easy. I've tried to ambush this one before once. It went badly."

Bianca was finally able to get rid of her "relatives" the day after the failed Hungarian assault. At her suggestion, her supposed uncle and aunt ventured outside with her the next morning, sharing in the general glee of the Citadel's inhabitants that another of Emeric's ploys had failed. They headed toward the walls, wanting to see the now-ruined moles.

Their path, as Bianca ushered them along, took them by an old stone-walled building that had suffered a fair amount of damage from cannon fire since the siege began. Some of the stones were now loose, held in place by wooden bracing. The night before, under cover of darkness, Bianca had smeared the stones and the wood supports with the special ointment she'd made up. Then, softly spoken the necessary incantations over them.

She accompanied her "uncle" and "aunt" on their promenade, chatting with them cheerfully. As they neared the wall of the old building, she stopped suddenly and went down on one knee.

"My shoe's got something in it. I'll catch up with you."

They continued on. When the moment was right, Bianca murmured the final words of the incantation.

It all worked very nicely. Following the principles of contagion and similarity, the wooden supports gave way and almost sailed toward her victims' heads. The loose stones followed, completing the work.

By the time Bianca's screams brought passersby to help her in her frantic attempts to remove the debris, her "relatives" were quite dead. The face and skull of her "aunt" were so badly crushed as to be unrecognizable.

❖   ❖   ❖

Four priests, standing already at the fortress walls and inspecting the ruined moles, seemed to flinch as one man. Two of them raised hands to their heads, as if in sudden pain.

"And again!" hissed Eneko.

"Who *is* she?" wondered Diego, lowering his hands slowly and a bit shakily. "And where is she hiding?"

"I don't know. But we must start searching for her in earnest. This creature *must* be stopped."

Chapter 68

Something about the whole situation made Erik nervous. It just didn't feel right. "The rest of you stay back here. Deploy scouts on the ridge. Kari, Basil, Dimitris, let's go forward."

The hut appeared deserted. A low stone structure, a mere single room, it didn't appear to have many possible hiding places. And except for the long moon-lit shadows of the ridgeline they were advancing down, no close hiding places. Erik sniffed. It was a balmy night and warm air was full of the scents of wild thyme. So why could he now suddenly smell something totally out of place in the Ionian air?

Ice. Sea ice. And something he'd last smelled with Abbot Sachs and Chernobog's vessel. Like too sweet an incense. It made him want to sneeze.

It also made him very tense. The hilt of the tomahawk slid into his hand, and he walked forward alertly.

A shot rang out, from the hut ahead of them. Erik dove to the left. Basil screamed and fell. Kari's pistol boomed. The glamour used to hide the ambush wavered and was gone. Erik, yelling like a banshee and running for cover, threw the tomahawk. It hit the target dead center, splitting his skull. The arquebus he'd been aiming at Erik went off. A flurry of other shots followed.

There was more fire from the ridge where the rest had waited. But Kari, Dimitris and Erik, saved by a premature shot, were back in the rocks.

"Basil?"

"He was shot in the stomach." The Corfiote pointed. "Look down there, Erik!"

The last of the moonlight shone on at least fifty steel helmets coming up the valley.

"We'll go over the top, past the hut. They're coming down to look for us now. Just stay put."

"Fan out!" shouted an enemy officer, now so close Erik could have almost cut his throat.

"They'll be running down the hill," Erik whispered. "They might try to come back up when they see the squad down there."

A few hundred tense heartbeats later and the pursuit was heading off down the hill. At a loping dog-trot the three went upward. Erik had a chance to see young Basil. Someone had cut his throat in passing. Erik could only be glad. He'd have had to give the youth battle-mercy himself otherwise.

"Present for you," said Kari, handing him his hatchet. "Now let's get out of here. Dimitris is bleeding."

They ran on, finding it hard going in the dark. Fortunately, thought Erik, it must be as hard for the enemy . . . but it didn't seem to be.

"There's a dog or something with them," panted Dimitris. "It's following us. I heard it."

Pausing, Erik listened. He heard a baying howl, quite close, very clear. No other barks answered. And by crashing through the maquis, the dog was way ahead of its human support. "Kari, you go ahead with Dimitris. He needs help. I'll deal with this dog. We won't shake them while they've got the dog."

"You be all right?"

"It's only one dog. I'll see who follows it. Might be worth leading them astray a bit."

Soon Erik realized that the dog was definitely after him. And, just as he was turning to look for a good spot to deal with the beast, he ran into a neat ambush.

He nearly got three bullets in him—and would have if Thalia hadn't yelled "hold!"

"Erik!" It was some five of his own men, and Thalia.

"Rearguard," said Giuliano. "The others are already ahead. We were just setting some booby traps to slow them down. Watch it. There is a cliff over there."

"Dog behind me," panted Erik.

And then it was onto them. Gaunt, pale in the starlight, yelping with hunting bloodlust. Erik saw the bullet hit it . . . but it did not stop. It sprang straight for his throat. Erik barely had time to grab the creature's paws, and stop it.

It was incredibly strong, and almost slimy. Hot, carrion-scented breath washed over him as it snapped furiously. Another shot rang out, with no obvious effect. The creature turned to bite at his hands. Erik dropped and, putting both his feet into its gut, gave the pale hound the full benefit of a flying mare. The dog hit a limestone boulder on the edge of cliff with a sickening crack.

And it got up in a single bound.

Thalia threw her bird-net. The creature tumbled in a tangle of meshes, snapping and yowling as if in pain. "Quick! Over the edge!" yelled Giuliano, grabbing one side of the net. He and Erik heaved and the net bag flew over the edge. Erik heard it bouncing and yowling on its way downward. He hoped it was a long, long way.

"Let's get out of here. We can set booby traps further on."

They hadn't gone more than a hundred yards when Kari hailed them. "Deal with the dog all right?" he asked cheerfully.

They'd taken every precaution to lose the scent, even if that demon-dog survived the fall. Down to the coast they'd gone, and walked in the water; then, come out into a stream, which they'd eventually left by way of an overhanging tree and then up onto some rocks.

Erik's feet were still very wet. And he was grim. He'd lost two men. Basil, who had been with him, and Luco, who had fallen in the skirmish with the rest of the group. And Dimitris's wound would keep him out of combat for weeks. What was more, he knew very well that they'd gotten clear by luck. The enemy were becoming more cunning.

Back in the forward camp, Erik found their peasant hostage—with a bump on his head and tied very securely. "He tried to make a bolt for it," explained Theo.

"Not surprising, that," said Kari, taking out his knife. "He's not going to have another chance."

The peasant's eyes widened with horror. Not at the sight of the knife. He didn't even seem to notice that. At the sight of Erik.

Erik looked back at him, dispassionately. "We'll have to move. But first we'll have to deal with this traitor. Show that no kind of money is worth this."

"I did not do it for money. I would not touch their filthy money. But they have my son, lord. They said they would kill him if I didn't bring you."

Erik's eyes narrowed. "Where do they have your son?"

"Please, lord. He is only a little boy. Four years old. Don't blame or hurt him."

"We do not make war on children," snapped Thalia. "Traitor."

His eyes blazed at her. "What could I do? They held my boy. They still hold him," he said bitterly. "They'll kill him. They'll think I betrayed them."

Erik saw a way to snatch a victory out this debacle. "Where is this child being held? We'll get him out."

The peasant prisoner gaped at him. Stammered. "But . . . but . . . I . . ." Words deserted him.

"Where is their base?"

"Kanakades."

"While they hunt us, we'll visit them," said Erik, with a savage smile. "They won't be in a hurry to trust peasants again, because they'll think you betrayed them. And they'll be a lot more wary. When you have to leave guards everywhere you have fewer men to fight with. Cut him loose, Theo."

"But Erik . . ."

"I can outrun him anyway. If we go along the other side of the Ropa, we should manage to avoid them."

The peasant made no attempt to run when they cut him loose. "I can show you where their patrols are." He paused. "If you save my son . . . well. I understand. My life is yours. But not my boy's. He is innocent."

"You've cost us two good men. And a good bird-net. And you've put some demon-dog onto our trail. As Thalia said: We don't make war on children. Or on peasants. But we'll expect blood-price from you for each of them."

"It was a very good net," said Thalia, quietly. "The priest blessed it. It fed us well."

Erik suspected it was not the knotted cords that had troubled the dog. The thing had not been worried by the bullets after all. It had been those blessings.

"It was an excellent net," Erik told her. "And one of the best throws I've seen. We must find you another one, since that's what stopped that creature. Although next time we'll try prayer, too."

Having someone who knew where the patrols were made getting to the Croat encampment very easy and very fast. They could see their pursuit beating the bushes across the valley, but there were only two men in this camp: the cook and the remount escort. They weren't prepared for trouble.

The peasant sprinted for the ruined house on the corner, calling "Spiro!"

There was a moment's silence. And then a scream. A terrible cry.

Erik and several of the others ran toward him.

The peasant was on his knees, clutching at a piece of torn, embroidered cloth. There were a few bone fragments scattered around him. A partially gnawed femur lay in front of the man.

Erik closed his eyes. "God have mercy on his soul," he said hoarsely.

Eventually, the man stood up, his face a deathly gray. "He gave my son to the dog." He looked at the bones; looked at the remains of the little waistcoat. "The bloodstains are dry already." His voice began to rise. "My boy has been dead since I left. I swear before God and all the saints that I will kill that blond man. I will spill his life for the life of my son. *I will kill him!*" he shrieked.

"No." Thalia spoke. Her voice was flat. "You will pay back the blood-debt first."

She picked up the gnawed thigh-bone and pushed it into the hand still holding the scrap of the waistcoat. "Go. Go find your kin. Your brothers. Your cousins. Your friends. Hunt them through the maquis. Find them and show them these two things. Show them the tooth-marks on his bone. Tell them what you did, and how the Hungarians repaid you. And then bury these remains of your son. Bury them in the churchyard with honor, because he died with honor. You have not lived with it."

He looked at her for a long, silent moment. Then nodded and turned away.

"You are just going to let him go?" asked Ambrosino. "He betrayed us, after all. We can't have peasants thinking they can do that and get away with it."

Erik looked at the Venetian. Of all of the recruits, this one had fitted in least well. Ambrosino kept himself to himself. "He's suffered enough. Under the circumstances I might have done the same," said Erik shortly.

"And I reckon within two weeks the story will have spread to every peasant on Corfu, Uncle," said Giuliano, somberly. "You don't understand what it feels like. But I do. That man will suffer until he dies."

"And most important of all," Thalia said grimly, "no Corfiote peasant will aid them again. Not for fear or for money. You Venetians don't really understand us. The Hungarians can stay here a hundred years after that story gets told, and it won't matter. They will never crush us, and in the end, we will kill them all."

"All right. Let's turn these horses loose and get out of here," said Kari. "I'm not enjoying this like I thought I would."

PART IX
August, 1539 A.D.

Chapter 69

"You're a fool, Emeric." Even in such a gorgeous voice there was only one Hungarian in the entire kingdom who would have dared to say that. The speaker was petite, curvaceous and almost edibly beautiful. She was perfection itself from her musical laugh to her cascade of lightly curled, fine dark hair. Her skin had that bloom to it that spoke of youth.

Emeric of Hungary would have found a nest of angry vipers more attractive. His great-great-aunt habitually chastised him. She also never failed to assist him in his schemes. She had, she had admitted once, a fondness for him because he was the only one of her blood in which magical skill had manifested itself.

He waited. There was no point in rising to her bait.

"You should have come to me for assistance first. I would have advised you to stay away from Corfu."

"Jagiellon seemed to think it would be an easy conquest, by the money and materiel he arranged. He is not aware that, far from being his cat's-paw, I have had intentions to begin conquests to the south for some time."

Elizabeth, Countess Bartoldy, laughed musically. "My dear boy. The fertility rituals on Corfu go back to prehuman times. Something that ancient, which keeps its base of believers, has a power reservoir the size of the ocean to draw on."

"I haven't seen any signs of great magic yet."

She dimpled. "Corfu's is a passive kind of magic, tied to the earth of that place. Very difficult for invaders to deal with. I do have something that will work, however—because it is not in contact with the earth. Wait."

She returned sometime later carrying a glass jar. A large jar, a cubit in height. She carried it with a negligent ease that betrayed her great strength. Emeric peered into the cloudy fluid within, and then wished he hadn't.

"An experiment of mine," said the Countess. "I constrained a fire and an air elemental to mate. It is not a natural occurrence. This is their offspring, somewhat prematurely removed. I have placed certain magical constraints on the creature, as well as enhancing its power."

Emeric looked warily at it. "Just what does it do?"

The countess smiled "It is a bringer of fires. And, of course, winds. Sickness, too, is one of its aspects. But the core of its ability lies in dryness. An island—surrounded by water to contain it—should be the ideal place to release the thing."

Benito yawned, cracklingly. "Sorry, Marco. It's not your company, honest. It's just . . . well, I have been working like a dog, and I haven't had much sleep lately."

Marco patted his shoulder. He noticed it was rock-like, stretching at the shirt. "You're working too hard. Everyone from the admiral to my father-in-law says so. Benito, one man, doing the work of a common laborer because he doesn't have the skills to build ships or clad them, isn't what Venice needs. She has plenty of good men working hard, but we need your brains."

Benito yawned again. "Why? Are we out of cannon-balls?" He grinned and raised a hand pacifyingly to his brother. "Seriously, Marco. I have a problem here. Everyone expects me to lead like a *Case Vecchie* born. Giving orders, seeing that things are done. And I don't know how. I might be a direct blood relation of men who are great leaders of men, but I grew up among the canal people as a thief. The only way I know to lead is by example. So: I want these ships built. I don't shout at people. I challenge them to keep up with me. And when the carpenters say: 'That's caulker's work,' and sit back and say 'we can do nothing until they've done,' I pick up another balk of timber and ask, "Do you think this is *Casa Vecchie* work?' "

Marco grinned at him. "And the result is that you need new shirts. You've put an inch on your shoulders since you started here."

Benito pulled a rueful face and felt the tight seams on the shirt. "Yeah. I'm getting a bit heavy and bulky for the old upper-story work, Marco. Not so good for squirming in tight little holes. So, tell me, what's the news from the outside world? Any news from Mainz?"

Marco shook his head. "This kind of heart condition is not something that changes from day to day, Benito. Apparently the Emperor's physicians say he seems to be recovering a little. Of course he is struggling to breathe and his chest gives him a great deal of pain. But this may ease, and if there are no further recurrences . . . he may yet leave his bed again one day. But commonly, I'm afraid, when these problems start, they do recur. We can only pray for him."

Benito knew there were millions of people throughout the Empire doing just that. And there were very few indeed who would be privy to the detail Marco had just given him. Most of the citizens of the Empire would only have heard rumors that the Emperor was not well. But the Holy Roman Empire felt the tremors of an uncertain future run through it—as did all of Europe and much of the world beyond.

Benito scowled. "And on other fronts? How are your attempts to contact Eneko Lopez coming?"

Marco sighed. "Not so well. We can't raise him, for reasons that aren't clear at all. Anyway, what I came to talk to you about was what you'd said to me about the undines and the tritons."

"Get anywhere?"

It was Marco's turn to shrug. "They're not like humans, Benito. They . . . well, they only live partly in the same world as us and they don't see things the same way. But Juliette wants to meet you. That's a step."

Benito smiled. "Sure. I'll sweep her off her tail with my charm. When do we do this thing?"

"Well, full tide is a good time," said Marco. "That's in about an hour."

"Sure. Where? At San Raphaella?"

Marco nodded. "We can take a walk up together. Or take a gondola."

Benito shook his head. "I'm supposed to be confined to this place."

"Only by your own decision."

"Yeah. But I'll pretend to abide by it," said Benito, suddenly looking an impish five years younger. "The roofs of Venice miss me. And I might as well enjoy them while I still can."

Benito found the undine's gaze quite disconcerting. He'd been forewarned about the bare breasts, and if he ignored the color, they were quite attractive. One might say, pert. And besides, he'd seen a few more than Marco, anyway. But her unblinking stare he found . . . scary. Those golden eyes actually seemed to be looking inside him, at something just below the skin.

Eventually she spoke. *"Mage Marco, you are sure this one is your brother? His flames, and the fire in this one are strange. Powerful. There is an echo of you about him . . . but you are water. Cool, healing waters. This one frightens me."*

Benito snorted. "Well, if it's all the same to you, green-hair, you make me nervous, too, just by the way you look at me."

Marco smiled and put an arm around Benito's shoulders. "Yes, Juliette. He is my brother. My half-brother, anyway. But he's been as close to me as a twin. And though at times he's as wild as fire, you can trust him to the ends of the earth."

Juliette didn't look entirely convinced. *"Spill a drop of your blood on the water then,"* she said to Benito.

Benito shrugged, took out the Shetland dagger and tried to prick his thumb. Hard work had calloused it, and besides, sticking a knife into yourself was never that easy.

"Do it for me, Marco."

Marco did, with all of a chirurgeon's practiced ease.

Benito squeezed the thumb. A red drop formed and splashed into the greenish chapel water. Juliette scooped some of it up in a long-fingered hand. Sniffed it. Tasted it. Looked penetratingly at him again.

Her next question startled Benito. *"Do you know the child Alessia?"*

Benito nodded. "She's on Corfu with her mother. It's where we wanted help to get back to."

Juliette regarded him keenly. *"Corfu! You mean Corcyra? Aieee!"* The golden eyes narrowed, still unblinking. *"Do you care for this child? Do you love her?"*

Benito blinked. "I . . . I don't really know her. I do care very deeply about her mother."

The look was now stern. *"I ask you again. Do you love this child? Will you guard her and care for her, if she needs it?"*

Benito had found the gaze of the Republic's chief Justice less disconcerting, less searching. Alessia was a baby, for heaven's sake. He'd hardly even touched one before her.

He remembered, suddenly and vividly, the warmth of her, the smell of her. She was Maria's kid. Of course he would love her. "Yes," he said, calmly.

Juliette continued to stare at him, but that flat golden stare seemed wary now. Benito noticed she'd edged away a little. *"The flame burns steady,"* she said at last. *"But it burns very, very hot. You must see to the child's welfare. I charge you with this. It is your responsibility."*

"And will you help us?" asked Benito, a little tired of the orders, the inquisition, the mysterious questions and references.

She nodded. *"I must. I will speak with the tritons."* And then she slipped away into the water with scarcely a ripple.

"Well," said Francesca, with a small, satisfied smile. "I have finally found the link between several of the trouble spots. It's so simple that I am disgusted with myself that I didn't think of it earlier. It's the local black market. The factions all buy extra supplies out of the Venetian storehouses from two men. A nice little link of bribery and blackmail for spies."

Manfred almost fell off the chair he'd been endangering by rocking on. "What? How much of this is going on?"

"I'm really not sure of the extent of it, Manfred," said Francesca. "But from what I can work out most of the Corfiote Libri d'Oro families are involved."

Von Gherens looked grim. "Hang the lot of them. It's treason."

Francesca blinked at the knight. "It's buying food on the black market. Hardly a capital crime."

Falkenberg rubbed the scars above his eye. "What you don't seem to grasp, Francesca"—he'd finally gotten to calling her Francesca—"is that it undermines the military capability of the Citadel to resist. You see it as a chain of blackmail that spies and traitors can use. We see it far more directly as shortening the period a fortress can withstand siege."

"Both apply," said Manfred grimly. "And it has to be stopped. And it is no use just cutting off the supply. Von Gherens is right. We need to make it clear that the buying, too, is a crime."

Francesca made a face. "I see what you mean. But the biggest problem is finding someone in the Libri d'Oro who *isn't* buying."

"And we're going to have to find out what this corruption has done to the supplies."

"You are going to have to do so quietly, without causing panic," pointed out Eberhard.

"It'll also upset the Libri d'Oro. Make the fomenting of treachery easier for someone," said Francesca.

"Without food, Francesca, there won't be any need for treachery to bring this place down. We've got water until the winter rains at least. I thought we had good rations for a year. It depends now on how far this stupid greed has undermined the capacity of the Citadel to resist. We've got a lot of people here, you know."

"I know. I pointed it out to you," said Francesca dryly.

❖   ❖   ❖

"Emeric is on his way back to Corfu." The words coming from Elizabeth's image had, as always, a faintly echoing air about them. "My plans are starting to come together nicely. So it is time for you to begin seriously undermining the Citadel. You have traitors in place by now, I assume?"

"Yes, mistress. I've managed to stall them, so far, although it's been difficult. They're mostly local noblemen. Corfiotes—the Libri d'Oro, they like to call themselves. Headstrong and amazingly stupid."

Elizabeth laughed gaily. "My dear Bianca, *all* petty noblemen are headstrong and amazingly stupid. If you think your Corfiotes are bad, wait until you meet the piglets who live in my part of Europe."

Bianca wondered if that was a promise. She'd visited the countess in her castle before, twice, but only for the brief periods of time needed to advance aspects of her training. At some point, though, it would be necessary for Bianca to take up residence with Bartholdy for an extended period. That would be a time that would be simultaneously exhilarating and extremely dangerous. Acolytes of Elizabeth, Countess Bartholdy, did not typically enjoy a long lifespan. But Bianca was determined—and confident—that she would be one of the few exceptions. Ultimately, the only exception.

The laughter having faded away, Bartholdy looked thoughtful. "I would have thought you'd be concentrating on the Venetians, though. The Libri d'Oro, when all is said and done, are simply parasites on Corfu. The real power is with their Venetian overlords."

"I have infiltrated the Venetians also, mistress," said Bianca hurriedly. "In fact, the wife of the captain-general is now my creature, and through her—if and when the time comes—I can subvert him. But that poses certain obvious risks, which I don't think we need to take at the moment."

She hoped Elizabeth would let pass the fact that the "we" in the last sentence really meant "Bianca Casarini." Elizabeth was hundreds of miles away, after all. If Bianca's schemes and manipulations backfired, she'd be the one to pay the price, not the countess.

But Elizabeth seemed in a good mood. "Oh, yes, I can understand that. Very well. Try your Corfiotes first. There's actually no great hurry, Bianca. I simply wanted to alert you, not have you start rushing about frantically. If your Corfiotes fail, you'll have time to develop your plots with the Venetians."

After the image faded away, and Bianca finished cleaning up the signs of the ritual, she examined the man lying naked on her bed. Paulo Saluzzo's face was locked in the same expression of stuporous satisfaction that she'd placed him in before she began the ritual. Although his eyes had been open the entire time, staring blissfully at the ceiling, he'd been oblivious to the satanic practices she'd undertaken in the very same room.

He was completely under her control, now. Bianca didn't usually bother to exercise that degree of magical control over her bedmates. She certainly hadn't bothered to do so with Aldo Morando. There was no need, as a rule. Sex itself, with most men, was enough to disarm them. But since Saluzzo needed to spend considerable time in her own house, unlike Morando or any of the Libri d'Oro with whom she'd copulated, Bianca had taken the time and effort to exercise the needed rituals on the man.

Besides, although those rituals were draining, they saved effort on the other end. She hadn't actually copulated with Fianelli's thug since the first few days after she'd murdered her "aunt" and "uncle" and seduced him. Saluzzo just *thought* she had. Indeed, he had the most vivid memories of wild and fantastic sexual activities, none of which had actually happened.

She laughed, softly. Deceiving Saluzzo was a small thing, of course. Once Saluzzo disposed of Fianelli for her, when the time came, she'd dispose of Saluzzo himself soon enough thereafter. And before too long, she knew, Bianca would have almost forgotten him entirely. Given the lifespan she intended to enjoy—eternity—she'd eventually forget him altogether. Still, she was discovering that she took increasing pleasure even in such small manipulations, deceptions and betrayals. Murdering the beggar boy had been almost ecstatically thrilling.

Such was the nature of her training and ambitions. She was very confident that she'd survive Elizabeth Bartholdy's regimen. Indeed, she intended to survive the countess herself.

Now, *that* would be a betrayal to cherish. Bianca even took the time, for a moment, to consider the ways she might use Elizabeth's corpse profitably. There had to be *something* immensely valuable to be squeezed out of that flesh.

Again, she laughed. No point bathing in the blood, of course. The one thing Elizabeth Bartholdy was not, was a virgin. Not in any sense of the term.

Chapter 70

Maria had taken to joining the Corfiote women in the weaving. After the incident in which she'd been arrested and hidden among them, she was accepted. And, she had to admit, now that Alessia was slightly older and sleeping through the night, staying indoors and being the good *scuolo* wife, shopping, gossiping, cleaning house, caring for the child . . . was far less active than she liked. It wasn't as if the house took much cleaning. Yes, Alessia did take a lot of time, and generate mountains of washing, but with Umberto working all hours and Alessia being a relatively easy baby—by comparison to Stella's children, who didn't sleep through the night until they were about four—Maria found herself wanting to be out, doing something.

Doing something to fight back. Weaving sailcloth would do.

Besides, she got on well with the Corfiote women. Most of the colonial Venetian women, even the *scuolo* wives, employed one or even several Corfiote girls in their homes. It was the largest difference in the way a Venetian *scuolo* wife lived in Venice and here. It also kept a gap between them and the local people. Working with them, Maria found she was absorbing the language in equal proportion to their respect. Here she wasn't a canal-girl who'd married a *scuolo* husband and gone up in the world. Here she was someone who they looked up to and who had earned their respect.

One of the women tickled Alessia. She gurgled. "She is a lovely child, Maria," said the woman wistfully. "I lost my first baby. The fever took him. I go to the temple to hope for another. But it may be better to only be blessed after this siege is over."

Maria lifted an eyebrow. "I think keeping your Spiro sober would be more worthwhile than the church."

The woman laughed. "Church, yes. But not the temple."

Maria was slightly puzzled. She'd seen them all at the chapel, at the Sunday communion. But she said no more.

"I accept that what you say is true, signorina," said Commander Leopoldo, a wry smile plucking at his lips. "But while it is true that a single young man like myself would seek you out and flirt with you . . . most people would assume that the prince would not take kindly to it."

Francesca lowered her lashes, smiling slightly. "Which is why you are cautious about it. Meeting me only occasionally and then keeping a safe physical distance, and well in sight of multiple witnesses. Believe me, I know men well. Not one of those watching will think anything more of these meetings than that you are brave philanderer."

The commander raised his eyes heavenward. "A stupid philanderer, more likely. Anyway. Just what does the prince want to tell me about?"

"The storekeeper. And a small coterie of clerks and guards. At first I thought it was just two of the guards, but we've pinpointed six now. They're running a black-market ring, selling extra rations to the Libri d'Oro families. Keep walking. You're supposed to be flirting with me."

His face was pleasant, but his voice was grim. "It's a hanging offense. I need names, Francesca."

"You need to go into this like a bull at a gate as much as a tavern keeper needs to give a drunkard a spare key to his cellar," she said sharply. "Eberhard pointed this out to us: If there is one thing we need even less than a shortage in the supplies, it's panic. Emeric has spies inside the Citadel, too. We don't need him to know, either. We want this quietly and efficiently done."

The young commander blinked. "I see I am in the hands of true professionals here. That sort of intrigue is not my forte, to put it charitably. All right. What do you want done? And can you walk a little slower? This hill is playing hell with my knee."

"Very well." She laughed—a musical sound, one that she had, admittedly, practiced. "This is my daily exercise too, Commander. In my former line of work, I could not afford to get fat and unfit. I probably still can't, for that matter! But even if I could, I've developed certain ingrained habits. One of them is walking a lot, and the other is walking fast. I apologize."

Again, the commander blinked. Like many people, she thought, Leopoldo found Francesca's bluntness about her former status as a courtesan—even a whore—more than a little disconcerting. Especially coming from a woman with such a close personal relationship with an imperial prince. But—also like many people—that same straightforwardness produced a certain level of trust and confidence.

She smiled faintly, watching the quick interplay of expressions on his face. "Now, today at about Vespers a cart will be taking extra food to various buyers. It will be going to Count Dentico's lodging—among others. The Count is the head of the pro-Byzantine faction of the Libri d'Oro. Among other things, his 'volunteers' have been making their way onto the guard on the north postern, by the Little Arsenal gates. No, we don't think it is a problem yet. But it would be a good idea if they were unobtrusively split up. Anyway, that's another matter. For now I think you want to work on catching the count's staff, and the troopers, red-handed. If you play things right you should be able to get the clerks, too. I doubt very much if that will net the real traitors—these things usually have layers within layers, like an onion—but at least it'll put a stop to one immediate and major problem."

She paused. "Falkenberg wants to know why you haven't established a curfew, and night patrols. I agree with him about this one. It makes dark doings much more difficult, if not impossible."

The commander took a deep breath. "I tried. The captain-general said they were unnecessary. However, while he is on the back foot with this, we'll institute them."

"That's a good boy. Let me have passwords and chits or whatever system you use, please. And I think you'd better leave the Knights as above challenge except for a password. When they're in full armor, that is, since it will be rather difficult to counterfeit or steal *that* armor. I think Falkenberg wants a patrol or two of them. He's worried about mines. And now, farewell, my admirer. That same sergeant will bring you word when I need my exercise disturbed again."

"They're going to be cracking down soon on the black-marketeering, I hope you understand," Bianca said to Saluzzo, stroking his chin. "And there's never any guarantee that treason will work."

The Florentine thug, lying next to her in the bed, smiled lazily. The feline smile had a very self-satisfied air about it. Saluzzo was firmly convinced that he'd just enjoyed an hour of sweaty, energetic and very enjoyable sex.

"Don't worry your pretty head about it, Bianca. Fianelli's about as charming a guy to work for as a slug, but there's a good brain under that ugly exterior. He's had it set for quite a while that if the black-market business goes sour, somebody else will take the blame. Nachelli and his two little cousins have been the go-between with the greedy Libri d'Oro, instead of us directly. Besides, not even Nachelli's dumb enough to get caught in a black-market sweep. He'll still be around afterward, to take the blame if the betrayal of the north postern doesn't work."

She frowned slightly, still stroking his chin. "What's to keep them from fingering you, if they're caught? Us, I should say."

Saluzzo's smile shifted from lazy to something equally feline, but far more savage. For a moment, Bianca felt the muscles in his arms and chest moving. The Florentine was quite a powerful man.

"Like I said, don't worry about it. I'll take care of the problem. Might have Papeti give me a hand. Won't take more than that, not dealing with Nachelli. The rent collector and his two goons-in-name-only won't be talking to anyone, trust me."

"Still . . ." Her hand moved down, beginning to stroke his chest. "There's Fianelli himself. I really don't trust him, Paulo—and neither do you, don't try to pretend."

The Florentine's eyes rolled sideways, to examine her face. The look in his eyes was not suspicious, so much as simply cautious.

"Ambition's a dangerous beast, woman. If I learned nothing else in Florence and Naples, I learned that much. That's why I'm living here, on this misbegotten little island in the middle of nowhere."

She chuckled throatily. "It's not *that* misbegotten, Paulo. Lots of potential here, actually—especially once the Byzantines or Hungarians are running the place. Their notions of accounting are a lot sloppier than Venetian ones, to put it mildly. In the right hands, run by somebody less narrow-minded than Fianelli . . ."

"It is a both a civil and a military matter, your honors," said Commander Leopoldo. "Which is why I asked if both of you could come. I am sorry to summon you so late and so urgently, but it is I think of importance that this be dealt with quickly—and as quietly as possible."

"You can't do this!" protested a stout, florid-faced man. "I am one of the Libri d'Oro! Governor, this man"—Count Dentico pointed an accusing finger at Commander Leopoldo—"charged his troopers into my home and seized me. All for some imaginary infringement about some goods my staff—without my knowledge—bought in good faith."

The commander's face was bleak. "We have a cartload of grain from the Republic's granaries. In bags labeled 'property of the Republic of Venice.' We have seven ducats in gold seized in the act of changing hands between Count Dentico's steward and the soldiers from the granary. The steward confessed to doing this on the count's express orders—and, besides, such amounts of money can only have come from Dentico himself. Pursuant to these findings, my men took trooper Dorte at gunpoint and drove the empty cart back to the granary. Storemaster *Capi* Tapani demanded the money. We have arrested him, too. My men have seized the records and are examining the stores of grain and other foodstuffs. As a preventative measure, we have kept all the *capi's* staff in custody."

He looked at the captain-general and the governor. "This is treason. Both buyer and seller endanger the fortress. But we don't want to create panic."

Captain-General Tomaselli looked excessively uncomfortable. Count Dentico was something of a friend of his. "These soldiers need to be dealt with harshly, according to military law. But the Count . . . well, my dear Commander. He's a nobleman and a loyal friend of Venice. One of the Libri d'Oro, as he says. We simply can't hold him accountable for the actions of his servants. Nor can you trust their testimony."

"He was feeding his horses and his hogs on it!" snapped the commander angrily. "Food that was meant to keep us safe from starvation during this siege turned into pig-shit."

The old governor sighed. "He's right, Tomaselli. If we let him off . . . if word gets out, and word will . . . ."

"How?" the captain-general said, in disbelief.

The governor looked at him as if he had failed to be able to write his own name. "The commander has used men, not waxwork dolls, to arrest these criminals. So when the word gets out, the commoners who have been battling along on the siege-ration will riot, for certain. As likely as not, even the troops would join in. Then we have riots within and war without. The Citadel's fall is certain." He gave Tomaselli a weary look. "Besides, as the Count is a civilian, I believe I have the final say. I will examine the evidence, and question the steward and the servants of the Count's household."

He turned to the commander. "Do you have them in custody? Good. If the evidence is as compelling as it seems, we have little option but to apply the ultimate sanction to all the guilty parties, equally."

Chapter 71

Emeric leaned back on the cushions of his traveling throne. "And so. How goes the siege in my absence? How is the situation in general?"

Dragorvich had not survived as Emeric's siegemaster without developing a fine understanding of his master's moods. The king was in a suppressed good humor. Plainly he had got what he was looking for. Dragorvich knew he'd been heading for the Carpathians—a long journey with only one possible destination: the Countess Elizabeth Bartholdy. The most beautiful—and some said the most influential—woman in Hungary. Emeric had brought more cavalry, and more men with him. But Dragorvich knew his master well enough to suspect that was not all he'd brought back.

He also knew Emeric well enough to know the king wanted triumph for himself.

"Not as well as when Your Majesty was here. However, pursuant to your instructions, we have now started three more tunnels. My engineers calculate that all four are now beneath the walls of the Citadel."

He cleared his throat. "Pursuant to your instructions, we've halted repairing the moles. But a few weeks should see them repaired. We simply await Your Majesty's orders on that. As for the rest, we've kept up cannon fire on the western outer curtain wall. It shows some signs of damage, but it is still far from being ready to fall. Night-firing from the ships has been kept up, more for the nuisance value than anything else. The Venetian gunners have range and elevation on the ship's cannon, so we cannot really use them for pounding the walls. Also, with the fortress on Vidos covering that flank, we cannot bring guns to bear on the northern side."

"That fortress must go."

The Count nodded. "It would assist us to have it taken."

"I'll think about it. Now tell me, Aldanto, have you caught Hakkonsen and his saboteurs yet?"

"We caught and killed two of them," said the blond man, flatly. "The hunt will continue."

"It had better."

He turned to the Byzantine admiral. "And the blockade?"

The Byzantine snapped his fingers. A lieutenant hurried forward with a pouch. "These letters were taken from a vessel we intercepted some days after Your Majesty took the fleet back to the Narenta. They indicate that Doge Dorma has no idea that the island has been invaded. He is, however, taking steps for the reinforcement of it." The admiral smiled. "Or he was going to. One of the steps he commands is recalling Captain-General Tomaselli and promoting the commander of the garrison, Leopoldo, into his place. No surprise there, of course. If Tomaselli hadn't been well connected with the previous Doge, he'd have been recalled long since."

Emeric gave a little crow of laughter. "I want those letters. We shall have to see to a way of getting them into the captain-general's hands. He may wish to change sides." He rubbed his hands gleefully. "Any news out of Constantinople?"

"The Golden Horn enclave still holds out. Vessels are not expected back from Trebizond yet, Your Majesty. The Greek emperor is nonetheless pleased with some of the prizes he has taken from the ships sailing from Acre."

The king muttered something about Emperor Alexius. It could have been "Useless ass." Then he turned to the Croats and Magyar. "And the peasants? Are they getting back to the land? I want yields as well as loot."

The Croat nodded. "I had to hang a few men to get the message home. But there are more of them working their fields."

The Magyar captain cleared his throat. "There are some of the Corfiote nobility we've caught—what the Venetians call the 'Libri d'Oro.' Most of them are inside the Citadel, but some were still loose in the countryside. They're not worth ransom, but I thought we might make them into collaborators, Your Majesty. They can find and drive the peasants for us."

The king nodded. "An excellent idea. See to it."

"Your Majesty . . . there are several towns, too. Fortified ones in the north. We have them under watch but they're not besieged yet. When the Citadel falls, of course, they will be easy to take. But in the meanwhile . . ."

"Offer them terms. Once we're inside the walls, we can change our minds, can't we?"

All the officers standing about laughed heartily. They knew Emeric well enough to know the king admired his own sense of humor—and frowned on those who didn't.

Emeric had chosen a bare hilltop overlooking the Citadel from the southeast for the ritual he had to enact in strict accordance to the instruction from Countess Elizabeth. Initially, he had been pleased at extracting help from her; now, in retrospect, he was no longer as pleased as he had been.

Elizabeth Bartholdy had a way of bringing the kings of Hungary under her control. Emeric had watched the effect on his own father, over the years. By the time his father died, he had been no more than a shadow of the man Emeric remembered as a boy.

He wondered just how many strings were attached to this particular "gift." Elizabeth never did anything that was not to her advantage. And, yes, he made use of the darker powers himself, but not to the extent that she did. Nor did he meddle with the powers that she dared to.

But . . .

He had the damned thing, after all, so he might as well make use of it.

He went out to his picked site in a grim state of mind. He ensured that his men would cooperate by stationing guards around a perimeter that was far enough away that no one would be able to see what he was doing except for his special assistants. Those assistants had been provided for him by Elizabeth, also. The ritual that needed to be enacted here could not be done by one person alone.

The weather had decided to cooperate, at least. Storm clouds gathered and built around Pantocrator. The wind whipped angry flurries of dust from where the assistants had been assiduously clearing every scrap of living matter, even lichen and tiny rock plants, until there was nothing but sterile, barren rock. Another was sharpening the bronze knife.

The patterns and sigils Emeric would do himself; he trusted such things to no assistant, even ones trained by Bartholdy. The fact that he kept such iron control over important matters, delegating them to no one else, was one of the things he thought his great-great-aunt respected about him. The brushes and pens for that work he kept in a special case—an ancient thing she'd given him many years before. It was made of hide and bone. The hide was curiously dark and iridescent, the bone . . . jet black. Neither part came from any earthly creature, and neither did the fangs, which served as a sort of semi-living lock and guardian. They opened only on certain words, treacherously closing on the hand if a mere intonation were wrong.

Of course, the king needed a suitable supply of ink. That was what the knife was being sharpened for. These rituals were designed to constrain the nonhuman and to protect him from it. They had to affect the homunculus he was about to release. Elizabeth had supplied the nonhuman blood from her captive stock. And Emeric and his assistants would have to give of their own to protect themselves.

So, when the knife had been honed to an edge that would wound the wind, each of them carefully slashed his forearm in turn, beginning with Emeric. Each of them funneled the scarlet blood that ran from the slash into the bottle that Elizabeth had prepared, while Emeric recited the guttural phrases Elizabeth had provided him. The sky darkened and the wind whirled around the hilltop, shrilling in their ears. There were two bottles now, one of red "ink," and one of black. Taking the first brush, Emeric began to paint the body and face of his first assistant with an intricate interweaving of sigils and symbols. The first went to build a fire in the center of the cleared place—only the fuel was bone, human and unhuman. When he was done with the last of them, and only then, did his most trusted assistant take the brush and complete the job on his master, Emeric. Then Emeric took up the knife and cut the first of thirteen protective circles into the bare earth.

At length, when the summer storm had formed into a huge dark tumbling mass, with Pantocrator shrouded in rain and distant thunder growling and cracking closer, they were ready. Stripped to the waist and painted—only their eyes showing in the masks of lines of alternating black and red—the nine began their chanting. The bone-fire was lit, the fungus that Emeric had piled atop it burning with a greenish flame.

Lightning lashed the earth, as if it was trying to strike them, but inside their protective circles it could not touch them. The assistants were made of stern stuff; though the very earth outside their hilltop smoked with the strikes, and the thunder threatened to shatter their eardrums, they did not even falter for a moment in their chanting.

Then, when the winds began to roar and the flames were near horizontal and the first heavy drops were splashing down onto the sun-dried earth, Emeric picked up the glass jar and threw the container into the flames. By the time the jar left his hands, the creature inside was fully aroused. The King of Hungary could sense the malevolent rage emanating from it.

The jar shattered. The liquid ran out of the fire in little coruscating, hissing rivulets.

The earth shook, angrily. If Emeric and his assistants had not been warned of the effect and braced for it, they would have been knocked to the ground.

And then the screaming began.

The scream seemed to go on and on; it pierced the

very brain. It was full of rage, and pain. And for one, terrible moment, even Emeric wondered if he had let something loose that should never have seen the light of day.

The mighty cloud above them was lit with sheet lightnings. And the rain, advancing moments before, slacked off. The scream thinned and faded, receding into the distance, leaving a strange taste in the back of the mouth, and somehow, in the mind.

Well. Whatever had been turned loose was no longer his problem.

Emeric stood triumphant, smiling toothily in the flickering firelight. The truth be told, high magics were something he followed by rote. He enjoyed the powers conferred on him, the use of which required no effort on his part, but he was always nervous about these tasks.

Suddenly the earth itself trembled. He was flung from his feet. The rock beneath the fire burst explosively, scattering flames and ash over them. The ground shook beneath them, again and again.

The ground shook like a dog, flea-bitten. "What was that?" Svanhild clung to Erik. *First the storm and now this!* She wished for Cahokia.

Erik patted her comfortingly. "Its just an Earth-tremor, dear. We have had them up at Bakkaflói, especially when the volcano at Surtsey has been active. In my grandfather's time, one knocked down half of Reykjavik. Either it is not a very big one or we are far from its center."

"Are we safe?"

"We should probably get out of this cave."

"But it is raining out there."

"It seems to be stopping now."

Manfred picked himself up from the battlements. "Who in the hell needs cannons? Another one like that and the walls will just fall down. Does this part of the world often get earthquakes?"

The captain-general nodded, staying sitting down. "They have been heard of before, yes." Manfred had been trying for tact, especially when listening to the captain-general's version of the destruction of the moles. He'd been struggling with a volcano of laughter. Instead he got an earthquake.

"Well, it is a lot less welcome than that storm will be, if it comes here off the mountain. I thought I was going to boil in my armor today."

Eneko Lopez and his companions came breathlessly up the stairs.

"Did you hear it?" demanded Eneko. "Or see anything unusual?"

"No. But I felt it," said Von Gherens. "Knocked me off my feet."

"Not the earth tremor. Just before that. The scream. The agony and the rage and hatred."

Manfred shook his head. "It wasn't from out here. We were watching the coming storm and then we had the 'quake. The storm seems to be breaking up."

Eneko took a deep breath. "Something very magical, and very, very evil has come to this island. Something that should not ever have been created. I fear for this place."

Count Dragorvich cursed. Then he swore. Then he kicked a rock. His adjutant kept well back. He had run to call the siegemaster, only to find the man striding to the mines already.

"All four, Tiepostich?"

The adjutant nodded. "Yes. We got two men out of the northern one. In the others we lost all of the sappers and we lost most of the bucket chain."

"Damn! Labor is scarce enough without this. And the king is not going to be pleased that we have to dig the tunnels again. We need to wait a few days before we restart too. There are always aftershocks."

Tiepostich knew that when the king was not pleased, one of Dragorvich's men was usually going to be heading for a slow death. He wondered if, this time, it would be him.

In the cave beneath the Citadel the rock moved, though not so much as a stalactite fell. But the priestess watched in horror as the sacred pool cracked across, and the water drained away into the rock.

She looked at the small altar with the half almond. Without a bride he would not help. The Goddess would defend, but this . . . this called for *him*. For the actual wielding of power.

But who would pay such a price?

Chapter 72

Francesca, Manfred thought, looked sour. She sighed. "I thought—as you wouldn't let me corrupt the black market for my own ends, as I wanted to—that we'd be better off getting rid of Count Dentico as the most dangerous of the lot. It appears I misjudged the nasty piece of work. He was such a pompous ass that he was thwarting, rather than aiding, the conspirators."

He eyed her uncertainly. Francesca was really in a rather foul mood, which was unusual for her. He needed to tread carefully here.

"That black-market ring had to go, Francesca. There were supposed to be siege rations for at least ten thousand souls for a year. Those stupid bastards were using the stuff like there was no tomorrow. Seven, eight times the ration per person. Wastage you wouldn't believe. Feeding animals on it. At a full ration now, the supplies will all be gone by December. Even on the slow cutback in rations that not causing panic demands, we're going to be eating boiled boots by March."

Francesca scowled. "Damned soldiers and their straight-ahead view of things." She gave him a look which was not entirely admiring. "Manfred, I *still* worry more about treachery tomorrow than starvation by next March. It's now blindingly obvious—to me, at least, if not you and Von Gherens and Falkenberg and—"

She waved her hand irritably, encompassing in the

little gesture all of the world's *damned soldiers.* "Count Dentico and that crowd of Libri d'Oro were just tools, being manipulated by someone else. Or, more likely, *several* 'someone else's.' There will be manipulators manipulating the manipulators, be sure of it, each layer of them better hidden than the next. And they'll have a more fertile ground than ever to do their work now, since the Libri d'Oro families have gone from a diet not far removed from the pre-siege one to a siege ration."

"Nine tenths of a siege ration, actually," corrected Falkenberg. "Do their souls good to fast a bit."

"It probably would," said Francesca. "Unfortunately, what it has done instead is to have made most of them angry and some of them desperate. They're blaming the Venetian authorities for their hardship, rather than themselves. There is still some black-market stock out there but the price has gone up sevenfold. And that's just making the people more bitter and revolt-ripe. I'm beginning to think we should have followed through on Falkenberg's ideas and hanged the lot."

The one-eyed knight grinned. "My old mentor had been through six sieges on the inside, and five major ones on the outside. You look at the bottom of all the usual suspects for why a fortress falls to siege, supply is usually the driving factor behind it."

"I'm worried that real trouble will break out now. I know there have been a whole rash of secret meetings among the Libri d'Oro families." Francesca sighed. "For that matter, the occasional exception like Leopoldo aside—the podesta is all right, too, if it weren't for his age—the Venetian upper crust in the Citadel doesn't fill me with great confidence either. Whenever you have someone like Tomaselli in a position of power in a small and isolated region like this, things get very rotten, very quickly. Venice should never have given him the post of captain-general in the first place, and, having done it, should have recalled him at least a year ago."

The soldiers in the room said nothing. What was there to say? On this subject, they all agreed with her.

Francesca never stayed in a bad mood for very long, fortunately. That wasn't so much because she had a naturally sunny disposition, Manfred thought, as the product of her long and rigorous self-discipline. The time he'd spent in Francesca's company—almost two years now, most of it in very close company—had made a number of things clear to Manfred about the once-whore, once-courtesan. Perhaps the clearest was that Francesca was the most formidable and capable woman he'd ever met in his life. Out of bed, even more than in it.

"Well," Francesca said, visibly forcing a little smile, "thank goodness young Leopoldo altered the duty rosters or I'd say the north postern was very insecure. But still, Manfred dear, I think we ought to consider extra patrols of Knights. Hefty patrols, not just a pair here and there. And I'm sure Leopoldo will listen to you if you suggest a few extra checkpoints."

Manfred nodded immediately. So did Von Gherens and Falkenberg. Whatever private opinion the two devout Knights of the Holy Trinity might have regarding Francesca's past, they had no more doubt than Manfred of her present competence.

Querini had a weakness for dice. And the cavalry captain's head was a lot less strong than he thought it was. The grappa had thoroughly fuddled it.

When he looked at the total of his losses he sobered up fast. "Ah . . . you'll give me time, surely?" If the siege went badly he might just die. That would be out from under this, at least. He'd lost several months salary, and was habitually in debt anyway.

The younger Dentico, now Count in his father's shoes, shook his head regretfully. "Can't do, I'm afraid. Since . . . the unfortunate happenings, we're having to watch things with the Army. You know my father was really killed because Tomaselli had borrowed heavily from him. It was a totally put-up job. We thought," said the young man, bitterly, "that Tomaselli was a friend of father's. So: no carried debts."

The cavalry captain was sweating now. "I . . ."

"Of course, if you could help us out on another matter that's been irritating us, we could let it go by for a while. We'd know we could trust you."

"Of course! Only too pleased to help. You know I organized those duty transfers you and the other fellows wanted so you could all be together . . ." Querini's voice trickled off.

"As it happens, Captain, it was about that that I wanted the favor. Some idiot's gone and shifted us around again."

Querini winced. "Commander Leopoldo has taken all the duty posting under his control. I can't do that again."

"Oh, there'll be no need to. I've got the June roster here. We'll just . . . cross out June and put in September. It's all in your writing anyway. And signed by the commander."

The sweat beaded on the cavalry officer's face again. "If Leopoldo finds out he'd . . . he'd . . . He doesn't like me anyway. I can't do it."

The young Dentico sighed and tapped the pile of chits. "Look, Leopoldo doesn't check every day, does he? The boys and I—well, I'll tell you the truth. It's Desarso's daughter. She's available and she likes a bunch. You know, some women just can't get enough. It's Adriano's birthday, and we thought we'd have a little party for him. But several of the fellows' fathers are real sticky about them being out, especially with this damned curfew. I mean, we understand why it's got to apply to the commoners, but it is ridiculous for us. So if you just slip this onto the duty board for the sergeants the day after tomorrow . . . we could forget this." He tapped the pile of chits again.

"It's done," said Saluzzo cheerfully, as he slipped through the back door of Bianca Casarini's house. "Within a fortnight, I'd say, maybe sooner. Hard to know, dealing with those idiot Greeks. But Fianelli tells me that Nachelli's cousin reported that the young Dentico handled Querini perfectly. He was there, watching, the fool. If it goes sour, the Greeks will finger him instead of us; through him, Nachelli—and me and Zanari will make sure that Nachelli can't finger anybody."

He laughed coarsely, pulling her to him and lifting her

onto the table by the door. The Florentine's hands were
already forcing up her skirt. "*If* it goes sour. It might very
well not. Best thing the Venetians did, executing the old
count. His son's smart enough to do the work right, and
dumb enough to do it in the first place."

She responded to his lustful embrace with feigned
enthusiasm. That was just a bit difficult, since Saluzzo was
obviously in a rutting mood. He wouldn't, this night, give
her the time to prepare the rituals that usually allowed
her to leave him to his own fantasies.

So be it. It was a minor inconvenience, after all, and
she could use the opportunity to advance another scheme.
"That still leaves Fianelli himself," she gasped, spreading
her legs. "I'd feel a lot better—*oh, Paulo!*"

The Emperor's hands shook as he held the parchment.
He screwed up his eyes in effort, and then handed it
to Baron Trolliger. "Read it for me, Hans. Damn this
ailment. I want that boy safe, and I am too weak to see
to it properly myself."

Trolliger read the agent's report aloud. The Emperor
pursed his lips. They were slightly blue, Trolliger noted.

"Two things," said the Emperor, tiredly, but breathing
slightly easier on the new medication. "One. I want an
attack on Emeric's borders with the Empire. Give him a
reason to come home. Second. Dispatch to Spain. If my
commanders there can spare the Venetian Atlantic fleet
as many extra men as the ships can carry. Rations too.
These generals. So literal."

The Emperor closed his eyes. "I hope Francesca is all
right. Sieges are hell on horses. And worse for women
and children."

"Sieges are hell for everyone," said Trolliger quietly.
He'd lost his younger brother, two sisters, his mother
and his dog in a siege that had spawned disease. It had
taken half his family, that plague. Except for the dog.
They'd eaten that. The baron still gagged every time he
thought of it.

"We've already got six light galleys ready for sea, Doge
Dorma," said the Admiral of the Arsenal. "Mostly," he

scowled at Benito, "because of that menace you have put in our midst."

Benito sipped his Soave, and smiled beatifically. "The admiral and I are the best of friends, really, Petro," he said innocently. "I've solved so many problems for him."

"Broken so many *scuolo* rules that the older masters want to murder him and the youngsters think it is a fine thing to do," growled the admiral. "I will say that this building program has been the better for it, though. Of course in the long term we'll regret it. You can't put the wine back into a grape when you want to."

Petro Dorma smiled and waved a hand pacifyingly. "Well, Admiral, how about if I took him off your hands? Of course, we'd want you to keep up the same rate of building, or we'll send him back."

The admiral scowled again. "We'll need an extra four laborers for the heavy lifting, but think of the tranquility! I don't think you'd need to send him back, Your Grace. The Arsenalotti are caught up in the patriotism of this young ward of yours now. I don't think I could slow them down. But what are you going to do with him? I can recommend a flea-ridden village a few miles from Eraclea. I have a grudge against the place."

"We want to send him back to Corfu, if we can. With three of those light galleys, some men, money and weapons."

Benito bounced to his feet, spilling wine. "I'm out of here! When do we sail, Petro?"

"Within the next two days. Your brother wants you to come and see him about 'special guidance,' Benito. As soon as possible. He said you could even walk, ride or come by gondola." The Doge raised his eyebrows. "I was not aware that you could get to him any other way."

Benito grinned. "You learn something new every day, Petro."

The blond-bearded triton Androcles was, as far as Benito was concerned, far less alarming than the undine had been. For starters, the look in those aquamarine eyes told Benito that the triton would probably delight in just the sort of practical joke that would appeal to

Benito. And for a second thing, if the nonhuman's eyes looked into his inner being, Androcles wasn't as deeply interested in what he saw there.

"Whoever advised you, advised you well. There is indeed something out there. Something to be avoided. A monster of slime and teeth. A parasite that likes to eat its victims alive. And it is working with the ships above, sometimes."

"Can you help us avoid it?"

The triton grinned. "I can. But will I?"

Benito shook his head mournfully. "Questions, questions. That's a hard one . . . as the camerata singer said to the bishop."

Androcles' shoulders twitched. He smiled and nodded. "He'll do, Juliette. The Lion seems to think that your efforts might get rid of this menace. And the truth be told, we don't like the thing. It stinks and befouls water even worse than humans do."

"Two days' time?"

The triton nodded. "We'll go and range the deeps in the meanwhile. We can taste the creature from a good many miles off, now that we have learned what it is."

Chapter 73

Dragorvich had been prepared for Emeric's fury at the loss of his mines in the earthquake. So he'd been relieved to find his master taking it all in relatively good humor.

"They may be unnecessary after all, Dragorvich. My agent within the fortress has widened a good chink in the enemy's armor. In the meantime, see if you can make the north causeway at least passable by footmen, and light cavalry at a pinch."

Dragorvich nodded, too relieved to ask many questions. "I've had men on the dark nights sneaking as far as they can and then swimming across, to clear caltrops. A few have been shot, but they paint themselves with mud first. They're difficult to see. The shingle should be safe for cavalry from that point of view, anyway. The causeway . . . give me a week, Sire, two at the most. It'll be good enough. We can make a covered way with green cowhides on top and some sandbags. It won't stop all the fire but it should make it possible for us to push a number of men across."

"That sounds excellent, Dragorvich. Don't make your preparations too obvious."

"Very well, Sire." He hesitated a moment. "I have a request. I know the policy is to get these peasants back onto the land, but I am desperately short of labor. If there is any trouble, can I have some of the trouble-makers? We'll put them in leg irons and use them up at the front. They're likely to die, but rather them than my sappers."

"An excellent idea. I'll let Ionlovich know. Don't spare them. They're not in that short a supply."

That had been ten days ago. Dragorvich had gotten his peasant-prisoners and had achieved all he'd promised. In the darkness his men had been readying the causeway to take a push of several thousand footmen, mostly Slav pikemen, and a number of Croat light cavalry units, who had been forming up since dusk. Dragorvich wished he knew exactly what the king had planned. It was plainly treachery from within the Citadel, and plainly on the northern side, presumably with someone on the postern there.

In the meantime, the new mines had been started anyway. He had reluctant Corfiote slaves to do that work now. And the cannons still kept up their volleys against the walls. The walls—so far—hadn't crumbled much. The trouble with bombarding Corfu's Citadel was that so much of the fortress was made of natural rock. You could eventually pound a breach in it, but it was harder than mortised stone.

Sergeant Boldo looked up at the duty rosters above him. The current roster had been made out by that ass, Captain Querini again, he noticed. Lazy bastard just crossed out the month. Oh, well.

"My name is there, Sergeant," said the young Libri d'Oro buck languidly. "See."

Sergeant Boldo shrugged, and handed the young man a curfew pass. "Password for tonight is 'nightingale.'"

This new system of Commander Leopoldo's was a pain in the bollocks. Still, orders were orders, and the man was reasonable. After the chaos of the first week, the commander had given week-passes instead of daily ones for those who worked nights, whom he—and some mysterious other—approved. The recipients had to learn the week's worth of passwords and two of the Arsenalotti masters had ended up in the brig for the rest of the night because they'd forgotten them. The sergeant had expected them to kick up a stink the way the *scuolo* usually did when they thought their territory was being infringed, but they'd been sour but reasonable about it.

Umberto got up for the midnight-to-dawn guard shift when Alberto Mavroukis tapped gently on the window. Alberto was one of those rare individuals who could fall asleep at the blink of an eye—at any opportunity—and yet had an internal clock that could wake him when he needed to. Alberto and Umberto were two of the ten masters from the Little Arsenal who were recipients of week-passes for this new curfew system. Though its purpose was to allow them to work late, it also meant he could sleep at home if he was on guard with Alberto. Sleeping next to a warm, soft-skinned Maria was infinitely preferable to sleeping in the north wall guard barracks.

The two walked down the dark cobbles. As luck would have it they ran into a bored, small-minded guard, who refused to accept their week-passes and insisted on taking them to his guard commander at gunpoint. The guard commander was in the throes of waking the next shift, and it took a great deal of Umberto's patience to get them, late, heading for the guard barracks on the north curtain-wall. The bells were already chiming for midnight before they were halfway down there.

"That bastard of a guard commander will probably make us sleep there next time," panted Alberto.

"He'll just chew us out," said Umberto, and saved his breath for running. The two arrived at the guard barracks.

Both realized immediately that something was very, very wrong.

The guard barracks was silent. It should have been full of people getting their gear off and lying down to rest, earlier watches griping about the noise.

Umberto looked at Alberto. Then he took the issue rapier out of its scabbard and walked forward into the lamplight.

The guard commander wasn't going to chew anyone out. Or make them sleep in the barracks. He lay in a pool of his own blood.

"*Merde!*" said big Alberto, in a very small voice. "What the hell do we do now?"

"Raise the alarm!" Umberto took a deep breath.

"Keep quiet or I'll shoot," said a voice from the shadows.

Umberto yelled. "*ALARU . . .*"

He felt rather than heard the shot.

As he fell he saw in a sort of strange slow way how the big caulker had grabbed someone with a pistol. He saw Alberto fling the willowy, elegantly dressed young man at a second man. And Alberto was bellowing at the top of his vast lungs.

Knight-Proctor Von Desdel and his patrol of ten knights were within a hundred yards of the guard barracks when they heard the shout, the shot and the yelling.

"That's inside the wall!" He was already urging his charger forward. "Sound that trumpet!"

Over on the Spianada, the Croats had heard the midnight bells without getting restive. The plan allowed the guards on the western outer walls to be changed and settle down before the northern postern would be seized. The biggest danger was the bastion on the northwestern corner. The king's artillery and the arquebusiers in the trenches were due to start a barrage on that when the charge started. The occasional cannon fire with its loading lulls allowed the sounds from the sleeping Citadel to carry well in the silent times.

They heard the trumpet. And the answer. And the bells begin to ring.

"Into those saddles!" yelled their captain. There was no time now to swing this whole thing into planned action. Now they must seize the moment—if it was there to be seized at all.

The Croats were some of the finest light cavalry in the world, with only the Ilkhan Mongols in serious contention in their portion of Eurasia. In many ways the Croats had the advantage over the Magyar—in speed, as scouts, and in tactical flexibility. The Croats had the first hundred and twenty men across the mole causeway before the Venetian cannon and arquebus fire began to make crossing it without heavy losses impossible. By the sounds above them, there was fighting on the north wall. But the traitors had at least prevented the barrage from above falling onto the galloping Croats.

And the gate was open! There were battle sounds from the watchtowers but they'd done it! If the Croats could get inside, they'd hold those towers, keep the gate open somehow, until the huge mass of Serb and Slav infantry who were waiting got in past the Venetian guns.

Yelling, the Croats spurred desperately forward, galloping horses spread out in a long race along the shingle. Then the first were in, under the raised portcullis, into the narrow roadway that led up into the Citadel.

And hurtling down on them, horses virtually shoulder to shoulder, were the famous Knights of the Holy Trinity. The sound of the metal shoes of those heavy horses on the cobbles was like thunder in the confined space.

In the moonlight and house-shadow-darkness, in the narrow lane, the Croats didn't know there were only ten.

There are places and times when light cavalry is superior to heavy cavalry—when maneuverability and rough terrain are factors, for instance. But one advantage that heavy cavalry always has is momentum. And armor—which adds to the momentum. In the narrow lane, neither terrain nor maneuverability offered any advantage to the Croats.

The Knights of the Holy Trinity hit them like a ten-pound hammer hitting a pin. Literally smashed the Croats back through the gate, riding down those that could not turn. The Knights wheeled and rode back in, preparing for another charge. A few of the later arrivals and some of the better horsemen who'd turned their mounts followed in on their heels, showing the advantages of the Croats' speed and maneuverability.

The portcullis crashed down behind them. The great gates were still open, but the heavy metal grid now had some thirty Croats trapped inside. Men were running out of alleyways, hacking at them, hacking at their unprotected mounts as they tried to fight the Knights.

And more Knights had suddenly arrived at the fray. Some half-armored . . . but too many.

The Croat captain knew the moment had slipped away. He never even saw that the great gates were closing. He did hear his lieutenant outside the gates yelling for a retreat. Inside the walls they'd die, he knew. But then, very few would live through the retreat either.

Umberto awoke to a blurry vision. At first he thought maybe he was dead and that Maria's mother . . . God, he'd loved her . . . was there, waiting for him. But would Heaven have so much pain?

Then he realized it was in fact Maria. Maria as he had never seen her. Maria with tears on her face, holding his hand as if she never wanted to let it go, with something so warm shining in her eyes that she looked like an angel. She'd looked at the baby like that; never at him. Until now.

"Maria?"

"Thank God!" He felt the pressure of her hand on his. "Umberto, don't you dare die on me."

"Try . . ." Things slipped away again.

It was some hours later that he awoke enough to make sense of his surroundings. He was in the hospital tended by the monks of Saint John, up on the hill.

"Did we beat them off?" he asked, wishing his head would stop spinning. "Alberto . . ."

"We did. We lost nearly fifty people, though. Alberto is fine, other than a broken finger. You two raised the alarm—because you slept at home. I am going to keep you there," said Maria, fiercely.

The seven surviving Libri d'Oro plotters attempted to look defiant when they were hauled before the captain-general and the governor. Only Flavio Dentico really succeeded.

"Kill us, then. You will get nothing out of us!"

The captain-general scowled. "We have torturers of sufficient skill to get the entire story out of you."

The old governor cleared his throat and turned to

Eberhard of Brunswick. "Perhaps you would like to explain to them?"

The *Ritter* nodded. "Your families and the families of the dead we have identified have been taken into custody. You may be fools and decide to wait for torture. But if you wish to save your families further pain . . . well, we need to know just who the spy is. Who in here has contact outside? This plot was orchestrated. I'm afraid we need to know this. And I'm afraid you *will* talk."

There was something really terrifying about the urbane, calm way he said it.

"What are you going to do with our families?" asked one of the younger men. It was plain that this effect of their actions had not been considered.

"They're in the dungeons below the fortress."

"They knew nothing of this!"

Eberhard raised his eyebrows. "Then suppose you tell us who did know of your treason. Singly, so we can check your stories against each other. At the moment the real reason for holding your families is to keep them alive. The people out there know who betrayed them. They're baying for Libri d'Oro blood right now."

Piece by piece the details of the plot appeared. A scant hour later troops were scouring the Citadel for Petros Nachelli, the glib, greasy former rent collector.

They found him, and the two cousins who served him as enforcers. But they weren't going to talk, not even under torture. Not without necromancy.

Captain Querini was tied to the chair. Commander Leopoldo was still half dressed, his face bloody, his tunic-jacket torn. He'd led the assault that had retaken the tower that held the portcullis levers, and he was furious about the loss of some of his finest men. He held the roster up to the cavalry captain's face and shook it furiously.

"You *testa di cazzo*! If it wasn't for a couple of *scuolo* sleep-at-homes who didn't come in to find they weren't on duty, we'd have lost the Citadel. As it is, I lost twenty-three men because of this!" He shook the piece of paper again. "You—!"

The captain gave a low moan. "I never knew. I was in my bed! I wouldn't have been in my bed if I known. I never meant any harm. . . . They tricked me. They lied to me. It was Dentico."

"You'll still hang."

Maria hadn't realized just how much the fireboat project had come to mean to Umberto until she'd sat with him the day after he'd been shot. Umberto was not a great communicator. His job and his home life—except when things were really boiling over and he would tell her—were two separate worlds. She'd followed progress in the yard more by snippets than anything else.

Now, weak and slipping into fever, he talked of little else but this. Maria passed an anxious day and an anxious, sleepless night listening to it. He was much the same the next day. She still dared not leave. Stella had come up to take Alessia for a few hours. Old Mrs. Grisini's Corfiote girl had come up with some food. A group of the Corfiote laborers' wives came with a small pot of sour cherry spoon-sweets. They were quiet—as befitted a hospital with a sick man—but each came and embraced her.

Maria sat there, biting her lip. She had never been hugged by this many people. They plainly thought he was going to die. The small pot of spoon-sweets sat there on the table beside her. She stared at it, eyes blurred with tears. She knew just how little they had, what sort of a sacrifice this was. She'd married Umberto to give Alessia a father. Now . . . she was going to lose him, too. For days he clung there, growing paler, growing weaker. Maria prayed. She prayed as she'd never ever prayed for herself.

It was late evening four days later, with Umberto tossing and mumbling, when two of the Corfiote women came in to the hospital. "You must come with us, Maria."

"I can't. I can't leave Umberto."

"If you don't, you will leave him at the graveside," said one of the women, brutally. "We have heard from Anastasia—the girl who works for Mrs. Grisini—that your house has been cursed."

"But what about Alessia?"

"The priestess said to bring her."

It was only when she got outside and well down the hill, that she came to realize that it was well after sundown. She was, she realized, dazed with exhaustion. "What about the curfew?"

The older of the two women shrugged. "We know where they patrol. And there are ways to pass. But it is difficult."

Maria was too tired to try to make sense of it all. She followed them to the cliff with the tall Italian poplar beside it. Ascended the ladder. Walked the winding cave trail into the inner chamber with its two altars, one white, one black. Looked at the cracked dry rock-cut pool where the water from the tiny waterfall now fell into a clay bowl drifted with flower-petals. At the huge, eminently female statue, terrible in its primitive beauty. Looked at the priestess in her simple white robe, with her long white hair in great waves around her. Looked into the compassionate eyes of . . .

Renate De Belmondo, the wife of the Podesta.

"Welcome, Daughter. The Peace of the Mother, the great Goddess be with you."

And the strange thing was that she'd felt just that. The hurt, the anger, the sadness had all receded, just as in her distant childhood memories, they had on those rare occasions when she'd turned to her own mother's arms.

The rest of the ritual, the soft refrains had not meant much to her. Except the priestess—who was also Renate De Belmondo in another life—had done her best with curse-exorcism.

"It may be best if you could move house, dear. There is lingering evil around you. Someone hates you very much, enough to spend a great deal of time cursing you. She is no witch, I think—but there is a great deal of magic here, and magic—"

She shrugged. "It is a tool. It often comes to the hand of those who do not know how to use it, yet succeed in doing *something* with it even in their ignorance."

Maria sighed. "Right now I'm living up at the hospital anyway. If Umberto lives . . . well, I'll try. I don't know how possible it will be."

"For your sake, your husband's sake, and for the sake of that lovely daughter of yours, you should."

When they returned to the small building on the north slope that was the monks' hospital, Maria fearfully hastened to Umberto's side.

He was still.

Maria felt as if her heart would stop. She put a trembling hand to his forehead. When she'd left it had been fire-hot.

It was cool.

Not deathly cold. Just . . . unfevered.

Maria didn't know how to thank the Mother. But she did it with all her heart anyway.

Umberto might have turned the corner, but to start him climbing the steep stair required a sickbed visit from Alberto, with his index finger strapped.

"How do you use a hammer with that?" asked Umberto weakly.

"Um. Haven't much, lately."

"What about the fireboats?"

"Old Grisini had another relapse and he's gone home. And well, Balfo, he's senior master after you, he said he couldn't see the sense of it. We'd never use them."

"*What?*" Umberto was struggling to sit. "I need to get down there! I'll tear his ears off, I'll—"

"You'll lie down!" said Maria crossly. "I'll tear any ears that need tearing."

"Maria, I've got to get down there! If we can deal with the enemy's fleet while they over-winter here . . . Most of them will have to be here, in the bay of Corfu."

"As soon as you are well enough to even sit on your own, I'll bring some of the lads up from the Little Arsenal to carry you down," promised Alberto. "Then we can carry you home."

Two days later they carried him down the hill. It started off with three big journeymen and Alberto, simply picking up the bed and carrying it out of the door. As they came out of the hospital, Maria realized that nearly every one of the Arsenalotti were there, from the masters to the Corfiote labor. And they weren't content to just carry Umberto. He had to travel shoulder high. Across the channel, across the Spianada, the Hungarians must have wondered just what the besieged had to cheer about.

Umberto didn't even have to tear ears. The issue was simply never raised and the Little Arsenal went back to hammering, sawing and working. In theory, Umberto was in charge of it. In practice he was still too weak and too tired. Maria was his eyes and ears, relaying orders, dealing with problems. The *scuolo*, as conservative as could be, would never have just taken orders from a woman. But Umberto's orders, relayed and made a lot more caustic by his wife—a different matter.

The only trouble was that Maria was not always inclined to just give Umberto's orders. Nor after the first few times did she say "Master Verrier says." She just told anyone from master to laborer to do it. And as they didn't know whether it came from Umberto or not, the Arsenalotti did it. Before two weeks were up, taking orders from Maria was so normal no one even thought about it. She was good at giving them.

For those first two weeks, Maria had had them knock up a space in one of the work sheds for Umberto. He was certainly not going to get home—or back—without carrying, and he was determined to be at the Little Arsenal. Maria did a trip to fetch Goat and the hens. One hen had disappeared, but the goat found more to eat in the shipyard than she had in Maria's own yard or than Maria had been able to scavenge for her.

PART X
September, 1539 A.D.

Chapter 74

The three light galleys Venice was sending to the aid of Corfu left without fanfare or fuss or any of the normal send-off. They left directly from the Arsenal sometime after midnight, with extremely select crews, a large supply of weaponry—and gold. Some fifteen thousand ducats worth, which would have made the small vessels a tempting target in any pirate's book. Led by the merfolk, the three ships slipped along the Dalmatian coast by night, pulling up, stepping masts and hiding on small islands by day. They laid up for two days with the mosquitoes in a swampy river mouth just north of the bay of Vlores, waiting for the merfolk to return with news of a safe route. The clouds rolled in, along with the triton, eventually.

"The water is clear of ships on this course," said Androcles, "because it's raining fit to raise the ocean level. You could sail within thirty yards of one of the carracks without anyone being the wiser. The galliots are all pulled up on the beaches. You humans don't seem to like getting wet."

They rowed on through worsening seas and squalls of rain. The light galleys had no real shelter for the rowers, and Benito found himself shivering. "Well, at least in this we should be able to land on the island during daylight," said Benito to the triton, who was pacing the vessel in the rolling gray sea.

Androcles shook his head. "No. The rain stops short

of Corfu. Any lookout will see you. You'll have to wait for nightfall." He looked up at Benito and chuckled. "The seas are getting heavier. Looks as if you aren't wet enough already, you might just join us soon."

Never was Benito so glad to see landfall as in the lee of that unnamed cape. The Venetian relief force was cold, wet, and bedraggled.

And on Corfu—undetected.

The hundred and fifty men who had landed there were handpicked as good seamen, with some knowledge of Greek—easy enough, as many Venetians spent time in the Greek possessions. They were all reasonably skilled horsemen, and were all combat veterans. What they weren't . . . was too sure where they were, where the enemy was, and just where they should go. Benito blessed the fact that at least it wasn't raining here.

He went down to the water's edge to bid farewell to the merpeople. Only Androcles had come inshore. "My thanks. We're in your debt."

Androcles grinned, his teeth pearly in the moonlight. "We'll keep it in mind." He looked at the three galleys. "What do you do with the ships now?"

Benito scowled. "I busted my ass building them and now we'll scupper them, rather than let the Byzantines have them."

Androcles shrugged. "Why not put them in the sea caves? There are some along the edge of the cape. You can only get in dry at low tide. If you take the masts down you should fit them. You will have to swim out of the cave, though."

Benito sighed. "I'm just about dry."

Most of the gear was off-loaded and skeleton crews of strong swimmers set out for the caves. They nudged their way forward into the darkness of the sea-hollowed limestone. "This is where we leave you," said Androcles. "Corcyra is another's territory, and this is too close already."

It was dark. They had to feel their way in, inch by inch.

"Trouble with sea caves like this, is that they cave in,"

said one of Benito's companion's cheerfully. "I went into one near Capri on my first voyage. They said it used to be a bigger one but it caved in."

"I needed to know that," grumbled Benito. "Reckon we can strike a light now? We're well into this thing and we've curved away from the sea. They shouldn't be able to see it from outside, and we need to work out how to anchor safely."

"It's as black as pitch in here. We'll need to chance it."

Someone struck a lucifer. A lamp wick caught.

Benito looked at the five Greek fishing-boats that were in there already. And at the people on them and on the shore-ledges. There were an awful lot of arquebuses, pistols, arrows and just plain rocks all ready to come their way.

Benito was extremely glad to recognize at least one of the vessels.

"Captain Taki! Spiro! Kosti! It's me! Benito!"

It was as near to inevitable that the caveful of fishing boats should have its own taverna, with a supply of the wine that Benito recalled so well.

"Why is this stuff so vile?" He demanded, eyeing the cup of russet-colored liquid. "And why do you all drink it?"

Spiro drew himself up in affront. "If you don't like our *kakotrigi*, don't drink it! I'll relieve you of the burden." He reached for Benito's cup. "It is a wine of the Corfiote character, and like us, it is hard to harvest. The grape clings to the stalk like we cling to our soil."

Benito held his cup out of reach. "I'm paying for this round. You snatch my drink when you're paying."

"Which will probably mean the end of the world is at hand, so you might as well drink it anyway," said Kosti.

"You're paying? I'd have had the *mavrodáphne* then," said Spiro with his wry grin. "*Kakotrigi* is cheap crap. But you get used to it. Even get to like it, if you drink enough."

And for a few cups they could have shelter for their

ships, and advice on where the Hungarian troops were. It struck Benito as a bargain.

"How did you make it back? Did you have any problems?"

Taki laughed and waved his arms expansively. "I told you I was the finest seaman around. We sailed rings around them."

"We came back in a patch of bad weather. We nearly missed the island," said Kosti.

"I hate to ask this. But just where the hell are we?"

Spiro rolled his eyes. "Great sailors, these Venetians. Masters of the Mediterranean. You're about a league and a half away from Paleokastritsa. And your dangerous friend is about four leagues away. Together with his blonde with the . . ." Spiro crooked his arms in front of him.

Benito grinned. This was going to be easier than he'd thought. He looked speculatively at the Corfiote sailors. "How are things going with Erik's private little war?"

Taki laughed shortly. "He doesn't have to do much anymore. The peasants are killing and sabotaging whenever they get the chance. Those Hungarians can't make up their minds what to do. One day it's reprisals and the next it's being nice to peasants. But the story is they ate a child from one of the villages down south. The father cooperated with them because they had his son hostage. And while he did that they ate the boy, like those Vinlanders did to old Cheretis' favorite goat. And fed the bones to their dog. There's this big yellow dog that goes about with 'em sometimes. People say it's no natural dog. Say it can be shot without being killed."

"That was Georgio's story," said Kosti. "Georgio once had a wild pig get drunk on fermented windfall apples in his master's orchard . . . and he tried to shoot it when it was sleeping it off. From about three feet away! He still missed it."

"Well, yes," admitted Taki. "But Serakis says he saw the boy's waistcoat and the thigh bone. Tooth marks right into it."

Benito scratched his chin, thoughtfully. "Doesn't sound like they're popular. So how do you think you lads and the other fishermen would feel about helping the Venetians do a bit of quiet raiding? Sink a few of those patrol vessels?"

"With our fishing boats? Are you crazy?"

"With the galleys. You spot them from shore. Dark nights we run out and sink 'em."

They eyed him with interest. Kosti's grin was feral. "Should make night-fishing around here safer," said Taki with a nod.

Even with a guide from the fishermen it was Erik's men who spotted them first. He plainly had scouts out. And any Hungarian patrol was going to have to deal with an ambush.

Erik himself came out to greet them. The Icelander was, Benito thought, looking as happy as he'd ever seen him. Obviously things were going exceptionally well for him with his Vinlander girl.

"Well, Benito!" He clapped Benito on the shoulder and grinned as he looked at the hundred and fifty men in the valley. "Is this all you bring me? And I had to part with perfectly good silver for your trip over!" Then he gave Benito an unexpected bear hug. Benito had never seen any real signs of emotional display from Erik. Perhaps this, too, was Svanhild. "Well done, boy."

Benito felt considerably taller. "I brought back the principal and interest on the silver. In gold. We've got arms for five hundred. We've got a secure hidden port and three light galleys we can use to raid the blockade ships. And there are more men coming, as soon as we have the ships. And now, let me introduce you to Captain Di Negri."

Benito pointed to the broad, curly-haired, swarthy man who was at the head of the column. The man stepped forward. "Knight-Proctor Hakkonsen? I am Fabio Di Negri." The two shook hands, sizing each other up. "I have orders from the Doge and the Senate to put myself under your command."

Erik raised his eyebrows. "That's good. And surprising, to be honest."

"I had to talk long and hard to get them to agree to it," said Benito, with a wry smile. "Fortunately Petro and, indeed, Venice know you."

"Well, Captain, you are going to be on your own anyway, a lot of the time," said Erik, comfortingly. "We've found the countryside won't really hide more than twenty in one group. I've three separate units working now already. With your men and the recruits we can bring in we should make the north virtually free of Hungary. We'll seriously affect them in the south too, I think." He turned back to Benito. "And you, Benito? Have they very sensibly made you have to take my orders too?"

Benito shook his head. "Actually, the Council of Ten has given me another assignment. Petro was opposed to it, but . . ." He shrugged. "I wanted to do it."

"What?"

"Trying to get the news back into the Citadel."

Erik winced. "Benito, things have tightened up a great deal since you and I came out. Largely, I am afraid, because of what we've been doing out here. It's nearly impossible to get within two miles of the Citadel. Emeric must have as many men patrolling around there as he has in the siege trenches."

"I'll have to go and have a look to see what I can think of."

Erik shook his head. "Something crazy, no doubt."

"Probably," said Benito with a yawn. "Meanwhile, can we get out of the sun and get a drink of water? I drank too much *kakotrogi* last night."

Erik laughed wryly. "Haven't you noticed how dry it is, Benito? The stream in this little valley has dried up. We're maybe half a mile from the nearest spring that's still flowing. The Corfiotes say it should be raining, now that we're into September. The rains started . . . and then stopped. We haven't had a drop since the day we had the earthquake."

Benito scouted, with Erik. And then with Thalia, pretending to be a peasant with onions to sell.

He watched for hours, trying to find the obvious chinks in Emeric's armor. He had to admit that the organization was slick. Still . . .

"What is that compound over there?"

"Corfiotes. Slave labor. They are taken from villages

where they suspect we have sympathizers." Thalia grimaced. "Mostly they get it wrong."

"They're not very well guarded. And they're marched up to the front lines every day."

"They have leg chains. The ones who are not working have a long chain threaded through all of the leg irons."

"Ah. I see. Do we know of a good blacksmith?"

Thalia turned to Giuliano. "Who is best? There are three making arrowheads and spear-blades for us."

"Gigantes, I think." The once-plump young son of an armsman smiled. "He used to make my plows. He was always coming up with new ideas that I didn't want."

"Do you think he could make me a set of manacles? And while I'm about it, provide me with some metal-cutting files."

"If you have the gold, yes. Files are precious."

"It's a mad plan!" snapped Erik.

Benito shrugged. "Of course it is. Do you think a sane plan would succeed?"

"No. But that's not the point. A breakout of those prisoners would certainly enhance our popularity even more. It's a good idea even if I don't like the way you want to do it. But look at the rest of it. It has one big flaw: Castles and fortifications are built not to be climbed. Trust me. I know about fortification."

Benito shook his head. "Erik, I don't try to tell you about hand-to-hand combat. Please don't tell me what I can or can't climb. I promise you that there are at least seven places where an upper-story man could get into the Citadel with ease. Of course they've got guards and I've got to get there. That's why I am going as one of the prisoners."

"It won't work. Look, after moon-down is the time they'll have their sappers sneaking over. The guards on the walls will shoot at anything that moves—or worse, if you're climbing, drop boiling pitch or oil on you."

"I know. Falkenberg told me. That's why I'm going in on the seaward side, near where we came down. I should be safe enough in the water."

"I forbid it," said Erik. "You're throwing away your life, Benito."

"I'm afraid, Erik, you can't forbid me to do anything," said Benito firmly. "Knowing for certain that relief is on its way will give the those inside the kind of fortitude that is worth an extra five hundred men. Those are my orders from the Doge."

He didn't tell Erik that what Petro had actually said was: *if you can let them know without killing yourself.* He wasn't planning on killing himself. If he died it would definitely be by someone else's hand. "What you can do for me is keep this sword. I don't think I can manage to hide it."

Erik looked at the rapier. It was plain he recognized the hilt. He'd been there the day it had been broken, and to someone like Erik weapons were as distinct as snowflakes. "That's quite an honor. What do you want me to do with it?"

Benito shrugged again. "Marco wouldn't appreciate it much. If I don't come back, have it for a wedding present that you can give to your firstborn son." He grinned at Erik's look of embarrassment. "If I do get away with this, you and Svan'll have to put up with a silver saltcellar or something instead."

Erik squeezed his shoulder. "It's a true Viking gift," he said thickly. "And our first. But I think—much as I envy this blade—I'd rather have the saltcellar."

"I'll do my best to see you get it."

Chapter 75

Benito had stripped down to match the slaves. The poor devils had nothing more than breeches, which mean that the Shetland knife, the three files, spare knives, and the manacle key had to be strapped to his legs. His body, face and the breeches were suitably covered in mud. His medal from the Hypatians he attached to the belt-line.

"If you're due a saltcellar, I'll have Manfred fly the Knots banner from the inner wall, north tower," whispered Benito in parting.

And then he was on his own. In what, he reluctantly admitted, were still his two favorite elements: darkness and danger.

Moving along the backs of the tent lines, once he'd dodged the initial sentries, was tricky. There were guy-ropes, and, on one occasion a soldier relieving himself. He moved silently, manacles bundled in sackcloth and on his back, closer and closer to his target.

At last he only had the palisade between him and the slaves. He lay there, trying not to shiver, and watched and waited, studying the movements of the guards. When he was satisfied at last, he took the moment and went up and over the eight-foot palisade like a chimney-rat under whom the fire has just been lit. Then he dropped, gently, from his full arms' stretch. This was the worrying part. There might be stakes or anything there.

He landed on something bony that swore at him in

Greek. It was the one thing he'd learned reasonably well
from Taki, Spiro and Kosti. As Spiro had explained, it
wasn't that fishermen were crudely spoken. It was the
fish. Fish don't understand otherwise.

"Shut up!" he hissed, in his now-passable Greek. "I've
come to help you get out of here." Which was true, up
to a point.

Sometime later, firmly manacled into the line, Benito
lay among the huddled-together-for-warmth prisoners
and pondered what he now knew. The prisoners had
no idea which place they'd be working in next. There
were, in toto, seven strings of twenty. The guards
came and took chainfuls at a time. There were several
strings out now. The prisoners—naturally—had wanted
to escape immediately. Another day or night working
meant a very real chance of dying. Benito had his work
cut out to persuade them to let him chance getting to
the Citadel wall.

His bait, however, was irresistible.

"Look—just running, you've got maybe one chance
in a hundred. But the resistance fighters out there, the
klepthes"—which meant bandits, but to the Greeks the
two were remarkably close—"they'll be waiting for my
signal from inside the fort. The night they get it, they'll
do two things. First, they want to raid one of the outposts
to the south. Second there'll be some, with horses and
donkeys, near the ridge with the holm-oaks. You get up
there, yell 'Kalimera,' and they'll try to get you away."

In the meanwhile, they took turns filing their manacle
chains the better part of the way through. The new-cut
metal would be plastered with dust and urine. If the opportunity arose, they'd probably be able to force them.

Morning came. Benito found himself sent to be part of
a bucket-chain, passing earth out of one of the mines. His
one worry now was that he was just that much stronger,
better fed and less exhausted than his Corfiote companions.
He hoped the bored, brutal guards wouldn't notice.

During that long, hot session one of the slaves died.
The guards took him out of the chain by the simple
expedient of chopping his foot off. "At least he was
dead," whispered the man next to him. "Zikos was alive

when they did it." And the mines were considered a lucky option.

That afternoon, Benito quietly swapped chains. "They've been in all day. They're bound to go out tonight to work on the causeway."

They did. The wrong one. He had to wait until the next night.

Benito no longer had to fake looking exhausted, hauling rocks and broken masonry to make walls for the troops to advance behind. They had hide shields to work behind, but these were poor protection against even arquebus fire. The guards stayed well back behind some sandbags. It was simplicity itself to slip his manacle and lie down when cannon fire made the guards pull their heads down. Then it was merely a quick wriggle and squirm through a gap and a scraping slide into the water. All too easy.

The water wasn't. It wasn't that cold, but it was still something of a shock. Benito began to ease his way, swimming very quietly next to the edge of the mole, so that his head, if anyone saw it, might be thought part of the stone fallen from it. The siege engineers had been using broken masonry from the town and there were any number of odd-shaped bits in the water.

Then, flipping onto his back, he began swimming away from the mole down the channel toward the sea. Oh, to be one of the merpeople! That thought put another into his mind: the creature that the merpeople said had been haunting the Adriatic. Benito decided maybe it would be a good idea to swim with his knife in hand. After all, it was dark and still here in the water.

When Benito's legs touched something moving in the water, he very nearly screamed. He would have if he hadn't swallowed water in his fright. Trying not to cough, he touched it again. It was a rope. A moving rope. Moving slowly toward the Citadel shore. Benito realized it sloped gently down. Someone was hauling something across—something quite heavy.

It almost certainly meant no good.

Benito swam in toward the Citadel, angling away from the rope. The rope was actually dragging something around to the south side. The shingle strip was very narrow here, and the original rock made up part of the corner tower. Benito eased out of the water, with that feeling in the middle of his back that he was in some arquebusier's sights.

The Citadel's builders had chopped and polished at the rock here so that the lower section was smooth. It did overhang slightly, though, and this brought Benito to where the load was being hauled. It wasn't a cave so much as another small overhang, also part of the original rock. Two men were straining to slowly pull something out of the shallows. It was plainly heavy. There was no way past, and besides, Benito had a feeling it might be more important than the mere news that Venice was on her way.

He waited, knife in hand, and watched. The moon was down and there was little light to see it all by. Just enough to see that the men were taking strain pulling the heavy weight up the beach.

The wind was cold and biting on his wet skin and wet breeches. Starting to shiver, Benito knew it was now or never. Two to one . . . and they might have swords or guns.

The first man was so intent on pulling he died without even knowing Benito was there. The second turned and managed to grab Benito's hand and draw his own blade. Benito had to seize his arm with his left. In the dark beneath the wall they wrestled desperately in absolute silence. The fellow was as strong as an ox. He was good eight inches taller and seventy pounds heavier than Benito. By sheer weight he was pushing Benito over.

What was it that Erik had said? "Use their strength. Get them off balance." Benito tried to foot-sweep the man. It was a dismal failure. Instead, Benito was thrown to the shingle and cobbles, and lost the knife. The Hungarian came diving in for the kill. Benito rolled and hit the fellow just behind the ear with a cobblestone-sized rock.

He hit him twice more. And then put some of the rope to good use, as well as the man's trousers as a gag.

Then he felt around and found the Shetland knife. Now to see what they'd been doing.

It was barrels! There were already five in the back of

the overhang and they'd plainly been surreptitiously drilling into the limestone. Benito was no engineer. Would the explosion have damaged the wall? He had no idea. But the barrels were a great deal easier to roll than to drag. He rolled them out toward where the latest one lay. All but one. That he pried at with the Hungarian's knife. He wasn't breaking his own! He liked that knife.

The barrel was full of powder. Black gunpowder, by the smell of it. Benito wished he had some way of striking a light—once he was a bit further away. He then had the bright idea of searching his captive and found a flint and steel. Now all he needed was a gunpowder trail and he'd have fireworks to celebrate his return home. Taking double handfuls of the stuff he crept along the wall strewing it. He made a line out to the barrels and put a pile of it against them. The only trouble was, of course, that he couldn't see what he'd done.

Still, he decided he'd used enough. Then it was lug the semiconscious prisoner—well, drag the prisoner—close to the postern. Benito looked longingly at it. It would be so nice and so easy just to go and knock on it now. But they'd probably shoot him first.

In the shadow of wall just short of the postern, Benito struck sparks into the powder trail he'd laid. It burned. It burned damned *fast*. Benito threw caution to the wind, dropped the striker and ran, jinking, farther away from the Hungarian lines, running eastward along the beach parallel to the wall. Running, there was a good chance the sentries on the wall would see him. If they saw him, they'd shoot at him first and ask questions later. On the other hand if he continued his slow progress, he'd either be blown up by his own sabotage, or spotted and shot in the aftermath of the excitement the explosion would cause. The shingle stopped, if he recalled right, and the cliff took over just beyond that.

There was a yell and a shot from above. Benito tried very hard to be small, and dove into the water. Water wasn't a wall or a sandbag but it deflected bullets. He was going to stay underwater as long as possible, and swim as far and as deep as possible, and not spend more time on the surface than he had to.

He came up in time to hear an explosion, but not the huge one he'd been expecting.

He risked a look. He could see men with brands, running down the length of the wall; running back in the direction he'd come from. He trod water, watching. Even from here he could see the barrels were still on the beach. They'd failed to explode. His powder trail hadn't worked. The explosion must have been the barrel he'd opened . . . obviously there'd been a powder trail to that too! That accidental powder trail had worked. Well, there was nothing for it now but to swim on. They'd not expect someone to go on swimming away from the Hungarian lines.

By the time Benito got to the ledge, swimming was just about too much of an effort. Once he'd hauled himself out of the water and onto it, his strength was gone. He was exhausted. Too tired to contemplate a sixty-foot climb on greasy limestone with anything but dread.

But it had to be done. It seemed like an awfully long way. Benito hugged himself, and danced up and down on the ledge trying to get warm. He wasn't succeeding well. But the sky was definitely paling—he wanted to be up this corner and over the wall before dawn or he was going to have a long wait on this ledge for nightfall. And he might be visible in daylight from the tower windows.

He began bridging his way up, one foot and one hand on either side of the corner, balancing between them. Fortunately it was a very nonstrenuous technique. A trick of balance, merely. Benito edged his way upwards toward the faint dark edge of the wall-top. He paused just below it, listening, although all he wanted to do was to get over that edge and rest. But there was no point in dying just yet. Not for the sake of a few dozen heartbeats.

Never had the top of even the most difficult building felt quite this satisfying to reach. Benito didn't walk away. He crawled to the stair . . . down it . . . To the deep shadows beside a building. He lay there for some time, trying to breathe quietly and gather himself up.

He was in, and almost home. Less likely to be shot,

anyway. But he didn't want to end up in jail again, either.

So: Where did he go? Getting into the governor's palace like this was not going to be easy. Tiredly, his mind turned automatically to Maria. She wouldn't mind if he turned up half dead on her doorstep. And then . . . well, maybe that husband of hers—or a note to Manfred. Or Francesca . . . or . . .

He was too tired to think coherently. He stumbled through the narrow lanes, the dawn bell competing with the Hungarian cannon. He passed a few soldiers, coming off duty, yawning. One of them made a comment, but Benito simply wandered on. He obviously looked mad or drunk, but harmless, because they didn't follow after him.

He got there. The door was closed—a drift of sand across the doorsill. The shutters were still tight, closed although the other houses were now coming to life. He knocked.

There was no reply.

He peered down the narrow passage that led to the back yard. That goat of hers had harassed passers-by from here. There was no goat, today. The place had that "nobody-lives-here" look.

Benito sat down on the steps. The doorknob was unpolished. The steps were full of wind-blown debris. Maria would never have allowed them to look like that.

A gray-haired old woman peered at him. "Who are you?"

"Uh. Benito. I'm looking for Maria and . . . and Umberto." Here he was, without even a shirt, in salt-stained breeches, his body and face muddy. He wished he'd thought to wash when he'd been in the sea. Some of it obviously had washed away, but he'd chosen that fine-grained clay that needed hard rubbing. She'd think he was some kind of lunatic. However, looking at the old woman, he could see she really didn't seem to be all there herself. She'd made up half her face. The effect was a little odd, especially when added to the unfocused-looking eyes.

She sniffed, looking about to cry. "They've gone. The

young man was shot. They've gone with that gorgeous baby. Like my baby. Babies always go . . ." She wandered off, seemingly having forgotten all about him.

Benito took a deep breath and pulled himself together. First things first. He needed to get off the street. He'd been plain lucky so far, but that couldn't last. Besides, the old woman's rambling had worried him. Upset him even more than finding the person he'd always relied on, known would be there as a last resort, wasn't. Could Maria and the baby Alessia be . . . dead? He swallowed and vaulted the gate into the tiny yard.

Definitely no one had been here for a while.

Benito sat on the back step and formulated plans as best he could. The worry had pushed back exhaustion. If there was no Maria he'd have to turn to his other friend.

The roofs.

Francesca got up early. In a relative sense, anyway. When she'd had the misfortune to have to survive life in the Red Cat she'd thought she got up early. Then along had come Manfred, and with him, Erik, and she'd finally understood that all things are relative. "Early" to a hooker meant before noon. To a knight in training it meant before dawn.

With Erik away she'd thought Manfred might ease back on the predawn training. But he seemed to treat it as an act of faith.

Now, with the sun peeping through the shutters in long golden streamers, was a far better time. She swung the shutters open. And screamed.

It was a perfectly natural reaction to seeing someone dropping from the eaves and into her bedroom. It took her a moment of hasty retreat to recognize the dirty, half-naked stocky man, who simply sat down on the floor.

"Benito!"

"Yep. Why do you get up so late? I've been waiting for you to open up for hours."

"Why didn't you knock?"

"And get shot through the shutters? I tried calling

quietly but you obviously didn't hear. Where's Prince Manfred?"

"Over at the exercise yard. I'll send someone for him. No, I'll go myself. Is Erik—?"

"Fine." Benito yawned. "Got any food?"

"In the next room. Look, help yourself. I'm going to fetch Manfred. I haven't even done my hair!"

She left at a run. Francesca never ran.

Benito got wearily to his feet, went into the next room, and found a bottle of wine and a small loaf. He didn't bother to try any further. Just flopped down in a chair in the far corner and drank wine straight from the bottle with a few hunks of bread to keep it company.

"He just dropped in through the window," said Francesca, unlocking the door. "I nearly died of fright."

Manfred grinned. "Made your hair stand on end, did he?"

She looked dangerously at him. "I came straight out to call you without even thinking of brushing it, Manfred."

"You're beautiful even with all your hair standing on end, Francesca. Now where is the boy?"

"I left him here . . . oh."

She'd spotted Benito, fast asleep, curled into the seat.

Manfred surveyed the boy. Mud. Bruises, scratches. And a pair of tired breeches. A three-quarters-full wine bottle still clutched and half of a dropped loaf on the floor beside him.

"I suppose he had to choose one of the good bottles," said Manfred, looking at it wryly. "The kid must be all in. He normally sleeps like a cat."

"Should we let him sleep?"

Manfred shook his head. "I'm afraid not. He can sleep once he's told us what is happening." He stepped over to the chair and began shaking Benito. The boy's skin was clammy to the touch. He was shivering faintly. "Here, Francesca. Get him a shirt and one of my cottes."

Benito woke with a start. An eyes-unfocused start,

reaching for a knife. "It's all right, Benito," said Falkenberg, beaming at him. "You're with us."

Benito shook his head, obviously trying to clear it. "Sorry. Wine on an empty stomach. And I was a bit tired. Thanks." The latter was addressed to Francesca, who handed him a shirt and cotte.

He stood up. Manfred noticed he was swaying. "Come on, Falkenberg, let's get him into those and he can sit down again."

"I can dress myself."

"Shut up," said Manfred, his big fingers struggling with buttons. "Or rather, tell us news. Francesca said you said Erik was all right?"

Benito nodded. "Yeah. Fine. He's looking like the cat that ate the cream. He's got his Vinlander, and he's got his insurgents, and he's making the Hungarians bleed."

"We've seen some of it from the walls, but I'm damned glad to hear it for certain." Manfred sat Benito down. "You've grown, boy. But my clothes are still a little big for you." That was something of an understatement. But at least he should be warmer. For an autumn day, it was warm. Benito wasn't.

"So: What happened to the plans for getting you over to Italy? Is the blockade just too tight? Or are there just no fishing boats?"

"I've been there and back. I came back with a hundred and fifty men to help Erik and news that the Arsenal is building a new fleet. As soon as they have the ships, Dorma will put to sea. There's a new war levy. They're recruiting mercenaries and calling for volunteers. The Old Fox himself has put up a thousand men."

Manfred blinked. "There and back . . . and back inside?" He looked at the wine standing on the floor. "And to think I begrudged you that. You deserve the entire bottle! In fact, make it a hogshead."

"I'd rather have some brandy. Listen—do you know what happened to Maria? My . . . my friend who told Erik. I went there first. It's all shut up."

Francesca smiled knowingly. "She's fine, Benito. She's down at the Little Arsenal. Her husband got himself shot by the Libri d'Oro traitors. But he's recovering slowly.

Look . . . is there anything else you really must ask him immediately, Manfred? Is there anything you really have to tell us, Benito?"

Benito shook his head. "Just was told to bring the news that relief was coming. It might be four, five more months though. And I left a prisoner at the southern postern. Oh. And to ask that you hoist the Knots banner at the inner wall north tower at sundown. Tell Erik he's getting a saltcellar after all." Benito stood up on this cryptic utterance. "I'm going to the Little Arsenal."

"Sit down. You need to rest," said Francesca firmly. "I'll go down and tell her."

Benito shook his head. "You'd frighten her silly. Besides," he added, grinning in a pale shadow of his usual impishness, "I've got to tell her that Kat wants to know why she hasn't written. And I have to check on the baby for her god-mama. Heh. If you'd met the god-mama, you'd know I don't dare delay."

Francesca shook her head disapprovingly, "I know men well enough to know I'd be wasting my time arguing. But Manfred, I think he needs an escort."

Manfred nodded. "And his own clothes. Everyone would think a fair had come to town, otherwise."

"I'm going *now*." There was a determined tilt to that chin and a feverish glint in Benito's eyes.

"Fine, fine," said Falkenberg soothingly. "We'll just get you a horse."

Benito closed his eyes momentarily. "Not a horse. Please!"

"Well, at least wash your face!"

Chapter 76

Maria was working on the looms on the upper tier, keeping a weather eye on the carpenters working on the next level down. The gates opened. Maria blinked at the sunlight on armor, then rubbed her eyes unbelievingly.

She got up slowly and deliberately, took Alessia from her crib in the shade, and walked down the stairs—being very careful not to stumble. Her knees felt a little weak.

Benito was grinning at Umberto, trying not to show his shock. The master-caulker had never been a big man. Now he looked as if a puff of wind would blow him away. He was gaunt and pale, and he looked at least twenty years older. "I hear you got in the way of a bullet, Umberto."

"The master is a hero!" said one of the other *scuolo*, affronted by this familiarity. "He saved the Citadel!"

Umberto's eyes narrowed, focusing on Benito. "Signor Valdosta?"

Benito nodded. "Just Benito Valdosta. Or as your wife would have it, just trouble."

"You got out? Maria told me you had been successful in getting out, that someone had signaled from the main island. Raftopo," he pointed to Benito, "this is the young man who bought your coracle, remember?"

The fellow nodded. "*Si.* I remember. Umberto wouldn't say what you wanted it for."

"We went over the wall to the island," said Benito. "How's Maria, Umberto?"

The former coracle-owner shook his head. A stolid oxlike thinker, he plainly ground everything to its finest. "If you got out, how come you're here?"

Manfred patted Benito on the shoulder. "Because he came back, of course. After he went all the way to Venice."

"In my coracle? Ha." The former owner looked as if people had all too often tried to put one over him.

"Hell, no—that sank about a mile away," said Benito. "Fishing boat to Italy. Small trader up the west coast and then a damned horse over the Apennines to Ferrara. Barge to Venice."

The *scuolo* wrestled with the implications of this. "You mean . . ."

"Back again, I see," said Maria. "You know, Benito, you're the original bad penny." But she was smiling broadly as she said it, and her eyes seemed a little moist.

He was looking like . . . Benito. At first she thought he had shrunk. The she realized it was just outsize clothes. Good clothes but enormous. The cotte hung like a dress on him, which was maybe just as well. The breeches he wore were muddy and salt-stained. His feet were bare and filthy. And his face . . .

She looked at it, remembering. It had lost a little of the youthfulness, and he was as pale as a nocturnal *Case Vecchie* gentleman. He was smiling at her, very oddly. "How's Alessia?" he asked. "Her godmother wanted me to ask."

She put a hand on his forehead. It was clammy but hot. "You can find out when you get out of the hospital, you idiot! He's feverish, Prince. Take him there before he falls over on us."

Benito obliged her by doing just that.

Manfred walked over to the commander's offices after they'd deposited Benito in the care of the monks. There were times for subtlety and quiet contact. This wasn't one of them.

"Commander Leopoldo's over at the south wall, sir. There's a bit of a situation there. We had explosions there early this morning."

Manfred laughed. *Benito!* "I'll go and see him there."

He went by horse, with Von Gherens, having had a sudden thought. He dispatched Falkenberg to go and keep a watch over Benito. The boy could easily be the target of whoever the spies in the Citadel were. The morale boost to the Citadel of having news from Venice was huge. That was why Manfred had told the men at the Little Arsenal what Benito had done. It would run like wildfire around the fortress. It would get to whoever was spying, too. Emeric wouldn't enjoy hearing that news.

"We think he may be some sort of trap," said Leopoldo, pointing to the man at the foot of the tower. "He's alive. We've seen him move. So why is he tied up? Who is he? And there are those barrels of what is probably gunpowder over there."

Manfred looked at the bound, trouserless man, and at the shingle strip with four haphazardly lying barrels on the beach. "Nope," he said with a grin and in a good carrying voice. "That's Benito's work. You can go out and collect the prisoner. I'll go out and fetch him if you like."

"That's a lot of black powder. If there is shrapnel in it and it goes off, Prince, you'll be mincemeat."

"I told you, Commander. My agent, Benito Valdosta, caught that saboteur last night, when my man was coming in from the Venetian forces. You should come up to the hospital and hear all the details."

"*Venetian* forces?"

"Hadn't I told you yet? The scouts for the Venetian relief force have arrived."

If the black powder in the barrels on the shingle had suddenly gone off, it could scarcely have caused a bigger explosion.

Hidden in some Aleppo pines in a rocky little defile, Erik surveyed the Citadel gloomily. It was still defiant, bathed in the last of the evening light, but he didn't see what he hoped to see. On the first day after the young tearaway left, he actually expected to see the banner of the Knights in that corner tower. When it wasn't hoisted, he'd given orders to move from all the localities Benito knew. Torture got information out of anyone. So did black magic. And Emeric used both.

The next day he still hoped. Tonight was merely a duty. The youngster was either a prisoner or dead, and most likely the latter. Erik thought about the sword Benito had left in his keeping, and sighed. He'd love to own it, but he'd part with it in a heartbeat if it could have spared the boy. He was so caught up in these morbid thoughts that he didn't realize that, flying above the north tower of the inner wall, was the famous treble cross of the Knights of the Holy Trinity.

"It'll be the most welcome saltcellar a bridal couple ever got," he said to himself, laughing in relief. "He must be down to two of his nine lives."

The slave breakout that night brought Erik sixty-two fanatical new recruits. But Erik's first priority was to feed the poor devils up a bit.

The Magyar officer shook his head. "They seem to have forgotten the meaning of trust. They won't even parley, Sire, let alone agree to terms. Early days—back in June—all they did when they saw our men was make sure the gates were shut and watch us. But now . . . Feeling has hardened, Sire. They're shooting on sight. Both Paleokastritsa and Kassiopi are still holding out. I've put men on watch, and they're in a sort of siege, but without cannon and a lot more men I don't see reducing either."

Emeric considered. "We'll play a waiting game, then. I don't want to take men off the siege here."

"Getting the heavy cannon to either of those two towns would be very difficult anyway, Sire. There is no road, just a donkey-track. It could be done, but it would take a lot of men and a lot of effort. Easier to starve them out. When the Citadel falls, they'll be forced to surrender."

Emeric nodded. "I see the peasants are coming back onto the land."

"The men and the older women are, Sire. You don't see a child except running away. Basically, hunger forced them out, but the lack of rain is worrying them."

Emeric snorted wryly. "I can only have it one way. The rain must stay away from the Venetians, too. So: What did you find out about the murder of those two Libri d'Oro collaborators?"

The Magyar officer scowled. "The peasants did it, Sire. But they swear it was some *klepthes*—bandits from the hills in the north. We really do have a problem with that. Our troops can't move singly. I have to send them everywhere in squads. I've tried torture. I've tried beatings. I've executed a few in front of their families. No one talks. So I tried a different tactic in Gastouri, with that second murder. We're twenty miles away from where I'd tried the last time. This time I pretended it hadn't happened. I told my men to go easy. To buy the locals drinks. To convince them we were simply taking over from Venice and that they'd find us far better masters. The peasants won't drink with us unless you hold a knife to their throats. I finally asked one old bastard why. He said we eat babies and feed our dogs their bones. I told him this was rubbish, but he insisted he'd been shown the gnawed bones."

"I don't want to go back there, Umberto," Maria said, knowing she couldn't tell him the real reason—that she was certain Sophia Tomaselli had put some kind of ill-wishing on the house and on him. For that matter, she wouldn't put it past the woman to try to get someone to poison them at this point. Living there just made her feel too exposed.

But none of those things would have made any sense to Umberto. "I know, it's getting colder down here. We'd benefit from living in a proper house again, but I'm scared. I won't take you there. I won't take Alessia there."

Umberto smiled. "Well. It makes a suggestion I have to make easier, Maria. I have here a letter from Master Grisini. He's not well. The honest truth is he's concerned for his wife's future if he should die. The captain-general would then reallocate his home. His wife should go back to Venice—in the normal course of events. Of course that can't happen right now because of the siege. Grisini is deeply worried that the captain-general will take a rather spiteful and petty vengeance by moving the old lady out. He could do it, too. However, the house is a very large one, and what Grisini proposes is that we—you and me and Alessia—move into the lower section. It's still bigger than our old house. The move doesn't have to be approved by anyone except Commander Leopoldo, and he's a reasonable man. If Master Grisini dies, we'll be 'sitting tenants,' the captain-general won't be able to evict us, and we can give house-room to old Mrs. Grisini until the siege is lifted and she goes back to Venice. The house is a lovely one, and Grisini is afraid if the *scuolo* losc tenancy of it we'll never get anything nearly as good again. He suggests we move four of the Illyrians into our old house, to stop fights with the Corfiotes down here."

Maria shrugged. "Umberto, old Mrs. Grisini isn't really in this world anyway. But if it means I don't have to take you and Alessia back to that house, fine."

"*Your* agent? You dared to do this without my permission?"

Eberhard cleared his throat. "Captain-General Tomaselli, while this place is a Venetian possession—Prince Manfred is *not* a Venetian subject. To be a bit blunt, he doesn't need permission to get his men to do anything. And he did, in fact, obtain *carte blanche* from the governor to get a message out. Signor Valdosta here was delivering a message to the Emperor of the Holy Roman Empire from the prince. That was his primary task, which he achieved. It was done on the prince's orders and with the prince's money. The fact that young Benito is a good citizen of your Republic and did his civic duty by reporting the matter to the relevant authorities there also, and returned with ships and men, was a bonus for Venice."

He paused. "I know you see this as an attack on the Venetian Republic. But please understand: To us it is a danger to the man who is second in line for the throne of the Holy Roman Empire. By comparison, the Emperor holds Corfu or even the Venetian Republic—though staunch friends—to be of lesser value. The reason that huge imperial efforts are going into relieving this siege is the prince. Our secrecy has nothing to do with a lack of faith in you personally, it was just that this matter was purely about Prince Manfred."

It spoke volumes for the influence that the older statesman had been able to exert over the captain-general that Tomaselli did calm down. "I hadn't thought of it like that. But nonetheless I should have been consulted! The security of this fortress is my responsibility. And any route this man followed could be followed by hundreds of enemy troops. The way must be blocked!"

Benito laughed. That made him cough. When the paroxysm finished he said, "I swam the better part of a mile in two sections, I climbed a sixty-foot cliff on the seaward side of the Citadel in the dark. Next thing the Magyar will be doing it on horseback and in full armor."

Eberhard patted Benito soothingly. "He's not well, Captain-General. I'm sure he'll show your men the spot when he's up. But it would not be easy for anyone else."

"I'll take you down it personally, Captain-General Tomaselli. I wouldn't dream of letting someone else assess the security." Benito went off into coughing again.

"He's fevered. I think we must leave him to rest. Come, Captain-General." Eberhard showed Tomaselli out and on the way shook his fist at Benito, behind the captain-general's back.

Manfred and Benito restrained themselves from sending Benito off into a coughing fit again, until the captain-general had mounted his horse and was clopping away.

"It is a good thing I insisted on Von Gherens staying outside," said Manfred, his shoulders still shaking.

Benito looked at Manfred. "It's an equally good thing I didn't tell him that Petro Dorma has decided to relieve the pompous ass of his post and promote Commander Leopoldo in his place."

"What! That would solve a hell of a lot of problems."

Benito raised his eyebrows. "Really? Do you think he'd believe me? It's not as if I can prove it. Captain

Di Negri has a set of orders signed by the Doge with the seal of the Republic on them . . . but I didn't see swimming in with them."

"I hadn't thought of that."

Chapter 77

Maria went to the door to answer the knock. It wasn't Anastasia, the young Corfiote girl who looked after old Mrs. Grisini. She always knocked firmly, and in a recognizable pattern. A pity; she'd have loved to ask her to mind Umberto and maybe even Alessia, if the old lady was asleep. She really had to go up to the temple again. Umberto was up—and then down—and she didn't know who else to turn to. But this was a very quiet knock. Tentative.

She opened the door to see Benito standing there. "What are you doing out of bed?"

"No one's asked me into one," he said with his old impish grin. "Even the monks have chased me out."

His face became earnest. "Maria, before I left Venice for the first time, Petro said I should come and see you and offer to baby-sit. Before I left Venice this time an undine called Juliette charged me with seeing to Alessia's welfare. I'm better. But I'm still forbidden drill or to do too much exercise. So I came to do what Petro and Juliette said I must. I've come to baby-sit."

Maria gaped at him. "You can't be serious!"

Benito shrugged. "As much as I ever am. Petro Dorma's no fool, as I learned eventually. And I sort of made a bargain with Juliette. So: Lead me to it. Tell me what to do, and you go out and get some time off."

Maria held her head and shook it, as if to check that it

was still attached to her shoulders. "Holy Mother! I don't believe this. Look, Umberto's not so good today, either. I've promised him I'd look in at the Little Arsenal, see how thing are going. I've, um, got another visit I really need to make. 'Lessi's asleep now. But would you stay with her and Umberto? If you mean it, that is?"

He smiled. For once, it was a smile with no overtones, no sense of anything hidden, and nothing of his mad recklessness in it. "I mean it. Like I said, lead me to it."

When Maria came back, guiltily, knowing that she'd been away for longer than she'd meant to be, she heard laughter from inside her new home. She found Benito had Umberto sitting up against the cushions in the bedroom, while he was executing intricate Venetian dance steps with Alessia in his arms.

"She's a better dancer than you are," said Maria, trying not to join in the laughter.

"She couldn't be worse!" Benito grinned. "I absolutely hated the dancing instructions that Dorma's mother made me suffer through. Marco now, he makes it look easy. Here, Maria. I think she's getting hungry."

"He even changed her, Maria," said Umberto wonderingly. "He's a braver man than I."

Maria thought Umberto was looking a great deal better than when she'd left.

Benito wrinkled his nose. "You've just got to switch your senses off, sort of. Make it just a job to be gotten through. It's no worse than a lot of other things I've done, and better than no few."

Maria shook her head at him. "Just when I think I know how your mind works, Benito, you go and surprise me again. I never thought you'd be any good with children."

Benito looked like mischief incarnate. "It's because they trust me. Nobody else does."

Maria snorted. "And that's no surprise!"

"Now Maria," said Umberto gently. "He's made me laugh. I'll say I feel better for it."

Maria gave Benito a reluctant smile. "Oh, he's not all bad. Just half bad. Now, I'm going to feed Alessia. Excuse me."

Benito gave her a little bow. "I'll take my leave, too, Umberto, Maria. I'll take a look in down at the Little Arsenal, Umberto. I want to see those boats."

"Come back and tell me what you think."

Maria walked him to the door. Bit her lip, looking at him. "Thanks," she said quietly.

He shrugged. "It's nothing. I'll come again, if you like. Umberto kind of surprised me. He's got interesting ideas about those fireboats."

That had surprised her too. "He looks better for the visit. But next time let me show you how to fold a napkin." It was a tacit admission that she wouldn't object to a next time, she thought, as she patted Alessia's derriere. "This is a mess."

"So was what I found there, believe me. I'll see you."

He probably wouldn't, she thought. He'd be off on his next madcap stunt, which would be far more interesting than looking after a sick man and a baby.

"And where have you been, young feller-me-lad?" asked Manfred, with a buffet that would have made Benito's ears ring for a good while if he hadn't ducked. "Enjoying the adulation of the admiring young women of the Citadel? Francesca tells me you're a very sought-after young bachelor."

Benito grinned. "It's hard being popular. If only you weren't seven sizes too big you could try it." He ducked again. "Listen, seriously, do you know about the project they've been busy with at the Little Arsenal? The fireboats?"

Manfred shook his head. "No. And whose project is this?"

"That's just it: The Arsenalotti have been at odds with the captain-general. So they've been doing it on their own. They've got nearly thirty of these things built. They reckon they've materials for twice that. They're smallish boats—long and slim and designed for speed. Umberto—Maria Verrier's husband—designed the things. I've just been down to have a look. The guy is good, Manfred. Those things, with a good following wind, will be like arrows."

"And just how are we supposed to launch these arrows?" asked Falkenberg, curiously. "Hold the beach while they're carried outside?"

"They've been built to be lowered over the wall into the water. He got the idea from Erik and me and our coracle stunt. Except they're making davits and winches. One of the men down at the Little Arsenal was showing me.

"And you say they've kept this in the dark?"

"Not deliberately. They were just looking for an opportunity to bring it up."

"With Tomaselli in charge, that won't happen," said Falkenberg. "Not that it isn't a good idea. Might be, at least. Take me down for a look in sometime, Benito."

Count Mindaug was scowling fiercely. Given the slight distortion always present in the summoned image above the blood-bowl, the expression made him look even uglier than ever.

"I hadn't thought he'd be this cautious, Elizabeth," Mindaug admitted. "By now, I'd expected Jagiellon to have intervened directly."

The countess decided that her silvery laugh would irritate Mindaug too much, at the moment. So she kept her expression simply serene. "Keep in mind, Kazimierz, that Chernobog is ancient, even if the shell he inhabits—that thing that used to be the prince Jagiellon—is still a relatively young man. For demons, 'ancient' and 'prudent' are almost synonyms. Even for a demon with a savage temper like his."

"True enough. Still—"

"Give it time. Which we have, by the way. Months yet, probably. The attempted treason failed, and my agent in the fortress informs me that any further attempts will take considerable time to organize. Unfortunately—or perhaps fortunately, given Chernobog's hesitancy—the woman who is running the Citadel's counterespionage work is extremely astute."

Mindaug's eyebrows rose. "A woman? Since when do Venetians—"

"She's not Venetian. She's one of the Imperials. Prince Manfred's leman, to boot, so she has plenty of influence.

Her name is Francesca de Chevreuse. The name she goes by, I should say, since I doubt very much it's her real one."

Now, the Count was shaking his head. For a moment, the tips of his sharp-filed teeth showed. "What is the world coming to? In the old days—yourself excepted, of course—women handled the gossip, not the statecraft."

Since Mindaug's mood seemed to be improving, Elizabeth issued her silvery laugh. "Don't be silly. Even in Lithuania, that's not true. Or have you already forgotten Grand Duchess Imenilda?"

"That was almost a century ago. Besides, she was Ruthenian. The Ruthenians have always been a peculiar lot. Meaning no offense." Elizabeth Bartholdy had quite a bit of Ruthenian blood in her own ancestry.

"None taken, I assure you. To get back to the point, Kazimierz, I really think you're worrying too much."

Count Mindaug studied her for a moment. Then said abruptly: "That may be, Elizabeth. But the fact remains that I now need to consider, seriously, the consequences of failure. If this trap of yours doesn't work—even if only because Jagiellon avoids it—I will be the one to face the immediate repercussions. Not you." He raised his hand and eyed it. "Granted, it's not the finest skin in the world, but it's the only one I've got. I'd just as soon avoid having it served up for one of the monster's meals."

He lowered the hand and brought his eyes back to hers. "I'll need to run, Elizabeth—which means I'll need a place to run *to*."

The countess ran a delicate fingertip across her lower lip, thinking. She was not surprised, of course, that the issue had finally come up. She'd already given it quite a bit of thought herself, in fact.

"You understand that I do not share your interest in territorial and material matters?"

Mindaug's pointed teeth showed again. "You're not *that* indifferent to them, Elizabeth. Or do you really think you'd be able to pursue your own interests—if you were a peasant woman?"

She laughed. "Point taken. Nevertheless—"

He was shaking his head. "I'm well aware that your

ambitions and mine are different. All the more reason, it seems to me, that there needn't be any clash between us. Even if . . . how to say it? Even if—"

"Even if you were residing in the Carpathians instead of Vilna—and trying to subvert my great-great-nephew and assume the throne of Hungary, instead of Jagiellon's."

"That's putting it bluntly. But . . . yes."

He waited, his face impassive.

Elizabeth thought a moment further, then shrugged. "I can't say I have any particular attachment to Emeric. He's easier to manipulate than you would be, but on the other hand . . ."

Mindaug finished the thought for her. "I'm smarter than he is. Which means I'd cause fewer messes for you to have to manipulate me out of." He left unspoken the obvious final clause: *assuming you could.*

But Elizabeth was not worried about that. And the more she thought about it, the more she could see a number of advantages to having Mindaug—if necessary, which she still didn't think it would be—taking asylum and refuge with her.

"Done, then. That *assumes,* of course, that our plans fail."

"Needless to say. I assure you, Elizabeth, that I'd much prefer to remain in Vilna, if at all possible. If nothing else, I'm too old to take any pleasure at the thought of a frantic race to get out of Lithuania ahead of Jagiellon's wrath."

"*Chernobog*'s wrath, Kazimierz. Don't ever forget who you're really dealing with."

For the first time, he laughed himself. "No chance of that, Elizabeth! It's why I approached you in the first place. A mere Grand Duke, even one as capable and vicious as Jagiellon, I would have been confident of handling on my own."

He glanced aside, as if looking over his shoulder. "I simply prefer to avoid the name, that's all. The Black Brain is near to me, and it never pays to do anything to tingle its attention. Speaking of which . . ." His hands began moving. "I think it's time to end this discussion."

Within seconds, his image had faded away.

PART XI
October, 1539 A.D.

Chapter 78

Diego sighed. "It is fairly certain that whoever the Satanist is—whoever *they* are, I should say, since there's certainly more than one—he or she is aware that we are hunting for them. This is the third place where we have found their foul traces, but never anything more. And they've been very cautious never to leave material we can trace to a physical place or person."

Francis nodded. "And venturing beyond the physical, here, where we are denied the protection of one of the wards, is nearly impossible."

Eneko Lopez went to a cupboard in the back of the chapel. "So. I think we should investigate this." He produced the dried-out bundle of herbs and other unpleasantness that someone had once tried to use as a curse on Maria Verrier.

"But it is a fake," protested Diego.

"I know," said Eneko. "But let us consider the very nature of Satan-worship. Its essence is to recruit more souls. Unlike demons who are content to devour, devils accumulate—and use their acolytes to accumulate. And whoever did this is ripe for accumulation. They—or parts of their coven—may already be drawn into this." He held up the bundle, a bit gingerly. "Here, we have physical traces. With some risks, we can use these to divine where they came from. And once we have that, we may catch some trace of our other tormentor. Or tormentors."

✧   ✧   ✧

By the time that the afternoon sun was sinking, the priests knew more about the "curse." One of the things they knew was that the maker knew absolutely nothing about how to stop themselves being traced by magic. The priests, patiently, set a watch on the suspected house. Curfew or no curfew.

It was after the midnight bell that they saw the various "visitors" arrive. Then the priests calmly went down the street and waited for the Knights' patrol.

"Just what are you doing out here, Father Lopez?" asked *Ritter* Wellmann. "It is after curfew, you know."

"We need some Venetian soldiers, too, *Ritter*. Please fetch some for us."

"To do what?" asked Wellmann.

"God's work, Brother."

"I'm supposed to be on patrol, not on missionary work."

Eneko Lopez was not amused. "You are Knights of God. Your oath is to serve Him first, *Ritter*. Send two of your men to fetch a detachment of troops and their officer here. *Now*."

Ten minutes later, an alarmed-looking lieutenant and some twenty pikemen arrived at a run. "I sent a message up to the fortress," said the lieutenant. "What is it? A mine?"

"Spiritually speaking, yes," said Eneko. "Follow me. The house must be surrounded and we must move in quickly. Wellmann, take the door down with your axe."

Ritter Wellmann was an artist with an axe.

Business, thought Morando, was booming. He always tried to think of other things at this stage. It required detachment. The carefully soundproofed inner sanctum he'd created in the cellar of this unobtrusive house had no less than five of the Citadel's leading social lights in it. And they were dressed exquisitely for the occasion, thought the confidence trickster, forcing down a snicker. Bianca Casarini was a true gem of a recruiter. The trade in information he sold Fianelli was even more profitable than the money he got directly from the women.

Since the curse incident—which had apparently even worked, to Morando's astonishment—Sophia was his to command. The one problem with her, and the other women she'd brought around, was that all of them seemed to derive more from the "sinfulness" of the ritual he'd invented than they did from the actual deeds. It was trying his imagination, not to mention at times his spine.

The other problem was getting the paraphernalia. Black candles had to be made; and he'd had to resort to stealing chickens to dye black. He had a fortune hidden under a paving stone in this room, but he still had to steal chickens, because they just weren't for sale any more. Tonight he'd used a cat. They seemed to like that, even if he'd felt rather sorry for the poor creature.

His supply of hashish was running dangerously low, too. He couldn't see replacing that until the siege was lifted or lost.

Still, the cellar was well hidden, and he had stores of food and water. He'd sit out the orgy of killing and looting that he knew would happen if the Hungarians won, with Bianca and Sophia to keep him company and provide him with pleasure. If the Venetians won . . . well, he'd farm Sophia and her friends a little longer and then it would be time to shave his beard and leave with a convoy heading to Outremer, to enjoy a rich retirement in Constantinople. Bianca had already agreed to come with him.

By the moaning and panting, he would soon be called on to chant some gibberish again. Morando had even made an effort with a grimoire he'd obtained years earlier to garner some real words and phrases.

"Grimoire" so-called, at least. Morando suspected the thing was probably a fake. Which was fine with him, when all was said and done. Playing with Satanism served his purposes, well enough, and Morando wanted no part of the genuine article.

And then Aldo Morando discovered the real fault with good soundproofing and a cellar whose only secret escape route took considerable time to open.

❖   ❖   ❖

They stormed in. Lieutenant Agra made sure he was the very first in through the door.

The room was a grave disappointment. It had a very ordinary table, a straight-backed chair, and a simple oil lamp, the flame wavering in the sudden disturbance. There was no one there. Nor in the single bedroom or the kitchen. But the priests seemed unperturbed, if in a hurry. They joined hands and chanted. As they did a misty trail of footprints appeared on the floor, ending at what appeared to be just another flagstone in the floor.

"Break it," commanded the short, slight priest with the eagle gaze. "Quickly. There is bound to be another way out."

The knight with the axe tried to put the edge of his axe into the crack. With a growl of impatience the priest took the axe from him and smashed it into the flagstone.

It split. The stone was set into a wooden frame full of lambswool. The knight took the handle of the axe and hauled and ripped the hidden trapdoor right out. Agra was down those smoke-shrouded stairs so fast he nearly broke his neck on them. At the foot of them, amid the screaming, despite the press at his back, he stopped.

He'd expected nearly anything but this.

The room reeked of smells, that of hashish prominent among them. Naked masked women, their breasts, groins and in at least one case buttocks painted with strange bloody patterns, clung to a man wearing a long cloak of black-and-red velvet, black boots, and nothing else. Not all of the women had the sort of bodies that the lieutenant would have paid to see naked. Even the smoky room lit with black candles could only do so much. It was the black altar and the headless cat lying with its neck in a bowl, though, that really got him.

At least, until the women went berserk. The lieutenant then discovered how well frightened and desperate women can scratch and bite.

Benito sat drinking some wine with Maria and Umberto in their small bedroom. Umberto sat against the pillows and Maria on the foot of the bed. Benito was sitting on the chair from the living room. Alessia was attempting to suck her toes on a rug at their feet.

Benito had been back every day to sit a while with Umberto and Alessia. Maria's initial surprise had given way to acceptance. But today she hadn't taken advantage of it to go out. Today she wanted to know what was happening. She was worried, and not without reason.

Benito grimaced at the wine. "I suppose the one thing we can be grateful for is that we've still got enough wine for a full ration. If it was good wine, we wouldn't have. The Libri d'Oro didn't want to buy it because it was so lousy. So even though the granary is down to an eighth full and the upper wells are running dry, we've got wine. If you can call it that."

Maria shook her head at him in irritation. "Benito, stop burbling about wine, and tell us what happened. You were there. You should know. The rumors in the lower town today are amazing! A coven of witches sacrificing babies and having orgies with demons and blasting priests and buildings to ashes—a high-class brothel—a cabal of female thieves. God knows what. People are claiming all sorts of things. I've even given in to curiosity and been to have a look, not that there was much point. There's a guard and a smashed-in door but you can't see anything else."

"Manfred says it's like a traveling players' version of a mixture between hell and a brothel down below in the cellar. They took him to see it. It's pretty tawdry in daylight, apparently, but the lieutenant who was testifying is thinking about becoming a monk after last night." Benito chuckled. "Apparently he saw a great deal more of a number of mostly unattractive women than he really wanted to. Anyway, it seems that some bored *Case Vecchie* women had initially gone to Morando because of his reputation as an astrologer and chemist and—ah—sexual physician. Apparently, no matter what else he can do, he's quite a lover, or at least, they think he is. And they, finding—at last!—a lover who wanted to hear gossip as much as they wanted to indulge in it, came in droves. Well. I guess five women isn't really a 'drove.' "

Maria snorted. "They're saying Sophia Tomaselli was right on the top of the heap."

"The captain-general is trying desperately to hush it all up," said Benito, nodding. "She's his wife, after all."

Both her eyebrows went up. "And the wife of the Salt Minister and of the largest oil exporter on the island. Come on, Benito! Everybody already knows all that. He might as well try to hush the sea. People are getting very restive about it. The *scuolo* are all for burning the Castel *a terra*."

Benito was silent for a moment. Then he said wryly: "Fortunately, they jailed the man and the women separately, because all the women came out singing one tune: It was a complete fraud, a put-up job by the Knights to discredit their husbands and allow the prince to take over. They'd been kidnapped, stripped, abused, and locked in the cellar. They wanted the Knights punished for the degradation by being thrown out of the sanctuary that Venice had kindly offered them—and the cowardly mercenaries who'd sold out to them shot."

"What!" Umberto had started upright. Alessia stopped playing with her toes. "You can't be serious!"

"Dead serious. And Tomaselli was ready to make it stick. Heh. It was pretty exciting, what with Lieutenant Agra having to be restrained and calling the captain-general's wife a whore and witch."

"Well, he was dead right!"

"Yes, well, as it pans out . . . half right. Morando lent her some of his occult books—those were fakes, too, Eneko says—and apparently she tried to cast curses on—ah—people she considered to be her enemies." He interrupted himself before he said the name, but Maria saw the guilty look in his eyes, and she knew who he was going to say. And although she had suspected it, having the evidence in front of her was enough to send her simmering temper into full boil. So that was, indeed, where the ill-wishing had come from!

But Benito was continuing. "Fortunately, old man De Belmondo was sick and we had the assistant podesta of Corfu standing in. He's one of the Libri d'Oro, but he did his law in Padua University and takes it pretty seriously. He pointed out that since it was the captain-general's wife accused, Tomaselli couldn't take part in the hearings. And he sent the guard off to fetch the other Justices, even De Belmondo from his sickbed. And, as I say, it was fortunate that they'd kept the man separate. He's from the north of Italy, originally. Milan, in fact—Pauline country. They burn witches up there on suspicion. His name—the one he goes by here, anyway, is Aldo Morando. He was so keen to prove he wasn't a man-witch or a Satanist, that he was spilling the beans as fast as he could. He was selling information and black lotos, and acting as a glorified pimp for that gaggle of rich women. They followed up several of his confessions, and found them all true. Then they had the brains, finally, to split the women up and question them individually. Then they came apart. Their stories didn't tally. Eventually, the truth became obvious."

Umberto shook his head, confused. "What? That he really was training witches in our midst, practicing black magic?"

"Well, no," Benito said. "That he was casting horoscopes, telling fortunes, dabbling in the occult mostly as window dressing for his real interest—getting information from one set of stupid, bored, sexually unsatisfied women to sell to whoever might be interested in it. The Justices called Eneko Lopez. And he said, although they'd hoped to catch real practitioners of black arts, that this lot were simply nasty, spoiled, bored, rich women."

"And what happened then?"

"Well, to make a long story short, Eneko had cut the legs out from under the Justices. It's not an offence to prance around naked in a cellar done up to look like a cheap whorehouse with astrological trimmings. And, while selling the stuff is illegal, simply using black lotos is also not a crime. As for participating in orgies and gossiping to your lover, well, the outcome of that is mostly up to the husbands, not the courts."

"What! You mean they've got away with this? The *scuolo* will—" Umberto was struggling to stand up.

Benito flicked up out of the chair and pushed him down, gently. "Relax! For starters, selling information to enemy agents is a serious matter. So is pimping. Morando is the one who's really to blame here, and they have him dead to rights. They even got him for chicken theft! And two of the ladies of Corfu high society are up for . . . prostitution. It appears that Morando was selling their favors for certain services he rendered—including Tomaselli's Sophia. But the cream of it is that Lieutenant Agra—the one who got so upset about being called a cowardly sell-out mercenary—has slapped a civil suit for defamation against them."

"So what's happening to them now?"

"Morando will rot in jail until trial in Venice. The treason part will probably have him executed. The others . . . well, they've been bailed. Released into the custody of their spouses. Except for the wife of the Salt Minister. She asked to remain in jail for her own safety, since he threatened to kill her." Benito shook his head, ruefully. "Not that I think, under the circumstances, those other women will find their husbands very, ah, 'protective.' Probably beat them to a pulp."

"So you mean that Tomaselli bitch is out there, free?" demanded Maria furiously.

"Calm down, Maria."

"*I will not calm down. I'll—*"

"You're upsetting Alessia." Benito had picked the baby up and was soothing her.

Maria pursed her lips and took a deep breath. "I am going out," she said between clenched teeth.

"Maria!" said Umberto, anxiously. "Promise me you won't do anything stupid. Please."

Benito had moved between her and the door. "Think of Alessia, Maria. You hurt Sophia, you're the one who will end up being punished. And by doing that you'll be punishing your baby. She'd rather have a mother at home."

"Get out of my way, Benito Valdosta. I'm not going to kill anybody unless it's you, for not moving. I'm going to talk to someone. A friend."

"I'm your friend."

"I need to talk to a woman. A man wouldn't understand. Now give me Alessia."

"I'll stay and take care of her. Just promise us you won't do anything crazy."

She laughed bitterly. "That's rich, Benito, coming from you. Just let me go, see. I'll be back once I've got this out of me."

Renate De Belmondo handed Maria a cup of steaming, fragrant liquid. "This tisane is a kind of magic too," she said with a gentle smile. "There are more and deeper magics than Eneko Lopez and his kind understand. There is magic in things they consider inert. There is power in people that they cannot detect. There are magics in love and hatred, too. Especially here."

Maria sipped the brew. It was soothing, there was no doubt about it.

"Vervain and a little heartsease. There are times and places for the picking of both. And it can only be done by one who has the great Goddess's hand about her." Renate looked sternly at her. "You must learn, Maria, to control and direct that anger of yours. Otherwise you'll hurt those closest to you."

Maria bit her lip. There was some truth in that, she had to acknowledge. Especially this afternoon. She knew that the source of the "curse" on her house was Sophia Tomaselli, even if she couldn't prove it. She'd heard some of what Benito had not told her—just what Sophia had said, to the Justices, to the curious gathered around as she and the other women were taken away. Vitriolic, to say the least, and Sophia placed all of the blame on being caught on Maria. And though of course it was not in the least logical, if you believed Sophia, it was Maria who had somehow *forced* her into the spy's service.

"It's . . . it's just the injustice of it all. It's not *right*!"

The older woman looked at her thoughtfully. "A sense of justice is a part of what makes us what we are. Some of us are willing to suffer ourselves to make sure there is retribution . . . even if it costs us. You are one like that."

Maria thought back to her single-handed vendetta against the *Casa* Dandelo, when Caesare wouldn't help— and Benito, the scamp, did. "Yes. I suppose so."

"But are you prepared to extract the cost of your retribution from others? From innocent parties. From your friends?"

Just the intonation said to Maria that this was a very important question. A question far wider than just the issues she'd run to Renate with. She paused to think. Maria thought of what Benito had said about Alessia. And of what she'd decided to do.

She shook her head. "No."

Renate smiled. Maria noticed that small lines eased from around her eyes. "The Goddess and her followers do not practice retribution."

"I don't think I can forgive that woman for what she tried to do."

Renate shook her head. "Neither could I. But our justice is based on restitution. And restitution finds no gain in mere retribution. Sophia Tomaselli was looking for retribution. She was quite content to hurt innocent parties in her quest to get it."

Maria sighed. "Yes. But . . . well, it was such a small thing. I mean she set out to attack everything—my life, my loved ones' lives, for something so small. So unimportant. Who on earth *cares* if some people think I'm more attractive than she is? Why would it make any difference to me? It's not as if I'm competing with her for anything! It's not fair."

Renate curled her lip. "Of course it is not fair. Such a person is an island of their own self-importance. The fact that their retribution is totally out of proportion, will not benefit them, and will hurt others, is irrelevant. You dared to slight the most important person in her universe. Anything is acceptable to punish you."

Maria paused for a while sipping the tea. This might all be true. But it didn't apply directly to her problem right now . . . did it?

"So what do I do about her, Priestess? I'm not having that woman on the loose to endanger my man or my child again. She might try anything. Poison. Thugs. Planting evidence to make us look like traitors."

Renate smiled. "I am only the priestess when I let down my hair and don the robes." She pursed her lips. "Of course, a charge of attempted murder should stick. I suggest tomorrow you swear one out. The fact that she used a weapon that she did not know wouldn't work, does not alter the fact that she tried. After all, if a man tries to shoot another and the weapon fails to fire, it is still an attempt at murder. She would be confined again in that case." The older woman took a deep breath. "Other than that, you must come to me every day now. I must teach you certain magics and certain rituals that will protect you and yours. I must teach you, too, how to control that temper of yours. How to break it to harness."

"Me? I can't do magic!"

The priestess stood up and put her hands on either side of Maria's head. "You already do magic. Magic that Eneko Lopez does not understand exists. Magic more powerful than he understands. An old, rough and elemental kind of magic, but strong."

She took her hands away and tugged at a sidelock of her white hair, a gesture indicating thought in the priestess who was also the governor's wife. "You know, I know a great deal about Sophia Tomaselli. In some ways we are very alike."

Maria shook her head vehemently. "You couldn't be more un-alike!

Renate twinkled. "I think that's a compliment. But there are some similarities that Eneko Lopez would see. For example: We are both aristocrats at the apogee of our social setting. We both turned to other sources of comfort after we arrived here. We both, I believe, did so for the same reasons: We both wanted to get pregnant. I know Sophia has tried all sorts of 'treatments' and diets and consulted churchmen at some length. She fell in with a trickster. I . . . fell in with one of my maids. She was a Corfiote and felt sorry for me. There, but for fortune, went I."

Maria shook her head again, vehement. "No. Sophia cares for nobody but herself. It's a blessing she's never had a child. You care for everybody. I don't believe you'd have done something like trying to curse me and mine. That's not like you."

"I don't think I would have done what she did, no. And caring is what the sisterhood looks for: sisterhood. And that was why I was taken to the temple. That is why you were. And that is why she wasn't."

"The two things are not alike at all," said Maria, stubbornly sticking to her earlier contention. "The Mother is gentle—not sick!"

Renate shrugged ruefully. "Stella is inclined to sensationalize news, but still, yes, those women were seeking perversion. Probably some of it came out of their mothers telling them that the natural urges and pleasures of their bodies were bad, wrong, and evil. Therefore they came to conclude that evil gave pleasure. Possibly only because they were bored and their husbands were under the impression that if *they* were pleasured and pleased, it didn't matter if their wives were." She sighed. "I don't want to deceive you, Maria. The great Goddess . . . well, there is one aspect that does call for a willing sacrifice. And the spring ritual dance is conducted in the nude. But no men are part of it. It is done for a reason."

She stood up again. "Now, I think you're all safe enough tonight. Here." She took from her reticule a sprig of green holly. "Prickly thing. And full of the heart of green-ness. Put it above the door lintel. Not with cold iron. If it turns black—come running, and bring your child. And go barefoot if you can. Touching the earth, it will be difficult for any other magic to affect you."

Now she looked mischievous. "Don't tell Eneko Lopez that's why his spells don't work well here. Contact with the earth of Corcyra. The earth here drinks magic. The more they use, the less well it works. And the magic is reborn in other forms within the Earth. We use it."

"I want to learn."

"Very well. You must come to me, here. This hilltop was a temple before it was a fort. One of the entries to the inner temple is still here."

Chapter 79

He looked as though he might very possibly throttle her, thought Sophia. He hadn't said a word all the way back to their chambers in the east wing of the fortress. Now, with the heavy door closed behind them, he turned on her in fury.

"How could you, you bitch! How could you! I'm the laughingstock of the Citadel. I'll be the laughingstock of all Venice when the siege is over. I'll never hold another position of authority you—you— My mother was right! I should never have married you!"

She drew herself up. "Nico, I did this for you. I went to this man to try and see if there was something—anything—I could do to have the heir you needed."

He snorted disdainfully. "Ha. Yes. By turning yourself into a *puttana*! By sleeping with half my officers! Grand. You give me an heir that isn't even *mine*."

She looked down her nose at him. "Those are absolutely trumped-up lies, Nico Tomaselli! As if I would ever desire another man but you." She sniffed. "I thought it was a fertility rite. Harmless. And they . . . they made out we were having orgies and . . . and all I wanted was a baby for you." She burst into calculated tears. They had never failed her before.

But they did this time. He folded his arms, and not around her. "Even if it were true, it's not what people are going to say. Venice takes a dim view of these things.

That new Doge, Dorma, is very straightlaced. Why, he even exiled his own ward for his antics and they were nothing like being paraded through half the streets of the Citadel, screaming and fighting, stark naked. I don't know how I will ever hold up my head in Venice again!"

"Then don't."

"What choice do I have, Sophia?" he demanded. "What choice have you left me?" His weak man's rage was beginning to build again.

Sophia had one last card left to pay. One last token from Morando, which she'd been trying to think of a way to use for weeks. It had come, magically transported, her lover had said. He'd suggested she make a lever out of it. She'd hesitated, but . . .

Now she had no choice.

"I have to show you something. In my bedroom."

"I'm not interested right now."

"You will be. Come." She simply walked up to her room.

By the time he got there, she'd taken out the folded letter. "Here." She handed it to him.

He looked at the address. The seal. "Who opened a letter to me from the Doge?" he demanded.

"I did. Because I love you and look after you. Open it. See how well Venice rewards you for your loyal service after all these years!"

He opened the letter. She watched as his ruddy face turned pale. He looked as if he were about to burst into tears. "Who cares what they think of you in Venice?" she demanded. "Let us go where they will appreciate us!"

He bit his knuckle. "Damn Dorma. Damn him to hell. Leopoldo in my place! After all I've done here!"

It was entirely typical of her husband, Sophia thought contemptuously, that he never thought to ask her how she'd obtained the letter. But, not for the first time, she was glad he was a fundamentally stupid man. She was in desperate straits herself, now—with outright treason as her only option.

"Damn, drat, and blast the man for an interfering busybody!" said Francesca furiously. "I've had a watch on

Fianelli for *weeks*—and now, thanks to Lopez's meddling, I've lost him. He was gone before the soldiers got to his shop. Who cares about Morando? He was just a minor player, working for Fianelli."

Manfred patted her soothingly. "There, dear. Look at it this way—you'll have a splendid time finding him again."

If looks could kill, Manfred would have been ripe for burial. "It's not a game, Manfred!" she said, in such a tone that even he sat up straight. "Morando by himself was nothing. Fianelli was *dangerous*. He still may be. *Somehow* he was getting information out—Fianelli, *not* Morando—in a way that none of your clever men suspected, and that nothing you did uncovered. If he was getting information out, what did he get *in*? What *could* he get in?"

Von Gherens looked puzzled. "If you knew who he was weeks ago, why didn't you let us deal with him then?"

Francesca eyed him darkly. "Von Gherens, you are to intrigue what deportment lessons are to a brothel."

The *Ritter* thought about this one for a while. "Useful, you mean? So why didn't we deal with this spy weeks ago, Francesca? I don't get it, like the deportment lessons."

"I'd guess she was planning to start feeding him wrong information," said Manfred, yawning. "She'd have had Morando arrested quietly, and blackmailed him into turning on his former allies."

Francesca smiled on him. "You're proof it is possible for someone to learn even if carrying all that armor starves the brain of blood. That's one reason. The other was I wanted the final link. I wanted to know how he was getting the information out to Emeric."

Von Gherens rubbed his broken nose. "You should have talked to Eneko Lopez earlier, then. You could have helped each other. Each of you had what the other needed."

"What do you mean?"

Von Gherens crossed himself. "I mean Fianelli was the Satanist Eneko was actually looking for. He was using demonic magic to send the information. Eneko and his friends had detected him sending it, but couldn't find him. You found him, but couldn't work out how he sent it. You two should talk."

Francesca gritted her teeth. "I should have. And I will."

Captain-General Tomaselli was not the most effective soldier or administrator. Privately, he knew that. But he'd tried. He had been loyal to Venice. That they should promote that—that—*upstart* Leopoldo into his place was unbearable. It was unfair! And thinking of that unfairness, Tomaselli dwelled more and more on the unthinkable.

He could ask for a great deal, if he switched his allegiance to the Hungarians. He wouldn't have to soldier or administrate any more, things which he was not really good at. And Sophia would be out of jail. He'd been horrified when apologetic soldiers had come to fetch her again. Those damned disrespectful *scuolo* sluts! How dare that woman swear out a charge against Sophia? He'd taken small, but satisfying steps to have some of her family's ration reduced. After all, her husband wasn't working.

Now all he needed was a way to contact Emeric to make a deal.

He would talk to Sophia. She might have some idea how he could do it. She was the only one he could trust. It was clear to him now that the charges against her were all false; she'd been betrayed as surely as he had. And he could take her some decent food and wine again. He went as often as three times a day, anyway. Her trial . . . He'd have to reach a deal before then. They'd conspired against her thus far. The trial would be a mockery, of course, magnifying her small digressions into vast things as a way of getting at *him*. That was what was behind the whole thing, he now understood.

Well, he'd show them.

"What are you *doing* here?" hissed the man who opened the door for Fianelli. The secretary for the podesta glanced over his shoulder nervously, looking to see if there was anyone in the corridor behind him.

Fianelli shouldered his way past him. "Close the door, you idiot, instead of gawping at me."

Hastily, Meletios Loukaris closed the back door, which served as the delivery entrance for Governor De Belmondo's palace. That done, the podesta's secretary started hissing another protest. But Fianelli silenced him by the simple expedient of clamping a hand over his mouth.

Fianelli was not a big man, and fat besides, but the secretary was smaller still—and slightly-built. He had no chance of resisting Fianelli with sheer muscle. So be it. In a former life, in Constantinople, Loukaris had carried out several assassinations. Despite his initial nervous reaction at seeing Fianelli, the secretary knew that he was alone in the rear portions of the palace. He could kill Fianelli, then dispose of the body by—

But, as his hand slid into his cloak and closed over the hilt of the special blade he kept hidden there, he felt Fianelli's other hand clamping onto his wrist. The criminal boss was stronger than he looked.

"Don't even *think* of trying to use that needle on me, Loukaris. Forget those silly Byzantine political games. I'm a lot tougher than you'll ever be."

To emphasize the point, Fianelli hauled the secretary's hand out of the cloak and slammed his knuckles against the wall. The little needle-shaped stiletto clattered onto the tiles. Then, for good measure, Fianelli pounded Loukaris's head against the wall also. Twice, and hard enough to daze him.

When his senses cleared—and to his surprise—Loukaris saw that Fianelli was extending the stiletto to him. Hilt first.

"Here, take it back. You might need it later." Fianelli gave him a piercing look. "*We* might need it. We're still in business, Loukaris. The only thing that's changed is that you'll be hiding me, from now on."

Loukaris took the stiletto. He considered trying to kill Fianelli with it, for just an instant, but discarded the idea as if it were a hot coal in his bare hand. True, Meletios Loukaris had killed before. But his victims had all been aristocratic elderly men, and one woman, none of whom had Fianelli's criminal history and skills. The secretary had no doubt at all that Fianelli would overcome him—and then shove the stiletto into his own throat.

Quickly, he slipped the stiletto back into its special pouch. "This is *dangerous* for me. If anyone spots you—the alarm's out all over the fortress—"

Fianelli was faster that he looked, too. His fat, heavy hand cracked across Loukaris's cheek. "Shut up. You'll hide me in your own chambers. Nobody ever goes in there except you, do they?"

"The maid," complained Loukaris, rubbing his cheek. Fianelli's slap had been hard enough to really *hurt*.

The criminal boss grunted. "We'll figure something out."

A horrid thought came to the secretary. "What about your men? I can't—"

Fianelli waved his hand. "Don't worry about them. It'll just be me. They've made their own arrangements, whatever they are." He grunted. "Not that I care. If they get caught, they have no idea where I am since I never told them about you."

He jerked a thumb forward. "Now show me the way to your chambers."

By the time they got there, moving carefully through the corridors of the palace, Loukaris had already figured out the solution.

"She only comes in once a day. Always in the early afternoon." Sullenly, he went over to a very large free-standing dresser and swung the doors open. The dresser was full of clothes, since the secretary to the governor fancied himself something of a dandy. "You can hide behind the cloaks and stuff. There's room in the back, and the lazy slattern never looks in here anyway."

"Good enough." Slowly, Fianelli's eyes scanned the room. By the end, he had a crooked smile on his face. "You'll have to share the bed. Unless *you* want to sleep on the divan. No way I'm going to."

The secretary grimaced. The bed wasn't really that big, but . . .

He'd already more or less resigned himself to the inevitable.

✧   ✧   ✧

By the end of the evening, his resignation had become complete.

Fianelli forced him to watch the ritual he used to conjure up the image of their mutual master, King Emeric of Hungary. Loukaris had never known that Fianelli was a sorcerer, in addition to everything else.

"Still in business, like I said." Fianelli seemed very satisfied. He'd also forced Loukaris to clean up the traces of the ritual. "I get the wall side of the bed."

"You can have all of it." Loukaris almost gagged on the words. It had only been chicken blood, but he felt like he might vomit. "I think I'll sleep on the divan."

"Smart man," murmured Fianelli. The squat criminal boss gave the podesta's secretary a look that combined menace and complacency. And well he might. To Loukaris, he looked like the King of the Frog Demons—contemplating a fly.

Chapter 80

"The Barbary corsairs and the Genovese are uneasy allies, Grand Duke," said Count Mindaug. "They're traditional enemies. Of course, both sides hate the Venetians like poison but still . . . It is a fragile alliance. Alexius may be a weak reed, but he is being a very effective stopper to the Dardanelles."

"And what news have you from the Holy Roman Emperor, Mindaug?"

It didn't surprise Mindaug at all that Jagiellon knew of his secret messenger from Germany. His communications with Hungary were far more carefully orchestrated. "The Emperor is worse. He took the news that his nephew is trapped on Corfu by Emeric's men as reason to find more energy, to organize things. But now he is sliding again. His campaign against Emeric is a measure of the man."

"Why? It seems quite a small campaign."

"It is meant to be. The Emperor knows he is dying. He doesn't want his heir to take over with a huge war on his hands. A conquest of Hungary would be an immense war, even for the Empire. This one is designed to cost Emeric a great deal—but it will do so only if he doesn't react to it. The Emperor knows that Emeric simply cannot leave such an incursion alone, when it becomes clear what ignoring it will cost him. Frankly, in my opinion, because Emeric believes himself the greatest commander alive, he would be unable to ignore any challenge, however insignificant, that threatened what he holds. The effort, I should guess, is to get him to withdraw from Corfu to protect assets closer to home."

Jagiellon's black eyes stared into nothingness. Then he turned to Mindaug again. "And have you progressed at all with your researches into the magic of Corfu?"

"In one respect, yes. I have been investigating the works of one Trigomenses Commensus. He has recorded various nonhuman interviews, attempting by virtue of their long lives to piece together early history. It appears that, back when Corfu was part of the mainland, it was the center of a fertility cult, long before the area was overrun by invaders—perhaps the Dorians. The nonhumans he questioned—dryads, undines and satyrs—regarded the place as sacred, too. It is an old place."

"I know that it is an old place, once regarded as being of great power. I can feel no trace of any great power there now, myself, though. Yet my slave and the shaman are not succeeding in their quest there. They are being magically hampered, but I do not know by what or exactly how. It is like wrestling smoke! I need to find the source of this and know if it can be harnessed. This began as an exercise in attempting to flank the Holy Roman Empire. It has become a search for whatever it is that can even thwart the magic of the shaman. He is an adept of great strength."

"I was coming to that, Grand Duke. Commensus' interviewees all agree: Power there requires a connection to the earth."

"You mean I would have to physically go there?"

"At least in spirit, my lord."

Mindaug held his breath, doing everything in his power to keep his mind blank. This was the moment for which he and Elizabeth Bartholdy had schemed for so long.

"Yes," grunted Jagiellon. It was all Mindaug could do not to let his breath explode in a gust. There had not been a trace of suspicion in the sound.

"Yes," Jagiellon. "I think you're right. Risky, but—worth it, to shackle that power and bend it to my will."

❖   ❖   ❖

"It's *infuriating,* mistress," snarled Bianca Casarini. "And I don't have any choice—I *have* to hide Fianelli's men from the Venetians, even if it's in my own house."

Elizabeth laughed. "Having three louts lounging about your house would try the patience of a saint. Which you are certainly not." The countess cocked her head sideways. "I assume you've taken steps to bring them under control."

The last words served to ease some of Casarini's foul temper. "Oh, yes. One of them—Papeti's his name—has been lusting after me for some time. So now he thinks he's succeeded—and the one whom I did seduce is furious about it. The right two words from me, and they'll cut each other up."

"And the third?"

Bianca shrugged. "He's just a slug. Seems interested in nothing much beyond sleeping, drinking and eating. I haven't bothered with him, since I need to keep my magics to a minimum. I have to be careful here, mistress, sharing a small island with Eneko Lopez and his damned priests. They can't do much because they're afraid to work without their wards. But they're still accomplished adepts, especially Lopez."

"Yes, I understand. Well, that should be enough. My plans look to be coming to fruition. For the moment, just stay out of sight."

Before she'd even had time to finish erasing the traces of the ritual, Bianca heard a ruckus erupting in the rooms downstairs. A brief one, but very loud, ending in a cut-off scream.

"Those *idiots,*" she hissed, hurrying from her bedroom. "They'll make the neighbors curious."

When she reached the bottom of the stairs, Bianca saw that her "two words" wouldn't be necessary after all. Papeti's body was lying on the floor, bleeding all over the tiles. Saluzzo, red-faced, was crouched over the corpse cleaning his knife on Papeti's blouse.

He hadn't even heard Bianca arrive. The Florentine's eyes were fixed on Zanari, the third of Fianelli's thugs.

Zanari was standing in a nearby archway, with a very nervous look on his face.

"She's *my* woman," Saluzzo growled. "Don't forget it, or—" Angrily, and despite having already cleaned the blade, Saluzzo drove the knife into Papeti's ribcage again. The corpse jerked under the impact.

Saluzzo spotted Bianca then. Leaving the knife stuck in the body, he rose and took two strides toward her.

"Paulo, what—"

Saluzzo was a powerful man. His slap sent her sprawling on the steps. The next slap, on the back of her head, dazed her.

Fortunately, perhaps, since the pain when he seized her by the hair and began dragging her up the stairs would have been considerably more agonizing otherwise.

"*Bitch.* I'll teach you!"

By the time they reached her bedroom and Saluzzo flung her onto the bed, Bianca had recovered her senses. Furiously, she began muttering the words that would destroy the man. Saluzzo didn't even hear them, he was so consumed with anger combined with lust.

Before she finished the incantation, though, Bianca had suppressed her anger. The situation, she realized, was ideal for a different use of magic. Someday, she might well have to flee her house in a hurry—a task that would be made considerably easier if Saluzzo remained behind to attack her pursuers with demonic fury.

That, of course, would require turning him into a demon—the shape of one, at least—which could be done, under the right circumstances.

These were the right circumstances. Rage and lust, combined, were the key raw ingredients.

"I'll teach you to fool around with anyone else," Saluzzo snarled. He'd already hoisted her skirts and forced her legs apart. Now, he slapped her again and started untying his breeches.

"Paulo, please!"

Another slap. "Time for your lesson, slut."

The period that followed was unpleasant. Even painful, toward the end, as Bianca's murmured incantations began

effecting the first transformations of Saluzzo's form. But
Bianca had been through worse in the past, and would
face still worse in the future. Immortality, as the countess
often remarked, had its price. Many prices, in fact.

Fortunately, Saluzzo was raping her on the bed—still
better, on a bed in the upper floor of her house, almost
twenty feet above the soil of Corfu. Had he been assaulting
Bianca on the ground itself, her magics would have drained
away. The more so, since the sort of transformation she was
carrying out on him was closely connected to earth magic.
It was not quite the same as making a golem, but close.

"What's the matter, Eneko?" asked Francesca, leaning
forward in her chair. "You look suddenly ill."

"You cannot sense it?" The priest's voice was brittle;
his temples held in both hands.

Puzzled, Francesca shook her head. "Sense what?"

"The magic. That is a hideous spell being used. The
one who uses it—it's the female, this time, not Fianelli—is
reckless beyond belief. I'd never dare use a spell that
powerful here on Corfu, without wards—not that I'd
ever use that spell anyway—because . . ."

He croaked. Surprised, Francesca realized it was the
sound of strained laughter.

"Of course, I imagine she's not concerned with the
danger of attracting demons. Since she's one herself, in
all that matters."

Magic was something Francesca knew very little about.
So she focused on what, to her, was the key point. "You're
sure it's a woman? Not Fianelli?"

Eneko raised his head slowly, staring at her through
eyes that were nothing much more than slits. "Oh, yes.
There's a succubus—of sorts—loose in this fortress, Francesca. And she's even more dangerous than Fianelli. More
powerful, at least, when it comes to magic."

Francesca leaned back in the chair, her lips pursed.
"A woman. Could it be Sophia Tomaselli?"

Before Lopez could respond, Francesca raised her
hand. "Yes, Eneko, I know the fetish she placed in
Maria Verrier's house was a fake. But perhaps that was
just a subterfuge—a way to protect her from charges of

practicing *real* witchcraft, in case she ever got caught."
Francesca chuckled, throatily. "It's the sort of thing I'd
have thought up."

Eneko's smile was thin. "At a rough estimate, Francesca, you are eighty times more intelligent than Sophia
Tomaselli. But it doesn't matter. You forget that Pierre
went to see her in her cell, after she was arrested. The
Savoyard's the best witch-smeller I've ever met. He
says, quite firmly, that while the Tomaselli woman is evil
enough, in a multitude of small and petty ways, she's got
no more demonic power than a carrot."

Francesca must have looked a bit dubious. Lopez's smile
became still thinner. "Please, Francesca. I have learned
not to second-guess you when it comes to intrigue and
espionage. Please don't try to second-guess me when it
comes to magic. Whoever the female is, it is not Sophia
Tomaselli."

Francesca spread her fingers in a gesture that, subtly,
indicated assent. More precisely, that she was beating a
demure but hasty retreat.

"I wouldn't dream of questioning you, Eneko!"

The two of them laughed, abruptly.

"Still," Francesca continued, "I think we should start
with Sophia Tomaselli. We should question Morando
again also, of course, but I doubt he'd say anything. If
this mysterious woman—"

"*Female*, Francesca—not 'woman.' Trust me. The
distinction, if you understood it, would be even more
important to you than to me."

" 'Female,' then. If this female is an accomplice of
his, at this point he'd never tell us. Even that she exists,
much less her identity."

"Why? He seems eager enough to tell us everything
else."

"Because Morando is expecting he'll be executed,
when he's returned to Venice. A traitor's death, too, his
legs broken first." For a moment, she glared. "Thanks
to those idiot men! That includes you, Eneko! A lesson:
Never tell a man you're going to execute him, if there's
any chance he might still have information you want. You
just eliminated any motive for him to keep talking."

Eneko scowled. "He was guilty of—"

"*Who cares?*" Francesca slapped the armrests of her chair with exasperation. "Why does a whore have to keep reminding priests and devout knights that justice belongs to the Lord? Ours is the province of practicality, damnation!"

Eneko's lips quirked. "I believe it's 'vengeance' that belongs to the Lord, Francesca, though I understand the point. Nor, by the way, have I ever called you a 'whore.'"

She shrugged. "It's just a word. Means nothing to me, to be blunt. And to get back to the point, Morando won't tell us anything because perhaps the only hope he has left—however faint it may be—is that his accomplice, if she remains at large, might somehow rescue him from his predicament. Yes, yes, it's a very faint hope—criminal associates are hardly noted for their personal loyalties and devotion. But, who knows? There might be some deep tie between them. And, even if there isn't, a man expecting a noose will hope for anything."

"Ah. That's why you think Tomaselli would know—"

Francesca shook her head. "We should question her also, but I doubt we'll get anything useful. The problem in *her* case being somewhat the opposite. Too much talk instead of too little. That woman is driven by spite more than anything else. At one point in her interrogation, you may recall, she named half the women in the fortress as being witches participating in regular Black Sabbaths. She had Maria Verrier copulating with Satan himself, while the podesta's wife—" She threw up her hands. "Ah, never mind! But you see my point. How reliable is the information given to us by a woman who'd insist that Renate De Belmondo—at her age!—was . . . well. You remember. You were there."

Lopez grimaced. He'd been present for most of Tomaselli's interrogation. Sophia, hysterically, had swung from protesting complete innocence at one moment to claiming, in the next, that she was the least guilty of several thousand women in the Citadel. The accusations she'd made regarding Maria Verrier and the podesta's wife had been particularly grotesque.

"I see your point. But, that being true, what do you mean by suggesting we start with Tomaselli?"

"We need to start tracing Sophia's associations. Not by asking *her*, but others. I'll have Mouse start working on that."

"Mouse" was the nickname Francesca had given to the best agent she'd started employing, since she arrived on Corfu. Eneko had met the man three times, but could never quite remember what he looked like afterward. When he'd commented to Francesca to that effect, she'd simply looked very smug.

"I'll tell Mouse to start with Stella Mavroukis, Maria's friend," Francesca mused. "That woman knows all the gossip there is to know about this island. Kérkira and the Citadel, anyway."

"What would you like me to do?"

"Eneko, would you be able to recall—precisely—when each instance of this 'female magic' took place?"

Slowly, Lopez nodded. "Yes, I think so. Diego sensed it, too—and sometimes Francis and Pierre—so we can compare our memories. Yes. I should be able to reconstruct it. What good will that do?"

"Maybe none," replied Francesca, shrugging. "But you never know. This sort of work is like trying to piece together a broken tile. The more pieces you have, the more likely it is that you will succeed."

Prince Manfred came into the room, at that point. His cheerful smile vanished like the dew under Francesca's glare.

"And *you*! If I succeed in piecing this all together—I *will* expect you to exercise your power and offer Morando a pardon. A commutation, at least. So that he can confirm whatever my suspicions are."

"What are you talking about? Piece what together?"

"*Manfred!*"

"Yes, darling. Certainly."

Eneko laughed. "These are the times when I know celibacy is a blessing."

"*Eneko!*"

"Sorry, Francesca. It's true."

❖   ❖   ❖

His lust satiated, Saluzzo's anger had faded also. He sprawled across her limply.

"Paulo, he *forced* me," Bianca said, in a pleading tone. "He held a knife to my throat."

Saluzzo grunted. The sound was skeptical, but Bianca could sense there was no longer any danger that he would strike her again.

That was good. She was having a hard enough time as it was, restraining her fury. The bastard was *heavy*.

Her hands began stroking his back. Saluzzo would think she was still trying to placate him. In actuality, she was trying to determine if her incantations had succeeded.

Yes. She could feel the small nubs of the wings, just under the shoulder blades. They'd remain vestigial, until she spoke the words of power.

Double-checking, her left hand stroked his brow. Yes, she could feel the slight nubs there also.

Unfortunately, her apparent caresses were stimulating Saluzzo again. His own hands began moving. Bianca resigned herself to another unpleasant few minutes. There was no way, in the circumstances, to do the rituals needed to allow Saluzzo to wallow in his own sexual fantasies.

So be it. Immortality had its prices. At least he wouldn't be as rough this time.

Although—

"*Ow!* Paulo, you have *got* to start trimming your fingernails."

A bit puzzled, he raised his head and glanced at his fingernails. "How did they get so long?" he wondered.

"You're careless, that's how." She took the sting from the reproach by nuzzling him. "Just keep them trimmed, will you?"

She decided it would be best not to comment on his toenails. Those would be getting shorter soon, anyway. Shorter, wider, and much thicker, as his feet began to change. In fact, she'd have to take steps to slow down the transformation. Even a thug—and this one was Florentine, after all—would start wondering why he was walking around on hooves.

PART XII
November, 1539 A.D.

Chapter 81

"And how are you doing at fending off the pursuit of the young ladies of Corfu, young man?" asked the governor's white-haired wife as they talked in a break during the soiree that was Corfu Citadel's attempt at maintaining a facade of normalcy in spite of the siege. The attempts were pitiful, looked at from one angle; but, after being under siege for half a year, the defenders needed them.

Benito decided he liked Renate De Belmondo, even if he'd rather have been having a glass of wine down with the Arsenalotti. "Oh, I'm not trying too hard."

That was true enough. He simply wasn't interested. Other than their physical charms, the "young ladies of Corfu" lacked salt. If he'd said the moon was green, they'd have agreed with him.

It had amused Benito at first to be considered a prize. But it had come as a shock to realize that more than one of the delicately bred young damsels of Corfu's high society, never previously in a man's company without a duenna, would happily lift her skirts on the floor of her parlor for the mantle of his name, his position with the Doge and his reputation as hero. As an actual person he was unimportant. He could have been a hunchback or a pygmy able to speak in short grunts only. It was his position that made him valuable—grandson of the Old Fox, second son of Valdosta, friend to the Doge, brother to the Young Lion, confidant of Prince Manfred.

Political power, a coin he held as debased to the point of worthlessness, was the true gold to them.

Then there were the real hero-worshipers. They were almost worse.

"He was complaining about the lack of spice here only yesterday, Contessa," said Manfred, grinning at Benito.

She waved her fan. "Well. If it's 'spice' you're after, I would think you'd want to consort with the ladies of our little covey of degenerates and try one of their Roman-esque orgies. Except that they seem to be keeping a very low profile, these days. They used to be the glitter of these little affairs."

Benito snorted. "I think I want a girl to chew me out, not chew me up."

The contessa smiled. "The best kind, those. They probably remind you of your mother."

He shook his head. "You obviously didn't know my mother, Contessa."

Before this conversation could go into details about his mother, Benito was glad to see Von Gherens bump-ing through the butterfly crowd, like a steel bumblebee. "Prince Manfred," he said without bothering to excuse himself for interrupting. "Emeric's doing an inspection of his troops. It looks like he's planning something. You'd better come and have a look."

"Very well," said Manfred. "You'll excuse me, milady."

"You coming, Benito?" asked Von Gherens. "There is someone I want you to see."

So Benito went along, tagging behind Falkenberg, who had been doing an uncomfortable job of bodyguarding. He knew it was a put-up job that Manfred had organized to save himself from sitting through a second hour of a hard seat and bad music. Well, Benito didn't mind being out of there either.

"As it happens, Emeric really is out and about," said Von Gherens to Benito, "and we really do want you to look at one of his companions. We think we last saw him in Venice. We'll go down to the main gatehouse. You get the best view from there."

The late autumn air was cool and dry, and that dryness lent great clarity. The enemy trenches and earthworks across on the Spianada were so visible it was possible to see the rough mortaring between the stones. Von Gherens looked to a knight staring across from the battlements. "Are they still there, Klaus?"

The knight nodded. "Yes. They're just at that end of the rampart. They should move across soon."

They waited. And, sure enough, men moved from one earthwork to the next. It was a pity that accuracy on the cannons was so imprecise, and that the king and his generals were out of range of arquebusiers. "There."

The blond head stood out clearly against the dark background. Benito squinted. If only it were closer! He gritted his teeth. "It could be Aldanto. Damn his soul to Hell. It could be."

"Klaus here is long-sighted. He saw him in Venice, during the troubles there. He says it is him. By the walk."

"If Erik was here, I'd say we'd have to stop him going out to look," said Manfred. He glanced at Benito. "No, Benito. *No.*"

"I'm not doing anything useful here. Besides sitting with Umberto and 'Lessi."

"No, Benito. No," repeated Manfred firmly.

Benito shrugged his shoulders. "I'll see you later. I want to go and look for something in among my gear."

"So," said Emeric, glaring at the Citadel, which, after all these months, still refused to fall. "We've lost four ships. All at night. All in the north. And at last count—"

His voice was rising dangerously. "—over two hundred horses. And more than seventy men." He pointed an accusing finger at Caesare. "You said you'd catch Hakkonsen. You and that yellow dog of yours. As far as I can work out, the situation has simply gotten worse. So, my involuntary and so-far-useless ally. *Where is he?*"

Caesare looked at Emeric with empty eyes. "We have a traitor at last. We will have either him or his woman soon. And given the kind of man he is, we will have him if we take her."

Emeric looked at him with narrowed eyes. "Where did you find a traitor? The peasants are terrified of the idea. They'd rather die. We've tried."

"Word has spread that the Libri d'Oro we captured are being reestablished on their lands."

"Ah. That policy has played handsome dividends. It is always easier to corrupt the leadership than the people. And it achieves more."

If Benito had remembered he had it, in the early days after Caesare turned out to be as false a hero as possible, he would have burned it. But it had stayed tucked away somewhere in his gear at the *Casa* Dorma. He certainly wouldn't have brought it along to Corfu. But, as he'd been sitting in jail, some anonymous servant had packed it along with just about anything he owned that was reasonably presentable. So, it had come into the governor's palace in the Citadel, along with a corded bag of other clothes and bags of grain and spare weaponry and whatever else he could carry easily. He'd seen it while looking for spare stuff Maria could cut up to make winter clothes for Alessia. The fabrics that the *Casa* Dorma had clad the younger Valdosta ward in were the absolute finest. Finer than Maria could dream of buying. And, damn her pride, she wouldn't take money.

When he'd found the silk scarf, he'd decided that he wouldn't give that to Alessia. Some residual trace of Aldanto might cling to it. Maria might just recognize it, too. She noticed clothes. And if she wouldn't take money from Benito . . . she certainly would have nothing to do with Caesare, in any shape or form.

But Benito remembered how Luciano Marina had used Maria's scarf to give them some idea whether she was alive or dead. Perhaps Eneko Lopez could do the same. With the scarf in a pocket, Benito went in search of the Basque priest.

He wasn't at the Hypatian chapel. In fact, it took Benito some time to track him down. He spotted Father Francis first. He was trying to be unobtrusive, but definitely up to something. Benito didn't disturb him in whatever it was. He walked on, and ran into another of the tight-knit group; this time it was Diego. And around the third corner, Lopez.

"Father Lopez, you don't do this well," said Benito calmly, as he walked past.

Eneko Lopez was a man of deep faith and great patience. So he didn't swear at Benito. He did turn around and let his breath hiss between his teeth. He gave Benito a look that would have turned many a man's wavering footsteps back to the paths of righteousness.

"Valdosta! This is difficult—and we're trying to be unobtrusive."

Benito looked about calmly, and pretended to catch sight of something on one of the rooftops. He leaned back casually against the wall and stared at it, while speaking very quietly out of the corner of his mouth. "Well, Father Eneko, it looks like I'd better teach you how to do that. It's something bad men do well. Good men, by the looks of it, do it badly. I was taught by one of the worst. I think you all need lessons and I'd be glad to help."

Eneko Lopez sighed. "Let me get the others, Benito. We may as well go back to the chapel. You may have a point. And what we're hunting is not just bad, but evil to the core."

"I'll see you there."

Back at the Hypatian chapel Benito explained. "If you look like you belong, no one looks twice at you. If you look like you're doing something perfectly ordinary, for a reason anyone can figure out without even thinking about it, no one is interested. On the other hand, if you skulk, all in the same habits, and look at a building furtively while muttering, you stand out like a bunch of daisies in a coal scuttle. At least one of you needs to move out of these clothes. Become a seller of something. Beads perhaps."

They all looked dubious. He sighed. "Let's work this out. How long does this—whatever it is that you're doing—take you?"

Francis answered immediately. "About three hundred heart-beats, to detect sorcerers. Perhaps a little less, in the case of the female one we're after. She's powerful and skilled, but careless."

"The night-soil cart."

All four of them blinked at him in confusion. "What?"

asked Eneko, after a moment. "Can you explain that rather remarkable statement?"

"It trundles along all the streets, stops, people load their buckets, and it trundles on. Easy to stop it in the right spot. It stinks, so no one stays near it longer than they have to. It's the perfect cover for anything one of you wants to do. As for the other two of you—one of you should get a shill and argue religion with him. Stop and argue at whatever point you need to stop. The shill can argue, loudly, drawing as much attention to himself as possible. You do your ritual, while you just nod and frown."

"And the third?" Eneko asked.

"Ah, the third one can stop and preach at passersby; say something a little bizarre, or preach about the end of the world coming soon. Then he can do a few moments in prayer. He'll look like any other religious lunatic, and no one ever pays any notice of them."

"It appears Aldanto taught you well," said Eneko, dryly.

"Yeah. Well, he was using us for his work, or he wouldn't have. He was like that. Look, that's what I wanted to talk to you about." He pulled the scarf out of his pocket. "Can you tell me if the owner of this is on the island?"

Eneko Lopez looked at the scarf. "It is possible. It requires the same spells we use to trace anything that was once the property of someone else. Why? Who does it belong to?"

"Caesare Aldanto." His voice was flat.

Lopez looked askance at Benito. "I thought he had drowned, young man."

"He's been reliably reported as alive. In fact, I *think* I recognized him myself, today, at a distance. He was also reported heading back to Odessa. I want to know if he's really here. If he is here, Manfred, Francesca and Eberhard will want to know for the implications that it will have on the situation."

"Odessa!"

Father Francis looked at the piece of bright cloth. "It would explain the Chernobog traces, Eneko. Perhaps he is an emissary."

"I thought he was just an opportunist and a traitor," said Eneko, slowly. "I thought we'd dealt directly with all of the demon's vessels. Why do you think he's here?"

"We think we saw him from the battlements. Hard to tell . . . but the way he walked, the posture, the head-color, and the fact that he was seen in Constantinople some months before all this blew up." Benito shrugged. "That's why I'm asking."

Eneko took up the scarf. "This could be exceptionally dangerous. We're deprived of some of our usual protections. Still . . . we know that we have come here to confront him. Let us try this thing, taking courage in faith."

Benito watched as they prepared. The scarf was placed over a chalice of holy water. The wards placed . . . Uriel too. Even if the archangel did not respond, he would still be there. Then, all of the priests placed a hand on the cloth.

Benito's Latin did not extend to much beyond "Deus," so he didn't recognize anything they were chanting.

Suddenly, the scarf burst into flames. Not ordinary flames, either; these were greenish, and altogether nasty-looking.

The only sign of alarm was in the widening of their eyes. The priests fell back a step, and began chanting something different; it *sounded* different, too, harsher, and confrontational— Benito got the impression of swords being drawn, though no weapon was in sight. The water in the chalice vaporized with a violent hiss, as the flame changed color, this time to a dark, glowing purple. At this point, a horrible scalp-crawling howl arose from the flame itself, a howl that cut right through Benito's head.

The chalice melted in part, and the burning shred abruptly gathered itself into a ball. Then it started moving; it bounced off the table and rolled rapidly out of the door.

"Stop it!" yelled Eneko.

As soon as it was outside, the flames gathered new life, and the ball doubled in size in the blink of an eye. Without thinking, simply obeying the priest, Benito did one of the most stupid things he'd done in a lifetime of doing stupid things. He stamped on it, grinding it into the earth.

The Saint Arsenius medal on his chest grew hot, briefly. Then Benito stepped back from the ash fragments. The dead ash fragments.

Eneko grabbed him with one hand, holding up a relic in the other. *"Let that which cannot abide the name of Christ depart!"* he commanded.

"It has already gone, Eneko," said Diego. He looked wonderingly at Benito. "You are both a very crazy and a very lucky young man. You just *stood* on a demonic emissary of Chernobog."

"It must have been weakened and limited by the holy place, by the holy water and the blessed vessel," said Francis in a shaky voice.

Benito examined the soles of his footwear and shrugged. "Well, my holy medal got hot, but I can't say it even scorched my boots."

Eneko held out a hand. "Let's see this medal," he said grimly.

Benito took it out from next to his skin. Eneko examined it as did the others.

"It is an old one . . . and undoubtedly genuine," said Eneko, thoughtfully. "How did you get a real Saint's relic, Benito?"

He raised his eyebrows. "It was given to me by the Hypatian monks in Messina, after I did them that little favor."

"I don't think they realized what a valuable gift they gave you," said Diego, "or what a powerful one."

"Or how well it would serve the church," said Eneko, exhaling a little sigh of relief. "Forgive me, Benito. 'Stop it' was meant for my comrades, not for you."

Benito shrugged. *He* was quite certain that the Hypatians of Messina knew exactly what they had given him; after all, it was meant to reward someone—even a thief—for returning some rather valuable property. And just perhaps, because you never knew with the Hypatian magicians, they might have gotten an inkling that he would be going into spiritual and magical danger. "It worked. And I'm the one who got you to try this in the first place."

"Well, you have your answer. Caesare Aldanto is here, indeed. And he is possessed by the Black Brain, Chernobog."

The priest sighed. "This calls for more than we four can do. This calls for the Knights of the Holy Trinity. Perhaps true steel and faith can destroy this thing as magic cannot."

Benito took a sideways glance at the man. He appeared in earnest. There were times when Benito wondered whether the intense Basque cleric was in the real world or not. "There is a siege out there, Eneko. A whole army between Aldanto and the Knights."

"If he is destroyed, Chernobog will be one factor removed from the siege." Lopez sounded earnest—but also resigned. After all, how was even a single Knight going to slip out unnoticed?

Benito shook his head. "I wouldn't mind doing it, Eneko. But it is a question of how."

"If it means going outside the wall, then it must be done," said Lopez.

"Fine. You tell Manfred to let me go. He's already forbidden me to try. I haven't said I am going to listen, though." He paused. "You know, there *is* one Knight out there already. Erik Hakkonsen. And if *he* knew Aldanto was alive, and worse, a minion of Chernobog—"

He let that percolate into Lopez's mind. "Still, you have to talk Manfred into letting me go over the wall or I can't tell him."

Eneko sighed. "I will. If in that brief encounter I divined it right, then he is seeking something in country-side. Erik could perhaps deal with him. Ideally, I should like to be there. While this is a perilous foe—like all slaves, it would lack most of the strength of Chernobog. It would still be very dangerous. Certain relics could limit it. That medal of yours, for instance."

Benito looked down. "And to think I nearly didn't tie it to my belt when I was disguising myself as a slave."

"It is a sailor's talisman. It might just be what kept you afloat," said Francis.

Mindaug noticed that the Grand Duke was distinctly short of breath. And that his jowls beneath the mask were almost gray. He hardly seemed to hear the news that the Venetian Atlantic fleet had been forced to retreat from the pillars of Hercules.

He wondered what had just happened, but knew that he would never learn. Jagiellon would never, ever tell a subordinate about anything that had given him so much as a moment of weakness.

Manfred rubbed his chin. "Getting out there . . . Well, Eneko. You have a spy—no, two, you say—with some ability at black magic to catch. Who is more important? And can your companions do it without you?"

Eneko Lopez pursed his lips and thought a while.

"Chernobog is a great threat. On the other hand . . . the cunning of these magicians, whoever they are—is almost worse. I suppose this fight is against Emeric and his minions first. And we need four for the cardinal points. But . . ."

"But me no buts, man of God," said Manfred, firmly. "I'll have Klaus on watch. If we get a chance again like today where we can maybe get Emeric and Aldanto . . . we'll sally. Speed and steel. We can get away with it at the moment. The captain-general isn't playing the role he was since his wife got herself into trouble."

Being a fugitive hampered Fianelli's movements, thought Emeric, studying again the latest reports his agent had sent through. But the man was capable and had found a safe hideout. So. It was time to destabilize the military structure of the enemy from within. Fianelli had mercenaries still on his payroll.

The commander must die. And so should this Benito Valdosta. He'd become an icon in the Citadel. A symbol. Well, he'd be a dead symbol, proving how long Emeric's arm was.

Chapter 82

Only a flicker of movement in the window saved Benito. He rolled just in time. The crossbow bolt was buried to the flight-feathers in the bed. Benito stared at the bolt. Felt his neck; looked at the broken glass; got up and went over to the mirror. His neck had a fine cut from the touch of the barb.

A crossbow was slow to reload. By the time the bastard in that tree reloaded, Benito was going to be shoving his rapier right up the place the would-be assassin deserved it.

But by the time he got there . . .

There was no one in the tree. No one anywhere around. In fact, there might just as well never have been anyone there at all. Except for that crossbow bolt in the pillow.

Ten minutes later, Benito, crossbow bolt in hand, was in Manfred and Francesca's chamber.

"Manfred. I worked with him for years. This," he held up the bolt, "stinks of something Caesare would organize, if he didn't do it himself. He can't fly, so this must be something a hireling did. But I'll bet it was at his orders. He and his master know we found them. Now they're out to kill me, personally. Well, I won't sit still while they do it. And I don't care what you say about it."

"You could be right," said Francesca. "Indirectly, at

least. It would have been Fianelli who gave the actual order, though, not Caesare. He's still somewhere in the Citadel, and his three goons have evaded capture also."

She turned to Manfred. "My dear, you are going back to living in a Koboldwerk shirt, now that they seem to be turning to crude assassination. You're a target, too."

Manfred rubbed his jaw thoughtfully. "Look, Benito, I understand what you're getting at. But . . ."

"But this fortress is flue-full of conspirators, spies, and traitors. I don't know who, or what, to trust—sweet Jesu, man, what can I do if I can't even be safe in my own bed?"

Manfred winced. Benito kept going while he had momentum. "Aside from anything else, out there, they seem to have sorted out the treachery problem. I'm safer running with Erik than I am here. Besides, if we get the chance I want Aldanto's head." He knew what his voice sounded like, and he moderated it before Manfred decreed he was too emotionally involved to go safely. "Look, it might not be Aldanto, but all the signs point that way, and I agree with Eneko. Get rid of this assassin, this agent of Chernobog—whoever, or whatever he is—and we'll get rid of half the menace."

"*Will* you let me finish?" asked Manfred irritably. "What I was trying to say is the story of your exploits getting in and out of this place is now common property. You can bet your last penny that Emeric has had a full report. You can bet you're being watched. You can also bet that Emeric has done his damnedest to make sure you don't use those ways again. We've seen the beach patrols. The small-craft screen. It's a lot harder. The chance of you making it into the slave encampment, never mind out again, has vanished."

Benito shrugged. "I'll have to think of something else then."

"What I was going to suggest is that we do this the old-fashioned way. Von Gherens and I were just saying we are letting the enemy have too much leisure to do what they feel like. Those causeways are basically both repaired. We're going to lose what advantage the water gives us when they are able to attack in large numbers at will.

We thought we might use one of these misty mornings we've been having to damage their little causeway, and make Emeric concentrate on defending his siege camp more. From this side, as well as Erik's side."

Manfred grinned. "So what do you say, young fellow? Get you on a good horse and have a little gallop. I won't promise to take you to the other edge of Emeric's camp, but in the chaos, mist, and few nice little fires . . . We'll dress you up as a Croat horseman and you should get yourself to the far side and out easily enough. It'll beat this swimming or sailing, eh?"

Benito groaned.

"It sounded like a good plan to me," said Manfred, a little defensively. "Given the mist and the fact that there hasn't been a sally except in response to an attack, they won't be expecting it. Von Gherens was just saying their entrenchments on the Spianada are too central. Emeric wanted the space to marshal his cavalry, no doubt, but it'll work in our favor."

"It's the horse part I was groaning about. I fall off the damn things."

Manfred chuckled. "There had to be something you weren't much good at."

"I can't dance. And Marco says I can't cook, either."

Francesca gave a little snort of laughter. "But a little bird told me you can change diapers," she said mischievously.

Manfred stared incredulously at Benito and then burst into laughter.

Maria listened to Benito in silence. Her expression grew more severe as he talked.

Then she stood in silence, looking at him for a while. Finally she said: "I don't suppose anything I say will stop you."

"No. I just stopped by to say good-bye, and to see Alessia and Umberto. I had to stop and see my favorite baby."

Maria shook her head. "Have you ever even touched another one?" She sighed. "Wait here. I want you to take something with you."

She came back a few minutes later with a wheel-lock pistol. "Kat gave it to me. You take it with you. And promise me this. If you get close to Caesare, blow his guts out before he gets too close. Remember, he'll mislead you with his talk. Don't give him a chance. And don't miss."

Clinging to the saddle, Benito cursed all horses. There had to be a better way to travel fast overland. Had to be!

Chariots. Or cutting canals everywhere. Or . . . *anything*. Trained giant serpents such as there were reputed to be in far-off Africa. Or dragons, as in far-off Qin. Or flying carpets. *Anything* but an idiot animal that went up and down in order to go forward.

True, the gallop hadn't been as bad as he'd expected. True, too, a grinning *Ritter* had had to haul him back upright when he'd started that slide down the side of the horse during the charge. But—like the raid on the Hungarian camp—it had been pretty successful.

The Hungarians were totally unprepared for those inside the Citadel to take the offensive. The men had settled into the humdrum of siege. Cannon fire every now and again. Daytime arquebus fire to slow down any signs of repair work on the walls. Otherwise sit around. Sleep if you could. Play dice. Eat. Keep a weather eye behind for an officer. The assault would come, when they had to go in and face enemy fire, but for now . . . the worst you had to fear was a work party or being part of the outer perimeter guards and patrols. That was dangerous. This was just military routine.

Sleep while you could. Even in the front trenches, a good two thirds had been in dreamland. The night workers on the causeway were already pulled back. The sea-mist was blowing and swirling. It would burn off in an hour or two, having given the cracked, dry earth no relief.

The mist swallowed sound quite well. The Knights' scouts had advanced cautiously, on foot, with their trumpets in hand. Seventy or so yards back, the Knights, a hundred of them, had come forward at a walk. They'd been able to get right onto the causeway—and the scouts off the far side—before the trumpet had called them to charge.

Yes, it had all gone well. Benito hoped the retreat had gone just as well. He hadn't stayed around to find out.

Instead he'd discovered the two drawbacks to Manfred's plan. The one was that he was still very close to the Hungarian camp and it was now full daylight and the horse was a lot more in control than he was. The other drawback was trotting. Now all he had to do was find Erik without the two downsides killing him.

He decided the best thing for it was to abandon the horse. He must be at least a couple of miles from the camp now.

A shot boomed from a nearby hillside.

Benito abandoned the horse by falling off into the dry broom. Up the hill he saw two Corfiotes scrambling for cover. Lying there, trying to catch his breath, Benito decided that the Croat's headgear had to be the next to go, before he was killed by own side.

Falkenberg came running in. "Leopoldo's been shot! A crossbow again."

Manfred's chair fell over as he sprang to his feet. "Damn! We should have expected this." He started heading for the door.

Von Gherens blocked his way. "Not without plate armor. And that Koboldwerk mail shirt. And Francesca, he's to stay away from all windows until we find this crossbow man. Leopoldo may live. Benito was lucky. Next time we may not be so lucky."

Francesca nodded and steered the prince back to a chair. "It's left a power vacuum, Manfred. The captain-general hasn't been near his office for two weeks. He's just abandoned things. Commander Leopoldo has been running the defense of the Citadel since then."

"And much better run it has been," Manfred said grimly. "You say he's not dead?"

"Well, not yet. He's being taken to the hospital."

"Is he conscious?"

"He was a short time ago. Cursing ferociously, in fact."

"Go there, Von Gherens. Get him to appoint a successor, if he's *compos* to do so. One of his junior officers will fill the post on seniority otherwise. And that may be a poor idea right now."

Von Gherens came back a little later. "The opium seems to be making him think clearly," he said with a wry smile. "He's just nominated Falkenberg to fill his shoes."

"But Falkenberg isn't part of the Venetian forces," protested Francesca. "The captain-general is bound to kick up a fuss."

Eberhard of Brunswick cleared his throat. "You could second him to the service of Commander Leopoldo, Prince. That would be completely legal."

The one-eyed Falkenberg grunted. "If this means I have to take orders from Tomaselli, forget it."

Eberhard smiled. "Well, technically you'd be taking orders from Leopoldo, as you would have to be seconded directly to his service. And Leopoldo would be taking orders from Tomaselli. We could persuade him to be too ill to pass them on. Of course this does presuppose Leopoldo staying alive. If he dies, it is another matter."

"You really could have trusted me with the sword, Benito," said Erik. "I would have given it back to you. I think."

Benito blinked. Svanhild was definitely giving Erik a sense of humor. Which was strange, as Benito didn't think she had had much of one to share. Perhaps it was just that the Icelander was so much happier.

"I needed it, Erik. Otherwise I'd have trusted you. Truly. But there is someone I have to deliver the sharp end of it to."

"And who would that be?"

"A mutual friend who had a crossbow bolt delivered to my pillow a couple of days back. A blond fellow with excellent classical features that the girls all admired. At least, they used to. I'm not sure what he looks like after all he's been through."

Erik's head shot forward like a snapping turtle. "Aldanto! He's here?"

Benito nodded. "And he hasn't changed except for the worse, either. He's joined up with another old friend that you've met before. With your old tomahawk."

The look in Erik's eyes was something that gave Benito a shiver. "I want him."

But Benito was not about to back down this time. "You'll have to stand in line, Erik. I've got a claim on behalf of my mother, my brother's wife's family, and Maria. Not to mention myself. And this time I intend to get him. If I fail, he's yours."

Erik looked speculatively at Benito. "He doesn't play by the rules, you know."

"I know.

"So should we play tag with him?" asked Erik, with a foxlike look. "I'll find out where he is. Our network of informers is unbelievable, especially since your jailbreak." He grinned at Benito. "Your status on this island is at a level that'll never survive the reality!"

Chapter 83

The middle-aged man looked about nervously. "You're sure we can't be seen or overheard?"

Caesare Aldanto shook his head. "The dog would have detected anyone, Ambrosino. He can smell out the smallest trace of life over as much as two hundred yards. And we simply cannot be seen through the solid walls of the olive-press. You are satisfied with what you have heard from Count Quatrades?"

Giuliano Lozza's uncle nodded. "Yes. I was surprised, to tell the truth."

The empty-eyed blond shrugged. "Why? King Emeric wants an income off the lands he conquers. He'll need vassals who understand local conditions, local peasantry, and how to get the most out of them."

Ambrosino's eyes were wary. "I would have thought he would have given the land to his own nobles, Signor Aldanto."

"There is enough. And as you have seen, Count Quatrades is well treated." If Aldanto sounded indifferent, it was for a good reason. He was.

"And protected?" Ambrosino asked sharply. "The peasantry have become violent. If there is one thing these peasants should never have been allowed, it is encouragement to rebel. To take up arms. The Venetians have planted and nurtured a seed in this war that will be impossible to put back into the seed-pod. I've said as much but they don't want to listen to me."

The Magyar captain who had accompanied Aldanto laughed coarsely. "King Emeric has a way of dealing with that. There are always more peasants."

"Nonetheless. I want that estate in the Ropa valley, but I also want a full-time guard of least twenty men stationed there. And five thousand ducats." He raised his chin; clearly, he was not going to be bargained down.

Aldanto nodded. "We have brought the gold. The bags are behind you, on that press-shelf."

Greed overrode the man's nervousness. He looked into a number of the bags eagerly, spilling gold pieces.

"We have had engineers from the army repairing the villa on the estate," said Aldanto, smoothly. "You could go there now, if you can tell us where to find Hakkonsen. Or the girl."

Ambrosino snorted with contempt. "You'd need a lot of men to take Hakkonsen in that spot. It's got three ways out, and he has good lookouts. Hakkonsen is planning a raid on Trembolino in two nights. You could ambush him."

"And why is he going to attack Trembolino?" asked the Magyar captain suspiciously. "That's where we are based!"

"I believe," said the middle-aged man slyly, "that they wish to kill a certain blond man. A man they call Caesare Aldanto."

The empty eyes gazed at the Corfiote aristocrat. "Why?"

"It appears that they want to repay some old scores with you, milord," he said, picking up every loose ducat and carefully putting them back where he had gotten them.

"That is an aspect I had not considered," said Aldanto. "Are you privy to the detail of Hakkonsen's plans?"

The man closed up the bags. "No. I'm not part of this raid. My nephew Giuliano is. I could have asked him, but I thought it best not to excite comment. We've had a bit of a falling out. Milord, if you could try and spare him? He and I have argued about the way things are being done, but he is still my sister's son."

"Of course. Families do have their differences, but blood is still thicker than water." Aldanto spoke with the ease of one who does not care what he promises. "Would you be able to guide, say, five of my men in, while the bulk of Hakkonsen's troops are trying to find me? We could be waiting for them when they return, with all the advantage of surprise."

The man coughed politely. "Five men? You would need fifty, milord."

"The five will do to open the path. We will have a hundred men out of our camp without it appearing too deserted, Signor Ambrosino; a hundred men, in blackened cuirasses. What's left will give them a fight, while we do our business."

Svanhild clung to him. "Couldn't someone else go, Erik? I worry so about you, my precious man."

Erik hugged her. "I worry about you, *elskling*. But I am going with that young rascal. He has the luck of the devil, so it should be fine."

She kissed him, but frowned, just a little. "I do not approve of Benito. He is not enough respectable for you, ja. And altogether too wild."

Erik patted her soothingly. "Never mind, love. When all this is over, my time of service to the Godar Hohenstauffen will be near an end, and we can go home and never see him again. He reminds me of Manfred a few years back, in many ways. And you don't disapprove of him, do you?"

"Oh, no. But he is a prince," she said, kissing him. The kiss turned into a longer kiss.

Outside the cave—which the Vinlanders had made unrecognizably comfortable, and Erik still felt terribly guilty about having to have Svan live in—someone cleared his throat. "Time to go, sir."

Erik recognized the apologetic voice. Lozza.

He had to smile to himself. Giuliano Lozza. Fat and unfit. Undisciplined and obsessed with revenge.

Then. He was now lean, athletic and tough as whipleather. Also now Erik's chief arms instructor. What a difference six months could make.

The curious thing was that Lozza hated to kill. He was, Erik admitted, better with a rapier than Erik would ever be. His father, possibly the greatest master of Bravura style, had started training him when he barely breeched. Giuliano used the weapon like other men used their fingers. He had the reflexes, and he had the strength. He just didn't like to kill. Erik was terribly afraid that such a weakness would kill him one day.

It was why he always paired Giuliano with Thalia. For one thing, Giuliano *would* kill anyone who came near her. He was as protective as a mother hen about the peasant girl. And Thalia, with her new net—carefully blessed—and the knife-skills Giuliano instilled into her, did not hesitate. Ever.

A strange relationship. Erik had never seen either so much as touch each other. She still called him "Master Lozza."

He kissed Svan for a last time and parted from her.

"Take care," she called after him.

"Do my best."

They rode through the darkness; Benito, as usual, clinging to his horse and swearing. Horses, even the most docile-natured, like the one they'd mounted him on, seemed to know Benito was not a rider and that he was afraid of horses. They sensed his nervousness and that made them skittish . . . which made Benito worse.

"Doesn't it seem odd, Benito, that Caesare Aldanto is out here, instead of with the main army?"

"Damn this animal," said Benito, in his mildest comment so far. "He's probably out here up to no good, Erik. Someone to be murdered, or spied on, or stolen from."

"And who do you think that could be, my young friend?" asked Erik, dryly.

"You or me at a guess. Probably you. Of course, he probably doesn't know who he's hunting."

Erik cantered a few more yards in silence. "I'll grant him this. He was very good with a sword. And he's not afraid to use it."

"Good with a sword he was indeed," Benito acknowledged grimly. "And if I get a chance, Erik, I won't give him an opportunity to use it. He's a master of dirty fighting. And one of the things he taught me was to never try to be fair in a fight. Kill your opponent before he kills you."

He ground his teeth, angrily. "I intend to return the favor of that lesson."

Caesare Aldanto might have been far more successful at seizing control of the canals of Venice had he been able, then, to select men as he did now. But he had perceptions of their natures and ability now that he didn't have then. The men he'd brought along for this expedition were killers. The most effective he could cull from an army. He'd principally stuck with cavalry since moving fast would be of the essence.

The other four accompanying Ambrosino into the defile should all have been hanged long ago. In a proper army, with the discipline to take half-mad killers out of their ranks and dispose of them, they would have been. These four would not only cheerfully perform atrocities on the defeated and the peasantry of the defeated, they'd perform them on their own comrades if they got the chance.

They reached the first sentries. Ambrosino called the password.

"Who's that with you?" asked the sentry.

"New recruits. Good men all."

"We can use . . . ahh!"

And they moved on. The yellow dog pressed against his flank. They talked as minions of the same master did: without audible words. The shaman sniffed. *The net-woman, she has been here, curse her name.*

I'll deal with her. Or the troops will.

Erik looked at the fires, at the sentries, not quite lazy enough in the darkness, and peered through the gloom at the horse paddocks. Something prickled his awareness. He looked at the horse-paddocks again. It was like ice water running down his spine.

"There's something wrong here. That's half the number of horses reported."

Benito looked. "Caesare!" he took Erik by the sleeve. "Mount up now. Let's get out of here. This smells of Aldanto and ambush."

Erik nodded. "Tomorrow is another day. We've got him tagged now. The country-people will tell us where he goes. We'll choose the time, not him."

"Svan will be pleased to have us home, unbloody."

Somewhere in the distance a horn sounded. It didn't mean anything to them and it was a good distance away.

"The Vinlanders are in the cave to the south there." Ambrosino pointed. "The others use the caves lower down. The very bottom cave is water-filled. It's their water supply and something to be very careful of. The valley over there is where the horses are kept. It's another way out. They can also go over the back there, but only on foot."

"Guards on both?"

"Of course. Hakkonsen leaves nothing to chance."

"Except you." Aldanto turned. "Sylarovich. Bring the cavalry up to that point. Tell them that any man that even so much as allows a harness to clink is dead. You saw the exits. Split three units of twenty off the troop. When I sound the horn, they must ride as fast as possible for each exit. Kill any guards and seal them off from escapees. The other forty are to take the caves, especially the top one. And tell them about the lower cave. We should have at least an hour to clean this lot out before the rest come back from the camp, very pleased with themselves. We should surprise them nicely."

Full dark, and Erik's nerves were on edge. They rode into the narrow gully that Erik had designated sole entry to the camp. Erik, at the head of the file paused . . . waiting for the request for the password.

Silence. And then distantly, a scream. Arquebus and pistol shots.

"*Ride!*" yelled Erik. "Ride! All of you get out of here!" But he himself was spurring his horse frantically, riding into the defile. Kari and his brother took off after him as if their tails were on fire.

Benito turned to the rest. "You heard him. You— Alexander. Take some of the boys to the top way out. And *Gino*. The other half of you to the valley way."

Alexander hesitated, and his horse curveted and danced sideways. "We need to follow our captain."

Benito aimed a blow at him. "You need to obey his orders! Now *move!*"

"Alpha group will go with me," Giuliano said calmly. "Omega takes the bottom way, and Theta, you will ride around to see if survivors need help. If there is nobody there, dismount and set up an ambush. Lower the horse-barriers. They will not ride out of here." These were the groups used in raids. They were each twenty strong. They were used to working together and each had its section leaders.

Perhaps it was that, or Giuliano's calm that did it. The troop split fast. As soon as they were on their way Benito began kicking the horse, to get it to follow. Erik and not the other horses. His will triumphed, to his surprise. Maybe the animal thought it was going to pasture down in the valley bottom. The stream had stopped flowing; but, thanks to the water-cave, they had water there and some grazing. Donkey loads of stolen Hungarian oats had added to that.

"Thalia, Georgio, Stephanos, Gigi, Marco. You will take the inner guard post. Stop any of them escaping and buy time for us if we need it to get out," said Giuliano Lozza, taking charge.

"Mikalos will go instead of me," said Thalia. "That calls for shooting. I can't shoot."

"Don't argue."

"Or what, master?" she said calmly.

"Please, Thalia." Giuliano wasn't quite begging.

"No."

Chapter 84

Svanhild had gone down to the horses, restless with a bright moon overhead. They were upset about something. She loved horses, and especially the steeds of the Magyar, which were superb. She'd talked with Erik about taking some home to the great plains beyond Cahokia. Apparently the Magyar steeds were bought from the Ilkhan and crossed with an old war-horse breed. She'd certainly never seen their like.

She walked among them in the moonlight, murmuring a bit of praise here, patting a neck or a flank there. Then she heard the thunder of galloping hooves. Erik must be back. So early? Something must have gone wrong. She gathered her skirts in order to run back toward the cave.

A group of cavalry thundered past her, heading for horse-paddocks she'd just come from. She ran for the cave and her brothers. She could see Bjarni, already out, sword in hand, running toward her, yelling and beckoning.

The main body of Caesare's cavalry had waited until the two blocking groups were past. Caesare mounted his horse. The yellow dog had gone ahead, scrambling up a steep limestone edge, claws scrabbling for a hold on the rock. It would attempt to deal with the guard on the upper footpath.

The shaman basically had to get out of the way. Horses

tried to trample the shaman if they smelled or saw him. The iron horseshoes were painful. Lead bullets the creature found harmless, but cold iron he liked not at all.

Now Caesare pushed forward and saw in the moonlight how things hadn't waited to begin going wrong. Those idiots going down to valley floor had broken open the horse-corrals. And ridden straight past his target! Horses, panicky and confused, were running back toward the camp.

He could see her, blond hair streaming, running in the moonlight. She'd never get to the men pouring out of the cave. As they began to charge into the little valley, Caesare saw her turn and look back.

And stop. Even amid all the other noise he heard the whistle she gave. The twist of horses that the rush of cavalry had released . . . stopped too. And, as a group, they began galloping toward her. They had less than half the distance to cover that Caesare did. And they had no riders to weigh them down.

Caesare knew that this one would have no trouble riding bareback. She'd get away!

He called for the shaman. The shaman was closer! Sliding and scrabbling, half falling, the yellow dog came down the slope from nearly straight above her. He would end virtually at her feet.

As, in dust and flurry and snapping teeth, the yellow dog cascaded toward her . . . Caesare saw that the horse herd was nearly at the woman. And then he realized what he'd done.

"GO! Leave her! Stay away!"

But the steepness of the slope meant that for all the pale creature's snarling and scrabbling the shaman-dog still ended up actually hitting Svanhild. It half knocked her over. The lead stallion reared.

Chernobog, looking through his slave's eyes, didn't understand horror in human terms. But he felt the slave's horror nonetheless, when he saw the blond woman and the yellow dog fall beneath the flailing hooves. The horror of failure. The horror of knowing what his master would do to him, when the woman died. Which, with iron-shod hooves pounding her as they tried to reach the yellow cur, was an inevitability.

The yellow dog, yowling with pain, exploded out of the side of the horse-mass. Straight toward Caesare.

The Magyar cavalry's horses felt just the same way about the yellow dog as the Corfiote guerillas' horses. Horses and humans had been together a long, long time. There was a deep bond between them. Only the true dogs hate the betrayer more. More than half of the main body of the cavalry charge, including Caesare, were unseated as the Hungarian horses tried to kill the yellow dog.

Erik arrived at a scene of pandemonium. It was apparent that Caesare's raid had run into more resistance than he'd expected. Part of the problem was horses. There were riderless horses, at least forty, milling in the narrow valley.

Standing in the middle of the slope were three Vinlanders. They were defending something against a considerable force. Defending it well, by the rampart of bodies. As Erik galloped toward them one Vinlander fell. Screaming like a banshee, Erik struck the flank of the attackers. He was vaguely aware of Kari and his brother beside him.

There were a good fifteen or so Magyars attacking the remaining Vinlanders, but the sudden furious attack drove them off, just as the second to the last Vinlander collapsed. Only big Bjarni remained standing. And it was plain that it was only sheer force of will that kept him up. "Erik," he croaked, his breath bubbling. "Svan. Take her home . . ."

Erik was already kneeling beside the crumpled form on the ground, his heart swelling until he thought it would choke him. He took her up, tears pouring down his face as he felt her bones grating against one another, felt the pulpy flesh moving in ways it never should. Gently, he called her, holding her. "Svan! Svan!"

She stirred in his arms. The horse hooves had left her body bruised and broken, the skull half-shattered. Her long blond hair was soaked with blood, looking black in the moonlight. "Erik." It was barely a whisper. "You came. Love you. Stay with me . . ."

He could not see for tears. "I'll never leave you, Svan. Never."

❖   ❖   ❖

When Benito and the others burst on the scene, Kari and his brother were desperately defending Erik, who was holding someone. Svanhild, Benito guessed, seeing the long hair in the moonlight. Erik seemed oblivious of his own impending death. Then, just as the impetuous Kari fell, Erik put his burden down. Stood up, picking up a sword from the ground as he did so. Even from here, Benito heard his scream. It was both heartbreak and pure rage.

And with Bjarni's great sword in his hands—a weapon so long it had had to be slung across the Vinlander's back—Erik went berserk.

Benito had heard of berserkers before. Now he realized that the magnitude of the truth defied the stories. In berserker rage Erik literally split a horse's head. Hewed two more attackers apart.

From downslope Benito heard Caesare yell: "We want him alive!"

Stupider things have been said, but not often. Benito didn't care. He was too busy fighting his way down the hill toward Caesare.

The thing that was Aldanto's puppet master saw through the puppet's eyes how one man could turn a battle. And that, far from being trappers, his troops were now surrounded, by men who knew the terrain. By men who were determined on vengeance, too. And in the middle of his Hungarians was a man seemingly possessed of superhuman strength, unstoppable, who was cutting down seasoned warriors like a scythe through cornstalks. Somehow this man had turned the situation from one where they outnumbered their surprised foes . . . into a developing rout.

He heard someone yell: "Just keep out of his way! He can't tell friend from foe."

The only trouble with this advice was that the newly arriving Corfiote irregulars were herding men toward their berserker. And fear—and the stupidity that it brings—was killing them fast.

It was time to intervene. The slave still had considerable

skills, one of them being with the sword. And if need be, Chernobog could draw on reserves of strength that might kill the slave. Later.

Then there was someone in his way, between him and his target. Someone who had once been a nobleman, by the ragged finery, and the dark wavy hair, not showing the rough crop of the peasantry. He was clean shaven too, which in itself was unusual, among these spiky rebels.

The slave had many "duel" assassinations to his credit. This fool would be one more. Chernobog allowed the reflexes of the slave to take over.

And came within an eighth of an inch of losing the slave's life. An accident, surely? The slave's one real attribute had been that he was a truly great swordsman. Chernobog, seconds later, realized that it was no accident. The swordsman had looked like he'd be another provincial aristocrat—full of delusions about his swordsmanship, and short on real skill or practice. A quick kill. A soft man, despite being lean and sun-browned. Chernobog could see it in the eyes. Doe's eyes. He could see it in the face. The fine lines there were those of someone more accustomed to a lazy smile than to anger. The slave Caesare was a lion to such men.

Except . . . this time the prey was a lot better with a rapier than Caesare Aldanto ever had been, or could have been. The swordsman's movements seemed almost effortless, fluid. Yet the blade moved faster than Chernobog's slave physically could. Caesare was driven back, forced back down the hill toward the opening of the lowest cave, the water-cave, fencing with one who could kill him in a heartbeat.

It also took the Black Brain very few of the slave's heartbeats to realize something else: The master-swordsman didn't *want* to kill.

So he lowered the sword point. Took the blade itself in his left hand and held the hilt out to the man. "I surrender!" he called out.

As the master-swordsman stepped forward to take the sword, Caesare stabbed him with the stiletto shaken from his sleeve. It struck something hard and skittered, cutting—but not, as intended, piercing the heart.

As he did this Ambrosino, the traitor, shouted and rushed to him, and grabbed at him. "You promised you wouldn't kill him!"

Caesare hit the traitor with the butt, and pulled back the stiletto to stab again.

Something hit him so hard he sprawled yards away, the stiletto gone. He'd been hit by the lead weights of the bird-net that the yellow dog had so dreaded. The woman threw herself over the fallen swordsman, protecting him with her body. Caesare staggered to his feet, snatching up the rapier he had pretended to surrender, from where it had fallen conveniently near at hand. She was now trying to pick the swordsman up.

So be it. Two for the price of one.

Then, a voice like doom behind him.

"Aldanto."

Caesare turned, slowly, and realized it was Erik Hakkonsen. Hakkonsen was at that final stage of berserk, when sanity returns—just before the berserker collapses.

Hakkonsen was bleeding from a dozen wounds and swaying with exhaustion. He was also intent on killing Caesare, even if it meant dying himself.

Hakkonsen, had he been in the peak of physical shape, would have been very evenly matched to the old Aldanto. Now his muscles were quivering with fatigue. And yet a will, a spirit harder than adamantine made Erik Hakkonsen drive Caesare back, back toward the water-cave.

One quick double twist-disengage, riposte, twist . . . and Erik's sword fell, clattered to the rocks.

"Die!" Caesare lunged forward. Somehow Erik managed to move so that the sword passed between his arm and ribs. He trapped the blade, holding Caesare's sleeve. The tomahawk came up.

The part of Caesare that was elsewhere used powers that could only be released in fleshy contact. A coup de grace of spirit world . . . only hampered by this place. Magical force, huge amounts of it flowed through from Chernobog, to the slave, and then into the Icelander. Coruscating rivers of power that should have burned and shattered the victim. Should have, but did not. Instead it seemed to flow through him and into the earth of Corfu.

Nonetheless, Hakkonsen fell back as if flung by some great force. He lay sprawled on the ground like a puppet with severed strings. The dry grass he lay on smoked.

"There's still me, Caesare."

The tiny part of Caesare that remained Caesare saw Benito Valdosta. An older, broader but not taller person, yet a very different boy from the one who had once idolized him. Benito had plainly hurt his one arm, as it was tucked inside his shirt.

"See this sword, Caesare Aldanto? It's my father's. Carlo Sforza. The Wolf of the North. He'd eat five of you for breakfast. I'm going to cut your head off with it."

The boy-man stalked closer. "You think you're a great swordsman, Aldanto."

"What's wrong with your arm, Benito?"

"Cut the tendons back there. The fingers aren't working. But that's all right, because I only need one hand to fence with you. If I hadn't cut it, I'd tie it behind my back."

Sheer bravado, Caesare was sure. Benito had always been prone to that mistake. He had the mental edge on the boy.

The boy was close now. Barely three yards off and walking in. *Fool.*

Benito stopped, just about within reach of a lunge. "I thought I told you not to brag when you fought unless you had a reason," said Caesare.

"You did." Benito smiled mockingly. "But I didn't always listen. You also said this business of saluting your enemy before you fence with them was an opportunity to kill someone, while they're sticking to fencing etiquette. But I've got a salute to give you from Maria."

Benito raised his sword.

As Caesare began to lunge . . . something slammed into his chest with the force of a mule kick, driving him down. His rapier went flying.

Dazed, Caesare looked up to see Benito drawing a wheel-lock pistol from the shirt where he'd hidden it—holding it in his supposedly maimed hand. The boy had fired right through the fabric. Some part of Caesare felt an odd little pleasure, then, realizing how much he'd taught the boy in happier days.

"It's Maria's," grunted Benito, holding the pistol up. Smoke was still drifting from the barrel. "It seemed a nice touch to me, you swine."

The cave was just behind the puppet, Chernobog realized. The puppet's vision began to blur. It was dying. But if he could lure the boy close enough . . .

Benito stepped in, hefting the sword.

Chernobog's power built—

And fled, hastily, from the mind and soul of the slave. The sword itself was blessed! And there was something about the boy himself—some strange *virtue* that would not allow the magic to even touch him.

Benito wished he could just turn away. But Caesare had always taught him: *Finish it. Be sure.*

And then the dying man spoke. The voice sounded . . . ecstatically joyful.

"Benito. Thank God! Kill me. Kill me, please. Kill me before it can get to me again. Please. Please! If you ever loved me—"

Suddenly something huge, black and slimy with a barbel-fringed long-fanged mouth launched out of the water. Benito barely managed to dodge aside, cutting at it.

Caesare didn't dodge and it seized him. The water closed over the monster and the blond assassin.

There might be a battle going on, but Benito sat down. There wasn't much of a battle left anyway. Caesare had been lying with his "I surrender," but the Hungarians had been similarly fooled. Unfortunately for them, it had been a case of "No quarter," after Caesare's treacherous about-turn.

Chapter 85

Some time later—probably somewhere near midnight, Benito guessed by the height of the moon—they were taking stock. Erik lay wrapped in a blanket beside Svanhild. His wounds were bandaged and the stump of one finger cauterized. He lay as still as death, his breathing weak, bloody and bubbling, his pulse, which could only really be felt in his throat, tremulous and faint. The physical wounds, even the one to the lung, he might survive. The greatest physical danger was that he had nearly bled himself white. But everyone knew it was that final magical blow that left him in the coma from which Benito doubted he would ever wake.

He looked dead. Svanhild was. It had seemed right to put them beside each other.

The cost to the insurgent camp had been high. All but one of the guards had been killed. Of the fifteen men and three women left in the camp—besides the Vinlanders—one survived. Of the Vinlanders—only Bjarni and Kari and two of the *duniwassals* might yet live. The youngest of Kari's brothers had been one of those who'd been in camp as part of Svanhild's guard.

There were some dead and some injured among the raiding party too, but by comparison they'd suffered lightly. Erik's berserker attack had cost the Hungarians dear in sheer numbers and in panic—trapping them between a human threshing machine and guarded exits.

The Vinlanders had cost the enemy at least thirty men.

It would take daylight and a collection of body parts to say just how many Erik had killed in his frenzy.

Of the hundred Magyar who'd galloped into this place, not one had escaped. Some thirteen were wounded. Some would die. A number had retreated into the store cave. They were still holed up there. The Corfiote irregulars were collecting firewood while they watched the cave mouth.

And there were three prisoners. Two who had surrendered to the guard on the upper way out. And Ambrosino.

Giuliano Lozza had bandages around his chest, but he'd very much taken charge of the camp. And now he came to his uncle.

"I always looked up to you. Trusted you, Uncle," said Giuliano quietly. "But my Eleni didn't. And neither did Thalia. They both tried to warn me in their ways. And both of them saved my life from the results of your treachery." He took a golden locket—a large one—perhaps three inches by two. There was a gouge through the gold-plate, revealing the harder metal underneath. The locket was so indented that it would never open again.

"One day I'll have her picture repainted. It was all I had left of her. There's a piece of my baby son's hair in there, too. You babbled on about family, about blood ties, about how important it is to support your own, no matter what. And then you betrayed us to the people who killed your kin."

"I . . . asked them to spare you. I tried to save you."

"And you killed our comrades. And now I am your judge, jury, and executioner. I find you guilty, guilty by all the gold in your pockets. Gold was worth more to you than blood. More than honor. I find you guilty of treason, of murder. Do you want to make your peace with God before I carry out the sentence?"

Ambrosino looked disdainful. "You'll never kill me. You haven't got the guts. You don't even kill rabbits on the hunt. You'll get someone else to do your dirty work."

"I'll do it," said Thalia.

Ambrosino gave her a look that was full of more contempt than if he had spat on her. "Peasant slut."

Giuliano put a hand on Thalia's shoulder. "It is a pity in a way that I am going to execute you. Otherwise I would challenge you to a duel and cut you into doll rags for insulting a good woman. And you know I could do it. But I am going to execute you as the ranking officer of this unit of the Venetian Corfiote Army. I am giving you a last chance to pray."

This time, Ambrosino spat.

Giuliano Lozza drew his sword and ran him through.

Ambrosino's mouth gaped wide widened. "You did it! You bastard! You—"

He coughed blood; his eyes rolled up. Giuliano withdrew the blade and turned away from the dying man.

"May god have mercy on his soul. Throw his body with the other carrion." His voice was hard. "Our own we will bury with honor. This lot we will dump outside their camp."

"There are the wounded. And the ones in the cave," said Benito. "What are we going to do with them?"

"Kill the lot of them," said one of the peasant-recruits. "Cut the throats of the wounded and the prisoners. Best way of dealing with vermin."

"What do we want?" asked Benito calmly. "A few more dead Hungarians? Or a lot of frightened ones? If you ask me, scared ones will make them weaker than a few more dead bodies. They sent their best, with a traitor, to ambush us. They were outnumbered by a smaller group of men. I don't see them telling their commanding officers that, though! By the time they get back, there will be thousands of us in the hills. I reckon we offer them a choice. They can live, stripped bare-ass naked, or they can die and we'll strip their bodies."

"Strip them?"

Benito grinned nastily. "They all wear those stupid helmets and that sash over their cuirasses. I suppose we can be grateful this wasn't a full-armor mission—they'd have been harder to kill—and I don't think armor is easy for people who've never worn it. I need a group of men in those clothes. I want anyone who sees us to take us for Magyar. And if we do that once, is there any reason for the Hungarians to assume we won't do it again? Fairly good chance we'll get some of them to shoot at each other. And they'll never be sure that patrol they see over in the distance . . . is it really their men over there?"

Giuliano nodded. "It makes every kind of sense. We'll make them nervous about everything. There'll be accidents."

"Tell me about it!" said Benito. "I nearly got shot by our supporters for wearing a Croat hat."

Giuliano sighed. "Well. We must get to it. Get those uniforms, get out of here. We need to get this camp broken and moved before dawn. My traitor uncle might have told them how to find this place as well as just showing them, and they might come looking. Moving our wounded is going to be difficult."

He sighed again. "Most of them are going to die, I'm afraid. We lack medicines or surgeons and quite a few, like Erik, can't ride. We can't abandon him. He is our leader. And he's a symbol of some fear to Emeric, or he wouldn't have sent this Aldanto hunting."

Benito shook his head. "Giuliano, Erik is not ever going to get better. Neither are a good three of the others, in their case for simple medical reasons. But Erik . . . My brother is the physician, and I wish he was here now, but I'm sure that what is wrong with Erik is magical. There is only one person that I know of on this island who could treat that: Eneko Lopez, or his companion Francis. And they're inside the Citadel. Erik meant a lot to you men out here, didn't he?"

Giuliano nodded. "He is a legend. More now, I suppose. The peasants refer to him as the ice-and-fire man. Or the hand of God."

"Right. I want to break into the Citadel—again. I'm beginning to feel like a ball tossed between inside and outside! I'll need at least fifteen, maybe twenty volunteers who are prepared to do something insane to keep Erik and the other badly wounded alive."

"Signor Valdosta, you always do the insane," said Thalia, who had come up quietly behind them. "I will volunteer. I owe you and Erik my life. I was not sure if I was grateful at the time. But I have decided I am glad to be alive after all."

"I wish you'd call me Benito. Everyone else does."

"She insists on calling me 'master,'" said Giuliano. "No matter how often I have said that we're comrades-in-arms now. And of course, yes. I am with you too. I owe him my sanity, my life, and it was my blood-kin that betrayed him."

"The bad news is that I won't take either of you. You've got to take over here, Giuliano. Recruit to replace what we've lost. And you, Thalia, you've got keep him tough. He's too nice for this. But he is also too valuable to waste. He's a good man."

"I know," she said quietly. "You and Erik saved my life. But he gave me back myself. My dignity."

"I'm an olive-grower," said Giuliano irritably. "Not a saint or a soldier."

"You're also the best man for the job. And as Doge Dorma was silly enough to invest me as a captain in the army of the Republic, I hereby give you a field-brevet to lieutenant. I'd do more, but as a captain I am limited to promoting you to below me. And I wish the two of you would stop wasting time and get a priest to marry you, as I don't think either of you will settle for anything less."

There was an uncomfortable silence.

Thalia looked down and wrung her hands. "It is too soon. Master Lozza will mourn his wife and child. I will mourn my man. Someday he will marry someone from his own order."

Giuliano looked Benito in the eyes. "I'll thank you to keep to your own business, Benito. Thalia . . . and I, both lost precious people."

Benito shrugged. "You both also nearly died tonight. And I'm not blind or stupid. This is a war. You could both still be killed while you fuss on about not hurting the other one's feelings. I don't think either of you didn't love your spouses. I just think you're hurting each other now. As for this difference in rank: Worry about it if you're still alive at the end of the war."

Giuliano put a hand gently onto Thalia's arm. "I don't wish to hurt you, Thalia. You were hurt enough."

"You are hurting me now," she said with a sniff. "You . . . all the other men in the camp. They make suggestions. Passes. You just taught me to fight. They mock you, too. They are scared to do so in the open because of your swordsmanship, master."

"If I married you, would you stop calling me master?"

She gave a watery sniff. "You don't want to do that."

"Actually, in among the ten thousand other things Erik's injury has forced on us, I want to do *that* most. But I don't want to hurt you more than you've been hurt. I don't expect much . . ."

"Would you two, hug, kiss, and get on with it," grumbled Benito. "I've got a crazy plan to go through with, and I need to find a wagon and something to hide the wounded in. And I've got some bodies and prisoners to strip, and some blacking to clean off the breastplates."

"Is that an order, sir?" asked Giuliano, putting his hands on her shoulders.

"Yes. And you, too, newly promoted sergeant. It is about time we had a few female sergeants. They're naturally good at telling men what to do."

"Yes, sir," said Giuliano, putting his arms around her. She folded into them as naturally as breathing. "You're good at managing people's lives, Benito."

"Yes. I wish I'd been as good at managing my own. Now, do you think anyone in that crowd speaks Hungarian?

Chapter 86

Late the next afternoon a wagon, escorted by a mounted patrol of Magyar, joined a number of other wagons heading into the camp. Erik's raids had forced Emeric's troops to dig earthworks and station guards, but a wagon with a Magyar driver and a military escort excited no comment. It didn't even get stopped. Benito reflected that Erik had missed some wonderful opportunities.

Benito put his earlier time within the Citadel to good use. He'd stood on the inner battlements making sure he'd get through the ruins of the town and the maze of tent-areas belonging to the different units of Emeric's army. Eberhard of Brunswick had stood up there with him while he watched, and had explained the interactions between the various tribes and nationalities in Emeric's kingdom. To the old statesman, those were potential danger areas of misunderstanding to be avoided.

To Benito they were something to be used. The Magyar, the elite of the army, Emeric's pets, weren't very popular, according to Eberhard. If you had to choose for least love lost between two groups, the levies from southern Carpathia detested the Magyars most. The Slovenes came a close second. And in the watching of detachments moving to and fro to the front, Benito knew where these two groups were encamped. They were on the southern end of the Spianada, behind a half-screen of buildings that the officers of both sets used for slightly

751

more comfortable quarters—just out of cannon-shot. There was an open patch that both sets of troops used as a parade ground.

Benito took his set of "Magyar" there with the wagon and parked it on the edge of the parade ground. His men dismounted. Some played dice. Some just lounged against the wagon. It was covered with a tightly tied-down tarpaulin. Benito hoped the poor devils inside weren't roasting as the afternoon sun blazed down.

Nobody came over and talked to them, except for one Slovene officer. Benito didn't understand a word. However he could offer a pretty good guess.

Stephanos, with his few words of Hungarian, was posing as the group officer. Stephanos snapped one word—"orders"—with as much arrogance as he could muster and jerked his thumb at the ornate pavilion on the hill. Benito thought he could have done a better job, but then he had to give Stephanos credit for looking the part. The man had been a taverna owner at the start of the war. In younger days, however, he had spent some years in Rugosa as a clerk, working for a Venetian buyer—who couldn't operate there, and had needed a trusted man. Stephanos was a positive graybeard to Benito, but he had the posture and attitudes of someone who is used to being respected.

Stephanos's Hungarian, unlike his Illyrian, was limited, and certainly wouldn't fool a Magyar trooper for an instant. But it worked fine on the Slovene.

Benito got to drive the wagon, with Nico. Nobody seeing Benito ride would have believed him to be a Magyar cavalryman. Just after dark they set out for the northern causeway. It meant crossing the entire front—but the Croats were on that side. They had two fluent Croat-speakers from Istria, whom Benito had recruited from Captain Di Negri's Venetian volunteers.

One of the wounded from inside the covered wagon groaned. "Shut him up!" whispered Benito hoarsely.

They were approaching the two earthwork and masonry fortresses that had been constructed to deal with any sally. By the looks of it, a lot of work had gone into these since Benito had left.

They stopped the wagon just short of one of the forts. The two Croat speakers dismounted. Benito held the wheel-lock pistol between his legs. If things didn't work now . . . It would mean they'd failed to fool the guards. Then it would be whether they retreated, and tried to leave the Hungarian base in the morning—because there'd be no leaving now—or decided to rush the causeway forts. Having looked at the causeway and the improved forts, Benito knew that one in ten of them might make it.

Halfway. Before the Venetians started shooting.

The two returned and said something in Stephanos's drilled-in Hungarian. The twenty fake Magyar dismounted, grumbling suitably, looking hangdog. A number of grinning Croats had turned out to take the horses and watch the Magyar's discomfort. The Magyar and the Croats had a healthy respect for each other. That didn't mean they didn't enjoy seeing the other lot suffer.

Really suffer. Proud Magyar having to do manual labor—off their precious horses—which had to be left with the Croats' flea-bitten nags, was a sight to be enjoyed.

Mocking cheers and jeers followed them struggling to haul the heavy wagon by hand along the causeway. Dragovich's engineers had built a snaking set of ramparts along it, and the farm wagon had to be backed and hauled around these. Several of the engineers and a group of sappers actually gave them a hand.

Tch. What a degradation for the crème de la crème. It served them right for being stupid enough to be caught drunk on duty. They were lucky the punishment was so slight. If it had been the king who'd caught them, they wouldn't just have to take a load of gunpowder casks to the front for Count Dragovich. The sappers might have wondered why they hadn't been told about this latest plan. But, in an army—especially Emeric's—nobody ever told common soldiers anything.

Since Manfred's sally, a forward post had been added to the defenses. By the looks of it, the Venetians had been pounding them. The wagon would certainly go no further.

The officer from the forward post emerged and snapped

something caustic. Probably: "What the hell are you doing here, you idiots? Get that damn wagon out of here!"

The poor fellow wasn't expecting a blow to the head with a knife pommel. The Corfiotes and Venetians moved fast, into the forward post. Now there was no time for subterfuge. Just violence.

Benito and the eight cutters didn't wait to see how it went in there. He flung off the Magyar helmet and tore the sash off and joined in cutting the cords that held the cover, flipping it over so the carefully chalked inner lining of the canvas sprang onto its banner-support poles.

Benito just had to hope shots being fired in that forward post would be taken as normal around here. In the meantime he had a stretcher to carry. Erik and the other three couldn't run themselves.

They started running forward. Benito just hoped the shooting would only start in earnest after the wagon got to burning. The wagon was neatly jammed across the causeway, supporting a banner of the winged lion of Saint Mark.

Shots rang out from the walls. They'd been seen. *"SAN MARCO!"* yelled Benito, with what breath he could spare. The other runners were shouting too. He looked left, back at the causeway. The wagon was burning merrily. The chalked outline of the Lion of Saint Mark reflected back golden.

They were almost at the corner tower. And then round it. Now the Hungarian forces were firing too. "Press against the wall. *San Marco! San Marco! A rescue!*"

"Who in the hell is down there?" bellowed someone from the wall.

"Valdosta! Wounded men! Help!"

"Valdosta?"

"San Marco! Help us! We've got wounded men."

The north postern spilled light. Benito saw pikemen come hurrying—but wary, and with their pikes ready. "Valdosta?" yelled someone from their ranks.

"Here!" Benito waved a hand. "Help us."

"It's all right boys! It's him. It's the madman!" Benito recognized the voice of large Alberto, Umberto's Arsenalotti friend. The Citadel's pikemen surged forward, grabbing them, grabbing stretchers, shouting "Valdosta." Cheering. Even laughing.

Benito didn't feel like laughing. Only eighteen of his band of heroes were here to enjoy the cheering.

Jagiellon prepared his favorite dish for the shaman. There were properties about it that would help to heal the shape-changer, even if the skin was only that of a palace servant. In the meanwhile, the shaman huddled in a corner in his feather-and-bell-hung spirit cloak. He sat there shivering, making the bells tinkle, and flickering his fingers across the surface of the tattooed *Quodba*-drum.

The noise—which reverberated outside the mere physical plane—was an irritation, but Jagiellon ignored it. He had no choice if he wanted to retain the services of this very powerful shaman. The shaman was enacting a kind of self-healing and pain-stilling. He was, despite his formidable skills, still a primitive man. Or something near that anyway. Right now, Jagiellon could have killed him effortlessly. The shaman was in too much agony to care.

But Jagiellon needed to send him back. Whatever it was about Corfu that hampered his own magics was powerful, intensely so. Jagiellon could not afford to let it fall into Emeric's hands. He knew that Emeric was a cat's-paw for someone whose interest in mere geographical possessions was limited: the sorceress across the Carpathians.

Soon, therefore, the shaman must go back. The power of Corfu would be centered on a specific place. The shaman must be the first into that place. The slave was useless now. His wounding had been physical and dire, and Jagiellon was not sure if he was going to bother to repair him.

Chapter 87

"So I was thinking," said Marco, "maybe I could try to contact Benito."

Sister Evangelina shook her head. "Even our most powerful mages cannot contact Eneko Lopez. Corfu seems to have become an island in a magical sense also. Besides, Eneko Lopez advised you not to try scrying out of the confines of the Venetian lagoon, did he not?"

Brother Mascoli smiled gently. "According to my researches, Corfu has always been a magical island."

Marco looked stubborn. "Look. The danger with my scrying was that the focus of my vision was too wide, that evil can enter and attack me. I can defend myself now. I've been practicing, as you know. With Kat, whom I know and love, I can narrow that down. Eneko didn't say 'never,' he said only in a case of dire need. I think there is now need."

Mascoli nodded. "And blood connections are always stronger. There is a magical resonance between them. But still, Marco, even if you could narrow your search and only reach Benito, and protect yourself, Corfu cannot be reached."

"I grant there is need," said Evangelina, "but is it dire?"

"I believe so," said Marco quietly. "I believe Benito needs me."

✧　　✧　　✧

"Is there anything that can be done for him?"

"God willing, yes." Eneko Lopez scowled. "Although here on Corfu . . . But we will do our best."

Manfred let one of his meaty hands rest on Erik's forehead—a surprisingly gentle gesture for so big and powerful a man. "I owe you a debt I can't ever repay, Benito. May God forgive me for letting him go. Or I should have gone with him."

He shook his head. "What a mess, Benito. I always thought . . . other people died in combat. Since this siege started, I'm beginning to realize that 'other people' can be your closest friends."

"If Eneko succeeds then he's going to need close friends, Manfred. She's dead. Caesare's men, or at least their horses, killed her. I didn't know Erik like you did. But . . . before this happened he was very much in love. He—they—were about as happy as a couple can be. When he got there, she was dying already. He went berserker. He killed half the Hungarians himself. Then Caesare nearly killed him with this magical blow."

"And what happened to Caesare Aldanto? I swear this world isn't big enough for both of us to live in." It was said with a calm assurance that was no less terrifying for its calmness. All the more so, coming from a prince of the Holy Roman Empire.

"I shot him. I think he's dead. Some monstrous eel thing took him down into the water."

"Chernobog's minion!" exclaimed Brother Francis. "The hagfish."

Manfred put a big arm around Benito. "You shot him? Well done! Are you sure you hit him?"

"Certain. I wasn't more than three yards off. I shot him in the gut. Liver and spine would have been hit too."

"How did you get so close? Melee?"

"I did what he taught me. Distracted him. Convinced him I was going to fence with him. And then I shot him when he thought I was dead meat."

"Well done!" repeated Manfred. "He never taught you anything better in his life. Now, you look exhausted." He managed a grin. "These jack-in-the-box visits to the

Citadel are all very well, but they're not good for you. Go and rest. I'll sit with Erik."

"I'll just go to see Maria . . . 'bout Caesare."

"You're swaying on your feet. She'll have the news by now or I know nothing about women. And I'll send Von Gherens down to tell her you're fine, but that you're in bed. Your own, alone, asleep."

Benito chuckled. "Not that she cares. But I suppose it will keep."

Benito slept a full twenty hours. He hadn't realized just how exhausted he was. Now up, washed—in salt water, as fresh water in the Citadel was under severe rationing—and dressed, he carefully checked, unloaded and reloaded Maria's wheel-lock pistol. Then he set off to see her.

"It's the bad penny again, Umberto," said Maria.

"And it is good to see him. If we had ten bad pennies like this youngster, Emeric wouldn't have a siege!" Umberto waved to a chair. "Have you come to see my daughter again?" he asked, with an attempt at a stern look. "I tell you I want a respectable *scuolo* husband for her, Benito, not someone everyone calls 'the madman.'"

"Where is she?"

"Mrs. Grisini and her maid have taken her out for a walk. The old lady is a little crazy too. I've sat with her a few times when Anastasia has been sick. She . . . sees things. But she's harmless. And she adores 'Lessi. I don't normally let her alone with her, but Anastasia is very good with both of them."

"And where's the goat?"

There was an awkward pause. "We sold her. We just couldn't find enough food for her any more. I couldn't bear to kill her myself. She was a black-hearted menace, but she was twice the guard that a dog would have been. Have you heard that Sophia Tomaselli escaped? The guards claim it was witchcraft."

Maria sighed. "I suspect it was simply money. They've searched all over. Even searched the captain-general's apartments, at his invitation. Anyway, let's talk about something else. Is it just as dry out there?"

"Just about. You can still find water underground or in the bigger rivers. But even the olives are suffering." Benito took out the wheel-lock pistol. "Here. I'm returning it with thanks. It did exactly what it was supposed to do. I think he's dead, and if that woman is around she might get vindictive. You might need it. Careful. It's loaded and primed."

She took the pistol. "You killed Caesare?"

"Yes. I think so, anyway."

Maria nodded. Seeing her husband's frown, she shook her head. "Good riddance, I say! I'm sorry, Umberto, I'm just being honest. Caesare Aldanto was an evil man. He did terrible harm to me and Benito and Marco, and lots of other good Venetians. Best that he is dead. He'd only go on doing it to other people."

Umberto nodded. "I agree with you on this one, my dear. You told me how he deceived our Garavelli cousins. But he was supposed to be a great swordsman and a fighter. How did you . . . ?" He smiled apologetically at Maria. "It'll be a story to tell the other *scuolo* masters. Young Benito here is one of the favorite sources of stories. I must tell you, Benito, it has done my prestige and popularity no end of good with all the wild journeymen and apprentices, that I am Valdosta's friend."

Maria snorted. "That lot are as bad as he was."

Umberto smiled. "They are the ones who really believe in my fireboats. The masters mostly say the authorities will never use them. That they will say we wasted the materials." He sighed. "They would work. It is my dream to see that they get the chance to work. Well, tell us about this Caesare."

"I had Maria's pistol in my hand inside my shirt. I pretended the hand was injured. I boasted a lot about fencing. About the sword. And then when were close . . . he lunged."

Benito lunged himself, demonstrating.

The glass in the small window shattered. A black crossbow bolt sailed through the space Benito had just vacated and hit Umberto squarely in the chest.

Maria still had the pistol in her hand. She turned and, as you might point a finger, fired.

❖   ❖   ❖

By the time the guards arrived, Umberto was dead in his wife's arms. His hand was still holding Benito's.

There was a blood trail outside, from next to the low wall where the killer had hidden.

"They found him," said Benito quietly. "He was hiding down in the ruined houses near the Kérkira side of the outer wall. Your shot shattered his right hand and hit him in the gut. He'll die. It's amazing he got that far. They've been questioning him, hard, as they reckon his time is short."

Maria held Alessia and rocked her. "Who was he? Why did he kill my husband?" Her voice was hard, bitter.

"His name is Zanari. A mercenary from Apulia who's been working for Fianelli."

Benito looked down, and bit his lip. "He shot Umberto by accident. His orders were to shoot me. Only I moved, imitating Caesare. That bolt was meant for me. I'm sorry, Maria. I'm really sorry. All I ever seem to bring you is sadness."

Her eyes were luminous with tears. "No, Benito. I still believe this is that woman's hatred. I'm learning that here on Corfu, magic goes further than the chants and words and symbols that Eneko believes in." She closed her eyes briefly. "I'm scared for Alessia, 'Nito."

Benito patted her awkwardly. "We'll do what we can, Maria. Francesca is hunting. She always finds, eventually." He cleared his throat. "We, um, I've been down to the Little Arsenal, talking to the *scuolo* and the workers. They want to arrange the funeral. Your husband was a much-respected man, Maria."

Maria stood there, tears now pouring from her eyes. Slowly, as if her head was too heavy to move, she nodded. "He wasn't . . . like you. Bravura. Just solid. Good. Not clever, but wise; he used every little bit of intelligence he had, and used it like—like the artisan he was. And he was kind, so kind; you would never believe how kind. I wish . . . he could have seen his fireboats used. He put so much into that project."

Benito squeezed her shoulder. "He was a damn fine

man. I started out intending to hate his guts. Only . . . well, I couldn't."

Maria nodded again. "His fussing used to drive me mad at first. I wasn't used to being a 'good little *scuolo* wife.'" She gave out a half-sob. "I guess I'm not any more."

"Well, there is a pension. And I know you won't take money from me, but for Alessia . . ."

She shook her head firmly. "No, Benito. Anyway, right now what we need is food—and all the money in Christendom can't buy much in the Citadel right now. Thanks to old Grisini, Alessia and I have a place to stay. It was a kindness that has repaid itself already, I suppose."

Alessia squirmed and grumbled in Maria's arms.

"Is something wrong?" asked Benito anxiously.

Maria shook her head. "According to Stella—who should know—she's starting with teething pains."

Alessia gave a niggly bellow. Maria rocked her to try and soothe.

"Can I hel—"

Both Benito and Alessia cut off their vocal output on the instant. And both of them seemed to be staring right through Maria.

Then Benito shook himself, like a wet dog. "Weh! What an experience!" He took a deep breath. "Marco and Kat send their love and their condolences, Maria."

"What?!"

"I've just had a magical communication with my brother," he said, absently. He looked—not dazed, exactly, but certainly deeply preoccupied. Obsessed, even; there was, of a sudden, a strange look in his eyes, a fire that was nothing like that crazy look he used to get whenever he was about to go off on some wild excursion.

A magical communication from his brother?

"But—" she began. "Benito, how—"

He shook his head violently. "Look Maria, I must go. I need to see Manfred and Eneko straight away. I'll be back later to see if there is anything you need. I'll come and baby-sit for a while, maybe, if you need to go out."

There was a furious knock at the door. It was a panting Alberto. "Maria. Come down to the workshops quickly! There's a fight between the Illyrians and the Corfiotes again."

"Me?"

"They listen to you, Maria. They're used to it. Oh, Jesu, Maria, if you don't come someone is going to get knifed!"

She swore a sailor's oath, halfway between anger and weeping. "Oh, God's Teeth—I'll come! Go on, Benito."

Benito went. But he was privately certain that Maria would be spending a fair amount of her time at the Little Arsenal, even if Umberto was dead. And that would be no bad thing. She would need something to keep her mind off her grief for a while.

And maybe that would keep her from blaming *him* for Umberto's murder.

Chapter 88

"Rome must hear of this!" said Mascoli excitedly.

Evangelina shrugged. "The requirement is a powerful magician, with a nonhuman, demideity in support, who has a blood relation on Corfu. I don't think it will help Eneko much."

Marco blinked. "You know, the strangest thing was that I was talking not just to Benito, but to someone else as well. A sort of person."

"Human?"

"I think so . . . although its thoughts seemed somehow formless. It was sore, hurting; just an annoying ache. I soothed it."

Eneko Lopez stared intently at Benito. "A blood bond! And with such a one as Marco Valdosta. Powerful indeed."

"Yeah. And the news was pretty powerful too, even if none of it was good. The Atlantic fleet still being held outside the pillars. The fire in the Arsenal. The heavy snows in Bohemia, so the imperial forces have made poor headway into Slovenia and Hungary."

"To say nothing of the Church failing to prevail on either the magical defenses or the earthly authorities of Aragon and Genoa." Lopez shook his head. "We never did have much influence with Barbary."

"Anyway. What I wanted to say was—if crisis struck—or if we found out something, could I contact him?"

Eneko shrugged. "Magical ability tends to run in families. The Valdosta—given their long association with the Lion—are known for it. And with the working of metals . . . so are the Dell'este. Sforza? Well, not that I know of. But we could try, with us supporting you. It might be dangerous because of the warding problem. We could try. If the need was great."

"Signor Valdosta," said Alberto, diffidently. "It would mean a great deal to all of the *scuolo* from the Little Arsenal if you'd say a few words at the funeral. We . . . well, Umberto derived a great deal of pride and pleasure from having his family associated with the *Casa* Valdosta. It would be a mark of respect."

Benito found the last part of that statement compelling. He found the rest of it an alarming burden. "I don't think I've ever met a man I came to respect more than Umberto Verrier," he said quietly. "And I've met all sorts from priests to princes. But . . . well, me? Alberto, the honor of the *Casa* Valdosta belongs with my older brother. He got all the honor and I got all the wildness."

Alberto shrugged. "Everybody expects a young *Case Vecchie* to run amok," he said tolerantly. "But what counts with us is that when the real trouble came, you were there. We've heard from one of the Venetian sailors who fought their way back with you, how you worked in the Arsenal." He took Benito's hand, turned it over, looked at the calluses and smiled.

"That's not the hand of an idle nobleman, signor. We *scuolo*, we're guildsmen. We respect a man who labors, we respect the fact that you've been first in the fight for us, and we like it that you can work and drink just like us. We're proud that the *Casa* Valdosta chose to be the friend of one of the *scuolo*. It would be a good thing for his widow, too. It will do no harm that some people see the mantle of the Valdosta is there to protect her."

Benito raised his eyes to heaven. "It's a pretty thin mantle. And don't say that to Maria. She doesn't believe she needs any protecting. Tell you what, Alberto. I'll ask her."

"I'm sure she'll agree."

Benito was certain she wouldn't.

He was wrong. Maria nodded, when he said that they'd asked him to do a eulogy. "It would have meant a lot to him, 'Nito. He really liked you. He was very proud of you, you know." She sniffed. "He even asked me to be nicer to you."

Benito found his reply had got stuck behind the lump in his throat. But he nodded.

The little Hypatian chapel was full to the wall-bulging point. The Little Arsenal's *scuolo*, the Corfiotes, the Illyrians, men, women and children . . . Today there was no fighting among them. Today they'd come to pay their last respects, to commit to God and the earth one of their own. To show to his widow, whom they'd come to respect, and love too, how much they'd valued her man.

Sibling Eleni conducted the service, giving comfort with the old words. The air was full of incense. It was getting in his eyes. After the homily, Benito had to stand up and speak. Facing the court had been easier. He swallowed.

"Umberto Verrier . . . When I was asked give this eulogy, I struggled to get the words I wanted to say about this man. So: I came here last night. It's not a place I come to often enough. My head stayed empty. I knew what I wanted to say about Umberto, but not how to say it. And my eyes wandered to the icons. Then I saw a face that had something in it that reminded me of Umberto. I saw the same look as I have often seen on the face of the man I was proud to call my friend, in the face of the Holy Saint Peter. The face of man that you know is as solid and reliable as the rock beneath your feet.

"When I first met Umberto, we hauled baulks of timber together at the gate where our ships landed. It took me very little time to realize that here was a man who spoke not with his mouth but with his hands, and that those hands knew exactly what they were doing. Umberto wasn't a great talker. He was a man who did, instead. And like the rock, he was a man you could rely on and trust. Because he was what he was. As good and solid as a rock."

Benito had struggled to start speaking. Now the words

came easily, painting a deep and full picture of Umberto, of the treasure that this husband had been to Maria. Benito had not realized what effect the quiet, small *scuolo* master craftsman had had on him. He was always just there when Maria was. Solid. You almost didn't notice him, until he wasn't there.

If Benito felt like this now, how then was Maria bearing it?

The pallbearers were all *scuolo*. Alberto had been polite but firm in his refusal of Benito's offer. "You can speak for him. But we carry our own."

They laid him in the grave and gave him into the embrace of the earth. And the world seemed a poorer place, full of dust and ashes.

Maria stood white-faced and weeping at the graveside. Work-roughened hands touched her, awkwardly, gently. Hands trying to say what the *scuolo*, the Corfiotes, the women and Illyrians could find no words for.

Benito did it himself. Words were too inadequate.

She turned to him. "Thank you," she said, quietly. "You said the right things about him."

"I wish that bolt had hit me instead," he said. "I'm worth less than he was. Maria, if you need anything, or need help with 'Lessi . . . I'll be there."

She nodded.

He was not too sure what she was agreeing with.

Erik opened his eyes at the end of what seemed like a long, long tunnel of grayness. He looked up into Manfred's face.

"Are you dead as well? Did I fail you, too?" The voice was a dry, cracked whisper.

"No. You're alive thanks to that mad scamp Benito. I must talk to Uncle about a barony for the boy, at the very least. Maybe on the border of Aquitaine. It'll do him and the Aquitaines good."

Erik blinked. "Where am I?"

"In the hospital, in the Citadel."

Then the despair washed over him. "She's dead, Manfred. She's dead. I promised I would never leave her. I must go to her."

A firm hand pushed him down onto the bed. "She's dead. You're alive and you're going to stay that way. Because you are my hearthman. I need you here. I order it."

Manfred knew the Icelander was still on the border between life and death . . . And the direction he took now was very uncertain. But he had never seen Erik cry. Tears welled up in those gray eyes, drowning them. Then Erik swallowed, tightened his jaw and said in a quiet voice:

"Very well. Duty remains, Manfred." He paused. "To every life there comes a season of happiness. I have had mine."

The baby wailed, and Maria tucked sweat-damp strands of hair behind her ears, then bounced Alessia in an attempt to soothe her. She might as well have tried to stop the tide; she got no more result than when she'd tried to feed the poor mite a moment ago. Maria felt her own irritation building to an irrational anger, and did her best to control it.

"I know you're teething, child," she told the youngest member of the Verrier family wearily, "and I know your poor mouth is hurting. But you've been so good up to now, can't you suffer in silence?"

She heard a familiar step at the door. It was Benito. "I tried knocking but the competition was drowning it out," he said with a smile. "I was down at the Little Arsenal and Alberto's wife was there. She told me Alessia's teething and giving you a hard time."

Maria nodded tiredly. "I'm nearly at my wit's end with it."

Benito produced a jar from his pocket. "I came here via the monks at the hospital. Brother Selmi said this might help."

"What is it?"

Benito grinned. "I don't even look like Marco, Maria. It's no use asking me. I told him what it was for, I told him how old she was, and I told him that if it did her any harm I'd feed him his own cassock. He seemed a bit taken aback that I'd offer a man of the cloth violence."

Maria raised her eyes to heaven. "You're impossible, Benito."

"Well, he seemed to think his cassock was safe. Let's try it anyway. It's in a honey base and it has cloves in it, but that is all I know." He opened Alessia's mouth and rubbed a fingerful onto the sore gums. "I wish I had ice for her. But the nearest is over in Illyria."

"Which you are not to fetch!" He was quite capable of deciding to do that.

Benito chuckled. "Only if this doesn't work, which it seems to be." He held out his arms. "Alberto's wife said you've been trying to quiet her half the night. I'll be glad to take her for a bit until she falls asleep. Which probably won't be long; I bet she's tired herself out to nothing, with all that crying."

"She's tired me out, if nothing else," Maria admitted, letting Benito take the baby from her arms.

"It'll pass, according to the brother at the hospital. The truth to tell, I think he was glad of a teething baby problem that he could help with, rather than malnutrition and siege wounds he can't."

Maria watched as Benito moved with a sort of slow, catlike walk that Alessia always seemed to find comforting. She was still amazed at how good he was with the child, and how frequent and constant he'd been about visiting 'Lessi. He seemed to have no problems about the fact that she, Maria, was using him as a mere baby-sitter. His arrival usually signaled her departure. He wasn't just coming to see her.

The truth was she was uncomfortable about her feelings for Benito. Umberto's death was still recent and raw. She'd been troubled about it when Umberto was alive. Now . . . she was careful to keep her distance.

But he was very good with 'Lessi, seeming to derive a deep satisfaction from looking after her. She'd never have thought it of him, although there was a tender side to the younger Valdosta. He just tried not to ever let it show. Perhaps it was having to survive on the canals after his mother had been killed. He'd been very young.

She sighed. He still seemed completely oblivious to the fact that Alessia could easily be his child. Probably was, in fact. Had no one ever explained to him about how long a pregnancy was? Or had he just deliberately excluded the idea?

"She's out, poor lamb," said Benito quietly. "Shall I put her down in her crib?"

Maria nodded.

PART XIII
December, 1539 A.D.

Chapter 89

"Benito!" the panting Arsenalotti porter yelled. "You'd better get yourself back to Maria Verrier. You're needed there. Somebody's kidnapped her baby."

"Who?" he snapped, the chill grip of fear on his throat. "Who took her?"

The Corfiote porter shook his head. "Don't know, nobody knows. Some says it's more witchcraft, some reckon it is something to do with a Hungarian spy, some blame the captain-general's wife. It's every rumor you can think of going through the Citadel like a fire. No ransom note, no clues, no nothing. But there's guards and that Eneko Lopez, looking."

Benito felt stark horror. Eneko Lopez and the Satanists he was sniffing for! And a missing baby. It added up to things he didn't like to think about.

When he got there, out of breath, he found a crowd of Arsenalotti, an officer of the Citadel guard, Eneko, and Francesca, too.

"The baby vanished some time between when you left Signora Verrier and about half an hour ago," Eneko said curtly, raising his voice a little to be heard over the crowd of Arsenalotti. "You don't remember seeing anyone hanging around the outside when you left, do you?"

Benito shook his head.

"Whoever took her didn't leave a note, and hasn't tried

to contact us," said the guard officer. "Unfortunately, that doesn't rule anyone out."

"They must have been around, watching," said Benito numbly, "If they took her that soon after I left."

The guard officer nodded. "We just don't know where to start, milord."

"Have you asked Anastasia?" Seeing the officer's blank look Benito explained. "The girl who looks after old Mrs. Grisini. In the upper floors of the house."

Maria shook her head. "She's up at the hospital, Benito. Just lack of food, I think. I found her passed out on the stairs the day before yesterday. The old lady was still pottering around and hadn't even noticed. The old lady is also up there, at the hospital. She has arthritic pains and it turns out she's been taking poppy-juice tablets to help her with it." Maria made a face. "It appears she's been taking too many of them. Washing them down with grappa on the quiet."

"Well, that leaves her out," mused Benito. "I'd wondered. She's always been potty about Alessia."

"About babies in general," said Maria. "She lost her own, from her first husband. Poor woman. I can't blame her entirely for her tablets and grappa. She's had a miserable life."

Benito shrugged. "Well, my sympathies, but I want to find Alessia. I'm just glad to have her excluded because I'd worry about what she might do to a child. She always seemed as mad as bedlam to me."

Maria pursed her lips. "She made some bad decisions. That first marriage of hers . . . poor, short but happy. Then she married Grisini. It was childless and—on her side anyway—more for sustenance than affection. The childlessness obsessed her a bit. But she'd never have hurt a baby. It can't be her, anyway. She was being looked after up at the hospital, the last I saw."

"If we knew roughly where Alessia had been taken to, we'd have a pretty easy time finding her," Benito said. "She's going to wake up in a strange place with her gums hurting, and she's going to start right in screaming. We'll set the Arsenalotti kids to listening for a baby where there shouldn't be one."

"If we knew roughly where she was." Francesca pondered that for a moment, while Benito turned away from the window and slumped down into another chair. "So who'd want a baby? Especially one that's likely to give them away?"

Benito thought about that for a moment.

"If I were some kind of agent, or someone wanting a baby for a ritual, the last thing I'd pick to kidnap would be a teething baby," Francesca persisted. "You can't reason with it, and you can't shut it up without hurting it. You can't even shut it up *by* hurting it. So what if this isn't a kidnapping, as Maria thinks it is? Who else would want a baby?"

"Who would want a baby—except a mother?" He looked up to see Maria nodding thoughtfully.

"Somebody who lost a baby already? And maybe can't have any more?" Francesca pursed her lips and sat up a little straighter. "And you've got a little china-doll right here, about as pretty as anybody'd ever want. All right, that makes sense. But who?"

"Remember, Benito, we are probably looking for someone who isn't entirely well balanced, but it's also probably someone too careful to give herself away by disappearing with it. Lord only knows why they took the baby—"

Benito felt a finger of ice trace the line of his spine. "You don't—you don't think they'd hurt her, do you?"

"Not if it was someone looking for a baby to care for. They'd try to look after her."

"Which leaves harming her by accident." His heart sank again. "Saints. If the baby starts fussing again, wakes up and starts crying—"

It was around dusk when the young Corfiote boy came panting in. "Down near the southern wall! There's a building that's been pretty well wrecked in the shelling, milord. No one living down there. But I heard a baby!"

Benito got to his feet. "Let's go."

Maria struggled to keep up.

Emeric's bombardment had turned from being largely focused on the front wall to working on the morale of the besieged by shelling the buildings inside the wall.

The result was that the forequarter of the city, inside the southern curtain wall, was largely uninhabitable with many damaged buildings. It was to this part that the boy led them, into a small square.

"It was here I heard it, milord."

At precisely that moment, a baby cried. A fierce howl of pain and frustrated anger. Benito knew that it had come from directly overhead. He knew that cry, knew that baby-voice. It was his baby, his little girl—

Anger he'd been carrying around inside since the abduction exploded into a white rage.

He went up through the skeletal remains of the building without a thought to fragile masonry. But at the third floor level he was confronted by a piece of staircase that was plainly newly fallen. This stopped Maria, but it didn't stop him. Not for an instant. He climbed across on tiny stubs of masonry, willing them to be big enough to hold him.

He gained the landing. "Get someone with some planks!" he called back to Maria. He pushed open the door at the top.

The room here was virtually intact. And leaning over the cradle at the far side of the room was a woman they'd supposed safe in the hospital. Mrs. Grisini's hair was awry, gray straggling locks hanging about her face. Her eyes, looking up from Alessia and into his, were unfocused, the pupils wide. She saw him and screamed in competition with Alessia.

"It's all right," said Benito, trying for an air of reassurance. She looked mad enough to do anything and Alessia was right within her grasp. He walked slowly forward, making no hasty movements.

She screamed again, and snatched the infant from the cradle, holding it so tightly against her that the baby howled in protest at this mishandling.

Benito froze where he was. She edged away from him, step by step, until her back was against the outer door that had once led to another room. Before Benito could stop her, she kicked the door open and dashed out onto what was left of the structure.

Torches and lanterns lit her eerily from below. She

looked like one of the condemned souls in the Holy Book. "Get away!" she cried, her eyes wild, waving her free hand at him. "Get away from me!"

Benito walked toward her, through the broken masonry, then out into the room one slow step at a time. "I won't hurt you, signora," he said, as quietly and calmly as he could and still be heard over the baby's screams. "I've just come for my little girl."

His heart pounded painfully in his chest, and his throat was too tight to swallow as she backed up another step. A cool, reasoning corner of his mind was calculating footing, the length of his own lunge, the amount of safe wood still behind her. The rest of him wanted to shriek and grab for his baby, now.

"You can't have her!" The woman said, shaking her head violently. "She's mine, not yours, she was meant for me. I saw it in the dreams!"

"What dreams, signora?" Benito asked, edging another foot closer. The wood creaked dangerously underfoot, and the whole building swayed again. He made a drastic revision of his safety margins.

"The dreams, the holy dreams," the woman babbled, clutching her hand in her hair while the baby subsided to a frightened whimper, as if she somehow sensed the danger she was in. "She's mine, she was meant for me—"

He was almost within reach—

Suddenly she looked over his shoulder, as light poured from the door behind him, and her eyes widened still further. "Benito?" Maria called. There was a murmur of shocked and frightened voices, and someone stifled a cry of despair.

"Stay back!" he warned sharply, as the woman took another two steps backward onto wood that moaned under her weight.

"Signora," he said urgently, recapturing her attention. "Signora, the dreams. What about them? What did they tell you?"

She transferred her attention from whoever was behind him back to his face. "You don't care about the dreams," she said accusingly. "You just want my—"

The wood gave.

Benito made a desperate lunge as the woman shrieked and teetered on the brink of the gulf, one arm flailing wildly, the other still clutching the baby. He reached her—she fell, just as his hands brushed the cloth—

He grabbed for it and held, as he was falling himself.

A blow to his chest knocked breath and sense from him, but he had a handful of fine linen fabric, and he held onto it past all pain and sense. The universe spun, then came to rest again.

He was dangling face-down over the street, three floors down to the cobblestones. With one hand and both legs he held on to the timber-strut that had saved him. The other hand was clutched in the linen dress of the little girl-baby, who was likewise dangling head down over the empty darkness, howling at the top of her lungs.

He edged back until his chest was supported by the timber, then drew her up. Only when she was safely cradled against his chest did he breathe again.

And held her carefully, like the precious thing she was, murmuring her name over and over, hardly daring to believe he had her back safe. He might even have burst into tears of his own at that point, but suddenly the others were on him, hauling him to safety, praising him to the skies. Arsenalotti, Arsenalotti wives everywhere, pounding his back, touching his sleeve, crying over the baby. Maria, her face as white as fine porcelain held Alessia, and stared down at her, fierce tears in her eyes.

No one seemed to be thinking about old Mrs. Grisini. Benito tilted his head to look down; and then, wincing, looked away. The torchlight showed enough. The crazed old woman's body was a broken ruin.

In the crowd below, Bianca Casarini turned and began walking away. She was disgruntled, a bit, at the failure of the scheme—but not excessively so. It had been Fianelli's idea in the first place, not hers. Emeric's servant was now desperate to do *anything* that might placate his master, given that all the other attempts at treason and sabotage had failed. No matter how petty the attempt might be.

Under pressure, Bianca had agreed to inflict the dreams on the old woman. She hadn't wanted to, herself, because she could sense the net thrown by Eneko Lopez and Francesca de Chevreuse closing steadily around her. But Countess Bartholdy had insisted.

"I can't afford to have Emeric get suspicious, this close to success. Which he will, if Fianelli reports that you are suddenly balking. So do as Fianelli wants, Bianca."

"Yes, mistress."

Well, she'd made the attempt—and the attempt had failed. Now the net would be closing more tightly still. It was time for Bianca Casarini to prepare for her escape.

Chapter 90

"The entire point of the exercise is not to surrender," said Captain-General Tomaselli. "It is to waste time. We know Venice is coming to our rescue. We know they have been delayed."

Manfred was pleased to note that the captain-general seemed to have accepted the de facto situation that first Falkenberg and now Erik had simply assumed control of the military of the Citadel. Erik, especially Erik these days, was someone people tended not to question if they could avoid it. Besides, Erik had produced the letter from the Doge brought by Benito, putting him in overall command of "Any Forces in support of the Republic of Venice, who are still at large on the Island of Corfu."

Somebody might argue they weren't at large. But so far no one had been that stupid, not even Captain-General Tomaselli. Ever since his wife's escape from prison, Tomaselli had been a very subdued man. All the more subdued, Manfred thought, because he clearly had no idea what had happened to her. Francesca had Tomaselli under constant observation, and she was sure the captain-general had no contact with his wife.

Manfred knew that Francesca herself was puzzled by Sophia's ability to stay hidden, in such a relatively small place as the Citadel of Corfu, and was getting worried about it. Some of the possible implications were . . . disturbing.

Manfred shook off the thought. Erik was speaking.

"It is a possible idea," the Icelander agreed.

Falkenberg chuckled. "We'll send old Eberhard out. If there's anyone in the whole world who can turn 'please pass the salt' into a three month negotiation, it's him."

"We have to be wary whom we send," said Erik grimly. "Emeric's middle name should be 'treachery.'"

"Well, you're not going. He wants your head," said Manfred firmly.

"And you're not going either," said Von Gherens. "Too valuable as a hostage. Send Falkenberg or me. They don't know us, and we can observe the military layout on the ground."

"I think I should go," said the captain-general. "I am high-ranking but expendable."

Manfred blinked. That had been in his mind, but he'd kept his mouth shut about it. "Very well. I'll ask Eberhard. The old man has been feeling underutilized."

When the captain-general had left, Francesca stood up. "I must go and talk to Eberhard too. This has interesting possibilities for espionage."

"A parley?" Emeric smiled savagely. "Such a thing presents some opportunities. Yes. Raise a truce flag. We can use the time to move materials onto the causeway without hindering cannon fire."

"Sire." Dragorvich hesitated. "You don't think they're using this to buy a respite? This would be the first time for many months that the western half of the citadel will not be being fired on."

Emeric shrugged. "I think it worthwhile. Aside from anything else, we can see if their delegation is worth taking hostage."

Dragorvich kept silent, of course. But, not for the first time, he reflected that the king of Hungary was ultimately something of a fool. Emeric always thought rules were for other people, without ever once considering that his own behavior might bite him back. There was a good reason, after all, that civilized nations considered diplomatic envoys untouchable. The Mongols were utterly fanatical on the subject. They had, on three occasions that Dragorvich knew of, destroyed entire kingdoms for breaching that rule of war.

They were met by a delegation of Magyar officers. "His Majesty will not receive you with weapons. Weapons are to be left here."

Falkenberg, in full armor, creaked to Eberhard of Brunswick. "It is to be hoped that he doesn't want us mother-naked, as I hear these Magyar cavalry have to go now."

By the pinched lips and dull red faces, Falkenberg hadn't made any new friends. Eberhard of Brunswick smiled sweetly. "Now, *Ritter*. Accidents will happen when you are foolish enough to give Carlo Sforza's son trouble."

"The story will be a matter of interest to the brother-hood of Knights. I'm sure it will elevate the status of the Magyar no end," said Falkenberg, calmly putting down his sword. The Knight knew he was playing to the gallery watching from the walls. Plainly the Magyar knew it too. But by the looks of the bright eyes . . . it might not make any difference in a minute.

Fortunately, a factotum from Emeric turned up to escort them down the causeway to the king.

"Sire. This was given to one of the guards by the Venetian officer," said the factotum, handing Emeric a slip of parchment.

It read: *Contact me. Deal.*

Emeric smiled wolfishly. "Well. Captain-General Toma-selli. Maybe his wife did pass on that little letter to him."

"Additionally, the elderly imperial . . . who I accompanied when he went to relieve himself, asks that Your Majesty consider a private deal. The man said he has magical word from his master. The Emperor wants his nephew intact. For which he is prepared to pay a quarter of a million ducats and also Your Majesty's former territory of Ceská, and to withdraw from the districts of Soporon and Vas."

"What!" Emeric started forward. "What did he say?"

The Factotum repeated himself faithfully.

"Damn him! *Damn him.* He's letting me know what the Emperor is doing. Trying to draw me back to Hungary. Ha! Well, I'll play him at his game. The Citadel is so close to starvation I'll win soon enough anyway. Then I'll take back Soporon and Vas—and take Ceská in the bargain. "

"My principal fear about your plan, my dear," said Eberhard to Francesca, "is that it may backfire on us. I think we may just have told Emeric what a valuable card he has to play in Manfred."

Francesca shrugged. "Surely he's figured that out for himself by now, Eberhard."

The older statesman shook his head. "Emeric . . . I have serious doubts about his sanity, Francesca. He thinks himself vastly clever, and vastly superior. He has welded the fractious elements of the Hungarian kingdom into a unit. But his decisions are sometimes . . . odd. There is a theory that the Emperor has that someone else in Hungary is pulling his strings. It may well be true. I did very little time in Buda, and I've never been so glad to leave anywhere, not even the weather in Ireland. His capital is a pretty place—with a monster corrupting it."

"I can see I still need to stop thinking like an Aquitaine," said Francesca. "But I was sure we'd get an approach from his spies. Soon."

"We may," said Eberhard. "But first we'll get the attack. Emeric simply agreed to everything. You don't negotiate like that when you're in earnest. Trust me. Negotiations are one thing I've done so often that I know exactly how genuine ones feel. Erik is preparing for Emeric to break the truce."

Falkenberg yawned. "It was long, boring and windy and dusty." He grinned nastily. "The dust was getting to Emeric, too. Now, is there any wine? Eberhard rationed me on Emeric's. I wouldn't buy horses from that man."

"Who? Emeric? Erik never *bought* any of them." Benito had come, full of curiosity, to nose out what he might.

"No. Eberhard of Brunswick. He kept that dickering

going all lifelong day, when we had no intention of surrendering—and Emeric has absolutely no intention of abiding by the terms he offered us. Man's a snake. Dresses like a pimp, too."

"Well, how long have we got before fighting resumes?" asked Manfred. "We've probably given the outer wall another two weeks' life with the work we've done to it today."

Falkenberg shrugged. "Eberhard insisted on until sunrise tomorrow to consult his principals. I suspect Emeric will try an all-out assault about an hour before the truce is over."

As events proved he was wrong. The assault came at midnight. It was overcast and as black as the inside of a cat out there, and Emeric obviously found the opportunity too good to miss.

Erik's men had also found the opportunity too good to miss. Since sunset, they had been outside the walls digging pits in the shingle and covering them with sailcloth and more shingle. The oil and pitch pots had been heating since dusk.

Sometimes a bad reputation is a serious impediment to treachery.

Chapter 91

Two days later, after the failed attack, the approaches Francesca had expected arrived. They arrived in a way she'd never expected, however—from someone she'd liked and trusted, who had given her a great deal of information: the little Greek secretary to the governor, Meletios Loukaris.

Francesca had put a lot of Manfred's money into watching. And she'd put a lot into the gossip grapevine. It had brought her a fair amount of information, but not the kingpin. Not yet. Now the gossip chain brought in another piece. The captain-general—having withdrawn from social life of any sort since his wife's arrest, and become almost entirely reclusive since her escape—was hosting a gathering. It couldn't really be counted as a party; the guest list was comprised of the worst bores among the *Case Vecchie* and Libri d'Oro. No women were invited. Francesca had a very good idea of the guest list for someone who hadn't seen it. An interesting group to choose for a party . . . and now on her watch-list.

"The awkward question," said Francesca, "is whether De Belmondo is involved, because his secretary is."

"Test him," said Von Gherens. "Tell De Belmondo we're going to arrest the man. And watch the secretary to see if he runs."

Francesca screwed up her face in disgust. "The thing I think I hate most about you military people is your crude attitude toward espionage. I was going to feed De Belmondo some information—confidential, and absolutely not to be repeated—and see if the Hungarians got it."

"And what were you going to tell him?" asked Manfred.

"I've been trying to think of something," said Francesca irritably.

"I think we should arrest this secretary and make him talk," stated Falkenberg.

Francesca shook her head. "The trouble with that, Falkenberg, is that some people will keep their tongues, even under torture. And you would make a feeble torturer, anyway."

Falkenberg tugged his moustache. "And why is that, milady?"

"Because there is a great deal you wouldn't do."

Falkenberg nodded. "True enough. But I've usually found that it's not what I would do, but what the ones being interrogated believe I am going to do."

Manfred sighed. "Look, Francesca, we'll do it your way—until tomorrow sundown. Then we do it Von Gherens' and Falkenberg's way. We'll tell the governor we're going to arrest the man at dawn. And arrive at midnight. If he's packing we know where we stand. If not, we put my one-eyed frightener on him. I just don't believe we can play around with this."

As it happened, they didn't need either step. Good fortune finally favored them.

De Belmondo came to see Manfred a little later, just after Francesca had left for her walk. The timing was too precise to be coincidental.

"Prince Manfred," said the old man, uneasily. "Forgive me intruding on you like this. But this morning one of the Libri d'Oro, a gentleman by the name of Alexander Konstantis, came to see me in secret." The old man looked embarrassed. "He and I share an interest in the collection of naturalistic curiosities. He is an avid collector of birds' eggs. Under this pretext he came to see me, privately, and not in the office. He, ah, has something of a reputation as a malcontent. I think he just likes to argue, but that is easily misconstrued. Alexander was invited to a gathering at the captain-general's rooms last night. Now, Signor Konstantis doesn't like Captain-General Tomaselli, and very nearly didn't go and only decided to do so to give the cloth-head—in his words—a good mocking. He found himself part of a group of very unlikely people. Either very wealthy landowners or people with a reputation—like himself—for being malcontents. His curiosity was pricked and he decided, instead of just enjoying himself, to find out why the captain-general wanted to mix the likes of him with those."

The old governor shook his head sadly. "The purpose of the gathering was treason, I'm afraid. Tomaselli sounded each of them out, and Alexander played along when it came to his turn. He is astute, and in his words Tomaselli is as subtle as a charging bull. He was invited to stay on after many of the others had gone home. Then it came down to open treason. Tomaselli pointed out that Venice had not only failed to protect their estates but also had armed the peasants. He gave details of water and food stocks. He argued that the Citadel must fall, and that all within would lose everything, even their lives. He offered—conditional to the surrender of the Citadel—that his allies would retain lands and privilege, under Emeric."

"I see," said Manfred.

De Belmondo smiled. "My nasty-tongued friend said he'd go along, that he had both the perfect plan and method, but that he wanted some guarantees first. In writing. And Tomaselli was much struck by the goodness of this idea!" De Belmondo snorted and shook his head. "As if Emeric would abide by a piece of paper! Anyway, they're due to meet again an hour after Vespers at the captain-general's rooms in the Castel *a terra*. Alexander thinks that action is imminent and so we need to take steps. Unfortunately, I don't know what parts of the army the captain-general may have suborned. But I was sure it wouldn't be the Knights, as you are outsiders."

"We'll be glad to assist," said Manfred. "I think we'll need some witnesses, Your Excellency. And I think that the only reason that the captain-general has resorted to civilians is that he has very little following in the army any longer. If he ever did."

De Belmondo looked around uneasily. "Very well. Now, Prince Manfred, I have a very awkward request. Do you mind not telling Francesca de Chevreuse about this?"

This sent ideas racing through Manfred's head. But he allowed no sign of his perturbation to show. "Certainly. But why?"

The governor pulled at his earlobes. "Well . . . someone has told me she may possibly be a spy."

"Interesting," said Manfred, keeping his urbane expression. Eberhard would have been proud to see how well he'd learned. So would Francesca. "And who told you this?"

"My secretary, Meletios Loukaris. De Chevreuse has been pumping him for information, and tried to use him to set up other informants."

Manfred couldn't keep a straight face any more. He grinned. "You're quite right, De Belmondo. She *is* a spy. Or at least an agent. She's been working for my uncle—and for me, of course—since we came here."

"Are you sure that is her true allegiance?" asked the old man doubtfully. "I mean, in this revolting world of double-dealing and treachery, it is possible for a person to serve two masters."

Manfred nodded "Indeed, it is. Which is why I want to show you these." Manfred produced the letter from Emeric, offering to Manfred safe conduct—and setting out the terms. "This was delivered this morning in response to a trap set by Francesca and Eberhard of Brunswick. I think you must agree that he is beyond suspicion? He has been one of the Emperor's finest and most trusted statesmen for many years."

De Belmondo sighed. "Treason and treachery all around us. Who brought this to you?"

Manfred looked steadily at the governor. "Your secretary, Loukaris. Who has been an agent of Francesca's and provided her with several other informants. This man didn't serve two masters. He served three."

❖   ❖   ❖

It was, Eneko Lopez admitted, an effective way of being unobtrusive. And as he'd felt he could not ask any of the others to take the night-soil wagon duty, he at least got to sit down. This weather had been troubling the old wound, and that made walking and standing painful. Nothing that could not be borne, but it was still a relief to sit. And Benito had been right. No one stuck around the wagon, or paid it any more attention than they had to.

And then he had to leave the wagon in hurry. They'd found him—at last! Fianelli must have been laughing at their earlier efforts. Given where the demon-user had been hiding all this while.

"We have him. We have him absolutely pinpointed! The magic use was unmistakable!"

Erik Hakkonsen looked at the cleric skeptically. "And why have you come to me, Eneko? You are very capable of arranging for Satanists to be caught."

"Because this is within the Castel *a mar*. Inside the governor's wing."

"The governor himself no doubt," said Erik, dryly. "Or maybe his wife. Yes, Eneko, no doubt after the last performance, which I've heard all about, the governor's wife. Reputedly the kindest women on the Island. You're getting like Sachs, Eneko. Witches under every cobblestone."

Eneko Lopez's single line of eyebrow lowered fractionally, but he kept his even tone. "Actually, Erik, it is the governor's secretary we suspect. A man named Loukaris. Or rather, someone hiding in his chambers, as he wasn't there when the magic activity took place."

Erik made a face. "Hmm. Awkward. But better than the man's wife being a black magician, I suppose."

The stern lines on Eneko eased. He shook his head and smiled easily. "Saintliness shines out of her, Erik."

"He just dropped dead, Mam'zelle." The tail was one of the best Francesca had hired. Right now he was also one of the most distressed. He'd been following the Count Timeto, one of the guests at the captain-general's suspicious little gathering the night before. "Franco or I had him right under our eye almost every moment of the time. He went in to try to see Governor De Belmondo this morning. I was at the door when he spoke to the governor's secretary.

"And what did he say, Mouse?"

"He wanted an appointment with the governor. Now! He was very insistent. The secretary lied to him. Loukaris said he would check to if the governor was available. Franco followed him. He went into his own chambers and nowhere near Signor De Belmondo. And then he came back and told the Count that the governor was out."

Mouse took a deep breath. "I was following the count. Not too close, not too obvious. There was quite a crowd in the courtyard and it was easy. But when he got to the gates . . . There was no one near him and he just fell over. He was dead, signora. They took him to the hospital, but he was already dead. And no one killed him." The small spy crossed himself.

Francesca bit her lip. "Mouse, do you know where Benito is?"

The spy looked startled. "He was nowhere near, signora. He was on his way to the armory."

"I need to see him. Ask him to come here."

"*Si.* But why, signora?"

"A good spy like you should never ask questions like that." But she had a soft spot for the little nondescript man. He'd brought her so many interesting titbits. "My elders taught me how to play politics and manage spies. Benito's master taught him how kill people."

"He is a soldier, signora," said Mouse, looking doubtful. "The Count was killed by magic, I'm sure of it."

"Benito might be starting to become a soldier. But Caesare Aldanto was an assassin. And Benito learned a lot from him."

A few minutes later, Benito appeared. He looked wary. "What is it, Francesca? That's a thief you have running your errands, by the way."

"I know. Benito. If Caesare had wanted someone to die, without making it obvious, how could it be done in a hurry? Let me tell you what happened." And she explained.

Benito raised his eyebrows. "There are a couple of possibilities. But the most likely . . . Well, Caesare told me that if you push a very sharp, thin-bladed stiletto—actually, a sort of lethal pin—into the victim's heart, the bleeding is almost all internal. The strange thing is there is apparently no more than a momentary pain, especially if the victim is corseted up like a woman, or used to momentary aches and pains, like someone who's elderly or out-of-condition. The blade is pulled out, and the victim can continue walking for a good few heartbeats while the killer escapes. Get someone to examine the corpse, carefully."

One of the guards was suitably corruptible, and Mouse was sent on another errand. Francesca had to wait impatiently.

Benito was right. De Belmondo, at least, was in the clear. Why else would the Count have been murdered?

"It's a good thing not all De Belmondo's informants are so trusting that they'd talk to his secretary," said Manfred, when she told them the story. "Or Alexander Konstantis might be dead, too. And for once, just once, I know more than you do, dear. You see, De Belmondo really *was* out of his office. He was seeing me. While that wicked spy his secretary had told him about was away!"

Erik came in from the office of the garrison commander. "I have news for all of you. Eneko has found Fianelli."

The actual arrest, coming after all those months of looking for Fianelli, was almost an anticlimax. Thanks to Alexander Konstantis's inspired meddling, those who had conspired with Captain-General Tomaselli were caught, red-handed, in possession of documents from Emeric, with their names on each. Eneko and the Knights burst in on the secretary's chambers at the same time, so that Loukaris could not get warning. They caught him and his master, Fianelli, who had been hiding like a boll weevil right in the middle of his hunters.

"Well, Francesca. You should be pleased with yourself," said Manfred, patting her on the back.

She looked at him, consideringly. "What I have found

is a series of strings and levers pulled by an evil man. I
can't call Emeric anything else. I'm just afraid of what
else there is."

Eneko nodded. "This drought, for example. It is
undoubtedly magical and undoubtedly the product of
Emeric, although I had not realized him capable of
such great magics. And the female Satanist is still at
large, don't forget."

"So is Sophia Tomaselli," grumbled Manfred. "How
can a woman that dimwitted have evaded us for so
long?"

That evening, as she studied again the records she
had slowly compiled, it was Francesca who felt herself
to be dimwitted. Never more so than the moment she
realized the truth.

"Of course!" she exclaimed, slapping the table with a
combination of exasperation and triumph. "How could I
have been so *stupid*? It's right there in Eneko's records—
once I match it properly against every else! Especially
the inheritance records! The creature inherited the house
within days after her aunt and uncle were killed—and
they were killed, according to those same records, at the
same moment that Eneko and Diego remember a terrible
burst of black magic."

Manfred raised his head from the pillow. He'd been
lying on the bed, a bit disgruntled because—very common, lately—Francesca was working at her desk instead
of being her usual seductive self.

"What are you talking about?"

Francesca ignored the question, too busy scrabbling
furiously through the mass of papers piled on her desk.
"Yes! And again! That little boy who disappeared—another
burst of satanic magic—and he was known to beggar on
the same street where she lives!"

More scrabbling. "Her name's everywhere in these
records, now that I finally have my senses. *Everywhere.*
Always seeming—taking each thing at a time—like a minor
and insignificant figure. But—"

More scrabbling. A paper held up triumphantly.
"Yes! She was known to be a friend and confidant of

Sophia Tomaselli!" Scrabble; another paper; scrabble; yet another.

Francesca rose, a paper clutched in each hand. Her eyes were slitted. "*And* she was noticed, twice, in the company of one of Fianelli's thugs. *And* in the company of Aldo Morando, on one occasion. All small incidents, buried in the mass. But taken as a whole, it's obvious. I have been so *stupid*."

Manfred was on his feet, now, reaching for his armor and weapons.

"You won't need those," Francesca muttered. "She's just a woman, Manfred, not a Magyar cavalryman. Besides, the Venetian authorities will do the arrest."

He shrugged, continuing what he was doing. "Eneko says she's a 'female,' not a woman. I've encountered a monster in the Basque priest's company, once—so I think I'll do it my way."

Impatiently—no moving Manfred, in a stubborn mood—Francesca waited till he was done. By the end, she was even in a good mood about it.

"Might be just as well. I need to get confirmation from Morando—and, for that, I'll need you to intimidate the Venetians into allowing me to offer him a commutation of his sentence." She patted Manfred fondly on the cheek—with only two fingers, that being the most she could get past the cheek guards. "You do look *so* impressive in full armor. You would even if you weren't a prince. Come, dear."

Morando had been half-asleep when his cell was suddenly invaded. He woke up instantly, however—as a prisoner condemned to death is bound to do when he finds his cell occupied by almost every major figure of authority in the area, several priests, three Knights of the Holy Trinity in full armor—and a beautiful woman.

Francesca de Chevreuse, in a dramatic gesture, drew forth several slips of paper from her gown. She handed one each to the podesta, the commander of the garrison, one of the priests, and the hugest of the Knights.

"I've written a name on those slips, Morando. The same name on each one. If you can match that name—it's the identity of your accomplice, the one you've been keeping a secret from us—you'll live. If you can't—or won't—you'll be executed. Here. Today—not later in Venice. So forget about the possibility of being rescued if Emeric takes the Citadel. Not that he wouldn't kill you himself anyway."

She grinned at him mercilessly. "In honor of Venetian authority, we will use the traditional Venetian method of execution. It begins, I believe, by breaking the legs. Then—though I'm not sure about this, it's all too ghastly for a delicate woman to contemplate—they do something with your innards."

Morando swallowed. He *did* know the procedures used by Venetians when they executed someone who had truly and genuinely infuriated them. Traitors being right at the top of the list.

It was, indeed, too ghastly to contemplate.

"Bianca Casarini," he croaked.

Slips of paper were studied briefly. A moment later, the cell was empty again.

Chapter 92

Bianca detected the coming soldiers when they were still some distance away—and had sensed the presence of Eneko Lopez even sooner. She had, many weeks earlier, established a faint degree of mental control over the urchins who were always in the streets, and who served her as unwitting and unconscious human alarm signals.

"That's it, then," she murmured to herself. "It's time to hide."

The thought was neither hurried nor frantic. She'd prepared for this moment, and prepared well. Three weeks ago, working mindlessly under her control, Saluzzo had finished breaking a hole through the rear wall into an adjoining house. The residents of the house, an elderly couple, had never noticed a thing—being, also, under Bianca's compulsions.

She'd slide through the hole, pass through the house, and be out on another street and heading for Morando's hideout before Lopez and the soldiers could finish breaking down the front door.

She rose and took a small bag from the side table in her bedroom. She'd had the bag ready for days, with all of her essential instruments and ingredients in it. Moving quickly down the stairs, she smiled savagely.

Then they'll have Saluzzo to deal with. And the fools came at night, to boot! In the darkness, the mindless thing he becomes will be twice as dangerous.

Saluzzo was slumbering on a divan in the front room, as he usually was, these days. He spent most of his time lately doing nothing but eating and dozing, awash in the reveries Bianca provided him. He'd grown a bit fat and soft as a result, but that didn't concern Bianca. The transformation he was about to undergo would make "fat and soft" completely meaningless.

She strode over, placed her hand on his face, and sent a jolt of sheer agony blazing through his head. Then, stepped back quickly.

Sputtering and yowling, Saluzzo scrambled to his feet and stared at Bianca. He was simply confused, at the moment.

His confusion vanished, as Bianca slapped him across the cheek. Then, spit in his face.

Rage came instantly to a man like Saluzzo. His face contorted with fury, looking even uglier in the light cast by the single lamp in the room. He took a step toward her, his big fist raised.

Perfect. Rage was essential to a full transformation. All that was needed now were the words of power, words that had never been intended to be shaped by human lips, but which Bianca had long practice in uttering.

Again, Saluzzo yowled with pain. A yowl, this time, that went on and on and on—and, as it continued, started changing in timbre and tone, within seconds sounding more like the scream of a beast than a human being.

Bianca sped from the room. She had perhaps a minute to escape, while Saluzzo's body was paralyzed by the changes it was undergoing. By then, the semi-mindless demon-shaped beast he'd have become, tormented by the agony of muscles, nerves, and bone wrenched into new shapes and the unfettered, pain-charged anger she had invoked, would not be able to think at all, much less clearly. By then, also, the soldiers would have started breaking in the door and the Saluzzo-monster's rage would have a different target.

And what a shock they would have, when their steel and iron weapons and armor did not protect them.

❖   ❖   ❖

Outside, on the street, Eneko Lopez fell to one knee. His hands clasped his head as if he'd been struck by a sudden and ferocious pain-lance straight into his brain.

The Venetian soldiers paused, as did Manfred and Erik. The arresting unit was still some twenty yards from the Casarini house. There was a full moon out, this night, so the house was clearly visible.

"What's wrong, Eneko?"

The priest seemed unable to speak. Manfred could see that his face was tight with pain. It also seemed pale as a sheet, although that could have been the effect of the moonlight.

Erik waved to the sergeant commanding the ten soldiers. "Go on. There's no time to waste."

The sergeant and his men continued forward, two of the soldiers hefting axes while four others held torches aloft. Erik knelt alongside Eneko. Manfred couldn't, because he was wearing full armor. His Icelander bodyguard, as he usually did given the choice, had opted to wear nothing more than half-armor for the occasion. Erik had learned to fight in Iceland and Vinland, and never was really comfortable in the heavy Teutonic armor favored by the Knights.

"Can we do anything, Eneko?" he asked.

The priest shook his head. Then, slowly, withdrew his hands from his temples. When his eyes caught sight of the soldiers—now standing before the door, raising their axes—they widened. And his face, impossibly, seemed to grow paler still.

"Oh, dear God—*no*. Erik, get them away from that door! They will be no match for—"

It was too late. The door shattered from within, not a second after the first axe landed. *Something* erupted out of it. Because of the darkness, it was difficult to see it clearly. Manfred could only discern a thing of scales and wings and horns and talons, with a face like a gargoyle's, shrieking fury.

The soldier holding the axe was smashed aside, by a taloned paw that shredded his throat in passing. A backhand blow from the same paw sent the other axe-wielding soldier sprawling, knocking down two other soldiers with him, their torches scattering.

The monster took a stride forward and crushed the sergeant's skull, its talons stripping away the helmet as if it were a mere skullcap. Then, to Manfred's horror, seized the sergeant by the shoulders as he collapsed and *bit* his head in half. The fangs sheered through the poor man's skull and brains like a knife through cheese.

The creature flung the sergeant's corpse aside and spit out the top part of his head, then spread its huge arms and bellowed with rage and a kind of hideous, triumphant glee.

Still, the moments the demon had taken to kill the sergeant had given the rest of the soldiers the time to back away. Back away *frantically*. Two of them dropped their weapons and simply ran. The remaining soldiers stood their ground, more or less, but they looked about as confident as five-year-boys facing a tiger in full fury.

Manfred felt calm settling over him, a calm so profound it was almost serenity.

"There's always adventures when you're around, Eneko," he said cheerfully, drawing his broadsword. "Erik, get that creature's attention for me, if you would."

Manfred stepped forward, holding his sword in both hands, the huge blade gleaming in the moonlight. From the corner of his eye, he could see that Erik was hesitating. Not surprising, of course—the Icelander was supposed to guard the prince from danger, after all, not draw the attention of monsters upon him.

"*Now*, Erik." Manfred's voice was soft, but the words came like iron. The commanding words of a prince, when all was said and done.

Erik stared at Manfred. And then, felt calmness coming over him as well.

He knew, finally, in that moment, what he had begun to suspect for some time. If Manfred survived his life—no telling *that*, of course—he would become one of Europe's great legends.

So be it. Erik Hakkonsen had been charged with guarding a prince, not just a man. He could hardly complain if, in the end, the man lived up to his station. A true prince was not simply an heir; he was also charged with protecting his people.

Erik drew his tomahawk, stepped forward and hurled it. Unerringly, the weapon flew toward the demon—unseen by it in the dark of night—and struck the creature between its horns.

Had Erik been using the proper Algonquin tomahawk he'd once had, that strike might well have felled the monster itself. As it was, the blade sank into the skull but didn't succeed in splitting the creature's brains. Not too surprising, of course. The thing's skull was considerably thicker than the little brain remaining within.

The demon screamed with pain and fury, its vaguely boarlike face swinging toward Erik and Manfred. Erik thought the eyes gleamed red; though it was difficult to be sure of color, in the dim moonlight.

Manfred took another step forward. *"Come to me, beast!"*

Still screaming, the demon sprang off the stoop and hurtled down the street toward Manfred. Its wings were spread fully now, and flapping. They were not sufficient to lift the great, heavy thing off the ground entirely, but they enabled it to race forward at an inhuman speed.

An instant later, the horrible creature was leaping in the air, sailing down upon Manfred like a hawk stooping on a chicken.

A very large and dangerous chicken. Manfred's great shoulders hunched and he swept the sword across, chest-high to the demon.

"DIA A COIR!"

It was an incredible sword-strike. The blade severed the monster in half. The upper half, still screaming, bounced off Manfred's lowered helmet and shoulders and spilled on the street behind him, almost at Eneko's feet. The lower half, gushing ichor and intestines, flopped backward.

Eneko Lopez stared at the thing writhing in front of him, the boar's face with its tusks still gnashing, the taloned paws scrabbling at the cobblestones.

He raised his crucifix. "That which cannot abide the name of—"

He never finished the sentence. *THUNK.* Manfred's sword removed the monster's head entirely, sending it rolling down the street like a loose cannonball. Erik hurried after it, muttering something about lost tomahawks.

THUNK. Manfred's sword, driven straight down with both hands, pierced the monster's spine and pinned the torso to the street itself. Whether by luck or simply the prince's great strength, the tip of the blade wedged itself between two cobblestones.

Meanwhile, working both fearfully and frantically, the soldiers were hacking the lower part of the demon's body into pieces. It was hideous work, if not particularly dangerous—though one soldier was knocked off his feet by a reflexive kick from one of the monster's flailing legs. Fortunately, the leg ended in a hoof instead of talons, so the soldier suffered nothing worse than a bad bruise.

The demon's torso was still twitching, but more feebly now. Eneko looked down the street the other way and saw that Erik was returning—his tomahawk in one hand and the demon's head held by one bat-shaped ear in the other. The head's maw was still gnashing, and, as the priest watched, made an attempt to bite Erik on the leg.

"Stupid," Manfred grunted.

Sure enough, Erik set the head down on a nearby stoop and proceeded to smash out all its fangs with the tomahawk. Three quick blows, delivered with all of Erik's skill with the weapon, and there really wasn't much left of the thing except blood and bone fragments, held together by strips of hide.

Not that Erik was probably planning to mount it as a trophy, anyway. Manfred glared down at his sword.

"Damnation," he growled. "It's going to take me *hours* to sharpen it properly. Eneko, sometimes I think you're more trouble than you're worth."

The priest rose to his feet, scowling. "We're not finished yet, Prince Manfred. This"—he pointed at the demon's carcass—"was just a tool. The real monster is still inside."

Eneko looked at the shattered door, feeling immensely

frustrated. "Or not. Probably not, any longer. That's why the creature set this thing loose. I sensed the incantation—as horrible as any I've ever encountered—which is what sent me to my knees."

Manfred's bull-like strength was put to use again. Even for him, withdrawing the sword was a struggle. But, within a few seconds, he and Erik were pushing through the entrance into the house. Their weapons ready, with Eneko and his crucifix coming right behind.

And, as Eneko had foreseen, it was too late. Bianca Casarini was gone.

Within a minute, they'd found the escape route she'd taken. But the elderly couple living in the adjoining house seemed comatose, and their own rear entrance was wide open.

After looking down that street, Manfred stated the obvious. "It's nighttime. She could be anywhere, by now."

Chapter 93

As soon as she entered Morando's cellar from the secret entrance, and closed the wall behind her, Bianca felt a thrilling surge of triumph. Her plans were working—and working perfectly!

She'd be safe from discovery here. The Venetian authorities in the Citadel had, weeks earlier, sealed the front entrance to Morando's domicile. They'd had to, in order to put a stop to the constant stream of curious visitors. That meant no one would even think of reopening the cellar and looking in it again.

Only one danger remained, and she'd deal with that now. Bianca went directly to the altar, not bothering to look around. The altar was a fake, true enough, but put to Bianca's use instead of the charlatan Morando's, it would serve her purpose.

Quickly, using the tools and ingredients in the bag she'd brought with her, she performed the necessary ritual. Not like the much more difficult scrying in blood she needed to use to speak with her putative mistress, this was a simple thing—communication by fire. Nothing that the powers of Corfu would be able to touch or hinder.

She kindled the flame of a candle made of the rendered fat of an unbaptized baby; then bent over the flame, cupping her hands about it, and whispered a single name.

This was a mild incantation, not something she had any

fear that the cursed Lopez would be able to detect. In and of itself, simply a communication—and with someone whom she'd prepared long ago for the purpose.

In his cell, Morando suddenly awoke, gasping for breath.

"Bianca?" he whispered. "Is that you?"

He saw the image of her beautiful face emerge, seeming like an apparition in midair. She was smiling gently.

"It's me, Aldo. But keep your voice down."

"Thank God!" Then, speaking softly: "Listen, they still don't know anything about you—and they say they'll commute my sentence to ten years on the galleys. So with your help—"

"*Nothing*, Aldo? They don't know about the secret entrance to the cellar?"

He shook his head. "No, I kept that from them. The only—"

He got no further. Bianca said some words he didn't catch and a sudden sharp pain stabbed through his chest. He gasped, clutching his chest with both hands.

Dimly, through the pain, he saw Bianca's smile widen. "Poor Aldo," she said. "That's the needle you're feeling. The one I implanted below your skin months ago while you were sleeping—and then numbed the nerves in the area, so you'd never sense it."

Her mouth worked, speaking more words. He knew it was an incantation of some kind, though he didn't understand the words themselves. "It's working its way into your heart now. Don't be concerned, though. I don't have time to enjoy this properly. It'll all be over within a minute."

The agony was now too intense for speech, or even screaming; the shock, even more so. He simply gaped at her, until he died.

In Casarini's abandoned house, Eneko Lopez broke off his part of the search they were conducting. His hands started to fly to his temples, again. But, this time, his frustration and anger was so great that he slammed them against a wall instead.

"*May the saints blast the monster! She's doing it again!*"

He leaned against the wall, shuddering. His face full of concern, Manfred took a step toward him.

Then, suddenly, the priest whole body grew rigid. "Wait," he murmured. "Something is happening . . ."

Perhaps a minute later, Eneko pushed away from the wall and turned toward Manfred. To the prince's astonishment, there was a smile on the priest's face.

A very, very, very grim smile. "I shall have to do penance for this, of course," said the priest. "Vengeance is, indeed, the province of the Lord. Still, I can't help but treasure this moment."

As she turned away from the altar, smiling broadly with satisfaction—treachery was *so* sweet—Bianca was startled by a sudden motion in the darkness of the cellar.

Sophia Tomaselli's face loomed in front of her. Bianca barely recognized the woman. The once-fastidious *Case Vecchie* looked like a hag. Filthy, her hair disarrayed—and with a hag's contorted grimace.

"You bitch! This is *my* refuge!"

Too late, Bianca saw that Sophia held a heavy candlestick in one hand—and was raising it to strike.

She threw up her arm to block the blow, but her recent use of two powerful incantations had left her very fatigued. She couldn't get the arm up in time. The brass candlestick smashed into her forehead like a mallet, sending her dazed and half-conscious to the floor.

Consciousness returned perhaps thirty seconds later, pain leading the way.

She couldn't breathe!

Her hands flew to her throat. There was something—

It was a silk scarf, she realized. Digging deeply into her throat, cutting off all air and blood. Somewhere behind her, Sophia Tomaselli was holding the thing, strangling her as Bianca had once strangled a niece.

"You stinking slut! Aldo's mine, not yours!"

Tomaselli's words came in grunts, sounding more like

something uttered by a peasant than a noblewoman. "Besides," Sophia hissed, "there's not . . . enough food. I'll share it . . . with Aldo . . . when he comes . . . but not *you.*"

Bianca was frantic now. The situation was absurd. How could such a pathetic creature as *Sophia Tomaselli* possibly be a threat to her? But the fact remained that the hag was in such a frenzy that she'd kill Bianca if she weren't stopped.

Automatically, Bianca started to utter the incantations that would destroy the creature—only to realize, then, that whether Sophia understood what she was doing or not, strangling a sorceress is perhaps the safest way to kill her.

She couldn't speak a word! In fact, her mind was becoming so fuzzy from lack of air that she wasn't sure she could have remembered the words well enough to incant them properly, even if she had been able to speak.

Bianca went into a paroxysm of terror, writhing and twisting on the floor. But everywhere she went, Sophia stayed on top of her—like some hideous leech, sucking out her life.

Desperately, she planted her hands on what part of Sophia she could reach. Nothing more than her hips, unfortunately, which were protected by the woman's tattered but still richly thick garments. The pain touch worked much better on bare skin—especially skin with a lot of nerves close to the surface. Even if she could have clawed her way past the fabric to Sophia's buttocks, she'd only have been touching fatty flesh.

Still, Bianca used the last of her strength to send agony pouring into Sophia's body as best she could. And a great deal of agony it was, too, despite the handicaps. Bianca Casarini was fighting for her life, and the agony she summoned was driven by a will to live that had sent her into every foulness imaginable, for years.

It was perhaps the worst thing she could have done, not that she really had any options. Sophia's body arched like a suddenly drawn bow from the excruciating pain—but her hands, clenched by the same agony, never let go of the scarf. The silk that had been choking

Casarini now collapsed her windpipe completely, crushing it into ruin.

Bianca spit out blood, feeling her life going with it.

I can't believe it! Sophia Tomaselli!
I WANTED TO LIVE FOREVER!

"She's dead," Eneko said grimly. "I felt the monster dying. I knew the moment she was gone."

He knelt and crossed himself, then kissed the crucifix, reverentially—and yet, Erik thought, with some other emotion as well. Guilt? Regret? Though Erik could not imagine what Eneko Lopez could possibly have to feel guilty about, at least in this instance.

"How did she die?" asked Erik.

After he rose to his feet, Lopez shrugged. "That, I couldn't tell you. I am not clairvoyant, you know. I could simply sense the monster's frantic attempts to use magic to forestall her death—somebody or something was killing her, that much I know, though I couldn't tell you who or what—and her eventual failure."

His expression was grimmer than Manfred had ever seen it—and Eneko was a man given to a grim view of the world. "'Vengeance is mine, sayeth the Lord,'" he heard the priest murmur. "Still . . . the beast died in great despair as well as fury. It was fitting."

And you shall *live forever, Bianca Casarini. Oh, yes, most certainly.*

Confused, Bianca opened her eyes. She was more confused, then, by what she saw.

First, because all the images seemed duplicated—no, multiplied, many times over.

Oh, you'll get accustomed to compound eyes soon enough. Perhaps unfortunately, from your point of view. Not mine, of course.

The strange voice seemed to be coming from all directions at once. Bianca's eyes moved over the . . . landscape?

Hard to tell. It just seemed like a world made of cables. A kind of enormous net of cables. Dirty-white in color, stretching to what seemed like infinity. She sensed that the effect was not simply caused by the weird multiplication of her vision.

A reddish glow somewhere to her left drew her gaze that way. Dully, she stared at it for a while. How long, she couldn't say. She seemed to have difficulty determining the passage of time.

The color of the glow changed, slowly; shading from red to yellow to, eventually, a particularly loathsome shade of yellow-green. The color of slime, if slime were as hot as lava.

Also the color she'd once seen, in a glimpse she'd gotten of the Great One. The eyes that weren't eyes at all, but something that had reminded her at the time of staring into bottomless, volcanic cesspools.

Welcome, Bianca Casarini! Welcome to eternity!

Realization finally came to her. She opened her mouth to scream.

Tried to, rather. She had no mouth. Looking down, all she could see was a proboscis of some kind, where she'd once had a nose.

Looking down still further, at her body, she saw that her lungs were now on the outside, red-veined and pulsing.

Oh, yes, that. I'm afraid that certain physical laws still apply here. On this level, at any rate. There are quite a bit more than nine, incidentally. How many? Hard to say. Depends on which mathematical formula you use.

She tried to scream again. The only effect was to make her proboscis grow more rigid—and cause the lungs to pulsate quicker.

Yes, yes, I'm afraid so. Volume to surface-area ratios, that sort of thing. All very tawdry, I'm afraid. It also means that discreet little spiracles won't do the trick at all. So I've had to modify your lungs a bit.

It does make you hideously ugly, true. But, then, that's now the least of your problems. I'm afraid Crocell lost his sexual appetites long ago—and wouldn't care in the least if you were still as comely as you were.

Paralysis was giving way to terror. Bianca's eyes now ranged down the rest of her body.

There were *way* too many legs, and she was quite

sure that wasn't simply a function of her strange new vision. Skinny, weirdly jointed, *hairy* legs.

Six legs, to be precise. I'm something of a stickler when it comes to tradition. Very conservative, actually, despite my reputation as a rebel.

Ah. Here comes Crocell, now. Give him a nice run, would you, Bianca? I have to keep him well-exercised, for the rare occasions when I let him out.

She sensed the vibration first. Looking down, she saw that her feet—*feet? what were those horrid claw-like things?*—were planted on one such cable. The cable seemed to be undulating. As if some great weight had been placed upon it.

She twisted her body—awkwardly, since she was unaccustomed to its new shape—and saw that a monster was moving toward her along the cable. Like a great spider, except for the face.

It was the face that finally broke what was left of Bianca Casarini's self-control. For some reason, the sight of a middle-aged man's face on such a monster—except that he possessed mandibles as well as jaws—was more horrifying than anything else.

Worst of all, was the look of bleak despair in the man's eyes. Utter and complete despair, such as Bianca had never seen before—not even in the eyes of her own victims.

Crocell was a much *better cheater than you were, Bianca. Oh, much better. That's why he gets a privileged position here. So to speak.*

As I said, I even let him out now and then. A privilege which, I'm afraid, you'll not be enjoying.

Bianca fled down the cable, shrieking silently. She could feel the cable thrumming beneath her feet, under the treads of something much heavier than she.

Oh, please, Bianca! Have no fear—after he sucks out your juices, I'll replenish them again. It's agonizingly painful, of course, but not terminal in the least.

If only she could scream!

No, no, not in the least bit terminal. Even though you were planning to cheat me, I'm not at all vengeful. Despite what you may have heard.

If only she could scream!

You wanted eternal life, Bianca Casarini. And now you have it.

If only she could scream!

As food.

PART XIV
January, 1540 A.D.

Chapter 94

"They've landed on Vidos Island!"

Like everyone else, Benito scrambled out of bed and rushed for a viewpoint of the island off to the northeast of the Citadel. Benito eyed the beached vessels on the island with impotent fury. The castle's defenders were firing, but it was obviously too little and far too late.

Vidos Island had guarded the northern sea access to the Citadel. Now, with the island obviously under heavy attack, the people of the fortress realized that there would be no place that would be entirely free from cannon fire. There would be no respite. The cannon from Vidos would not be able to hit the Citadel, but the Byzantine fleet would now be able to sail into that area and shell the Citadel without coming under direct fire from both flanks.

Benito strode off in search of Manfred. He found him standing with Erik contemplating the situation grimly. "They're in the outer walls of the island already," said the Icelander. "The keep might hold out a while, but it won't be for too long."

"And they'll be able to harry the northeast too." Benito sighed. With Emeric's latest increase in bombardment on the city itself, rather than just the walls, much of the population had taken to at least sleeping over there. True, very few people had been killed by the cannon fire, but it was frightening and hurt morale. Knowing there was no place that they could truly get away from the possibility of a cannonball killing them—or, worse, their children—was going to dent morale even further. Emeric was slowly chipping away at the spirit of Citadel with starvation and fear.

"We need to strike back somehow."

"A sortie is out of the question," Manfred said. "You two have forced Emeric to invest more in defense than he has in attacking capability. The shingle out there is a set of death traps for horses."

"Then let's take it to the bastards by sea," urged Benito. "We've got the fireboats. If the keep on Vidos hasn't fallen by tonight, they'll have all their carracks bunched around the island, firing ship's cannon at the keep."

Manfred cocked his head at Erik. "You've looked at those cockleshells. What do you think?"

Erik nodded. "Almost all of their larger cannon are on the carracks. The cannon on those carracks are what they've mostly been using to harass the Citadel from the sea with anyway. Burn them and you'll reduce their marine gunnery to a pitiful effort."

"But will it work?"

Erik shrugged. "Those little boats are works of shipbuilder's art, Manfred. They've got one weakness: they were built to run straight with the wind. If we can row them to a point where they're directly upwind, leave each of them with a slow-match and a dead bearing . . . well, it is going to be a question of how well we aim and how well we can judge the slow-match time. You'd be aiming a small boat at a small target a long way away. Most of them would miss. Still, it's worth trying. We're not going to get as many Byzantine ships so close together again. Get one of those little sailing bombs in among them and we'll likely see a fair number catch fire."

Benito compressed his lips. "We're *not* going to miss. Not if I have to ride those little ships all the way in myself. Call it Umberto's legacy. The Little Arsenal has about fifteen longboats. The Byzantines would either have to up anchor and out oars in the dark, or, with the light galleys beached at Vidos, launch. It's the better part of a mile . . . but with a start and twelve rowers we should do it."

"What are you suggesting, Benito?"

"We lower longboats. Give each team two fireboats to tow out. The enemy are going to be focused on Vidos. We should be able to get really close—they're firing and the muzzle-flash will be easy to see. Set the fireboats on their line, leave one man to each, have him jump overboard at the last moment. With luck, the longboats will recover the aimers."

"Why does someone need to stay with each fireboat?"

"Because they don't have steerage if they aren't moving quite fast." He saw the puzzled look on Manfred's face. "Just take it from me or Erik. That's how it works, Manfred."

Manfred looked at him with a strange expression. "You'll need men who are tired of life, Benito. The longboats won't be able to hang about looking for anyone."

"Manfred, we're starving. We're down to four cupfuls of water a day per man. You don't have to be tired of life to volunteer for this—you have to want, desperately, to live." He shook his head. "The people down at the Little Arsenal are furious about Umberto's murder. They're tired of being powerless to do anything. A lot of them— especially the caulkers—swim like fish. The caulkers have to, for when there's a sprung plank. There's only so much you can do to repair a ship from the inside, and if the ship's on the water it means diving with a rope around your waist and some wadding. I'll get volunteers all right." He sighed. "I'll get too many."

"You know I will not assist in the war of one Christian soldier against another," said Eneko Lopez. "Regardless of what vileness Emeric delves into or what Chernobog does, most of Emeric's troops and the Byzantine soldiers are of our faith."

Benito held up his hands pacifyingly. "I'm not proposing you do anything that kills anyone, Eneko. All I was hoping for was some way to save good men from drowning in the darkness. Like the glowing winged Lion on the sails of the great galleys."

Eneko Lopez looked at him with those penetrating

eyes, and apparently decided in Benito's favor. "Tell me what you are planning. I suppose I should be grateful that a fiendish mind like yours is on the side opposing Chernobog and the Devil-worshipers."

Benito told him. Eneko Lopez shook his head. "And you have thirty men prepared to do this?"

"I think at last count even places on the longboats were double-subscribed." Benito looked at Eneko consideringly. "You know, Father Lopez—everybody always lectures or preaches to me. Antimo said it was my face. Now I'm going to do the same for you, seeing as you've also done it to me." He grinned wryly. "Fair's fair, after all. You priests, Justices—even princes—seem to think you have the monopoly on a sense of justice. It isn't like that at all. I promise you the scuolo, the boat-people, hell, even thieves, have a sense of justice. Of what is right. It may not always be what the priests and others think is right, but they believe in it. And they're prepared to pay a high price for what they believe in. The Arsenalotti are angry and frustrated about this siege, and about the murder. Umberto was a quiet fellow, but he was theirs. He'd stood by them, he'd bled for them. Maria too. The Corfiotes think more of her than they do of the governor, for instance. They're bitter about her loss. She's even won over the Illyrians. I've got men who can't swim volunteering. I had four times what I wanted for the fireboats. Now, are you going to help me keep these men alive or are you going to get sanctimonious with me?"

Eneko Lopez looked at him in silence. Then he drew a deep breath. "I stand humbled. You know, those of us who fight the battle for the human spirit do so because we believe in its potential. We are, after all, made in the image of God. But sometimes we spend so much time isolated and only dealing with the bad that we forget. Yes. Some luminescence can be magically contained in small bottles. It is not without cost, but I suppose if you fail and the Citadel falls . . . evil will have its day unchecked."

"I'll take the bottles with gratitude," said Benito. "But as for 'unchecked,' Eneko, short of clearing Corfu of people, Emeric is just going to meet unending resistance, whether we're here or not. Erik sowed the wind out there. Emeric is reaping the whirlwind."

The wind was to the southeast, blowing dust from Corfu's once green fields across the Citadel. "It's not natural," grumbled one of the Corfiotes. "It should be blowing northwesterly."

"And it should be raining, too," said his friend with a dry smile. "And then we could row twice as far and get wet from above with fresh water and below with salt. Stop complaining, Dimitros."

His companion continued blackening his face. "I need something to keep my mind busy. This is crazy!"

"Have your tot of grappa, and let's get on with it."

One by one, the small boats were lowered into the sea. In tense silence now, the little flotilla began running out toward the muzzle flashes around Vidos. The inner keep had no large cannon. The Byzantine vessels were perfectly safe.

But some good admiral had still deployed a couple of small galliots to patrol. Benito thought his heart would stop when one of them loomed up through the darkness.

"What ships?" called the watchman on the prow.

"Tell them we're some Greek name, we've sprung a leak and we're taking water," whispered Benito. "And then we row like hell. We have to board them."

Obviously, at least five of the longboats had had the same idea. The small galliot was a twenty-oar vessel—but she was quartering the wind and the oars were shipped. Abandoning all stealth the longboats closed fast.

Shots rang out . . . and then they were on board, desperate Venetians and Corfiotes, outnumbering the crew, boarding from several vessels. The silence they'd hoped for was a lost dream. Now all they could do was move fast.

Benito had volunteered for the fireboats. The *scuolo* liked him too much to tell him he was an inexperienced amateur seaman. Besides, he was lucky. And crazy. They needed that, too.

A caulker grabbed him by the shoulder. "Come, milord.

The lads are getting the sails up. We'll deal with this ship. You get to yours. There'll be trouble coming."

Benito scrambled over the side of the galliot and onto the fireboat assigned to him. Someone handed down the slow-match. "Go Valdosta! Go!"

The darkness ahead was Vidos. With the fireboat's sixteen feet of oil-and-gunpowder-laden hull accelerating beneath the belling sail, Benito did what steering was possible. Then he put the rudder into the bracket. She'd run straight now, but any lookout attracted by the shooting out at the galliot could hardly miss her. Just as he thought that, Benito realized that the carracks at anchor were firing now, not at Vidos Castle keep, but at them. Salt spray flying, Benito touched the slow-match to the fuse. It sputtered and lit. Taking a deep breath, Benito dove overboard.

The water was chilly. As he came up the night sky was suddenly lit by an explosion and a plume of flames. One of the fireboats wasn't going to get to the fleet.

Benito tugged at the bottle tied to his waist. "Fiat lux!" he spluttered.

There was light. There were other lights in the water, mostly farther back toward the Citadel. And the oil from the cannon-hit fireboat was burning on the water—much too close for comfort. Benito took a desperate look around, wondered how long he could hold his breath and swim underwater, and resolved he'd drown before he burned.

Then a longboat with the boatswain calling stroke, as if this were a regular trip out to a carrack at anchor, came out of the darkness and hauled him inboard. "I might have known you'd be the closest to the enemy," said a wet Erik, grimly. "We've lost a good few men, and the galleys are going to be after us. Look."

Benito saw a galley silhouetted against the flames. Saw the muzzle flash. And laughed helplessly. "That's the one we captured, Erik. It looks like the boys are trying to take it home."

There was huge explosion and flash behind them. The men at the oars pulled. The little boat raced toward the Citadel. Vidos might fall, but, as Benito peered back at the pandemonium of fireboats exploding, he knew

Umberto's idea made sure it hadn't been a cheap victory for King Emeric.

It was a fitting repayment.

It was morning before they could see just exactly what the damage had been. Benito already knew the cost. Four men had not been picked up. One, Dimitros, had ridden his fireboat right in, while his longboat team, rowing frantically behind, had screamed at him to jump. Only God knew what had been in his mind now; presumably he was explaining himself to the recording angel, trying to persuade him that it hadn't been suicide. In attacking the galliot, now beached on the northern shingle beside the *San Nicolo* and *Dolphin's* hulks, the Venetians and Corfiotes had suffered nine wounded and five killed.

They'd seen that some of the Byzantine fleet had burned last night. But now at first light every survivor (who wasn't in the hospital) of what was being called "Umberto's revenge" was on the northern wall looking out. Counting ships.

There was silence. "Lord and Saints," said someone awed. "If we could come along now with four great galleys we'd hold the sea!"

That might have been something of an exaggeration. But the carrack fleet was considerably reduced. The fire had taken—or made the skippers run up onto Vidos—at least fifteen carracks, the bulk of the cannon-bearing vessels.

But it was the flag on the outer walls of Vidos castle that brought a cheer that must have rung right across the bay between them. When the fireboats had struck, the besiegers must have run to the shore. The island's trees had also caught fire, and the galleys and smaller craft the enemy had landed with must have had to either be rescued or burn. And the surviving soldiers had used the opportunity to retake the outer walls. How long the small garrison could keep the winged lion flying there was another matter, as the gate must be smashed. But it was a heartwarming sight, nonetheless.

A gunner from the walls of Vidos celebrated first light with a round into a largely intact carrack.

But looking at the cheering men and women on the Citadel, Benito couldn't escape the fact that they were all gaunt. The siege had now lasted more than eight months. Starvation might beat them yet, even if they'd just singed Emeric's beard for him.

Chapter 95

"We still hold total military superiority here on the island. We've still got some several hundred men on Vidos, and the barricade the defenders have put up on the gate's ruins can't hold."

General Krovoko was trying to put the best face on the situation that he could, but he was going to have to tell all of the truth, and he knew it—as he knew of Emeric's propensity to kill the messenger. "But the Byzantines are whimpering. With the bad weather most of their fleet was here in the shelter, so, naturally, we used them for the attack on Vidos. It was a fiasco. They were anchored in close formation off the southern side of the islet. When they saw the fireboats, several captains tried to run."

Anger crept into his tone. "If they'd just stayed put we'd have lost half as many vessels. In the dark, in panic, they ran into each other, fired cannon into each other, ran aground or just plain ran. Three of the vessels ran all the way to the Albanian shore and one of them was wrecked. We had a ship, burning, make landfall at Kommeno point. The local people killed most of the crew before the cavalry arrived. We lost nineteen carracks, and three galleys, with fire damage to another four vessels. We're down to seven carracks. The blockade, with nothing more than the Narenta galliots and that handful, is worth little, Sire."

General Krovoko was done with his report. Now he

waited, fatalistically, for the sky to fall on him. Emeric pushed himself back in his throne. "I know. But that's not really what concerns me. The Atlantic fleet hasn't come home and we know that the eastern fleet is still sitting in Trebizond after their attempt on the Dardanelles. It's the steady trickle of losses here on the island that worries me, especially as the weather, and the lack of ships, limit my fetching more troops."

Krovoko shook his head. He was a little surprised to find himself still alive and discussing the matter. "Sire, the countryside is definitely hostile, the insurgents in the north must number in the hundreds, and although we've taken Kassiopi, Paleokastritsa still holds out. The place is inaccessible and the locals have managed to resupply when the insurgents have attacked the forces we have there."

"But the island grows drier. Lack of water must be affecting them."

General Krovoko nodded. "What we really is need a safe place to rest our men. This campaign of raids and ambushes . . . it's wearing them down, Sire."

Emeric looked thoughtful, but offered no comment.

The Magyar cavalryman pointed to the map. "We can land men here, on the mainland, near this lake. Make a base for accumulating supplies and let the troops rest. We have more men than we need for the siege, and less than we need to hold siege and subdue the island. They'll be safe from the Venetians or even Corfiotes."

The Narenta pirate captain muttered in his dialect. It was, by the tone, something derisive.

Emeric looked coldly at him. "What was that?"

The pirate captain looked uneasy, but stood his ground. "I said that would be escaping from an angry cat into the lion's den. That is Iskander Beg's land. The Lord of the Mountains will not like it."

Emeric pinched his lips into a harsh line. "He doesn't have to like it. I've tried to contact him, to reach an agreement with the bandit. Well, he doesn't wish to treat with me. I would have preferred to bring my men here by land, but the mountains have too many places where ambushes are easy. But the land next to the lake is gentle. With the lake behind us, the sea in front, this should be an easy strip to hold. I like the idea. See to it, General. It will act as one side to the pincer I want to work on the coastal strip. I'll leave the bandit chief to his mountains. We'll hold the lowlands from here to Montenegro in the next few years.

"Now onto other affairs. We must press the attack on the Citadel hard now. Let drought take the rest of the island."

"We've walled and entrenched the moles," said Dragorvich. "The troops can move forward protected. The front wall is crumbling. Give us another two weeks' cannonade, Sire. A determined push will take the first curtain wall."

"You can have a few weeks. I want them pounded into submission. At the end of February—or at the latest, early March—we must be in. The Venetians will doubtless make something of a push in the spring with whatever ships they have ready. We'll want at least three weeks to repair and reequip the Citadel against that attack."

"We're down to third-rations." It was so dry that Maria and the other horta gatherers were not finding much to gather. Winter was not the best time for wild greens anyway, but there had always been something. . . .

But with this many women, and a restricted area to hunt in, it was getting less easy by the day. The sound of the cannons was by now such a normal part of the background noise, that it was only its stopping that they would have noticed. The attack on the walls now was relentless. The Hungarians had so increased their forward positions and fortifications that they could sally and attack the walls repeatedly with relative impunity. Food ships and water carts arrived for them each day. Here inside it was relentless starvation and less in the water ration by the day. Maria's biggest worry was having milk for Alessia. Two of the other women's breasts had already dried up. Too little water. Too little food. Alessia now weighed less than she had two months ago.

Maria could not weep for Umberto anymore; she dared

not waste the water on tears. What would she do if her milk dried up? It was a constant nagging fear.

"I know it's risky," said Benito, irritably. "But we're on our last legs here. If we actually knew when they were coming, it would make the world of difference. Come, Eneko. Please."

The cleric nodded, wearily. "Very well. We'll try again."

But there was no response.

Marco had an almost overpowering compulsion to make contact with his brother. But both Mascoli and the Strega sage Du Catres who sailed with them advised against it. They had, to be precise, forbidden it utterly. Marco had insisted on going on this voyage. "They'll need healers and food more than soldiers," he'd said. Finally Doge Dorma had given permission for him to go. Under conditions. The first was the shield of mages who accompanied him. The second was that Kat remained in Venice, at least until the siege was lifted. Dorma made it very clear that he would prefer it to be until Marco returned.

The priestess looked at the half-almond on the altar, and wondered. There was only one candidate. She had explained everything, as best she could. She had instructed, without demanding, without, as far as she could tell, even hinting. The candidate must choose of her own free will; that was the law. But would she? Would she even see the need?

She must. She must. Or they would all die here. Perhaps, even, the Goddess, and the Cold God.

Yes. Perhaps even them.

PART XV
March, 1540 A.D.

Chapter 96

"Back!" shouted Erik. "Back to the inner curtain-wall!"

Maria watched as the knights charged again, making space and time for the footmen and others to pull back without endangering the wall. Benito was out there, somewhere. Rearguard, setting explosives with the Knights' bombardier. She herself had only just gotten up here, having led the women up from the wall by the Little Arsenal. Toward the end, they'd been reduced to throwing cobbles and bricks at the enemy. The arquebusiers had shot out their powder. Blades were blunted and nicked. And yet there always seemed to be more foes.

Maria closed her eyes to pray, then opened them, looking at the scene below. Already the bulk of the Hungarian forces were pouring in through the breach in the outer wall. The inner wall, which enclosed the Castel *a mar* and the Castel *a terra*, was higher than the outer curtain wall—but it certainly wasn't thicker. And the wells in the upper part of Citadel were long dry. True, they'd all taken part in the filling of the huge cisterns up in the Castels . . . uphill all the way, carrying water ewers. But when that was gone, there would be no more.

According to Benito, the water available might last the ten thousand people inside the Citadel two weeks. The cisterns had been intended for the garrison only. On wet, verdant Corfu, the wells and the two springs in the inner citadel never ran dry.

Except now. There was an evil thing out there, as the high priestess had explained. A spirit of dryness, fire and death. A thing that caused green life to wither just by its existence.

Maria sighed. First her home. Then Umberto. And now this. They were being devoured slowly. She made her way through the crowded streets and to the hospital and the Hypatian chapel, where some women and the children who were too young to fling rocks had been sent when it was realized this was an assault that might actually succeed. Stella had taken Alessia and a number of other *scuolo* and Corfiote children so that the younger women could go to help on the walls.

She found Stella at the chapel, looking stunned and crying. "Alberto—he's missing! They tell me he was shot. He was with the rearguard. There was no one to bring him in. Dear God! Dear God!"

For once her children were silent. Big eyed. Scared, even the ones too young to fully understand.

Maria couldn't find words, so she simply hugged her, hard. The older woman clung to her. Maria swallowed. "Stella. You . . . you stood by me, when, when Umberto and I were new and friendless. You were there when there was that curse and others avoided me. You've stood by me. I'll help as much as I can."

Stella pulled away, despair warring with anger in her face. "God's Death, Maria, don't you understand? We're all going to die here. My man. My babies. All of us. We'll either die of thirst and starvation or the Hungarian monsters will get us."

Maria picked up Alessia. The little girl hung listlessly in her arms. "I'll do something. I have to."

She turned and walked out of the chapel. A horrible thought had just crossed her mind. If there had been no one to bring Alberto in . . . where was Benito? He was with the rearguard. Benito would always choose the hardest, the riskiest task. He would be in the front of the vanguard . . . and at the back of the rearguard. Maria went searching.

Eventually she found Erik and Manfred. The prince's armor was dented. His visor was now up and there was blood oozing from a small cut above his eye.

"Prince Manfred. I'm looking for Benito."

He looked a little annoyed that someone should trouble him at this stage. At the mention of Benito's name, though, the expression eased.

"Last I saw of him was when we were returning from that final sortie. He and a couple of others—a big fellow and another man—were lighting the charges to the houses on the road. Have you seen him, Erik?"

Erik frowned. "No. And he's supposed to report to me. Check with the gate guards. Wait. I'll come with you. That'll get answers."

Very shortly, Maria knew the worst.

Seven of the rearguard hadn't reached the gate. Alberto and Benito were both among them.

Benito. Gone.

What little remained of the bottom of her world crumbled and fell away, leaving her hollow and utterly, utterly alone.

She turned blindly from Erik, not hearing what he said, and walked away. Alessia whimpered and nuzzled weakly, but Maria had no milk to give her. Maria's eyes remained dry. There were no tears to cry now. The time for weeping was over.

She'd lost Umberto . . . He'd not been her soulmate, perhaps, but he'd been someone she'd gone from liking to loving. And now she'd lost the man she'd truly loved, too. Benito was gone. She hadn't even had a chance to say good-bye to him, much less tell him—well, much of anything. Except that he was a fool. Which he was. And that his wildness was going to get him killed.

Which it had.

And very soon she'd lose her baby, too. Alessia was dying, slowly, of hunger; the worst of all possible deaths. Even being spitted on a Hungarian spear was better than this, dying by inches.

And that was when she knew what she had to do.

It came to her, all of a piece; not as a blinding flash of revelation, but settling over her like a blanket. Certainty. And perhaps it was folly equal to Benito's, or insanity, and perhaps her soul would be damned, or perhaps it just wouldn't work at all . . . but there was only one person here who could and would do what she was about to. Therefore, she would do it. She had nothing to lose, now. Except Alessia, and if she did not do this thing, Alessia was lost anyway.

There was only one way forward. Squaring her chin, Maria walked determinedly through the frightened crowds, onward and upward to the Castel *a mar*—

—to see the high priestess. To tell her that she was ready to become the bride of the master of the black altar.

The guards recognized her; let her pass unquestioned. It all happened very quickly.

Renate was waiting for her, her hair loose, her white robe on.

"If you had not come—" The priestess looked exhausted, and seemed twenty years older than when Maria had first come to the island.

"Well," she said. "I did."

They took the passage down from the Castel to the hidden temple.

"Merde! They've come up the side!"

Struggling with the weight of Alberto—he might no longer be fat, but he was still large—Benito took a side street. Alberto was plainly in shock, but was doing his best to hobble, supported by the smaller man. The road was unfamiliar to Benito, but the sound of hooves galloping up the street was not. He hauled Alberto over a low wall and they hid as a troop of Croats rode past. Lying in the shadows, Benito suddenly realized that he had in fact seen the house across there before. It was dilapidated-looking, with a smashed door that was now boarded over.

The last time he'd been there, there'd been a guard on it, to keep away the curious from the house of the "black magician," Aldo Morando. He'd been there to look at the fraud's cellar. It might do as a place to hide. Alberto needed his leg tended, needed to rest. The gates of the inner curtain wall were bound to be closed by now. They were stuck on the outside, and Benito had a feeling getting in might be next to impossible, even for him.

"Come. We must hide better before the footmen start searching for loot."

Alberto, wincing and trying not to cry out, struggled up, leaning on Benito. "God. I can't. Leave me, Valdosta."

"Can't do that. That gabby wife of yours told me to look after you, big man. Come on. There's a place just over there."

It didn't take Benito long to pry away the boards sealing the doorway. Inside, Benito found the place much as he remembered it. Even with Morando in prison people had been too superstitious, after the initial curiosity, to come here. The trapdoor, as he remembered, was in the passage. He hoped it wasn't too damaged to put back.

Only when he looked in the passage . . . the broken door wasn't there. He had to get down on hands and knees to find it. The knight's axe had split the thin stone, but someone had put it back together again and smeared dirt very carefully in the crack.

Benito used the faithful Shetland knife to lever it up. Someone had nailed the split wood together again also.

Who? And why?

The whole thing smelled of trouble. But could it be worse than the Hungarians?

He helped Alberto to the stairs. "I can crawl," said Alberto through gritted teeth. "You close it."

Benito did so, as Alberto edged his way downwards. It was as dark as Stygia in here. There was also a bad smell. Nothing very strong, just the trace of corruption that came from a putrefying corpse or carcass not buried deeply enough.

Suddenly, someone struck a light on the far side of the garish cellar. And Benito knew at last the answer to the mystery that had been plaguing Maria.

Sophia Tomaselli looked a lot more like a storybook witch now. Her once magnificent hair was wild and tangled. She wasn't wearing any clothes. She'd painted herself with something . . . black now, anyway. Some of the patterns were smeared.

She had a wheel-lock pistol. She was also swaying

drunk—which was presumably why they'd made it this far.

She blinked owlishly at them. "Two of you. What's wrong with him?"

Benito really hadn't had time to look. He'd been just ahead, running for the gate when Alberto had gone down with a scream. He knew the man had been hit in the lower leg. He was in pain and bleeding. "I don't know. I'll have a look." He spoke in as level a voice as he could manage.

Sophia's eyes narrowed. "You! You're Valdosta. The wonderful hero." She snarled that out in such a way as to make it abundantly plain that whatever he was in her opinion, it was neither wonderful nor heroic.

"I need to see to his leg," said Benito calmly.

He might as well not have spoken. "Come over here. Come here or I'll shoot you." Her voice was ugly with triumph. "My prayers to the Devil have been answered. I saw how she looked at you, that *scuolo* puta . . . Baby-sit! Ha."

She stepped over to the altar and took up a knife. "Now we're going to have the true sacrifice." The little giggle that followed had a half-insane flavor to it. "The one that Morando was too scared to do. But I'm not afraid! I promised if he let me destroy her I would give him the old sacrifice. Killing you will do both. First I'm going to cut . . ." She gestured obscenely with the knife in her hand, for the first time pointing the pistol at the roof and not them.

Benito threw the Shetland knife. By now, the once-stocky boy had the shoulders and chest of a very powerful man. The blade went right through her thin chest, stopping only when the hilt slammed into the flesh. Sophia was flung backwards onto Morando's mock-altar.

Benito already had his rapier out, and was running forward. But . . .

She wasn't going to vent her spite on anyone ever again. From the amount of blood, the Shetland knife had split her heart.

"Holy mother of God! Let's get out of here!" Alberto was already trying to crawl up the stairs again.

Benito looked at the dead woman. Death had eased the lines of hatred, fear and misery from her face. "Stay there, Alberto. She was crazy and now she's dead."

"She said she prayed to the Devil to destroy Maria. That she promised human sacrifice . . ."

"And look what it got the poor silly bitch. Don't worry, Alberto. The best priest I know examined this place and said it was all a fake. A complete fraud. She was crazy and she believed in it, but it's nothing for us to worry about. Your leg and the Hungarians out there are a lot more serious." Benito tugged at his knife, struggling to free it from the bone.

"But you did come here. Here of all places."

Cleaning the knife on the piece of black velvet that Morando had used for his pseudo altar cloth, Benito shrugged. "Maria says this is Corfu. Magic here happens. And so do coincidences."

He took up the lamp and the knife and started toward Alberto. And then stopped, his eyes caught by something to the side. "Well, I'll be . . . No wonder she could hide out here! Morando must have been prepared to do just that. There's more water and food stashed in here than there is in the whole Citadel. This was a false wall."

Benito walked over to Alberto and started gently cutting the fabric away from the bloody mess. A bit of bone protruded from the jagged wound. Benito sucked breath between his teeth. "I wish I was my brother. I *really* wish he was here. I think you've got a open fracture of the fibula. I'll have to see what the hell I can find for a splint. And let's see if that woman left any of Morando's wine. I could use a cup myself, actually. Even *kakotrigi* would do."

Alberto managed a weak laugh. "*Kakotrigi* is like this place. You get used to it. Get to like it."

The hagfish had swum as close to the edge of the shingle as it dared. If anyone had looked down from the walls now, they would have seen the sinuous shape of it in the clear azure water. Fortunately, the fury of the attack—as seen through the eyes of the shaman's hawks—was on the front wall. The Hungarian forces had gained a foothold

*inside the broken wall, and men were starting to pour
through the gap and up onto the walls. The shaman was
able to change into the other form and lope ashore. Shaking the water clear of its fur, it ran to where the wall
was pounded into steep rubble. Here, with no defenders,
it gained entrance. With the fleeing townspeople, it ran
through the inner curtain-wall gates.*

*It began searching. Tasting the air. Relishing the fear,
hating the crowd.*

On the slope behind Corfu town, Giuliano Lozza mar-
shaled his men. He was de facto commander of the Corfiote
irregular army, because he had the most soldiers by far.
The Venetian captain had had the sense to recognize an
unstoppable local force and go along with it. And across
the island, so had everyone else. The story of the naked
Magyar having to walk back to camp in the buff spread
from village to peasant to fishermen. Greeks loved to laugh,
and their sense of humor could be a bit rough.

This man Lozza was no foreigner, they'd decided. This
was someone who spoke their language and knew more
about olives than any Libri d'Oro they'd ever met. He'd
even married one of their own, a peasant woman.

Once they'd called him *Loukoúmia*—fat little sweet-
meat. No one did that any more. Not since he'd given
a very pointed but nonlethal lesson in swordsmanship to
one idiot who had dared put a hand on his wife.

"We beat neither our women nor our olive trees on
Corfu," he'd said firmly and finally. It was a local peasant
saying, too. That was the final and vital detail. Women
asked their menfolk why they hadn't joined.

Giuliano had nearly three thousand men, men with
everything from old boar-spears to new and recently
acquired Hungarian arquebuses. And torches.

Waiting. Like the great banks of heavy cloud that
hung seemingly just off shore. The rain never came. The
Corfiotes were going to.

When the Hungarian units had begun pulling back
three days ago, Giuliano had known this was to be the
big assault. He'd begun sending out word, and the Corfiotes had come.

Giuliano was a master swordsman. He knew he was outnumbered and that the enemy had the edge in professionalism and equipment. But he also knew that it was not the strength of the swordsman that wins the day. It was the timing of the stroke. With the Hungarians sweeping into the outer Citadel, now was the time for the stroke. Loot, or the desire for it, made the Hungarian encampment virtually empty. The artillerymen were sitting around, disgruntled at not being able to join in the spree. The cannon would have to be moved now. All they got out of this was hard work.

And Giuliano Lozza.

Chapter 97

"The circle is unbroken. Out of life comes death, and out of death, life."

Maria looked at the point in the rock, engraved with a circle—the symbol of the mother—and surrounded by spirals so old that time was weathering them away. From the middle of that circle the water of the sacred spring had flowed—apparently unceasingly, for millennia. Now, as she watched, a tiny drop slowly formed and dripped down to the clay basin that stood in for the cracked holy pool.

Maria put Alessia down beside the cracked pool. The baby girl was too listless to go anywhere. Too listless to even cry. Maria turned with sad eyes to Renate. "You'll see her safe to Katerina, Holy Mother?"

Tears streaked the older woman's face. She nodded. "This can fix things, Maria. If you are willing."

Maria shrugged. "It is too late for me. Benito's dead. It'll be too late for Alessia soon. So what do I have to do?"

"Drink the water of the holy pool. Take up the almond. Offer yourself as a willing bride. I will do the rest."

Maria stared up at the figure of the Mother, the old, old figure cut out of the living rock. Legs like barrels, fat thighs that stood for the plenty She provided, the cleft of Her mystery, overhung with the great belly of fertility, the huge domes of pendulous breasts, the round ball of a head, featureless except for a hint of carving that might have been hair, a mouth. How old was She? Who had carved Her? Was there still any power in Her at all?

Maria tried to feel something from that figure; all she could feel was her own despair.

Well, even if nothing happened, there would be a few drops of water.

She went to the basin; raised it to her lips, and drank. With the taste of sweet water still on her tongue, she walked the two steps to the altar, and took up the half almond.

Her fingers touched it, with a shock.

Her hand closed involuntarily on it, and she whirled, to stare at the Mother.

Gathering about the shapeless form were tiny, dust-like sparks. Only they weren't dust, they were sparks of golden light, more and more of them with every moment, outlining the figure, then enshrouding it, enveloping it in a blanket, a haze of gold, the color of corn, the color of wheat, the color of life . . .

A sigh eased from her; she closed her eyes, and let the power lead her where she needed to go.

The yellow dog found the cliff entrance to the temple-cave by nose. There was only woman-scent coming from it. And, for the first time on this accursed island, also the strong, heady smell of powerful magics. Unless the other had sent a woman . . . he was here first. The only problem was that the cave mouth was up there, and the yellow dog form was not good for climbing trees. He wondered briefly if he should assume his human form, but decided against it. That was by far the most vulnerable.

He hesitated. By the intensity of the magics up there, time was not on his side. He changed into the hagfish form. This body did not like the dry, but it could climb like a snake.

He ignored the screams of people who saw the huge, oily-black monster twining its way up the graveyard poplar, and oozing into the cave mouth. Soon it would not matter.

It was dusty and dry and spiked with stalagmites here,

so the shaman assumed the doglike form again. His nose led him, hastening, up the narrow labyrinthine passages, panting and slobbering a little.

Yes. This was what he had been sent to find. To the shaman's senses, the entire place pulsed with power; throbbing like a racing heart. The master's advisor, Mindaug, had said the master needed to be physically present to claim this. The shaman wished he knew how to do so himself.

He ran into the temple chamber yowling in triumph, ready to fight.

There were two humans there. An old woman with long white hair, unconscious and crumpled on the floor. And a baby—dying, by the smell of it.

He could feast later. The shaman's nose told him there had been three. He quested for that third, to rend, to kill, with the magical energies in this place growing around him. To his eyes the place was full of sheets of green light.

She wasn't here—yet she had not left.

The shaman gave a half-vulpine, half-canine sort of shrug and began the ritual to call his master's physical presence here.

It was as if all solid things had become shadows. Maria, with the almond in her hand, her firm chin up and heart hammering, walked down steps of light set into the shadow.

She could not have said how long she walked, but she came at length to a great hall. At the far end were two thrones. A tall man stood up from the left-hand throne and walked toward her, palms out. On his right hand rested the other half of the almond. A tall man, made of shadows, as the Mother had been made of light. Shadows, but not evil—the restful shadows of twilight, the dark before dawn. And yet, she sensed there was a great deal concealed by those shadows, and she willed them away.

"Greetings, bride." He seemed to be looking through to the inside of her. He did not seem to notice that his concealment was melting until he stood before her unveiled. "Your spirit is very beautiful."

He was black-haired and gray-eyed; lean, pale, grim-looking. She set her jaw. Just because she had agreed to this, did not mean she was going into it blindly. Oh, no. All right, the marriage with Umberto, not unlike this one, had worked out—but she'd known Umberto, hadn't she? This—*Person*—she knew nothing at all about. So before she took the last irrevocable step, she had to know. She would do it, yes, but she still had to know.

"Just exactly who are you?" she demanded. "Husband," she added, as an afterthought.

It took the man aback. In fact, he literally stepped back a pace.

"You are a willing bride?" The pale-visaged man showed both surprise and a hint of doubt.

Maria nodded, feeling completely out of her depth, and brusque with it. "Yes, of course I am. The priestess said that without a bride the Mother could only resist, passively. That without a bride you would not intercede. Look," she continued, in growing irritation, "my baby was dying. My friends are dead or dying. The man I loved, Benito Valdosta, is dead. I was too proud to tell him that I loved him, and now he's dead. The whole island is dying. Somebody had to do something, so I said I would do it. I knew I had to be willing and I had to be fertile, of childbearing age. I didn't know I had to know all about it."

Just like a man! Assuming, she supposed, that because things had always gone a particular way, they always would go that way! Just proving Gods could be as dense and intransient as humans.

"I'm a new acolyte, and somehow or other nobody got around to telling me what I'm supposed to be doing. The priestess assumed I knew everything already, I suppose, and I assumed she'd tell me sometime and never got around to asking. I knew that to take up the almond, to become the bride, meant I would die. But if that was what it took to get you to help, I was willing. You are going to help us, aren't you?"

Perhaps that last came out a bit aggressively, but—oh, *stupid* man-God! Why was He just standing there, as if none of this mattered to Him? Was He going to act, or not?

He seemed altogether startled, now. "It is not that I did not wish to help. It is just that I cannot. My only connection with the Mother is through her embodiments. You are the embodiment of the Mother. The things above the earth are hers only. I have no power there, but I can lend my strength. I always have willingly given my help to my Mother."

Maria was now more confused than she'd been before. "I don't understand," she repeated. "Just who are you?"

He blinked, slowly. "I am the Lord of the underworld. Aidoneus is the name I am sometimes given."

"The devil?" He didn't seem evil. Just distant.

He shook his head in violent negation, the first time he'd shown any sign of emotion. "No! Shaitan's realms are elsewhere, and I want none of his kind of darkness." He spread his hands, as if in apology. "The spirit world is a complex place. All things are possible here. And none."

Well, that was certainly unhelpful. It was like arguing with Eneko Lopez. "It all seems to be shadows," she said doubtfully.

He nodded, more certain. "This has been called Shadowkeep, at times. And Hades, which is nothing like Hell. More often, simply the realm of the dead. Some of the dead leave here to go on to other realms, but all are here at least for a time. Time is meaningless to the dead. Of course, you are not dead, so you are not outside of time."

She wrinkled her forehead. She thought the point of this was that she died; this was getting more confusing by the moment. "So am I not dead?"

He shook his head. "No. Only a living one can be the living embodiment of life. One day you will die, but you are not destined to do so for many years. You will stay down here and be my wife. And the Mother Earth will be fertile and grow, because I can lend Her my strength."

Stay here and be his wife? Was that what all this bride business was about? To be a real—wife? To a God? Or something—

Well, she'd accepted dying. And you could get used to anything.

She shook herself all over, and one thing swam up out of her sea of confused thoughts. Alessia. What was going on out there? Or up there? Or wherever "there" was?

"Alessia—my baby?" Surely the Lord of the Dead would know if Alessia was dead? Or if the Hungarians had broken through . . . there'd be many dead, including Stella.

He looked past her, his face gone indifferent again. "Your child is lying beside the sacred pool in the temple of the great Goddess. There is an evil creature of darkness, a cursed one, sniffing at her." He sounded as if it all meant nothing to Him. Actually, it probably didn't.

But she reacted with outrage. "But—but you're supposed to help! Renate was supposed to take her away! Why didn't she? She's not going to kill my baby, is she?"

He looked into the middle distance. He was plainly seeing things in the shadowy places. "The priestess lies within the portals of the underworld. She has expended too much opening the way."

Outrage was no proper word for what she felt now. All the sense of betrayal, all the despair, all the anguish that had brought her here welled up inside her and spilled out.

"*You're supposed to help!* You—you cold fish, you're supposed to be stopping all of this! That's the bargain! That's why I came here!" Maria knew she was screaming, although in this strange place it didn't seem so. The sound was curiously deadened.

He looked at her as if she was a child to whom he had already explained the situation. "I need to be asked. And death and life need to be joined so the circle can be complete."

"Well, *I'm* asking you. Do something! Now!" She stamped her foot. This sound too was faint and thin. More like the memory of a sound.

For the first time a flicker of expression ran across that cold face. It was hard to say what it was. But his voice was somehow warmer, more interested. "You remind me of my first wife. Kore was from before the humans came. She brought fire and light into this place. We had some terrible fights, as I recall. She also had a quick temper like yours." He sounded nostalgic.

Maria felt her fury rage against the flatness of the man, and the place. "Listen, you! I'll make your life a misery for all that long life you've said I'd have, unless you do something now! About my baby. About the siege. About Renate. *NOW!*"

Her voice seemed louder somehow than it had when she'd shouted earlier. And edges to everything seemed sharper, clearer.

"You have a beautiful, strong spirit," he said, with what could almost be a smile. He reached toward her and she saw the hands were like Benito's brother's hands. Long and shapely. And the almond seemed to glow. "Come. Join me then, avatar of the great Goddess. Join me and then I can do this 'something' you demand."

She reached out her hand, opening it to reveal the almond. Her hands were work-calloused and rough compared to his. "Doing something is always better than doing nothing," she said firmly.

As their hands clasped, the two almond halves touched. She felt them draw toward each other.

Click . . .

The seed began to swell and then burst into growth. The roots were wriggling against their clasped hands and leafy shoots came questing upwards. And Maria found she could see things in the strange shadows of this place. People and places, myriads of them.

"It's a strong tree. The strongest I have seen in centuries," he said. His voice was definitely warmer now. And somehow he seemed less inhuman. "Let us plant it."

"It needs light, and earth and water," snapped Maria. "Not shadows. And I need to get on before it is too late for little 'Lessi."

The place was definitely lighter. "Then get on. Make earth and light and water for it." His voice was deeper, stronger and more powerful now. And there was definitely a gleam in those gray eyes.

It was a test of some sort, she knew. And she had no idea what to do. She looked into the strange shifting shadows, looking for a place for it.

Instead she saw Alessia, lying still and pale. Renate just

beyond, fetal and breathing so faintly you could hardly see movement in that frail chest. And a great yellow-furred dog-creature. It was scratching symbols with undoglike precision on the stone floor of the temple. Drool hung down from its jaws.

She searched her memory of all the things the priest-ess had said, desperate for a clue. All she could think of was Renate saying calmly: "Use your anger. Channel it with your will."

She looked around at the pale, shadowy hall. Either she was getting used to it or it really was more substantial and more clearly defined than it had been. There was a dead piece of wood there, in the middle of the floor. She channeled her will at that place.

Let there be earth, rich fecund . . . earthy, steaming with the scents of morning, as she remembered it from the forests of Istria. That wonderful earth that could support a hundred thousand mighty trees, growing strong and tall and straight.

Let there be sunlight, as warm as a lover's caress, as golden as . . . as the morning sun on the wings of the Lion. Oh, she remembered that, too, that sunlight that was so full of life you could drink it like wine, light that touched hurt and left healing behind it.

Let there be water, cool and clean and refreshing as the water in the temple had been that first time she'd gone to pray for Umberto. Water, oh blessed Jesu, let there, of all things, be water!

She felt the power answer to her will; where it came from she did not know, but she launched it as she had launched a thousand rocks at the enemy, as she had launched herself into this voyage, as she had launched Alessia into life—

By the hotness of her anger at wrongness of all this, by the love she held for all of them, let them *BE*.

And . . . *they were.*

The earth-smell, that had been so strange to her when she first came to the forest, tickled her nose with its lush scent. Sunlight welled around the dead stick, coming from everywhere and nowhere. And there was a mist, curling, lush with water, around the remains of the last bride's tree. And suddenly, the hall seemed very small to contain such richness.

He actually laughed. "I'm grateful you left me some hall! Come, let us plant this tree, and see to your need."

They walked forward into the sunlight, off the cold flags and onto the loamy earth. Using their free hands they dug a hole into it, and then put the seedling into the soil. The rootlets actually started reaching through their fingers and pushed hungrily into the earth. It was growing, growing even as they formed the soil around it.

"It will be the finest tree I have had here in many millennia." There was respect there; interest, too. Still holding her hand, he turned to point earthy fingers at the shadows. The yellow dog was howling there. "Let us see what happens with the half-jackal first—the cursed one. In a way it is protected from me. It cannot die."

In the shadows Maria saw the creature now for what it was: No dog. One removed from the dog-line. A cross between gray wolf and golden jackal, a howling half-domesticated creature from the wet northern forests that *could* have been the father of humankind's four-footed loyal companion.

Could have been. It had once fawned and guarded, and pretended loyalty. And when the man and the woman had left it to guard their most precious thing, it had eaten the child. The one they had trusted was cursed, cursed to live until it had been forgiven for the betrayal that was now long forgotten by men. But the memory and the shame were with all dogs—whose ancestors were cousins to it—and man's other ally, the horse, forever. The hyena they would hunt and hurt as often as possible. They could hurt it, even if they couldn't kill it.

There was also a shadowy person in there. Someone who had taken the cursed creature's name. The shaman had taken the form and with it the curse. He thought not being able to die a good thing, and cared nothing for the rest.

"How do we deal with it?"

The lord of the dead shrugged. "We protect your babe, and that is all we need do, for now. The great Goddess is dealing with it already, as She does with all those who work magics here. This is the place of the great Goddess. You know what the earth of Corfu does to foreign magic. The greater the magic—the faster it will draw that power. The creature relies on magic for its being. It would have been dead millennia ago if nature were to have run its course. The magics it uses now would kill it—were it not unkillable for magical reasons. The more it does, the more the earth of Corfu will draw that power that sustains it."

She understood now. The Goddess was absorbing anything worth having from the creature, and the longer it remained, the more She would take. Even the curse that kept it alive would be affected.

It was diminishing itself.

Still—this was that passive defense again, and that was not enough. "Surely there is something I can do," she said, feeling her anger welling again.

The God shrugged, very much amused. "You are She. And my power is yours. Take it up, my bride."

And she did.

Chapter 98

The shaman paused, as a wave of weakness came over him. Just a few more lines and Jagiellon himself would arrive here. He could rest then. He started to scratch symbols again. He shook himself, trying to focus his tired old eyes.

And then it came to him. He did not ever feel tired. Not in this body. And as for the ill-effects of age . . . the curse that had been laid on the yellow wolf-jackal had stopped the creature knowing those.

At last the shaman understood the nature of Mindaug's trap, and Mindaug's treachery. The shimmering half-materialized form of the master felt it too. Now the shaman knew why he had found the stink of magic everywhere. This place was a fertility temple. A mumi-place. The whole damned island was that. And the shaman, who was old past the reckoning of most men, knew that new life was a cyclic thing. It needed death. Life and death were one big wheel. The very soil here was sucking him dry, rotting him away like decomposing leaves in winter, to fuel new birth. The more magic he used in trying to fight it, the faster it was happening. It was swallowing him, and it would have swallowed the master . . . because their own magic was the fuel used.

A trap! He could sense his master's shriek, and his own thoughts shrieked in answer. All of it—a trap. Laid by the traitor Mindaug to supplant Jagiellon, working with his ally the Hungarian witch-countess.

But Chernobog had not yet fully materialized. The demon could still—barely—withdraw from the closing jaws. The shaman felt him fading away, leaving his servant behind. Behind, and alone, and sucked nearly dry of magic.

The arthritic, near-toothless, rheumy old wolf-jackal dragged and swayed his way to the cave mouth. It was a long way down, and the sight of the hagfish had brought people, and knights in armor and on horseback.

The wolf-jackal didn't care. Even pain was better than death. By the time it had dragged itself to the water, hounded over the wall and attacked afresh by the Croat horses, it was yowling and shrieking with agony.

The curse assured that the wolf-jackal wouldn't die, although the pain was not ameliorated. The magic of Corfu meant that each time his body repaired itself he was closer to the real death. Every spell, every twist of enchantment he controlled was drawing it out of him. He abandoned what magics he could. The shaman knew Jagiellon would not help. He must have suffered too, and wouldn't dare use magic to help the shaman.

Falling into the water and assuming the shape of the hagfish kept the shaman alive, but did nothing for the pain. And it was not the great beast it had been, oh no—it was a little, little thing, a wraith of the monster it had been, struggling feebly toward the deeper water—

—and two hawks hit the hagfish in the shallows, gouging at it beak and claw in their new-freed fury. Had they been creatures of the earth, not sky, the island of Corfu would have freed them long ago.

They were goshawks, torn from their native forests, forced to fly over water, stranded here. Their fury knew no bounds.

But behind that fury was Another, who lent speed to their wings and strength to their talons and beaks and when the shaman tried to strike them, knocked it back into the water, yet would not let it escape. The hawks savaged the hagfish with rage—the rage of goshawks protecting their young, for that Other told them, deep in their half-made hearts, that this *thing*—this *outrage*—had menaced young, had *eaten* young. They were going to avenge every young thing it had ever taken in its long, long life.

And so they did, as the Other hauled it back from the depths and protected them from its ever-more-feeble assaults. They tore at it and tore at it, until there was nothing left to tear. Nothing, but blood slicking the water like oil, and shreds of flesh, and the taste of its vileness in their mouths.

Then, that Other gave them some strength as their own began to fail. Lifted them, lofted them back to the land. And showed them a place—forest. Not like theirs, but like enough. And it soothed them with the promise of game to hunt and sweet water to drink and no one to disturb them, ever again.

Go. Build a nest. Raise young, and prosper.

And so they went, flapping heavily away through the hot, heavy air, bird-wise, and with the wisdom of birds, letting go of their rage and forgetting the thing that had bound them. Except not quite; keeping enough that they would never allow themselves, or their young, to be bound, ever again.

Maria took a deep breath, and flexed her hands, and the Lord of the Shadows now turned and pointed to a shadow that nearly made her sick. "There is the thing that is causing the Mother much pain."

It was hideous. Anger and pain radiated out from the little fetal-creature. It had wings, crumpled and twisted and deformed. It would never fly. But the small wings beat furiously, thrashing away the mere pressure of their gaze, that hurt, that burned it like acid. It was trapped by the magical confines of this place. It floated above the earth, a creature without weight—but still pinioned here, above Corfu. Pinioned with chains of blood—the nonhuman blood of its parents.

Her first reaction had been horror. Now she felt simply pity.

"It's just a baby!" she objected.

"Of sorts, yes." He waited—perhaps to see what she would do.

Not destroy it—blessed Jesu, it didn't know what it

was doing! No, she had to—heal it? Help it? "What can I do for it? It's not on the earth of Corfu."

The Lord of the Underworld shrugged. "It's some-where between death and life. That puts it in both of our realms. We can see it, and it can see us."

The anger, hurt and bitterness flowing from it were almost too much to bear. "Whoever did this must be a monster," said Maria, recognizing the unborn fetal thing for what it was.

"Elizabeth Bartholdy." There was a brief shadow moment of a beautiful woman. Plainly the twisted, warped creature saw it, too, because it howled in frustrated rage.

"How do we help the poor creature?" she cried, feel-ing its pain deep inside herself. It was a baby—only a baby—forced to do what it was doing.

"Remove its bonds. Remove just one of the sigils in its parents' blood. Wash them away." In the shadow now she could see the spidery tracings on the rocks of a blood that had never been red.

"With what? There is no rain or water because of the poor thing. If it would let it rain . . ." Maria sniffed. Swallowed. "I won't cry," she choked. "This is no time to cry!" She had to do something, not dissolve in tears! Crying wouldn't help—

"Why not?" the Shadow Lord asked, quietly. "Tears will wash as well as rain. It won't live, you know. It only survives in this sort of half existence because of the magics worked on it."

"I won't cry because it's soft to cry." She paused, feel-ing a strange stillness come over her. Like that blanket of understanding that had settled over her, letting her understand what she needed to do, a new understanding stole quietly over her in the stillness. "Maybe it needs something soft."

"Yes?" the Shadow Lord said, a hint, just a hint, of encouragement in His voice.

"I don't think it's ever had care or any love." She thought of Alessia, how even so loved a baby as she had nearly driven her mother mad a time or two.

"This isn't its fault. It's just a baby. A baby doesn't

mean to make you miserable when it's hurting. It just doesn't know how to do anything else. And it's hurting, it's hurting so much, from what that awful woman has done to it!"

This time, it was rage that followed the words, it was despair, for all the children that had died because of those horrible people out there, for this poor little thing that had suffered the tortures of the damned, been forced into birth. No baby ever *asked* to be born, but this one had been tormented into existence, and nothing would make it better except to be ushered out of life—

Maria wept for it, a mother's tears. The tears fell down and into the shadow.

And the silvery blood-writing boiled. There was a brief moment of movement, of wind and of fire.

And then there was a surcease of pain.

The rain began. The clouds, so long held back, swept in, swept over the hawks in their new forest, so that they held up their heads to the falling rain and drank in the sweet water that washed away the foulness on their tongues. It swept over the peasant women who set out jars and bowls to catch it. It soaked into the earth, that drank it with a million thirsty throats, and sent it down into the streams, into the unseen crevices of the rocks, with the sound of life renewing, at last.

"It is in my kingdom now," said her new husband. "I have put it where it belongs."

"What else must we do?" asked Maria tiredly.

He shrugged. "The Mother's place has rain at last, and will heal. *It* has got its people again, and they love it. It is in a magical place with those that perished giving birth to it. They blame it no more than you; and now they can cherish it. With that, it will heal."

"What about the siege?"

"Ah." Tall already, he seemed to grow taller. And grimmer. "War is death's kingdom. *Mine*, not Hers."

"Hah," Maria replied, feeling anger giving her back her strength. "Maybe so. But I'm going to help."

Chapter 99

Erik was on the battlements of the inner curtain wall, organizing and trying to prevent panic. Most of all, wishing silently that the inner walls had been built as the outer had: to withstand cannon. But the outer walls had been rebuilt not fifteen years back. This inner wall was probably a century old.

The outer wall had stood up to months of pounding. The inner wall would last weeks at best. Which was more time than they had water for, anyway.

A cannon across on the Spianada boomed. They must be mad! They should move them up first . . . a second, then a third cannon spoke. And Erik realized they were firing into the outer city. Into their own troops. Peering out to the enemy encampment on the other side of the Spianada, Erik's jaw dropped. For the first time since Svanhild's death he began to laugh. It was harsh sound, but it was laughter nonetheless.

The Hungarian camp was burning. Not as if from a little brave band in a small patch, but across a wide front. It must have taken thousands of men. And more and more of the Hungarian artillery fired into the Hungarian troops in the Citadel. If they spiked those guns before retreating . . . the inner citadel would last as long as its water held out.

Erik wondered whether this was Venice's forces at last. Like the rain, those had just never seemed to get here.

Manfred came up behind him, helmet under his arm and grinning like the cat that had eaten the cream. Von Gherens was just behind. "Well, Erik. What do you think? Half of them seem to be running back to camp. Are we going to sortie again?"

Erik shook his head. "The cannon-fire is doing it for us. As soon as it stops—"

A cold wet something hit him on the nose. Then another hit his cheek. "I don't believe it! It's raining!"

The rain came down in a gray, hissing curtain. So heavy that the view of the Spianada and then the section of the Citadel outside the inner curtain suddenly disappeared.

Manfred, Erik and Von Gherens stood there, rain driving in their faces, plastering their hair down, grinning at each other.

"Come on, you pair of loons," said Von Gherens. "Your armor's getting wet."

Behind them the Citadel was echoing—despite the rain—to cheers and cries of *"San Marco!"*

Erik was the last to leave the battlements.

He looked out at the rain, but he saw her face. And no one in the downpour could tell rain from tears anyway. He hadn't been able to weep, since that early moment in the hospital. Now, here, alone in the rain, where no one could see him, he could. Somehow it lifted a weight from his soul.

Giuliano saw the first heavy drops splash on the dusty earth. Like Erik he gaped. But he'd lived here all his life and he knew that when it rained here, it rained in earnest. "Sound the retreat," he said to the young Venetian with him.

"But sir, we still have some cannon to spike!"

"Believe me, Nico. They won't be using them for a while anyway. Look at that rain. This place is going to be fetlock deep in mud soon. And this rain will cover the retreat beautifully, eh, Thalia?"

She smiled at him, eyes like stars. "Good for the olives, too."

She was a jewel past price.

✧   ✧   ✧

The cannonball must have hit the house, because even in the cellar they felt the impact of it. Flakes of black paint fell from the ceiling. Alberto looked owlishly at Benito. "I believe I'll have that second drink after all. No sense in dying sober."

In Benito's informed opinion, if the next cannonball came right through into the cellar in two heartbeats' time and hit Alberto . . . he still wouldn't die sober. Yet he'd suffered Benito's rough surgery stoically. The wine might have helped. They hadn't eaten much in the last while and a little wine went a long way.

"Air holes, but no view," grumbled Benito, passing the bottle over. "No wonder the woman went mad in here."

"You ask me she was mad to start with," said Alberto phlegmatically. Once he'd got over his shock the big man had rapidly reconciled himself to staying down here for a while.

Benito hadn't. He'd been pacing the cellar like a caged animal for the last while. Being pinned down would kill him as surely as bullets or swords, he decided.

"Alberto. I'm going to have a look outside."

In the temple cave, Alessia stirred. The rock beneath her moved slowly, slightly, readjusting from the terrible stresses that had been put on it and were now washed away. The crack that split the holy pool healed. Water, rising from a deep artesian flow, began to drip slightly faster. And, as the rains beat down outside, faster still. The drops became a trickle and the trickle became a stream. The clay bowl overflowed. The pool filled up.

The healing and the magic in this place affected other things, too. Alessia woke up. She got to her knees; then, waving her arms for balance, stood up. It was no great height. She took little swaying baby-steps forward.

And fell into the pool.

Another baby might have drowned. But this child was hemmed in by certain protections. She sat up, wet through, and screamed. And screamed. She wanted her mother.

She wanted her mother NOW.

And if her mother is not there to care for her—she just has to touch running water to call me or my kin to help.

So had the undine Juliette stated at her christening. Alessia hadn't understood the words at the time, of course. Nor would she have now. But in a pinch, the new baby-sitter would do. He was big and warm and smelled nice.

Not like Mother. But nice. Familiar.

Benito had eased the trapdoor up very cautiously, ears straining for the sounds of danger. Instead he heard a peculiar drumming noise. He couldn't place it at first. It was a long time since he'd heard rain on the roof.

"Hey, Alberto!"

"What?" asked the big *scuolo* man, warily. He'd bet Alberto had the late Sophia's wheel-lock at the ready.

"It's raining out there! Not just raining. Bucketing it down."

"No! After all this time!"

"I'm going out."

"You'll get wet," said Alberto with a laugh.

"Yeah. But so will anyone else. It's nearly as black as night out there."

"I'll stay here and look after the wine. I can't run and you'll probably need to."

Benito realized very shortly that "rain" was an understatement. It was as if the heavens were trying to catch up on the whole dry winter in one fell swoop. Even in a final assault on a beleaguered city, troops would be reduced to seeking shelter in this. He stalked up the narrow street, seeing no one. Benito felt he could hardly have seen someone across the narrow street, it was sheeting down so hard.

And then he realized he was seeing someone after all, walking toward him. As he turned to shrink back against a doorsill he realized this was a very strange someone. The woman wasn't wearing any clothes, except for a crown of water lilies. And even in this light, her hair was green.

In spite of his attempt to hide she obviously knew where he was, and beckoned imperiously at him.

"You! Your daughter needs you. Come."

"Who are you?" he said warily.

"I am the Crenae of the spring within the hill. And your daughter wants either her mother or you. Our kin promised we would help if she was in need. Besides, she is nearly shaking the holy mount with her screaming. Nothing we can do will comfort her."

"Er, I'd help. But you've got the wrong person. I don't have any daughters."

The cold rain was soaking Benito. It didn't seem to perturb the nymph. "Yes you do," she said firmly. "Juliette examined your blood."

"Alessia?" The rain was getting in his eyes. "She's *my* daughter?"

"She certainly isn't your son!" snapped the nymph. "Now come. We must go to the cliff on the side of the Castel *a mar*. She is in a cave there."

Benito's mind groped at the thought of Alessia as his daughter. He'd thought—Caesare—

Suddenly it all clicked into place for him. The timing—Maria's sudden determination to marry Umberto—

And, the truth was, the baby didn't look in the least bit like Aldanto. In fact, now that he thought about it . . .

He pushed it all aside for a later time. "Got a place I can climb the inner wall in this?"

"The gates are open. The people of the city have pushed back the attackers."

"What? I must go and tell Alberto!"

"Your daughter needs you, *now*. She is very young and very unhappy. I have left my sister with her, but she is screaming the place down."

Benito shrugged. "Let's go, then. I'll send someone for him."

On the way to the gates, the rain slackened off slightly. It looked to be a mere lull in between waves of heavier downpour, but Benito realized the Venetians were making the most of it. Troops were marching down to the outer wall, set on doing what repairs they could. Ordinary people were hastening to their homes and lodgings to see what the Hungarians had left. Benito was pushing against this tide when a wet-haired, red-eyed woman grabbed his arm. Benito hadn't even recognized Maria's friend Stella without her permanent smile.

"Signor Valdosta!" Her face was a map of misery. "My Alberto? You haven't seen him? Even, dear God, his body . . ."

He squeezed her shoulder. "He's fine. He's got a broken leg, that's all."

Stella simply dissolved on his shoulder, clinging to him. "Where is he? I'll murder him! I've been so worried. So unhappy—"

"I hid him. Now look, he doesn't know what's happened out here and he's scared and has a pistol. For God's sake, don't get yourself shot getting to him."

She nodded. Her smile was back in full-force. "I'll call. He'll recognize my yelling at him, for sure. Where is he?"

"You know the house that guy was using for his orgies with the *Case Vecchie* women? The fake magician, Morando? I know you went and had a look."

She nodded. "I even got a peek into the cellar, where they did . . . that stuff."

"Well, we hid out in that cellar. The trapdoor is closed and it has been mended. It's in the passage. And as I said, for heaven's sake, be careful. He's armed and scared."

She kissed him. "Bless you, Benito Valdosta! I will be careful." She started to hurry with the tide of people.

He grabbed her shoulder. "Uh. Stella."

"Yes," she turned.

"He's also a bit drunk."

"I'll break his other leg for him!" she said, with cheerful savageness. "And you'd better go and find Maria. She'll be worried sick by now."

"Will you come on?" said the nymph, tapping her foot impatiently. Benito realized, as he hadn't in his preoccupation, that no one else seemed to notice his strange escort. Well, Marco said that the undine Juliette had done much the same thing to the audience in the church at Alessia's christening.

She led him to the cliff. The hagfish had broken away

part of the concealing tree, and Benito could see the cave. "I can go with water-flow. You will have to climb up there."

The limestone was wet. The handholds and footholds were tiny and rounded. It didn't matter a damn to Benito. He kicked off his boots, and began to climb. Reaching the cave, he wondered for a moment just where to go. The cave was dark. But then he realized that all he had to do was follow his ears.

A hundred heartbeats later he was holding and comforting a small, cold, wet child against his wet but exertion-warm body. "Why in hell didn't you dry her?" he snapped at the two nymphs.

"We don't know much about human babies."

"What sort of gratitude is this?" demanded the other crossly.

Benito sighed. "Look, I'm sorry. I thank both of you. Now I must dry her, warm her up, and find her mother. What was she doing here?"

"You'd better ask her," said one nymph, pointing to the curled body of Renate De Belmondo. "She's been starting to stir." And with that, they slipped away into water that Benito would have sworn could not hold a minnow.

Benito looked around the temple, and took the finely woven cloth off the altar-stone. He stripped off Alessia's wet clothes and, using the Shetland knife, cut the altar cloth into a sort of poncho for her. Cut a strip to make a nice belt. He took off his own soaking-wet shirt too, and tossed it onto the altar-stone. He'd be better off without it.

There was no food down here, and 'Lessi was undoubtedly hungry. The whole of the Citadel was. But she could at least drink. He took a tiny clay bowl from beside the altar and helped her to drink. It seemed to do her a great deal of good, and she'd warmed up nicely against him. She started settling down for sleep. Loved, cared for, and with not a worry in the world. Benito put her down carefully.

Then he took a double handful of water and splashed it on Renate De Belmondo's face. He did it several more times, adding more sacrilege to the large number of incidents he'd already managed.

She moaned. He tried shaking her. She opened her eyes. He sat her up. Then, remembering something Marco had said, put her head between her knees.

Chapter 100

Renate De Belmondo had been in the service of the great Goddess for nearly forty years. She came to the temple almost every day. The sounds here were as familiar as her husband's breathing. The fountain bubbling and the sounds of the tiny waterfall cascading into the sacred pool were like the voices of old friends. Even in her giddy and confused state they comforted and caressed. She tried to sit up. The someone who had been holding her head between her legs helped her to lean back against the wall. Then it came to her, as she tried to focus her eyes. The fountain had been reduced to oozing droplets, the cascade to accumulating drips falling slowly into the clay bowl instead of the rock pool. She blinked and then screwed her eyes up, willing them to focus. The pool swam into clarity.

It was brimful. And the glad cascade was running stronger than she'd ever seen it. She breathed a sigh of relief. At least their troubles were over.

Then, as a very angry male face leaned into hers, Renate De Belmondo realized that *her* troubles, on a personal front, might just be starting. And being nearly seventy and the high Priestess of the great Goddess weren't necessarily going to help.

"What was 'Lessi doing down here?" he demanded angrily. "And where the hell is Maria?"

It was a question she really didn't want to have to

answer. She struggled to focus her mind, to draw on some of her powers. She looked at him. He was bare-chested, and muscled like a stevedore across that chest and those shoulders. When she'd first met Benito Valdosta he'd looked like a mischievous imp of a young man. Now . . . he looked like some kind of dangerous wild beast.

"Men are not allowed in the Mother's temple. You will be curs—"

He shook her again. Respect for persons or places was not with him. "I want Maria! And as for your God-forsaken temple, I'm here because *you* left my daughter where she could drown. The nymphs from your private water supply—that you've been enjoying while the citadel's people went thirsty—called me because my daughter has an undine for a godmother."

She put her hands to her head. "Please don't shout. You must leave now. I understand why you came, but the great Mother Goddess's temple is forbidden to men. I see you have committed various sacrileges—I am sure unknowing, because you are still alive. But you must go and never return. Be assured there was no water here before the rite, and the baby was in no danger. Now go. You will leave Maria's child here. I have sworn by the great Mother that I will see that she is taken to Katerina Valdosta."

Benito took a deep breath. Renate De Belmondo saw deeper into people than most mortals, if not as deeply as the undine Juliette. She saw the wildfire in there. Wildfire accepts no limitations.

"She's my child, too. I always thought she was Caesare's baby. It doesn't matter to me anyway. Long before I knew, the undine asked me if I loved her. I do. She as good as told me I was the father then, but I didn't understand."

The words were tumbling out of him in no particular order, but Renate was used to hearing hysterical words tumbling out of distraught women, and managed to make sense of them, or at least, as much sense as *could* be made, since she had no idea of who, or what, most of the people he was talking about were.

"She told me it was my responsibility to look after

Alessia. I accepted it then and I accept it now. I'll look after her if anyone but her mother is going to. Maria told me about Katerina and babies. Kat might be better when she has her own, but for now I'm keeping her. As for you: 'Lessi was cold, wet, and miserable and whether you admit it or not, in danger while you were supposed to be looking after her. I'm keeping her. Try if you can to stop me."

He stepped over to pick her up.

Reluctantly, Renate called on the power of the great Goddess to prevent it.

And realized that absolutely nothing was happening. Benito picked up the baby, and cradled her as naturally and easily as any mother.

"The great Goddess obviously feels the justice of your claim," said Renate, reluctantly. "But I did promise her mother. I must admit she thought you were dead."

"Where is she?" said Benito, in a calm voice that Renate could feel paper-thin skin over a volcano of emotion.

The priestess took a deep breath. There was no avoiding it. "She has gone to be the bride of Aidoneus."

Benito gave her a flat stare that said: *If you thought one man and an altar cloth were sacrilege—I haven't even started yet.*

"I'm more patient than Maria, but not that much. We're in the middle of a war. Maria only married Umberto for Alessia's sake. And now you come with a cock-and-bull story about Maria getting married—now—and just abandoning Alessia. *Merde.* I'm going to find her if I have to pull the Citadel and every person in it apart. I'll start right here if I have to."

Renate held herself in stillness, and acknowledged the justice of his words. If Maria had known he was still alive—she would never have gone. Renate had not tricked her, but . . . there it was.

"Maria went, as a willing sacrifice, to live in the underworld with Aidoneus, the Lord of the Dead. Believe me, she only did this because . . . because she believed you were dead, and that her baby was dying. She did this to save Alessia. To save the island."

"Sacrifice. You killed her."

It was not a statement. It was a death-sentence. Renate saw it in his eyes.

"She's alive. I did not touch her. I swear by the great Goddess, as Her high priestess." He looked at her without understanding. "She is alive; only a living bride can go to the Lord of Shadows. She will probably live a very long time; the last bride must have been nearly a hundred before she died in the body. It is magic, Benito. She has gone, living, into the Underworld."

She shook her head. "I'm sorry Benito. There is nothing you can do about it. She's alive. But there is no way back."

Benito looked at her with eyes of flame. "Hear me . . . Priestess," he spat the word out. "I want her back from wherever you've hidden her. Alive, unhurt, *now*. Or there won't be any priestesses, or any temple. I'll hunt down all of you. And I won't send you to any play-play Lord of the Dead. I won't be stopped. WON'T."

The baby wailed at his anger, interrupting his tirade—he suddenly had to turn his attention back to the child, which would have been comical, except that it wasn't. There was heartbreak for him. He just hadn't figured it out, yet. "There, Alessia. It's all right. I'll fix it."

"You aren't letting yourself understand, Benito Valdosta." Renate had gathered herself by now, and stood straight, looking him directly in the eyes. "The Lord of the Dead is as real as your brother's Lion, or Eneko Lopez's Saint Hypatia. His kingdom is just as real. The magic that allows a living bride to serve as the channel for his power is as real as that which allows your brother to serve as channel for the Lion, or Lopez as the channel for his angels. The choice was hers to make. She has gone to spend the rest of her life in the Kingdom of the Dead. The real dead. You can kill me. I won't even try to resist. You can kill every priestess on the island. You can destroy the temples of Mother, of the great Goddess. All it would take would be enough gunpowder."

Somehow, that was starting to get through to him. Perhaps it was her conviction and her steadiness. Perhaps it was the Mother, reaching him past his anger.

"You could be an inhuman monster to make Emeric

look pleasant," she continued, sternly. "Massacre dozens of innocent women. It wouldn't make any difference to Maria. Believe me, I didn't want to make this happen; in fact, I didn't make it happen at all, it just did. The priestesses and devotees have been dreading it. We are a peaceful fertility cult, and we have never taken an unwilling woman to be the bride. But there has to be a bride, an opposite for the Lord of the Underworld, just as there has to be a male as well as a female for fertility. And it has to be a fertile woman. I love my husband dearly, and still, I would have gone rather than Maria. But I couldn't. There was only one among us who could, and did, at the crucial moment."

She took a deep breath. His anger was fading, but the bleakness that was taking its place was painful to see. "Accept it, Benito. Accept it as you have accepted your daughter. No one comes back from the Kingdom of Aidoneus. She is trapped there until her body is returned to be buried with honor in the sacred glade. I'm very, very sorry, Benito. There is really nothing you or I can do, other than accept it and honor her sacrifice."

There were tears in Benito's eyes. But his voice was rock steady. "You can accept it. And the consequences. I'm not going to. I'll keep trying to find a way, if I have to study magic until the day I die." He pointed an accusing finger at her. "She wasn't due to die. You did this to her. I'm not finished with you—or this place—but I need to get Alessia out of your hell-hole. Besides, I want to mourn among decent people and not with a murderess. You can run if you like. But it won't help you."

Renate was a high priestess and not without pride. "I won't run. And I'm just as unhappy as you are."

"Ha."

"Benito, this was her choice; she was a willing sacrifice."

"Alessia and I aren't willing. And if I can't get her back, I'll at least see there are no more victims. I will clean up this rotten mess if it is the last thing I do."

He turned on his heel and walked away into the darkness, toward the cave-mouth, holding the baby in his arms.

◇   ◇   ◇

He was scarcely out of sight when the two nymphs came sinuously out of the pool. "It had to be that one's lady-love, didn't it? You humans are such fools."

Now that Benito had gone, Renate allowed herself the weakness of tears. "She was willing, and she thought he was dead."

One of nymphs looked at her with disgust. The other stamped her foot. "And now he's going to blow up the sacred pools, dig up the glades, burn the groves."

"The great Goddess has always had the power to stop that. We endure."

One of the nymphs said dourly, "And who do you think the current embodiment of the great Goddess *is*? And how do you think she's going to respond to your requests for help, when she sees who you want help against? Especially if she thinks you deceived her about him being dead."

"I didn't know!"

One of the nymphs rolled her eyes. "You could have found out, though. Minor magic. And Aidoneus would have known. I've been through a fractious bride-period before. But that woman's lover was a fool and as ordinary as dung. This one . . . he's been on a knife-edge between good and evil—or, worse, what he's probably going to inflict on Corfu. The kind of narrow intolerant 'good' that's worse than evil, even."

"I don't see what you expect me to do."

"Nothing. As usual," said the one nymph cattishly.

Renate sighed. "If they could only talk. It's . . . it's all just a terrible misunderstanding. We all did it for the best."

"Well, let him talk. Let him go and see her."

Renate shook her head "Aidoneus can see out through the shadows and together they can affect all things living and dead, but short of being in the land of the dead they can't see each other. They can't talk."

"So let's send him there," said the one nymph, tugging at a tangle in her hair.

Renate drew herself up. "We don't kill."

The nymph clicked her tongue at her. "Oh, you don't

have to be dead to go to Shadowkeep. That's the easy way. It's been done the hard way before a couple of times and by different ways, but you short-lifers have probably forgotten."

The one nymph turned to the other, cocking her head. "What do you think, Sister? Acheroussia?"

The first nodded. "If the limnaiad there is willing."

Renate sighed again. "Well, let me at least make sure the rituals of spring still happen this year."

"Very well. We'll ask Valdosta if he wants to visit the Lord of the Dead, and make arrangements with she of lake Acheroussia."

Chapter 101

"It's my opinion," said Benito stiffly, "that even the Paulines are too lenient with witchcraft and magic. It's time they were both eliminated. I'm sorry you don't see things my way, Eneko. But I'm not going to let that stop me."

"The Church believes we will achieve more by a degree of tolerance, Benito."

"Tolerance is well and fine, Eneko Lopez. But tolerance doesn't mean making doormats of ourselves. The price of our tolerance is that they practice their religion within the constraints of our law and our society. If they step outside it—and if human sacrifice isn't stepping outside it then the Church, law, and society need a wake-up—I'm not going to sit back and turn a blind eye, even if you are."

Eneko Lopez shook his head. "I think you're allowing personal unhappiness to affect your judgement, Benito. This is not exactly 'human sacrifice.' Of course, the Church frowns on it."

Benito stood up. "You can continue to dance around this, Eneko. I'm not going to."

He walked out, down toward the sea. Part of him longed to simply fling himself off the walls and down into it. To make an end of sorts. But . . . well, there was Alessia. She depended on him. And, right now, he depended on her. And there was work to be done.

As he was passing a street fountain, now gurgling with

water—the Citadel had water, if not food—he heard someone call. He turned to see the Crenae nymph he'd followed to Alessia's rescue beckoning to him. "Valdosta."

"Alessia? Is she all right?"

"There are less-well-guarded crown jewels," sniffed the nymph sarcastically. "Anyway, you're worrying about nothing. The priestess wouldn't hurt a child, not even for her own life's sake."

"A matter of opinion," said Benito angrily.

"Not really," said the nymph. "We see deeper into the spiritual side of you humans than you can. And our sister Juliette would not allow harm to come to Alessia. Since her mother sacrificed herself for the island, we of nonhuman kind feel repayment to her child is the great Goddess's justice."

"Good. Now, if you'll excuse me I have a poplar tree to fell. The first part of *my* justice."

The nymph plainly realized just which tree he was speaking about. She winced. "Retribution won't help, Benito. And you will hurt many of those who are trying to help the child. Our kind depend on the protection of the Mother Goddess. Maria is the living embodiment of that Goddess."

Benito shrugged. "That's what you say. As far as I can work out, De Belmondo at best helped Maria kill herself, deprived Alessia of her mother and me of my anchor. I don't look on what I am going to do as revenge. I'd call it prevention of this ever happening again. As for the nonhumans: You're long-lived. Don't tell me this hasn't happened before. Don't tell me it was always a case of siege and starvation. You let probably miserable women do this, time and again, leaving broken hearts and spirits in their wake—for your benefit. You were content to benefit from their misery. You just let it pass. You had your chance to do something. You didn't. Now you must suffer the consequences."

The Crenae-nymph wilted back somewhat from the sheer force of his bitterness. There was some justice in what he said. Most of Aidoneus' brides had gone to him deeply unhappy.

"If we arranged it so that you could speak to Maria . . .

you could see that we and the priestess spoke the simple truth. Would that be acceptable to you? She isn't dead, Benito Valdosta. Just beyond the reach of mortals, creating life and light into the shadow world so that it may be reborn into ours."

Benito shook his head. "I only look stupid, nymph. I'm not gullible. You nonhumans are masters of illusions. I'd want to see, touch and be sure this was Maria, before I trusted. And then I'd bring her home."

The nymph bit her lip. "You could try. She—like you—doesn't belong in the Kingdom of the Dead. Aidoneus can do nothing to stop you. She is there by her choice. And while glamour may work on other people—we know it doesn't work on you. You can see us."

"Probably because you choose to be seen. The honest truth is that I don't trust you, I certainly don't trust that priestess of yours, and I don't trust this great Goddess cult. Show me and I might change my mind. It's not likely, though."

The nymph nodded. "Very well. We'll arrange it. You will need to take a boat to the Acheron and then go to Acheroussia, the lake of lamentation."

"You tell me where and when, and I'll be there," said Benito. "I'll have to break out of here, and I'll have to take a bit of care about that. I've got responsibilities now."

The nymph lifted a shoulder. "Then why don't you wait? The Venetian fleet is coming tomorrow and with it your brother, the mage Marco. You can give Alessia into his care."

"Very well. I'm going to go and read up on this Acheroussia and this Aidoneus. I never saw the sense in book-learning before. I'm beginning to understand its purpose. Your tree and your temples have a respite. But it is a temporary one. And I'm going to take steps to see that just killing me won't get your lot off the hook." His expression left no doubt about the reality of that threat.

In shrines across the island, women enacted the rites of spring, danced the star dances, to the sound of the reed-pipes. And this year the embodiment of the great

Goddess, She who is fertility and new life, responded with a vigor not seen for many a century.

Renate had the satisfaction of knowing that the new avatar was the strongest for many years. The women who had gone as willing brides weren't usually of the caliber of Maria.

She also knew that Maria had brought a dark cloud to rest over the old religion's centuries of invulnerability. From time immemorial the great Goddess's place had been something immovable in the face of changing times.

Now it met a force that would not be stopped.

"I told you I would help," Maria said, stubbornly, but with no little pride.

He laughed; she was a little startled. She hadn't expected a laugh out of him. "So you did," he said. "So—you, whose magic is of the earth and life—what is it that you think you can do in war?"

Maria paused, and thought, and remembered a certain legend she'd heard, sung by a troubadour at Kat's wedding-feast. The man had run out of love songs, and, in desperation, was trotting out some wildly inappropriate ballads.

This one was about Saint Joseph of Arimathea, and his staff, and a thorn-tree.

"I'll show you," she said, taking a deep breath, and gathering in her power.

She began on land, for everywhere in Emeric's camp there was wood. Tent-poles, wagon-wheels, gun-carriages. Where the blessed rain fell on them, she reached with her power, woke up the wood, and reminded it that it had been alive once, and growing. She passed over the land with her power, and His, stretched out in a great shadow behind her. And where her shadow fell, whatever could grow, did. Whatever had once grown, grew again. On the plains of desolation, a carpet of flowers grew.

And trees. Many of them. Growing out of what had been Emeric's weapons of war. Which he would not be moving again any time soon, if at all—for out of life, comes death, and his mighty cannons were not faring well at all beneath her rains.

Now she turned her attention toward the siege on the water. True, water was not her province. But eventually, all ships come to land—or have earth aboard them, in the form of ballast. And where earth was, so was she . . .

Beside her, the Lord of Shadows laughed, and laughed, and laughed.

Emeric looked at the stream of muddy water creeping into his ornate gilded pavilion and swore. It had been raining now for five days. Sometimes it had slacked off to a drizzle. But mostly it had just poured. The homunculus Elizabeth had provided had plainly been destroyed. Emeric had to regard any magician who could do that with respect. The resultant rain was making the siege into a disaster. The Spianada was a quagmire. The accursed Venetians used the chaos ensuing when the Hungarian cannon were turned on Emeric's own men, and the burning of the camp by raiders, to retake the outer curtain wall.

They probably couldn't hold it . . . if the rain let up. But the rain was altering everything. The rain had flooded the mine; it had also flooded the gap between the moles, washing one away and making the other unstable. Emeric had insufficient tents for his men after the fire, and the mosquitoes had used the rain as a time to catch up on a winter's worth of breeding. The night air hummed with them. Emeric could only hope the Venetians in the Citadel and the insurgents in the mountains were suffering just as much. But apparently the sea breezes gave the Citadel some relief, and the higher places were never as bad.

What was truly worrying were the reports of disease starting to break out in the crowded quarters. It appeared to be some sort of cyclic fever. What the locals called "malaria." It was apparently something they'd mostly lived through as children. Emeric's troops largely came from areas where it didn't occur. Without that childhood immunity, the soldiers who caught it often died.

A rider came galloping up through the rain. "Sire, the Venetian and Imperial troops have landed in Sidari. We think at least twenty thousand men."

Emeric closed his eyes. "Call the admiral."

"He is coming up the hill, Sire."

Emeric and the admiral looked at the hulls of the galleys. They wouldn't be sailing anywhere in those vessels.

The dead wood had started to sprout. Sprout? That was too mild a word for what was happening. It was growing before his very eyes. Roots were creeping down toward the earth. Shoots were edging out of the twisting wood toward where the sun would be if it stopped raining.

"If they were touching the shore, this is what happened. Even if they weren't touching the shore, this is happening in the holds, where the ballast is. With the fireboat attack and then this . . ."

The admiral shrugged. "I don't have a fleet any more. The galliots have almost all been pulled up and won't be sailing again. Unless you want to start building from scratch, that is. The timber is turning back into woodland. It's plainly magical."

Emeric snarled in frustration. "It is magic. Very powerful magic." He sighed. "Very well. We need to start ferrying my troops across to our camp over on the Illyrian shore." He already knew what would be happening to the wooden wheels of the gun-carriages. Emeric saw defeat looming. It was time to snatch what he could and run.

Maria was learning how the shadows of this place intersected and related. They shifted and moved in something like a great, complex dance, but she had as yet to find exactly how the steps went or hear the music they moved to. She found she could see into places distant and remote, if not quite as Aidoneus did—at will—at least with increasing clarity.

Some of them led into this place, too. It was vast beyond all imagining. Here she could walk into the shadows, walk among the dead—even talk to them.

The intensity which they'd had in life was gone, and now they gave her great deference as the lady of the living and bride of the king. She discovered she could find people just by desiring to do so. They were considerably less frightening than she'd thought they would be. And somehow, no matter where she was, the almond tree remained in sight.

She'd expected to find Umberto, or Erik's Svanhild, but—

"Not here," the Lord of the Dead, said, divining her thought before she could speak it. "Not now; they came here, and passed on, to their own place. Your Christians all merely pass on, and the followers of Allah, and of other gods. Only those who believe that death will bring them here, to me, remain with me. Every man goes to his own afterlife, according to his beliefs. And every man sees me as his beliefs dictate."

He looked over his kingdom, musing, a little smile on his lips. "You would be surprised to hear what your Christians see me as."

That made her blink. "Saint Peter?" she hazarded.

"Sometimes. Sometimes." And he would say nothing more than that.

Time down here seemed to have little meaning, but Maria found there was one person she had not been able to find. She supposed Aidoneus might be keeping Benito aside. She was at first embarrassed to ask. He was dead, and she'd made her choices. But she wished she could just tell him . . .

She asked instead for help in choosing the right shadow to see Alessia. Aidoneus would be a patient lover, she thought—if he was going to be a lover at all, in that sense. He seemed to have infinite time to attend to her, to talk to her, to listen. He was, she decided, much like Umberto in some ways—except that he allowed her space, too. But now Aidoneus took her hand again, and directed her eyes into a pattern of shadows.

She could see Alessia as if she was leaning over her crib. But the place was unfamiliar. It was very grand. It must be Renate's apartments. She tried to move her view outwards to see the priestess, wishing she could thank her for her care.

Something resisted that change in focus.

Maria tried again.

The resistance held firm, but she recognized the person behind it now: Aidoneus.

She let go his hand, still staring into the shadow. It blurred, becoming one with a myriad of other shadows. She squinted at it, wrinkling her forehead in effort. It was like staring into the brightness of reflected sunlight on the water. But she saw now. Saw through it. Saw Benito pick his daughter up and hold her.

She turned away, after staring for a long, long time. She turned to Aidoneus. "You knew."

He nodded. "I number the living and the dead. I know each by their inner flames. Each and every one is different. I know the when of their passing if not the other details that the fates weave. Sometimes there is doubt. A place where the thread is thin. That one's thread is like a cable."

From a high vantage point, Iskander Beg watched. The Lord of the Mountains was waiting. Very few of the invaders would return to Hungary.

Jagiellon had known before he arrived in Count Mindaug's chambers that the treacherous advisor had fled. Still, there were ways of extracting information even from walls if one were as powerful as the Grand Duke was.

Mindaug had plainly planned it well. Every volume of his precious library was gone, too. Jagiellon set about the magics that would let him know where Mindaug had gone. Eventually a face appeared in the blood-filled bowl. A very beautiful woman's face.

Elizabeth Bartholdy.

So. Much was now clear to the demon who lurked within Jagiellon. The Grand Duke of Lithuania had a new enemy, it seemed. Not "new," exactly, for he'd always known that the Hungarian sorceress was hostile. But he hadn't realized, till now, that she was such an active opponent; a player herself in the great contest, it seemed—and a major one.

Her motive was clear also, and it was not the normal drive for conquest. Elizabeth Bartholdy was, in her own way, more interested in the spirit than the flesh. She thought to tap the power of the one whom not even Chernobog would name, without paying the inescapable price. And might even have grown powerful enough to have done so, had she succeeded in trapping him. Bathing in the blood of virgins prolonged her life. Bathing in the blood of Chernobog . . . would have prolonged it for a very long time, if not perhaps eternally.

Grand Duke Jagiellon ordered servants to sterilize Mindaug's quarters, clean away every trace of the traitor. Then, when they were done, ordered his soldiery to sterilize the rooms still further, smearing the walls with the blood and brains and entrails of the servants. Then, when that was done, he ordered that wing of the palace burnt to the ground.

The bonfire produced a memorable stench. The flames, despite the feverish efforts of the soldiers, singed some other portions of the palace also. But Jagiellon was indifferent. A few charred timbers here and there were a small price to pay for power. He need no longer fear that Mindaug might have left some magical links behind.

Jagiellon's fury had ebbed by then, in any event. There was always this to look forward to: The skin of the beautiful Hungarian sorceress would make a memorable meal, someday in the future, with Mindaug's as the appetizer.

The triumphal fleet sailed into the anchorage off the Citadel of Corfu, led by three light galleys and a number of fishing vessels. It was a small gesture, but a significant one.

Amid the cheering, Marco was one of the first ashore, looking for Benito among the emaciated defenders. He found him, with a baby on his knee.

"Ah. Godfather," said Benito with a tired smile. "The man I need. Here. Have her."

"Er."

"Stella here will help you with practical details like feeding and cleaning," said Benito, putting a hand on her shoulder. "As for entertainment, Brother, you're on your own. She sleeps a lot, luckily for you. And she likes to dance. Even my dancing. Although she probably won't by the time I get back."

"But . . . where are you going? What happened to Maria, Benito?"

"I'm going to try and bring her back from the Kingdom of the Dead."

Marco grabbed Benito as he began to turn. "Maria was my friend too, 'Nito. Now tell me exactly what you're planning to do and what has happened."

Marco was unprepared for the tears streaming down Benito's face.

Chapter 102

"I'm going to Hades," said Benito grimly.

"Hades?"

"Apparently where this cult sent Maria to."

"You mean Hell?"

"They say it isn't the same at all. Just the Kingdom of the Dead. Except that she is alive in it. I want to bring her home."

"Are they telling you the truth?" Manfred asked doubtfully.

Benito shrugged. "It's a chance I'll take. I'll try anything. The nymphs seem quite earnest about it. The entry is on the Greek mainland. The Byzantines are nominally at least in control, but I can get a fishing boat to take me across without causing any upset, I reckon."

"I will accompany you," Erik said firmly. "For two reasons, Benito. One is that you've come with me, and been my spear carrier, and borne me away on my shield when I needed that. The other is that I also lost someone precious. I would give anything to see her again. Anything at all."

Benito took a deep breath. "I don't know, Erik. I don't know if they'll allow it. And even if you do find Svanhild . . . she is dead, my friend. Maria is somehow alive down there. They tricked her into this. I'm going to get her back if I can."

Erik smiled sadly and put a hand on Benito's shoulder.

"I know this. But you must understand. Even if the chances are tiny, we must take them. Even if I can only speak to her, I will accept that. The loser must accept what terms he can get. And Svan . . . there were so many things I still wanted to say."

Manfred lumbered to his feet. "Well, I have to tell you this. This time, you're not—either of you—going off on this without me."

"I cannot permit it. It is too risky," said Erik, automatically.

Manfred squeezed his shoulder. "Erik, you are my bodyguard and my friend. But the dangers of the halls of the dead don't relate to the body. The dead don't touch the body. They can't. What they can damage and destroy is the mind and the heart. To be honest with you: Your mind and heart are a lot more fragile than mine."

"You don't have a mind to damage, above your belt," said Erik grumpily, a spark of his old self asserting itself. "But I cannot take that chance."

"I'm not actually giving you the choice, Erik," said Manfred with simple finality.

Benito realized, then, just what power rested in the House of Hohenstaffen. The Emperor ruled millions in the Holy Roman Empire . . . but it wasn't just because of being in line to the throne that Manfred could speak so. Erik had always seemed to order Manfred around. For his own safety and good, of course. But when he wanted to exercise it, ultimate authority rested with Manfred. It always would.

"We'll have to do this quietly," said Manfred. "Or I'll have to go through this pointless argument with everyone. Organize it, Benito."

"The Acheron? You want the *Nekromantio Arheas Efiras*?" asked Spiro. "Don't do it Beni'," he said, for once in earnest. "That's a bad lot of fakes that. They prey on the fact that if you've lost someone—you're miserable. Easy victim. They're parasites, bloodsucking ticks. Once someone's time comes; they're gone." He put a hand on Benito's shoulder. "Come and have a drink with me and talk it out. I'm buying this time."

Benito was touched. Spiro's ability not to pay for wine was as legendary as the fact that he would never be serious. Now he offered to do both.

"Thanks, Spiro. Not this time. And I'm not going to the *Nekromantio*. Maria was taken before her time. I have talked to the nonhuman waterfolk. They say there is a way that I could go, on a lake called Acheroussia. And neither you nor anyone else can stop me. Apparently if it isn't my time, the Lord of the place can't touch me. Of course, he might not help either."

"Well, we'll take you. Land you quietly. The truth is the Byzantine officials aren't locals and the locals aren't about to tell them about a fishing boat from Corfu. A Venetian galley would be another matter."

Benito nodded knowingly. "Exactly what I thought. So: Can I hire a passage over?

Spiro nodded. "Taki will say yes."

Chapter 103

Manfred spent the trip over-polishing his armor. Polishing it to a mirror-gloss. Manfred was methodical about weapons and armor, without the fanaticism that characterized some Knights. This was excessive and unlike him.

Finally Erik asked why he was doing it.

"Cleanliness is next to godliness. And where we're supposed to be going to . . . I thought I could use a bit of help."

Erik snorted. "In your case, I think it is futile."

"My nurse used to tell me about the gray hosts when I was a gossoon," said Manfred. "Bright steel was supposed to banish 'em. I thought it might be useful."

From the hilltop, they could see the lake. Its dark waters were long and narrow, and a patch of cold mist clung to the middle. But it looked depressingly like a very ordinary lake.

They walked down to the edge where the limnaiad awaited them with a bag of old, old coins. She pointed at a seemingly ordinary boat rowing toward them. "Charon. You will need the obols for the ferryman. Don't expect the other side to be anything you recognize."

Erik shrugged. "I can see the other side from here. It looks very much the same as this side."

"There is more than one other side to the Acheroussia," said the limnaiad, in a cool voice. "You'll see."

Benito opened the bag and counted the coins. "Three is not enough," he said, sternly. "I want eight."

The limnaiad pouted. "They said you wouldn't know."

"The more foolish them, whoever they were."

"The Crenae."

"I wonder how well they do in dry fountains. I saw some ways of draining this lake, on the way here."

"Don't pay the ferryman until you get right across," said the limnaiad hastily.

The beach of black sand seemed to stretch to the far horizons. The only mark on it was the keel of the ferryman's boat. And looking back they could only see mist.

"You won't need the rest of that," grumbled the ferryman, as Benito put the purse away.

"Return fare."

The ferryman snorted. "I've never had one."

"We'd still hate to get back here and find you weren't going to take us because of it," said Manfred cheerfully.

They walked onward, in toward the gray gloom of the interior of Death's country. The way ahead was funneled by tall, glassy black cliffs. And then they came to an end point, a place where only three trails led on. One steep, rocky and draggled with straggly thorns, and seeming to peter out a few hundred yards on. The second, wide and well cobbled, went on into the middle distance. The third seemed to lead off into a valley winding up toward the cliff-top.

"Where now?" asked Benito, looking at the three trails.

Erik took one look. "The narrow one. The hardest one. Mortals are not supposed to pass."

"It would be," said Manfred with a groan. Climbing a steep path in armor was pure misery.

Upward and ever upward the trail wound. Eventually they came out at a misty gray plain.

"Do we have any idea where we're going next?" asked Manfred.

"To look for the dead, I suppose," said Benito.

"We're already among them," said Erik slowly.

Benito realized that the gray mist around them was full of shifting forms, almost seen . . .

Out of the corner of his eye he could see faces. He could also see the expression of eagerness on Erik's face.

Benito took out a small crock sealed with wax from the bag he'd carried with him. He opened it and poured the contents into a dish.

"What's that?"

"Colyva. Taki insisted I bring it. He said it feeds the souls of the dead and they'd be more likely to leave us in peace." Taki had had no trouble in believing they were coming to visit the dead. The captain had stayed sober the whole trip and Benito had seen him crossing himself and fingering an amulet repeatedly.

"What is it?" Manfred looked curious and hungry enough to steal morsels off the plate set for the dead.

"Wheat, pine nuts, almonds and raisins. And pomegranate seeds. I had the merry devil getting hold of those. All soaked together in honey. Each part of it has some significance, but Taki was pretty vague about it. It's as old as Greece, he said."

"If the dead don't want it, I could use it," grumbled Manfred.

But the dead did. Kin came first. And then friends.

Erik looked for Svanhild. But she wasn't there.

He peered forward, into the distance.

Manfred looked oddly at his friend. "Erik. You remember you said you'd never leave her?"

Erik nodded. "My vow. I wish . . . I wish I had not broken it. I will doubtless go to the place of oathbreakers."

Manfred shook his head. "No," he said solemnly. "You won't. She promised the same, didn't she?"

"I think so. In her dying breath."

Manfred took a deep breath. "I think you've been looking in the wrong place. I don't think she'd come here; this place is for the people that believe in it. She's gone somewhere else. And she's waiting for you. But I think—"

he added, warningly: "That if you try to get there too soon, she's going to have some sharp words for you."

"The Lord of the Dead has sent me to fetch you into his presence," said one of the shades. "But only you may come into the presence of the living Embodiment of the great Goddess. She wishes to see you, and Aidoneus cannot refuse her."

"I want to see her, too. But what about Manfred and Erik?"

"They must remain here. No harm will come to them. No harm can."

Benito walked through shadows. At length, he came to a great hall. In the middle of it, in a patch of sunlight, stood an almond tree in full blossom.

And standing in front of it were two people. Not the insubstantial shade-people of this place, but real people. One of them was Maria. Benito gave a glad cry and would have run forward, seeing her there. But something stopped him.

"I can put unimaginable distances between us should you even take one step further forward," said the stern-faced man at her side. "The avatar of the Mother, the great Goddess, She who is the earth of Corcyra wants to speak with you. Speech I will permit. Nothing more."

"I've come to fetch her. She doesn't belong here in this prison."

The Lord of the Dead shook his head. "She came willingly. She has to honor her bargain."

"Did you, Maria?" asked Benito calmly.

She nodded. "I thought you were dead, Benito. Alessia was dying. I thought I could save her and the island."

Benito grinned. "You told me I wasn't allowed to die without your permission. You think I'd dare disobey? Seriously, Maria. They tricked you into this on false pretenses. That's no bargain. A bargain takes honor on both sides, Lord of the Dead."

Maria turned to Aidoneus. "You knew he wasn't dead."

Aidoneus nodded reluctantly. "Yes. I told you: I number

the living and the dead. I can see the ends of the threads of destiny. I can see his end and I can see yours. Yours is far. Further than earthly time would allow. You must be remaining here in the underworld. Our time passes differently, and does not wear out the flesh as fast."

Maria's eyes narrowed. "But when you asked if I was a willing bride, I told you that was why: Because Benito was dead. You deceived me. *You cheated!*"

Aidoneus was silent for a long time. Finally he spoke. "Yes. I do cheat, but only by allowing people to cheat themselves. I wanted you. Your spirit is bright and strong. Many of the brides who have come were barely able to sustain themselves, never mind sun and light and flourishing life."

"The compact is for a willing bride," said Maria. "You told me that. You asked me if I was willing. Twice! You knew that you were deceiving me. That's why you tried to stop me seeing Benito in the shadows."

The Lord of the Dead held up a hand. "You gave me three reasons for being willing." Aidoneus pointed to Benito. "He was dead. Your baby was dying. And the siege was killing your friends."

Benito's eyes narrowed. "You know that Maria is destined to live for many years. Just exactly when is Alessia's time?"

"It is some time into the future," said Aidoneus calmly. "I may not tell mortals the exact time or place of their dying. I also may not lie."

"So you cheated a second time," accused Benito.

Aidoneus nodded. "But the third reason would have been true. The weave of fates was altered by her coming here."

"So does one third of a compact make it valid?"

Maria pursed her lips. Then, rubbed her square chin. "I don't cheat, Benito. It makes it one third valid. Because I was willing for that reason."

Benito sighed. "Agreed. But that still makes you mine for one third, 'Lessi's for another. Doesn't that outweigh the other?"

Maria sat silent for a while. She looked from Benito to Aidoneus, biting her lip. "Benito. You've just come all the way to the Kingdom of the Dead for me. No one else could do something like that. But fair is fair. One third of my life is Aidoneus'. He—and Corfu—need me."

The Lord of the Dead looked at her with eyes of longing, and sadness. "I'll accept that," he said quietly. "I did cheat. But I also gave fair return."

Maria nodded. "You did. But can *you* accept it, Benito?"

He started to reply immediately. Always the quick-witted one, Benito was. But then—perhaps for the first time in his life—stopped to think first. *Really* think.

He thought for quite some time.

In the end, it was the quietly sad, longing face of Aidoneus that gave Benito his decision—and, perhaps most important, allowed him to accept it calmly. For all that the two didn't look at all similar, there was something about Aidoneus that reminded Benito of Umberto Verrier. Lonely men in middle age—insofar as that term could be applied to someone like Aidoneus—who always did their duty. Including, when the need arose, sheltering and caring for a woman that a younger and more flamboyant man had not been able to do. Or willing to do.

Benito still felt that he was responsible for Umberto's death. That aching guilt had never left him. Until now, when he made his decision. The first truly adult decision he thought he'd ever made in his life.

"Yes, I can accept it." Benito shrugged. "I'd be a damned liar to say I liked it, Maria. But I thought I'd lost you forever and completely. Two thirds is a sight better than none at all. I see Aidoneus' point. I'd take one third if that was what I could get. How about eight months with me . . . and four down here?"

Aidoneus actually looked nonplussed. "I thought you'd refuse. Very well. I accept also. Maria will spend the four months of winter with me, the rest of the year with you."

Maria looked at him with a curious expression. "You've grown, Benito. I'm still not sure if I want a man—even for eight months of the year—who doesn't know if he's a wolf or a fox."

"I'm neither, Maria. I'm me. And I'm yours if you want me. I'll have you under any terms. Take me or leave me."

Maria bit her lip again. Then, nodded. "I think I prefer Benito to wolves or foxes."

Aidoneus sighed. "Very well. A bargain is a bargain. But this is my kingdom. There is a last clause to our agreement. Go back to your friends now. Maria can follow you out. But if you look back before you reach the far shore you have lost her forever." Aidoneus' voice was full of grim certainty.

Benito looked at Maria. "It's a deal. But how do I know if Maria is following us out?"

"You can turn and have a look," said Aidoneus with a raised eyebrow. "Or believe. She cannot make any sounds out there, away from the tree."

"You're cheating again, of course."

Aidoneus smiled wryly. "Yes."

Benito shrugged. "My companions can't turn either, I suppose?"

"It doesn't mean as much to them as it does to you. It is possible for them. But no, they can't turn either."

Benito took a deep breath. "You're on."

"What happened?" demanded Manfred.

"She doesn't belong here, and he cheated to get her—on two of three counts. But he did keep his side of the bargain on that third count. So Maria will spend four months of the year here. She can come out now, following us—but only if I don't look back to see if she is following. Not until I get out on the further shore. And you two can't turn around either."

"That's impossible," said Manfred.

Benito shrugged. "It's the terms I've got. It's better than no terms at all. But I have one request, Manfred."

"What?"

"Walk in front of me."

"If I walk behind you I can try and stop you turning."

Benito shook his head. "Manfred, you said you owed me for bringing Erik back. That I could ask for anything. Well, this is what I ask."

✧   ✧   ✧

They marched. And marched. Even the final black beach sands seemed endless. The ferryman held out his hand. "Pay me."

Benito snorted. "You'll get our fares on the other side."

"Show me the money."

Holding the ancient coins firmly, Benito held up four obols.

"Isn't that one too many?"

"Play fair," said Benito boredly, and sat down. He did not even twitch his head.

The sunlight on his face was the sweetest thing Manfred had ever felt. The boat slid into the shallows . . . and Benito, still not turning around, held out the four obols.

"Can I keep the change?" asked the ferryman grimly.

"Play fair," said Benito, climbing onto the beach, without so much as a glance. Both feet firmly on the beach he turned, and took Maria into his arms, out of Charon's ferry.

He kissed his love slowly and long. Her lips were warm, as was her body pressed against his. They stood like that for a very long time.

Manfred leaned back against Taki's bulkhead and grinned at Benito and Maria. "I take my hat off to you, Benito. I'd have looked. I'd have had to."

Benito grinned. "I didn't need to look."

"You've got faith," said Erik seriously.

"Actually, Erik, what I had was Manfred walking ahead of me. You've got well-polished armor, Prince."

Manfred laughed until the ship shook. "The Fox's grandson, all right!"

Maria stuck her tongue out at him. "No. He's just Benito. My Benito."

Benito smiled at Maria, lovingly. "I could see you the whole time, Maria, dearest. All the way. I wished I could have told you not to look so worried. He cheated. I never said I wouldn't. For you I would do anything."

Epilogue
Spring, 1540 A.D.

Now that the relief effort was fully underway, the Citadel was allowed a day of celebration, of feasting, of laughter. The feast was of course entirely brought from the ships. It was not very good food, but there was enough.

"Governor De Belmondo is retiring, as soon as Venice sends a replacement," said Marco. "The doctors have told the old man to quit or die in harness, soon. The siege took a toll on him and he's nearing eighty. But he'll stay on in Corfu. He has a small estate in the south."

Benito snorted. "Him, I can deal with. But his wife I'd prefer to see back in Venice, if not Vinland."

Maria pinched his arm. "You're not being fair, Benito. I've told you."

Benito's expression hardened slightly. "I've heard you. I'm never going to entirely agree with you. But I agreed to let it be."

"You're impossible, Benito Valdosta," said Maria. It was plain that there'd still be some stormy exchanges on this one. But Marco noticed she still held his hand, firmly.

"So who will they send to govern us?" asked Alberto, plainly keen to move the subject away from this area.

Marco laughed. "He's come to talk to you, O new head of the Little Arsenal. I was in magical communication with Venice from the ships this morning. Benito has been nominated to be interim deputy governor by the Senate; and to repair the war ravages here, the Senate has voted a budget allocation of half a million ducats."

"Deputy Governor!" Benito gaped. "Me? Are they crazy?"

Marco shrugged. "The Senate was adamant, apparently. For the moment, given De Belmondo's age, they mostly want someone whom they trust to keep Corfu Venetian—and, despite your hair-raising reputation in some other respects, you now have a rather towering reputation as Venice's man-in-a-pinch."

Benito was still gaping. Marco smiled and patted him on the shoulder. "Don't worry, Benito. It's just temporary until the Senate can finish wrangling over who they want as a permanent governor to replace De Belmondo. If it makes you feel any better, Petro told the Senate they were out of their minds. He proposed you for temporary captain-general, instead. But the military types had fits over that idea."

That brought a grin to Benito's face. "And well they might! I'm never going to be their favorite in peacetime. But I've got the perfect candidate for the job: Giuliano Lozza."

"Now that the supply distribution is well in hand," said Manfred, "we'll be heading onward to Jerusalem. A part of the fleet is going east to Canea. There'll be other vessels there, and we can go on to Ascalon."

Manfred looked sad. "I've a need to do some praying for my uncle, who may well not live much longer. And the business of politics goes on. So: We'll be loving you and leaving you, Benito Valdosta. Unless you'd like to come along. I've always a space for you in my company."

Benito felt the earnestness behind those lightly spoken words. He thought back. Command and siege had made Manfred grow. He was no longer likely to challenge Erik's watch-keeping ability. "I'd enjoy it. But I think Venice and Maria would prefer me to stay put awhile. I'll be here when you come back. They also wanted me on the fleet that is set to deal with the Aragonese, Barbary corsairs and the Genovese, too. Strange, to be wanted—and not just by the Schiopettieri, for a change."

Everyone laughed. "Benito, I have to agree with Maria: You were born to be hanged," said Francesca.

Erik squeezed Benito's shoulder. "I really don't feel party-like, yet. I'll be back, to collect Bjarni and the other Vinlanders—except Kari, who insisted on coming with us—and to collect what remains of Svanhild's things.

Honor demands I must return them to her kin in Vinland. You'll take care of them for me?"

Benito nodded. "They're managing to feed Bjarni, at least, Erik. If he comes out of it . . . I'll take care of him."

Erik mustered a smile. "I couldn't think of a better caretaker."

Benito assumed a look of injured virtue. "I'm respectable these days. I'd be a married man if the church would agree."

"I think the authorities are mistaken in that. Still. I think I have learned. Those who are truly joined, neither man's laws nor God nor death really put asunder. Words and rituals don't really seem to mean that much."

"Are you entirely mad?" demanded Giuliano, looking at Benito as if he had offered him a lifetime in purgatory instead of the highest military position on the island. "Who would look after my olives? No! Thalia and I," he put a possessive arm around her, "are going to grow good eating kalamatas, not little lineoleas. I've got a new vineyard in the planning, too."

"I could have told you that he wouldn't do it," said Eberhard quietly, when Giuliano had walked away. "Cincinnatus."

"What?"

"You'd benefit from some history lessons, young Benito," said Francesca. "Giuliano Lozza could be a great condottiere if he wanted to. He doesn't. All he wants is a few acres of olive trees, some vines and a wife to make plump with his spoiling. Give him a pack of noisy children, too, and he'd be happier than any king. There are some people who just don't want power, or adulation, or even too much money."

Benito laughed. "You know why?"

"No."

"Because it is his for the asking. So, if I can't have Giuliano, who do we make captain-general? Leopoldo will do for now, while he recovers, but he's good, and ambitious. Venice will move him on for sure. You're all off to the Holy Land. So who am I left with?"

"You can always do double duty while you look for someone else. And why don't you make Thalia the minister of agricultural reform? You'd get Giuliano that way. And if the island really needs him—Giuliano will be there."

"That should give the surviving Libri d'Oro the hissy-fits," said Benito, with a look of pleasure.

"When they discover what you're planning on doing about tenant farms," said Manfred cheerfully, "you might just *need* Lozza."

Benito grinned evilly. "No. We'll do it slowly. It's like cooking lobsters. If you start with cold water then they don't flap and snap like they do when you try to drop them into boiling water. But the system as it stands is a recipe for insurrection."

"As we saw during the siege," said Eberhard. "But you may find that loosening the bonds will lose Venice this island."

Benito shrugged. "The system as it is will definitely lose it. I plan to work on ties of trade and blood instead."

"You'll make a good deputy governor," said Manfred with a chuckle. "Keep the taverns in trade anyway."

"For four months of the year," said Maria sternly.

Benito looked at her. There was a sadness in his eyes, but acceptance, also. He put an arm around her. "It's not every husband—in all but name, anyway—who gets a four-month holiday."

Spiro came up with a Venetian glass of tawny liquid in hand. "Here you are Beni. *Kakotrigi*. You'd better get used to it, if you're going to be our governor."

"That's your third," said Maria, taking it herself.

Benito shook his head. "I should have said it is not every man who *needs* a four-month holiday. *Ow!* I was only joking, Maria! You'll get 'Lessi wet if you pour it over me."

Maria looked sternly at him. "I have walked among the dead and asked them secrets hidden from ordinary mortals, Benito Valdosta. And among them I found out your weakness. Tonight, I am going to tickle you."

The last part was said with a Maria smile, full of promise, full of loving. An older Maria, confident at last of herself. Of being loved enough. Of being someone who no longer felt insecure about her station, about being a canaler with a *Case Vecchie* man. She had something now that made her realize just how irrelevant these things were.

Maria pointed a finger at Spiro. "You. Fetch us two more glasses of this—this *kakotrigi*. I didn't like it much at first sip, but I'm finding it better and better."

"It grows on you," said Benito, putting his arm around her again. "Part of the magic of this place."

Eneko Lopez tasted the wine. "Rough magic," he said with a grimace.

"But good and strong," said Maria, laughing.

In the high valley in the shadow of Pantocrator, the faun played on his panpipes a part of the ancient dance that is love, life, death, joy, sorrow and Corfu.

CHARACTERS

Principal Characters

Aldanto, Caesare: Sellsword, spy, Milanese of aristocratic family; formerly a Montagnard agent, now enslaved by Jagiellon.

Bartholdy, Elizabeth: Hungarian Countess, great-great aunt of King Emeric of Hungary; a sorceress, appearing to be about twenty years old.

Casarini, Bianca: Florentine resident on Corfu; follower of Elizabeth Bartholdy.

De Belmondo, Renate: Wife of the Podesta, priestess of the Mother Goddess.

De Chevreuse, Francesca: Courtesan, formerly of Orleans.

Emeric: King of Hungary.

Hakkonsen, Erik: An Icelander, and bodyguard and mentor to Manfred.

Jagiellon: Grand Duke of Lithuania; possessed by the demon Chernobog.

Lopez, Eneko: A Basque cleric and ecclesiastical magician.

Manfred, Prince, Earl of Carnac, Marquis of Rennes, Baron of Ravensburg: nephew to the Holy Roman Emperor.

Mindaug, Kazimierz: Count, advisor to Jagiellon. A student of western magic.

Montescue, Katerina (Kat): Lodovico's granddaughter, married to Marco Valdosta.

Shaman of Kandalaksha: His name remains a closely guarded secret. He is the servant of Jagiellon.

Thordardottar, Svanhild: only daughter of a powerful Vinland trading house.

Tomaselli, Nico, Captain-General: Venetian Military commander of Corfu.

Tomaselli, Sophia: wife of the captain-general.

Valdosta, Benito: grandson of the Duke of Ferrara, illegitimate son of the condottiere Carlo Sforza; ward of Doge Dorma.

Valdosta, Marco: grandson of the Duke of Ferrara.

Verrier, Maria: former Venetian canaler, married to Umberto.

Verrier, Umberto: Master in the Caulker's Guild.

Verrier, Alessia: Daughter of Maria.

Minor characters

Bartelozzi, Antimo: Agent and advisor to Enrico Dell'este.

Beg, Iskander: Illyrian chieftain, know as the Lord of the Mountains.

Bespi, Fortunato: Former Montagnard assassin, now bodyguard for Marco Valdosta.

De Belmondo, Alexio: Podesta of Corfu.

Dell'este, Enrico, Duke of Ferrara: The Old Fox. One of Italy's leading military tacticians; grandfather to Benito and Marco.

Dorma, Petro: Doge of Venice. Head of the commercially powerful House of Dorma.

Dorma, Angelina: Petro Dorma's younger sister.

Evangelina, Sister: A Hypatian Sibling.

Falkenberg, Ritter: A Prussian Knight-Proctor. Master of siege-craft.

Fianelli, Marco: A Corfiote criminal; and a spy for King Emeric.

Hohenstauffen, Charles Fredrik: Holy Roman Emperor.

Kari: Half-Osage tribesman. Hearthman to the Thordarsons.

Kosti: Fisherman, crewman on Taki's boat.

Leopoldo, Commander: Commander of the garrison, Corfu Citadel.

Loukaris, Meletios: Secretary to Podesta De Belmondo.

Lozza, Giuliano: Son of Flavio Lozza, a legendary master-at-arms. A plump olive grower.

Mavroukis, Stella: Maria's gossipy friend.

Mavroukis, Alberto: Stella's husband; a Master in the Little Arsenal of Corfu.

Mascoli, Brother: Hypatian priest of St. Raphaella.

Montescue, Lodovico: Head of the formerly powerful House Montescue.

Morando, Aldo: Swindler, fake Satanist.

Nachelli, Petros: Rent-collector and go-between for spies.

Saluzzo, Paulo: A thug working for Fianelli.

Sforza, Carlo: The wolf of the North, Milan's chief condottiere. A military legend.

Spiro: Corfiote sailor, fisherman, crewman on Taki's boat, friend of Benito.

Taki: Skipper of a fishing boat.

Thalia: Peasant woman, first female sergeant in Venetian Corfiote forces.

Thordarson, Bjarni: oldest son of a powerful Vinland trading house.

Thordarson, Gulta: Third son of a powerful Vinland trading house.

Trolliger, Baron Hans: One of the Holy Roman Emperor's courtiers and advisors.

Von Gherens, Ritter: A Prussian Knight-Proctor.

GLOSSARY

Aquitaine: An independent kingdom in western Europe; it comprises parts of what in our universe would be called France and England.

Armagh, The League of: A loose alliance of Celtic/Nordic states.

Arsenalotti: The workers at the Arsenal, Venice's state shipyard.

Ascalon: A port in Palestine.

Bacino: Harbor basin.

Barducci's: A tavern well known for music.

Bretagne: Brittany. An independent Duchy, part of the league of Armagh.

Carnac: Capital of Celtic Brittany.

Capi: Roughly the equivalent of a lieutenant.

Carreta: A pony/horse trap.

Case Vecchie: Great houses; the Venetian aristocracy.

Cassone: A carved chest.

Chrysostom, John: Charismatic preacher associated with Saint Hypatia, at the breakpoint between this universe and ours; born 349 A.D.

Colleganza: A collective trading venture.

Cotte: A surplice-like garment, the predecessor of coat.

Curti: Literally, "short"—the Case Vecchie who had not been ennobled for many years.

Dalmatia: The eastern coast of the northern Adriatic Sea. Once the source of much of Venice's timber.

Ferrara: City-state in the Po valley in northern Italy; famous for steelworking, particularly swordsmiths.

Fruili: Region to the northeast of Venice.

Galliot: Small galley.

Golden Horn: Venetian trading enclave in Constantinople.

Hohenstauffen: The ruling house of the Holy Roman Empire.

Hypatia, Saint of Alexandria: Patron saint of the Hypatian order. Neoplatonist philosopher and librarian of the great library at Alexandra. Her saving of the Library from the mob instigated by Cyril the Patriarch of Alexandria is the breakpoint between this universe and ours.

Ilkhan Mongol: The Mongol khanate.

Istria: Peninsula to the south of Trieste. A Venetian possession.

Jesolo: The marshes to the east of Venice in the Venetian Lagoon.

Koboldwerk: Cunningly wrought chainmail made by dwarves.

Libri d'Oro: "Of the Golden book"; landowners; the Greek aristocracy of Corfu.

Longi: Literally, "long"—the Case Vecchie who had been ennobled for many generations.

Marangona: The bell which rang for half an hour from dawn to summon the Arsenalotti to work. Also rung for national emergencies.

Misericord: Thin dagger intended to penetrate joints in armor.

Narenta: Large river on the Dalmatian coast. A pirate lair.

Negroponte: Venetian trading outpost on the east coast of Greece.

Outremer: Originally "outré mer"—beyond the sea. Refers to the East, on the far side of the Mediterranean.

Paulines: The faction of Christianity taking its lead from the writings of Saint Paul. In this universe, the dominant religious faction in the north of Europe. More hierarchical and militant than the Petrine faction.

Petrine: The gentler, more tolerant southern faction of the Church.

Poignard: Dagger.
Podesta: Governor.
Ritters: Teutonic Knights.
Scaliger: The ruling house of Verona.
Schiopettieri: Mercenary soldiers under the control of the
    Lords of the Nightwatch (Signori di Notte); Venice's
    equivalent to a police force.
Scuolo: Guilds.
Surcoat: Loose sleeveless garment with insignia normally worn
    over armor.
Trebizond: Venetian trading outpost in the Black Sea.
Veneto: The region of northern Italy which includes Venice.
Veneze: People of Venice.
Vinland: North America.
Visconti: The ruling house of Milan.

FOOD

Kourabiedies: Almond cookies.
Stifado: Lamb or kid stew, on Corfu, commonly with quinces.
Loukoúmia: Turkish delight.
Sultanína glykó: Spoon-sweets (grape preserve flavored with
    rose geranium).
Melanzane alla finitese: Crumbed aubergine 'sandwich' of
    melted cheese.
Risotto con finocchi: Rice dish with fennel.
Kakotrigos: A grape variety which clings to the vine. Made
    into a tawny wine on Corfu called Kakotrigi.

The following is an excerpt from:

A Mankind Witch

by Dave Freer

available in hardcover from
Baen Books, July 2005

Prologue: Players various.

Biscay, July 1538

Cair clung to a spar floating in the open ocean, out of sight or scent of land. The rain had stopped now, and, as the spar rose with the swells, he looked around for other wreckage. Other heads in the water.

He saw nothing but white-capped gray sea.

The loss of his crew cut more deeply than the loss of his ship.

He drifted. And clung. The cloud-tattered morning turned to a slate-skied afternoon. There was no longer hope left in him. Just relentless determination, beyond any logic or faith.

And on the wings of evening, a dragon came out of the sea-mist.

Lying, bound with coarse rope, on the ribs in the bow of the longship, Cair knew that it had been no dragon. A dragon would have mercifully devoured him then and there.

"They say," said the prisoner next to him, in broken Frankish, "That you are a man-witch. That any other would have drowned. They found no others, nor any sign of your ship."

Cair let none of his instinctive scorn show. Primitive superstition! Instead he said nothing, keeping as still as he possibly could in his patch of relative warmth.

He remembered little of the rest of the voyage. It was blurred with fever and exhaustion. But he was aware that the other prisoners avoided even touching him.

Telemark, Kingshall, July 1538

"The poor girl. I feel so sorry for her. She's stunted, you know. They say . . ." and the honeyed voice of Signy's stepmother dropped, but not so low that it couldn't be heard clearly through the thin wooden wall. "It's the *dokkalfar* blood on her mother's side . . . The woman died in bearing the girl. That's a sure sign of the ill-fortune that goes with meddling in *seid*-magic. And only the one scrawny girl-child, Jarl. Anyway, it is not important. She is of the royal line even if she probably will never bear children. She's far too small. She spoils her complexion with sunlight. And she has no womanly skills. I mean, look at her embroidery! It's appalling. No, your master would be wise to look elsewhere."

Signy's nails dug into her palms. She dropped the frame of crooked stitchery that confirmed the truth about her skills with a needle. She knew perfectly well that she had been supposed to hear every word.

That it was meant to wound. That didn't stop it hurting. The Dowager Queen Albruna seldom missed the opportunity to try and belittle her . . . And seldom failed to do so. It wasn't hard. Signy knew that she was no one's idea of a shield-maiden. She was too small, too wiry, and as gifted with 'womanly' skills of fine weaving and delicate stitchery as a boar-pig. She couldn't even see her threads in linen-work, let alone do it. But, by Freya's paps, she sooner die than let the queen-mother see any sign of how her barbs stung.

She scrambled to her feet in a tangle of limbs, kicking over a footstool. That was normal too. Her stepmother hadn't said that Signy was as graceful as pregnant cow on an ice-patch—yet, but she would, as usual. Then the shaming, half-true stories would follow.

Albruna could enjoy needling her step-daughter. King Hjorda wouldn't care: He'd take her if she had two heads and tail. He wasn't interested in Signy as a woman: she was merely wanted as a claim to the throne of Telemark. As long as her brother was unwed and without heirs . . . she had value. And if that vile old goat Hjorda could get a son on her, he'd have a better claim to the throne than Vortenbras did. She was a very valuable trading piece at the moment, and Albruna was holding out for a high price. Signy knew that that was why she was still here, an old maid of twenty-four. She was waiting for Hjorda to increase his offer. Albruna would go on belittling her, pretending to try and put Hjorda off, until the price went up enough.

Signy spat, trying to rid her mouth of the sour half-vomit taste that the thought of her father's old foe engendered. She touched the wire-bound hilt of the dagger in her sleeve. She'd sworn on both Odin's Ring and Thor's hammer, that she'd see King Hjorda dead in his marriage bed. Her father's honour demanded that. Then she would die herself as her own honour required. But not for the first time she wished that she really was the *dokkalfar seid*-witch's daughter that Dowager-Queen-Mother Albruna accused her of being, every time she wanted to make sure the princess had not friend in the royal household. If Signy had had any powers, dark or no, she'd have turned her step-mother into a rat in a nest of vipers long ago. The Gods knew, she'd tried. But her participation in any charm, any piece of *Galdr*, guaranteed that it wouldn't work. She could make any charm backfire, let alone fail

"Come now, Your Highness," said Jarl Svein, his voice as smooth as oiled silk, "A princess of the Blood of two ancient houses, no matter how suspect the blood-lines are, is a jewel of value."

Abruna gave her characteristic sniff of disdain. "I've always had my doubts about her blood. Seriously, King Hjorda would be wiser to look elsewhere. How can someone of our lineage be so graceless? She's as clumsy . . ."

Signy had been told to wait until she was called to meet Hjorda's emissary. But she knew what was coming next. She'd rather face the inevitable whipping than stay a moment longer. After all, what was one more whipping? They hurt less than words anyway. She could be in the friendly comfort of the stables in a hundred heart-beats. She darted out of the door of the antechamber . . .

To have her passage blocked by a large woman with thick butter-milk-blond braids "Where do you think you're going?"

Such an insolent question from a thrall-wench! Signy raised herself up to her full height, and did her best to look a Princess in every one of those meagre inches. Even as she did it, she knew she was failing. "It is none of your business, Borgny." she hoped she'd kept the quaver out of her voice.

Mainz, late October, 1538

"It's already snowing in the North, Uncle," protested Manfred. "Surely it'll wait until summer. Or at least Spring." There was not much hope in his voice. When the Holy Roman Emperor made up his mind, even Prince Manfred of Brittany obeyed. He was even learning to do it with not more than a token protest.

"You're big enough to keep out the cold," said Charles Fredrik, dismissively waving his own large hand at his oxlike nephew. "And I want this sorted out before spring comes and more trouble starts. You, Erik and Francesca will travel together to Copenhagen. Francesca, it will be your unenviable task to soothe the Danes down. The Knights of the Holy Trinity are still the bulwark of our defence against the Grand Duchy of Lithuania, and, with Jagellion on the throne, we need them more than ever. The last thing I need is them involved in a messy little land-squabble with the Danes up in Sweden.

At the moment the Knights are subdued because of the way they were used in the Venetian affair. They know they came very close to feeling the full weight of my wrath. The Abbot-General has agreed that there is a problem in Skåne. He has agreed to allow you to act in his name there, provided that we also deal with the Danes." He grimaced. "Which may be more tricky than knocking a few Knights' heads together, Francesca. They are stiff-necked about that independence of theirs, even if they are a vassal state. It's not something that you would be advised to mention."

Francesca, or, as she now styled herself, Francesca de Chevreuse, although this was not the name she'd been born to, shivered artistically. "Your wish is my command, my Emperor." She dimpled, looking at him her eyes provocatively half-lidded. "Forgive the shiver. It's the thought of all that ice and snow, and me without any good furs to keep it from my skin." The former Ventenian courtesan was a voluptuous warm-creamy-skinned beauty. She liked to show that skin, and was well aware that even the Emperor liked to look at it.

Charles Fredrik chuckled. "We'll have to see that you are appropriately equipped. We can hardly have our Imperial special emissary turning blue in public. See to it, Manfred. Let Trolliger have the reckoning. Why do I get the feeling that suppressing them militarily might have been cheaper?"

Francesca acknowledged this with a smile and a small bow. "I shall try to restrain Manfred from spending more than the cost of a troop of cavalry, Your Highness."

The Emperor shook his head. "I hope you absorbed the lesson, nephew."

"What?" asked Manfred, rubbing his solid jaw. "Never to go shopping with Francesca? My purse learned that a while ago, Uncle."

"Beside that. Explain to him, Francesca."

She turned to Manfred. "He means I have not wasted my effort on fighting the inevitable, the Emperor's orders, but instead got the best out it that I can."

"Huh," said Manfred, gloomily. "What can I get out of it? To think I asked for you to send me away from this pile of stones before winter set in properly. I had somewhere warm in mind, before the Bishop General insisted on me coming back to some freezing Chapter-house in Prussia. Even Erik got chilblains in that first winter."

The Emperor turned his attention to the third person present at the interview. Erik Hakkonsen had not said anything yet. But then the tall, spare Icelander seldom said more than he had to. The Clann Hakkonsen of Iceland had provided personal bodyguards for the heirs of the Imperial House Hohenstauffen's *Wanderjahre* for centuries now. They were far more than mere bodyguards. They were the final arms-instructors and mentors for the princelings. Their loyalty was not to the Empire—Iceland was part of the League of Armagh, owing no fealty to the Holy Roman Empire, but to the House Hohenstauffen, personally. It meant that they, and only they, treated the scions of the most powerful Imperial house in the world like troublesome children, from time to time. Charles Fredrik knew that he owed his personal survival—and the survival of the Empire—to Erik's father. Erik had done as much for Manfred. When the Hakkonsen spoke, the Hohenstauffen listened. But Erik just shook his head and smiled wryly. "He still complains too much, Godar Hohenstauffen. Even if that affair in Venice did help him to grow up a bit. A bit of hard riding in the cold will be good for him."

Norway, Telemark. All hallows eve. A convocation high on the barren vidd.

The hag spat into the balefire. Green flames leapt as the stream of spittle hit the burning fungus. She wiped her chin with the back of her broad hand, and then turned again to face the *Draug* she had raised. Needs be it must be one of dead of this place. Midgard's dead for information about Midgard, after all. She'd brought the body up here, after her slaves had hauled it out of the bog where she'd laid him, face down, with his throat cut.

And they thought that his body lay in his ship-mound in honor! A seeming was quite adequate to fool these Midgard lice. And she was the mistress of seemings.

"Speak," she ordered.

The *Draug* gurgled horribly at her. Her hard green eyes narrowed as her son stepped forward, ready to cuff the dead thing. Bah. Blows, even blows from one such as he, could not hurt the dead. But she could. Her *galdr* would burn it like a whip of fire. She waved her hulking child back, back to his *Björnhednar* guards.

She raised her arms to begin the chanting . . . and realized that the *Draug's* defiance was merely a problem of the cut throat. Or maybe it was defiance of a sort. The *Draug* hated her, hated her with a helpless fury that could drive it to act even against the pain she could inflict with her *galdr*-chants. She took a handful of clay and mended it. "Now. Speak. Defy me if you dare. What is it that holds us back? Why did the raid fail?"

"The *Draupnir*," he croaked. "The oath."

Of course. It was obvious now. The oaths sworn on that thing would be binding, even if the swearer had no intent of honoring them. She should have guessed. But the thing had that about it which repelled her. Odin's temple yard was not a place she went to if she could possibly avoid it. The one-eyed one's priests were less affected by seemings than others, even if she'd seen to it that the present high incumbent was near to blind with cataracts. With certain protections her son should be safe from it. And if not—well they would find a way to break the oath. Or cause it to be broken.

Lightning split the sky, and the thunder echoed among the high places. Big drops began to hiss on the balefire. Now that she had what she needed, Bakrauf began dismissing the spells that had given theDraug the seemings of life. It fell like a child's broken doll, tumbling onto its side by the fire. The face of the dead kinglet was twisted into the rictus of a smile. She considered it, thoughtfully. *Draugar* thus compelled could not lie. She kicked the body,

and gestured to the *Björnhednar*. "Take him back.
I may need him again."

She turned away, the firelight glinting briefly on
the cunningly wrought silver ornaments in her ears.
They were perfect, down to the last hair, and no
small part of her power over the *Björnhednar* rested
in them.

Then she strode back downhill, away from the stone
that marked the gateway between her place and this,
back towards the halls of men in the valley below.
Behind her, her son followed. The pelting rain and
even the hail did not worry her. Troll-wives have no
objection to rain. It is bright sunlight they avoid.

CHAPTER 1

"You speak Frankish?" the Karl-translator asked, when the guards deposited him in front of the throne in the high thatched hall.

More fluently than you, thought Cair. But he put on a show of concentration. Nodded earnestly. "I have small." Cair was still not even sure where he was. Some remote little Kingdom in the Norselands seemed a fairly sure bet. But now came the difficult bit. He had to lie, and lie fluently.

"Vortenbras King he says have you kin who would pay *blot* . . . blood-price for you? Ransom." Faced with Cair's blank look, the Karl tried again. "Give him money for you."

Cair wrinkled his forehead in a show of effort. "You tell him-King, me poor man." If word went out that some Norseman was demanding a ransom for Cair Aidin . . . Well, even in fleets of the corsairs there were a good few who would pay for him . . . Dead. If word got to one of the Holy Roman Empire's spies that the Redbeard was a prisoner here—they would pay generously. Very generously. They would keep him alive too. Their torturers were good at that. Dead people felt no pain. When he'd last heard, the Republic of Venice also was offering five hundred thousand Ducats for his head. "Me poor man," he repeated. It would mean slavery, but that was better than the alternatives. He would have some chance of escape from slavery. And for some obscure reason the slaves here appeared to be left entire. The threat of castration might have persuaded him to try his luck at escaping from the gilded but carefully guarded cage they would put a high-value prisoner into, instead. However, he'd made sure of that already—all that happeed to slaves was a branding. And, once branded, slaves didn't appear well guarded at all. Perhaps the Norse trusted to the remote wildness of this place.

The bearlike man on the throne spat disgustedly at the translation. Bellowed something obviously derogatory in Norse. It was like enough to Frankish to have a haunting familiarity. "What him-King say?"

"Vortenbras King say you too old for good Thrall. Not enough work in you before you go die. And too small to plow with."

Too old! He was thirty-five. Not a young man, true. But in his prime! Then Cair understood the implication of the second part of the statement. He'd heard of that, yes. Poor places where they plowed with teams of men or women instead of horses. They did that in the high Atlas, apparently. But for one such as he to be put to such a use by these primitive barbarians!

The hulking bear of a man snapped an order. Cair found himself being dragged backwards—by the hair—by his translator. He had to turn and follow, stumbling. He was going to have to learn this language. Fast. And he was going to have to restrain himself from killing idiots like this hair-dragger.

"Where are you taking me?" he asked.

"To be branded. Then," and the disdain showed in the man's voice. "You go to be woman's slave. Signy."

Cair thought—by the tone—that the last word was probably some kind of Norse insult.

"What your name, slave?" demanded the stable-master in mangled Frankish, looking down at him, as he sprawled on the soiled straw he been shoved down onto.

His new-burned flesh throbbed. Cair added that to the reckoning. But right now he had to survive until that reckoning came due. And that meant that he had to stop being a Corsair admiral—and become an anonymous slave. He was not Cair Aidin until he stood on the deck of his own ship again. The barbarians couldn't pronounce his name anyway. He bowed his head. "Cair, Master." He would be that, and think of himself as just that, until he was free.

"A good name for a thrall," The stable master grunted. "Get up. Move dung," he pointed to a wooden shovel. "And learn our tongue."

Cair, the new slave, shoveled horse-dung. That was another thing they'd pay for, when he escaped. But for now he was content to bide his time. To study his captors and the place he was captive in. When he made his break, he intended to be successful. And, if he had to bring half of the Barbary fleet here, he'd burn this place around their ears. The 'palace' and its halls were wooden. The roofs were thatch. They'd burn well. They thought that being this far from the coast would save them. Nothing would.

But after a few days of captivity, Cair—the new thrall—was somewhat less sanguine about it all. The first thing that struck him was that they'd scarcely give a slave at this much liberty if escape was a real possibility. He soon realized that, beside the brand, there were other trammels set on a thrall. And one of them was that, here in the north, he was a small, unarmed fellow. Among the corsairs he'd been of average height. It was not something that had worried him, previously. With a sword in hand, or a ship to command, he was the equal or the better of any other man. Here he was utterly forbidden to even touch either a ship or an edged weapon. A few older, very privileged thralls had belt-knives. Small belt-knives.

Besides being a mere small unarmed slave-thrall, the bottom of the Norse social order, he also found he was at the bottom of the pecking order for slave-thralls. He was a woman's slave. And not just any woman. Signy.

You didn't, it would appear, go any lower, around these parts. Being the lowest of the low meant that you got the worst of everything, from sleeping quarters to food, if you could call it that. They were teaching him the job with a good supply of buffets, blows and occasional buckets of filth. And even others thralls were free to hand out a good beating if they felt like it.

On the second day, still struggling with the language, and still wracked by the last chill of fever,

Cair found this out the hard way. He wasn't even too sure what he'd done wrong. All he knew was that he was getting a fiercesome beating with a broken stave for doing it. And the fact that he'd dared to strike back was making it worse. The thrall doing the beating was heavier, taller and better fed than most of them. He was one of Queen Albruna's slaves—not supposed to be in the stables at all. The other thralls stood and cheered and jeered. There wasn't much entertainment in the stables. Certainly no one lifted a hand to stop it.

The fight was going badly. And then it was going worse. The big fellow kneed him in the crotch, and, as Cair's head came forward, he cracked it down against one of the stalls.

Cair swore, amid the blur of pain . . . and then the hitting stopped.

Cair managed to stand upright. Blood was streaming from his nose, and the world was definitely out of focus. But the big tow-haired thrall was no longer laying into him. And the stable was oddly silent. Cair closed both eyes and then tried opening them again. His vision was still far from normal, but he could see the Thrall, stretched out full length on the stable floor. His head appeared to have turned into a heavy wooden bucket.

That was quite enough for Cair. He was plainly either dead or concussed, and in either case he was going to sit down. Now.

He slumped against the wooden stall partition. He was vaguely aware that some of the other thralls had hauled the bucket head away. But he felt too sore and sick to care. And no-one had come to drive him to his feet and to work again. He drifted away to somewhere between concussion and sleep.

He awoke to find someone kneeling next to him. Lifting his head. Holding something to his lips. "Drink this."

He sipped. It was a clay dipper of water. He tried to work out who it was giving this nectar to him. The light was bad in the stable by now, not that it was wonderful at any time, but evening was plainly close.

It was a woman. Not a thrall he'd seen before. A scrawny lass that had plainly been crying. He sipped some more and then tried to sit up. Quite involuntarily, he groaned.

"You've taken quite a beating, by the looks of you," said the woman, critically. Not particularly sympathetically, but kindly enough. "Can you stand up?" she asked.

Cair tested his limbs. "I think so. I'll try."

"Good," she said. "This is Korvar's stall. He doesn't like being put elsewhere. Come. Up."

She hauled at his arm and he staggered to his feet. She made no attempt to support him, but he did manage to grab the stall edge and steer his way out. The woman appeared more concerned at fussing around the stall, and leading an elderly warhorse across to it, than watching what he was doing, so he sat down again. But his head was clearing, slowly. She patted and soothed the horse. "Next time don't bleed in this stall," she said to Cair, sharply. "The smell of blood gets Korvar overexcited." She leaned over and kissed the horse's muzzle. The horse twitched and sneezed. She laughed. "There, you big old silly. Settle now." Eventually, she came out of the stall, and looked critically at Cair. "There is some horse liniment I made up for strains up on the shelf in the corner. I've found that it helps a bit for the bruises. Then you'd better get across to your quarters, before you get another beating."

It was only after she'd left that it occurred to his muzzy mind that she'd addressed him in Frankish. Not just Frankish but good Frankish. Spoken as a highborn noblewoman would, not some stable-girl. But he'd thought no more of it. His head throbbed and so did his ribs. He'd roughly slathered some of the horse-liniment on himself. It burned in the raw places, and woke him more thoroughly, but perhaps the herbs in it would do him some good. He'd staggered over to the stinking hovel where he'd been told to sleep. It was small, dirty, crowded, smoky, full of vermin . . . and oddly silent when he'd crept in. He'd found a space easily enough, and slept.

Getting up the next morning was even more torture. The bruises had set, and for all that it was midsummer, it was still cold at first light. He chewed on his coarse rye crust and supped the weak, sour small-beer handed to them in the garth outside the kitchen. In the kitchen, the morning's work had plainly begun well before, and the noise was enough to make him retreat from it. He chewed cautiously. His mouth was sore. Looking around he realized that he stood in a little island of silence, while the other ragged Thralls jostled and talked—in muted voices, true, among themselves. And across the yard he caught sight of the tormentor of yesterday. He had a dirty bandage around his head. And the minute his eyes locked with Cair's, he shied away.

Cair's own head had bled, and his hair was matted with dried blood. But it was only when he'd helped to lead the horses out to the paddocks down beside the water, and took the opportunity—along with one of the other two Thralls, to wash his face in the cold water that he could wash it clear gingerly. And peer at his reflection in the water. He didn't think—all things considered, that he looked that terrifying. So on the way back up to the stables, he ventured to ask what was going on. The other man who'd bothered to wash had spoken peasant Frankish to him yesterday. He was presumably a Frankish prisoner taken on one of the local's raids. "Why is everyone behaving as if I have the plague this morning?"

"I haven't done anything to you," said the other thrall, warily.

"Except kick me and trip me face down into the dung heap yesterday," said Cair.

The thrall held up his hands pacifically. "But I didn't know, then."

"Didn't know what?" asked Cair.

"That you were a manwitch." Even after the rudimentary wash by the lake-side, the man's face was none too clean. The dirt was the only bit of color on it, right now.

Cair was about to deny this latest piece of ridiculousness when it struck him that it might be useful. These were pagans, after all. They weren't likely to accuse him of trafficking with the devil. "Who told you?" he asked, doing his best to look threatening. He raised one eyebrow, a trick he'd practiced and used to some effect on prisoners himself. If this was the only coin he had to play, well, then he would play it with skill.

The thrall's eyes widened, and looked ready to bolt. "I saw, yesterday, what you did to Eddi. And I've heard from Piers that one of the other new captives says you were floating on the sea, miles from the land."

Now, thought Cair. All I have to do is find out what I "did" to Eddi, who was presumably the person who had given him the bruises that hurt so devilishly this morning. Whatever it was, Cair hoped the bastard was at least half as sore as he was. He ached. Even his aches had aches. He could use any reputation that would stop this from happening again. There were a few tricks he could use to foster the story. There were a fair number of things a civilized man knew to be science that these ignorant pagans would take for magic. But for now he kept his mouth still and let the tongue of rumor speak instead. From experience, he knew that it always spoke louder than any mere man could. He and his brother had cultivated rumors of the Redbeards' uncanny successes, and of the folly of resisting them, for that just that reason. Even the Venetians were inclined to run, and, when cornered, surrender rather than fight. It always made for easier victories, if the victims were half paralyzed with fear before they even went into the fight. Logical thought did not come into these things, thought Cair wryly. "See you behave yourself today, and you won't get what you deserve. I'll stay my vengeance. For now."

The thrall nodded so eagerly that his head was in danger of parting from his shoulders. "Nobody will give you trouble. I promise."

"Good. Now show me what I am supposed to

do around here. I don't want more beatings." He saw, instantly that this had been the wrong thing to say, and rectified it immediately. "My powers are low now, too low after my magics at sea, calling the King's ship to me, to undertake great workings again. But I can still manage to deal with the likes of Eddi. Or you. However, I have been here for a greater purpose than to waste magic on thralls if I don't have to."

The thrall nodded. "We'd better go and muck out then. Signy never says anything, except if the horses are badly looked after."

There was that name again. He'd taken it for a Norse insult the first time he'd heard it. This thrall and the others in the stable yard put a fair degree of disdain into it. Yet she was apparently a Princess. "Who is this Signy?"

"The old king's daughter. King Vortenbras's sister. Half-sister."

It was curious that these slaves would even dare to treat someone that high-born with anything but the very greatest respect, or even omit a title. They certainly spoke the name of Vortenbras's mother with hushed deference. It appeared that how much respect a thrall got from his fellows was largely determined by who owned you. Thus the sooner he, Cair, got himself transferred to the service of some more important personage, the better. It would make life more comfortable, until he could escape.

"They say that she is a *seid*-witch," said the thrall with disdain. "Or at least the Queen does. But I never saw any sign of it."

❖   ❖   ❖

During the rest of the day, Cair gradually pieced together a great deal from his new informants, Henri, once a fisherman from the coast of nearby Helgoland, and Thjalfi, their half-witted companion-in-labor. Thjalfi had no problem repeating the story, over and over again, of Eddi and the bucket. It would appear that Thjalfi had, prior to Cair, been Eddi's favorite kicking-target. By the way the moonling smelled, Cair wished that Eddi had kicked him into the water. Thjalfi had no Frankish, but he was slow of speech as well as wits, and he repeated things endlessly. As a learning tool he was a noisome asset. If Cair understood Thjalfi right, Cair had called Eddi "Buckethead" and a string of strange and obviously magical words. And the bucket had come from nowhere and landed on Eddi's head.

The Berber-coast obscenity Cair had yelled at Eddi, hadn't been 'buckethead'. But it did sound similar. Luck and a falling bucket had been on his side. Now he just had to capitalize on it.

From Henri he learned a great deal more. King Vortenbras of Telemark's hall was some fifteen leagues from the coast—for just the reason that Kdir had surmised. Once the small Norse 'kingdom' had had its seat on the coast. And inevitably had raided far and wide . . . and brought down the wrath of the Danes and Holy Roman Empire on its King's Hall. Now, with the Royal Hall tucked into the mountains, beside what had been an ancient Holy site, silver coming from the mountain mines, and a treaty with the Holy Roman Empire, Telemark under King Vortenbras was a growing power. Rumor had it that the limits of this power irked the King. He was looking to stretch them, folk said.

Then, as the afternoon drew in, Cair got another surprise. As he was carrying in a load of straw, a woman spoke in Norse, plainly giving some instruction. Cair felt that he ought to know the speaker. He peered up from under his load, and saw Henri and Thjalfi bowing. "Ja, Princess Signy."

It was the woman he'd taken for a thrall-wench the night before.

Her dress was indeed shabby for a noblewoman, but in the clearer light he could see that it had been, at least once upon a time, a good riding habit. She wore some jewelry too. Poor stuff, but if he had noticed those bracelets he'd never have mistaken her for a thrall. Her hand rested on the head of one of the hunting dogs that seemed to slope around everywhere in this place. She was inspecting the stable, and pointing to a tag end of a halter-rope buried in the bedding straw. Cair was standing a great deal closer to it than she was, and he could barely see it. The woman must have eyes like a hawk.

She was a slight little thing compared to most of the women he'd seen here, fine boned, they called it back on Lesbos, where he'd grown up. Her hair was so strained back and tightly braided that it was virtually invisible from the front. He put down the net of hay. Bowed, considering the ramifications of his encounter last night. What had a noblewoman—who had plainly been crying, been doing in the stables after the household was abed? Cair was a thinker. Life, especially to a master of ships and men, was a chess-game and you had to think at least five moves ahead if you wished to win. "Pick that up!" she snapped at him—in Frankish. "Don't you watch where you put things down, Thrall? They told me I had a new stable-Thrall that spoke no Norse and was too old for good work, but didn't expect you to be an idiot too. I suppose I should have. They always give me the insolent, sick, lame and lazy. I don't care elsewhere, but you'll learn to do proper job with the horses or I'll have you whipped. Even if I have to do it myself. And learn to speak Norse."

Picking up the hay, hastily he did his best to bow again. But she was no longer paying any attention to him. Instead she'd gone with Henri to inspect some saddle galls on the rough-coated bay. Her voice as she talked to the horse was now as gentle as it had been waspish a minute ago. And, if she'd recognized him, she'd not given any sign of it.

Afterwards, when she'd left, Cair found himself doing some further cleaning of the two stalls that the Princess had been dissatisfied with. He'd already come to realize that her section of the huge stable was cleaner by several degrees than the other parts. He was also aware that the horses in this part of the stable were old. Several of them were definitely beyond work.

Henri grumbled. "It's only those of us in the stables that she makes work. Those house-thralls of hers are the laziest bunch of sluts you've ever met. The Queen's women work their fingers raw. But not Signy's. No. Half the time they tell her what to do. And the Queen lets them! But I'd swear the Mistress spies on us down here. Look at Vortenbras's men. Half the day they can sleep in hay-loft. The only time I thought I'd try that she turned up and nearly pulled my ear off. And we get the worst food and everything."

"That is going to change."

Henri blinked at him. "No, it's not. The King doesn't love his half-sister."

Cair stared pointedly at him. "I have my powers. Do you want your head in a bucket?"

Henri gaped at him. "You mean . . ."

"I mean the Princess Signy wants her horses cared for. A fine and beautiful noble lady must have what she desires." Cair was much more observant than his fellow peasant horse boys. He'd looked up, just briefly, a few moments before. Above the stalls, the roof-beams had been layered with rough timber to make a sort of ceiling and junk store. The timber didn't fit too well. And through one of the cracks Cair had glimpsed a piece of embroidery that he'd seen earlier.

END OF EXCERPT from
A Mankind Witch, **by Dave Freer,**
available in hardcover, July 2005,
from Baen Books

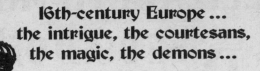

16th-century Europe ...
the intrigue, the courtesans,
the magic, the demons ...

a historical fantasy series from masters of the genre

◇◇◇◇◇◇◇◇◇◇◇◇◇◇◇◇◇◇◇◇◇◇◇◇◇◇◇◇◇◇◇◇◇◇◇◇◇◇◇

The Shadow of the Lion

Mercedes Lackey,
Eric Flint & Dave Freer   0-7434-7147-4 ◆ $7.99

Venice, 1537. A failed magician, a fugitive orphan, a reluctant prince, a devious courtesan, and a man of faith must make uneasy alliance, or the city will be consumed by evil beyond human comprehension.

This Rough Magic

Mercedes Lackey,
Eric Flint & Dave Freer   0-7434-9909-3 ◆ $7.99

The demon Chernobog had almost seized absolute power in Venice until the guardian Lion-spirit awoke to protect his city. But the Lion's power is limited to Venice, and Chernobog has allied with the King of Hungary in besieging the island of Corfu to control the Adriatic. Far from the Lion's help, Manfred and Erik organize guerrillas, as Maria discovers the island's ancient mystic powers. If she can ally with them, she may be able to repel the invaders—but not without paying a bitter personal price.

A Mankind Witch

Dave Freer   (HC) 0-7434-9913-1 ◆ $25.00

In an alternate world where magic works, the Holy Roman Empire still rules Europe, and the Renaissance has come, with very different results. Norway is still pagan, and a sacred relic, the Armring of Telemark, has been stolen from Odin's temple. Without it, truce-oaths cannot be renewed and bloody war with the Empire will follow. Signy, the older stepsister to the King Vortenbras is accused. When she disappears, most think it proof of her guilt. Her only partisan, the Corsair-Captain Cair, knows that she had been carried off and is determined to find and rescue her; he will not only find that magic is very real, and dangerously so, but that he himself has a natural talent for it.

◇◇◇◇◇◇◇◇◇◇◇◇◇◇◇◇◇◇◇◇◇◇◇◇◇◇◇◇◇◇◇◇◇◇◇◇◇◇◇

Available at local bookstores everywhere!

Or, use secure, easy *online ordering* at:
www.baen.com

If not available through your local bookstore, send a check or money order for the cover price(s) + $1.50 s/h to Baen Books, Dept. BA, P.O. Box 1403, Riverdale, NY 10471. Include a full name & address for shipping. Delivery can take up to eight weeks.

ELIZABETH MOON

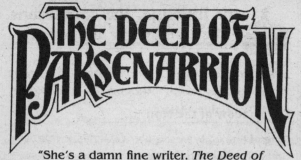

THE DEED OF PAKSENARRION

"She's a damn fine writer. *The Deed of Paksenarrion* is fascinating. I'd use her book for research if I ever need a woman warrior. I know how they train now. We need more like this."

—Anne McCaffrey

By the Compton Crook Award winning author
of the Best First Novel of the Year

Sheepfarmer's Daughter	0-671-65416-0	$5.99
Divided Allegiance	0-671-69786-2	$7.99
Oath of Gold	0-671-69798-6	$6.99

or get all three volumes in one special edition:

The Deed of Paksenarrion	(HC)	0-7434-7160-1	$26.00
	(trade PB)	0-671-72104-6	$18.00

The Legacy of Gird	0-671-87747-X	$18.00

Sequel to *The Deed of Paksenarrion* trilogy, now in an omnibus trade edition containing:

Surrender None and *Liar's Oath*

Available at local bookstores everywhere!

Or, use secure, easy *online ordering* at:
www.baen.com

If not available through your local bookstore, send a check or money order for the cover price(s) + $1.75 s/h to Baen Books, Dept. BA, P.O. Box 1403, Riverdale, NY 10471. Include a full name & address for shipping. Delivery can take up to eight weeks.

ERIC FLINT

ONE OF THE BEST ALTERNATE-HISTORY AUTHORS OF TODAY!

RING OF FIRE SERIES:

1632 31972-8 ◆ $7.99 ____

1633 (with David Weber) (HC) 7434-7155-5 ◆ $7.99 ____

1634: The Galileo Affair
(with Andrew Dennis) (HC) 7434-8815-6 ◆$26.00 ____

Ring of Fire (ed. by Eric Flint) (HC) 7434-7175-X ◆$23.00 ____

Grantville Gazette (ed. by Eric Flint) 7434-8860-1◆ $6.99 ____

Mother of Demons 87800-X ◆ $5.99 ____

Rats, Bats & Vats
(with Dave Freer) 31828-4 ◆ $7.99 ____

The Rats, the Vats, & the Ugly
(with Dave Freer) (HC) 0-7424-8846-6 ◆$24.00 ____

Pyramid Scheme
(with Dave Freer) (PB) 7434-3592-3 ◆ $6.99 ____

The Course of Empire
(with K.D. Wentworth) (HC) 7434-7154-7 ◆$22.00 ____

The Warmasters
(with David Weber & David Drake) 0-7434-7185-7 ◆ $7.99 ____

Mountain Magic
(with David Drake, Ryk E. Spoor & Henry Kuttner)
0-7434-8856-3 ◆ $6.99 ____

THE JOE'S WORLD SERIES:

The Philosophical Strangler 0-7434-3541-9 ◆ $7.99 ____

Forward the Mage
(with Richard Roach) 0-7424-7146-6 ◆ $7.99 ____

Crown of Slaves
(with David Weber) 0-7434-9899-2 ◆ $7.99 ____

(more Eric Flint!) ➔

MORE...
ERIC FLINT

The Shadow of the Lion
(with Lackey & Freer)   0-7434-7147-4 ◆ $7.99 ____

This Rough Magic   (HC) 0-7434-7149-0 ◆$26.00 ____
(with Lackey & Freer)

Wizard of Karres   (HC) 0-7434-8839-3 ◆$22.00 ____
(with Lackey & Freer)

The World Turned   (HC) 0-7434-9874-7 ◆$24.00 ____
Upside Down (edited by David Drake, Eric Flint & Jim Baen)

THE GENERAL SERIES:
(with David Drake)

The Tyrant   (PB) 0-7434-7150-4 ◆ $7.99 ____

THE BELISARIUS SERIES:

with David Drake:

An Oblique Approach   87865-4 ◆ $6.99 ____
In the Heart of Darkness   87885-9 ◆ $6.99 ____
Destiny's Shield   57872-3 ◆ $6.99 ____
Fortune's Stroke   31998-1 ◆ $7.99 ____
The Tide of Victory   7434-3565-6 ◆ $7.99 ____

AND DON'T MISS THE CLASSIC AUTHORS OF SF
EDITED & COMPILED BY ERIC FLINT —
NOW BACK IN PRINT FROM BAEN BOOKS!

Randall Garrett
James Schmitz
Keith Laumer
Murray Leinster
Christopher Anvil
Howard L. Myers

If not available through your local bookstore send this coupon and a check or
money order for the cover price(s) + $1.50 s/h to Baen Books, Dept. BA, P.O.
Box 1403, Riverdale, NY 10471. Delivery can take up to eight weeks.

NAME: _____

ADDRESS: _____

_____

I have enclosed a check or money order in the amount of $ ____

DID YOU KNOW YOU CAN DO ALL THESE THINGS AT THE

BAEN BOOKS WEBSITE

?

✓ read **free sample chapters** of books (Schedule)

✓ see what **new books** are upcoming (Schedule)

✓ read entire **free Baen books** (Free Library)

✓ check out your **favorite authors'** titles (Catalog)

✓ catch up on the **latest Baen news** & **author events** (News & Events)

✓ **buy** any Baen **paperback or hardcover** (Schedule & Catalog)

✓ read **interviews** with authors and artists

✓ **buy** most any Baen book as an **e-book**, individually or an entire month at a time (WebScriptions)

✓ **communicate** with some of the coolest fans in science fiction & some of the best minds on the planet (Baen's Bar)

GO TO
WWW.BAEN.COM